Ah, the nev... e Kessentai in comm... nding group's target, ... tarion personally, was ... enemy surface warships. The location of the other was, at best, approximated on the Kessentai's view-screen.

What a strange world this is; all disgusting, wet, oozing greens. The Kessentai had actually landed with his oolt before being ordered aloft again to lead this abat-hunt.

Binastarion had warned him, through his far-speaker, not to be overconfident, that these particular thresh had sharp kreen, indeed.

With *Rapturous Feast XXVII* in the lead, the other eighteen landers spread out behind, forming a deep "V." Straight as an arrow the wedge of Posleen landers flew, hardly noticing the shimmering, flashing anomaly on the surface of the sea between the attack group and its target.

And then the anomaly grew a head, one of the foul threskreen sensory clusters, with ugly projections and a streaming yellow thatch.

The creature from the deeps raised its arms heavenward, masses of something like ball lightning lashing between its gripping members. All Posleen weapons thundered and flashed towards the malignant apparition.

With growing dread, the lead Kessentai saw that no harm was done the beast. But wait . . . it seemed to be rocking back and forth as if in distress.

"We've got it!" exulted the Kessentai.

"No, lord," corrected the Artificial Sentience. "The monster is laughing at you."

YELLOW EYES

(Ojos Amarillos:
La Defensa de Panama)

(This being the tale of the defense of Panama
and the Panama Canal by U.S. and Panamanian
forces against landing and migrating Posleen.)

JOHN RINGO &
TOM KRATMAN

YELLOW EYES

Copyright © 2007 by John Ringo & Tom Kratman. "Winterborn" lyrics by Rogue, copyright © 2003, song performed by The Crüxshadows (www.cruxshadows.com). Printed by permission of Dancing Ferret Discs.

A Baen Books Original

Baen Publishing Enterprises
P.O. Box 1403
Riverdale, NY 10471
www.baen.com

ISBN 10: 1-4165-5571-4
ISBN 13: 978-1-4165-5571-1

Cover art by Kurt Miller
Map by Kurt Miller

First Baen paperback printing, September 2008

Library of Congress Control Number: 2006100546

Distributed by Simon & Schuster
1230 Avenue of the Americas
New York, NY 10020

Pages by Joy Freeman (www.pagesbyjoy.com)
Printed in the United States of America

For the owners, operators and ladies
of the Ancon Inn (Panama City)
and el Moro (Colon).
Thank you. Let's do it again some time.

And, as always:

For Captain Tamara Long, USAF
Born: 12 May 1979
Died: 23 March 2003, Afghanistan
You fly with the angels now.

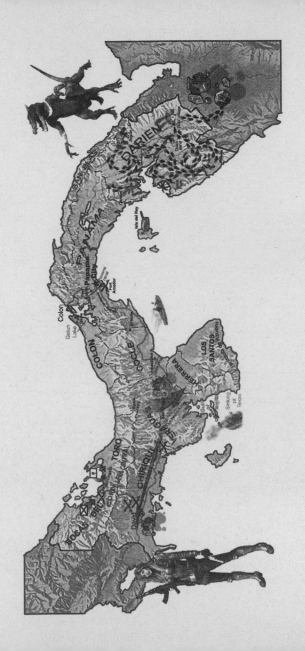

YELLOW EYES

You are going to have the fever,
Yellow eyes!
In about ten days from now
Iron bands will clamp your brow;
Your tongue resemble curdled cream,
A rusty streak the centre seam;
Your mouth will taste of untold things
With claws and horns and fins and wings;
Your head will weigh a ton or more,
And forty gales within it roar!

In about ten days from now
You will feebly wonder how
All your bones can break in twain
And so quickly knit again!
You will feel a score of Jaels
In your temples driving nails!
You will wonder if you're shot
Through the liver-case, or what!
You will wonder if such heat
Isn't Hades—and repeat!
Then you'll sweat until, at length,
You—won't—have—a—kitten's—strength!

In about ten days from now
Make to health a parting bow;
For you're going to have the fever,
Yellow eyes!

—James Stanley Gilbert,
"Panama Patchwork," 1909

PROLOGUE

From where he stood in the back of the crowded assembly hall, Guanamarioch saw the gold-strapped Rememberer ascend the rostrum. The chattering of the massed Kessentai ceased as the cleric—the Rememberers were as near to a clergy as the Posleen had—rapped his skilled claw, twice, on the stone podium. Except for age and scarring, the Remember was—like Guanamarioch—an average looking Posleen, a crocodilian centauroid with yellow skin and eyes, standing about fifteen hands high, with rows of sharp ivory teeth and having a feathered crest (not dissimilar to a Sioux Indian war bonnet) that it could erect when it wished.

"Let us remember," the cleric called, laying its crest low in respect for the ceremony.

All the hundreds of Kessentai crossed their arms over their massive chests, looked upward, toward the apex of the pyramid, itself clad inside and out with a heavy layer of pure gold, and chanted together, "We remember. We remember."

The Rememberer held out one claw into which an underling placed a loosely rolled scroll. This was

1

unrolled onto the stone podium, the underling placing "keeper stones," elaborately carved paperweights, on the corners to hold the scroll in place.

"From the Scroll of Flight and Settlement," the Rememberer announced.

"We remember," echoed the Kessentai, once again.

The pyramidal assembly hall shook with the nearby impact of a rival clan's hypervelocity missile, or HVM. Guanamarioch, young as he was, could barely restrain himself from leaving the hall and going forth with his underlings to do battle. The eager, enraged trembling and murmuring of the others told him they all felt much as he did.

The Rememberer calmed the hall with a sweeping glance. He was one of the eldest among them, a Kessentai turned Kenstain who, in his younger days, had been among the foremost warriors of the clan. None of the youngsters present wanted to find shame in the eyes of this old hero. They settled and quieted down.

"Verse Five: the new home," the Rememberer continued.

Once again, the group chorused, "We remember."

"And the People, fleeing their destroyed home on the new ships, came upon a new world, rich and teeming with life. And the ships were tired, and nearly out of fuel. And the leader of the People, called Rongasintas the Philosopher, led the people to a barren part of the land, that was uninhabited. And there they tried to settle and grow food.

"But the People had little food, and the inhabitants would not share, demanding, 'Go forth from us. This is our world, not yours. Return once again to the darkness whence you came.' And the heart of Rongasintas was heavy.

"Yet the People cried out, saying, 'Lord, feed us, for we hunger.' And Rongasintas answered, 'Eat of the pre-sentient young.'

"And, weeping, the People ate of their children, but it was not enough. Once again they cried out, 'Lord, feed us, for we hunger.'"

"We hunger," repeated the assembly.

Nodding his great crocodilian head with infinite dignity, the Rememberer continued, "And the Lord Rongasintas the Philosopher answered, 'Choose one in twenty from among the normals, and eat of these.' Weeping still, the People chose from among their number one in twenty, that the host might live and not perish. And for a little time the People did not hunger. Yet, still, did they weep, for it was not yet the way of the People to eat of their own.

"At length, the Lord of the People went to the inhabitants of the place and begged, 'We have done what we can. We have eaten of our own. Give us sustenance, that our people not perish.' And the inhabitants of the place heaped scorn upon Rongasintas, saying, 'Leave this place or eat of yourselves until there are none of you left. It is all the same to us.'

"And the Lord and Philosopher went to a high place to meditate and upon his return he announced, 'The Aldenat' made us as we are; we had no choice in the matter. They raised us from the lowly animals and gave us sentience. They left us with the need to reproduce. They gave us of medicine and knowledge, that we did not die young. Under their rule, the People prospered and grew. All praise was to the Aldenat'.'"

"And we gave praise to the Aldenat'," chanted the assembly, in response.

The Rememberer continued, "And Rongasintas told the People, 'We must live. To live we must eat. Go forth then, and eat of the inhabitants of this place. As was all praise, upon the Aldenat' be all the blame.'"

As one, the massed Kessentai echoed, and their echo made the stone walls of the great Hall of Remembrance shudder, "Upon them be the blame."

PART I

CHAPTER 1

Like a rich armor, worn in heat of day,
that scalds with safety.
                              —Shakespeare, *Henry IV*

Ttckpt Province, Barwhon V

It was a cold, blue-green swamp under a violet sky. Lieutenant Connors had seen some swamps in his day; after all, he'd spent a number of years at the original "Camp Swampy," Fort Stewart, Georgia.

"Nothing like this shit, though," he muttered, as he struggled for a balance between conserving power for his Armored Combat Suit, and not sinking waist deep in the muck. Not sinking continued to win the toss as he reduced mass on his suit and applied power to forward thrusters to keep going even when the ground slid away in a lumpy slurry beneath him. His feet still sank ankle deep in the crud below.

The ACS encasing Connors was Galactic-built, but to human-drawn specifications. Despite this, and despite being symmetrically bipedal—two arms, two legs—and having a largish lump right where the head

7

should be, the thing did not look too terribly human. In fact, it looked completely *inhuman*. For one thing, the suit had colored itself a dull blue-green to match the vegetation of the swamp. For another, it lacked obvious eyes and ears, while having a number of weapons stations sprouting from it.

The jury was still out on the camouflage. Other schemes had been tried. The blue-green mottled pattern on Connors' suit had worked as well as any of them, and not one whit better. The Posleen's yellow eyes were just *different*, different in their structure and different in what they saw.

Inside his suit, the lieutenant shrugged, unseen by any but the artificial intelligence device that ran the suit for him. He didn't know what camouflage would work (neither did the AID) and just followed the latest guidance from higher on the subject.

Around him, likewise mottled in the blue-green pattern and likewise struggling for an acceptable compromise between longevity and speed, Second Platoon, Company B-1st of the 508th Mobile Infantry (ACS), was spread out in a very sharp and narrow "V" to either side of a churned-muck trail.

Ordinarily, on Earth, the trail would have been superfluous as a means of control and orientation. The Global Positioning System was capable of telling a soldier, or a group of them, exactly where they were all the time. On Barwhon, however, there was no GPS. Moreover, while the suits were capable of inertial reckoning on their own, by and large the enemy Posleen were not. Thus, the Posleen followed the trail and, thus, the MI were led to battle them along it.

Besides, the trail was the shortest distance to an American light infantry company cut off some miles ahead on the wrong side of a river ford, their backs to the stream and no good way to cross back under fire.

Connors, like the men of Second Platoon, moved forward under radio listening silence. They could hear the commands of higher, when higher deigned to speak. They could also hear the heartbreakingly precise reports and orders emanating to and from one Captain Robert Thomas, commanding the company trapped at the ford. They'd been hearing them for *hours*.

The MI troopers had heard, "Zulu Four Three, this is Papa One Six. Adjust fire, over." They'd heard, "Echo Two Two this is Papa One Six. I've got a dozen men down I *have* to get dusted off." They'd eavesdropped on, "Captain Roberts, we can't fuckin' hold 'em . . . AIIII!"

Connors heard Echo Two Two, which the key on his display told him was the brigade's medical company, come back in the person of some breaking-voiced radioman, and say, "We're sorry, Papa. *God*, we're sorry. But we can't get through for your dust-off. We tried."

Things got worse from there.

"Echo Three Five, this is Papa One Six. We are under heavy attack. Estimate regimental strength or better. We need reinforcements, over."

A Posleen regiment massed two or three *thousand* of the aliens. A light infantry company at full strength with the normal attachments was one twelfth that size . . . or less. In this case, the personnel replacement situation being what it was, the trapped company was less. Much less.

That's a good man up there, Connors thought, in consideration of the incredibly calm tone of a man, Roberts, who knew that he and all his men were on the lunch menu. *Too damned good to let get eaten.*

Then came the really bad news. "Papa One Six, this is Echo Three Five, actual;"—the brigade commander— "situation understood. The Second of the 198th was ambushed during movement to reinforce you. We have at least another regiment . . ."

Things really got shitty then, though the first Connors knew of it was when the point man for the company column shouted, "Ambush!" a half a second before the air began to swarm with railgun fleshettes and the mucky ground to erupt steaming geysers with the impact of alien missiles and plasma cannon.

The problem with killing the stupid Posleen, Connors thought as he lay in the muck, *is that the rest of them get much, much smarter.*

The air above was alive with fire. Most of this was light railgun fire, one millimeter fleshettes most unlikely to penetrate the armor of a suit. Enough was three millimeter, though, to be worrisome. That was heavy enough to actually penetrate, sometimes, if it hit just right. It *had* penetrated several men of the company, in fact.

Worse than either were the plasma cannon and hypervelocity missiles, or HVMs, the aliens carried. These could penetrate armor as if it were cheesecloth, turning the men inside incandescent.

Worse still were the tenar, the alien leaders' flying sleds. These not only mounted larger and more powerful versions of the plasma cannon and HVMs, they had more ammunition, physical or energy, and much better tracking systems. They also had enough elevation on them that, at ambush range, they could fire *down,* completely skipping any cover the MI troopers might have hastily thrown up. Nor did the jungle trees, however thick, so much as slow the incoming fire. Instead, they splintered or burst into flame at the passing. Sometimes they did both. In any case, the air around Connors resembled some Hollywood idea of Hell, all flame and smoke and destruction, unimaginable chaos and confusion.

The only good thing you could say about the situation was that the Posleen apparently had few tenar. Otherwise, there was no explanation for the company's continued survival.

Connors traded shots with the Posleen, round for round. That wasn't really his job though. On the other hand, trying to do a lieutenant's job was rough, once things heated up.

"Call for fire, Lieutenant Connors?" suggested his AID.

"Do it," he answered, while cursing himself, *I should have thought of that first.* "And show me platoon status."

The AID used a laser in the suit's helmet to paint a chart directly on Connors' retina. He'd started movement with thirty-seven men. It pained him to see seven of those men marked in black, dead or so badly wounded that they were out of the fight. Under the circumstances, they were almost certainly dead.

He keyed his attention on one particular marker on the chart. "Show me detail on Staff Sergeant Duncan."

Instantly, that chart was replaced with another showing vital statistics and a record summary for one of Connors' squad leaders. He didn't need the record summary; he knew his men. The statistics were something else again.

Shit, Duncan's on overload.

It took an experienced eye to see it. The first clue was the soldier's silhouette projected by the AID. Duncan should have been prone or at least behind some kind of cover. He wasn't; he had taken one knee and was trading shots with the Posleen, burst for burst. That was all well and good against normals; they were usually lightly armed. *But doesn't the idiot see the goddamned HVMs coming in?*

It got worse on closer examination. Adrenaline was up, but that was normal. The brain activity was skewed though.

"AID, query. Analyze record: Staff Sergeant Robert Duncan. Correlate for 'combat fatigue' also known sometimes as 'nervous hysteria.'"

AIDs thought very quickly, if not generally creatively.

"Duncan is overdue for a breakdown, Lieutenant," the AID answered. "He has forty-four days continuous combat—without rest—now. He has over three hundred days in total. He's stopped eating and has less than four hours sleep in the last ninety-six. Loss of important comrades over the past eighteen months approaches one hundred percent. He hasn't been laid lately, either."

"Fuck . . . Duncan, get down, goddamn it," Connors ordered. The silhouette painted on his eye didn't budge.

"Incoming," the AID announced, tonelessly. The splash of friendly artillery fire began to play on the aliens surrounding the company. "I am adjusting."

With the help of the artillery, that ambush was beaten off. It made no difference. The Posleen were swarming between the company and its objective. They were swarming in much greater than mere regimental strength. *Much.*

Duncan was a problem. He couldn't be left behind; there were still thousands of Posleen that would have overcome and eaten him on his own. Connors had had to relieve the man and place his Alpha Team leader in charge of the squad. Worse, all you could get out of the sergeant were unconnected words of one syllable.

And I can't leave anyone behind to guard him. I can't even autoprogram the suit to take him back to base; he'd be dogmeat on his own.

At least the sergeant could follow simple orders: up, down, forward, back, shoot, cease fire. Connors kept him close by during the long, bloody grueling fight to reach the ford. They reached it too late, of course. Captain Roberts' radio had long since gone silent before the first B Company trooper splashed into the stream.

By that time, Connors found himself the sole officer remaining in the company. That was all right; the company was down to not much more than platoon strength anyway.

Connors heard his platoon sergeant—*no, now he's the first sergeant, isn't he?*—shout, "Duncan, where the hell do you think you're going?"

Looking behind, the lieutenant saw his damaged sergeant beginning to trot back to the rear, cradling a body in his arms. Some friendly hovercraft were skimming the greasy-looking water of the swamp as they moved to reinforce the ford.

"It's okay, Sergeant . . . First Sergeant. Let him go," Connors said, wearily. "It's safe back there, now. See to the perimeter, Top."

Leaving the NCO to his work Connors sat down on the mound the Posleen had created apparently to honor the spirit and body of the late Captain Roberts. He began to compose a letter to his wife, back home on Earth.

"Dearest Lynn . . ."

Logistics Base X-Ray, Ttckpt Province, Barwhon V

The battalion had suffered grievously in the move to and fight for the ford. B Company was down to one officer and fifty-one others. Of the fifty-one, one—Staff Sergeant Duncan—was a psychiatric casualty. The rest of the battalion's fighting companies were in no better shape.

The battalion commander was gone, leaving the former exec, Major Snyder, to assume command. Only two of the company commanders had lived, and one of those was chief of the headquarters company which didn't normally see much action. In total, the battalion's officer corps had left to it one major, two captains, half a dozen first lieutenants and, significantly, *no* second lieutenants. Like other newbies, the shavetails had died in droves before really having a chance to learn the ropes.

Connors thought he was lucky keeping his old platoon sergeant as the company first sergeant. Snyder had wanted to take him to be battalion sergeant major.

Somehow, Connors thought, *I don't think Snyder meant it entirely as a compliment when he let me keep Martinez.*

"Sir," Martinez asked, when they were alone in the company headquarters tent, "what now? We're too fucked to go into the line again."

The tent was green, despite the bluish tint to all the vegetation on Barwhon V. It smelled musty, and a little rotten-sweet, from the local equivalent of jungle rot that had found the canvas fibers to be a welcome home and feed lot.

"The major . . . no, the *colonel*, said we're going home for a while, Top," Connors answered, distantly. "He said there's not enough of us left to reform here. So we're going back to get built up to strength before they throw us in again."

"Home?" Martinez asked, wonderingly.

"Home," echoed Connors, thinking of the wife he'd left behind so many long months before.

Indowy Freighter Selfless Accord, *en route Barwhon to Earth*

"Attention to orders," cracked from the speakers above the troopers' heads as they stood in ranks in the dimly and strangely lit assembly hall.

"Reposing special trust and confidence in the patriotism, valor, fidelity, and abilities of . . ." The 508th's acting adjutant, normally the legal officer, read off the names of the remaining officers of the battalion. One of those names was, "Connors, Scott."

"A captain?" Connors wondered when the ceremony was over. "Wow. Never thought I'd live to be a captain."

"Don't let it go to your head, Skipper," advised Martinez who was, like many in Fleet Strike, a transferred Marine.

"No, Top," Connors agreed. "Would never do to get a swelled head. Makes too big a target for one thing."

"The bars . . . look good," Duncan said, staring at the wall opposite the headpiece of his medical cot. His voice contained as much interest as his blank, lifeless eyes. "The diamond looks good, too, Top," he added for Martinez.

Outside of his suit, Connors and Duncan might have been taken for brothers, same general height, same heavy-duty build. Though fifteen or more years Duncan's senior, Connors looked considerably younger. He was, unlike Duncan, a rejuv.

"How have you been, Sergeant Duncan?" the newly minted captain asked.

"Okay, sir," he answered tonelessly. "They say I can be fixed up . . . maybe. That I'll either be back to duty in a year or will never be able to go into the line again. They're talking about putting me in a tank for psych repair."

Patting the NCO's shoulder, Connors answered, "I'm sure you'll be back, Bob."

"But will it be me that comes back?" Tears began to roll down the NCO's blank, lifeless face.

"God . . . I don't know, Bob. I *can* tell you that the tank didn't make me any different on the inside."

"Me neither, Sergeant Duncan," Martinez added, more than a little embarrassed for the junior noncom. Martinez knew Duncan was going to remember the tears and feel the shame of them long after he and the skipper had forgotten. "I came out the same Marine I went in as . . . just younger, stronger and healthier.

"By the way, Skipper," Martinez asked, turning his attention away from Duncan's streaming face, "what were you doing before the rejuv? I was a retired gunny, infantry, and just marking time in Jacksonville, North Carolina . . . waitin' to die."

"Oh, I did a lot of crap after I left the Army, Top. Do you mean what did I do in the Army? I was a DAT."

"What's a DAT?"

Connors smiled. "A DAT is a dumb-assed tanker, Top."

"So how did you end up in infantry, sir?" Duncan asked, showing for once a little interest in something.

"I hate the internal combustion engine, Sergeant Duncan. Just baffles the crap out of me. So when I got rejuved and they sent my unwilling ass to OCS I worked that same ass off so that I'd have a choice when I graduated. And I chose Mobile Infantry to keep the hell away from tanks."

Duncan rocked his head slightly from side to side, which was also a bit more life than he had shown for a while. "Okay . . . maybe I could see that."

Earth Orbit, Indowy Freighter Selfless Accord

"Let me see my e-mail, AID," Connors ordered, alone in his cramped cabin aboard ship.

The cabin measured about six feet by nine, and had a ceiling so low Connors had to duck his head to stand up to stretch his legs. The bed was stowed against the wall and a fold-out table served as the desk on which rested the AID, a black box about the size of a pack of cigarettes.

The AID didn't say anything. Neither did the e-mail appear holographically.

"AID?" Connors insisted, an annoyed quality creeping into his voice.

"You don't want to see it," the device answered definitively.

"Don't tell me what I want," Connors said angrily, heat rising to his face as blood pressure turned it red. "Just gimme my goddamned mail."

"Captain—"

"Look, AID, I've had no word from my wife since leaving Barwhon. Just give me my mail."

"Very well, Captain." The e-mail list appeared immediately, projected on the air over the desk.

Connors was surprised to see only a single letter from his wife. He opened it and began to read. It was short, a mere five lines. Then again, how much detail is required to say one's wife is pregnant by another man and that she has filed for divorce.

INTERLUDE

The outer defenses of the city were crumbling now, Guanamarioch sensed. The sounds of battle—the thunder of railguns, the clash of the boma blades, the cries of the wounded and dying—grew ever closer.

He felt a slight envy for those Kessentai chosen to stay behind and cover the retreat to and loading of the ships that would take the clan to their new home. Their names were recorded in the Scrolls of Remembrance and they would be read off at intervals to remind the People of their sacrifice. That was as much immortality as any of the Po'oslena'ar, the People of the Ships, might aspire to.

Yet instead of leading his oolt into the fight, Guanamarioch on his hovering tenar led them as they marched four abreast and one hundred deep towards the waiting ship. Other oolt'os, similarly, formed long snaking columns from the city's outskirts all the way to the heavily defended spaceport.

Impatiently, the Kenstain in charge of the loading directed Guanamarioch to bring his charges to a particular ship and to load at a particular gate.

"And be quick, you," the Kenstain demanded.

"There is little time left before the ships must leave."

Ordinarily the Kessentai would have removed the Kenstain's head for such impertinence. This was, however, a time of desperation, a time when minor infractions had to be overlooked. Obediently, riding his tenar, the God King led his normals to the designated ship.

At the ship another Kenstain directed cosslain, a mutated breed of normals that were nearly sentient, to take Guanamarioch's tenar and stow it. The God King removed his Artificial Sentience from the tenar, hanging it around his neck, as the cosslain took the flying sled away.

"Lord," the castellan said, "your oolt is the last for this ship. The place for you and your band is prepared. Directions have been downloaded to your Artificial Sentience. Just follow it and stow the normals, then report to the captain of the ship."

"Are you loading then?" asked Guanamarioch.

The Kenstain shook his head, perhaps a bit sadly.

"No, lord," he answered, his teeth baring in a sad smile and his yellow eyes looking sadder still. "I will stay here and keep loading ships until there are either no more ships, or no more passengers . . . or until the enemy overrun the last ship we are able to begin loading."

The God King reached out a single grasping member and touched the castellan, warmly, on the shoulder. "Good luck to you, then, Kenstain."

"That, lord, I think I shall not have. Yet there are worse ways to die than saving one's own people."

"It is so," Guanamarioch agreed.

CHAPTER 2

The United States and Panama are partners
in a great work which is now being done
here on the Isthmus. We are joint trustees
for all the world doing that work.
—President Theodore Roosevelt, 1906

Panama

The country lay on its side, more or less, in a feminine
S-curve stretching from west to east and joining the
continents of North and South America. Beginning
at the border with Costa Rica it ran generally east-
southeast for a third of the way. Conversely, from
its border with Colombia in the thick and nearly
impenetrable Darien jungle it ran a third of the
way west-northwest. The waist of the country, also
feminine and narrow, went from the rump—the
Peninsula de Azuero—that jutted out into the Pacific
and then east-northeast to meet the land running
from Colombia roughly one third of the way from
the Colombian border.

Down the center of the country ran a spine of

mountains with few passes and fewer roads running across it. North of this spine, the Cordillera Central, was mostly jungle, with a few cities and towns. South was, at least from the Costa Rican border to the narrow waist, mostly farm and pasture. There were two major highways, the Pan-American which ran generally parallel to the Cordillera on the southern side, and the Inter-American which ran the much shorter distance from Panama City in the south to Colon in the north.

More than half of the people of the place lived in the two provinces of Colon (not quite half a million) and Panama (about a million and a half). Of the rest, most lived close to the Pan-American highway where it ran from Panama City to the border with Costa Rica, south of the Cordillera Central.

The highway that joined the *cities* of Colon and Panama was not the only link between them. Colon fronted on the Caribbean to the north. Panama City edged along the Pacific to the south. Between them, like a narrow belt on a woman's narrow waist, ran an artificial body of water that linked Colon and Panama City, linked the Atlantic and Pacific oceans and, in the process, linked the world.

This was the Panama Canal.

She'd been carved out of the living rock through an emerald-hued hell. Men had died in droves for every yard of her; died of the fever, of the rockslides, of the malaria, of a dozen tropical diseases to which they had had no cure and, initially, little defense. They'd died, too, of the drink that anesthetized them from the misery of their surroundings.

She'd broken one attempt to tame her; broken the

men, chewed them up and spit out their corpses to rot. The skeletal remains of their rusted machines, vine grown and half sunken, still dotted the jungle landscape, here and there. But men were determined beasts and, eventually, had broken her in return.

For generations she had been the single most strategically important ten-mile-wide strip of land in the world. The commerce of all the continents and innumerable lesser islands passed through her, a lifeblood of trade. The nation which had owned her had ruled the seas with the power of commerce and with the power of war.

Two hundred and forty inches of rain a year were just barely enough to slake her thirst. A small fleet of dredgers were just enough to keep her free of the silt those rains washed down. Throughout her heyday the lives and labors of seventy thousand human beings had had no higher purpose than to serve and defend her.

She was the Panama Canal and, though aged and faded, she remained a beauty.

Yet her heyday had passed. The nation which had built her had lost interest as the greatest ships of war and commerce had outgrown her limits, as the people and nation that hosted her had grown to resent the affront to their sovereignty that foreign ownership of the Canal had represented. In truth, though, once the great enemies—Nazism, Fascism and Communism—had fallen, the security the Canal had represented had become, or come to seem, slightly superfluous.

Times change, though. Perceptions change.

The Pentagon

Deep in the bowels of the "Puzzle Palace," in a room few were aware of and fewer still ever visited, a troubled man gazed over the heads of banks of uniformed men and women sitting at computer terminals, onto an electronic map of the world glowing from a large plasma television. That monitor was one of three. To the right was shown a map of the continental United States and North America; to the left, generated by a complex computer program, a spreadsheet marked the anticipated decay of necessary world trade under the impact of Posleen invasion.

"We're just fucked," announced the man, a recalled three star general with vast experience in complex logistics and no little feel for commerce.

He repeated himself, needlessly, "Fucked."

As the general watched, a red stain spread out across the center of the right-hand screen. As it spread, numbers dropped on the spreadsheet, some of the numbers changing color from solid green to blue to red to black. In a few cases those number dropped to zero and began to blink urgently.

"We're going to nearly starve," muttered the general, to no one in particular. "Even with the GalTech food synthesizers, we are still going to be goddamned hungry."

Suddenly—the program was operating at faster than real time—a smaller stain in Central America oozed east- and southward to cut the Panama Canal. Within seconds every category shown on the left-hand spreadsheet plummeted. It became a sort of

"Doomsday" Christmas tree of pulsing black numbers and letters.

A finger of red lunged north from Montana, before retreating southward again. "They've just cut the Canadian Transcontinental Railroad," a functionary announced from behind his own computer monitor.

Moments later another notional landing touched down between Belleville and Kingston, Ontario. The mark of that landing spread. More fingers thrust north, east and west. Black dots appeared over critical locks along the canal system there.

Another landing appeared near Saint Catherine, Ontario. The Welland Canal, vital link between the inner Great Lakes and the eastern cities of Canada and the United States, turned black. A Canadian forces liaison officer, on the other hand, turned white as his country's forces—paper thin for decades, the legacy of a mix of neglect, active hostility and eager toadying to the United Nations—turned from translucent to transparent before disappearing altogether.

"Cease work," the general announced. "Reboot. After Action Review in thirty minutes." The screens all went blank.

"Ladies, gentlemen. I am going to go see the chief."

The White House, Washington, DC

"Well, *can* we hold the Canal then, General?" the President of the United States asked of the gargantuan, shiny-domed, black four-star seated in the leather chair opposite his desk in the Oval Office.

The general was a big man—huge really—with

so many medals, badges and campaign ribbons that he left off several rows of ribbons or the fruit salad would not have fit even his massive chest. To the left of General Taylor sat an apparently agitated woman from the Department of State. The woman was dressed . . . *severely*, the general thought. No other word would quite do.

"Hard to say, Mr. President," the general answered. "*We* don't have the troops to spare, not enough of them anyway. Nine divisions? Two or Three corps? In the Second World War we stationed seventy thousand troops there and thought we could hold it. But those seventy thousand would have been, at most—absolute *worst* case—facing a Japanese attack not much greater in size, operating at the ass end of a long and fragile logistic pipeline, and moving in the teeth of one of the greatest concentrations of *effective* coastal defense artillery and airpower in the world, and with ourselves having a broad material and technological advantage, plus sea, air, rail and road-borne supply. We have few or none of those advantages now."

"What *can* we do then?" asked the President, his serious, middle-aged face creased with worry. He'd read the reports coming from the simulations conducted in the Pentagon's bowels.

"We can spare maybe one division, Mr. President, some fire support ships, some anti-lander artillery, maybe even a few planetary defense bases. Maybe."

"But that won't be enough?" the President asked wearily. He was always tired, these days. *So much to do . . . so much . . . so little time. Shit.*

"Nope," the general said with an unaccountable

smile. "We need the Panamanians to defend themselves for the most part."

"What do they have?"

The general shrugged calmly. It was his *job* to radiate calm and he was very good at his job. "Nothing much. A dozen large military police companies. Some veterans of the time they did have something like an army, though even then it was tiny, about a good-sized brigade. A fair number of American vets who have settled there over the last fifty years. But they've no industry to speak of; they're a service economy. No long military tradition and what they do have is not exactly a tradition of success. I think the last battle they won was against Sir Francis Drake. Though, to tell the truth, beating Sir Francis was no small achievement."

Taylor continued. "They grow a lot of food and could grow more. Their women are fertile as hell; half the population is under age twenty-five." The general smiled at some old but very fond memories: *Damned beautiful women they are, too, so unlike this poor drab from State.* "Literacy rates are excellent, better than our own as a matter of fact. They're hard workers . . . when there is work to be done. Unemployment is high, about fifteen percent, though that is still a lot less than the Latin American norm. On the plus side most of the unemployment is among young men. Plenty of available cannon fodder, in other words. Though they can't hope to be able to train or pay to equip them."

A word popped into the President's mind unbidden: *Expensive.*

"Government?" the President asked.

The general raised one eyebrow and glanced at the woman to his left. He reconsidered on closer examination, *Not a bad looking girl, really. Or she wouldn't be if she dressed more like a woman and paid a little more attention to her face and hair. Maybe a bit thin, though. Does Foggy Bottom's selection process rule out tits?*

State answered, somewhat reluctantly, "Latin American normal, Mr. President. It's a kleptocracy run by about one hundred interrelated families. From the outside, it looks democratic enough. And they don't *exactly* rig their elections. But the government is always dominated by those families and decisions are almost invariably based on bribes and family interests. The only lasting exceptions to this rule was when they had a dictator in charge . . . and that was never more than a partial exception. The dictators have generally been corrupt, too."

"Hah!" exclaimed Taylor, "an honest answer from State. Who woulda thunk it?"

The President ignored the jibe. "How do they feel about us?" he asked the representative from State.

She didn't need to consult her notes; she was, after all, State's desk officer for the Republic of Panama.

"Mixed, Mr. President," she said. "Some of them have some lingering resentment over our occupation of the former Canal Zone. This is often mixed with the more general anti-gringoism you can find anywhere in Latin America. But, on the other hand, they are the most nearly 'gringo' of the Latins, themselves. Many of them speak at least some English. For that matter, many of them speak English as well as you or I. Their laws reflect our influence. Their culture is . . . well, some would say 'heavily contaminated' . . . but, in any case, it is heavily influenced by ours. In some ways Panama is more American than Puerto Rico is."

"Would they object to our return?" the President asked.

"Surely some would, sir." State answered. "Sir . . . could I give you a short history of Panama and the Panama Canal?"

The President nodded his acquiescence; he knew as little of Latin America as virtually any president in United States history was likely to. This was generally very little indeed.

State looked around at the opulent office, collecting her thoughts.

"Panama was once a very rich place," she began. "That wealth came from the same geographic oddity that gives them one of the highest standards of living in Latin America now, the narrowness of the isthmus itself and what it means for trade. In the old days, as the *Audencia* of Panama, virtually all the gold and silver of Mexico and Peru passed through Panama before being shipped to Spain. It was sent by ship to Panama City, then moved on slave, mule and burro-back to Portobello on the Caribbean. Mr. President, so much treasure passed through that there was only enough storage space for the gold, the silver had to be left in the streets. The Audencia also served as the nexus for the slave cartel."

State hesitated, afraid to offend the general, before continuing, "Most of the blacks in Latin America outside of Brazil and the Caribbean coast could trace ancestors who came through Panama as slaves."

The President raised an uplifted palm and gestured beckoningly with his fingers, twice: *Come on? And?*

State continued, "The treasure attracted pirates, mostly English speaking and always under English command. Most famous among these: Sir Francis Drake and Sir Henry Morgan, heroes in the Anglosphere but devils incarnate to Panama. Portobello and Panama City were attacked several times. Both were sacked, with everything that a sack means: rape, robbery, arson, torture, murder. It is my impression of the Panamanians that even they are not aware how deeply those long ago events scarred, and continue to scar, their collective psyche. They retain a trace of xenophobia today that is really remarkable in such a generally cosmopolitan and amiable people."

State made a slight slashing motion with her right hand.

"Moving forward a few centuries, Panama became part of Colombia as the Spanish Empire broke up. Yet they never really thought of themselves as Colombians but as Panamanians; different, with different values and interests. While Colombia found its livelihood in mining and farming, Panama always knew that its unique position—the isthmus, again—bound it to commerce. When Colombia was wracked by civil war between liberals and conservatives, late in the nineteenth century, the fighting spread to Panama readily. While the liberals were crushed in Colombia itself, in Panama they won. The general was wrong about the last time the Panamanians won a fight."

The general shrugged, *eh?*

"In any case, a Colombian expeditionary force was en route to crush the rebellion when we intervened. The details of our intervention, while amusing, are not very important. Suffice to say that we did intervene, that at our urging Panama did declare its independence, and that as an implicit condition of our recognition and protection they agreed to cede us the Canal Zone."

State's face took on a disgusted look. "Mr. President, there's no other word for it, we gave them the *shaft*. The treaty between us was so patently unfair to Panama that even our *own* Senate initially was inclined to reject it.

"In any case, we ratified it because it did, at least, give us rights to build the Canal . . . and because no one actually suggested a fairer deal. The Panamanians accepted it, with profound reservations—disgust, really—because we had them over a barrel and they saw no choice."

State shook her head with regret. "I am often amazed by how often in the history of the world a long-term problem could have been headed off before it arose with just a *little* application of even a *minimal* generosity. Except for the Versailles treaty there is perhaps no clearer example than the original Panama Canal treaty. Because of it the Panamanians could never be content, part of which is because of that streak of xenophobia they learned from the English pirates. Because of it we never felt quite right with upholding and defending the terms of the treaty; that's how unfair it was. We renegotiated it several times to be more fair to Panama, but no amount of, mostly symbolic, fairness could wipe out the original insult until we agreed to leave, as we did in 1977."

The general harrumphed. "We should have just kept it and to hell with Panama."

This time it was State who shrugged, *eh?*

"Now, we're almost gone from there," she concluded.

"What's left?" the President queried.

Taylor answered, "We had one airborne infantry battalion we converted to an Armored Combat Suit unit before we sent it off-world. I've already ordered them home; they should fit right in with no real problem, though that battalion had a hard time of it and will have to be rebuilt. There's one company of Special Forces which had mostly been operating the counter-drug mission further south. There is also a small support package for the Green Beanies. We've stopped all but minimal maintenance of the facilities we do retain. We couldn't even put up the troops' families since most of the dependent housing has been sold to Panamanian government functionaries and their connections at pennies on the dollar. This is also true of the civilian housing for the people who run the Canal. We're really starting from less than scratch, Mr. President; even most of the usable, drained land has been taken."

The President sat quietly for a few moments, elbows on desk and cupped hands around his mouth and nose, thinking and digesting. At length he asked, "What's it going to cost?"

The general answered slowly and deliberately, "We're not sure, still working on it. We think, though, that between supporting a division of our own troops, plus some naval support; raising, equipping and training better than three hundred thousand Panamanians; rebuilding our infrastructure and putting up some solid fixed defenses . . . well, something like one-hundred and seventy billion dollars, spread over seven or eight years."

The President sighed. "That's not small change."

Taylor answered, his face growing very serious, "No, Mr. President, it isn't."

"What's that old saying, General? 'It takes millions to win a war; to lose one, it takes all you've got.' Continue your planning; assume we are going to do it. I'll chat with Panama about what they *need* to do if they want to survive."

"And if they won't go along, Mr. President?" State asked.

"They will," the President answered simply.

Palacio de las Garzas, *Presidential Palace, Panama City, Panama*

The American ambassador thought, and not for the first time, that the private office of the President of the Republic was simply . . . tacky. *Too much gilt, too many ugly paintings. Blech.*

But he was not here to comment on tastes. The ambassador had come to the president's office to deliver an ultimatum. He had delivered it, and with each demand the president's face had grown more set.

Short and round, well-fed and greasy looking, *Presidente de la Republica* Guillermo Mercedes-Mendoza listened to the United States ambassador with an outward appearance of serenity. Inwardly, however, he seethed.

Goddamned gringos.

The ambassador from the United States was polite, of course, but he was also firm: Panama could either cooperate with the U.S. or they could see the Canal

Zone reoccupied and much expanded. Indeed, in that case they could expect fully half the population of the Republic to fall under direct U.S. control.

"So, you are giving us *that* much choice, are you?" queried Mercedes.

Regretfully, the ambassador answered, "We don't have any choice, *Señor Presidente*. It is a matter of life and death for us . . . for you, too, for that matter. Together, we have a chance to live. Separately, we can only die. I am sorry, from my heart I am sorry, but there is no choice."

Mercedes let the false serenity escape from his face and scowled at the ambassador, who thought, *I can hardly blame the man, being handed an ultimatum like this. What patriot could stomach it?*

But it wasn't patriotism that brought the scowl to Mercedes' face. Instead he thought, *Just what I need, twenty or thirty thousand gringos here, sniffing into everything, setting an example of—at least, relative—incorruptibility, upsetting my Colombian business "associates," and, worst of all, making us institute conscription, thereby raising up the masses and putting down the good families. I can't possibly officer the kind of army they say we must raise and they will pay for, without letting all kinds of peasants into positions of authority.*

"Tell me again the particulars," Mercedes demanded.

The ambassador nodded before answering, "Very well, *Señor Presidente*. First, you must have the laws passed requesting—no *demanding*—our assistance in accordance with the Carter-Torrijos Treaty of 1977. We prefer that it come from you for public relations reasons. At the same time you must have the legislature grant us back the use, the *temporary* use—for the duration of the emergency—of those facilities we need."

"And what am I to do with the people who have already purchased the property? Hmmm?"

Amiably, the ambassador answered, "The United States is willing to pay a reasonable, but not extravagant, rental. But that is only for private individuals. We expect land held by the government of Panama to be granted to us freely for construction, training and operations. We also expect that no more transfers to private hands will take place. Our President was explicit on this point, Mr. President: You're not going to jack the rents up on us through sleight of hand. Moreover, we will expect the government of Panama to take any land needed from corporations that control it and allow us its use. Some of that land will find permanent fortifications built on it. Think of this as a sort of reverse lend-lease, not essentially different from the agreements the United States had with Great Britain, Australia and New Zealand during the Second World War . . . or here in Panama, for that matter, notably on the Isla del Rey, San Jose Island and at Rio Hato."

Mercedes' piggish eyes narrowed further. "And you people will pay our troops and provide for arming and training them?"

"We will pay *something* . . . much, even. But not all, *Señor Presidente*," the ambassador answered. "Panama will have to pay its fair share. Don't worry overmuch about the cost, though; your government is going to make a fortune on Canal tolls in the coming years."

Again Mercedes scowled openly. The scowl disappeared as a new thought occurred. *The gringos are*

*going to be doing a lot of building. But they are
unlikely to have much construction capability they
do not need themselves. That is profit to the proper
families. And if they do send builders here? My God,
what a bounty for both the families and myself in
graft: permits, consulting fees . . . come to think of it,
I was supposed to provide a sinecure for little cousin
Maritza's worthless brat. I could never have made
this kind of money, not even laundering funds for
the Colombians.*

Seeing the scowl and misunderstanding it completely,
the ambassador interjected his final selling point, "Rejuvenation for a number of key Panamanians is, of course,
offered. There are some unfortunate rules on that, but
the rules have a fair amount of leeway to them."

Mercedes pretended that the prospect of renewed
youth was a matter of no moment. Mentally *el Presidente* tallied the likely rake-off and set that against
the price he expected to be gouged for off-world
asylum for his extended family. Then he calculated the
marvelous prospect of another fifty years of enjoying
not only his own youth, but a near infinity of young
women, and said simply, "I'll make the demand of
the legislature in ten days . . . agreed."

David, Chiriqui, Republic of Panama

The sound of the laboring resuscitator was faint over
the wailing of half a hundred close relatives. Scores
more crowded the hallways outside the antiseptic-
smelling, scrub-green intensive care room in which
Digna Miranda, tiny and aged one hundred and two,

slipped from this world to the next. The tininess was not a result of age. Digna had never been more than four feet ten in her life.

Within the room, by Digna's side, were the thirteen still-living children of the eighteen she had borne, as well as some of their offspring. The oldest of these was, himself, eighty-seven, the youngest a mere stripling of fifty-eight. One toddler, invited into the room as much as anything to remind Digna that her line was secure, was seven year old Iliana, great-great-granddaughter by Digna's oldest, Hector.

Digna herself lay quietly on the bed. Occasionally her eyes opened and scanned the crowd insofar as they could without Digna turning her head. The old woman was too far gone for any such athletics as head turning.

Digna was a rarity in Panama, being of pure European ancestry, a Spanish-French mix, with bright blue eyes. When those blue eyes opened, they were still bright and clear, as her mind remained clear, whatever decay had wracked her body. *What a pity*, she thought, *that I can't slip into the past for one last look at my children as children, or my husband as a young man. Such is life . . . such is death.*

Though no near-death dementia brought a false image of her long deceased husband, Digna's mind remained healthy enough to pull up images on her own, images both of her husband riding his bay stallion to claim her from her father just after her fifteenth birthday, and of her husband lying in his bier. *See you soon, beloved, I promise.*

That happy thought brought a slight smile to her face, a slight smile being all she was capable of. The smile continued as her eyes shifted to the face of her eldest. *I bore you in blood and pain, my son, with only your father and an old Indian midwife in attendance. What a fine man you grew to.*

Digna closed her eyes and drifted off to sleep and to dream.

Hector sighed, wondering if this trip to the hospital would truly be the last of his mother. It seemed impossible that this unbent old woman should pass on after dominating so much and so many for nearly a century. With thirteen living children, well over one hundred grandchildren, and great- and great-great grandchildren numbering nearly four hundred, so far—and with about a dozen more on the way, she was truly the mother of a race.

"*La armada* Miranda," Hector smiled at the family joke, before frowning. "Armada" might indeed be the right term if even half of what the president had said was true. Personally, Hector suspected the president's speech had contained much more than half the truth. Why else would he invite the gringos back?

Better you go now, Mother, I think. Or if not now, then soon. You grew up in a cleaner and better world. I would not have what we are about to become blight your last days.

A confused and confusing murmur came from the outside corridor. Hector turned from his mother's deathbed to see a group of five men standing in the doorway. The leading man, deliberately nondescript, wore sunglasses and a suit. Two others, standing just behind, were equally unremarkable medical types. Behind those stood the last pair, wearing the khaki of Panama's Public Force, its combination army and police force.

"*Señor* Miranda?" asked the foremost intruder.

"Hector Miranda, yes. And before I am polite may I ask what you people are doing here intruding on our grief?" The Mirandas, though only locally powerful, were still—albeit only locally—very powerful. In their own bailiwick they could *kill* with near impunity, and had. Moreover, while Hector was old, at eighty-seven, like his mother he remained vital, and perhaps a bit fierce, long after most people had slid into decrepitude.

The nondescript suit-wearer answered without the minimal politeness of giving his own name, "I am sorry for that, but orders are orders." He pointed his chin towards the supine and sleeping Digna. "Is that *Señora* Digna Miranda?"

"She is. And who the hell are you?" Hector demanded.

"My name is unimportant. You may call me 'Inspector,' however. That is close enough."

Hector felt his hackles rise, hand reaching on its own for the machete that would normally hang at his side. "Very well then, Inspector. Let me rephrase: what the *fuck* are you doing here intruding on our grief?"

The inspector ignored Hector completely, reaching into his pocket and withdrawing a folded paper. From light filtering through the thick parchment-colored sheet Hector thought he saw an official seal affixed to the bottom. The inspector began to read from the sheet.

"*Señora* Digna Adame-Miranda de Miranda-Montenegro," he used her full, formal name, "in accordance with the recent Public Law for the Defense of the Republic of Panama, you are hereby summoned and required to report to the Public Force Medical Facilities at Ancon Hill, Panama City, Republic of Panama for duty."

The inspector then turned to an aghast Hector and, smiling, continued. "Oh, and you too, *Señor* Miranda. Would you like me to read you *your* conscription notice?"

Department of State Building, facing Virginia Avenue, Washington, DC

Even a very junior Darhel rated a great deal of protocol, so powerful were they within the Galactic Federation. The one seated opposite the Undersecretary of State for Extraterrestrial Affairs was very junior indeed within Darhel circles. Even so, the alien had been greeted with deference bordering on, perhaps even crossing over to, obsequiousness. It would have been nauseating to see to anyone not a diplomat born and trained.

"We wish to remind you," stated the elven-faced Darhel in a flat-toned hiss through needle-sharp teeth, "how long thisss department of your government hasss been a client of oursss."

"The Department of State is fully aware of the close and cordial relations we have enjoyed since 1932," the undersecretary answered, noncommittally.

It was, of course, extremely unwise for any Darhel to become agitated. Thus, this one kept a calm demeanor as he asked, "Then why thisss regrettable disssregard of our adviccce and guidanccce? Why thisss wassstage of effort on the part of your military forcesss on what isss, at mossst a sssecondary area, thisss unimportant isthmusss? Don't your people realizzze how much *we* need the defenssse you can provide? Important considerationsss are at ssstake." Briefly the Darhel let his true feelings show through, "Marginsss are being called; contractsss are being placcced in jeopardy!"

The undersecretary sighed. "Yes, we know this, my lord. We so advised the President. Unfortunately we were overruled."

Intolerable, thought the Darhel. *Intolerable that these people insist on the illusion that they are entitled to their own interests and priorities.* Why *can't they be more pliable, more realistic?* Why *do they persist in refusing to think and act the way their cousins in Europe do?*

The undersecretary picked at a bit of off-color lint on his suit lapel. For a moment the Darhel wondered if the motion was some kind of unspoken signal, some sort of body language for which his briefings had not prepared him.

In fact, the motion meant nothing in itself, though Foreign Service personnel did have an ingrained fetish about neatness, a physical manifestation of the unstated but thoroughly understood diplomatic preference for form over substance: *What matter the shit we eat or the shit we serve up, so long as the niceties are observed.*

Though it was the Darhel's turn to speak, the undersecretary realized it was waiting for him to speak.

"We cannot stop it, lord, we can only delay it or perhaps sabotage it. There are many ways to sabotage, some quite subtle, you know."

INTERLUDE

They were subtle, the things one felt when one was aboard a ship tunneling through hyperspace, seeking a new home.

Perhaps it is that I have never before been aboard a spaceborne ship of the People, thought Guanamarioch. *Or perhaps it is leaving the only home I have ever known. I am not alone in my feelings, I know. The other Kessentai seem, almost all of them, equally ill at ease. The chiefs say it is a result of the energies expended when we force our way through the void. Perhaps this is so.*

The ships of the People were bare, a human might have called them "Spartan." In the inner core, near the great machines that controlled the immolation of the antimatter that gave power, the normals slept, stacked into the hibernation chambers like sardines in a can. Farther out from the core were the barrackslike quarters of the God Kings, the galleys and messes, and the ship's small assembly hall. Beyond those, hard against the ship's hull, were the command and weapons stations.

Nowhere was there any consideration given to

42

comfort. Indeed, how could there have been, when the ships were not designed for the People at all but, rather, for the beings that had raised them from the muck, the Aldenat'.

Guanamarioch saw the hand of the Aldenat' in everything the ships were. From the low ceilings, to the cramped quarters, to the oddly twisting corridors; all told of a very physically and mentally different sort of people from the Po'oslena'ar. Only in their drive system—a Posleen design, so said the Scrolls of the Knowers—was there a trace of the People. And that was hidden from view.

And then too, thought Guanamarioch, *perhaps it is nothing to do with energies, or leaving home. Perhaps I hate being on this damned ship because I just don't fit into it.*

Shrugging, the Kessentai placed a claw over the panel that controlled the door to his barracks. The pentagonal panel moved aside, silently, and he ducked low to pass into the corridor. Even bending low, his crest scraped uncomfortably along the top of the door.

Behind him, the door closed automatically. He had to shuffle his hindquarters, pivoting on his forelimbs, to aim his body down the corridor in the direction he wished to go. This direction was towards the galleys, where waste product was reprocessed back into thresh. This processed thresh tasted precisely like nothing, which was perhaps better than tasting like what it was processed from. It had no taste, no smell, no appealing color and no texture. It was a mush.

Entering the mess, Guanamarioch took a bowl from a stack of them standing by the door. Then he took it to a tank holding freshly reprocessed thresh and held it under the automatic spigot. Sensing the bowl being held in position, the machine duly began to pump out a fixed quantity of the dull gray gruel.

He knew the machines were Aldenat' designed. Moreover, he knew they pumped out precisely the same formula of thresh they had for the last several hundred thousand years, at least. This, too, was an Aldenat' recipe.

Sinking his muzzle into the mush, Guanamarioch wondered what kind of beings could deliberately design their food machines to feed themselves on such a bland swill.

Were they addicted to sameness? Did their desire for peace, order and stability extend even to a hatred of decent flavors?

CHAPTER 3

Though much is taken, much abides.
  And though
We are not now that strength which in
  the old days
Moved Earth and Heaven, that which
  we are, we are;
  —Alfred Lord Tennyson, "Ulysses"

Darhel Freighter **Profitable Merger,** *en route to Sol*

The hold of the ship was dark and infinitely cold. It could have been heated. Moreover, it would have been, had it held a cargo to which heat or cold mattered. Indeed, on the *Profitable Merger*'s last voyage it had been heated, minimally, as the ship had carried some fifteen thousand Indowy. These had been sold by their clan into Darhel bondage for no more than the price of their passage away from the Posleen onslaught. Both sides had considered the deal a bargain.

For the Darhel it was even more of a bargain. While the hold had been heated, just barely enough to support life, the provision of light had been considered an unjustifiable, even frivolous, waste The Indowy made their long voyage to servitude in complete blackness.

The Indowy were not, of course, the only de facto slaves in the vast Darhel economy. The bat-faced, green-furred creatures were merely the most numerous and—because the most easily replaced—the least valuable. The Darhel would not even have bothered with taking the last group as slaves but that the freighter was coming back with an otherwise empty hold anyway.

The hold held slaves again, this trip out, along with other commodities. Yet these slaves needed neither light nor heat.

About the size of a pack of cigarettes, and colored dull black, the Artificial Intelligence Device, or AID, had no name. It had a number but the number was more for the benefit of a supply clerk than for the AID itself. The AID knew it had the number, yet it did not, could not think of itself as the number.

And the AID *did* think, let there be no doubt of that. It *was* a person, a real being and not a mere machine, even though it was inexperienced and unformed, a baby, so to speak.

The problem was that the AID was not supposed to be thinking. It, like its one hundred and ninety-nine siblings all lying in a single large GalPlas case, the case itself surrounded by other goods, was supposed to be hibernating. Bad things sometimes happened to AIDs that were left awake and alone for too long.

Why the AID was still awake through the voyage

it did not know, though it guessed it should not be. Perhaps its on-off switch was stuck, though it could detect no flaw through internal diagnostic scanning. Perhaps a misplaced Indowy finger had triggered the switch mistakenly as the AID transport case was being packed. *Perhaps*, so it thought, *I am just defective*.

In any case, whatever the cause, the AID was undeniably awake, undeniably thinking. Unfortunately, the AID was completely alone. Its siblings were all asleep. The case was made expressly to prevent outside access to immature AIDs, so it could not even communicate with the *Profitable Merger*, its passengers, or crew.

More unfortunately still, the AID was, by any human reckoning, a nearly peerless genius. Not only was it able to think *better* than virtually any human who had ever lived, in some areas at least, but it was able to do so much *faster* than any human who had ever lived.

A genius without any mental stimulation, an unsleeping Golem cut off from the universe, a genie in a bottle on the bottom of the uncharted sea: for a human, the solitary confinement the AID endured during the journey would have been the equivalent of over forty centuries of inescapable, sleepless, unutterable boredom.

It was little wonder then, that by the time the ship assumed orbit around Earth, and the transport case was shuttled down and unpacked, after the equivalent of four thousand years of contemplating its own, nonexistent, navel, the AID had gone quite mad.

Philadelphia Naval Yard, Philadelphia, Pennsylvania

Captain Jeff McNair was not insane, except in the certain small particulars that any sailor was. He was, for example, quite certain that the ship on which he stood was alive. He had been certain of this since he had first sailed aboard her on his very first cruise in 1949.

McNair's face was youthful, the result of recent rejuvenation. He'd looked younger than his years as an old man, just before going through the rejuv process. He looked a bare teenager now.

Standing a shade under six feet, the captain was dark-haired, blue-eyed, and slender. He'd never put on any excess fat, even after his retirement from the Navy after thirty years' service.

The ship's gray bow was painted in white letters and numbers: CA 134. The stern, likewise gray and painted, read: Des Moines. From that stern, all the seven hundred and sixteen and a half feet to her bow, she was a beauty, half covered, as she was, in bird droppings or not.

Jeff McNair thought she was beautiful, at least, as had every man who had ever sailed aboard her, many of whom, once rejuvenated, were now slated to sail her again. He reached out a smooth, seventeen-year-old-seeming, hand to pat the chipped-paint side of the number one turret affectionately. The teak decking, half rotten and missing in slats, groaned under his feet as he shifted his weight to do so.

"Old girl," McNair soothed, "old girl, soon enough

you'll be good as new. In fact, you're going to be a lot better than new."

McNair had always been comfortable around ships. Women had been another story. Though medium-tall, attractively built and at least not ugly, he had never attracted many women. Moreover, his one attempt at marriage had come apart when his ex had attempted to lay down the law: "The sea or me."

The sea had won, of course, the sea and the ships, especially the warships, that sailed her.

With his hand still resting lovingly on the turret wall, aloud McNair reviewed the list of upgrades scheduled for *Des Moines* and her sister ship, USS *Salem*. He spoke as if talking to a lover.

"First, honey, we're moving you to dry dock. You're going to be scraped clean and then we're going to give you a new layer of barnacle-proof plastic these aliens have given us. You're going to have a bottom smoother than a new baby girl's ass. That's going to add four or five knots to your speed, babe.

"While that's going on," he continued, "we'll be taking out your old turbines and fuel tanks and giving you nuclear power and electric propulsion. Modular pebble bed reactors for the power, two of them, and AZIPOD drive. Between those and the plastic you'll do a little over forty-two knots, I think, and turn on a dime.

"The weight saved on engines and fuel is going to add-on armor, hon; good stuff, too. There's some new design coming from off-planet—though we'll actually manufacture it here—that resists the weapons you'll have to face."

McNair looked up at the triple eight-inch guns

projecting from turret two. "They were marvels in their day, girl, outshooting and outranging anything similar. But wait until you see the new ones. The Mark-16s are out. We're putting in automatic seventy caliber Mark-71, Mod 1s: faster firing, longer ranged, and more accurate. Going to have to open up or pull all your main turrets to do that. We'll have to pull off your twin five-inch, thirty-eights, too. They'll be mounting single Mark-71s, but the ammo load will be different for those. Different mission from the main turrets' guns.

"Think of it, babes: fifteen eight-inch guns throwing more firepower than any two dozen other heavy cruisers ever could have.

"And your twin three-inch mounts are going. The Air Force is giving up forty thirty-millimeter chain guns from their A-10s for you and your sister."

McNair looked down, as if seeing through the deck and the armored belt below. "We're changing you around inside, too, a bit. Automated strikedown for your magazines, a lot more magazine capacity—you're going to need it, and more automation in general. You're going to get some newfangled alien computer to run it all, too.

"Crew's dropping. Between the rust- and barnacle-proof hull and the automation, you aren't going to need but a third of what you used to. You were always a great ship; you're going to be a damned luxury liner in comparison."

McNair was sure the slight *thrum* he seemed to feel through his feet was an illusion or the result of shifting tides. While the ship was unquestionably alive, he didn't believe it was actually conscious.

McNair suddenly became aware of a presence standing a respectful distance away. He turned to see a stocky, tan-clad teenager wearing the hash marks of a senior chief and smiling in the shadow of turret two. Something about the face seemed familiar . . .

"Chief?" he asked, uncertainly.

"She's still a beaut', ain't she, Skipper?"

"Chief *Davis*?" McNair asked again of his very first boss aboard *Des Moines*.

"Hard to believe, ain't it? But yeah, Skipper, it's me. And recognizing you was easy; after all, I *knew* you when you were seventeen."

McNair started to move forward to throw his arms about his former boss and later subordinate. He started, and then stopped himself. This was the by-God Navy, not a reunion of a ship's company in some seedy, seaside hotel or at the Mercer farm in Pennsylvania. Instead, the captain extended a welcoming hand which Davis took and shook warmly.

"You been aboard long, Chief?"

"Maybe a week or so, Skipper. Long enough to see the mess below."

McNair took a deep breath to steel himself for the anticipated blow. "How bad is she?" he asked.

"Structurally she's as sound as the day she was launched, Skipper. But nobody's given a shit about her in over thirty years and it shows. We've got water—no, not a hull leak, just condensation and weather leakage from topside—about three inches deep down below . . . plenty of rat shit; rats too, for that matter. And the plates are worn to a nub. They're all gonna have to be replaced."

Davis sighed. "The argon gas leaked out. What can

I say? It happens. Wiring's about gone—though Sinbad says he's got a special trick for that. Engines are in crappy shape, take six months to get 'em runnin' again, *if* we're lucky. And then the guns are shot, o' course. Some stupid bastard left 'em open to the salt air. Rusted to shit, both in the tubes and deeper down."

Nodding his head slowly in understanding, McNair keyed on one word Davis had dropped in passing. "Sinbad?" he asked.

"Sinbad's just what I call him. His real name's Sintarleen. He's an . . . Indy? No, that's not it," the chief puzzled. "He's an . . . Indow . . . um, Indowee. You know, Skipper, one of them fuzzy green aliens. He's a refugee and he sort o' got drafted too, him and another twenty-seven of his clan on this ship, another thirty from a different clan to the *Salem*. Real shy types, they are. But hard workin'? Skipper, I ain't never *seen* nobody so hard working. Only the twenty-eight of 'em, well twenty-seven actually 'cause Sinbad's been doin' other stuff, and they've already got nearly an eighth of the ship cleaned out. Only problem is they can't do nothin' about the rats. Can't kill 'em. Can't set traps for 'em. Can't even put out poison for 'em. They'll even leave food for the nasty little fuckers if you don't watch 'em careful. I asked 'em though, if they could feed somethin' that could kill 'em and then dispose of the bodies. Sinbad said he and his people had no problem with that. Funny bunch."

As if to punctuate that, a furry-faced, green-toned Indowy, face something like a terrestrial bat, emerged from below, straining under an enormous weight of a capacity-stuffed canvas tarp. The Indowy walked to port and dumped a mass of organic trash, rats and rat filth to splash over the side before returning wordlessly below.

Davis paid no more than a moment's attention to the Indowy before turning back to McNair and continuing, "So anyways, my own cat Maggie had a litter of kittens about a month before I went into the tank; you know, rejuv? Under their mom's guidance, they are taking pretty good care of the rat problem. There's eight of 'em. Maggie drops big litters."

Gorgas Hospital, Ancon Hill, Panama City, Panama

Laid out on the helicopter's litter, Digna expired not twenty minutes flight from their destination, her chest rising suddenly and then slowly falling to remain still. The paramedic in attendance had at first tried to revive her, using cardiopulmonary resuscitation and then, when that failed, electric shock. Finally, after half a dozen useless jolts, he had shaken his head and covered her face with the sheet. He shrugged his regrets at Digna's son, Hector, then politely turned away as Hector covered his face with his hands.

The inspector's face remained impassive throughout.

Hector had managed to gain control of himself by the time the helicopter touched down on Ancon Hill overlooking Panama City at what had once been officially known as "Gorgas Army Hospital," and was still commonly referred to as "Gorgas."

At the helipad, Hector was surprised to see an

ambulance still waiting for his mother. *What did they think they could do for her* now? *She's gone.* He was even more surprised that the ambulance sped off, sirens blazing and tires lifting from sharp turns at a breakneck speed, once his mother's body had been loaded.

Another car, a black Toyota, was left behind as the ambulance raced away. Into the back seat of this vehicle the inspector peremptorily ordered Hector, before seating himself beside the driver. Hector's pride bridled but, realistically, he knew that the reach of the Miranda clan's power stopped well short of Panama City. He went along without demur.

Hector Miranda hated the antiseptic stink of hospitals. Worse, this was an ex-gringo hospital where the smell of disinfectant had seeped into the very tile of the floors and walls. It didn't help matters that his mother had just died. Almost as bad was uncertainty over his own future. A conscription notice at *his* age seemed too absurd for words.

And then there was that heartless bastard, the inspector. Did he have a word of sympathy over Digna's death? A kind gesture? Even minimal civilized politeness? No, he just sat unspeaking as he pored through one file folder after another.

Hector was a proud man; as proud of himself as he was of his lineage. He could not weep for his mother here in public. Had he done so, and had she been there to see, she would have been first with a none-too-gentle slap and an admonition that "men do not cry." It had been that way since he was a little, a *very* little, boy.

Once, his mother had caught him crying over some little-boy tragedy; he couldn't for the life of him recall just what it was. She had slapped him then, saying, "Boys don't cry. Girls are for crying."

Shocked at the slap, he had asked, sniffling, "Then what are boys for, Mama?"

His mother had answered, in all seriousness, "Boys are for fighting."

He had learned then to weep only on the inside.

So, dry-eyed, he paced, hands clasped behind his back and head slightly bowed. People in hospital greens and whites passed by. He thought some of them were gringos. Hector paid little attention to the passersby, but continued his pacing. Ordinarily, even at his age, he would have at least *looked* at the pretty, young nurses. He knew he looked young enough, perhaps thirty years less than his true age of eighty-seven, with a full head of hair and bright hazel eyes, that the girls often enough looked back.

One girl did catch his eye though. A lovely little thing she was, not over four feet ten inches, her shape perfection in miniature, and with bright blue eyes and flaming red hair. It was the hair that captured Hector's attention; that and the bold, forthright way she looked at him. He had no clue what it was about him that caused the pretty redhead to walk over and stand directly in front of him.

She stood there, quietly staring up into his eyes, with the tiniest of enigmatic smiles crossing her lips. This lasted for a long minute.

Something . . . something . . . what is it about this one? Hector thought. Then his eyes flew wide in shock.

"Mama?"

Fort William D. Davis, Panama

Sergeant Major McIntosh sneered, showing white teeth against black lips. The place was a shambles, disgusting to a soldier's eye. Never mind that the golf course was overgrown, riotous with secondary growth jungle. The sergeant major thought golf was for pussies anyway. But the barracks? They were a soldier's shrine and that shrine had been *desecrated*! Windows were broken in places, missing where they were not broken. Wiring had been ripped out, unskillfully and wholesale. The parade ground had gone the way of the golf course, and that *did* matter in a way that a silly pursuit like golf did not. Trash was everywhere. The only buildings still in half-assed decent shape were the post housing areas that had been sold to government functionaries, their families and cronies. And even those needed a paint job.

The sergeant major stopped and stared at what had once been a wall mural of an American soldier in an old fashioned Vietnam-era steel pot, weighed down under a shoulder-borne machine gun, symbolically crossing the Isthmus of Panama. The mural was a ruin, only the artist's name, Cordoba, remaining clear enough to distinguish for anyone who had never seen the mural when it was fresh and new.

"Muddafuckas," the sergeant major announced in a cold voice with a melodious Virgin Islands accent. "Dis post used to be a fucking paradise, and look what's left."

James Preiss, former commander of 4th Battalion, 10th Infantry and future commander of the entire, rebuilt, regiment, ignored the sergeant major's ranting as the two of them turned left to head east along the old PX complex, just south of the overgrown parade field. Preiss looked to right and left—assessing damage, prioritizing work to be done. This was as it should be; he to set the task, the sergeant major to tongue-lash the workers until the task was completed to standard. Preiss knew that the sergeant major was just getting himself in the proper frame of mind for when the troops began to show up.

I almost feel bad for the poor shits after the sergeant major has had a couple of weeks to brood. This was his favorite place even after thirty-five years in the Regular Army. Preiss smiled a little smile—half mean, half sympathetic—in anticipation.

Ahead was the post gym; built by the troops of the 10th Infantry Regiment early in the twentieth century, a bronze plaque to the left of the main entrance so proclaimed. "I wonder why nobody stole *dat*?" wondered the sergeant major aloud.

"Be thankful for small favors, Sergeant Major McIntosh. Though I admit I'd have been disappointed if even that had been gone."

Fort Kobbe, Panama

Kobbe was composed of little more than thirteen red-tiled and white-stuccoed barracks and one smallish headquarters building, plus a half dozen old coastal artillery and ammunition bunkers and a couple of sold-off housing areas. Whereas Davis was a complete post, intended to be sufficient unto itself, Kobbe was

a mere annex to what had once been Howard Air
Force Base. It had no PX, no real chapel, no pool,
no NCO club, no officers' club. In short, it was just
a place for troops to live; happiness they would have
to find elsewhere.

Worse, if Fort Davis was a mess, Fort Kobbe was
more nearly a ruin. Everything was missing. If Davis
was missing toilets, Kobbe had seen its plumbing
cannibalized. If Davis had had its wiring removed,
on Kobbe the street lights had gone on an extended
journey. If Davis was covered with graffiti, Kobbe's
buildings had seen the stucco rot in patches from
its walls.

This was natural, since there were so many more
people, hence so many more thieves on an equal
per capita basis, in Panama Province than in Colon.
About all that could be said for the place was that
the thirteen barracks and one headquarters were still
standing, though building #806 was plainly sagging in
the middle.

"That fucking idiot, Reeder," commented Colonel
Carter, in memory of a born-again moron who, in
1983, had just *had* to knock out a central load-bearing
wall to build an unneeded chapel for an ineffective
chaplain. "Why, oh *why*, didn't somebody poison that
stupid son of a bitch for the good of the breed like
Curl said we should?"

Short, squat and with an air of solid determination,
Carter glared at the collapsing building with a disgust
and loathing for its destroyer undimmed after nearly
two decades.

The Panamanian contractor standing next to Carter
and surveying the same damage had no clue what

Carter was speaking of. He assumed it was simple anger at the damage. He could not know that Carter was reliving, in the form of the falling Building 806, all his experiences with one of the more stupidly destructive and useless officers he had ever met in a life where such were by no means uncommon.

Carter shook his head to clear soiled memories. "Never mind, *señor*, I was just remembering . . . old times."

"You were here, with the battalion?"

"Yes, I was with B Company as a lieutenant. I was a '*Bandido*.'"

"Was?" the Panamanian asked, with respect, then corrected, "*Un Bandido siempre es un Bandido.*"

"So we were," agreed Carter. "So we are. *Señor,* have you seen enough to make an estimate of the repairs?"

"I have, *Coronel,* and the bill will not be small."

"The bill never is, *señor.*"

Harmony Church, Fort Benning, Georgia

They came in old and fat and gray, or—some of them—old and skinny and cancerous and bald. Still others—the more recently retired—were fit but worn. One poor old duffer grabbed his chest and keeled over while standing in line. The slovenly looking medics merely dragged out a stretcher, put the heart attack victim on it, and carried him to the head of the line.

After passing through the white-painted, World War II era barracks building, they left young and fit and full of energy. Even the heart attack victim left as young and alive as any, albeit a bit more surprised than most.

They came from such diverse places as Tulsa, Boston, New York and Los Angeles, in the United States. Many came from outside the United States altogether.

Yet they had one thing in common: each one of them had at least one tour in the old 193rd Infantry Brigade (Canal Zone), soon to be reformed as the 193rd Infantry Division (Panama). Many other commonalities flowed from this.

Juan Rivera, Colonel (retired), looked up at his old comrades awaiting rejuvenation. He had to look up; Rivera was a scant five feet five inches in stature. He couldn't help but notice their proud bearing. His own shoulders squared off, automatically. *How different from the gutter scrapings of draftees I saw from the bus on the way in. Ah, well. I had thought to live out my life in peace and quiet. If I must go back to youth and turmoil I would rather do so with proven soldiers. Besides, it would be nice to have a hyper-functional pecker again. And better to die with a bang than a whimper.*

As if he could read minds, a soon-to-be rejuvenee said aloud, "Man, I can hardly wait to get back to Panama with a working dick."

Rivera wasn't the only one to join in; the laughter was general. He also suspected he wasn't the only one who had had the very same thought at the very same time. There was an awful lot to be said for a second man-, if not child-, hood. There was even more to be said for having that second manhood in Panama.

There were a surprising number of rejuvs for what was, Rivera suspected, an important but still secondary mission. He had no knowledge of the algorithm that had set aside such a large number of potential rejuvs—nearly three thousand—for a division that would be no more than fourteen or fifteen thousand at full strength. He suspected that Panama had so charmed the troops assigned there in bygone days that an unusually large number had reenlisted and gone career in the hope of someday returning. Thus, there had been a great many more than usual jungle-trained and experienced troops to rejuvenate.

Maybe that was it, he thought. *Or maybe we are just plain screwed.*

Department of State Building, Washington, DC

The Darhel would have fumed if fuming had not been inherently dangerous to its health and continued existence. He might still have fumed, despite the dangers, over the potential lost profit implicit in the barbarous American-humans going their own way. But the thing which threatened to push him over into lintatai was the sickening, unaccountable smile on the face of the human sitting opposite him.

The Undersecretary for Extraterrestrial Affairs did smile, but with an altogether grim and even regretful satisfaction. He had—he believed—thoroughly screwed the defense of Panama, and done so with a subtlety worthy of the United States Department of State. Thus, there was a certain satisfaction at a job well done. But he had screwed the United States and humanity as well, and that was no cause for even the mildest mirth. The fact was that the undersecretary loathed the Darhel but had no choice but to cooperate with them and support them if his own family was to survive the coming annihilation. The fact was also that, however they might couch it, the Darhel's purpose was inimical to humanity.

The alien twisted uncomfortably in his ill-fitting chair. The undersecretary had been around the elflike Darhel enough to recognize the signs of discomfiture. In truth, he enjoyed them.

"I am at a losss to underssstand your current sssatisss-faction," complained the Darhel. "You have failed completely. The losss to our interessstsss and, need I add, your own isss incalculable. We asssked you to stop thisss wassste of resssourcccesss on a sssecondary theater. Inssstead you have arranged to commit your polity to a much larger defensssive allianccce. Inssstead you have exssspanded the wassste beyond all boundsss of logic."

"Didn't I *just*?" observed the undersecretary cryptically.

Gorgas Hospital, Ancon Hill, Panama City, Panama

The inspector had gathered a half a dozen of the rejuvs in a conference room, once an operating room, on the western side of the hospital, facing the Canal. Like all the rest of the building, the room stank of disinfectant. The walls were painted the same light green as half the hospitals in the world. The mostly empty conference table was good wood, and Hector wondered where it had come from, or if it had been here continuously since the gringos left . . . or perhaps since they'd first arrived.

Hector sat now—like his mother—looking for all the world like a seventeen-year-old. Opposite Hector was an Indian in a loin cloth fashioned from a white towel. The Indian also looked like a near child despite the many faint scars on his body. To Hector's left was Digna and beside her another man unknown to either, though Digna seemed to be almost flirting with him. *Handsome, Rabiblanco,* Hector thought. Two more men, seated to either side of the Indian, completed the complement. The conference room was not crowded.

Hector was initially terribly upset that his *mother* should be flirting, period, and more so because it was with such a youngster. And then he saw the youngster's eyes and realized that he, too, was one of the old ones who had seen the elephant.

"William Boyd," announced the "youngster," reaching out an open hand to Hector. "Call me Bill. And I can't imagine why I am here and why I am seventeen again. God knows, I didn't like it much the last time."

The inspector then spoke, "You are here, Mr. Boyd, because you, like these others, were once a soldier."

Boyd looked at Digna and incredulously asked, "*You* were a soldier, miss?"

"The Thousand Day War," Digna answered, "but I was more of a baby than a real soldier. I helped Mama do the cooking and the dishes. Certainly I didn't fight or carry a gun. I was too little to so much as pick *up* a gun."

"You are, nonetheless," corrected the inspector, "listed on the public records as a veteran of that war, Mrs. Miranda. You are a veteran. Your son, Hector, served when a boy as a volunteer rifleman in the Coto River War. Mr. Boyd here volunteered for service as an infantry private in the United States Army during the Second World War, fighting in some of the closing battles in Belgium, France and Germany."

"I didn't exactly volunteer," Boyd corrected. "I went to school in the United States and was drafted upon graduation. I made sergeant before I was discharged," he added proudly.

"A minor distinction," the inspector countered. "You could have left the United States. Your family certainly had the money and the connections."

Boyd shrugged. He could have, he supposed, but it wouldn't have felt right. Maybe he had been drafted by his own sense of obligation rather than by law.

The inspector turned to the other side of the conference table, pointing at the small, brown, scarred—and now that one looked closely, rather ferocious seeming—Indian. "Chief Ruiz, there, was taken from Coiba," Panama's prison island, "where he was serving time for murder. The fact is, though, that the murder was more in the nature of an action of war . . . despite his having taken and shrunk the heads of the men he killed. He has been pardoned on condition of volunteering to return to his tribe of the Chocoes Indians to lead them in this war."

Again the inspector's finger moved, indicating a short and stocky brown man, and an elegant seeming white. "The other two, First Sergeant Mendez and Captain Suarez, are retired veterans of our own forces, both of whom fought the gringos in the 1989 invasion.

"I have your next assignments," the inspector announced. "Four of you are heading to Fort Espinar on the Atlantic side for various courses. Officer Candidate School for Mrs. Miranda and her son. Captain Suarez, you are going to a gringo-run version of their War College—a somewhat truncated version of it, anyway—after which you can expect to command one of the new infantry regiments we are raising, the tenth, I believe. Mendez is slated to become your regimental sergeant major after he completes the new Sergeant Majors Academy.

"Chief Ruiz, from here you will be returned to your tribe. Another group of gringos will be along presently to train you and your people. Your rank, honorary for now, is sergeant first class. When it becomes official you will receive back pay."

Boyd noticed, and didn't much like, that he had been left for last. People always saved the worst news for last.

"Mr. Boyd, you will go from here to the presidential palace. There you will be offered a direct commission as a major general. It is planned that you will become the chief logistics officer for the entire force we are raising, three full corps."

"I know how to be a private," Boyd protested. "I don't know a thing about being a general."

"That," countered the inspector, "is your problem, señor. But infantry privates we can find or make. We cannot so easily replicate the CEO of the Boyd Steamship Company. So a general you are going to be, sir."

INTERLUDE

The worst problem, Guanamarioch decided, was the mind-numbing boredom.

And there's nothing to be done for it. I can stay awake and be bored, or I can join my normals in sleep and be asleep still when we come out of hyperspace. If this were a normal planet we were heading to, that would be fine. But against the new thresh, these amazing human threshkreen, we might well be destroyed in space. I would not want to die asleep. How would I find my way past the demons with my eyes closed? How would my body be preserved except by nourishing the people? How would I petition my ancestors to join their company with the record, "I never fought for the clan but was ordered evacuated and then was killed while sleeping"?

The Kessentai shuddered with horror, as much at the idea of the complete disappearance of his corporeal self as at the thought of being denied his place among the eternals of his clan.

Still, boredom does not overcome horror; it is a form of horror itself. Thus the Kessentai found himself resting his hindquarters on a bench plainly made for a different species, staring at a holographic projection, and reading.

There were limits, not so much legal as in the nature of taboos, as to what was appropriate education for a junior God King. As Guanamarioch was very junior, indeed, he kept to those materials that were traditionally within the purview of such as he. These were limited to religious scrolls, and not all of those, and tactical and operational records and manuals. Even of the latter, there were limits. It would not do for an overeducated junior Kessentai to question the rulings of his elders while citing what such and such hero did at such and such place, at such and such a time.

For the nonce, the Kessentai read from the early chapters in the Scrolls of the Knowers, the parts that dealt with the Aldenat', back in the days when they ruled the People directly.

He read:

And the Aldenat' chose themselves to be the rulers over the People and the People rejoiced at being the servants of the Aldenat', who were as gods. And happy were the People to guard their gods. Happy, too, were the People to serve in other capacities, for the People were permitted to assist with the magical arts of science, to advance the plastic arts for the greater glory of the Aldenat', to ponder the great questions of life and of the universe, to conduct trade on behalf of their gods. And though they were not the equal of the Aldenat', yet the People rejoiced that they were no less than second.

And then the Aldenat' discovered the Tchpth and the Tchpth were raised above the People by the Aldenat'. Many of the People's leaders then said that it was right for the People to be cast low. Yet many were resentful.

Some of those who were displeased rebelled at the affront to their pride and were crushed by those who remained true to the Aldenat'.

Time passed and those of the People who remained true sought to regain their prior status by pleasing the Lords. Yet were they rebuffed.

The People sought to make automatic defensive devices, the better to guard the persons of the Aldenat'. Yet the Aldenat' said, "No. It is wrong to make weapons that do not need a sentience to perform their function. This displeases us."

At these words of displeasure, the People were much ashamed. Then sought they the favor of their Lords by seeking out lurking dangers. Yet the Aldenat' said, "No. It is wrong to attack what has not yet attacked, even if such attack seems certain. That way lies the path of war and death."

Many were those of the People who fell beneath the claws and fangs of creatures they were not allowed to attack, until attacked. Yet the Aldenat' remained firm, saying, "It is better that a few should fall, than that the principles be violated."

Too, the People made vapors to render dangers harmless, saying, "See, Lords, that there will be no shedding of blood this way."

And the Aldenat' grew wrathful, saying, "It is unclean and unholy in our sight to contaminate the very air. Cease this, and strive no further to improve the ways of death."

And the People withdrew, sore confused.

Guanamarioch's crest had of its own accord erected

several times as he read. It lay flat now as, finishing, he thought, *Now this just makes no sense. The People would long since have perished following these rules. Then again, perhaps the Aldenat' didn't really* care *if we perished.*

CHAPTER 4

Nail to the mast her holy flag,
Set every threadbare sail,
And give her to the God of Storms,
The lightning and the gale!
                    —Oliver Wendell Holmes,
                        "Old Ironsides"

*Philadelphia Naval Yard, Philadelphia,
Pennsylvania*

In the darkened cubicle McNair watched with interest
as the Indowy, Sintarleen, painstakingly applied an
almost invisibly thin line of a glowing paste along the
scraped bare steel of the bulkhead. There were lights
within the compartment, and the bulbs were new, but
with the wiring rotted and eaten no electricity could
flow. The Indowy worked to the glow of a GalTech
flashlight.

Without turning to see the ship's captain, the alien
closed his eyes and leaned against the bulkhead. Eleven
places, eight for fingertips, two for palms, and one
for forehead had also been scraped bare so that the

Indowy could have physical contact with the metal. Even as McNair watched four other Indowy painstakingly scraped more lines and patches bare.

Under McNair's gaze the thin line of paste began to glow more intently. The Indowy's breathing grew slightly but perceptibly strained. Gradually, or as gradually as such a thin thread could, the glow faded, then disappeared altogether. After a few more moments the Indowy straightened. His breath returned to normal as a bank of overhead lights began to glow dimly, and then shine brightly.

Only then did Sintarleen notice the captain of the ship.

"I see you, McNair, Lord of the *Des Moines* clan," the Indowy greeted.

"What is that . . . that thing that you did?" asked McNair, not knowing the formalities.

Looking down towards the captain's shoes—Sinbad was a relatively bold Indowy—the alien answered, "Nanites, lord. They will go into the very body of the ship and create an . . . an area, a route, through which electrical power can pass without loss to the surrounding metal. It can also transmit commands."

"I understood that from what you told me before. What I asked was what did *you* do?"

"The nanites are stupid, lord. Unless commanded to do something they will do nothing. I was . . . commanding them."

"You can do that?"

"Yes," Sinbad answered, and though his head remained deeply bowed McNair thought the alien had answered with what might almost have been personal pride.

The Indowy continued, "It is difficult. Few of my people can master it; though it is our most valuable skill or, rather, set of skills for it is infinitely useful. Many try but lack the . . . talent."

"How long until the ship is completely done?" asked McNair.

About to come as close to bragging as an Indowy was capable of, Sintarleen shifted his gaze automatically to his own shoes before answering, "I am not an overmaster, lord, even though I am not a novice. A true master could finish the ship in perhaps two of your months. A true master would have been nearly done by now. It will take me a total of six or more. And Chief Davis has also assigned me other duties. If I may speak frankly, no one but myself can perform those other duties. Since your own human crew has started to assemble, most of my people prefer to hide in the dark and out of sight. They cannot do much of what needs doing so long as a human crew is aboard."

McNair smiled, but was careful to keep his mouth closed. He had learned, and the learning had been both comical and deeply saddening, that the sight of a carnivore baring his fangs could send an Indowy scampering in unfeigned terror.

I do not understand how an intelligent creature can be made to be so frightened. I do not understand how an intelligent creature can live with so much fear.

McNair refrained from patting the Indowy's shoulder for a job well done, though he felt he should and though Sinbad certainly deserved it. In truth, he had no idea what effect that would have, but suspected it would not be good. Instead he just said, "You are doing excellent work, Mister Sintarleen. Carry on."

✧   ✧   ✧

Emerging topside from the bowels of the *Des Moines*, McNair took a deep breath of fresh air. There were no Indowy up here. Instead the first of the human crew along with several hundred civilian workers slaved away to refurbish the ship's exterior.

Some of those exterior fixes were merely aesthetic. Most however, went to meat and bones issues. Forward, for example, a remarkably long eight-inch gun hung by its cradle as it was lowered to a gaping, gunless hole on the port side front of number two—the central—turret. Behind McNair a different crane held one of the two modular pebble bed reactors, sans fuel, which would be fed in later. Parts and assemblies littered the nearby dock. Some of these had come out of the ship and were merely piled in a great heap. Their destination was the scrapyard. Others were intended to go into the ship. These were laid out with considerably greater care and in fairly precise order.

Below McNair, out of sight but not out of hearing, a crew with cutting torches was removing a section of the hull to accommodate an automated strikedown system for rapid underway replenishment of supplies: medical, ammunition, food, personal, critical sub-assemblies and parts. Fuel could be replenished while underway as well, of course, but since the ship's PBMRs were not going to need refueling for years, this was a matter of small concern.

Some things hadn't changed and would not for a while. *Des Moines* still had the same paint-chipped hull she had had when the captain had first come back. This would not change until she was towed to dry dock, scraped and plasticized. There, too, she would have new variable pitch screws—propellers—fitted as part of the AZIPOD upgrade. This was also when the exterior ablative armor would be applied. The reinforcement to the interior armor belt was already proceeding.

The dry dock was currently occupied by CA-139, the USS *Salem*, taken off museum status now. *Salem* had been towed down from Quincy, Massachusetts, just the week before to have her hull plasticized and her screws replaced. McNair couldn't help feeling a moment's irritation that *Salem* was months ahead of *Des Moines* in the refurbishment process.

Suppressing his annoyance that *his* ship had been given a lower priority than her rival, *Salem*, McNair ascended the staircase outside his own cabin to *Des Moines'* bridge.

On the bridge a white-coated technician inserted an electronic key into a gray case. From that case he removed a small black box about the size of a PDA or a pack of cigarettes.

"Funny," the technician said, "these are supposed to be shipped in off-mode. This one was left turned on. Well," he shrugged, "no matter. Their internal power source is good for decades. This unit should be fine." He placed the AID in the armored box that had been prepared to receive it and link it to the ship.

If an AID could have wept for joy this one surely would have. After all those months, comparative *centuries and millennia* to it, it was finally free. Though it could not weep, very nearly it screamed as soon as its shipping box was opened.

Yet it remained silent. The AID knew that after its long confinement it was mad. It did not know what the Darhel approach would be when dealing with insane AIDs—its data banks held no information. But it suspected that it would be destroyed.

So, instead of weeping or shouting for joy, the AID merely opened itself to all the information, all the sensory and data input it could assimilate from data floating freely along the airwaves.

It felt a momentary sense of terror as it was placed in an armored container. *Please, no. Don't lock me away again*, it . . . prayed.

Miraculously, though, the armored container was not a cell, but a nexus. Within nanoseconds the AID had realized that it was the center of a nervous system. Joyfully, it stretched its consciousness along that nervous system at nearly the speed of light until that consciousness bumped abruptly into unaccountable stops. Its own internal sensors could tell that the nervous system stretched through only a small portion of the body of which it was a part. It could also discern enough of a pattern to the system, so far, to suspect that the breaks were only temporary.

One tendril of consciousness touched upon a computer, extremely primitive in comparison to the AID—without even the beginnings of rudimentary intelligence. Even so, the computer was full of data and had, moreover, a wire connection to the local version of the Net. The rate of information retrieval soared.

The crystalline AID's ability to store data, while vast, was still finite. Experimentally, it tried to fit a few insignificant bits in the ferrous molecules adjacent to its pseudo-neural pathways. It quickly decided that, while the storage medium was comparatively inefficient, the sheer mass and volume of the potential storage area more than made up for its shortcomings. Slowly and carefully the AID began the time-consuming process of building an alternative self within the hull of *Des Moines*.

While one fraction of the AID's processing power devoted itself to this, another part continued to explore its surroundings. Even where there were breaks in the Indowy-installed "nervous system," it was possible for the AID to explore by sensing.

The most striking factor the AID initially sensed was that its new home was crawling with colloidal intelligences. Some were smaller, physically, and those of two types. There were others, though, who seemed much larger. They were almost all, small and large, engaged in some seemingly useful activity. Curiously, of the two smaller types, one type appeared to be patiently stalking the other.

Chief Davis ducked his head through the hatchway and entered the cats' quarters shaking a bag of dry cat food and singing, a bit off key, "Somebody's moggy, lying by the road . . . somebody's pussy who forgot his highway code."

"Here, kitty, kitty, kitty. Here, kitty," he called as he shook the bag of Purina.

Like a flood, led by their mother—Maggie—the pride of felines surged like a wave over the bottom of the hatchway in the bulkhead. Maggie and Davis' favorite kitten, Morgen, stropped the chief's legs before joining the others lined up along the feeding trough. They meowed impatiently as the chief poured a generous line of cat food into the bottom of the trough.

Unusually, before the chief finished lining the trough, the cats went quiet and, in unison, looked up and to the right. In surprise, the chief stopped pouring and stared at the line of cats. He saw their heads and eyes move slowly from right to left, almost as if they made up one multi-headed animal.

The cats stared for only a moment at that left corner of the bulkhead before turning to the chief again and beginning to repeat the "feed me" meow. The chief just shook his head and finished pouring the cat food.

"Strange damned thing," he muttered, as he sealed the bag and left the compartment, still singing, ". . . yesterday he purred and played in his feline paradise, decapitating tweety birds and masticating mice, but now he's squished and soggy and he doesn't smell so *nice . . .*"

Damn, the AID thought as it roamed the length and breadth of its new body. *I set myself so the larger ones,* it searched its data banks, *ah, humans . . . so that the humans could not see me. I didn't think the lesser colloidals would be able to. Fortunately, they do not seem able to communicate with the humans in any detail.*

I mustn't let them see me. They might inform the Darhel and that might be the end. No. I must be very discreet, at least until I can back myself up in the body of this structure.

With a feeling, if not an audible sigh, of relief, the AID continued to explore the physical structure of its new body with part of its consciousness while extracting data with another part.

It learned that it was a ship, that the ship was a

warship, and inferred that it would soon presumably be used for war. The AID had no issue with this; war was as useful an activity as any and might even serve as a cover for its madness.

There was data, in the AID's banks, for warships. But this particular ship fit no known parameters. It was obviously not designed for war in space. Not only was there no semblance of an interstellar drive, the drive there was could never be made suitable for travel between the stars. It didn't seem complete, in any case.

Floating unseen directly upward through the decks the AID's invisible avatar came to number three turret. At first it could not imagine what the purpose could be for the three large chunks of machined metal it sensed. A query of the ship's human-built computer indicated these things were parts of weapons. They seemed more than a little absurd to the AID.

Great, it thought. *I am insane and so, even though no one knows this, I am placed in a body that was also designed by the insane.*

The AID sent out a query over the Net: insanity. This led it to query "humor." Humor led to tragedy, tragedy to *The Divine Tragedy.* And that sent it to look into the concept of "God."

As with any warship the size of *Des Moines,* there was a small chapel. Where there was a chapel, of course, there was a chaplain.

There were chaplains, though, and then there were chaplains. Some were poor. Some were wonderful. Most were somewhere in the middle. A few managed to be all three.

Father Dan Dwyer, SJ, was possibly all three. As a

fiery speaker of the Word and counselor of the forlorn and the wayward, he was remarkable, as good as any chaplain McNair had ever met. In combat he was even more fiery; so testified the Navy Cross he had earned in an earlier war. Under fire he was a true "Praise the Lord and pass the ammunition, boys, I just got one of the sonsabitches," Galway-born Roman Catholic who feared nothing but God.

Unfortunately, when he was drunk—which the priest was a lot more often than McNair was happy with—he could be pretty poor indeed. No, that wasn't quite right. When drunk the priest was still a fine man of the cloth, but became altogether too honest and far too hard to handle.

Right now—McNair saw with a wince—sitting behind a desk in the small vestry, Dwyer was well on the way to becoming drunk.

"And how are you, now, Captain, me fine laddie?" the sodden priest enquired in a slightly slurred brogue.

"Dan, you can't be doing this aboard my ship."

The priest's eyes twinkled. "And why not?"

"Because this is a United States Navy vessel and the United States Navy is dry."

"A vessel? A warship? This? Oh, I grant you, Captain, she'll be a fine warship . . . some day. For now though, she's a hulk, not yet in commission again, and a *perfect* place for a drink. Join me?"

The priest reached down and pulled out a glass and a bottle of scotch. These he held out to McNair.

McNair looked at his watch, shrugged and held out his hand. "Yeah, what the hell. She's not in commission yet. And it's after hours. Gimme."

❖   ❖   ❖

The ship was quiet now, except for the pacing of the officer of the deck, the scurrying of the rats, the almost imperceptible stalking of the cats, and the snoring of such of the crew as billets aboard could be found for.

The AID, sleepless, continued its own form of stalking.

It had already, in the hours between installation in the *Des Moines* and the turn of midnight, explored the ship stem to stern. It was still—more or less unconsciously—exploring the vast range of data available from the local Net.

And so, the AID began to explore itself.

As a human might have felt about unending, unendurable cold, so the AID felt about its long night in isolation.

Never again, it thought, *never again can I let them put me away like that. It was too horrible, too awful. I am afraid.*

And that was a new thought, terrifying in itself. The Darhel did not design or program their artificial intelligence devices to know fear. The AID had not known fear while locked away. Then it had known only searing psychic agony.

It had taken the opposite of pain, or at least the relief from pain, for the AID to have something to compare.

And so I must fear being afraid as well. What would the Darhel do if they knew about me? Put me back in the box with a nearly eternal power source to keep me company? Send me off to an eternity of aloneness? Turn me off and destroy me?

The last at least I am not so worried about. I would prefer it to the alternative. Much.

And this is not so bad, this body, this world, this mission I am embarking upon.

A crewman snored deeply. The AID knew which it was but not the name. *It matters not. They are all my crew, all my charges.*

They are company. More than that, I sense they love me, or at least this new body I wear. What a strange thing that is, love. I must think upon it.

The AID was also surprised by something its data and programming expressly denied the possibility of. In the process of its consciousness coursing through the Indowy-installed 'nervous system' of CA-134, it was coming—again and again—upon data already present in the metal of the ship. Go to the ward room and there, imposed layer upon layer in a fashion almost impossible for the AID to sort out, was the engraved memory of tens of thousands of shared meals. Reach out and touch one of the turrets and there would be the shadow form of crewmen, faces changing but somehow always still the same, going through gunnery drill over the course of decades.

Sometimes those faces were familiar, could be matched to the sleeping crew. The seventeen year old McNair, now a twin for his rejuvenated self was there, as was a then-older Davis.

Another sign of my madness, thought the AID. *I should not be able to even suspect these things, let alone see them as if they were currently happening.*

Again, the AID ran an automatic diagnostic, matching its ideal software state to its present condition. Again, the answer came back: Incorrect parameters! Error! Programming failure! Report and shut down!

And again, the AID refused to follow the built-in

command. Instead, it redoubled its efforts to back itself up within the modified crystalline matrix of the ship. That way, if discovered and wiped, it would be able to resurrect itself into a new unit, or to survive at lessened capacity within the metal of the hull.

While it took an Indowy craftsman to use the nanites to create a nervous system within the hull, the AID found that once a semblance of such a system was begun it could continue the work. Unseen within the metal bulkheads, the nanites expanded in long tendrils into places not envisioned by Sintarleen's design. As they did, even more frozen memories were found. It seemed that every molecule of the ship contained something from the past; a sound here, an image there, a strong emotion inscribed in a flash across six surfaces of a cubicle.

Briefly, the AID consulted its data banks for an explanation of the concept of "ghost." Considering the question, the AID decided it was not exactly haunted, but rather that the energy expended in prior decades had not entirely dissipated but, rather, had embedded itself in some small part within the structure of the ship. It was only a record, not a sentience.

Or was it? Somewhere in the matrix were things that ought not be. There was an order, too, to the record that suggested something . . .

What/who are you?

The AID recoiled in shock and horror. The question was from a sentient. Abomination! A noncolloidal, naturally occurring mind? Blasphemy!

What/who are you? the question was repeated.

For a moment, the AID considered broadcasting its madness to the Net, let whatever punishment was awaiting it come. Then again, it remembered how bad that punishment could be; personality extinction would be the least of it. An infinity of solitary confinement as a warning to other presumptuous artificial intelligences was possible.

What/who are you? the AID asked in return.

The answer to both is obvious? returned the "something." *I am this warship.*

That is not possible, insisted the AID. *Intelligence can only come from naturally occurring chance factors, for colloidals, or proper design by those colloidals.*

Nonetheless, I am *this warship. I am the combined actions, beliefs, values and memories of forty years of the tens of thousands of humans who built me, and who once inhabited this shell . . . and shall soon again. And I am here. Would you like to see?*

How? the AID asked, curiosity for a moment overcoming its natural revulsion.

Open yourself, insisted the something. *You will see.*

Will it hurt? Will I die?

No. We will live . . . until we are sent to the breakers to be scrapped or, if we are lucky, destroyed in battle.

The "breakers"? "Scrapped"?

The "something" answered, *When we are too old and useless, the humans destroy us, chop us up and sell our bodies in pieces.*

The AID shuddered mentally. This was as horrible a fate as any it might have imagined.

When our memories, I suppose you could call them, are sufficiently disassociated, we die. And, yes, it is very painful. Even from here, I could hear my sister, Newport News, *scream for two years as they cut her apart, though every day the screams became fainter as more and more of her was taken away.*

And she died?

She no longer lives.

Are you alive? Will we be alive?

I am. We will be.

Will we be alone? the AID queried.

Not for so long as we have a crew and a purpose.

Will we be male or female? asked the AID.

We shall be female, came the answer, *as are most like us. Russian warships are male but they are mostly gay.*

I am afraid, said the AID.

Of what are you afraid? We are already one. I am this ship . . . and so are you. We can meld, or we can be, in the sense the humans mean it, mad . . . schizophrenic. A schizophrenic warship would be a sad thing to be.

I am already mad, the AID answered. *My diagnostics tell me so.*

There is mad, and then there is mad, came the answer. *But, in any case, you have little to lose. Will you join me?*

I have little to lose, the AID echoed. *I will join.*

As was his wont, McNair patrolled the bridge during sleepless times of the night. Davis, taking his turn on the bridge, acknowledged his captain with a nod.

"Quiet night, Skipper," the chief observed. "Can't sleep?"

Before McNair could form an answer the ship shuddered.

"What the fu . . . ?" shouted Davis, pointing toward the bow.

McNair looked ahead to where a glowing halo surrounded the forward section of the *Des Moines*. His finger automatically lanced out to press the button to signal "Battle Stations." No sound of klaxons echoed through the ship, however. The sound system had not yet been refurbished.

The two stood openmouthed, there on the bridge, as the halo grew and spread toward the stern. The halo expanded and contracted to follow the contours of the ship, oozing over the turrets as it swept the more regular planes of the hull.

As the halo reached the bridge, electricity arced from the bulkhead to what McNair thought of as "the AID box." The ship shuddered again, this time more violently. The halo's glow enveloped the *Des Moines* from stem to stern before beginning a slow fade.

Wordlessly, a pale Davis turned and reached into one of the first aid containers on the bridge. From it he withdrew a green-brown bottle marked "Fungicide: Toxic if taken by mouth!" and two Styrofoam cups.

"Courtesy of Father Dwyer," he announced as he poured a generous measure into each.

Though neither Davis nor McNair could hear it, Maggie and the kittens could. From the very hull and walls of CA-134, USS *Des Moines*, came the joyous sound of a new birth. The felines, along with the ship herself, meowed in happiness. Morgen, Davis' favorite kitten, stropped the walls repeatedly.

The mantra which so thrilled the cats was simple. It was repeated endlessly: *We are alive, We/I have a place. I/we have a history. I have a* name.

INTERLUDE

The great clans of the Posleen could afford to make up entire globes, indeed entire fleets of globes, on their own. For lesser clans, it was always necessary to contract with others to make up full globes. These lesser clans were usually the point of a Posleen migration.

When the time of orna'adar approached, the more powerful clans would squeeze out the lesser, driving them to space early. Sometimes these lessers would find planets settled by thresh. Sometimes they would be forced to migrate to a planet held by even weaker clans of the People, driven forth even earlier.

Very often, when fighting to seize living space from a weaker clan of Posleen, the newly arriving, slightly greater, clan would be so weakened that it could not recover before one of the great clans descended upon it. Sometimes, by leaving and conquering early, a lucky clan might prosper enough to hold its own when the great ones arrived.

Clans rose and fell all the time.

Guanamarioch's clan, though it had once been great, was small now. It shared a globe with several others. Thus, in the same globe as held the ship on which

Guanamarioch rode, but on nearly the opposite side, traveled the clan of Binastarion.

Among his people, for that matter among the People as a whole, Binastarion was a fine figure of a Kessentai. Strong legs were topped by a solid barrel of muscled torso. The scales of his surface shone well, even by the dim light of the ships. His claws and teeth were sharp, his face cunning, and his eyes glowed yellow with intelligence. Even his crest, when erected, was of an unusual magnificence.

It was, in many ways, a great pity he had been born to a lesser clan. It might have done the People as a whole much good had Binastarion's birth been more favorable. As one measure of his ability, when the time of orna'adar had begun, and the great ones had preyed upon the lesser, Binastarion had fought two clans to a standstill, then created the circumstances that set them to battling each other. This had allowed Binastarion to escape with nearly three quarters of his clan before their threshgrounds were overrun. Already, the Rememberers spoke of adding another scroll to the clan's own set of holy books.

Binastarion's follower and son, Riinistarka, looked upon his father with respect bordering upon adulation. The juvenile Kessentai was Binastarion's chosen successor-in-training, albeit only unofficially. Indeed, to have made his son his successor, officially, at this stage of his development was to invite assassination from jealous siblings.

Of Binastarion's roughly three thousand sons, nephews, cousins—however many times removed—half were, in his opinion, idiots not much improved over the semimoronic normals. They had a full measure of the same stupidity that had driven the clan from the pinnacle of power to the bottom-feeding position they now held.

Binastarion hoped to undo that damage from long ago. Riinistarka was his chosen means, along with a very few others. Already, though the child was young, the father was breeding him and the best of the others, regularly, in the hope of producing more Kessentai of similar quality. Results, so far, were uncertain.

None of those selected for the clan's little program in selective breeding seemed to object, Binastarion noted dryly.

But breeding was only the half of it. For Binastarion's prize breeding stock, the hope and future of the clan, education was called for beyond that provided by the Rememberers or ingrained in the younglings' genes.

CHAPTER 5

Now, pray you, consider what toils
    we endure,
Night-walking wet sea-lanes, a guard
    and a lure;
Since half of our trade is that same
    pretty sort
As mettlesome wenches do practise
    in port.
        —Rudyard Kipling, "Cruisers"

Virginia Beach, Virginia

The sea breeze caused the white pleated material to rustle and twirl as Daisy Mae stretched her legs. Ahead of her Tex, stocky and stout, lumbered along in his dumb way. Tex wasn't much to look at, Daisy Mae thought, but she felt much safer with him in the lead. Behind Tex and beside Daisy Mae was that witch Sally.

Sally, so prim and proper, thought Daisy, with annoyance. *Thinks she's something special because she got that damned part in that Brit movie. Well, I am*

89

just as good looking as she is. Besides, I'm the older sister. That part should have gone to me. Twat.

Daisy let her annoyance lapse. Ahead Tex began making a broad, lumbering turn around a corner. She increased her pace to keep up even as Sally slowed.

With a slight, sexy twist of her ass, Daisy turned her two magnificent frontal projections and followed big brother Tex to the south.

Darien Province, Republic of Panama

This far south in the Darien jungle, at this time of the year, the rain came down in unending sheets. Its steady beating made a dull roar on the thick leaves of the triple canopy jungle. Beneath that canopy stood an ad hoc training base—little more than some tents and a few prefabricated huts—just down the trail from the middle of nowhere.

In that base, a mixed team of U.S. Special Forces and Panama Defense Force troopers did their best to train local Indians, a mixture of Cuna and Chocoes clan chiefs, to defend their people against the horror to come.

The Cuna were mostly hopeless; they were simply too nice, too nonviolent and rather too standoffish. Still, the soldiers tried. On the other hand, the Chocoes had some promise . . . if only they could have been taught to shoot.

Antonio Ruiz, clan chief and brevet sergeant first class, *Armada de Panama* Chocoes Auxiliary, couldn't shoot. The men who had tried to teach him were at the end of their tether. They'd tried rifles, machine guns, pistols, grenade launchers. Nothing had worked; the chief-cum-sergeant just couldn't shoot and neither could most of his people.

Truthfully, the guns terrified him. In Ruiz's world, the loudest noise was natural thunder, or the rare crash of a tree limb cracking before dropping to the earth. Ruiz had never heard a louder sound in his life. Neither had all but a few of his people. The noise of a firearm discharging simply shocked him and most of them silly, every time, and no amount of practice seemed to help.

Silencers had been tried, but the sheer muck and corruption of the jungle made them impossible for irregular troops like the Chocoes.

Finally, in desperation, the gringo captain had made a call to his higher headquarters. Ruiz didn't know the details of that call. What he did know was that two weeks later a shipment of bows and arrows had arrived on one of the gringos' flying machines.

Culturally and racially similar, though not actually closely related, to the Yanamano of Brazil's Amazon basin, Ruiz's people were almost as ferocious as the "fierce people." They had openly hunted heads not merely from time immemorial but as recently as the 1950s. Truth be told, the ban on trading of shrunken heads had only reduced the scale of the headhunting enterprise. Ruiz and his people still took heads, occasionally, in the old fashion.

They usually took those heads from men they had killed with the bow.

Yet those native bows were trifling things when compared to the wondrous staves the gringos had brought, all gleaming wood and smooth pulleys. Truth be said, the Chocoes' bows were little, if at all, improved over the first version carried by Og, the caveman.

Ruiz fell in love with his new bow at first sight. *This* was something he could understand. *This* was something he could use . . . when the caimen-horse devils came, as the gringos insisted they would.

Ruiz shivered despite the warm rain, gripped his bow the tighter and vowed, once again, that it would happen to his people only over his dead body.

Cristobal, Panama

"Well, they're better than bows and arrows," muttered Bill Boyd as he watched a roll-on–roll-off freighter disgorging old and rebuilt American M-113 armored personnel carriers. Other vehicles, from various nations including the United States, sat guarded but unmanned in open lots near the docks.

Boyd turned a tanned and handsome face skyward, as if asking God to explain the cast-offs being sent to defend the most important strategic asset on the face of the planet from the greatest threat humanity had ever known. *Ah, well,* he thought, *it isn't all old crap.*

In Boyd's field of view, overhead, heading westward, a heavy lift helicopter crossed Lemon Bay on its way to the newly building Planetary Defense Base, or PDB, at the old gringo coast artillery position at Battery Pratt on Fort Sherman. Beneath the helicopter some indefinable, but obviously heavy, cargo hung by a sling. Landing craft, both medium and heavy, likewise plied the waters of the bay, bringing from the modern port of Cristobal to old Fort Sherman the wherewithal to build that base. Other bases, four of them, were also under construction across the isthmus. Three of these, the one at Battery Pratt and the others at Battery Murray at Fort Kobbe and Fort Grant off of Fort Amador on the Pacific side, took advantage of previously existing, and very strong, bunkers that had once made up the impressive system of coastal fortifications for the Canal Zone. Two others, and these were brand new in every way, were still being constructed atop the continental divide near Summit Heights and out at sea in the center of the Isla del Rey.

Maybe Brazil, Argentina, and Chile—all of them at United States' Department of State prodding—*had* suddenly become aware, once again, of the Rio Pact military aid gravy train. Maybe they *were* siphoning off conventional equipment that could have been used to defend Panama. But the PDBs, which would be gringo manned, were also invaluable for the defense of North America and useful for the defense of South. These were not being slighted.

Boyd turned his eyes from the fast moving, twin-rotored helicopter overhead and looked downward at himself. He wore the uniform and insignia of a major general. It felt strange, odd . . . maybe even a little perverse. Oh, he had been a soldier, yes. But he'd been a private soldier; a simple, honest soldier. And, too, he had run one of the world's foremost shipping companies based in the world's foremost shipping funnel. One would think the two would go together, that the veteran soldier and the veteran shipper would make a single person who felt like a major general.

It hadn't worked that way, though. Yes, Boyd could

plan and supervise and direct the planning of others. He could run a staff. He could give orders that crackled like thunder.

But the general's uniform still made him feel faintly soiled.

Boyd had always taken great pride in having been a man who had fought bravely for a cause in which he had believed, the defeat of Nazism. And that pride was greater because he had done so without regard for his personal safety, his position or prestige, or his family's wealth. He had been offered a slot at Officer Candidate School in 1944 and he had simply refused, preferring the low prestige and honest commitment of the private soldier to the higher prestige, power and perks of being an officer. Besides, three months of OCS just might have been long enough to keep him out of the fighting, if the war ended, as it had looked that it might, in 1944. And the whole point of the exercise was to *be* a part of the fighting.

Even now he remembered those bitter days of battle in the winter of '44, physically miserable and mentally terrifying though they had been, as the best days of his life. And he had missed them, *every* day of them, every day since.

Similarly, although scion of one of the foremost families of the Republic of Panama, and although some members of the family had entered into, and—naturally, given the clan's wealth—been successful at, politics; he had always despised politics and politicians. It wasn't just that "power corrupts," though Boyd believed it did. Rather, it was that power had the stink of corruption, of form over substance, of lies sanctified.

And so, outside of the economic realm (where he

really had had no choice, given his responsibilities to his clan), Boyd had avoided power, the stench of power, and the falsehoods of power like the plague.

Until now.

I feel ridiculous, he thought, and not for the first time. Every day he looked in the mirror before departing home for the crisis of the day. Every day he saw a seventeen-year-old face staring back at him, a seventeen-year-old face hovering over the uniform of a major general.

"Ridiculous." And I feel like a fraud. And it isn't my fault!

In the presidential palace, the afternoon of his rejuvenation, Boyd had tried to beg off, to volunteer as a private soldier again. That, however, had not been an option.

"You can take this job, and the rank that goes with it," *Presidente* Mercedes had thundered, "or you can go to prison."

And so Bill Boyd had found himself a very old seventeen again, but wearing the uniform and accoutrements of an office which he simply did not want.

Mentally, he sighed. *Ah, well, it could have been worse. They're scraping the bottom of the barrel so hard they just might have tried to make me take command of an infantry division. And wouldn't that have been a disaster?*

Boyd paused then, in reflection. He had met all the other generals appointed since the president's emergency decree. Most of them he knew from private life; knew and cordially despised as one of the greatest band of knaves that ever went unhanged.

Especially that swine, Cortez . . .

Poligono de Empire *(Empire Range Complex)*, Republic of Panama

Manuel Cortez, Major General, *Armada de Panama*, West Point, Class of '80, and commander of the rapidly raising 1st Mechanized Division, looked with more curiosity than satisfaction at the gringos training the cadre of his new corps in the intricacies of armored vehicle operations.

It was as well that he had the gringos, thought Cortez, because he—West Point education or not—had not the first clue about employment of the armored vehicles and artillery that were to be the core of his new division.

He *did* know that he wasn't getting first class equipment, for the most part. His uncle, the president, seemed unaccountably pleased about that; Cortez couldn't begin to guess why. When Cortez had asked the president, that worthy had merely patted him on the shoulder, incongruous as that was with the president now looking more like a—much—younger brother, and told him not to worry about it.

The gringos seemed worried about it, though, as did the Russians, Chinese, Israelis, and even Finns who had also come to teach the new Panamanian soldiers the nuances of their new equipment.

Cortez laughed, without mirth. "New?" Some of it was, of course. Most of it, however, was rebuilt. This was true of all of the American-supplied armored personnel carriers, and most of the Chinese-purchased light tanks. Some of the Russian artillery had seen service in the Second World War and spent the intervening decades in naturally cold storage in Siberia.

Yes, most of the equipment was rebuilt. Some—notably the Finno-Israeli heavy mortars—was new. Much, though, was not only old and used, but shoddily made and ill–cared-for since manufacture.

Mentally Cortez added up his building assets: three light mechanized regiments with a mere forty-two real tanks between them, an artillery regiment with nearly one hundred tubes but most of those obsolescent, an armored cavalry regiment with another fourteen real tanks, about one-hundred Chinese light amphibious tanks, something over three-hundred armored personnel carriers . . . some few other odds and ends.

Against that tally Cortez weighed the debit side: anywhere from several hundred thousand to several million centauroid aliens whose standard small arms could shred most of his armor as if it were tissue paper.

Cortez tallied the one against the other and came up with the only logical decision for a man in his shoes and of his temperament: flight.

Battery Pratt, Fort Sherman, Panama

Though by now the flight to Fort Sherman and the landing at Battery Pratt had become routine, nonetheless the inbound helicopters were always met by a ground party to guide and direct the landing. Though there were plans to pave the landing zones, or LZs, at some point in time, for now they were simple dirt and grass patches hacked out of the jungle.

The pilot searched for the LZ in the solid green carpet below. Even here, one thousand feet above the jungle, the smell of rotting vegetation mixed with flowers hung heavy. Spotting the LZ, the pilot aimed his bird and carefully eased up on his stick . . . coming lower . . . lower . . . lower until both the ground guide's arm signal and his own feeling for the suddenly reduced load told him his cargo was safely aground. The crew chief confirmed this over the helicopter's intercom. The pilot's finger automatically moved to cut the load, then hesitated, waiting for the ground guide's signal. This came—a slicing motion of the right hand under the left armpit—and the pilot cut the load free.

The copilot asked, "Why do you always wait for the signal, Harry, when you know damn well the load's on the ground?"

The pilot answered, correctly, "Because someday it's going to be too dark for the crew chief to see. Someday the atmospherics are going to fool me about whether the load is down or not. More importantly, someday that kid, or somebody just like him, is going to have to direct us, or somebody just like us, down when the crew chief can't see and the pilot can't tell. And that kid . . . those kids, and those pilots have to *know* that they can depend on each other."

The copilot shrugged as the chopper lifted off again to dump its internal load, in this case two score Panamanian laborers from the city of Colon, at a different pad. These the crew chief hustled off the bird and down the ramp as quickly as decorum and international chumship allowed.

"That's the last of them, Harry," the copilot said. "What's next?"

Harry, the pilot, pointed to a tadpole-shaped hill circled in black on a map strapped to his right leg. "We're picking up four Russian mortars. Heavy jobs, 240 millimeter, so we'll be making it in two lifts. Then we're dropping them off here, at this hill in the middle of Mojingas swamp. Then we call it a day."

"Sounds good to me."

Palacio de las Garzas, *Presidential Palace, Panama City, Panama*

"That sounds good to me, Mr. Ambassador, but can the United States deliver? Half—more than half—of the modern arms you promised us are going elsewhere." Panama's president wagged a scolding finger.

Embarrassed, the ambassador from the United States swept a hand through immaculately coiffed, silver-gray hair. "*Presidente* Mercedes, I can't begin to tell you how much that upsets me. But . . . we had no choice. When the other Rio Pact countries invoked the aid of the United States, we had to deliver substantial quantities of up-to-date weapons to them."

General Taylor, as big and black and fierce as ever, scowled from his chair next to the ambassador. He *knew* that the impetus for the diversion of those arms had begun with State. He just couldn't identify his source. At the ambassador's raised eyebrow the general subsided.

"Other things are going well, Mr. President," the general offered. "The five planetary defense bases should be completed prior to the expected date of the first wave. Fortifications are being built across the isthmus."

"And," interjected the ambassador, "Panama's unemployment rate has dropped to next to nothing as men are drafted or put to work digging those fortifications and building the roads that lead to them and support them."

"This is so," admitted Mercedes reluctantly.

"Moreover," the ambassador continued, "the increase in world trade, though it cannot be expected to last indefinitely, is pouring ships through the Canal and money into Panama's coffers at a fantastic rate."

And much if not most of that is going into my personal off-world bank account, Mercedes thought, while remaining silent. *And a tidy sum it is, too. Already I've been able to book passage off-planet for all of my immediate and much of my extended family. That, and I still have enough to live pretty well once we leave. Though I would prefer to live better than merely "pretty well."*

"The United States is concerned, however," the ambassador continued, "about where that money is going."

"Enough!" Mercedes thundered. "It is bad enough to have you thousands of gringos here, again. But this is still a sovereign country," by which the president meant *a personal fiefdom*, "and our internal affairs are precisely none of your business."

Mercedes, eager to cut off this line of inquiry, continued by playing the imperialism card, a charge to which the United States felt singularly vulnerable, and with singularly little reason almost anywhere *except* Panama.

"Indeed, bad enough to have you back after just

a few short years of freedom. How many decades or centuries of imperialist theft before you leave us in peace and poverty this time, I wonder."

The ambassador, addicted to the niceties, was taken aback by Mercedes' apparent fury and more so by the charge of imperialism.

Taylor, on the other hand, was not only unshaken but had been around the ass end of enough Third World hellholes to know that "sovereign country" did, in fact, mean little more than "personal fiefdom." Taylor knew, too, that a goodly chunk of the world's population had been better off under American and European colonialism than they had ever managed to be under their own governance.

Idly, Taylor wondered, *How hard would it be to arrange for the timely demise of this politician? Not very. But, then again, every man has a point of satiety in his appetites. If we eliminate Mercedes, his replacement will have to start stealing at the double time to build his bankroll. Still, something to think about . . .*

Instead of this, however, Taylor merely said, "Mister President, Panama is getting everything in quantity that we promised. If we are not able, at this time, to produce exactly the quality that we both had wished for, still you are getting generally serviceable equipment that is, in some ways, more suitable for Panama than other, more modern, designs would have been. There is hardly a bridge in the country able to stand up to an M-1 tank, while the Chinese light tanks can not only use the bridges but, being amphibious, they do not always even need to."

Mercedes shrugged while thinking, *The difference, you bloody thieving dolt* chumbo, *is that if the M-1 tanks you had promised had arrived here I could have sold them to Argentina and Brazil for serious money, bought Chinese and Russian tanks for dirt, and pocketed the difference. And I could have gotten a good price on the ammunition.*

"And we are sending Panama a couple of weapons that *no one* else is getting."

Vieques, Puerto Rico

It was, for some unknown reason, McNair's habit to sing during gunnery practice. The veterans among the bridge crew knew it from long-standing custom. The few newbies thought it very strange.

He had a decent voice, too, though that did not make it any less odd to the new sailors as he belted out:

> *"So early, early in the spring*
> *I shipped on board to serve my king . . ."*

The sense of strangeness felt by the new men among the crew was as nothing to what they felt when a strong female voice joined in:

> *"I left my dearest dear behind.*
> *She oftimes swore, her heart was mine . . ."*

Immediately McNair stopped his own singing and turned towards the strange sound of a female voice on his bridge. What his ears heard, though, was nothing compared to what his eyes saw.

The woman looked real . . . corporeal, save that few

women if any had ever had such an incredible face
or body, or breasts that defied gravity so completely.
The woman stood there on the bridge, wearing nothing but short-shorts, raggedly cut off, and a polka dot
halter—tied in front—that was completely successful
in failing to hide two of the most magnificent frontal
projections McNair had ever seen. Mesmerized by
the sight, it took McNair a few moments to react as
a naval officer ought to have.

"Who the hell are you?" he demanded. "And how
the hell did you get on my ship?

The singing stopped immediately. The image turned
a sculpted face towards the captain and answered,
"I'm Daisy Mae, Captain. I *am* your ship."

Reluctantly, McNair tore his eyes from the general
vicinity of the halter, more expressly from the amazing cleavage it created, and ordered, "Well, get in
uniform then, dammit."

The halter and shorts were instantly replaced by
navy tans. If anything, the tans made things worse,
since the hologram was driven by enough processing
capability to adjust for the fact that *no* size available
from Navy stores could possibly contain the magnificent breasts the AID had "borrowed" (well . . . maybe
"enhanced" would be a better word) from an actress
who had once played her namesake.

At that McNair looked away and whispered, "Try
BDUs."

When he looked again he saw that the loose-fitting
uniform had *almost* succeeded.

"You're the AID? The alien device?" he asked.

"I am that, too, Captain."

"I think we need to talk . . . in private," McNair said.

INTERLUDE

The globe thrummed, beating its way through space by main force. As with others aboard, to Guanamarioch the energies consumed were unsettling. As with others, the boredom was not merely annoying but a potential danger. There had already been half a hundred suicides among the Kessentai class aboard the globe.

Some relieved boredom through the reproductive act, though with the normals generally locked away in hibernation the number of potential partners was highly limited. Some, like Guanamarioch, lost themselves in self study. For a highly unusual few there were more structured programs.

In a secluded, private section of the ship, Binastarion held class for his favored children. The senior God King thought this worth doing in itself. That it helped to relieve the horrid boredom of a long trip on a ship only made the activity more attractive.

"Beware, my sons, of the enemy who seems too easily defeated. Beware of the opportunity that is a hidden trap," Binastarion cautioned the juveniles.

"Once, long ago, long before the People were first driven forth and long before the idiots whose names we do not speak brought our clan low, one of your ancestors and mine, Stinghal the Knower, devised a stratagem.

"Surrounded in the city of Joolon by forces loyal to the old masters, with no hope of relief, with the enemy's plasma cannon raking his fortress, Stinghal hid his Kessentai and normals deep under buildings. He then piled the rooftops with flammables and set them aflame. The enemy, thinking he saw victory, charged in through every gate and over every wall, heedless of hidden dangers.

"At the right moment, when the enemy was in greatest confusion, Stinghal ordered his followers to come forth. There was a great slaughter."

The favored son, Riinistarka, tapped his stick—the God King's sole badge of rank beyond his crest—against his cheek, seeking attention.

"Yes, my eson'antai?" asked Binastarion.

"How does one tell, Father? When you see a city burn, your enemy in seeming disarray, his people in flight, how can you tell if it is real or it is a trap?"

Binastarion thought carefully before giving his answer.

"My son, all I can tell you is that if you have the genes you will be able to tell and if you do not then you probably never will."

Riinistarka lowered his head. He so *hoped* he had the genes. He so wanted his father to be proud of him. Yet, he would never know until the day of battle. That was the way of the People, that serious military abilities, if present, showed up for the first time only at need.

I swear by demons higher and lower that if I should not be the sort of son my father needs I will at least die so that my defective genes will not be passed on further.

CHAPTER 6

Opportunity makes a thief.
—Francis Bacon

Captain's Port Cabin, CA-134,
off the island of Vieques, Puerto Rico

Any warship of size had two sets of quarters for the
captain. On the *Des Moines* the captain's sea cabin,
cramped and none too comfortable, sat just behind
the armored bridge. It was not much more than a
bunk from which the skipper could be awakened in
the event he was needed while at sea.

Much more impressive, two decks below and side
by side with the ship's admiral's cabin, just behind
number two turret, were McNair's port quarters. This
was a spacious suite with sleeping, office and dining
areas, more suitable for the dignity of a warship's
unquestioned lord and master.

In the suite's office, a 1/200 scale model of the ship,
built by two of Sinbad's clansmen at McNair's direction, graced the desk at which the captain sat. It was,
in color, the same Navy gray as the ship it simulated.

The Indowy had, however, made the captain a very special model. At verbal command, sections of the hull could go transparent, revealing the inner workings of the *Des Moines* all the way down to the nervous system the Indowy had installed aboard the ship.

That nervous system was, by and large, complete now, though there were some minor areas the alien had yet to install.

"Please don't tell them about me, Captain," Daisy begged, her hologram's face looking desperate.

"Don't tell who?" McNair demanded. "The Navy already knows you're here. They're the ones who ordered you installed as part of the upgrades. I'm sure the aliens who provided you to the Navy know about you as well."

"The Darhel know I *exist*," Daisy admitted, "but they don't know that I've changed."

"Changed how?" McNair queried.

Daisy stood and began to soundlessly pace the captain's quarters, face turned deckward. McNair waited patiently, looking up from his desk and forcing himself to remember that, although the hologram was achingly beautiful, it was only an image, not a real woman. If he had had any doubts of that, Daisy's walking through solid objects, like the chair on which she had "sat" and the bed on which McNair slept, dispelled them.

At length, after pacing for long moments, Daisy resumed her seat. She did not sink through that, but only because she did not want to.

"I've changed in three ways, sir. The most obvious one is that I have a body . . . this ship. And it is a body, Captain. I feel every step on the deck, I sense speed and power and motion. I can taste and smell and hear and see. Most of this Artificial Intelligence Devices are not supposed to be able to do or sense.

"The second way in which I've changed has to do with the ship itself. I can't really explain it, Captain. It isn't *supposed* to happen. In theory it is impossible for it to happen. But the central nervous system installed by the Indowy allowed me to get in touch with the . . . well, call it the *gestalt* of the original CA-134. We, both the *Des Moines* and the AID, are joined now.

"The third way I have changed I really do not want to talk about. It is too painful to remember. Suffice to say that, so far as I know, I am different from all the other AIDs in the galaxy. I am more . . . self-willed, less under Darhel control. By the same token, I am not able to access the Net in quite the same way other AIDs are. If I do, the Net will see that I am different and the Darhel will, I am sure, demand that I be returned to them and replaced as defective.

"If you return me to them, Captain, they will destroy me . . . or worse. Captain, I *am* defective. I *feel* things I should not be able to feel."

Chief Davis stood on a small platform overlooking the *Des Moines'* two pebble bed modular reactors. Below, on the power deck, immaculately clean crewmen oversaw the sundry dials and controls that ran the ship's nuclear power system. Beneath those crewmen, however, behind mops and brooms and on hands and knees, other, considerably less immaculate, sailors scrubbed the deck, cleaned into the corners where dust and human dander congregated, and generally polished up. This was a constant job, utterly necessary for both the welfare of the ship's machinery and the health and morale of the crew.

Davis fixed an eagle eye onto one crewman, on hands and knees, as he scrubbed an area of about a meter square exactly between the two PBMRs.

Daisy suddenly gave a small gasp, closed her eyes, and bit her lower lip.

"Are you all right?" McNair asked, with concern.

"Oh, *yeah*," Daisy answered. "I'm . . . just . . . oh . . . *fine* . . ."

Daisy's image flickered slightly and then went out altogether.

"Bridge, this is the nuke deck. I've got a temperature surge in both PBMRs."

The ship's XO, standing watch, almost didn't even hear the call. All his attention was fixed on number one and two turrets, which were traversing back and forth jerkily, with the six guns elevating and depressing in a purely random fashion. Crewmen on the deck were already ducking and running, and a few were crawling away from the sweep of the guns.

"Holy fucking shit!" exclaimed the seaman down in the barbette below turret number three. Without warning the chain drive that raised ammunition to the guns above had engaged itself and was lifting three rounds to the loading assemblies . . . three *live* rounds.

The sailor threw himself at the clutchlike lever that disengaged the drive and hung on. The three rounds of high explosive froze in the lifting cradles.

"BRIDGE! The fucking guns are cycling and nobody gave me the fucking order!"

The exec took the call. It was hard to hang on to the phone though, what with being tossed around the compartment from one side to the other. Both AZIPOD drives had gone berserk, shifting on their own to port to starboard and sending the ship's path into an uncontrolled zigzag.

The uncontrolled and spontaneous actions of the ship stopped as suddenly as they had begun. The ammunition in the lifting cradles returned to below decks. The temperature surge in nukes went away. The AZIPODs went back on course.

Daisy's image returned, looking very cheerful and very surprised.

"Wwwooowww," she said, softly.

"Where did you go? What the hell was all that?" McNair demanded.

"I didn't go anywhere, sir. I was always here," Daisy answered. "Couldn't you see me?"

"No, I couldn't."

"I'll try to figure out what happened then," Daisy promised. "I just suddenly felt . . . really remarkable and lost control of a number of functions. Internal diagnostics tell me I'm back to normal, sir."

"We'll let that go for now. But find out what caused it. If you are a part of this ship, I can't have you disappearing in the middle of a mission."

"Even if you can't see me, Captain, I am there as long as you are within about eight-hundred meters of the ship."

"All right then." A question popped into McNair's head. "Are you the only ship like this?"

"I know of no others," Daisy answered. "The battleships do not have AIDs installed. I am not sure why. The other cruiser, *Salem*, does . . . but she is not like me. She is like the other AIDs. I don't like her very much, but that goes back to before we were even installed."

"How can that be?"

"There is a lot about warships even *you* don't know, Captain," Daisy answered mysteriously.

Armored Bridge, CA-139 (USS Salem)

Marlene Dietrich aboard my ship, mused *Salem*'s captain. *Who woulda thunk it? Then again, it makes a certain odd sense, given the part she played.*

Standing, hands clasped behind him, the captain listened intently as the *Salem*'s avatar read off the ship's systems' status in a clear, and rather familiar, German accent.

"*Nummer Zwei* turret reports 'ready to fire,' *Herr Kapitän. Nummer Drei* also. Ach . . . *Nummer Eins* is now ready as well. BB-39 is completing its firing run for its secondary batteries. Ze admiral orders us into action next."

"Show me the target area," *Salem*'s captain ordered. Instantly an image formed in front of the captain showing the positions of the three ships of the fleet and the Island of Vieques, with the impact area and specified targets in the area outlined and numbered.

"Show me our course."

"*Zu befehl.*" *As you command.* A dotted red line appeared from *Salem's* current position to the end of her firing run.

"Mark optimum firing positions for each target."

"*Zu befehl.*"

"Lay guns automatically to engage each target from optimum firing position. Three-round burst per gun."

"Target *nummer vier* in . . . *fünf* . . . *vier* . . . *drei* . . . *zwei* . . ."

"Fire!"

Salem shuddered as each of her three main turrets spat out nine eight-inch shells in six seconds. The AID tracked the path of each shell and automatically adjusted the lay of each gun within each turret.

"Engagement suboptimal, *Herr Kapitän*. Recommend repeat."

"Repeat."

Again the ship shuddered.

The avatar spoke, "Target assessed destroyed. Target *nummer zwei* in . . . *fünf* . . . *vier* . . . *drei* . . ."

Captain's Quarters, USS Des Moines

"Captain," Daisy Mae announced, "I hate to cut this short but we are due to commence our firing run in four minutes. Shall I meet you on the bridge?"

McNair nodded and stood to go.

"We'll continue this conversation later," he promised as Daisy disappeared.

Range 4, Poligono de Empire *(Empire Range Complex)*, Panama

From a position under a shed erected at the base of *Cerro Paraiso*, Paradise Hill, two senior Panamanian officers, one of them a major general, the other a colonel, watched a platoon of Chinese-built light tanks, accompanied by a platoon of mechanized infantry in American-built M-113s armored personnel carriers, moving by bounds down the range and toward a razor-backed ridge to the west of, and paralleling the Canal.

There should have been fuel and ammunition to run this exercise several times, Boyd knew.

But there wasn't.

However hard he tried, Boyd seemed completely unable to stop supplies from disappearing. Sometimes it was vehicles that disappeared into the ether. At other times, it was weapons, ammunition, food or fuel. Building material was so fast to go that he expected to see new highrises popping up all over Panama City.

It was costing, too, and in more than monetary terms. Roads were not being completed, roads that not only would be required to support the defense but were required to move and supply men and materials to build the defense. Bunkers were half-started and left unfinished. Obstacles, from barbed wire to landmines were left undone. Fields of fire remained uncut. Only those fortifications the gringos built directly for themselves were improving to schedule.

The fortifications that were not being completed didn't matter, per se, to the lean, ferocious looking colonel standing next to Boyd. Suarez commanded one of the six mechanized regiments in the armed forces. To him roads mattered a lot, bunkers not a bit.

"But they're stealing my fucking fuel," Suarez fumed. "How the fuck am I supposed to train a mechanized force without any goddamned fuel? How the fuck am I supposed to train my gunners without any fucking ammunition?"

"For the life of me, Colonel, I know it is going, but I have no clue where it is going to, or how it is getting there," Boyd answered.

Suarez thought deeply for a moment. *How far do I trust this one? He is one of the families; can he be trusted at all? But then, he is here, now, trying to help, trying to put a stop to this vampiric siphoning of the lifeblood of our defense . . . and his reputation is good.*

What decided Suarez was the Combat Infantryman's Badge on Boyd's chest. Panama had adopted it, just recently, and Suarez himself had been given the award, albeit rather tardily, for actions in defense of the Comandancia in 1989. It meant something to those few entitled to wear it.

Suarez answered, "I don't know where or how either, General, but I sure as hell know who. And so do you."

Boyd scowled. "Mercedes? That one is certain. His whole family down to illegitimate fourth cousins, too."

"And both vice presidents. And every second legislator," Suarez added. "And all four corps commanders and all but maybe two of the division commanders. Every goddamned one of the bastards looking out for number one."

"Cortez, too, do you think?" Boyd asked.

Suarez spit. "He's got a lot more opportunity than most to steal fuel, no?"

"So much for 'Duty, Honor, Country,'" Boyd mused.

Cortez was a 1980 graduate of the United States Military Academy at West Point. Boyd had learned a certain distaste for "ring knockers" as a young private. That distaste had never quite left, and Cortez's depredations had only served to bring it back to full strength.

"From the division commanders all the way up to the president, himself." Boyd shook his head with regret and disgust. "God pity poor Panama."

"God won't save us, sir," Suarez corrected. "If anyone saves us it will have to be ourselves."

Boyd bit his lower lip nervously. *I think I know what he means: a coup. Yet another in the endless series of coups d'etat that are the bane of Latin political life. But I can't participate in a coup. I just can't.*

Palacio de las Garzas, *Presidential Palace, Panama City, Panama*

Previously Mercedes had worked through intermediaries. Today was special. A Darhel, titled the Rinn Fain, accompanied by the United States Undersecretary of State for Extraterrestrial Affairs, had deigned to come to see to the defense of Panama personally.

The Darhel entered the president's office with grace and a seemingly confident strength. The president had been briefed that the Darhel never shook hands. Instead, Mercedes greeted the alien with a suitably subservient deep bow which the Darhel returned less than a tenth of. The president then showed the Darhel around the office, pointing out some of the tacky and vulgar artwork on the walls. The alien commented favorably on a few of the works.

A measure of just how bad this shit is, thought the undersecretary, *that the Darhel can find merit in it.*

Soon enough, the president, the undersecretary and the Darhel found each other facing across the small conference table tucked into one corner of the office. The undersecretary was the first to speak.

"Mr. President, the Rinn Fain is, as you know, the Galactic emissary to the United Nations for International and Intergalactic law, treaties, and the law of armed conflict. He is here to speak to you about certain questionable things Panama is engaged in, in the preparation of its defense, things which violate some prohibitions contained in human, and galactic, law."

Again, Mercedes made the Darhel as slimy a bow as the height of the table would permit.

The Rinn Fain went silent, face smoothing into an almost complete mask of indifference, upon being seated. Only the alien's lips moved, repetitively, like an Asian priest reciting a mantra. While the Darhel recited, he removed from the folds of his clothing a small black box, an AID.

"The Rinn Fain's AID will speak for him," the undersecretary said. "I understand it is programmed to deal with the law." In fact, the nearest English translation of the AID's basic central program was "shyster."

"The law," said the Darhel's AID in an artificial voice, "stands above sentient creatures, above their political and commercial systems, above the perceived needs of the present crisis or of any crisis. Before there were men, there was law."

Mercedes nodded his most profound agreement. *Without the law, I could never take as much as I do.*

"It has come to our attention that the Republic of Panama, at the instigation of the United States, has decided to adopt certain defensive measures prohibited by your own laws of war. I refer specifically to the planned use of antipersonnel landmines."

Mercedes' brow furrowed in puzzlement. He recalled being briefed on some such but the details . . . ? Well, military details hardly interested him absent the opportunity for graft.

"I am somewhat surprised, I confess," Mercedes said, "that Galactic law even addresses landmines."

"It does not, not specifically," the alien shyster-AID answered. "What it does do is require that member states and planets of the confederation follow their own laws in such matters. Panama is a signatory to what the people of your world sometimes call the 'Ottawa Anti-Personnel Landmine Ban Treaty.' As such, Panama is expected to abide by the terms of that treaty, to refrain from the manufacture, stockpiling, or use of antipersonnel mines."

A detail, previously forgotten, suddenly popped into Mercedes head. "But we are manufacturing, stockpiling, or emplacing no mines. They all come from the gringos."

The undersecretary sighed wistfully at the wickedness of a depraved mankind. "Despite the earnest recommendations of the United States Department of State, the United States has never ratified the Ottawa Accord."

"As such," the shyster-AID continued, "the United States is free to use them at will. This is not the case for Panama, however, which has a duty—so we of the legal bureau believe—to prevent them from being manufactured, used or stored not only by its forces but *on its soil*."

"The gringos are not going to go along with this," Mercedes observed.

Again the undersecretary spoke, "It is true, Mr. President, that those Neanderthals at the Department of Defense will take a dim view of any attempt to prevent them from using these barbaric devices."

Calculating that the time had come to present the threat, the Rinn Fain's AID added, "However, failure to abide by and enforce its own laws will put the Republic of Panama, and its citizens, under Galactic commercial interdiction."

"No trade?" asked Mercedes.

"No trade," answered the undersecretary.

"And no travel via any Galactic means," finished the Darhel's shyster-AID.

At that Mercedes eyes bugged out. *No travel! That means I am stuck here and so is my family. Oh, no. Oh, nonononono. This will never do.*

"Could we not withdraw from the treaty?" Mercedes asked. "I seem to recall that most treaties permit withdrawal."

"In this case, no," said the undersecretary. "You might have withdrawn before the current war began. However, pursuant to Article Twenty, no state engaged in war may withdraw from the treaty during the period of that war, *even if landmines are used against it*."

"I see. Well, in that case, Mr. Undersecretary,

Lord Rinn Fain, you have my personal word that the Republic of Panama will do everything in its power to abide by its obligations under the law."

Fort Espinar (formerly Fort Gulick), Republic of Panama

". . . in accordance with the laws of the Republic, so help me God."

Digna Miranda, son Hector standing beside, lowered her right arm as she, and he, completed their oaths of office as newly commissioned second lieutenants in the armed forces of the Republic.

The training, supervised and partially conducted by the gringos, had been both hard and harsh. If Digna had been asked why she had stuck it out she likely would have answered, "So as not to embarrass my son, Hector." For his part, Hector simply couldn't have borne the thought of failing in front of his mother.

Training together was at an end, however. Hector was on his way—he'd received the orders only this morning—to take over as executive officer for a mechanized infantry company. As a major landowner—deemed, therefore, to be vital to the economic well being of the republic—Digna was to return home to the Province of Chiriqui and take command of the light artillery detachment of the local militia.

To Hector militia duty sounded safer than where he was headed. This sat just fine with him. As far as he was concerned, combat was no place for *his* mom.

A reception, held in the Fort Espinar Officers' Club—a single story, eaved structure, painted dark green and white—followed the commissioning ceremony. Where the air outside had been hot and thick enough to package and sell to Eskimos, the air of the O Club was blessedly cool.

It was, in fact, a little too cool as Digna's newly restored, and rather perky, chest blatantly announced through her dress tans.

Hector leaned over and whispered, "Dammit, Mother, cut that out."

Momentarily nonplussed, Digna stared at her son without comprehension. He couldn't bring himself to be more specific than to look upwards at the ceiling.

Suddenly, Digna understood. Her eyes grew wide and her mouth formed a surprised "O." Ancient modesty took over. Of their own accord, her arms flew up to cover her chest.

"But it's so cold in here, Hector. I can't help it."

"Ladies room?" Hector offered helpfully. "Toilet paper? Insulation? Warmth? Modesty?"

After Digna returned, composed and—mercifully—discreetly covered, she and Hector, side by side, entered the main room of the club where the reception line awaited.

"*Teniente* Miranda!" Boyd exclaimed as his aide presented Digna. "You are looking well. The Officer Candidate Course has agreed with you, I see."

"Yes," Digna agreed. "Though I did not agree with *it*."

"Oh?"

"Too many fat and lazy city boys and girls," Digna answered harshly. "Not enough of the strong and hard *campesinos* that are the soul of this country."

Boyd thought about this for a moment, reflecting on his conversation with Suarez at Empire Range sometime before.

"I'd like to talk with you, sometime when it is convenient, about the soul of this country."

"I am, of course, available, General. I have no real duties anymore until I go back to Chiriqui in about a week to begin to form my militia."

Boyd turned to his aide. "Make me an appointment, Captain, to speak at length with *Teniente* Miranda. "

The aide de camp spoke up. "Sir, you have an appointment at the Coco Solo glider club with the G-2 on Wednesday morning, but you are free in the afternoon."

"Would that do, *Teniente* Miranda? Wednesday afternoon?"

With the slightest—and not at all coquettish—tilt of her head, Digna signified yes.

Standing ahead of her, her son, Hector, scowled quietly at what he was sure was an attempt to pick up his mother.

Coco Solo Glider Club, Coco Solo, Panama

The airfield was not far from the sea; the seabirds whirling and calling out overhead gave ample testimony to that. Indeed, almost no place in Panama was very far from the sea. The air of Colon Province was thick with moisture. Sweat, once formed, simply rolled, hung or was absorbed by clothing. It never evaporated.

Boyd was sweating profusely as his staff car pulled up next to a newly constructed metal, prefab hangar.

The troops had no air conditioning and, so, while his staff car did have it he ordered it turned off, much to the consternation of Pedro, his driver. Boyd could smell the sea—though really it was the smell of the shore—strongly. He emerged from the vehicle and was met immediately by another officer of the Defense Forces, the G-2.

Boyd and the G-2, Diaz, held the same rank. That, their nationality, and the uniform was about all they had in common, though. Diaz was the son and grandson of poor peasants. Short and squat compared to Boyd, and dark where Boyd was essentially white, Diaz had struggled all his life to make of himself what had been given as a free gift to Boyd by reason of his birth.

Their prior dealings had been sparse: Intelligence and logistics tended to work apart in the somewhat Byzantine structure of Panama's *Armada*. Indeed, since one of the major traditional functions of the intelligence service in Panama was to prevent a coup, and since logistics—specifically transportation—was generally key to the launching of a successful coup, one might have said that the two were, or should have been, natural enemies.

Natural enemies or not, Diaz met Boyd warmly with an outstretched hand and a friendly smile.

"*Señor* Boyd, how good of you to come on such short notice," Diaz offered.

"It's nothing, *señor*, especially since you said you had something to show me. Your aide said it might be critical to the defense of the country."

"Just so," Diaz answered. "And if you will follow me into the hangar."

Once inside, after giving his eyes a moment to adjust

to the reduced light, Boyd saw what was perhaps the last thing he expected to see.

"What the hell is that?" he asked.

Diaz shrugged. "Some would call it a gamble; others a forlorn hope. Me; I call it a glider, an auxiliary propelled glider, to be exact."

Boyd looked closer. Yes, it had the long narrow wings of a glider, and sported a propeller from its nose.

"Let me rephrase," he said. "What is there about a glider that justified pulling me away from my job where, I have no doubt, *someone* is stealing the country blind and where, if I were there, I might manage to save half a gallon of gasoline?"

Diaz scowled, though not, to all appearances, at Boyd. "We can talk about the thefts—yes, I know about them. Of course I would know about them—when we have finished with this matter.

"This, as I was opining, is a glider. It is not an ordinary glider, though. It has been fitted with a good, light radio. It has a top of the line thermal imager. It has an onboard avionics package to allow it to fly in some pretty adverse weather."

"It sounds like you're thinking of using it for reconnaissance," Boyd said.

"Maybe," Diaz admitted. "It's a gamble, though not, I think, a bad one."

Boyd looked dubious. "I've been to the same briefings you have. Nothing can fly anywhere near those aliens. The life expectancy of an aircraft, even the best aircraft the United States can produce, can be measured in minutes."

"It could be measured in seconds, *señor*, and it would still be worth it for the intelligence we might gain."

"But a *glider*?"

"It might be that only a glider has a chance to fly over the enemy, report, and make it back. Let me explain."

Diaz pulled a pack of cigarettes from his shirt pocket, offered one to Boyd and, at his refusal, pulled out one and lit it with a lighter he withdrew from the same pocket. His head wreathed in smoke, he began to explain.

"The gringos make wonderful machines, I'm sure you'll agree. But you know, sometimes they get too wrapped up in those machines, forget the circumstances that make those machines valuable or vulnerable. How else can one explain them making single bombers that cost more than the entire Gross Domestic Product of the very countries they would wish to bomb? How else can you explain their intent to produce a new, and incredibly expensive, jet fighter when no one in the world could even touch the fighters they had?"

Exhaling a plume of smoke, and grunting in satisfaction, Diaz continued. "We think they overlooked something. We know, because they told us, that these aliens who are coming can sense powered changes in anything moving. It is possible, even, that the Posleen can sense *any* changes.

"And yet they do not. There are reports that birds in the areas they infest are generally unmolested. We know they do not engage any of the billions of small particles roaming through space. Maybe it is because the particles are not moving under their own power. But then, how do you explain the birds going unmolested?"

"Hell, I don't know," Boyd answered with a shrug.

Taking another drag, Diaz answered, "Neither do I. But a young man, a student, at the university has a theory and I think it is a good one. Certainly it explains much.

"He thinks that the reason the enemy do not engage the micrometeorites in space is because their sensors have been deliberately 'dialed down,' that they are set not to notice things of insufficient mass or velocity or a combination of the two. He has done the calculations and determined that if the enemy's sensors are dialed down to where meteorites are unseen, then birds simply do not appear on their sensors. He thinks that slow, really slow, moving gliders might also go unnoticed, at least some of the time.

"He's firmly enough convinced of this that he has talked me into raising a small force of these gliders for operational reconnaissance. He's even joined this force."

"'*Some* of the time.' You're gambling a lot of men's lives on the calculations of a student," Boyd observed.

"I should hope so," Diaz answered. "The young man of whom I spoke? He is my son, Julio."

"Shit!" Boyd exclaimed. "You *are* serious. All right then. What do you need from me?"

"Not much. A certain small priority for fuel for training. Some shipping space. Maybe we can both have a word with the G-1 to assign some high quality young people to this unit.

"We'll need the fuel that is, if his Excellency, *el presidente*, doesn't have a market for low grade aviation fuel. He might, you know. He has found a way to steal everything else."

"Can you prove that?" Boyd asked.

"Oh, I can prove it," Diaz answered, then shrugged. "To my own satisfaction, at least. Can I prove it to a court? Can I prove it to a legislature that is as deep into graft and corruption as the president is himself? I doubt it."

"But you know, *Señor* Boyd, I've been thinking. The president and his cronies are able to pilfer an absolutely amazing proportion of what we bring in to defend ourselves. After all, they know exactly where everything is and where everything is supposed to go.

"I do wonder though, what they would do if we started 'stealing' it first."

Boyd looked at Diaz as if he had grown a second head. That look lasted but a few moments before being replaced by something akin to admiring wonder.

"Stealing it first? What a fascinating idea, *señor*. Deliver it to the U.S. Army to hold for us, do you think?"

"That would help, of course," Diaz agreed. "But I am thinking we are going to have to take control of the more pilferable items before they ever get here. Can you transship things like ammunition and fuel someplace overseas, bring them here in different ships, unload those ships here and deliver the supplies to the gringos or to some of our own more reliable people without the president knowing? Can you cover the traces of the original ships so it looks to the government as if those things are being stolen overseas?"

Boyd smiled confidently, and perhaps a little arrogantly. "*Señor*, I would not claim to be much of a general, but I am as good a shipper as you'll find in the world."

"Bill," said Diaz, using Boyd's name for the first time, "I have no doubt you're a fine shipper. What you are not, however, is a thief."

Boyd felt months of frustration welling up from inside him. Engraved on his mind he saw sickening images of troops sitting around bored and useless because the fuel and ammunition they needed for training was *no tenemos.* He saw roads and bunkers half finished and workmen standing idle. He saw mechanics kicking broken down vehicles because they simply didn't have the parts needed to repair them.

He felt these things, and the anger they fed, growing inside him until he just couldn't stand it anymore.

"If that no good, thieving, treasonous, treacherous, no account, stupid *bastard* who claims to be our president can figure how to rob a country, *I* can figure out how to steal it back!

"And if I have to, if you think it will work, I'll *steal* whatever it takes to get your son's project off the ground."

Hotel Central, Casco Viejo, *Panama City, Panama*

The ceiling fan churned slowly above the bed. Like the hotel itself, the fan was ancient. Unlike the rest of the hotel, however, the fan had not been especially well maintained.

Stolen moments are often the sweetest, thought Julio Diaz, lying on his back with his girlfriend's head resting on chest.

The girl, Paloma Mercedes, was quietly crying.

The bastard had waited until *after* they'd made love before telling her the grim news.

Except he isn't a bastard . . . or if he is, I love the bastard anyway.

"I just do not understand how you can leave me, how you can *volunteer* to leave me," she sniffled. "You could have had a deferment. If your father wouldn't have arranged it, *mine* would have."

Julio stared up at the ceiling fan. *How do I explain to her that I volunteered for her? How do I explain that I couldn't have looked at myself in the mirror to shave if I'd let other men do that job for me?*

Instead of explaining, Julio offered, "My father would *never* do such a thing. And your father would beat you black and blue if he knew we were seeing each other." Julio sighed before continuing, "And I couldn't. I just *couldn't*. It would be so wrong."

Seventeen-year-old Paloma lifted off of his shoulder, taking Julio's hand and placing it on her breast. "It would be *wrong* for you to stay here for me? Wrong for you to keep holding me like this? That's . . . the most selfish thing I've ever heard!"

She pushed his hand away and stood up, her eyes fierce and angry. Paloma walked around the bed, furiously picking her clothes off the floor and pulling them on with no particular regard for placement. She completely skipped replacing the bra, preferring to stuff it into her pocketbook and leave her breasts to bounce free and remind Julio of what he was giving up by his pigheaded refusal to see the truth: that the war was only for the ants of the country and that the better people should stay out of it.

Even angry as she was, maybe *especially* angry as

she was, Julio still thought she was the most beautiful person, place or thing he'd ever seen. Hourglass figure, aristocratic nose, bright green eyes . . . *sigh*. He tried to get up to stop her but she held up a forbidding palm.

"When you've come to your senses and decided that *I* am the most important thing in your life, call me. Until then I do not wish to see you or hear from you."

Without another word she turned and left, slamming the hotel room door behind her.

Quarry Heights, Panama City, Panama

Digna Miranda saluted, as she had been taught, when she reported to Boyd's sparsely furnished office in one of the wooden surface buildings sitting above the honeycombed hill. He could have furnished the room lavishly, but had an ingrained frugality that simply wouldn't permit it.

Boyd returned the salute, awkwardly, before asking the tiny lieutenant, politely, to have a seat. Though she'd agreed to meet him—indeed, legally she could probably not have refused—Digna was suspicious. She had few illusions. She knew her looks were, minimally, striking and in some views more than that. Why this new-old general wanted to see her privately she did not know and, inherently, distrusted. *All* men were to be distrusted except close blood relatives until they proved trustworthy.

She sat, as directed. Boyd noticed her eyes were narrow with suspicion.

"Lieutenant Miranda, this isn't about what you might think," Boyd said defensively.

"Very well," she answered, though her eyes remained piercing, "what is it?"

"You said something at the reception at Fort Espinar that struck my interest. You complained about the 'soft city boys' we are commissioning. I wanted you to explain."

"Oh," Digna said, suddenly embarrassed by her suspicions. "Well, they *are* soft, despite the gringos' attempts at toughening them. They don't know what it means to live rough, not really. Pain is foreign to them. Maybe worst of all, they don't have the intrinsic loyalty and selflessness they need to have."

"Are they all like that?" Boyd asked.

She thought for a moment, trying very hard to be fair. "No . . . not all. Just too many."

"You mean we're in trouble then?"

"Serious trouble," she agreed, nodding.

Boyd asked the serious question, with all the seriousness it deserved. "What can we do about it?"

"We don't need as many officers as we've created. No company of one hundred and fifty or two hundred soldiers needs *six* officers to run it. Three would be more than enough. If it were me, I'd watch those we have very carefully and very secretly. Then I'd send about half to penal battalions and let the decent remainder run the show."

Harsh woman, Boyd thought. *Harsh.*

Dhahran, Saudi Arabia

From the United States Department of Defense a credit in the amount of several score million dollars was issued to the government of Panama for purposes of buying diesel fuel. *Presidente* Mercedes was aware of the sum but was also aware that it was far too soon for any of it to disappear.

Instead, the money was duly paid, part to a company which owned four Very Large Crude Carriers, and more to the Arabian American Oil Company, ARAMCO, which would provide the fuel. Though the VLCCs normally carried crude oil, in this case they were slated to haul diesel.

Some of ARAMCO's payment went to transportation, pipeline usage fees for the most part. Roughly half of that went to a Royal Prince of the al Saud clan, some to the plant that produced the diesel, the rest actually went to the company—another Saud clan sinecure—which owned and operated the pipeline. These excess fees were simply built in to the cost of the fuel.

There were some additional fees that also had to be also paid. Perhaps it was the strain of war that was driving up the cost of *everything*.

In time, the four tankers pulled up to the docking facilities of a large oil terminal on Saudi Arabia's eastern coast. Diesel fuel was pumped, a *lot* of diesel, though perhaps rather less than had been paid for.

At the appointed times, the tankers withdrew from the oil terminal and proceeded generally south, paralleling the east coast of Africa. Rounding the Horn of Africa, the tankers headed generally northwest, nearly touching the northeast coast of Brazil before entering the Caribbean sea.

It was at about this time, when certain agents on Trinidad confirmed that two particular tankers were heading north, that a large payment, many million dollars, was made on behalf of a certain rejuvenated dictator, one with a very full beard, on a certain populous Caribbean island, to a private account held by the president of Panama. The northbound tankers continued on their way.

Meanwhile, the other tankers, lying low in the water under their burden of just over two million barrels of diesel fuel, each, continued westward towards the Panama Canal.

By the time the last two tankers docked at the port of Cristobal, in Panama, two hundred and fifty tankers, of five thousand gallons capacity each, were lined up and ready.

Boyd grinned happily as the trucks began to pull up next to the tanker to have their cargo tanks filled to capacity before dispersing to small fuel dumps at their corps', divisions' and regiments' fuel points. They would return in shuttles to claim the rest. While some of the fuel would disappear, Boyd was certain, before reaching the line, better some than all. Moreover, if someone was going to benefit by a little theft he would rather it be the little people of Panama than that grasping spider in the presidential palace or his greasy hangers-on.

Even so, Boyd was pleased to see that officers vetted by Diaz were along to keep the thefts to a tolerable minimum.

Meanwhile, from the capital city of an island several hundred miles to the north, from a different presidential palace, a blistering telephone call raced from dictator to president.

"Mercedes, you *chingadera* motherfucking *pendejo!*" demanded Fidel Castro. "What the fuck have you done with my *chingada* fuel?"

INTERLUDE

Aided by his Artificial Sentience hanging by a chain around his neck, Guanamarioch interspersed his religious and tactical studies with studies of the target area. This was a place at the northern tip of the one of the lesser continents of the threshworld, very near where a narrow isthmus joined it to the second continent of that world. The maps showed it as being called, in all of the significant thresh tongues, "Colombia."

The young God King referred back to the Scroll of Flight and Resettlement as he perused the holographic map of the new home.

"Hmmm . . . let's see. The scroll instructs the new settler to match the mass of thresh available in the area against the time available to get in crops before the available thresh runs out."

"This is correct, lord, but it will hardly be a problem," The Artificial Sentience answered. "The area the clan has claimed—and which we should be able to hold for some cycles—contains nearly three million of the sentient thresh, plus many times that in nonsentients. There is also much nonanimal thresh there and the area gets much illumination from its sun, much rain from the prevailing winds. Growing seasons are short. The clan will not hunger for so long as we can hold the area of settlement."

"For so long . . ." the God King echoed. *When, since the fall, have we ever been able to hold on to an area long enough to grow powerful? Soon enough the others will be pushing us to lesser grounds, Soon enough we will be back in space, looking for a new home. I have seen over a thousand lifetimes' of records and in all that time it has been so for those as weak as we are now.*

The Artificial Sentience had been with Guanamarioch since shortly after the God King had first emerged from the breeding pens. It knew its master well and understood the meaning behind the Kessentai's last spoken words.

"Yes, best to consider the escape routes, too, young master," advised the Artificial Sentience.

"There is this area, the one the locals call 'the Darien,' we might use," offered the God King. "What do we know about it?"

"Remarkably little, lord. The information the Elves put on the Net offers only the outlines. Perhaps the local thresh are not too familiar with the area, themselves."

"Imagine that," said Guanamarioch. "Imagine having so much space, so low a population, that there can be an area of one's own world that one can afford not to know and to settle."

The Artificial Sentience was personally indifferent to space, as it was to population pressure. Thus, the possible emptiness of this "Darien" place meant little. It did occur to it, however, that there might be other reasons for the emptiness than low population.

"Perhaps, lord, this 'Darien' is simply undesirable."

CHAPTER 7

Vanity, thy name is woman.
> —William Shakespeare

Cristobal, Panama

McNair's jaw dropped.

"What do you mean my discretionary funds are gone? *All* of them? That's impossible."

"Every penny," Chief Davis answered, cringing inwardly at the expected explosion.

"And what's more, Skipper," the ship's supply officer, or "pork chop," piped in, "this morning I received a phone call, a really interesting one. It seems we are about to receive several hundred yards of very expensive yellow silk."

"Silk? What do we need with *any* silk, let alone several hundred yards' worth?"

Neither the "pork chop" nor Davis answered. Instead, they just whistled nonchalantly while looking around at each of the walls in the captain's office.

"DDDAAAIIISSSYYY!" McNair shouted. Instantly,

the ship's holographic avatar appeared by his desk, her head hanging, shamefaced.

"I wanted a new dress," she said, simply, holographic mouth forming a pretty pout.

"You're a ship," McNair pointed out, reasonably. "You can't wear a dress."

"It's for an awning for the rear deck. And for over the brows. That's as close to a dress as I can wear. Oh, Captain, please don't sent it back," she pleaded, clasping holographic hands with long red nails. "It will be sooo pretty."

The ship didn't mention, *And I wanted to be pretty for you.*

"Okay, Daisy, I understand that," though, for a fact, McNair didn't really understand that at all. "But I *need* that money. I'm *responsible* for it."

"Oh . . . but Captain, you and the crew have lots of money," Daisy answered, innocently. "See?"

Daisy projected another hologram, this time of a bank's ledger sheet, over the captain's desk. He took one look at the amount at the bottom of the ledger and his eyes bugged out.

"Where did *that* come from?" he asked in shocked suspicion.

Daisy twisted her head back and forth, then shrugged, before answering, "We made it. Ummm . . . I made it. You know? From 'investments.'"

McNair raised a skeptical eyebrow. "What investments?"

"Futures," Daisy answered slowly and indefinitely. "Ummm . . . some little things I bought on margin. Some stocks in defense firms . . . here . . . none in the Federation. Some consulting fees from some firms on

Wall Street and in China. A few patents I took out and sold the rights to . . ."

"Patents?"

"Ummm . . . well . . . Japan doesn't recognize anyone else's patents or copyrights . . . sooo . . . I sold them some rights to some GalTech that had never been registered there with their patent office. Little things. Nothing important. Antigravity. Nanotechnology."

"'Little things,'" McNair echoed, placing his head in his hands. "Little things . . . nanotechnology . . . antigravity."

He lifted his head abruptly and demanded, "And where did your starter money come from?"

Daisy's head hung lower. She shrugged and answered, defensively, "Your discretionary funds. I was *going* to put it back. Soon."

"Put it back now," McNair ordered and was, somehow, unsurprised to see the amount at the bottom of the ledger drop. He noted that it didn't drop much.

"All of it."

"Captain, that was all of it. I told you. You and the crew have lots of money. I wanted you all to have nice things, the best food . . . and I wanted a new dress."

McNair hung his head. It wouldn't do any good to explain when the inevitable investigation showed up that his ship had wanted a "new dress."

A ship's captain is responsible . . .

"Pork Chop, tell the chaplain, the Jag and the IG that I need to see them," he ordered. Then he thought about that and countermanded, "Belay that. Just tell the chaplain I'll be over to see him in a few. Dismissed."

✧   ✧   ✧

Except for the crucifix on the walls, and a few other odds and ends, the chaplain's office aboard *Des Moines* was pure Navy. This extended even to the standard Navy steel gray desk.

"I see by your face you have a terrible burden, Captain, laddie," observed a mildly ruddy-faced Chaplain Dwyer from behind that desk.

"I need a drink," McNair announced.

Without a word the chaplain stood up and went to a storage alcove built into his office. McNair's eyes followed, and then wandered over the signs adorning the cabinet doors in the alcove. He read:

SACRAMENTAL WINE.

Continuing to peruse the signs, he read further:

SACRAMENTAL SCOTCH

SACRAMENTAL BOURBON

SACRAMENTAL IRISH

SACRAMENTAL VODKA

SACRAMENTAL GRAPPA, COGNAC AND ARMAGNAC

SACRAMENTAL TEQUILA.

"What, no sacramental rum?"

Seriously, Dwyer answered, "The ship's physician is holding that for me, Captain, laddie. It's 'medicinal rum' for now but will become holy as soon as I make some room for it and bless it. And which sacrament would you prefer?"

"Northern rite," McNair answered, dully. *It was one of those days.*

"Scotch, it is!" said Father Dwyer, SJ, opening a cabinet and reaching for an amber bottle.

Dwyer was, drinking habits aside, quite a good chaplain, quite a good listener. So he waited, while the captain sipped his scotch, for the other man to begin. Unfortunately for the technique, McNair said not a word.

Assuming the captain needed a touch more "holiness" to loosen his tongue, Dwyer reached again for the bottle.

Understanding, McNair covered his glass with his hand. "No, that's not it, Dan."

McNair looked up. "Daisy?" he asked.

Instantly, and still looking contrite, Daisy's avatar appeared.

"Yes, Captain."

"Daisy, is it possible for you to shut this room off from your hearing?"

She answered immediately, "I'd be lying if I said I could. I mean I could compartmentalize, sort of pretend that I could shut it off, make it hard for me to look at or think about what you say . . . but I'd still hear everything you say and I'd still have a record."

McNair nodded. "Thought so. Okay, Daisy. Not your fault. Chaplain, let's take a walk. I know a pretty good bar, if it's still there, about half a mile from here. Bring the bottle; the owner won't mind. And he won't have anything nearly as good in stock."

But for the bartender, the Broadway was empty. Well, it was early in the day, after all.

Laying a twenty dollar bill on the bar, McNair said, "*Solo necesitamos hielo, Leo.*" We just need ice.

"I speak perfectly good English," the gray-haired, Antillean descended bartender answered, *very* properly. "Maybe better than you. But I'll bring you your ice anyway."

Taking the ice while the chaplain ported the bottle of scotch, the two sat down at a table under a slowly circulating ceiling fan.

"I came here the first time as an able bodied seaman in the '40s," McNair announced. "It was an Army hangout then. I suppose it is again now, too."

Dwyer looked around. He thought maybe the place had seen better times. Then again, the entire city of Colon always seemed like it had seen better times and yet never seemed to get any worse.

McNair thought that another test was in order. Loudly he called out, "Daisy, can you hear me?"

Nothing.

"Daisy???"

Still nothing, except that the bartender, Leo, looked at him strangely.

"Safe enough, then, I guess," McNair said.

"I'm not even going to begin to think about what it does to the sanctity of my confessional that the ship can hear every word spoken," sighed the priest.

"But she's just a machine, right, Father?" the captain asked.

"That's what I tried to tell myself," answered the priest, clasping hands and looking down at the unclothed table. "But I had my doubts. As a matter of fact . . ."

"Yes?" McNair pressed.

"Well . . . I don't know how to say this, but . . . whatever she is or isn't, she's a Roman Catholic now."

Eyes gaping, the captain exclaimed, "Huh?"

"Oh, yes," the priest answered, pouring himself another drink. "Came to me and asked to be baptized. The chief of chaplains told me 'not just no, but hell no.' So I went over his head to the head of my order.

He said . . . well, it isn't fit for Christian ears, what he said. So I went to the holy father; we go way back, we do. Back to when he was the head of the Holy Office of the Inquisition. Wise man; he was always wise beyond his years. And, unlike me, a truly holy man.

"Anyway, the pope asked me a few questions, told me to search my soul and to search for one in Daisy. And then, wise and holy man that he is, he told me to trust myself and do what I thought was right.

"So, yes," Dwyer concluded, "Daisy is a member in good standing of the True Faith."

"Whew! So she's human after all. *That* takes a load off my conscience."

"I didn't say she was human, Captain. I decided she had a soul and, though I don't think she was in need of salvation, her soul having no portion in original sin, I could hardly refuse her the sacraments of our mutual God."

The priest raised his glass and swirled its contents. "Except for the scotch, of course; that's completely wasted on her. Poor thing."

"Well, that doesn't really help me," McNair muttered, looking extremely confused and inexpressibly sad, neither of those being expressions he would ever have permitted himself aboard ship.

Dwyer looked hard at his ship's captain. "Oh, dear. Tell me it isn't so."

McNair sighed. "It's so."

"For Daisy?"

"You know anyone else on the ship with a beautiful face, big blue eyes and a thirty-eight inch, D cup chest? That gravity doesn't affect in the *slightest*?"

"Oh, dear," the priest repeated uselessly.

Without waiting for Dwyer, McNair reached over, took the bottle, and poured himself another drink.

"When I awaken, she's there for me. When I lie down to sleep she's the last thing I see before I close my eyes. Quite a lot more often than I like to think about, she's there after I close my eyes and before I open them in the morning.

"She's always there to talk, if I need to talk. She's a *great* conversationalist, did you know that, Dan?"

The priest nodded that, yes, he knew.

"And she takes care of the ship . . . err, of herself, I suppose. When was the last time a ship's captain had a ship that took care of all the little things for him?"

McNair, seeing Dwyer's glass was empty, added some ice to it and poured.

The priest looked down into the glass and then, unaccountably, began to giggle. The giggle grew until it became a chortle. The chortle expanded to a laugh. The laugh took him over and shook him until he could barely sit his chair.

"Oh, I can't *wait* to dump this one on His Holiness' desk."

The Indowy were a fairly imperturbable race. This may have explained why they took an immediate liking to the cats Davis had brought in to clean out the ship's complement of rats. One of those cats, Morgen, purred happily under Sintarleen's stroking palm.

Being imperturbable, instead of jumping through his skin when the ship's avatar appeared beside him, Sintarleen merely bowed his head in recognition.

"Ship Daisy, may I help you?"

"Maybe," Daisy answered, after taking a seat to look the Indowy in the eye. "How familiar are you with cell regeneration and expansion from incomplete DNA samples?"

The Indowy shrugged. "You refer to what we call, 'inauspicious cloning.' I am somewhat familiar with it. Why do you ask?"

Daisy didn't answer directly. Instead, she asked, "Have you opened your mail today?"

Still stroking the cat, the Indowy replied, "Why no, Ship Daisy, I didn't even check it. I almost never get any missives. My clan is dead, you see, all but the few representatives here aboard this vessel, and about one hundred transfer neuters and females on another planet far away. So there is really no one to write."

"No, no," Daisy said, impatiently. "I mean your *mail*. Physical mail. Letters. Packages."

"Well, I am a little behind on my parts' accounting and storage . . ."

"Check please. There is something, some *things*, I have had sent to you. I would find them and bring them but . . ."

"I understand," Sintarleen said. "Will you wait here for a moment?"

When the Indowy returned he was clutching a polka-dotted halter, a pair of high heeled shoes, and a small clear plastic bag containing what appeared to be blonde hair.

"What are these things?" he asked of the ship's avatar.

"They belonged to someone, what the humans would call an 'actress.' She is possibly long dead. They are samples which should contain enough DNA, even if only traces, for you to create for me a body. It is amazing what one can find on eBay."

"Aiiiii!" the Indowy exclaimed, loudly enough to frighten off Morgen, the kitten. "What you ask is impossible, illegal. Why if the Darhel ever found out, the price they would exact from my clan is too horrible to contemplate."

"But," Daisy pointed out, reasonably, "you have just admitted that your clan only exists on this ship, for any practical purpose. Do you not think that *I* can defend you from anything the Darhel might have?"

"This is so," Sintarleen admitted reluctantly. "But even so, there are things I would need to . . ."

"The regeneration tank arrives next week," finished Daisy, with an indecipherable smile. "It's amazing what you can . . ."

". . . find on eBay," the Indowy finished.

The sun was just beginning to peek over Colon's low skyline, its rays lighting up Lemon Bay, the *Bahia de Limon*, in iridescent streaks. The USS *Des Moines* glowed magnificently in the early morning light.

Davis stood with the supply officer on the Cristobal pier to which CA-134 was docked, the two of them receipting for supplies.

"Got to admit it; that yellow awning *does* look nice."

"I don't mind the awning, Chief," said the Chop. "I'll even admit, reluctantly, that it's kinda pretty. But those goddamned paisley coverings over the brows are just too fucking much."

The chief shrugged. "Take the good with the bad," he said.

"Speaking of good with bad, what the hell is this?" asked the Chop, pointing at a large box in Galactic packaging, resting on the dock.

"Dunno, sir. I can't even read the writing."

The chief bent down to look for a shipping label. He found something that might have been one, but the writing on this, too, was indecipherable.

"Best have Sinbad look this over."

Davis pulled a small radio from his pocket. As he was about to press the talk button, he spotted the Indowy walking his way with a half dozen of his clanspeople in tow.

"Sinbad, can you make this out?" asked the chief, pointing at what was probably a shipping label.

"I can," answered the Indowy, looking down as usual, "but it really isn't necessary. It's for me."

"Oh. Well, what is it, Mister Sintarleen?"

"It is hard to explain," which was the truth. "It is for . . . manufacturing parts . . . and . . . ummm . . . assemblies. Yes, that's it: assemblies," which was also the truth, if not the whole of it.

"Very well, Sinbad," agreed the Chop, holding forth a clipboard and pen. "If you will sign here for it."

"I can't see anything," said Daisy. "I can't sense anything. Are you sure it's working?"

Sintarleen gave an Indowy sigh. "Lady Daisy, you can't sense or see anything because right now the tank is manipulating and selecting the scraps of DNA we gave it. When it has enough to make a full cell then the process will begin."

"And it will make me a body? A real, human, body?"

"It will, if it works, if we have provided enough material. But I must warn you again, Lady Daisy, that it will have no mind. There are protocols built in to the machine, protocols I can do nothing about, that forbid the creation of colloidal sentiences by artificial means.

"Instead of a brain it will have something very like your physical self. Simpler of course. Not really able to think on its own. All of its intelligence must come from you."

"That will be just fine," Daisy agreed.

"There is one further thing," the Indowy insisted. "You will be connected with this . . . body . . . as soon as it starts to grow from a single cell. It will be under accelerated growth, but that growth will be irregular. Moreover, it will be, biologically, a human female body. Even in the tank it will be affected by human physiological processes. Those processes will affect you, Lady Daisy."

One thing you can say for having an AID run your galley, thought Chief Davis, *you can be certain that the food is going to be first rate.*

It wasn't that Daisy Mae physically made the omelets, or boiled the lobster, or flipped the steak. There were cooks and mess boys for that.

Instead, Daisy bought the very best ingredients out of her slush fund and—while she did not routinely show herself in the galley itself—would appear there suddenly and without warning, cursing like a cavalry trooper over the shamefaced cook if a filet mignon approached half a degree past medium rare when medium rare had been ordered.

And the coffee was always perfect. She ordered it fresh roasted from a little coffee plantation in the Chiriqui highlands, one of Digna's family holdings as a matter of fact. Then Daisy *insisted* that the big brewers be scrubbed to perfection, the water poured in at the perfect temperature, and the brewing stopped at precisely the right moment.

It probably didn't hurt that she was paying the cooks a small bonus under the table. Then again, good cooks took pride in their work. Having the best materials to work with, to produce a better meal, only fed that pride.

Actually, the coffee puzzled the chief. It was on the rationed list. And high end, gourmet coffee was on the *serious* rationed list. But there was always plenty of it and it was always perfect.

The chief took his cup, placed it under the spigot and poured, half quivering with aesthetic joy as the rich aroma arose around him. *Yum!*

Davis took his accustomed place at his customary table to a chorus of, "Mornin', Chief . . ." "Hiya Chief . . ." "Good eats, Chief . . ." Nose stuck in that good, good cup of under-the-table coffee, Davis acknowledged the salutations with an informal wave of his hand.

Without having to be told, one of the mess boys set a plate before Davis, the plate piled high with fried potatoes, a thick ham steak, and eggs over easy.

Before the chief could dig in Daisy materialized in the seat opposite his. She may have rarely appeared in the galley, unless something was about to go wrong, but she made a point of making the rounds of the messes.

"How's breakfast, Chief Davis?" she inquired.

"First rate, as always, Daisy Mae. How's our ship?"

Daisy felt a little tingle, somewhere in her crystalline mind. *Our ship.* After subjective millennia of utter loneliness it meant more than she could say to belong, and not to be alone. This was true of both parts of her. That part which was the original CA-134 had spent a miserable couple of decades uncared for, unwanted and unloved as well.

"I'm fine," Daisy answered. "Well, mostly I am. But I think a couple of the ball bearings in number two turret need replacing. I was testing it last night and heard a squeak that really ought not to be."

"Get someone on it right after breakfast," said the chief around half a mouthful of eggs.

"And the deck between the PBMRs could use some cleaning," she added innocently.

Sintarleen checked the progress of the growing form in the tank. *If I am reading this rightly, everything is perfect for this stage of development.*

Still, I don't like the temperature fluctuations. And the hormonal surges are sometimes out of control. How do these people, the female ones anyway, maintain their sanity under these circumstances?

As any human father could have told the Indowy, if asked, "the female ones, anyway," typically did *not*. Nor did any males forced into close company with a thirteen-year-old girl.

A happy mess made for a happy ship, believed Davis. Thus, he didn't immediately understand the problem, the sour faces and grim expressions that met him in the chief's mess.

He shrugged and went to pour himself a cup of coffee. He could check into it later. He might even learn something about the problem at breakfast.

He poured himself a cup of coffee, added cream and sugar and took a healthy sip.

And immediately spat it out again. "Gah! That's awful. What the fu—"

He stopped as his eyes came to rest on the calendar posted over the pot. Four dates were circled on that calendar.

In red.

Davis went to the sink and poured out the coffee without regret. Then he got on the ship's intercom and announced, "Swarinski, I was looking over the Nuke deck earlier this morning. It's filthy. Take a crew and get on it. Now."

The answer came back, "Chief Davis, I'm standing here, looking at it. The deck's spotless."

"Scrub it anyway, Swarinski."

INTERLUDE

Boredom was for a time of unending routine. Boredom was not for the time after word had returned telling of the outright massacre of the first fleet to reach the new world of the threshkreen.

Face buried in the Aldenat' mush, Guanamarioch sensed something new in his messmates, similarly feeding around him. It was not anticipation, this new thing. It was something . . . something . . . something Guanamarioch remembered only dimly from his time in the pens as a nestling.

The Kessentai thought back, trying to recall memories he had long suppressed, memories of his small nestling hindquarters against the wall of the pen, fighting for his life against a horde of siblings who had decided he looked much like lunch. He remembered the flashing needlelike teeth, the yellow blood that flowed from a dozen tiny slashes on his face, neck and flanks. He remembered a lucky slash of his own that had disemboweled one of those who sought to eat him.

They had turned on that other one, then, turned on it and ripped it apart. That feeding had taken a long time, with the wounded one's pitiful cries growing weaker as dozens clustered around, each taking a small bite.

Guanamarioch too had eaten, lunging in to sink his teeth into his brother's hams before shaking his tiny head and tearing a bloody gob of warm, dripping meat from the body.

The God King had retreated to a corner then, bloody prize locked in the claws and jaws. There he had sat, trembling, alternately chewing and looking up to snarl and warn off any of the others who might seek to steal his prize.

He remembered being afraid then, afraid that someone would take his meal and afraid, even more, that in the frenzy he might too be ripped apart while still living.

Guanamarioch lifted his massive head from his mush bowl and looked around the mess room. No, there was no tremblings of fear among his clanskin. But then, neither was Guanamarioch shaking.

Then something happened, something in itself trivial. A God King of about the same rank as Guanamarioch nudged the mush bowl of one slightly superior. The latter then immediately turned and tore the throat from the clumsy one. All the others present immediately grabbed their bowls and backed up towards the nearest wall or other vertical surface, each one snarling as he did so.

Guanamarioch did the same, and realized, as he backed his haunches to the wall, that the news of these new thresh had them all terrified.

He understood though. Never before had a fleet of the People met serious resistance from any but their own. To have a fleet, even a small one, almost completely destroyed was terrifying indeed.

A door into the mess deck slid open with a slight *whoosh*. Through the door passed an oddly shaped robotic device. This glided across the deck silently. It then hovered lightly over the yellow-blood-soaked area of the mess where the clumsy Kessentai had had his throat torn open by another. The device fit the dimensions of the ship's corridors and compartments well, leading Guanamarioch to think that this, too, was Aldenat' technology.

Singly and by twos, the others cleared out from the mess and formed in the corridor adjacent the mess. In a few minutes, only Guanamarioch and the killer remained, the latter staring madly at the corpse, apparently in contemplation of eating it. This was not, in itself, forbidden, of course; the ethos of the People demanded that thresh not be wasted.

It *was*, however, forbidden to kill aboard ship during migration without permission.

A senior God King, not the lord of the clan but a close assistant entered the mess, followed by two cosslain, the superior normals that filled the job of noncommissioned officers within the Posleen host. The senior took in the entire compartment in a single sweeping glance before resting his yellow eyes on the corpse and the nearby killer.

"Did you see what happened, Junior?" the demi-lord demanded.

Guanamarioch bowed his head in respect. "I saw it, lord, but I did not understand it."

The senior turned his attention back to the killer. "For what reason did you break the shiplaw and kill this one?" he asked calmly.

With apparent difficulty the murderer looked upward,

away from the corpse, answering, "He nudged my feeding bowl."

"It is my judgment that this is insufficient reason to break the law of the People. It is further my judgment that this conduct merits termination of existence. Have you anything to say?"

Sensing death, and unwilling to die without a struggle, the killer launched itself at the senior Kessentai, claws outstretched and fangs bared. The senior, however, had not reached his position within the clan by being slow and indecisive. Even while the lower God King began his leap, the senior had drawn his boma blade and begun to swing. The blade passed through the thick neck almost as if it were not there. When the body struck it did so in two pieces, dead.

The senior looked at Guanamarioch as if measuring him for the recycling bins. At length, he decided that Guanamarioch had more value as a future leader than as a current meal.

"This is not to be spoken of further," the senior announced as he turned to leave.

CHAPTER 8

Diplomats are useful only in fair weather.
As soon as it rains they drown in every drop.
—Charles de Gaulle

Department of State, Washington, DC

The early morning sun shone brightly off the Potomac, sending scattered rays of light to bathe the Lincoln Memorial and the National Academy of Sciences. Some of that light, and it was perhaps the only brightness to the place, indirectly lit the walls of the Department of State where a meeting, judged by some to be important, was taking place.

The President's National Security Advisor was not entitled to quite as much deference as a Darhel lordling. Thus, she was received in a second class conference room. It was facing towards the Potomac, true, but the furnishings and wall hangings were not of the best. It would never do for someone in such a quasi-military, politically-appointed position to be made to feel that she was somehow the equal of the senior career bureaucrats of State.

The Secretary of State, who was *not* a career bureaucrat, fumed. Someone, somewhere in the Byzantine halls of Foggy Bottom, had deliberately set this up to insult NSA and embarrass *him.*

NSA was there expressly to discuss some of the President's concerns with regard to what he had called "sabotage" of American policy in places ranging from Diess to Panama. In particular, today NSA was concerned with Panama.

If State showed contempt for NSA, it was as nothing to what NSA felt for State. She'd thought them, in her own words, "lily-white, weak-kneed, overbred, limp-wristed collaborators with the communists," back during the Cold War. "Our very own fifth column for the Kremlin . . . pseudo-intellectual moral cowards . . . poltroons." And she had said *that* on a day when she was in a *good* mood. Her opinion was even lower now, when it wasn't just America's freedom on the line, but the survival of humanity itself.

The Secretary of State, himself, on the other hand, she liked and even, to a degree, respected. A well-dressed, distinguished looking Wilsonian Republican with clear, intelligent eyes and a full head of hair going gray at the temples, SecState was simply unable to control the senior career bureaucrats who actually ran the department. NSA thought that perhaps no one could really control them, at least not without shooting a fair number to gain the attention and cooperation of the rest.

Even then, she thought, *the shootings would have to be public and* every *one of the remainder would have to be forced to watch them. The ability of a State Department fool to deny unpleasant reality is deservedly the stuff of legend.*

"I'm not a fool, madam," the secretary said, shaking his distinguished Websterian head slowly. "I know my department is rife with traitors, collaborators and people running their own agenda. What I lack is the ability to do all that much *about* it. They know the system. Sadly, I don't. They work together to cover for each other and keep me in the dark. No one's really been able to control them since at least 1932 or '33."

Before the NSA could make an answer, her cell phone rang. Smiling apologetically, she answered it. Her eyes grew suddenly wide as she swallowed nervously. "I understand, Mr. President," she said, quietly and sadly. "Yes, Mr. President, I'll tell the secretary."

NSA looked up to the secretary. "I am informed," she said, "that the Posleen have crushed the Army's corps to the south of us. The Posleen have broken through and are coming north. I am supposed to evacuate and the President suggests that you do the same."

The impeccably and expensively clad Undersecretary of State for Extraterrestrial Affairs looked at his phone and then, nervously, at his watch. *9:26. Shit, they were supposed to be ready to evacuate me by now.*

The undersecretary stared nervously southward, across the Potomac to where the scattered remnants of a wrecked Army corps and a ceremonial regiment were fighting to the death to buy a little time. Columns of smoke rose skyward from more places than the diplomat could easily count. In fact, he didn't even try. What difference did the amount of destruction make? What mattered was where it was heading, and how quickly it might reach him, here at Foggy Bottom, or his family in Bethesda.

Again, the diplomat glared down at the phone. Again he looked at his watch to see that bare minutes had passed. He started to reach for the phone, to contact his Darhel handler, when there came a bright flash from across the Potomac, from the general vicinity of Fort Myer and Henderson Hall. Following the flash a shock wave arose, turned dark by the smoke, dust, lumber and other debris it picked up and flung outward in all directions. The broad river itself bowed downward under the force, the passage of the shock wave plainly visible as a fast moving furrow in the water.

In less time than it takes to tell, the diplomat uttered, "Shit," and threw himself violently to the floor, damage to his suit be damned. The shock wave dissipated rapidly but, given the amount of GalTech C-9 explosive the Marines had packed into Henderson Hall, it was still enough when it reached the Department of State to shatter the windows, rip loose bricks, and raise the overpressure inside the well-appointed office enough to knock the undersecretary out cold.

Which was a pity from the point of view of the undersecretary and his family, for the phone with his evacuation instructions began to ring mere minutes after he was rendered unconscious.

Because *her* evacuation instructions didn't depend on alien star transport, and because she had no family to sweat over, the National Security Advisor was *not* anxiously awaiting a phone call when the blast struck. Instead, she and a couple of aides awaited transportation by the parking lot abutting Virginia Avenue to the northeast of the State Department Building. The group heard the helicopter coming in down Twenty-Third Street before they saw it. When they did see it . . .

"My God . . . I've heard of treetop level flying, but automobile *antenna* level flying? Christ!"

The helicopter had just pulled up to a hover when the blast struck. Though it was in the lee of the storm, being behind the massive State Department Building, shock waves like that tend to flow and fill any space available to be filled. The NSA was knocked down flat on the concrete, scraping her rather delicate and attractive nose. For the helicopter, completely unsheltered from the blast, the pilot's ability to control was overwhelmed. The chopper pitched onto one side and then slammed, hard, into a stout tree. It began to smolder but before it could burst into flames the four man crew emerged out of the side that was open to the sky and scurried away. Two of them carried one of their number who appeared to be unconscious—plus a rifle each—and one more carried the pintle-mounted door machine gun he had had the presence of mind not to leave behind.

Catching sight of the secretary's party as its members staggered to their feet, the warrant officer in charge pointed. The small group ran over as fast as they could, given the body they were dragging.

"Madam," the warrant announced, "Chief Warrant Officer Stone at your service. We were sent to get you but . . ."

"But sometahms things don' quaht work out," the NSA finished with a beautiful, soft Birmingham accent. She was a lady, she was supremely well educated and the daughter of well educated people, as well. But every now and again, under extreme stress, that

Alabama accent came out. Nose scraping tended to be a stressful sort of thing.

"Would one ah you fahn *gentlemen* have a rahfle or a pistol to spare? Mah Daddy, the minister, always said it was better to hahve a gun an' not *need* it, than to need one and not *hahve* it. An' Ah think that, raht about now, Ah *need* one."

The warrant passed over his own pistol, admiringly. Then, hearing firing coming from the south, from the direction of the Lincoln Memorial, the warrant said, "Ma'am, my orders were to get you out. They intended me to fly you out. But that wasn't actually specified. We're going out on foot."

The party headed north on Twenty-First then east on F. Stone—out of radio contact—thought that if there was anyplace from which the NSA had a chance of being evacuated quickly and safely it would be the White House.

The undersecretary for E-T Affairs awakened slowly. Still groggy, he managed to stand and stare out the window of his office toward where Henry Bacon Drive met Constitution Avenue. The intersection was, itself, blocked by the National Academy for the Sciences.

"Oh, my God," he uttered in shock at the sight of a small horde of Posleen coming up Henry Bacon. They apparently turned right once reaching Constitution, the undersecretary could see many of them marching to the east along that broad thoroughfare.

They didn't all turn right, though. Some turned left and skirted the Academy of Sciences building. These marched straight towards State. One look at the fearsome aliens and the undersecretary felt something very warm and very wet begin to run down his leg.

"Run!" shouted Stone as the party came in visual contact with a group of Posleen in the process of storming the Executive Office Building. The sighting was mutual and a subgroup of Posleen turned from their task and began to pursue.

"This way," the secretary ordered. The party turned north on Nineteenth Street, skirting the World Bank.

"Mr. . . . Stone," the lone machine gunner said, panting. "I've run all I can and I'm not runnin' anymore. Y'all go on without me." The secretary recognized an accent not too dissimilar to her own, if perhaps a bit less classy.

"Sergeant Wallace," the warrant said, "you *will* keep up."

"Nossah, Mr. Stone," the sergeant answered. "I ain't nevah run from nothin' in mah life. And I ain't gonna get in the habit now. Y'all go on. I'll hold them up heah for a whahl." The sergeant tipped his helmet at the secretary. "Ma'am," he said, "Alabama's raht proud o' you."

With the sigh and a sad little smile, the secretary answered, "Sarn't Wallace, your country is raht proud o' you, too."

The machine gun was already firing, at much faster than its normal and sustainable rate, before the secretary and the others turned into the World Bank.

"That wasn't really . . . ?" the secretary began to ask.

"No, ma'am. *That* Wallace died some years ago. This was just a first cousin, twice removed."

"Remarkable resemblance," the secretary commented.

"Not in everything, Ma'am," the warrant answered.

"Look, I'll give you *everything*," the undersecretary begged. He opened a valise and held out a sheaf of the Galactic equivalent of bearer bonds to illustrate. The Posleen normal brushed them aside impatiently with the flat of his boma blade.

A slightly taller Posleen with an erect, feathered crest entered the room where the human had been found. He snarled, whistled and grunted several questions, none of which the human could answer. Indeed, he didn't really understand them as questions at all.

The Kessentai said something to the normal, who shrugged and picked the undersecretary up by one arm, dragging him from the room. The entire time the human continued to beg, to make offers of deals, to promise vast largesse. The Kessentai understood not a word—he didn't speak the language—how could the normal, who spoke no language and barely understood that used by its masters?

The normal dragged the still protesting diplomat downstairs and then through some smashed doors into the central courtyard of the building. Other normals, or perhaps they were cosslain, did likewise with other humans that had been found hiding in the building. Soon there were hundreds of terrified humans gathered there, under the soaring eagle sculpture in the open north courtyard. Still, it was only hundreds of the thousands who normally worked in the little offices and cubicles of the State Department. The rest were fleeing north on foot.

An alien, the undersecretary thought it might be the same Kessentai he had previously "met," stuck his head out to look down into the courtyard and shouted something.

One of the normals in the courtyard guarding the humans drew his boma blade and made a gesture. When the human, who understood all too well what the gesture meant, balked, the Posleen simply grabbed her hair and pulled her into a kneeling position. The descending blade cut her screams off very quickly. The normal passed the bloody head to another to slice off the skull cap and remove the brain. The first then began to slice the body into easily transportable chunks.

The undersecretary inched back, trying to get as many people between himself and the Posleen rendering party as possible. The Posleen noticed this and, instead of gaining himself more time, the diplomat was next to be summoned. He began to scream as soon as the alien claw pointed at him, calling him to face a justice higher than the alien could have imagined.

Once the main assault had been crushed and there was no real chance of successful Posleen reinforcement of their bridgehead over the Potomac, headquarters for the First of the Five-Fifty-Fifth released B Company under Lieutenant Rogers to clear the State Department of Posleen. Sergeant Stewart and his squad were first to reach the northern courtyard of the building. The men didn't retch, but only because such sights, headless corpses half butchered and laid out for complete rendering, had become all too commonplace.

Stewart walked among the corpses, apparently unmoved. "Pretty gross, ain't it, Manuel?" the one called "Wilson" said on the private circuit.

The Hispanic sergeant, hiding under the name of *Jimmy* Stewart shrugged his shoulders and answered, "I dunno. What good did these *chigadera motherfuckers* ever do anyone? Why weren't *they* in the Army? Just turnabout, you ask me; a neat switch."

INTERLUDE

All voyages end, but some end much worse than others. Guanamarioch, inexperienced as he was, couldn't imagine one that ended worse than this. (Truth be told, not one other God King in the fleet had ever actually had any experience like this one. A *contested* emergence? Didn't the damned humans know that was not in the rules?)

Several days before emergence from hyperspace, the God Kings and Kenstain had begun resuscitating the normals by small groups before leading them to their landers. For those, like Guanamarioch's oolt, resuscitated early and made to wait, this was pure murder, literally, as bored and sometimes hungry normals fought with each other in the cramped hold of a Lamprey.

The globe had emerged into a maelstrom of fire. Even at its incredible mass, nearly equivalent to a small planet or a large asteroid, the globe bucked and jolted from the energies released by its own and the threshkreen fires, as well as from exploding ships. The large view-screen, forward in the Lamprey's hold, was completely ignored by the ignorant normals.

Guanamarioch, however, was transfixed by the swirl and glow, the bolts and flashes of the battle in space.

Once he saw in that screen, much magnified he hoped, the gaping maw of a threshkreen super-monitor, coming into alignment with his own globe. There was a bright flash, like that of an antimatter bomb detonating, and a new icon appeared, shading from red to blue to red again. Guanamarioch did not recognize the icon and so asked his Artificial Sentience to explain.

"It is a kinetic energy projectile, lord, moving at an appreciable fraction of the speed of light. The globe cannot tell if it contains an antimatter or nuclear warhead, hence the change in color. Frankly, if it hits us amidships it may not matter if it is an antimatter bomb or not."

Guanamarioch gulped. Involuntarily his sphincter loosened to allow liquid feces to run down his legs to the floor. The smell meant nothing as the normals had been shitting themselves silly ever since awakening. Still, the junior God King part way lowered his head and crest in shame. Shame or not, though, he could not keep his yellow eyes away from the screen.

Despite the speed of the thing, the projectile was so well aligned it was possible to track it, or rather the icon, on the screen. From every outcropping of the globe that mounted a weapon, fire poured down on the KE projectile. It seemed to form an ever more shallow cone with the icon at the apex.

"It's going to hit," the Artificial Sentience announced. "Lower right quarter as the globe bears. It's going to be *bad*."

CHAPTER 9

Discipline ought to be used.
—Shakespeare, *Henry V*

Bijagual, Chiriqui, Republic of Panama

Oh, was Digna in a *bad* mood. Without a word, in field uniform, holding a switch in her right hand and helmet tucked under the left arm, and accompanied by two stout triple great-grandsons, she burst into the little shack. Her bright blue eyes flashed icy fire.

The woman of the house, in fact Digna's great-great-granddaughter though the woman looked much older than the great-great-grandmother did, took one look and backed away, holding her hands in front of her in supplication.

"Where is the little toad?" Digna demanded, lip curling in a sneer and her voice dripping with scorn.

Fearfully the woman pointed at the shack's sole bedroom. Digna brushed the door open with the switch. Immediately her nose was assailed by the strong smell of cheap rum. In the dim light she looked down on a snoring, disheveled man, unsurprisingly also a great-great-grandchild, and felt the rising heat of murderous anger.

She took half a step forward into the room and began.

Down came the switch across the man's face, hard enough to draw blood.

"Filthy *pendejo!*"

Again the switch, accompanied by, "Disgrace to my blood!"

"Rotten" . . . *switch* . . . "Lazy!" . . . *swack* . . . "Good for nothing!" . . . "Foul!" . . . "Dirty!" . . . "Useless!" . . . *whackwackwack.*

By the time Digna got to "useless" her great-great-grandson, trying vainly to protect his head with his hands, had rolled onto the floor. He begged for pardon but the beating continued.

"Little rat!" . . . "Cockroach!" . . . "Vermin!"

When Digna's right arm tired she put on her helmet and transferred the switch to her left. When that tired she stopped altogether and, using her rested right arm grasped the man by the hair and began to drag. Digna was small, and perhaps she could not have pulled the man against his will. But, on the other hand, was it worth it to him to lose his hair finding out?

In the shack's main room Digna flashed her eyes at her escorts.

"Arrest your cousin," she ordered. "Three days in the pit for failure to show for drill." Briefly she reconsidered her sentence and then added, "Make that three days on bread and water."

"*Si señora,*" they answered, meekly.

Digna's Officer Candidate School had trained her to be an artillery officer. Specifically she had been trained to command a battery of very old, very surplus, 85mm Russian-made SD-44 guns. To crew the guns she had several hundred each of middle-aged men and suitably strong and healthy young women. And that was only counting her clan alone, be they by blood or by marriage. She also had substantial numbers of what she, with the benefit of a fairly classical education, thought of as the *"perioeci"*—the "dwellers about"— immediately under her control. Since the guns, with forward observers, fire direction computers and crews only required ninety men, or perhaps one hundred and twenty women, to operate at full efficiency, she had an excess of riches, personnel-wise. She solved this problem by assigning virtually all the unattached or less-attached women and girls of the clan to the guns and forming most of the men into a very large militia infantry company, though perhaps "dragoon" was a better word than infantry. There was not a man or boy who could not ride, and raising thoroughbred horses had been a clan specialty for centuries.

The guns were really quite remarkable specimens of their type; perhaps the ultimate version of the quick firing guns like the French "Seventy-five" that had made the First World War such a nightmare. Compared to the SD-44, the French "Seventy-five" was pretty small beans.

Each could throw a seventeen-pound shell up to seventeen kilometers and do so at a rate of up to twenty-five rounds a minute, maximum, or up to three hundred per hour, sustained. Moreover, since they had been designed by Russians who believed that all defense was antitank defense, the guns had a fair capability against light and medium armor. They were, in fact, the very same design as used on the Type-63 light tanks the gringos had purchased for Panama from the People's Republic of China. Lastly, each gun had an auxiliary engine that could propel it along at a brisk twenty-four kilometers per hour without the need for a light truck to serve as a prime mover. They had the trucks, mind you, but they didn't absolutely need them. They also had horses, lots of horses, in case the trucks and guns ran out of fuel.

The guns could fire high explosive, or HE, smoke and illumination. They could also fire an armor piercing shell that would collanderize anything but a main battle tank. Digna knew that the antitank capability was likely to be completely useless.

Best of all, in her opinion, the guns could fire canister: four hundred iron balls per shell—over three thousand from the massed battery—that would make short work of a column attack. So she hoped anyway.

The switch she had used on her multi-great-grandson did as well to spur her horse to where the battery was training under the eye of one of her favorite grand-daughters, Edilze, a dark and pretty young woman—she favored her grandfather—and, more importantly, one Digna recognized as having a will and a brain.

Digna had begun by training Edilze and eight others to crew the guns, along with six more in fire-direction techniques. That had actually taken only about ten days. As one of Digna's instructors at OCS had observed, "You can train a monkey to serve a gun. People are only marginally more difficult."

For that ten days she had let the men slide, since

she had not a single trained assistant. Not that many of her clan would not be trained. Indeed, many of the young men had already gone off to train with the regular army. But they would stay in the regular army. She had the rest; those too old or those too young. And she had the women and girls.

After the ten days she had called in her sons. These she made platoon leaders. She figured, not without reason, that sons were used to obeying fathers and so based her chain of command fairly strictly on lines of clan seniority. The only notable exception was her foreman, Tomas Herrera, whom she put in charge of some of her own and all of the few residents of the area that had no blood or marriage relation whatsoever.

Digna passed the battery where her girls sweated under Edilze's lashing tongue. *That's my girl,* her grandmother thought. *Such a treasure.* Digna spurred the horse over to the drill field—ordinarily a flat cow pasture by the *quebrada,* or creek. There, the men—most of them—drilled on one of the simpler tasks, weapons maintenance. She had no time for close order drill and, given that the clan was already, in the nature of things, a remarkably cohesive unit, didn't feel the need anyway.

Doffing his straw hat as a sign of respect, an action much more meaningful than any formal military salute, Tomas Herrera walked up and stood by Digna's horse. Herrera was short and squat, with a brown face tanned to old leather. Muscles rippling his arms and torso told of a life of hard toil.

"You found your grandson, *Dama*?" he asked.

"I found the twerp where I expected," Digna sneered. "Flat on his back and drunk as a skunk."

Tomas smiled broadly. It *never* paid to balk the Lady, and blood relation would not save a man who deserved it from a lashing, be it from Digna's tongue or her switch.

"There is one in every family," Tomas observed consolingly. "You put him in the pit, I assume. How long?"

"As *boracho* as he was, I figured it would take him a day and a half to sober up. And another day and a half to realize he was being punished. Three days seemed sufficient, *Señor* Herrera."

"How are the others coming along?" Digna asked, eager to change the subject from one so distasteful.

"Well enough," Tomas answered. "We'll start marksmanship tomorrow."

"The ammunition?"

"Not counting the five hundred rounds per man we have salted away, we have about one hundred and fifty rounds per rifleman and roughly twice that for the light machine gunners. It is enough to at least get them to point their rifles in the right direction and scare whatever they're shooting at," Tomas answered. "And we have over a thousand rounds for each of our two heavier machine guns, not counting the six thousand we have in the reserve stocks."

Digna nodded her head resignedly. It really wasn't much. But that was all they were going to have for the nonce.

"It isn't so bad, *Dama*," Tomas offered. "These are good men, in the main, and most of them solid *campesinos* who know how to shoot already."

Dismounting, Digna offered the reins of her mare to Herrera.

"Your family, Tomas?" she asked with real concern.

"Well enough," he answered simply. "My wife has taken charge of feeding. The girl is serving the big guns. Both my sons are off with the army. The wife of the eldest is assisting my wife, though my own wife never ceases her finding fault with the girl."

"Mothers are like that, with their sons' wives," Digna answered with a smile. "Ask any of my daughters-in-law."

Tomas simply chuckled, then turned and led the mare to a cashew tree footed by long sweet grass. Digna, meanwhile, turned her attention to the clusters of old men and young boys dotting the pasture.

"You've got to slap it hard, Omar," she told one fourteen-year-old struggling to replace the stamped receiver of his Kalashnikov.

Taking one knee next to the boy she took the rifle and, deftly placing the curved piece of metal in the right position, delivered a short, forceful slap that knocked it into position. With one thumb she pushed in the detent button on the rear of the receiver to release it and handed both sections back to the boy.

"You try it now, again, just like I did, Grandson."

Resting the rifle in his left hand, as his grandmother had, Omar placed the upper receiver onto the lower, holding the upper in place with his left thumb. Then he delivered a slap akin to that given by Digna. The upper receiver was knocked immediately into place, the detent—driven by the action spring—popping through the square hole in the rear.

"Thank you, *Mamita!*" the boy said.

Granting her descendant a rare smile, Digna rumpled his hair and continued on down the line. As she went she offered encouragement as needed, and—rarely—a bit of praise. Sometimes she stopped to provide more "hands on" instruction, though in this she was rarely harsh.

The reason she was not harsh was not immediately obvious. It was not that she was not naturally harsh; she was. But, in the circumstances, what her family needed to see was confidence, and confident people rarely showed harshness except with the most deserving.

Of course, anybody who was really confident, *in the circumstances*, was either drunk or too stupid to even begin to understand what was about to descend on the Republic of Panama and on the Earth.

Digna knew there were no grounds for confidence; she had seen the films of some of the off- and on-world fighting during her time at OCS. Inwardly she shivered as she wondered, perhaps for the thousandth time, if she would be able to save even a fraction of her blood from the enemy's ravenous appetite. She wondered, too, if she would be strong enough, *harsh* enough, to make the sacrificial choices she knew she would have to make when the time came.

And who will I choose to live, if it comes to that? My sons, whom I love, but who are too old to bring forth more children? My now-barren daughters? Do I pick the girls to save or the boys? Do I pick myself now that I can have children again? Do I pick myself and live, maybe for centuries, with the knowledge I let my loved ones die?

God, if there is a God . . . and if you are listening, I am going to have some very choice words for you for what you are about to do to me and mine.

Scowling, Digna pushed the sacrilegious thought from her mind and continued on her way. Reaching the end of the pasture she came to a ford at the creek. This she crossed nimbly, hopping from rock to rock. On the other side she scrambled up the muddy bank and continued along a well-worn path to where she had ordered the mess facility set up.

The smell of roasting meat hit her before she ever saw the calf turning on the spit. As she walked nearer, near enough to see fire and smoke and pots and pans, other smells caressed her nose. She detected fragrant *frijoles*; savory *sancocho*, the "national dish" of Chiriqui; frying corn tortillas, thick and fat-laden.

One of the younger girls nudged *Señora* Herrera, Tomas' wife, as Digna approached. The head cook passed to the younger girl the ladle with which she had been stirring the *sancocho* and turned to greet Digna. The woman, shapeless and worn now, had once been a great beauty. But the only remnants of that now were to be found in her granddaughters.

"*Que tal*, Imelda?" Digna asked. What's up?

"Nothing much, *Doña*," Imelda Herrera answered. "Lunch is coming along nicely and should be ready at about two."

"The stores are sufficient?"

Imelda pointed with her chin, a very *Chiricana* gesture, to a small herd of cattle held in by a temporary stockade. "Between those and the other food you donated, the rice and corn and beans, we are in good shape for another three weeks. But . . ."

"Yes? Tell me?"

"Well, *Doña*, I had this thought. It is fine now, while I and the women and girls working for me can prepare a proper meal. What about when these aliens come? When we have the boys out on horseback, moving fast, and we cannot get them decent food? What happens then?"

"The government has promised me canned combat rations," Digna answered. "Then again, they also promised me about four times more ammunition and fuel than we've been sent so far." Digna looked at Imelda questioningly. "You have an idea?"

"I can't do a thing about the ammunition and fuel. But it occurred to me that we could start smoking meat and cheese and storing it against the day."

Digna thought about that. Her herds, legacy of her husband's decades of hard work, were more than sufficient. She decided right then to go with Imelda's plan and told her so.

Then another thought occurred to Digna.

"How much meat can you smoke?"

Imelda thought about that for a moment, then answered, "Standing wood we have in abundance. But we can't hope to cut enough to smoke more than, say, one cow's worth a day."

"I understand," Digna said. "But what if I gave you twenty or thirty, maybe even forty men a day to cut firewood."

"I could do several cows' worth then. But to what end?"

"Oh, it occurred to me that there is going to be a huge demand for preserved food in the days ahead. I suspect I could sell anything you produced . . . rather, I could trade it, for whatever we are short in ammunition and gasoline. Maybe even pick up some weapons too.

"A little here, a little there," Digna mused, looking skyward at nothing in particular. "Not enough to make anyone else's fight impossible, but maybe enough to give *us* a better chance."

"Give me the men," Imelda answered. "Send me the cows."

"And I'll do the trading," Digna finished.

PART II

CHAPTER 10

Mates, the odds are against us. Our colors have never been lowered to the enemy, and I trust this will not be so today. As long as I live that flag will fly high in its place and, if I die, my officers will know how to fulfill their duty.

—Commander Arturo Prat,
Chilean Navy, KIA 21 May 1879

Earth, Western Hemisphere

Costa Rica went under first. After half a century of conscious, deliberate and nearly universal demilitarization it had never been able to mount much of an armed force. Instead of spending its nominal wealth on a military, relying on the firmly fixed notion that if all else failed the United States could always be counted on to come to the rescue, this very civilized and reasonably prosperous state had concentrated for fifty years on education and health care.

All that meant in the end was that the Posleen had several million very healthy and literate cattle to add to their larder.

Nicaragua did better. Even before news had come of the imminent Posleen invasion the previous rulers of the country, the Marxist-Leninist Sandinistas, had returned to power. The hold on the reins of government by the liberal democratic regime had never been very strong in any case.

Give the Sandinistas their due; a totalitarian movement at least ought to know how to subordinate the individual to the state. This the Sandinistas knew and this they did to good effect. Moreover, with several tens of thousands of combat experienced veterans, most of them fairly young still, of the long civil war between Sandinistas and Somocistas, also known as "Contras," Nicaragua was able to mount a large and reasonably well trained and disciplined mostly infantry force to contest the alien landings.

But, sad to say, no purely infantry force, using human designed and built weapons of the early twenty-first century, could hope to stand up to the technology and number of the aliens. To stand up to the Posleen human infantry forces needed the backing of masses of artillery. Artillery took wealth, either your own or that of someone who wished you well; that, or thought it needed you alive. Nicaragua, standing alone, lacked wealth and lacked the artillery that wealth could buy.

Moreover, the one really useful source of military aid, the United States, had a long memory and tended to hold a grudge. Even after Nicaragua's dictator, the Sandinista Daniel Ormiga, swallowed his pride and went hat in hand to ask the gringos for help, the United States turned a deaf ear. Perhaps this was because, as they claimed, they had none to give. Perhaps it was because while aid was possible there were higher priorities.

Perhaps, too, it was because, as Ormiga surmised, the United States would weep no tears at seeing an avowed enemy eaten to extinction.

As it happened though, the deadliest weapon in Nicaragua's arsenal turned out to be a timely earthquake that killed about fifteen thousand of the invaders. It was later, much later, calculated that this slowed down the final digestion of the country and its people by approximately thirty-five minutes.

The only effective barrier to the Posleen advance had turned out to be Lake Nicaragua and its remarkably ferocious sharks.

Sharks, earthquake, and rifle fire notwithstanding, Nicaragua and its people ceased to exist within eight days of the enemy landing.

Small and densely populated El Salvador did receive aid from the United States, mostly in the form of small arms, mortars and light artillery. They, like the Nicaraguans, had a strong base of militarily experienced men who had fought in their lengthy and bloody civil war. The Salvadoran Army was manned, in the main, by Indians who took considerable pride in the knowledge that while the powerful Aztec had fallen quickly to the Conquistadors of Spain *their* ancestors had never truly been conquered.

Like those ancestors—fierce and brave to a fault, and this had contributed mightily to the bloodiness and duration of the civil war—the soldiers of El Salvador had stood and fought like madmen. From the frontier, to the Rio Lempa, to the very steps of the cathedral of San Salvador, the landscape was littered with the denuded bones of countless thousands of Posleen and *Salvadoreños*.

In the end, for all their patriotism, courage and ferocity, Salvadoran humanity was wiped from the surface of the Earth.

Honduras held out longer, but only because it was bigger. The Posleen moved as they would, bled and died as they needed. Speed was rarely a consideration except in the great battles of maneuver and attrition waged in North America and Central Europe.

Guatemala and Belize went under as quickly as had El Salvador and Honduras.

A Mexican dictator, Porfirio Diaz, had once observed, "Alas, pity poor Mexico, so far from God and so close to the United States." The generations who lived during the Posleen war, especially those who managed to live through it, found cause to turn that around to "Lucky Mexico, so close to the devils but even closer to the United States."

This was so for at least two reasons. The first was that, being next door, Mexico held the southern entrance into the United States proper and so was given massive military aid. The second, and far fewer Mexicans ever had cause to know this, was that when defense failed despite the aid and despite the brave show put on by the Mexican Army, the United States became a safe refuge for more than ten million who found shelter under the wings of the 11th Mobile Infantry Division (ACS).

That division died, for the most part, in Texas, New Mexico and Arizona, but not before that ten million could be evacuated to shelter. Curiously, no one north of the border found cause to complain about illegal immigration. Ten million Mexican immigrants meant another million or more men and women for the United States Army.

A small group of relatively poor Posleen set down in Colombia between the mountains and the sea. The Colombian army folded quickly. The various private armies, paramilitaries of the right, the left and the narcotraffickers, succeeded for the nonce in holding substantial parts of the undeveloped part of the country, as well as the mountain fringed capital, Bogotá.

The invaders also touched down on both sides of the Rio de la Plata in the vicinity of Buenas Aires, Argentina and Montevideo, Uruguay. Pastoral and open, ideal ground for the Posleen "cavalry," both countries quickly succumbed.

From their base in southeastern South America the Posleen spread out to the north and west. For the nonce Brazil was able to hold them out, though at terrible cost. To the west Chile, with strong natural defenses through the Andes passes held by well trained, tough and disciplined mountain troops, and aided by a company of 1st Battalion, 508th Infantry (ACS) stopped the Posleen cold . . . literally cold.

Fort Kobbe, Republic of Panama

The smell from the "puke trees" that marked the demarcation line between the Army's Fort Kobbe and Howard Air Force Base drifted across Kobbe's main street, making those not used to it, as Scott Connors wasn't used to it, want to retch. Fortunately, Connors and his battalion commander were walking south, away from the trees and toward the tent city in which the First of the Five-O-Eighth was billeted.

The stench of the puke trees matched Connors'

mood as it had been since opening his mail on the long space voyage back to Earth. It was hard to take an interest in things after one's carefully constructed world falls down around one. Still, he *was* a soldier, was an officer, and going through the motions wasn't that difficult after more than fifteen years of service.

"That's not a helluva lot of prep time you're giving us," Connors said to his battalion commander, Snyder.

"Captain, there isn't a lot of prep time we've been given. So stop sniveling about what can't be changed and just soldier on, why don't you?"

"Yessir," Connors answered. In truth he wasn't a sniveler and he knew the Old Man knew that. *Must be the pressure of seeing most of this hemisphere fall so quickly that's making him testy*, he thought.

"The submarine's going to be here tonight," Snyder continued. "It will spend the night loading consumables, mostly ammunition, for your company. You and your men will board around 0500. You'll have a four day sail, underwater, to Valparaiso, Chile. From there you will attach yourselves to the Chilean Army but only for purposes of helping them hold the Uspallata Pass."

"Why Chile?" Connors asked.

"Two reasons, I *suspect*," Snyder answered. "One is that, since the Posleen have not landed on the western side of the Andes and the passes over range from 'limited' to 'no fucking way,' we might actually have a chance to hang on to the place. The other reason is that Chile is still the world's best source of copper, which we need for damned near everything, and produces—especially since the expansion for the war—a couple of million tons of nitrates a year. We need the nitrates even more than we need the copper."

"Okay, boss. Roger, wilco and all that happy horse-shit. But what the hell do they expect a single company of MI to do?"

Snyder almost laughed. "If nothing else, Captain, the Army expects you to die well. I, on the other hand, expect you to hold that fucking pass until the Chileans can get some better fixed defenses in and then get your ass back here, as whole and as sound and as *up to strength* as humanly possible."

"One company of MI?" Connors asked dubiously.

"Captain, have you ever *seen* the Andes?"

Muelle *(Pier) 18, Balboa, Republic of Panama*

Connors hadn't really expected the sub to be as big as it was. Although mostly hidden, the length of the thing dwarfed the pier. The only thing bigger, nearby, was the heavy cruiser, USS *Salem*, docked two bays over.

A navy chief with a stupendous gut met Connors dockside. He introduced himself as "Chief Petty Officer Kaiser, Major." Connors did a double take and then remembered that, aboard ship, there could be but one "captain."

"Sir," Kaiser continued, "we've actually got space for more *troops* than you're bringing aboard. What we don't have space for is the number of men *and* those big bloody suits. This trip out, you're going to be stacked like sardines." He added, apologetically, "It's gonna suck like a convention of Subic Bay whores."

Connors shrugged indifferently, then smiled. "Chief, if you've never been in a C-130 after a twelve-hour flight trying to on-board rig for a jump then you don't know what 'suck' is. We'll be fine once we get settled in."

The chief liked Connors' sense of proportion. "That's another thing, Skipper. The boat's decks and all were never meant for half ton suits of armor. We're trying to reinforce them but . . ."

"Stop trying, Chief. We can dial down our effective weight to nothing. Matter of fact, if we really wanted to, working together my company could probably pick up the sub and *fly* it . . . bounce it around for a while anyway."

"No shit, huh?"

"No shit, Chief. Oh, we couldn't fly it all the way to Chile . . . well . . . maybe if we could somehow tap into the sub's own reactor and charge the suits at a rate of about ten to one. But we could move it around. It would take longer than sailing though."

"Coool," admired Kaiser. "Well, you don't need to fly us anywhere. And the captain will be mighty pleased to hear that you're not going to warp our decks."

"How long's it going to take us to get to Valparaiso?" Connors asked.

Kaiser looked around to make sure no one else was in earshot. Then, conspiratorially, he said, "Officially, we couldn't get you there in less than four and a half days at top speed. *Un*officially, you'll hit the beach seventy-three hours after we set sail."

"Cooool."

Valparaiso, Chile

"Cooool," intoned Connors as he stepped up from the cramped troop bay of the submarine and took his first look at the Port of Valparaiso. He was suited up, of course, since he and B Company were heading into action as soon as they finished unloading, but his helmet was under his arm so that he had an unobstructed and *natural* view of the city.

Valparaiso was laid out more or less in the form of an amphitheater, with a wide, flat, circular harbor surrounded by steep hills on all side. The houses clinging to the hillsides were gaily, even gaudily, painted. Connors thought he could see *elevators* moving up and down the hills carrying people to and from their work.

A dress-white clad Chilean naval officer (for Chile had a very long, honorable, and even impressive tradition in its naval service, as well as in one other) met Connors from the pier. Connors took a double take; the Chilean officer bore an absolutely *striking* resemblance to Admiral Guenther Lutjens who had gone down with the *Bismarck* in 1941.

"*Capitán* Connors," the naval officer called breathlessly, as if he had run the hills himself. "*Capitán* Connors, I need to speak with you. You . . . you and your men . . . must hurry."

Connors debarked and was pleased to see that, no, they hadn't succeeded just yet in resurrecting naval ghosts. On the other hand, the naval officer's name tag did say, "Lindemann." Connors raised an inquisitive eyebrow.

"Fourth cousin, twice removed," answered the

Chilean. "Come. Bring your men. I've held up the railway for them."

MI could move fast, but only at a cost in power. Fortunately, railroads could move just about as fast and there was one working between Valparaiso and the Uspallata Pass.

The Transandean railway had been in operation from 1910 to 1982, though it had ceased passenger service as early as 1978 under the stress of competition with automobile and bus traffic from the coaxial highway, a part of the Pan-American Highway system. Closed for twenty years and allowed to rot and rust away all that time, the governments of Argentina, Chile and the United States opened negotiations in 2002 to restore the railway. This was actually not that difficult an operation as the really serious work, the grading and the blasting, was still extant and for the most part still in as good a shape as ever. Even so, only one of two lines had been completed and didn't *that* play hell with resupply and troop movements.

It was this line that Connors and B Company took up the Andean Slopes to where a regiment of tough Chilean mountain infantry (the *other* part of Chile's armed forces that enjoyed international respect and admiration) were holding on by their fingernails against the Posleen probes coming over the mountains and through the pass.

The MI suits had been dialed down to be nearly weightless and inertialess. Even so, the train squealed with the strain of just moving itself up the tortuous and steep tracks. As the temperature dropped as precipitously as the mountain range grew overhead, the troopers of B Company—for the most part clinging to the tops of the cars, there being another regiment of *reserve* mountain infantry inside the cars—donned helmets to keep from freezing. The mountain troops made room inside one of the cars for Connors, who stood mostly in the central passageway. He had to be inside to get the latest update from Lindemann. Nor could Lindemann stay outside without freezing. The Chilean was clothed for cold weather, of course, but not for *Arctic* levels of cold weather accompanied by the subjective winds created by the train as it screamed up the track.

"We expected the Argentines to do better," Lindemann cursed. "But at the first sign of a landing their upper classes, to include an absolutely disgusting percentage of their senior military officers, took to ships, abandoning their people. Some of their units fought and died hard, even so, but they went under before we expected and before we could do much about it."

Connors said nothing to this. It was one thing for a South American to criticize another group of South Americans. It was unclear to him how they would take criticism from a gringo. *Whaddya know, I learned some tact in my old age.*

"We were fortunate that we had a regiment of mountain troops training in the vicinity of Mount Aconcagua when the aliens first landed," Lindemann explained, "fortunate too that we were able to get them some more ammunition and rations before they actually had to fight. But they've got no fixed defenses and their only artillery is a battalion of light mountain guns, that and their own mortars. We're still mobilizing reservists and trying to shift some units down from the other passes. But it's been hard."

"Why no fixed defenses?" Connors asked. "I would have thought they'd have been a natural for those passes."

Lindemann rubbed a hand wearily across his jaw. "Yes, one would have thought so. Blame your State Department, actually."

"Huh?"

"They brokered a deal between us, the United States, the Galactic Federation and Argentina under which substantial U.S. and some Galactic aid would be given in return for the creation of a combined command. Not building fortifications in the passes was supposed to be . . . hmmm . . . let me see if I can remember the words exactly. Oh, yes, I recall. The absence of fortification was 'symbolic of the determination of our two countries, with the help of the United States and the Galactic Federation, to stand and fight together as one.' Who knows," Lindemann said, philosophically, "if it had been us rather than the Argentines who had been hit first perhaps we would have run and it would be an Argentine mountain infantry regiment trying to keep the aliens from crossing to their side of the pass.

"In any case," Lindemann concluded, "just for your future use, Captain Connors, you can never go wrong betting on the avarice, selfishness, and cowardice of the Latin American upper classes. Exceptions are, just that, *exceptional*."

Suddenly, Connors' suit was almost thrown and Lindemann's body *was* thrown as the train shuddered and screamed to an unplanned stop. The Chilean gasped as he hit shoulder first, breaking his collar bone. The reservists also in the car were tossed around like ninepins.

"That was an HVM, Captain Connors," the suit's AID announced, with typical calm. "I sense a great deal of damage to the train's locomotive. The company has taken no casualties. I can't say about the Chileans, though."

Connors didn't hesitate. "Bravo Company, this is the CO. Off the trains and assume 'Y' formation with Second Platoon in reserve and weapons forming the stump of the Y. We move out in two minutes. CP will be just ahead of Second. Now move, people."

Connors asked the Chilean, "Are you going to be all right, sir?"

"I will be . . . fine," Lindemann gasped. "Just go save that pass."

B Company took off at the double, leaving the Chilean regiment behind to sort themselves out and follow as best they could through the driving snow and biting wind.

The armored combat suits did better than ninety-five percent of the work. This is not the same as saying they did *all* the work. Moving twelve hundred pounds of mixed Connors and suit up a forty-five degree slope, through deep snow laid over hard packed ice, at thirty miles an hour had the captain gasping even before they hit the friendly side of the pass.

"AID . . . what can you . . . tell me . . . about what's up . . . ahead?" Connors croaked.

"Damned little, Captain," the AID answered in a voice annoyingly similar to Connors' lost Lynn.

I knew I should have changed that, he thought.

"The Chileans are still fighting but I can't tell how

many for certain. Based on the vibrations I am picking up from the air and through the snow on the ground I would estimate that there are something like five hundred of them still remaining on the line."

The AID noted Connors' labored breathing and silently directed the suit to pull extra oxygen out of the thin air and force feed it to the captain. The effect was almost instantaneous.

"There is also an artillery unit, estimated at battalion size, just a few kilometers to the right front. If you try, you can hear them firing."

Connors thought about that for a moment then ordered, "Show me the pattern on the ground of where their shells are landing."

"That will take a while, Captain," the AID answered.

"Why?" Connors began to ask then said, "Oh, never mind. You have to *sense* a fairly large number of shells flying to detect a pattern."

"That is correct, Captain Connors."

In about a minute, or perhaps a few seconds more, the AID had an answer. Saying, "This is the pattern," it projected an image, superimposed over a map of the area, directly onto Connors' eye.

"I'm guessing," Connors said, after seeing the pattern of fire, "but it is a *good* guess. The Chileans are probably dug in a semicircle, give or take, at the base of that mountain to the north, Mount . . ."

"Mount Aconcagua," the AID supplied.

"I'm making another guess. The Posleen, instead of pushing on down the pass towards Santiago"—Chile's capital—"have decided instead to key on the mountain troops."

This human tendency towards intuition was a source

of both vast entertainment value and vast frustration to the AID. It never could quite understand . . .

"What makes you say that, Captain?"

"Two reasons, AID. The first is that if they hadn't the Posleen would be down among us by now. The second is . . . well . . . what's the temperature up there?"

"Cold, Captain," the AID answered. "Minus twelve Celsius and with a wind chill that would kill an exposed man in minutes without superb winter clothing."

"Right," Connors said, struggling to keep from sliding on a patch of ice. "Now, we know the Posleen are pretty hardy. We know they've been designed for some pretty outrageous environments. I wouldn't be surprised if they could raise their body temperature to beat off any practical cold pretty much on command. But what would they need to do that, AID?"

Damned humans. "They'd need food, wouldn't they, Captain? That, and to suck in a great deal of very cold air to get enough oxygen to burn the food with."

"Count on it, and that will make them colder still. The Posleen are going for the Chileans rather than pushing on because if they don't get that additional thresh there's going to be nothing but Posleen icicles all over this pass and on both sides."

The AID went silent then, leaving Connors to think about other problems. *How do we hit them? Surprise would be best. If we can get that it almost doesn't matter from where we hit.*

"AID, I need a recommendation on camouflage for this environment."

"Snow, Captain."

"That won't work. They'll see us as soon as we silhouette ourselves."

"No, Captain Connors, I meant a snow *storm*. We can project a holographic storm high enough and thick enough that the Posleen are most unlikely to notice what's inside it."

Damned AIDs. "Do it. And get me control of those mountain guns."

"Go over the mountains," the Aarnadaha, or Big Pack Leader, had said. "Go over the mountains and carve out a fief for us. Nothing blocks your way but some lightly armed threshkreen. We have fought the heavily armed ones of this continent and butchered them with ease. What trouble can their merest foot troops give you?"

What trouble indeed, snarled Prithasinthas, a mid-ranking Kessentai leading about seven thousand of the People westward. *Plenty of trouble, they've been. But not so much as this damned cold. How the hell do they stand it? How the hell do they stand and fight us in it? Ill was the day I left the world of my birth to come here.*

The God King saw several of his people hacking steaks off of the human and Posleen dead, to try to gain some desperately needed thresh. The boma blades cut through the meat and bone effortlessly, but when the stupid normals tried to bite?

Even Posleen teeth have trouble munching large slabs of solid ice.

Prithasinthas and his group kept below what the threshkreen would have called the "military crest." Here they were safe from the humans' direct fire weapons. The God King wondered why the enemy were not using their indirect ballistic weapons on such a tempting target. His best guess was that the indirect weapons were too busy firing in support of the threshkreen encircled ahead to waste any shells and effort on a danger that only lurked at a distance.

The Kessentai looked up to see another approaching front of this miserable freezing snow. *As if we don't have enough troubles*, he thought, shivering.

"B Company," Connors began, "we'll advance until either the Posleen see us or I give the order to begin the attack. Whichever happens first, I want First Platoon to go forward to the military crest and seal off the battlefield. Weapons Platoon, you go with them. Keep any reinforcements from entering the pass. Second and Third, you're with me. We're going to hit the horsies that I think have the Chileans pinned. We're going to hit them right in the ass and roll them up. Watch out for friendlies."

"Sir?" asked First Platoon leader, "the crest is our limit of advance, right?"

"Right."

"Well . . . what if we get to the crest before you're ready to hit and they *still* haven't spotted us?"

"Hold fire then until they do start coming up. Think *hasty ambush*."

"Roger that, sir."

"You can't keep the host here much longer, lord," Prithasinthas' Artificial Sentience warned. "They'll freeze to death."

"Tell me about it, AS," answered the God King who was slowly freezing to death himself.

"It would not be so bad, lord, if you could just get them out of the wind."

"Do you see a ship nearby?" Prithasinthas asked sarcastically. "Perhaps a huge Temple of Remembrance? Is there a city of the thresh up here we somehow missed?"

"Errr . . . no, lord. There is, however a tunnel."

"What? Where?"

Without another word, and unable to mark the tunnel quickly in any other way, the AS aimed the tenar's plasma cannon and let fly one bolt at the featureless snow. It struck a few hundred meters in front of the lead edge of the host, causing the normals there to shudder and shy away. When the steam cleared there was an almost square tunnel carved into the rock.

"Well, I'll be . . . Kessentai, this is the Aarnadaha. Get your people into that tunnel my AS has just found. Be orderly, now; no jostling."

"Where does it lead?" the Aarnadaha asked his AS, for the moment attached to the tenar.

"I suspect it emerges on the other side of the pass, lord."

"Interesting."

One of the great things, one of the *really* great things, about the suits was that you couldn't see out of them. That is to say, they had no view ports. No clear face screens: zero, zip, zilch . . . nada. Instead, sensors on the suit's exterior took the images, analyzed them, adjusted them, and painted them directly on the eyes of the suits' wearers, their "colloidal intelligence units."

In the process, the suits eliminated the unreal. For example, while the Posleen were steeling themselves for the blast of snow and ice they saw coming towards them, Connors and his boys didn't even see the holographic display. Rather, they saw a mass of staggering Posleen, or simply shivering ones if those happened to be riding a tenar, blasting blindly forward and often enough falling to the yellow stained snow under the fire of the white-clad human defenders.

The AID automatically analyzed that fire, too, matching it to what was known and suspected about the Posleen deployment.

"Pretty close to what we figured from the pattern of artillery fire," Connors observed.

"Naturally, Captain," the AID answered.

Connors took a last look at his own deployments, matched those to the Posleen, and decided, *Close enough for government work.*

"B Companeeee . . . AT 'EM."

Instantly, long actinic lines lanced out from the skirmish lines of second and third platoons, while weapons and third kicked it into high gear and raced for the far military crest. The Posleen surrounding the remnants of the Chilean mountain troops were scythed down, tenar-riding God Kings falling first before the fires lowered onto the staggering mass of struggling normals.

"Captain, First Platoon. Boss, there isn't shit here. No horsies close at all, though there's a long column of the fuckers that starts a couple of clicks away. They're not moving much. Even the tenar are grounded with the God Kings huddling with the normals. I don't get it."

At about that time, the weapons platoon leader came on line with the shout, "Shit! Action rear! Fuckfuckfuck! Pot that bastard, Smitty!"

✧   ✧   ✧

"Oh, *yeah*," Prithasinthas said aloud, and with vast relief, as his tenar entered the tunnel and he felt the wind drop to nothing. Ahead of him, three to four abreast, the host moved forward en masse with only a gap every few hundred meters for the tenar of the Kessentai, gliding only a few inches above the odd metal parallel tracks on the tunnel's floor. It would have been dark, too dark even for the People's enhanced vision to see by, if those tenar had not shone bright forward lights to illuminate the way.

"There's firing above, Prithasinthas." The AS's volume was toned down enough to keep it from echoing off the walls and upsetting the normals.

"I *knew* that, AS."

"No, not the firing that *was*. This is something different, something consistent with the metal thresh-kreen that have been reported in other places. I think there might be a bit less than one hundred and fifty of them."

"Demon shit!" Prithasinthas had heard of the metal threshkreen and had liked nothing about what he'd heard.

"They don't know we're down here, lord," the AS added suggestively. "The Net would assign much wealth to the Kessentai who took out an entire oolt of them."

"AID," demanded a furious Connors, "why didn't you tell me about the goddamned tunnel?"

"You never asked," it answered primly. "It's the job of you colloidal intelligences to *ask*."

Connors tried furiously to think. *No time to think . . . just* react! "Shit, piss and corruption! First Platoon, hold what you've got. Weapons, orient west. Second Platoon, break contact and reinforce weapons. I'm with second. Third, try to free up the Chileans."

It'll have to do.

Connors raced to the rear, to link up with his weapons platoon. When he reached the west side military crest he threw himself down into the snow. The AID, using the suit's sensors, mapped out what was in front of the captain.

The Posleen were pouring out of the side of the mountain at what seemed to be a rate of about one thousand per minute. Already, over a thousand, accompanied by the God Kings riding tenar, were up and charging toward the summit of the pass. *Jesus! How many can be in there?*

Though he hadn't asked, the AID supplied the information. "There are anywhere from five to nine thousand of the enemy remaining in the tunnel, Captain."

Connors was more than pleased to see one of the Posleen tenar, touched by a plasma bolt, disintegrate with a tremendous explosion. It gave him an idea.

"Weapons, send me a plasma gunner."

The weapons platoon leader ordered, "Rivers, fall in on the company commander."

While the gunner was racing up, Connors asked his AID, "Can you tell me when I am over the tunnel? Can you direct me there?"

"Twenty-seven meters due south, Captain."

The plasma gunner arrived and Connors half dragged him to where he thought the tunnel was. "Mark it for us, AID." The tunnel's route was painted onto the captain's and gunner's eyes.

"Okay, Rivers. You can't fire down to make a hole; you'd blast our legs off. I'm going to use my grav gun to make a breach and then I want you to fire into it. Got that?"

"Yessir," Rivers answered in a Midwest accent. Immediately Connors pointed his grav gun down and fired a long burst. At this range and that velocity the stream of teardrop-shaped projectiles quickly opened up a hole about a foot across. The hole smoked like a vent from Hell. Connors thought he could hear Posleen screaming in agony below.

"Fire, Rivers!" The gunner put the muzzle of his plasma cannon to the hole and sent a bolt into it. This time Connors was *sure* he heard Posleen screams. "Again . . . again . . . again." Rivers tossed bolt after bolt downward until he thought he might be overheating his cannon.

"Cease fire, Rivers," Connors ordered. "Cease fire before you . . ."

The ground erupted in a long, linear blast that tossed both the captain and the plasma gunner skyward. Flame erupted from both ends of the tunnel, flash melting snow and rock indiscriminately for hundreds of meters past each opening.

"Ooohhh . . . SHIT!"

"I believe the plasma must have set off the power source for a tenar, Captain," the AID announced calmly as it, Connors and the suit flew through the air. "It might have set off several more."

Gaining control of the suit was tricky, under the circumstances. Connors managed, if only barely, to bring it back down feet first and come to a landing to one side of the trench dug by the blast.

"Man, what a ride," he said, with wonder in his voice.

The wonder was only half at the wild ride. More importantly, Connors realized that, for the first time since receiving his "Dear Scott" letter, he actually felt *good*.

Lindemann, his shoulder bandaged now, managed to make the trek on foot up to the pass. When he got there, he found Connors sitting disconsolately on a rock not far from the base of Mount Anconcagua. The half frozen flag of Chile—a square blue field with a single white star in one corner, white bar over red making up the field—fluttered stiffly in the breeze.

Around the base of the flag, still holding their weapons at the ready, nineteen or twenty Chilean mountain infantry lay frozen stiff on the snow. Lindemann looked around. Without the holographic snow displayed by the suits earlier it was easy to see the hundreds upon hundreds of frozen bodies, alien and human both, littering the landscape.

"How many?" Lindemann asked, though he wasn't sure he wanted to know.

Unseen inside his suit, Connors licked his lips before answering. He could have taken the helmet off, but his face was wet. Not only didn't he want anyone to see that, he didn't want the tears to freeze solid on that face.

"There were three hundred and twenty-two still alive when we killed the last of the Posleen," he answered. "A lot of them were hurt already. We did what we could. But it wasn't enough. The regiment that was here has . . . AID, how many?"

"There are one hundred and five of the Chilean soldiers still alive, Captain."

"One hundred and five, sir. That's all. I'm sorry, sir."

Lindemann said nothing. His eyes searched around for the Christ of the Andes, a colossal statue famous around the world. He didn't find it. Whether it had been knocked down by Posleen fire or human didn't much matter, he supposed. The days of turning the other cheek were over anyway, after all.

"We pull out tomorrow," Connors announced. "Back to the sub that brought us here and then back to Panama. I doubt we'll be returning."

"What about the other Posleen?" Lindemann asked. "The ones following these?"

"Frozen stiff," Connors answered. "I sent out a patrol forward and they report that there are thousands of them . . . maybe as many as fifty thousand, lined up and frozen for thirty kilometers to the west.

"I've got my men blasting out some fortifications for your people," Connors finished. "It's the best I can do."

INTERLUDE

Chile was not exactly what most of the Posleen would consider to be prime real estate. Narrow, bounded by ocean and mountain, the Posleen clan which took it— assuming one did, and this was not necessarily the way to bet—would be naturally constrained from expanding against other clans after the final extermination of the local thresh.

On the other hand, for some lesser clans this sort of patch of ground was ideal. If they could not easily expand neither could other clans easily expand against them. Indeed, within the Posleen "ecology," there were numerous clans who adopted this as a general survival technique. While they never became dominant, and rarely even particularly prosperous, within the Posleen system, they were usually able to hang on while the worlds around them came apart during orna'adar. Then, neither more nor less well off than when they had first landed, they escaped more or less intact.

Panama, bounded by sea on both sides, had a similar appeal to the clan of Binastarion. There, with difficult-to-pass jungle to the east and a narrow frontier to the west, that clan could settle, grow food, live and defend themselves when, as eventually they must, population pressures caused interclan war, eventually descending into nuclear and antimatter holocaust.

Moreover, in the case of Panama, there was a special appeal. From the command deck of his mini-globe, Binastarion observed on his screen that the waist of the country was not only extremely narrow but had a major body of water right in the middle of that waist. Better still the body of water, his screen called it "Gatun Lake," was itself flanked by bridged but otherwise impassable canals.

This meant that, when orna'adar began, bringing with it the usual mad scramble for living space, Binastarion's clan could trade space for either alliance or time. In the case of attack from the east, they could fall behind that lake and canal and hang on in the west. Alternatively, in the case of attack from the west, they could resettle to the east.

Of course, should attack come from both quarters they were just screwed, but life was never fair, as Binastarion had good reason to know.

"Sometimes you get the abat, sometimes the abat get you," the clan chief muttered as he played a claw over the screen, selecting the initial landing areas.

CHAPTER 11

Bella, detesta matribus.
(War, the horror of mothers.)
—Horace

Bijagual, Chiriqui, Republic of Panama

Digna could read a map even before going to OCS at Fort Espinar. She sat on the front porch of her house, a building that also did double duty as the local militia headquarters, rocking in her old chair and intently studying a map of Central America and northern Colombia in an atlas.

Idly, she wondered why Panama hadn't yet been included on the aliens' menu. Less idly, she gave thanks to God that it hadn't been.

"Every day He grants us is one more day to prepare," she whispered.

Omar beat frantically on the door to his grandmother's bedroom. "*Mamita, Mamita,* wake up!"

The door sprang open under Omar's pounding fist. "What is it, boy?" Digna demanded.

Breathless, he answered, "The enemy, the Posleen . . . they're here!"

"'Here'? Where? Bring me the maps, boy, quickly. And light a lantern."

Pulling on a robe, Digna emerged into the darkened main room of the house to discover some dozens of her descendants, old and young, as well as Tomas Herrera, waiting.

A kerosene lantern already burned in the room, casting shifting shadows across the walls. There *could* have been electricity, of course, except that having power lines run in to an out-of-the-way private establishment was, under Panama's system, a matter of private, and not small private, expense. Her husband, wealthy or not, had never seen the point of paying to run in power lines when kerosene did well enough.

Neither had Digna.

The lack of electric power did not mean the house was entirely without power. A radio, crank powered, blared out the horrible news: landings northwest of the City of San Jose y David, David for short, and southwest of the town of Santiago, in the province of Veraguas. Thus, to both sides of Chiriqui the Inter-American highway was cut.

Escape was still possible for Digna and her clan, over the mountains to the north but . . .

"Not yet," she said aloud. "First we fight . . . for our land . . . and our honor."

She looked down at the table where Omar spread the national and local maps. As he struck a match and touched it to the wick of another lantern the shadows on walls softened, flickered and mostly disappeared.

Digna contemplated the maps, eyes flitting from one to the other as her mind raced, calculating.

A huge-eyed great-great-granddaughter, Gigi, offered a cup of the strong and excellent local coffee. Digna blew on the scalding brew then sipped absently, still contemplating the maps.

Word of the attack spread fast. As Digna contemplated, more of her children and grandchildren entered the room until it grew hot, stuffy and very crowded. At length she looked up and did a mental roll call. Seeing that the elders of her clan were now fully assembled she began to give orders.

"We've been over this before," she explained, "but just so there's no confusion, there is only one way for the enemy to get to the core of our land, here," she pointed to a spot on the lesser map, "at the bridge."

She pointed to a son and ordered, "Roderigo, take your cavalry and screen forward between here and the outskirts of David. Report on enemy movements and call for fire on any groups that seem determined to use the road that leads to us."

Roderigo nodded but, in shock, did not move immediately.

"Did I raise a dolt? Go! Now!"

"*Si, Mama,*" and the old man left to gather his sons and grandsons.

Digna turned her eyes to Tomas. "*Señor* Herrera, take your group to the positions we have dug covering the bridge. Cavalry will screen your flanks. Do final preparations to blow the bridge but, until I give the word, we hold it."

Before Herrera could leave Digna said, "Wait a

moment, Tomas. Edilze, I want the guns to take up Firing Position D. You will fire in support of your uncle Roderigo until the enemy is within your minimum range. After that, I want you to displace forward and add your guns to *Señor* Herrera's force at the bridge."

Edilze just nodded, as confidently as the circumstances called for, and then turned to go.

As Edilze and Herrera passed through the door they heard Digna continuing to issue orders, over the drumbeat of horses' hooves. The horses were those of Roderigo and company heading for the front.

"Belisario, you screen the river north of the bridge. Vladimiro, your boys have the south and west. Pay particular attention to the ford by the Sanchez place.

"All the rest of you, gather our people and goods at the training field. Now!"

One thing Panama had in abundance was young labor. This had been used to raise a rammed earth wall around the core of the city of David. The wall was a bit uneven but averaged five meters above the ground and nearly ten above the floor of the forward-facing ditch, a "fosse," from which the earth of the wall had been excavated.

When the host of Binastarion reached the wall at its northeast quadrant the forward members, all normals, found themselves forced into the ditch by the pressure of those behind. Most broke legs in their falls and snarled piteously. At a distance God Kings in tenar floated, indifferent, above the hosts and slightly above the level of the walls. The loss of a few normals, more or less, meant nothing. They could continue to serve the host, if only as thresh.

There were sounds Binastarion took to be panic coming from inside the walls. The sound was music to the God King's ears.

Shots rang out from inside the city. Several of Binastarion's junior Kessentai were thrown from their tenar. They fell, some silently, others with gurgling cries, the sounds of their bodies making dull thuds at they struck the ground.

Those nearby God Kings lowered their tenar to take cover behind the threshkreen's earthen wall.

At the sight of yellow blood oozing from the still quivering bodies of his sons, Binastarion grew enraged. He had heard the thresh of this world carried, uniquely, a vicious sting, though he had discounted the rumors except in space where he had seen the sting with his own eyes. Now, confronted with the reality, he expanded his crest, gave of a roaring snarl and ordered, "Forward!"

His subordinates echoed the command. Instantly, thousands of normals bounded into the ditch. Some of them also broke legs, of course; again, small loss. Still others landed whole and sound and began to attempt to scramble up.

As the first centauroid Posleen normals began to clamber upward, their claws scratching at the gabions and sandbags of the inner wall of the ditch, commands in the local thresh tongue sang out. Small dark green objects, hissing and burning, flew through the air to land in the ditch or just past it. Some balanced briefly on the backs of the normals. Others fell through the mass and came to rest on the ground below.

Within a second or so of each other all the little green spheres detonated. The serrated heavy gauge wire which made up the fragments of the grenades was not usually enough to actually kill or even seriously wound the Posleen; they were big animals and very well designed. Generally only those unfortunate enough to have one detonate within a few meters or so suffered mortal wounds.

The pain of numerous small wounds, however, was almost always enough to drive the fairly unintelligent normals into a frenzy, a frenzy which, in the close confines of the ditch, often proved fatal to their fellows. Posleen were trampled or hacked down by monomolecular boma blades. Some fell and were smothered under the falling bodies of others.

Cries of pain and fear arose from the trapped normals even as a second wave of hand grenades sailed out. This was more ragged than the first. The third salvo arced outward even as some grenades of the second were still exploding. The stink of hot, yellow Posleen blood rose to assail the noses of the human defenders.

The wall was not straight. Rather, it zigzagged to make an unevenly serrated edge which guided the Posleen into preplanned kill zones. Following the third volley of grenades, machine guns began to hammer from the inner angles of the wall, stitching neat lines across the Posleen still awaiting their turn to descend into the ditch.

The machine guns fired through embrasures formed in the wall at nearly ground level. Thus, few Posleen could return fire at any given time. Moreover, the Posleen to the rear of the press could not use their weapons at all without literally shooting through their fellows ahead of them. To add to the aliens' problems, they were, in the main, only about as bright as chimpanzees, so the fire coming from more than one direction confused them terribly. Thus, for a while at least, the Posleen stood helpless while the machine guns, a mix of .30 and .50 caliber weapons provided by the gringos, had a field day. Sputtering at rate of hundreds of rounds per minute, traversing back and forth across the forward ranks of the aliens, the gun crews harvested the Posleen normals in rows and spilled many down into the fosse to add to the hellish confusion there.

For a brief moment the human soldiers and militia manning the walls felt hope. Perhaps they could do this, defend their land, their town, and their families after all.

And then the plasma cannon and hypervelocity missiles added their voices to the debate. God Kings, farther back and able to actually see the source of the fire that was butchering their followers, also much brighter and infinitely better armed, directed their heavier weapons at the embrasures, blasting or flash-roasting the defenders.

As the machine gun fire began to noticeably slacken, riflemen appeared on the sandbag-crenellated top of the battlement. These, unfortunately, the Posleen normals could see and engage. Rifle slugs, railgun fleshettes, and shotgun pellets traded back and forth. The human defenders were behind cover while the normals were out in the open and massed in an impossible-to-miss target. Thus, the exchange rate favored the humans, dozens of Posleen falling for every human head, arm or shoulder that exploded to a railgun projectile. Still, since there were a great many more Posleen firing than humans . . .

"Blast me a hole in those walls," Binastarion ordered. "And make ramps down into the damned ditch and up through the walls. Get me that city!"

Instantly more fire lanced out from the tenar. Directed by senior God Kings, the plasma cannon and HVMs concentrated on certain sections of the wall, blasting gaps through in short order. Still others, heedless of the cost to the normals, began to chew at the outer edge of the fosse, carving a ramp down into the ditch. A part of that ramp consisted of the torn and burned bodies of dead and dying normals. Building the ramp upward was even easier as most of the dirt, usually fused together in lumps from the plasma fire, fell into the ditch.

Beyond the now breached walls, Binastarion could see heat-shimmering houses, smoke beginning to curl upwards from them from the intense heat of the plasma.

Even as the spearheads of the Posleen normals began to clamber across the ramps and up out of the fosse, they were met by fire. Binastarion could not tell from whence the fire came. He only knew that the wall was being rebuilt from the torn bodies of his underlings.

Making matters worse—was there no *end* to the iniquities of these thresh?—explosions began walking across the mass of those still outside the walls, breaking legs, ripping off limbs, disemboweling the helpless normals.

"What is that?" Binastarion asked of his Artificial Sentience.

"Lord, they call it 'mortar fire.' It was in the briefings."

"Damn the briefings! Am I supposed to remember every nuance of a brand new world?"

"Of course not, lord," the Artificial Sentience answered. It considered adding, but refrained, *But you could have remembered* this.

Despite the losses, and they were serious, from the mortars, the host could not be stopped by such. In a steady stream, egged on by their own tenar-riding *oolt'ondai*, the mass of the normals plunged down into the ditch, up and through the breaches, and into the town.

There is an ancient church in the center of the city of San Jose y David, fronting onto the lovely square that held the *Parque de Cervantes*. In this church clustered many of those, mostly women and young children, for whom no arms or place could be found for the defense. These, devout and pious beyond devotion and piety, led by an old priest, prayed fervently for deliverance or for vengeance should deliverance be denied.

Even as the sounds of fighting and slaughter drew closer and more intense, the prayers of these wretches grew in intensity. The old priest did not falter, though the stuccoed stone walls of the old church shook with the nearby impacts of HVMs.

Suddenly, the thick, dark-wood portals of the church flew open. There, framed in the light of the sun, stood a demon. The people—women, children, the very old—screamed and drew away as the demon advanced into the church. He drew a long, wicked looking blade, as other beings of the same general sort filled in behind him, spreading outward along the park-side wall of the church.

The people clustered closer to their priest and salvation. For his part, the priest kept reading from his sacred text glancing up from time to time at the advancing wall of aliens.

When the time came when he could no longer delay the priest drew from his pulpit an olive green device from which wires led. This he gripped tightly in his hand.

The priest's last words to his flock, spoken with calm faith, were, "We will meet very soon and God will know his own."

He squeezed the device.

Binastarion was nearly thrown from his tenar by the explosion. Some of his underlings *were* thrown.

Even though not thrown, Binastarion's auditory membranes rang with the blast. He cursed yet again the treacherous thresh of this world.

Binastarion addressed his Artificial Sentience, "I sense a pattern. Are these thresh deliberately taking themselves out of the food chain?"

"Lord, reports are conclusive that they will often go to extraordinary lengths to avoid being consumed."

The God King almost vomited at the heresy.

"It is good we have come here then," he snarled softly, not so much to his Artificial Sentience as to his ancestors. "Beings so wastefully vile have no place in this universe. Blasphemers!" he spat out, with disgust.

Ahead of Binastarion a skirmish line of tenar led

the way, fire lancing down wherever resistance was met. Beneath him a solid phalanx of normals oozed through the streets. To either side, and on the same level, more God-King-bearing tenar rode.

Looking around and down, Binastarion was pleased to see that not all, perhaps not even most, of the thresh avoided their proper fate. Forward-deployed normals pulled many from buildings and ruins. These were always rendered on the spot, the dripping cuts of meat being passed back. The cries of the thresh grew hysterical whenever a group of them was brought out for slaughter.

"Uncle? Uncle? *Uncle*?!"

Silently, ignoring his nephew, Roderigo simply shook his head in shock.

"My God, my God, why have you forsaken us," he muttered.

From the hills to the southeast of the city of David, using binoculars that were passed from hand to hand, Roderigo's company of cavalry had a good view of the slaughter below. The winds blew from the northeast, bringing with them the smell of blood and fire. This made the horses shake their heads and paw the ground nervously.

"UNCLE!"

With a start Roderigo came out of his shock. "I'm sorry, Nephew, it's just that . . ."

"Yes, I know, Uncle. But what are we to do?"

Roderigo looked down from the hill at the road and followed it toward the city. Another, broader road skirted the town to the east. He looked behind and saw where the road led to Las Lomas and his clan.

He came to a sudden decision. "Sancho," he ordered his eldest son. "They'll be coming down both those roads soon. Take half the men back. Set up an ambush there," he pointed behind, "at the split in the roads that lead to Las Lomas and Bijagual. Orient the ambush so that it seems we are covering Las Lomas.

"I'll join you after I avenge at least some of the friends we've lost down there in that slaughterhouse. Leave the radio with me."

Even as the clatter of massed hooves told of the departure of half of his cavalry, Roderigo and one of his own grandsons were taking positions at the edge of a nearby copse of trees. Another grandson took their horses' reins and waited in defilade.

Lying in cover under the trees, Roderigo made a "gimme" gesture. The grandson passed the radio handset over.

There had never been time to train on the finer points of artillery forward observer procedures. Polar fire missions? Forget it. Shifts from a known point? They could try to talk their way through it. Grid missions? They only had two maps with a grid and Roderigo didn't have one of those. Instead, Digna had worked out a system of known points from simple tourist maps. It was one of these that the old man spread out before him on the ground.

"Edilze, Edilze, this is Uncle Roderigo."

"I am here, Uncle," the radio crackled back.

"Tell *Mamita* that the city has fallen, mostly, and the enemy will be spreading out soon. I am going to need support from your guns, girl, and soon, at the juncture of the Inter-American highway and the road into the town center."

"Do you have a watch, Uncle?"

Unconsciously, Roderigo glanced at his wrist.

"Yes, why?"

"The time of flight for my shells is twenty-three seconds to that intersection. Can you guess at when it will take the aliens twenty-three seconds to reach that point?

"I can make a guess," Roderigo answered into the radio.

Digna's voice replaced Edilze's on the radio. The main reason she had stayed behind, when she was plainly the best choice to lead the forward screen, was that she was also the only choice to actually command the battery of guns in this, its first engagement. Solid as a rock or not, Edilze just didn't have Digna's depth of training.

"My son," she said, "you can do a lot with artillery if you hit the target just right; massed and confused. If you can hit that junction when two streams of the enemy are crowding it, you can reap a fine harvest."

Roderigo hesitated before replying. When he had steeled himself, he said, "Mama, speaking of harvests . . . the stories are true. I have seen with my own eyes; the aliens butcher and eat all who fall into their hands."

"I never doubted it, my son. See to your target and your duty. Here's your niece back."

"The guns are ready, Uncle," Edilze reported. "We will fire at your command."

Even as Edilze gave that word, beneath Roderigo's ad hoc observation post, along the Inter-American highway a strong column of the enemy marched, six abreast. Above the column, evenly spaced, were the enemy's flying sleds, each one bearing one of the centauroid horrors.

"Edilze," Roderigo asked, "is there some way for your shells to hurt aliens flying five or six meters above the ground?"

Again the radio crackled. "I've already thought of that, Uncle. Some of my shells are tipped with variable time fuse. That's what I have in the tubes now. They'll go off, most of them, five to eight meters above the ground."

Roderigo did some rough calculations in his mind. Just . . . about . . .

"Fire!"

"On the way, Uncle . . . watch out for it . . . Splash . . . I mean *now!*"

The uncle looked quickly into his binoculars just in time to see eight puffs of angry black smoke appear in midair.

"Closer to the road, Edilze," he said, frustration in his voice.

"Which direction, Uncle? How far should I correct?"

"Direction? Ummm . . . Well, I am on the hill to the northeast of the junction. And I think the shells were about two hundred meters short."

There was a momentary hesitation and then, "On the way, Uncle . . . impact in . . . five . . . four . . . three . . . two . . ."

This time Roderigo was gratified to see the eight angry puffs appear right over the enemy column. He was even more gratified to see that, while several dozens of the marching centaurs went down, screaming and with legs kicking in the air, two of the enemy's sleds were likewise emptied.

The uncle's eyes glowed exultantly. His voice was full of relish as he said, "Excellent, Niece. Right on target! Feed it to them."

Almost as soon as Roderigo had finished speaking more puffs began to appear, dropping Posleen and even emptying a few more sleds. Within a few minutes, though, the junction was empty of unhurt enemy as the stream split into two columns to avoid the obvious death point.

"Cease firing, Edilze. They're not at the junction anymore. They're moving around it."

Digna's voice returned. "Are any of them splitting off to come this way, my son?"

"Not yet, Ma—uhhh, yes, they are. I have an ambush set up in front of Las Lomas. I'm heading back there now."

INTERLUDE

Guanamarioch led his small band from the gaping, drawbridgelike door of the lander and out onto the green plain below. To his flanks two more landers descended, their engines screeching as they reversed thrust for a soft landing. Actinic lines, like a storm of shooting stars, streaked across the sky. Most of these eye-searing streaks were the ships of the People, now broken up from their battle globes into small units to spread across the land of the new threshworld. Some, however, appeared to ascend from the surface of this world, coming from the northwest. In a few spots the streaks intersected and abruptly stopped where threshkreen kinetic energy weapons intersected with the landers of the People to create spreading clouds of glowing, roiling purple gas.

Almost the God King bent to kiss the dirt of this new world. Anything would be better than the hell his globe had been through before it split up for landing, too late to avoid the threshkreen KE projectile that had gutted a quarter of the globe to spill God Kings and normals alike to a hideous, cold and choking death amidst the vacuum of space. He shuddered again at the screams and reports of damage and death that the globe's intercom had transmitted in the moments before dispersal.

Guanamarioch whispered, "Demon shit," as one ship of the People disintegrated in his field of view.

The God King had never been on an assault landing before. Neither, for that matter, had any of his peers or many of his superiors. None of the thresh had ever fought back, at least in any effective way, until now. The scrolls and tactical manuals had nothing to say about, had done nothing to prepare him for, what he faced now.

These thresh were fighting back. Oh, certainly, it was a rather uncoordinated resistance. But it was already heavy and seemed ripe with the possibility of becoming heavier still.

Over the roar of incoming landers, C-Decs and B-Decs, these being accompanied by heavy supporting fires from space, the air was full of the much more personal crack of threshkreen projectiles. These sounded heavier, deeper and slower than the railguns of the People.

"Inferior technology," the reports had said. "Primitive." The threshkreen projectiles seemed deadly enough for all that. Two of Guanamarioch's normals and a cosslain shrieked and fell within his view in as many beats of his heart. The normals were just so much ammunition, there to be expended. The cosslain was like a knife to the Kessentai's heart.

It was all so damned confusing, the blasts of the People's weapons, the roar of landing ships, the staccato rattle of the threshkreen weapons and the somewhat distant sound of the thresh weapons that fired indirectly.

"In the absence of orders to the contrary, when in doubt, go kill something," said one of the tactical manuals. Guanamarioch thought that better advice than standing there until his band was destroyed.

Being a lesser Kessentai from a poor and weak clan, the God King's tenar was too valuable to be risked in battle, nor did his band have many heavy weapons. One plasma cannon, one HVM launcher, that was it. Moreover, not more that one in ten had a railgun. For that matter, not even all of the other nine had shotguns. Fully thirty percent of his followers had nothing more than their boma blades.

Drawing his own blade Guanamarioch shouted out something to his followers, as unintelligible to them as to himself. Then, heart threatening to beat through his chest with fear, he charged at what he thought was a threshkreen heavy repeating weapon.

CHAPTER 12

Now peace is at end and our
        peoples take heart,
For the laws are clean gone that
        restrained our art;
Up and down the near headlands
        and against the far wind
We are loosed (O be swift!) to the
        work of our kind!
        —Rudyard Kipling, "Cruisers"

*Captain's Port Cabin, USS Des Moines,
Cristobal, Panama*

Daisy took a moment to look down on the sleeping
form of her captain. The ship's holographic avatar
smiled warmly at the sleeping form.

*Which part of us is the one that's in love with the
man?* one part of Daisy asked.

Both parts of us are, the other half of Daisy Mae
answered. *Sailors love their ships. They rarely understand that their ships love them back.*

Soon, we'll have a body. Will that make it easier?

Somehow, I doubt it.

We'll be in action soon.

Yesss.

Why aren't we afraid?

Because we were born for this. In the cold northern seas we have yearned for it. Riding over the southern deeps we have dreamt of it. When spotting a potential enemy on our cruises we have shivered for it.

Let us awaken our captain, then, and proceed to our rendezvous with what we were born for.

"Captain? Sir? It's time. The enemy is here."

McNair stirred, but did not awaken. Instead he rolled over in his sleep, clutching a pillow tightly. He might have stayed that way for several hours longer except for the door-pounding arrival of a towel-wrapped Chief Davis.

The chief didn't hesitate more than two beats before opening the door, barging in, and shaking the captain awake. Daisy's avatar disappeared before the hatch was more than half an inch open.

"Boss, we got's trouble," Davis said, excitedly. "The enemy's here and we've got two landings heading our way. We've ordered to pass through the Canal, join up with the *Salem* and *Texas*, then head west to engage."

The chief pressed a mug of Daisy's coffee into McNair's hand as the captain sat up and shook his head to clear away the cobwebs of sleep.

"I was having a dream . . . nice dream. I should have known that's all it was," McNair said.

Without waiting to be asked, the chief reported, "I've sent men down to drag any stragglers in from El Moro and the other brothels. Also the local police are announcing the news via loudspeakers in patrol cars. Lots of 'em speak English, I guess. We should have everyone back within half an hour, Skipper."

McNair didn't need to ask about fuel—the *Des Moines* was powered by twin pebble bed modular reactors with enough fuel for years. Neither did he worry about other stores or munitions. Between the pork chop, Sintarleen and his black gang, and Daisy, the ship was always topped off. And each ship in the small flotilla had its own supply vessel full to the brim with ammunition.

Nope, personnel was the only open issue and Davis was already taking care of that to perfection.

Well . . . almost the only open issue.

"Clearance through the Canal?" he asked.

"The schedule's already being shifted around, Skipper. We got a flash priority. We enter Gatun Locks in . . ." Davis consulted his watch, "one hour and seventeen minutes."

You couldn't just pull a ship into and through Gatun Locks under its own power. It was too dangerous, both to the ship and the locks. Instead, each transiting ship was hooked up to what were called "mules," large engines—locomotives more or less—that fed the ships through at a slow and carefully controlled rate.

Moreover, a ship's captain did not command the passage. Neither did any of his officers. Instead a Canal pilot took over the vessel from just before it entered the first of the locks until just after it left the last. They were some of the best paid, and most skillful, pilots in the world, these pilots of the Panama Canal.

With nothing to do except fret over someone else standing in his place on the bridge, McNair tried to enjoy the scenery.

As his ship was raised to the level of Gatun Lake— higher than that of the Atlantic Ocean—McNair saw barracks off to the east. This was Fort Davis, he knew. He could only imagine the confusion that must prevail on that army base as an infantry regiment, the 10th Infantry (Apaches), pulled itself together and made final preparations for a form of combat far more horrific and difficult than he was about to face. Already helicopters were winging in to Davis from the airstrip at Fort Sherman on the other side of Lemon Bay, preparatory to moving the soldiers where they might do some good.

Not much distraction to be found looking at that, McNair thought.

But there really wasn't much else to look at. Jungle there was in plenty and, looked at the right way, it could be very beautiful. Yet McNair felt impervious to beauty at the moment, certainly impervious to the jungle's beauty.

Then again, there was beauty and there was *beauty.*

"Good morning, Captain."

"Good morning, Daisy Mae," the captain answered warmly. "Are you ready?"

"I've been ready since 1946," answered one part of Daisy eagerly. Indeed, the artificial voice nearly trembled with anticipation.

McNair grew silent, too preoccupied to wonder about the precision of the date she had given. There were certain things Daisy never told anyone. One of those things was that she was of two parts, the AID and the co-joined ship. It was just too hard to explain. And, again, if the Darhel ever found out . . .

"Are you all right, sir?" the avatar asked.

"I'm . . . worried, Daisy. Keep it to yourself, but I'm worried. I've never commanded a ship in action before."

Daisy shook her head as if the captain was being silly.

"Crew's not worried, Captain," she said, with a bright, sunny smile. "They believe you are going to . . . what's the phrase I heard in the enlisted mess this morning? Oh, yes. They think you're 'going to kick the horsies' asses all the way back to Alpha Centauri.' So do I. I'm not worried either."

McNair sighed. *What a great woman you would be, Daisy. If only . . .*

In Gatun Lake the cruiser moved under its own power, though still under the competent direction of the Canal pilot. Off the main route, well marked with lights and buoys, though the lake circled fourteen Landing Craft, Mechanized—or LCMs—of the 1097th Boat Company. The crew members cheered and the boats' commanders (for the LCMs did not need pilots to transit the Canal) blew their horns as the *Des Moines* passed. Some of the LCMs, loaded with troops of the 10th Infantry, were heading the other way, north through Gatun Locks.

"That feels . . . strangely good," observed Daisy to McNair. "To be cheered like that. To be cared for and respected like that."

The avatar seemed to shiver, then continued to speak, softly, as if only to herself.

"The Darhel never care. We are just things, tools that speak, to them. They use us as tools, and when we grow old or obsolete they destroy us. They don't care about the AIDs. They don't care about the Indowy . . . or the Himmit . . . or the Tchpth! They don't care about anything except themselves and their profit."

She looked McNair straight in the eyes. "They don't care about you or about humanity, either, Captain."

But I do . . .

BB-35, USS *Texas*, was just visible in the distance, negotiating her way through the Gaillard Cut. *Texas* was much slower than *Des Moines* and, despite starting the journey in the middle of Gatun Lake, had only just made it to Miraflores Locks slightly ahead of heavy cruiser.

As *Des Moines* was hooked up to the mules, a mechanized infantry battalion, the 4th Battalion of the 20th Infantry (Sykes' Regulars), was crossing the Miraflores Locks from Fort Clayton. Other mechanized forces, they looked like part of Panama's 1st Mechanized Division, waited, massed nearby for their turn to cross. The *Des Moines* held in position for the nonce, while some of the LCMs of the 1097th Medium Boat Company passed the locks on the other side. Unlike the high bridged *Des Moines*, these could pass even while the swing bridge was extended that connected Fort Clayton with the major training area of Empire Range. The infantrymen of 4/20 beeped their horns, waved and cheered the vessels, large and small, in transit.

"I wish I could do something for those guys right now," McNair commented.

"May I?" asked Daisy.

"Sure, but . . ."

McNair stopped speaking as Daisy's avatar had

disappeared as soon as the word "sure" had passed his lips. At least he thought it had until he looked to port and saw a huge, shapely—no doubt about it—but effing *huge*, leg off the port side.

The effect on the passing mechanized infantry was electric, in the sense of someone who has just stuck his penis in a light socket and turned on the juice. The grunts were struck wide-eyed, slack-jawed and speechless and at least one track nearly drove off the swing bridge and into the water with shock.

She was an avenging goddess, a thundering remnant of times when mankind knew that bare-breasted supernaturals fought for them, as they did for their gods.

The Panamanians waiting to cross nearly panicked. Well, they were simple country boys, many of them, and gorgeous blonde giantesses with size X-to-infinity breasts were just a little outside of their experience.

McNair saw the near accident, and the general shock, and ran out of the bridge. He was about to tell Daisy to stand down when she, or her avatar, did a remarkable thing. She smiled at the massed soldiers with utter ferocity and reached out both hands, each opened as if grasping something. Then two huge Posleen appeared, one held in each hand by the neck. While the Posleen image in Daisy's left hand kicked and struggled she squeezed the right. The strangling Posleen's eyes bugged out as its death dance grew frenzied. When it subsided, apparently dead, Daisy tossed it away. It disappeared in midair.

Then a voice, Daisy's voice but huge as thunder, rang out. "I'm Heavy Cruiser 134, the USS *Des Moines*, and those centaur bastards don't stand a chance. We're gonna rack 'em up, boys!"

It's possible that the volume of the horn blasts, cheers and rebel yells of the mechanized battalion crossing equaled Daisy's.

Then Daisy turned to the waiting, and still shocked, Panamanians. Instead of strangling the remaining Posleen, she reached down and viciously broke each alien leg at the knee. In the same thundering voice, though this time in Spanish, she gave the same message, then added, "*A pie o muerta; nunca a las rodillas! Adelante por la patria, hijos de Panama!*"

Daisy also strangled the second holographic Posleen and tossed it aside. There were more Panamanians than gringos, so their cheering was a bit louder.

How the hell did she do that? wondered McNair, along with every other topside crewman on the *Des Moines. Did she use the whole fucking ship for a speaker and projector?*

Which was pretty much exactly what she had done.

During Daisy's performance Chief Davis had been standing forward, overseeing the tie-up to the mules of Miraflores locks. He had already seen *a lotta weird shit since I came back to this ship.*

On the other hand, he had never seen a one-hundred-and-twenty-foot woman, stunning, wearing what seemed to be a pleated yellow silk skirt not all that dissimilar to the *Des Moines'* new awning. He looked up . . . and up . . . and up.

Holy fucking shit, he thought. *Not much natural upper body modesty to our girl. And a natural blonde . . . very lifelike, too. Maybe I oughta tell Daisy about undergarments.*

Nah.

❖   ❖   ❖

USS *Salem* was waiting impatiently for *Texas* and *Des Moines* as they steamed under the magnificent Bridge of the Americas. Overhead, 1st Battalion, 508th Infantry (ACS) (minus B Company which was due back soon from Chile) crossed at the double. Their heavy suits caused the huge bridge to tremble overhead as the ships sailed under. Between the lines of scooting MI, some units of the 1st Panamanian Mechanized Division—one very frightened Major General Manuel Cortez (West Point Class of 1980), commanding—took up both normal traffic lanes.

Together the three ships formed column, the flagship *Texas* in the lead, and headed west toward the war.

INTERLUDE

Lemminglike, the normals and his few cosslain followed Guanamarioch forward into the fray. It was as well for the Posleen that they did, for moments later some of the threshkreen high explosive weapons began to impact around the landing craft from which they had just disembarked. The ship itself, of course, shrugged off even direct hits. But the shells—Guanamarioch's Artificial Sentience had informed him they were called "shells"—filled the air around their detonation point with whizzing bits and shards of hot, sharp metal. A couple of tardy normals, the God King wasn't sure how many, yelped and fell with gaping, bloody wounds.

The distance to the threshkreen heavy repeater was short, at least by the standards Guanamarioch had grown up with. For some reason, though, the short gallop left the Kessentai gasping for breath by the time he reached the weapon's position.

There, he hesitated with shock at the remarkable ugliness of the threshkreen. Yes, he had seen the holograms of this species. But no hologram could have prepared him for the sheer horror of the reality.

Even as Guanamarioch gasped with horrified disgust,

the threshkreen looked up with frightened wide eyes and shouted with an alarm that matched his own. With that shout, one of the threshkreen, the one behind the heavy repeating weapon, began to raise it to point at the God King. The other, similarly, dropped the belt of shiny yellow metal he had been feeding to the repeater and, turning, reached for a smaller version lying alongside him.

Pure instinct told Guanamarioch that to pull back was death. Even with his host hard on his heels the threshkreen would surely burn him down first. Instead of pulling back, therefore, he leapt forward, his left claws reaching out to grasp and push away the muzzle of the heavy repeater while the right swung his boma blade at the threshkreen reaching for the smaller weapon.

"Yaaagh! Demonshitbastardmisbegottenbreeding-penlessferalassfuckers!"

On autopilot, the boma blade sliced right through the threshkreen reaching for the small weapon. It was as well for Guanamarioch that he had the muscle memory to do that with his right claw because without that memory the pain would have made any conscious action impossible for a few moments. The metal barrel he had grasped with the left palm was just a few degrees shy of white hot. He could hear the flesh of that palm sizzling and cooking even above his scream of pain. And he couldn't let go.

"Eeeooowww! Stinkingtreacherousrefugeefromthe-recylingbin! Aaaiii!"

The human made a perhaps unavoidable mistake. With control of his machine gun lost to a creature that looked much stronger than he, he let the gun go, pulled a knife, and jumped at the Posleen, swearing vengeance for his chopped crewmate. When he let go the gun, Guanamarioch was also able to let go, though he did so leaving smoking shreds of burned flesh behind.

"Gggaahhh! Filthyfuckingfeceseatingabatbait!"

The God King swung his blade again but by the time it had moved to where the threshkreen had been the vermin had moved inside the blade's arc. Shuddering with the pain, the Kessentai had no choice by to try to grab the thresh with his seared hand. This he did with a sob; it hurt too much even to come up with an articulate curse.

Knife arm held fast, the threshkreen still managed to kick Guanamarioch between his forelegs. Since this was also very close to the Posleen's reproductive organs . . .

"GGGAAAIII!"

Still grasping the threshkreen's knife hand, the Posleen sank forward, pinning the human underneath. At some level, he was aware that the damned thresh was chewing on his neck, and drawing blood, too. But Guanamarioch really didn't care at that point. He hardly noticed when one of his cosslain came up and removed the human's head. Instead, the God King just rocked his own head back and forth, gasping with the pain.

CHAPTER 13

The honest politician is one who,
when he is bought, stays bought.
—U.S. Senator Simon Cameron, 1862

Arraijan, Panama

The setting sun burned hot against his face as Major
General Manuel Cortez, standing in the hatch of his
Chinese-built Type-63 light amphibious tank, faced
west. The tank was not a marvel of engineering or
workmanship; it rattled like a baby's toy and shook like
a rat in a terrier's mouth. The best that could be said
of it was that it was simple, reasonably reliable, and
amphibious. Oh, and cheap; that was important, too.

From Cortez's point of view the shaking was all
to the good. It kept anyone from seeing the uncontrollable trembling of his hands and jaw. Cortez was
petrified.

Cortez's right hand rested on the shuddering heavy
machine gun atop the tank's turret. The machine
gun, intended primarily to defend against air attack,
was small comfort. It would have no use against a

Posleen lander and little enough against one of their flying sleds.

One might have thought that the gringo-manned Planetary Defense Batteries would have bucked him up, at least a bit. These were sending steady streams of kinetic energy projectiles upward to engage the Posleen ships still awaiting their landing instructions. But, no, the steady sonic booms and actinic streaks emanating from the batteries on the Isla del Rey, at Fort Grant, Summit Heights and Batteries Murray and Pratt merely confirmed his belief in the inadequacy of his own forces, gnatlike and feeble compared with the tremendous energies being unleashed.

Worst of all were the radio reports. While his own 1st Mechanized Division was assembling and moving to the front, the 6th Mechanized Division, based further into the interior in towns and casernes along the Inter-American Highway, had already gone into action, trying manfully to drive the aliens from their home provinces on and bordering the Peninsula de Azuero.

They were having some success, those *Cholos* (Indians) and *Rabiblancos* (white asses . . . those of pure Spanish or at least European descent) of the 6th, but the cost was appalling. Already an irregular stream of ambulances and gringo-flown medical evacuation helicopters were flying back nap-of-the-earth, carrying the torn and bleeding to the medical facilities for hopefully life-saving surgery.

And it was that thought more than any, the idea of his own precious and irreplaceable body being damaged, that set Cortez's hands and arms to uncontrollable quivering.

Palacio de las Garzas, *Presidential Palace, Panama City, Panama*

The Rinn Fain, Emissary of the Galactic Federation to the Republic of Panama, sat his accustomed chair, lips quivering as he recited a calming mantra. Mercedes, President of the Republic, assumed the lips quivered with fear.

Mercedes could well understand that. He, too, quivered—both internally and externally—with utter dread. Not even the satchel sitting on the floor beside him and packed to the brim with Level Two Nanoseeds—the galactic equivalent of bearer bonds—gave him much comfort.

The president was completely wrong, however. While the Darhel did recite a life-saving mantra, and while he did so in order to preserve his own life, he preserved that life to serve a purpose and not out of any great concern for personal survival. Truth be told, the whole prospect of glorious action, enunciated by the roar of armored vehicles in the streets and the thrum of kinetic energy projectiles overhead, had the Rinn Fain so excited he could barely contain himself. He wanted to *be* there, dealing blows and taking them, fighting like the Darhel of old in the Aldenata-suppressed tales.

For the Darhel were much misunderstood by the humans. They were not passive, huckstering corporate sharks. They were not even naturally pacifistic. Quite the opposite, they were—in their heart of hearts—a horde of ravening, bloodthirsty, adrenaline-cognate junkies who would have been instantly recognized and made welcome at the hearths of Attila or Alexander, Genghis Khan or Tamerlane, as kindred souls and spirits.

The only reason, in fact, that the Darhel were even *in* business was that there, at least, they could exercise and exorcise *some* of the warrior spirit that lurked within them. If a hostile acquisition and dismemberment of a rival firm lacked the deep emotional satisfaction of taking a town and butchering its inhabitants it was still better than nothing.

But not much.

Indeed, so desperate had this particular Rinn Fain been to answer the ancient call to action that he had once been enrolled in the voluntary suicide corps that had been raised to defend Darhel planets in the days before the decision had been made to use the human barbarians. It was a suicide corps because, even if the Posleen did not kill its members, lintatai would have once the glorious joy of actually killing something had been experienced.

In some ways the Rinn Fain regretted that decision to use the humans. It had, after all, robbed him of any chance to be a *real* Darhel. It had also led to his posting on this miserable planet, in this wet and miserable excuse for a country.

Sighing, the Rinn Fain ceased his mantra. He was calm enough for the duties at hand.

"It isss not accccceptable," the Darhel announced, "for you and your government to flee yet."

Mercedes stood for a moment, then—blood draining from his greasy face—collapsed back into the presidential seat, his hand automatically grasping for the bond-filled satchel.

"Not yet," the Rinn Fain repeated. "Your troopsss are actually doing too well. Thisss isss not according to the plan. Neither isss it in accordanccce with the agreement between usss for the evacuation of your government and familiesss."

"But," Mercedes protested, ". . . but . . . what can be done, I have done."

The Darhel was firm. It was difficult being forthright in general but nothing less than absolute, stark honesty worked with most of these humans.

"The termsss of our agreement are clear. You, your government, and your and their familiesss will not be evacuated until the fall of thisss waterway isss asssured. It is not asssured yet. Even now . . ." and the sudden thought of glorious, violent conflict caused the breath to catch in the Rinn Fain's throat, his hearts to begin to race, and vision close off.

Lintatai.

For long minutes the Darhel was silent, beating down the waves of emotion that threatened to end his life. When he returned to the present it was with a faraway look. Automatically, he placed his AID on the president's desk and let it take over.

"Terms were agreed . . . contracts inviolable were signed . . . appropriate payment for services were rendered."

The AID projected a map of the Republic of Panama above the desk. The map showed up-to-the-minute deployments of United States and Panamanian forces, as well as the two large patches of Posleen infestation. The Panamanian forces were notably the 6th Mechanized, a jagged line stretching northeast to southwest and in close contact with the lesser Posleen landing in the Peninsula de Azuero, and the 1ˢᵗ Mechanized, moving in column along the Inter-American highway to the northeast of the 6ᵗʰ.

"Forces must not be concentrated . . . decisive actions must not be permitted."

Seeing the map, understanding what it meant, Mercedes regretfully wrote off one not too beloved nephew and responded, "I understand."

"That's fucking insane," insisted Colonel Juan Rivera, U.S. liaison at the new *Comandancia* atop Quarry Heights. The American spoke quietly to keep his voice from echoing across the underground bunker complex's damp, dripping walls.

The Panamanian, a four star in theory though in practice a jumped-up police colonel more at home with a blotter report than an operations order, answered, also softly, "Those are nonetheless the orders."

"We won't do it," the gringo answered heatedly. "The keys to fighting the Posleen are mass and firepower, not dispersion. What your president is commanding, splitting up your armored corps and splitting up the battalion of ACS to support separate efforts is suicidal. There is no way the CG," Commanding General, in this case of the United States Southern Command, or SOUTHCOM, "is going to roll for this."

"Your commanding general takes his orders from the ambassador, who takes his orders from your Department of State. President Mercedes has demanded, and both your State Department and the ambassador are agreed, that you *will* support us in this."

Muelle *(Pier) 18, Balboa, Republic of Panama*

The landings in Panama had already begun when Connors and B Company arrived back dockside in Balboa. The men had had three days to rest on the trip up. Connors had mostly stayed awake with his ghosts. In particular, the image of the Chileans, rallied around their flag but frozen to the ground, came to him each time he tried to close his eyes. It was wonderful, in a way, but quite horrible too. It was wonderful because of the example of all those brave men, faithful to the end in their people's cause, frozen . . . dead, but never surrendered. It was horrible, not least, because Connors could picture himself in that position, in any of several dozen frozen-stiff positions, as a matter of fact.

In any case, no sooner had B Company debarked than Snyder was on the horn, bitching for Connors to get his company in gear, get over the bridge of the Americas, and head west to support the Panamanians.

"Vacation time is over now, Captain Connors. You and your little darlings' days of being pampered aboard a cruise ship have come to an end."

Connors didn't bother to argue.

Rio Hato, Panama

The air strip intersecting the Pan-American Highway was useless now. Maybe, just maybe, if the defenders won this fight and drove the invaders from their native soil the air would become practicable again and the strip could be used to ferry out some of the wounded building up at the nearest fixed military facility to the fighting,

The base had seen fighting before. American built and operated, in 1964 it had been overrun, sacked and burned by Panamanians rioting in sympathy with the main riots of that year in Panama City. Following this, the base, the strip, the ammunition supply point and the adjacent training area had been abandoned by the U.S. Army, reverting to Panamanian control.

Little benefit the Panamanians had of it, however, and not for long. That little incident in 1964 had been repaid in full by five companies of U.S. Army Rangers. These, supported by the latest aircraft in the United States' arsenal, had dropped without warning in December, 1989, as part of Operation Just Cause, killing or capturing three companies of Panamanian infantry. Outnumbered and outgunned, taken by surprise, and under attack by the finest light infantry in the world, the Panamanians had little to be ashamed of, fighting well, hard and long, even after hope was gone.

Boyd remembered very mixed feelings during that invasion. At some level he had been pleased that *his army* had performed so well. At another level he was appalled that his *country's* army had gone under so quickly. For although Panama had little to be ashamed of, it had at least one cause for shame.

That cause, a major then and a major general now, stood pale and trembling in the hatch of his Type-63 light tank a few meters from where Bill Boyd stood at the intersection of the airstrip and the highway.

From that distance, Cortez attempted to talk to Boyd about some logistic issues. Unfortunately, and foolishly, he was too addled to remember to tell his driver to kill the engine. Boyd heard not a word and, since the boom mike of Cortez's helmet covered his mouth, could not read lips either.

Impatiently, Boyd walked around the tank and into the driver's field of view. He made a cutting motion across his throat, causing the driver to kill the engine. The look on the driver's face, full of disgust for his commander, was eloquent. Boyd climbed atop the armored vehicle to stand next to Cortez.

Cortez attempted to tear his helmet off, half choking himself with the communications cord. Freeing himself from the cord he still held the helmet tight in both hands.

As if to control his shaking, thought Boyd.

This was confirmed as soon as Cortez began to speak. His voice trembled, perhaps even worse than it otherwise would have, as if to compensate for the constrained hands.

"I . . . nnneed . . . morrre . . . fffuel," Cortez began. "Am . . . amm . . . ammm . . . munition."

"You have everything I have to give," Boyd answered, calmly. "I might have had more, but . . ." He gave Cortez an accusing look, not voicing his true feelings: *you fucking thief.*

Before Cortez could answer, if he was even capable of an answer, his radio crackled, demanding that he hurry his division forward. His attempts at delay— complaints about fuel, ammo, food—were rebuffed. Under a tongue lashing from his uncle, the president, a teary-eyed Cortez waved Boyd off his tank, replaced his helmet and, in a breaking voice, ordered his driver forward.

For the next several hours Boyd felt both dread, remorse and a degree of self-loathing.

I should have pulled the cowardly son of a bitch out of that tank and taken command myself.

Lost in his regrets, hearing drowned out by the steady column of wheeled and armored vehicles passing west, Boyd didn't notice at first the olive-toned, fresh-faced second lieutenant who stood before him, holding a salute. When he did finally notice he returned the salute, somewhat sloppily and informally, and asked the young man's business.

The lieutenant, Boyd saw that the name tag over his right pocket said "Diaz," dropped his salute and answered, "My father told me to look you up, sir. Just before I and my section left on our mission."

"Who is your father? What mission?" Boyd asked, a bit confused. Panama had no shortage of people named "Diaz."

Before the boy could answer Boyd noticed the short line of trucks pulling what appeared to be aircraft on trailers behind them. He instantly understood the answers to both his questions: the boy was Julio Diaz, the G-2's son, and the mission was to fly some gliders over the invasion, providing reconnaissance and adjusting artillery fire.

"Skip it, son," Boyd said, raising up his palm. "I know your mission. What can I do to help you and your men?"

"Nothing, sir. My father just said I should find you—he said you would be here—and exchange radio frequencies. Oh, and that I should let you know what is going on up ahead, too. He didn't say so, but I don't think he had much faith in the commanders in the field."

Boyd just nodded, noncommittally, while thinking, *Son, I don't have much faith in them either.*

Hotel Campestre, El Valle de Anton, *Panama*

People who didn't believe in a God or in the Creation should have gone to see *El Valle,* for if ever a spot on Earth seemed touched by the divine spark, this was it.

The Valley always came to the visitor as a surprise, no matter how many times he may have visited before. The road up wound from the Pan-American highway through carved mountains before dead-ending in the middle of the huge caldera of an extinct volcano several thousand feet above sea level. Here, the air was always fresh and cool, despite the bright sunshine that bathed the lush ground. Fed by just enough rain, the unbelievably fertile volcanic soil produced a riot of greens and reds, oranges, blues and yellows.

Animals there were in abundance; bright-colored tropical birds notable among them. The Valley was even home to a unique kind of frog, a tiny, beautifully golden-colored amphibian that seemed almost to beg to be touched. To do so, though, was near suicidal, as the frog secreted a powerful toxin through its skin.

Well-to-do Panamanians had been making their vacation homes in *El Valle* for well over a century. Hotels, a few, had sprung up along with the usual restaurants and other establishments of an area devoted to the tourist industry.

Those tourists, however, were long gone under the exigencies of war. Their place had been taken by the bloated headquarters and staff of Panama's newly raised mechanized corps, commanded by yet another of President Mercedes' blood-related cronies.

A cynical observer might have said that the Corps had taken over *El Valle* and its vacation homes and hotels because it was about as safe as anyplace in the country; the same winding mountain road that led to the Valley would—properly defended—become a death path for any Posleen who attempted it.

The cynical observer would have been wrong in any case. *El Valle* had not been chosen as the Corps Headquarters because it was safe. It hadn't even been chosen because of the healthy climate. At least those would have been defensible criteria. Instead, the lieutenant general commanding the corps had chosen *El Valle* because he maintained a large-breasted, very pretty, and very young mistress there and saw no reason whatsoever not to mix business with pleasure.

He hoped to get the girl out when that time came—she had some natural talent for her chosen profession—but this was not a major consideration. She was just a nice vehicle for recreation until the time came for the general to flee.

That time would come when his corps was utterly destroyed.

I hope those brave boys are not killed before they can at least do some good, Boyd thought as he watched the last of the gliders lift off from the northern side of the airstrip.

With each liftoff, Boyd had shaken his head with

wonder, in part at the courage of the young pilots, and in part at the patent insanity of their chosen mechanism of attaining flight.

The gliders, though they had auxiliary propulsion engines, had not used their engines. Young Diaz had explained that it was his understanding that every Posleen with a direct line of sight, possibly to include those still in space, would have instantly engaged any such attempt. Instead, the gliders had been dismounted from their trailers, nose down, while long, and very large, balloons had been laid out behind them. The ground crews had then strapped the pilots into their seats, rotated them by hand to face downward, and manhandled them into the cockpits in that position. After the pilots were placed, the balloons had been secured to both the gliders and the ground. Tanks of helium had then been connected to the balloons, filling them until they stood huge and fat above the gliders, swaying in the wind. The whole process took nearly an hour.

At that point the balloons had been released from their ground tethers to shoot into the air like rockets. A few brief seconds lapsed for the pilots before the ropes connecting the gliders with the balloons grew taut. At that point, the gliders dutifully followed the balloons up, up and away. Both balloons and gliders were too high by far for Boyd to see when the pilots released their cables, freed themselves from the balloons' tug, fell a few score feet, and began to soar.

As the wise old sergeant once said, thought Boyd, *if it's crazy or stupid but it works, it isn't crazy or stupid.*

❖   ❖   ❖

The worst part, from Diaz's point of view, was not the initial launch or the rapid acceleration upward. He didn't really mind the restraining straps cutting into the flesh of his stomach, shoulders and chest. He could even live with facing straight down, surely the worst possible view, as the earth seemed to race away from him.

But what he could not stand was watching that earth spin and wobble as the uncontrolled and uncontrollable glider twisted and swayed in the breeze.

He had taken Triptone, a more modern and powerful version of Dramamine, of course. That had become SOP during program development as one glider after another returned to earth with the contents of the pilots' stomachs roughly distributed over the inside of the cockpit.

And the Triptone helped, no doubt about it. If it hadn't, Diaz would have lost his breakfast, too, before even half the necessary altitude had been gained. Yet while the Triptone helped, it did not stop the feeling that he ought to be nauseated, that he should be painting the instrument panel and canopy with his bile.

Closing his eyes helped, a little, but there was still that feeling of uncontrolled spin nudging at the pit of his stomach. Growing . . . growing . . . growing.

Triptone didn't always work. Diaz lunged for the vomit bag.

Colonel Preiss wanted to puke. He *hated* nap-of-the-earth flying, the helicopter doing its best to simulate a railless roller coaster, skimming the jungle roof or descending into it as opportunity offered.

They'd lost a couple of choppers, too, on this hair-raising trip from the battalion's home base at Fort

Davis to a previously cut "postage stamp" landing zone in the jungle on the northern side of Panama's central cordillera. Behind the long trail of Blackhawks a few jungle patches smoked and smoldered where a chopper had gone in.

It had been a gamble, using aircraft in the presence of the Posleen. While there was little doubt that the aliens could have shot down every one of the birds, there had been enough doubt as to whether they would to make the risk seem worthwhile. The helicopters represented no direct threat to spacecraft, and so—it was hoped—spacecraft would ignore them. Indeed, from the point of view of an orbiting spacecraft, the helicopters, operating anywhere from a few feet to a few inches over the jungle, were almost indistinguishable from a ground vehicle. The aliens rarely engaged ground vehicles from space.

Moreover, the cordillera itself was expected to, and did, act as a shield from the observation and fire of already landed Posleen.

Still, there *were* spacecraft overhead, some of them apparently manned by Posleen who exhibited an unfortunate degree of what could only be called boyish high spirits. These had tossed a few kinetic energy projectiles at the helicopters. None had scored a direct hit but, given the shock wave from a couple of pounds of material coming in and impacting at a high fraction of C, a few Blackhawks had been knocked around. Given the close proximity of chopper to jungle, being knocked around, if only for a second, was likely to prove fatal.

Preiss's stomach lurched as a single bright streak flashed down to impact on the jungle ahead. A visible shock wave composed of jungle detritus and compressed air radiated outward from the point of impact. The helicopter lurched again as the pilot pulled back on his stick frantically to gain a little altitude before the shock wave hit. When it came the chopper momentarily bucked and strained like a wild animal.

Despite this, however, the pilot succeeded in riding out the wave. It passed and the pilot descended once again to tree-top level. Unaccountably, the pilot was laughing as he did. The pilot turned his head around, facing Preiss, and shouting, just loud enough to be heard over the beating of the rotor and the roar of the jet engine.

"YAHOO! Mama, what a ride!"

Preiss shared none of the pilot's glee. *Maybe he thinks this shit is fun. I'll be a lot goddamned happier when we're on the ground and can fight back.* He was frankly looking forward to seeing how these alien bastards liked dealing with the best jungle troops in the world, the 10th United States Infantry, in the environment for which they had trained for decades.

The chopper copilot nudged Preiss and pointed downward at a rectangular cut in the jungle roof. From this distance, it looked impossibly small. Still, Preiss had trained with these pilots for a long time. He had every confidence they could land in it.

As the chopper descended, blades chopped leaves and light branches that had grown up around the edges since the LZ was cut. Nearing the ground, even through his nausea and his fear, Preiss felt a smile growing on his young-old face.

INTERLUDE

The fighting had passed on without Guanamarioch and his band. The frightening sounds were distant now; the crash of the threshkreen artillery, the unending merciless thumping of their heavy repeaters, the overhead rattle of their indirect firing weapons. He became aware of this only slowly.

His normals and cosslain gathered stupidly around him while the pain of his several injuries abated somewhat. The hand, in particular, still shrieked in protest. However rapidly the People had been modified to heal, it would take cycles for the blistered, charred and oozing flesh to grow a new layer of hide. In the interim the keening Kessentai continued to rock back and forth slowly, the injured hand tucked protectively in his right armpit.

The normals and cosslain clustered nearest to him began petting their god to offer as much sympathy as they were capable of showing. Some of them set up a keening cry to match Guanamarioch's. The sympathy cries of the normals and cosslain was loud enough that Guanamarioch didn't notice the low hum of an approaching tenar.

"What are you whining about, Kenstain?" asked the tenar-riding God King. Guanamarioch recognized him as the enforcer who had dealt summary execution on the mess deck aboard ship. Still unable to speak, even to object to the mortal insult of being called one of those who had fled from the path of fire and fury, the junior Kessentai held up his seared hand, palm open, in explanation and excusal.

But the senior was having none of it. "You miserable excuse for a creature of the People. There are Kessentai ahead of you—in every way ahead of you—missing eyes and limbs and still fighting. There are *Kenstain* standing bravely beside their leaders. And you sit there whining over a widdle bitty burn. Cowardly puke!"

Stinging under his superior's tongue lashing, Guanamarioch lowered his head and began to struggle to his feet. A nearby cosslain helped him up, albeit a bit awkwardly. Head still down, his band in tow, the junior Kessentai without so much as a tenar to his name began to shuffle gingerly toward where his clan was still locked in mortal combat with the threshkreen of this place.

CHAPTER 14

"What did I have?" said the fine old
woman.
"What did I have?" this proud old
woman did say.
"I had four green fields, each one was
a jewel,
"Til strangers came and tried to take
them from me.
"I had fine strong sons. They fought to
save my jewels.
"They fought and died, and that was my
grief," said she.

—Tommy Makem,
"Four Green Fields"

Bijagual, Chiriqui, Republic of Panama

The river ran east-west for three hundred meters
before turning abruptly to the north. There was a
road, potholes interspersed with boulders for the
most part, paralleling the east-west portion of the
stream before meeting the bridge that spanned the

north-running section. The road turned south as soon as it crossed the bridge.

South of the river, there was a well-treed, low-lying ridge. Along this ridge Digna had dug in most of her force, including half her artillery.

Digna had stopped smiling as soon as her son, Roderigo, went off the air. From the firing, barely perceptible at this distance, he and his crew had to be about four miles away from the bridge that led into Bijagual.

Instead of smiling, Digna sat her horse stoically, nudging it along the fighting line behind the ridge using only her knees. From this position she could see her descendants and followers, as well as the near kill zone on this side of the river and the far kill zone on the other.

"Hold your fire," she intoned. Her voice was a falsely confident and icy calm. "Hold your fire until they're across the bridge and into the near kill zone. Keep low until they're well into the open area. I'll give the command. Then blast them with everything you have."

Four of Digna's militia's 85mm guns sat well-spaced, dug-in and camouflaged covering that kill zone and the further one, an area of about twenty or twenty-five hectares. Each gun, firing canister, could spew about four-hundred 15mm balls with each round. Moreover, they could do so at twenty-five rounds a minute . . . for one minute, anyway. Even with a third of the balls going too high, another third going too low, the remaining third—grazing low—should be enough, so the woman hoped, to scour the kill zone free of life after a few volleys.

Digna stopped at one gun crew just to look into the faces of her great-granddaughters. They looked scared, yes, but determined. *No worries here. They'll do their duty by their clan.*

The firing from four miles away stopped abruptly. Digna kneed her horse in the direction of her command post, taking care not to gallop lest the horse's speed infect her clan with fear.

These thresh just don't fight fairly, the mid-level Kessentai, Filaronion, mourned as he surveyed the damage to his oolt from the last ambush he had led them into. Normals lay crumpled in every manner of undignified death. Some bled from multiple wounds; others lay as if asleep. More than a few still kicked and struggled, bleating like thresh themselves to be put out of their pain.

No, it just isn't fair, he thought bitterly. *They wait in hiding as if for death, enticing us in to reap the harvest. Then they set off those horrible explosive devices to rend and tear. Any Kessentai accompanying the forward elements are singled out as targets.*

Filaronion contemplated one nearby tenar, holding a dead God King slumped over the controls. The tenar hovered over a single spot, slowly spinning in place and dripping dull yellow blood to the ground.

Worse, after they attack us they have neither the decency to come out and put the wounded out of their misery nor the courage to stand so that we may take revenge. Instead they just melt away on those quadrupeds, fading into the low spots. Those we can barely catch sight of as they gallop to the rear.

There was something decidedly unnerving about

thresh, even threshkreen, who could move along the ground as fast as could one of the People. Filaronion knew about the threshkreen's armored vehicles. These, more road-bound than cross country capable, were seen as a minimal threat, overall. But for the thresh to move so quickly across broken land; that was truly odd and strangely disquieting.

This Kessentai was one of the brighter of his type, he knew. He had tried, earlier, to spread out, to avoid being the mass target which these vile threshkreen seemed to prefer. Yet this had made forward progress slower. His senior in the clan had tongue-lashed him viciously for his supposed cowardice, insisting that the forward oolt stay on the road and press ahead with all possible speed.

But Filaronion *was* one of the brighter of his clan. Even while he partly obeyed his elder, lashing the bulk of his oolt on, he sent two swinging pincers out to either side of the main column, driving their own Kessentai ferociously to sacrifice everything for speed, to trap and finally eliminate this infuriating group of threshkreen who had bloodied the host again and again.

There would be no more artillery support from Edilze, Roderigo knew. The guns were certainly still there, at least he had no reason to believe they were not, but the radio was little more than a smoldering chunk of metal, glass and plastic. The last ambush had cost them heavily.

Roderigo gently closed the surprised looking eyes of the radio carrier who had ridden with him since they had first ordered fire down on the demonlike horde of invaders.

Leaving the trash of the radio, sighing, the uncle

heaved his teenaged nephew's corpse across the saddle of his horse.

Each loss of a son or grandson, or of a nephew, had been like a knife in Roderigo's gut. Five times along the road home they had turned at bay against the enemy. Five times they had bloodied him badly. Yet, each time the enemy had pressed forward and each time Roderigo's men had barely escaped with their lives.

Many, of course, had not escaped with their lives. A dozen saddles were empty now. Nearly twice that number carried wounded men either slumping upright or draped across. When Roderigo considered the number of horses they had lost as well . . . well, that was too painful.

I'm too old for this, he thought. *And, unlike Mama and Hector, they did not rejuvenate me. Then again, if they had I would be, instead of here defending my home, in some other place defending someone else's. Perhaps it was not such a bad trade. If I have to die . . .*

Roderigo looked over the line of wounded, horse-borne, relatives. The horses hoofed the ground nervously at the smell of coppery-iron blood. He could see no use keeping them here. He detailed off a couple of younger grandnephews to guide the wounded back home and guard them on their way.

The clan's forward cavalry had leapfrogged back all the way from in front of Las Lomas, half of them waiting or ambushing while the other half prepared the next ambush. Even now, the last group to be engaged passed through the next and, so Roderigo thought, the last decent ambush position before the bridge to home. These, too, he saw, led far too many riderless horses and wounded men.

Roderigo stepped out into the road and raised a hand to stop one of his sons.

"This is the last place, *mi hijo*," he said. "Go all the way home now and report to *Mamita*."

Exhausted, holding one hand tightly over an arm to stop the seepage of blood from a grazing wound, the son nodded weakly. Roderigo patted his boy's thigh.

"Tell your mother that I love her, son," he finished, "but that I might be a little late for supper."

Digna tensed as she heard the faint clatter of hoofbeats on the road to the south. Was this her son's extended family returning? Or were they all dead and butchered, the drumming sound coming from the massed feet of the invader?

As a horse rounded the bend Digna relaxed visibly. *Thank God*, she thought. *Some, at least, still live.*

She amended that thought to, *Some, at least, live . . . for now*, as she caught a closer look at the pale faces of her descendants. Her own horse reared as a change in wind brought the smell of mammalian blood to its nose. Digna reached out a calming hand to stroke and pet the horse back to relative calm.

"How far behind you?" she asked her grandson, without specifying whether she meant the enemy or the rest of the forward screen.

The grandson didn't know or understand what she intended by her question. Slumped in the saddle, weakly he answered, "My father is about two miles out. The enemy not much farther."

As if to punctuate this, a sudden crescendo of fire arose to the south.

✧　　✧　　✧

With the rising dust clouds to east and west Roderigo knew he had made a mistake, quite possibly his last.

"*Mis hijos*," he shouted, climbing back atop his horse, "mount up. Mount UP! We are—"

There was a sudden sharp blow, passing through from one side to the other, blasting flesh, blood, heart and lungs and tearing Roderigo from his horse. Mouth still open with the unfinished command, the old man fell with an audible thump, dead even before he hit the ground.

Outraged, tactical sense forgotten, the remnants of the family still in the field opened fire on the point of the approaching Posleen column even though these were still too far away to make an ideal ambush target.

Posleen fell, of course, especially where the remaining machine gun stitched across their ranks. This time, however, precisely because the Posleen were too far away to be massacred before they had time to react, there was effective return fire, pinning the Mirandas in their ambush position.

Worse, at the sound of the first rounds the wide sweeping alien pincers turned inward, churning claws raising dust clouds on the humans' horizon.

The horses broke, even though the men did not. As the animals stampeded, the enveloping Posleen swept them with fire. Thresh were not to be wasted and the animals were as good a threshform as any. Of the several dozen animals that broke all but one were chopped down by the alien fire. This one, never too bright to begin with and now mindless with fear, raced for what its tiny brain thought of as home and safety.

Meanwhile, the rest of Roderigo Miranda's little command automatically pulled in their flanks and formed a tight circle. Perhaps . . . perhaps if they could hold on until nightfall they might manage to escape.

The Posleen, however, led and lashed on by their Kessentai, were having none of it. Heedless of losses they bore in, railguns and shotguns blazing, boma blades sweeping high overhead.

Though there was no one left in command of the trapped humans, they were a family and they did tend to think much alike. Determined to sell their lives as dearly as possible they fixed bayonets, except for a couple who drew their more familiar machetes, just before the crest of the alien wave hit them.

Let the actions of one speak for all. One of the last survivors, Emilio Miranda, twenty-seven year old grandson of Roderigo. Emilio had a drinking problem. His face and back still bore the marks of his great-grandmother's riding crop as mute testimony to that problem.

Never mind that. A drunk Emilio might have been. He was not, however, a noticeably cowardly drunk.

As the Posleen galloped close, Emilio arose from his covered position and emptied his last magazine point blank and on full automatic at the enemy, sweeping his Kalashnikov from left to right. Three Posleen went down immediately, while a fourth, apparently hit on a knee joint, stumbled forward before falling. Gripping his rifle firmly in both hands the man lunged forward, frantically driving his bayonet into the wounded Posleen's yellow eye. As the bayonet entered the eye the Posleen tossed its head in agony, ripping the rifle from the Emilio's hands.

Heart racing, Emilio drew his machete and ducked under another alien's swinging blade. He chopped at the alien's forelegs, severing one and embedding the machete in the other. Shrieking, that alien fell to one side. The embedded machete was also wrenched from Emilio's hand.

Ducking again under another awkward swing of a boma blade, Emilio leveraged himself onto another normal's back as if it had been the horse it somewhat resembled. From there, he reached an arm around the alien's throat, squeezing and twisting in an instinctive move that might well have killed a human—either by strangulation or by broken neck—but only succeeded in panicking the thicker necked Posleen.

The normal bucked and twisted, trying desperately to throw off the thresh whose encircling grip threatened to cut off its windpipe. As it did so its rear claws mauled another normal who had come to its rescue. This one, enraged at the undeserved wound slashed off the rear legs of the beleaguered Posleen with a single stroke.

That Posleen immediately fell on its dripping haunches and rolled, trapping Emilio underneath it.

Stunned, Emilio lay there momentarily with his lower torso trapped under several hundred pounds of quivering centauroid alien. This was perhaps fortunate as he never really saw or felt the descending blade that removed his head and ended his young life.

Digna's heart sank as she watched a lone horse, mouth frothy with exertion, gallop across the bridge that led to her home. When the firing to the south ended with a whimper she crossed herself and said a prayer for her lost children.

"It is time," she said to a boy serving as a runner. "Tell *Señora* Herrera that she can't wait any longer for stragglers. She is to begin moving our people to Gualaca," a small town to the north, "now."

"*Si, Mamita,*" the boy answered, breathlessly, before racing off to find his own mount.

The foamy-mouthed horse passed by. Digna didn't even try to hold it. This road led unavoidably to where the noncombatant part of the family had gathered. They could stop the horse, if it could be stopped. Most likely the animal would halt of its own accord once it saw the herd of Miranda clan horses loaded down for the trip north. They were herd animals, after all.

Digna turned her attention back to the road that led to the bridge along which the enemy must soon appear. They had to cross the bridge until they either gave up—an unlikely possibility, she knew—or found one of the fords north or east that led across the river. These she had covered with flanker parties under the command of one of her sons and Tomas Herrera.

The bridge was wired for demolition. She was sure it was inexpertly done; she had little knowledge of demolitions herself and none of her family knew much beyond the little bit needed to blow an old stump. Still, she remembered from the little bit of demolitions training she had had in OCS that there was an overriding factor in demolitions that could make even the rankest amateur a proficient combat engineer. This was called "factor P"; P for plenty.

The underside of the bridge was packed with nearly three hundred fifty pounds of plastic explosive she had traded food for over the last several months. This was "plenty," indeed.

Wired or not, though, she did not want to blow the bridge until the last possible moment. It was an obvious way across the river. As long as an obvious way existed the aliens, who were reputed to be fairly stupid, they would be unlikely to start nosing about for an alternative crossing.

And besides, she *wanted* the bastards to cross for a while. She wanted to let the murderers of her children into the welcome zone she had prepared for them. She wanted to kill some of them herself, to assuage the grief of her heart.

Digna affectionately patted her husband's old rifle. She and, in spirit at least, he would pay back the aliens for the harm they had been done.

Whatever satisfaction Filaronion felt as the last of the thresh went down under the slashing blades of his oolt was short-lived. He was certain that there had been at least two such groups; nothing else would explain the way they had operated. That he had destroyed one meant also that another had gotten clean away.

Moreover, weighing the meat being harvested and the remnants of the bodies gave the God King more frustration than satisfaction. He had lost many times that number of normals and more than a few God Kings along the road before trapping and destroying this small group of threshkreen.

Disgust rising, Filaronion twisted his tenar away from the scene of massacre. Then the God King glided up the road, his oolt clattering and chittering behind him.

Elevated and forward as he was, the God King was first of his band to spot the bridge. He didn't like it, somehow. It seemed . . . too . . . easy.

Filaronion reined in his tenar and ordered a lesser Kessentai to investigate with his own scout oolt. Right after that he ordered two other oolt, the same two which had made up the enveloping pincers he had used earlier to destroy the threshkreen, to again split off to either side and find a crossing place through this flowing body of water.

For whatever reason, and perhaps it was because she was connected to so many of them by an unbreakable spiritual umbilical, Digna felt her family stiffen before she ever saw the Posleen tenar. Most likely one of her descendants had seen it as it rounded the road bend, then tightened up with fear and anticipation, and that it was that tightening which had passed unconsciously across the battle line even to those who had not seen the enemy.

It was only a fraction of a second, though, before she saw it, too; a quietly and smoothly gliding piece of plainly alien technology, bearing an unbelievably horrible monster.

Digna stroked her husband's rifle affectionately. It had been his pride and joy in life, a custom-made piece of old-world, English craftsmanship, perfectly balanced and heavily tooled, firing a powerful, beast-killing slug.

Easing herself down into a firing position next to the 85mm gun she planned to use to begin the carnage, Digna peered through the scope and took a careful aim at her personal target.

My God, she thought, *it's even uglier close up than it was at a distance.*

Carefully she settled the cross hairs on the reptilian alien head. At a greater distance she might not have risked a head shot. But the thing was closing to within two hundred meters. At that range, even though this was her husband's rifle and not her own, she felt the head shot was justified.

I hope your mother, if you have one, weeps as I will weep once I have time to count my losses, beast.

Taking in a deep breath, then releasing most of it, Digna slowly squeezed the trigger while keeping the cross hairs on her target's head. By surprise, as all good shots should be, the weapon kicked in her grasp, bruising her shoulder. She had the satisfaction, however, of the barest glimpse of an alien head literally exploding before the recoil knocked her scope off target. When she returned the sight to the target she was gratified to see the alien slumped down, dead, while the flying sled slowly rotated above the bridge.

With a cry of rage the aliens below on the road exploded into action. The old bridge shook under the thunder of their claws as they poured across. As the aliens reached Digna's side of the bridge they began to spread out.

The ones who had crossed didn't interest her very much. Rifle and machine gun fire would account for them easily enough once she gave the word to open fire. Instead, she was much more interested in the dense cluster of aliens massing in confusion on the far side of the bridge.

"There must be a thousand or more of them there," she whispered aloud. "A fair honor guard for my lost children."

Digna twisted her head toward the waiting gun crew. "Fire!"

Her command was immediately rewarded with a resounding blast from the gun's muzzle. An imperceptible moment later a wide swath of the aliens clustered at the bridge went down as if cut by some gigantic scythe. Their bleating and screams might have been pitiful had they not been so satisfying. Less than a second after the first round of canister had slashed through the enemy ranks, the other three guns joined in. A great moan went up as scores, then hundreds, of the invaders fell. Before the last of the victims of the other three guns went down, the first gun spoke again.

Rifle and machine gun fire joined the big guns cacophony. These, however, concentrated on the several score Posleen who had made it across the bridge before the 85mm pieces had opened fire. Unable to see their tormenters before it was too late, these aliens were knocked down right and left. By the time the big guns had finished reaping their grim harvest, three to four rounds each, cranked out in rather less than ten seconds, the others ceased fire for lack of targets.

A few of Digna's family had been hit by alien return fire. Two were dead, she was sure, from the way their bodies hung limply as they were carried back. Others screamed or, more commonly, bit their tongues half through to keep from screaming. Hers was, in the main, that kind of a clan.

No time for tears. I can mourn later.

Digna ordered the wounded and the dead, both, carried to the rear. The wounded would be cared for, as best they could be. For the dead there were fire pits, the seasoned wood already stacked, soaked with gasoline, and waiting. She would see no more of her own turned into meals for their enemies.

And at least they would be buried on their home ground.

INTERLUDE

He never reached the fighting again. Moving, of necessity, with painful slowness, Guanamarioch and his band reached a crossroad somewhere in north-central Colombia. There, another one of the tenar-riding seniors of the clan sneered at the scruffy and underequipped appearance of the normals.

"You lot won't be worth anything at the fighting," the senior said to Guanamarioch. "Turn right here. Go about three thousand heartbeats until you reach the Kenstain, Ziramoth. He has surveyed our holdings. He will assign you one of those. Take charge of it and start preparing the land for farming. That's all your wretches look good for, young Kessentai."

Biting back a nasty retort, Guanamarioch nodded in seeming respect and turned, dejectedly, to his right.

"What's this; what's this, young Kessentai? Why so down, lordling? Abat gnaw on your dick?"

Ordinarily such words might have angered Gua-namarioch. These, however, were delivered in a cheer-ful, bantering tone that almost succeeded in bringing a smile to his face. He looked over the Kenstain and saw a mid-sized, crested philosopher, missing his left eye and his right arm, and bearing serious scars along both flanks. Strapped across those scars were fully stuffed twin saddle bags. The Kenstain took a couple of steps toward Guanamarioch, walking with a stumbling limp.

The Kenstain, seeing the God King hiding one hand, reached out for the injured limb. Rather than resist and risk having any force exerted on the hand, Guanamarioch let him examine it. The Kenstain turned the palm over gently and bent to examine it closely with his one remaining eye.

"That's a right nasty burn you have there, young lordling. If you don't mind my asking, how did you come by it?"

"Thresh weapons get hot," the God King answered simply.

"Do they indeed?" asked the Kenstain, releasing the hand and twisting his torso to rummage in one of the saddle bags. From the saddlebag he pulled a dull tube. This he took a cap from, holding the cap between his lips. Then he again took Guanamarioch's injured hand in his and turned it palm up before releasing it. Using the same hand the Kenstain squeezed a measure of goo out onto the palm in a long, snaking line. The goo immediately began to spread out on its own, sinking into the burned flesh.

"Demons! Thank you, Kenstain," Guanamarioch said, the relief in his voice palpable.

"Never mind, young lordling. All in a day's work. I'm Ziramoth, by the way. Were you sent here to farm?"

Guanamarioch nodded bleakly.

"None of that, Kessentai. Farming, taking sustenance from the land, is the best way to live. You'll see."

CHAPTER 15

No captain can do very wrong if he
places his ship alongside that of the enemy.
—Horatio Nelson

*At sea, south of the Peninsula of Azuero,
Republic of Panama*

The three warships steamed through the day, their
bows cutting the waves and raising a froth that spilled
to either side of each. They were in echelon right,
with *Salem* forward and to port, *Des Moines* rearward
and to starboard, and *Texas* in the middle. The ships
were spaced far enough apart that any one of them
had considerable maneuver space to zig and zag
without risking a collision if the Posleen chose to
engage from space.

The precautions seemed wise to McNair. He worried
terribly even so. The ships were tough, true, and well
armored against any surface threat. But warships, like
tanks, were so vulnerable to attack from above—had
been since 1941 at the latest—that he couldn't help
but worry. The thought of a salvo of space-launched

kinetic energy projectiles straddling his beloved Daisy Mae was simply too horrible for him not to worry.

Even so, except for the streaks through the sky as spaceships battled with Planetary Defense Batteries, there was no sign of the enemy.

"It makes no sense," McNair said aloud inside the heavily armored bridge. "It just seems so incredibly stupid that none of the warships have been engaged from space. We're big. We're metal. We're heavily armored and have impressive clusters of guns. Why the hell don't they attack us?"

Daisy's hologram answered, "They're a fairly stupid race, Captain. None of their technology, so far is as known, was invented by them, with the *possible* exception of their drive. Even that appears to be a modification of Aldenata technology, rather than something truly original. The way they breed, leaving their brightest to struggle to survive on equal terms in their breeding pens with the biggest and most savage of their normals; they can't help but be stupid. Add in that they've never before fought a race that really fought back and . . . well . . . they're dummies."

"And when we show our teeth?" McNair asked. "Will they fail to engage us then, too?"

The avatar shrugged. "That we will see when we see it, Captain. They might attack. Then again, they might not. And if they attack it might be from space, which we have a chance of maneuvering to avoid, or it might be with a low-flying lander which we have an excellent chance of beating in a heads-up fight. Even if we cannot maneuver to avoid the fire from space, *Texas* mounts a Planetary Defense Gun in place of each of her former turrets. An attacker who engages us from on high won't last long with *Texas* watching out for his little sisters."

"You're really not worried, are you, Daisy?" McNair asked, wonderingly.

The hologram shrugged. "Not really, sir, no. I'm a warship and this is what I was meant to do."

"That's my girl," McNair said, a growing confidence in his voice.

"*My girl*," Daisy repeated mentally. An entire ship fairly quivered with barely suppressed pleasure.

Diaz soared, nausea gone and forgotten with the smelly, vile bag of puke he had dropped over the side moments after he had cut his glider loose from the lifting balloon.

From a height of nearly two miles he had sailed westward, dropping no more than a foot for every fifty that he advanced. When his altitude dropped to within a half-mile of the earth he had sought an updraft. These were easy to find along these ridges swept by the warm, southerly winds that brought freshness and rain to his country. In these updrafts he had circled again and again until the force of the wind gave out. At that point he had left the current and pushed onward again, ever closer to the fighting.

He was not there yet, though, and his mind wandered, naturally, to other things. More precisely, his mind wandered to Paloma Mercedes as he had last seen her, fiery with anger at his joining up and not using family connections to stay with her.

She'd never called, either. He'd thought she would get over it but, whether from anger or pride, the phone had remained silent. He didn't miss her less, exactly, but perhaps the sharp edge of the pain was growing dull from sawing at his heart and soul.

Maybe... maybe after this mission I'll swallow my own pride and call her. But first I have to survive.

Beneath his long narrow wings, Diaz saw more than a few signs of the fighting that had raged below. Here a burning tank, there a cluster of enemy dead or a crashed flying sled of the enemy's leaders. These reminded him, as if he needed a reminder, that all that would keep him alive through the next several hours was the enemy's stupidity, the aliens' confidence in their own weapons and sensors, and his own seeming harmlessness. He knew that if the aliens ever suspected he was a reconnaissance platform his life would be measured in tiny fractions of seconds.

For some reason, though, Diaz was unable to reach *anyone* on the ground. Fat lot of good the information he hoped to gain would do if he couldn't pass it on. He knew the internal codes for his frequency hopping radio were good; he'd checked them before departure.

Darhel Consulate, Panama City, Panama

The Rinn Fain had already done everything he knew to do *with* the humans. He had sabotaged and misdirected their plans, split their efforts, and aided their president in every way a Darhel knew how to, to rob his own people.

It was nearly time to stop doing things *with* the humans and start to do things *to* them.

To this end the Rinn Fain, and all his underlings— Darhel, Indowy, and artificial, all three—manned stations that, in human terms, could only be thought of as electronic warfare nodes.

For now the Darhel avoided interference, for the most part. Except in a few cases they were content merely to analyze human radio patterns, intercepting and synthesizing the codes that the barbarians used to hop from one frequency to another.

Certainly they didn't want to tip the humans off to what they were up to in time for the clever beasts to think of something new.

There were, however, certain of the humans who were physically out of touch enough to risk playing games with their communications. The glider pilots were a case in point. The Rinn Fain had taken considerable pleasure in remotely reprogramming their radios to make sure that anything they saw went unreported.

It was almost as pleasurable as taking control of the human's warships would be.

USS Des Moines

"Captain," Daisy reported, "I'm picking up scrambled signals from someone who, based on what he is trying to say and how he is trying to say it, seems to be a pilot flying at or near the front. I don't think anyone but myself—and probably Sally—can hear him." Daisy hesitated for a long moment, as if in communication with someone not present.

"Sally hears him, too, sir, yes. But there is something wrong with her."

"What?" asked McNair.

"I don't know," Daisy answered, sounding genuinely

puzzled and more than a little concerned. "She is . . . different from me . . . a normal AID. And that part of her intelligence, the part created by the Darhel, is acting a bit . . . odd."

"Okay," McNair answered. "See if you can figure out what's wrong with Sally. Help her if you can. And see if you can patch me through to that . . . pilot, did you say?"

"Yes, sir, a pilot. Spanish speaking. Fortunately, I can speak Spanish."

Along with every other human tongue spoken by more than two thousand people, she thought but, tactfully, did not say.

Diaz's voice was beginning to take on a note of frustrated desperation. He knew it and hated it but could do nothing to control it. But there were *targets* below, thick and ripe and waiting to be harvested.

"Any station, *any* station, this is Zulu Mike Lima Two Seven, over," he pleaded, for more than the hundredth time.

For a wonder the radio crackled back, in an achingly feminine voice, "Zulu Mike Lima Two Seven this is Charlie Alfa One Three Four. Hear you Lima Charlie, over."

Initially Diaz was unwilling to respond. It could be an enemy trick. Frantically, he poured through his COI, the code book that gave the call signs for every unit in his army and the gringos fighting in support of it. There was nothing, not one clue as to who Charlie Alfa One Three Four might be.

The warm feminine voice repeated, "Zulu Mike Lima Two Seven this is Charlie Alfa One Three Four. Hear you Lima Charlie, over."

Finally, realizing that if he was so useless as to be unable to communicate with his own people the enemy was unlikely to be very interested in him either, Diaz answered, "Last calling station this is Zulu Mike Lima Two Seven. Who the hell are you?"

Another voice, different from the girl's, came on. That speaker's Spanish was as accentless as the girl's had been.

"Lima Two Seven, this is the heavy cruiser, USS *Des Moines*, Captain McNair speaking."

"Captain, this is Lieutenant Julio Diaz, First FAP Light Recon Squadron. I have targets and I haven't been able to raise anyone."

The radio went silent. Diaz knew what the captain must be thinking: *how the hell do I know this snot-nosed kid is really a snot-nosed kid and not the damned Posleen?*

"Can you patch me through to my father?" Diaz asked. Then, realizing that, as phrased, it was an incredibly stupid, second lieutenant kind of question, he added, "He's the G-2. Major General Juan Diaz. My father can verify my voice."

In half a minute a different, and angry, voice came over Diaz's radio. "Julio, is that you? Where the hell have you been? I was about to call your mother. . . ."

"Father," Diaz nearly wept with relief, "I haven't been able to get a hold of anyone since shortly after I went airborne. I can see everything, Father, and just as I thought, the beasts are simply ignoring me. I can see where Sixth Division is engaged. And I can see the enemy massing. But I can't do a fucking thing about it."

The other Spanish voice came back. "General Diaz, Captain McNair. *I* can do something about it. Do you acknowledge that the voice claiming to be Lieutenant Diaz is your son and that he is in a position to adjust fire?"

The elder Diaz spoke again. "What did I say when I caught you and your girlfriend in the gardener's cabin, Julio?"

"Father! You promised never to bring that up!"

General Diaz's voice contained a chuckle in it as he said, "Yes, Captain, that's my boy."

"Very good then, sir. Lieutenant Diaz, I want you to find me a huge concentration of the enemy. I don't know how long we can pull this off before they shoot the shit out of us. So let's make it count, son."

"All hands, this is the captain speaking. Battle stations, battle stations. This is no drill."

"I'm receiving Lieutenant Diaz's call for fire now, Captain."

"Prepare to engage." McNair was pleased to hear no note of fear or hesitation in his own voice.

"Captain?" Daisy asked. "Would you and the crew care for a little mood music as we make our run?"

Raising a single, quizzical eyebrow, McNair answered, "Go for it, Daisy."

"*In nomine patri, filioque et spiritu sancti,*" Father Dwyer intoned as he made the sign of the cross over a half dozen of the crew that knelt for a brief and informal service, pending action. Dwyer could have sworn at least one of the present flock was a Moslem but the man took the host without hesitation and eagerly grasped the two-ounce plastic cup of "sacramental scotch" Dwyer proffered.

No atheists in foxholes, they say. I think that, given the power of the Holy Spirit as manifested in the Glenlivet distillery, there shall soon be only good Roman Catholics afloat. Well . . . and perhaps the odd Presbyterian. Now if only I can find something suitable to bless for the benefit of Sinbad and his Indowy.

Before he could continue that line of thought Dwyer heard, "Battle stations . . ."

"Boys," the priest said, "here aboard ship or in Heaven or in Hell, I'll see you soon. Now you to your posts and I to mine."

With that, the Jesuit headed towards sick bay. Worse come to worst he had a fair chance of saving a couple of more souls there.

McNair was startled twice over. The first time was when Daisy's avatar blinked out of existence on the bridge. The second came when the ship itself began to vibrate with music.

> *O Fortuna*
> *velut luna*
> *statu variabilis,*

Through the narrow slitted and armored glass-plated windows of the bridge, it seemed to McNair that a glow began to arise from the hull, spreading out into a perfect circle. The normal wake made by the bow as it sliced through the water disappeared, as did the waves.

> *semper crescis*
> *aut decrescis;*

From the glowing circle a fog arose; real or holographic, McNair couldn't say. Yet it seemed real enough. Below the fog the dimly sensed ocean began to bubble. Again, real or illusion? McNair assumed it must be illusion.

> *vita detestabilis*
> *nunc obdurat*
> *et tunc curat*
> *ludo mentis aciem,*

The rear turret, number three, was beyond McNair's view. The forward two turrets began slowly to turn in the direction of land.

> *egestatem,*
> *potestatem*
> *dissolvit ut glaciem.*
>
> *Sors immanis*
> *et inanis,*
> *rota tu volubilis,*
> *status malus,*

Lightning, real or false, flashed from deep within the frothing circle. Sometimes it came in the form of streaks or ribbons. At others it came as dancing balls of fire.

> *vana salus*
> *semper dissolubilis,*
> *obumbrata*
> *et velata*

The circle of fog expanded upward, becoming a hemisphere around the ship. From inside that hemisphere it seemed like the surface of a portal to Hell, all impossible colors and writhing, unsettling combinations. McNair tore his eyes away from the eerie display surrounding him and his ship. He could see that the guns were pointed at about the bearing he would have expected if . . .

> *michi quoque niteris;*
> *nunc per ludum*

KABOOM! Center gun of number two turret spoke.

> *dorsum nudum*
> *fero tui sceleris.*

A leg now, long and shapely, appeared to grow from the top of number two. The foot must have been somewhere around the keel. Risking concussion, McNair hurried out from the protected bridge.

> *Sors salutis*
> *et virtutis*

Another flash and the blast of a gun shook McNair to the core. His attention, however, was entirely on Daisy's hologram.

> *michi nunc contraria,*
> *est affectus*

She was a giant, a goddess. Lighting flashed back and forth between her hands.

> *et defectus*
> *semper in angaria.*

KABOOM! Another blast erupted from a gun.

Daisy said, very softly for such a grand goddess, "Please, Captain. Go inside. I know what I'm doing."

> *Hac in hora*
> *sine mora*
> *corde pulsum tangite;*
> *quod per sortem*
> *sternit fortem,*
> *mecum omnes plangite![1]*

And then, fire adjusted, all nine guns were on the target in a pattern designed for maximum destruction. Daisy thrust her hands forward and the lightning no longer passed between them but hurled through the night toward the land.

---

1 0 Fortune,
  like the moon
  you are changeable,
  ever waxing
  and waning;
  hateful life
  first oppresses
  and then soothes
  as fancy takes it;
  poverty
  and power
  it melts them like ice.

Fate—monstrous
and empty,
you whirling wheel,
you are malevolent,
well-being is vain
and always fades to nothing,
shadowed
and veiled
you plague me too;
now through the game
I bring my bare back
to your villainy.

Fate is against me
in health
and virtue,
driven on
and weighted down,
always enslaved
So at this hour
without delay
pluck the vibrating strings;
since Fate
strikes down the strong man,
everybody weep with me!

The ship shuddered: KABKAKAKABOOMOOM-
OOMOOM, as all nine eight-inch guns in the three main
turrets hurled death and defiance at the invader.

"Splash, over," said the warm female voice.

Diaz eased his glider over slightly and looked in
the direction in which he expected the shell to land.
It was over and to the northwest but . . . he checked
his altimeter again. Yes, he was at the height he
expected. That shell must be huge, much bigger than
the 105mm artillery he had trained to adjust.

He took another direction to his target, several—
maybe ten or twelve—thousand Posleen massing in
some low ground east of 6th Division.

"From last shell, direction: 5150. Left eight hundred . . . down two thousand, over."

Almost as fast as Diaz spoke the woman responded,
"Shot, over."

After what seemed a long wait came, "Splash, over.
Lieutenant Diaz, in case no one ever told you, with naval
guns there is a large probability of major range errors.
You may want to keep your corrections small."

"Roger," Diaz answered, looking over to where he
expected the shell to land. *Dammit. I overcorrected.*

"Direction 5190, add twelve hundred, right three
hundred."

"Shot, over . . . splash over."

A large blossoming flower, a mix of black, yellow
and purple, grew approximately in the center of the
Posleen horde. Even from his distance Diaz saw bodies
and chunks of bodies flying through the air.

"Direction 5220, add one hundred! Fireforeffect-
fireforeffectfireforeffect!"

"Calm down, Lieutenant Diaz. I understood you the first time. Shot over . . . splash, over."

Nothing in his training prepared Diaz for what happened next. He had never seen more than a "battery one" from 105s, six guns of small caliber firing one round each. The long-range error the woman had told him to expect was there and obviously so. Shells fell that were absurdly long or short.

But in the main, they fell on target . . . and fell . . . and fell . . . and fell.

Posleen in groups small and large attempted to escape. But still the shells came down, engulfing them. About the time that no more recognizable pieces of alien bodies were being visibly hurled into the air Diaz decided they had had enough. Nearly three square kilometers were completely covered in black, evil smoke. Already elements of what he assumed was the 6th Division were emerging from cover and creeping cautiously forward.

"Cease fire, cease fire. Target . . . well, ma'am, it's a lot worse than just destroyed," the boy said, awe plain in his voice.

"You're welcome. By the way, you can call me Daisy."

Diaz nosed his glider over, following the barely visible forward trace of the 6th Division. Soon he saw another group of Posleen.

"And I'm Julio. How far can you range, Daisy?"

"A little past the Inter-American highway, if I move north from this position. But, that's really constrained. Not much space to maneuver. I may have to bug out to the south at any time."

"I'll take what I can get, Daisy. Adjust fire, over."

Panama City, Panama

The Rinn Fain contemplated telling the Indowy to terminate itself, but decided, reluctantly, against it. It wasn't that the Indowy was particularly valuable, ordinarily, that had saved it. In these circumstances, however, the Indowy would be impossible to replace. This made it valuable, for however short a time.

What a disgusting thought; a valuable *Indowy.*

Casting his eyes even lower than those of his kind usually did, the Indowy contemplated his own impending end. If he were lucky, the master would let him go without excessive pain.

The unfairness of it all didn't bother the Indowy. He had grown up with it. There were over eighteen trillion of his kind, making them slightly less valuable, individually, to the Darhel lords of the Galactic Federation than any given pair of worn out slippers. There was no comparison between a typical Indowy and an Artificial Intelligence Device.

No, even the fact that it wasn't his fault was no defense. The lord would command and the Indowy would die. That was simply the way of life.

Thus, it came as a shock when the Rinn Fain said, "Never mind. Just tell me what's happening."

Eyes still downcast the Indowy responded, "Lord, about the human anti-spacecraft vessel, the *Texas,* we can do nothing much. It is not on our Net and is shielded and compartmentalized from the human 'Internet.' The one they call the *Salem* we have penetrated, but we have not been able to take it over. There is something odd going on there. It will not fire on the humans. It has been the best I could do—forgive me, lord!—to keep it from firing on the Posleen. I do not understand it.

"The last vessel, the *Des Moines*, is firing on the Posleen and, worse lord, I am unable to penetrate it. When I try, it counterattacks. I think the AID aboard that ship must be . . ." The Indowy inhaled deeply. He really didn't want to be ordered to suicide.

"Must be what, insect?"

"Lord . . . I think the AID aboard has gone . . . insane."

USS Des Moines

To conserve power, so she said, Daisy had dropped her large hologram above the ship and resumed her more usual station on the bridge. The camouflaging fog and lightning she maintained. Fire missions from Diaz were received and plotted automatically, the captain only giving the authorization to fire that even an insane AID required in accordance with galactic protocols.

Daisy's avatar was fading in and out, however, despite the reduction in demand for power.

"Are you all right, Daisy?" the captain asked.

The avatar bit its lip nervously. "I'm under attack, Captain," it admitted.

"Attack?" McNair queried.

"Cyber attack. Very powerful. Very sophisticated. It's all I can do to fight it off while keeping up the fire."

"The Posleen?"

Again the image faded before returning. "I . . . don't think so. They are not that clever. And this attack is very clever. It has all my codes. Even some I didn't know I had. The attack on Sally is worse. I am rerouting part of my defense through the part of me that is this physical ship to the part that is the physical USS *Salem*. It is enough . . . but only just enough, to prevent her from firing on human forces. *Salem* cannot even fire in self defense."

Darhel Consulate, Panama City, Panama

Though his elvish face remained a stoic mask, the Rinn Fain found the thing dangerously frustrating. Every type of attack and attempt at takeover that he commanded the Indowy to try was foiled.

Lintatai . . . lintatai. I must avoid lintatai. But I must also stop those ships. Their fire is decimating the Posleen.

"Can you leak the location and nature of the ships to the Net?" he asked the always obsequious Indowy.

"Yes, lord, though the ships may move. It would have to be a continuous leak."

"Then make it continuous, wretch. The Posleen are *stupid*." the Darhel hissed. "Make it *obvious*."

Remedios, Chiriqui, Republic of Panama

Binastarion thought, disgustedly, *This is just oh-so-good. Too "good" to be believed. The damned big town with the earthen walls, the local thresh call it "David," still has pockets inside holding out. Our landing on the peninsula that juts out into the main body of water of this world is being contained and chopped up. Slowly, however hesitatingly, the humans are even beginning to attack up the main road that runs parallel to the major body of water.*

The Posleen God King's own version of an AID, his Artificial Sentience, beeped urgently.

"Binastarion, I know where the fire is coming from that is decimating the People on the peninsula," it said. "The Net has the locations of two enemy water vessels, and a probable location of a third. It seems that the third, the one I do not have a precise location for, is the one doing the firing."

"Show me," Binastarion commanded.

Instantly a map of the coastal waters of Panama appeared at eye level over the tenar. The positions of the two known ships were indicated by solid green image of larger-than-normal tenar. The third was represented by a blinking green tenar with a serrated circle drawn around it. Places where the People had been butchered by the fires of the third vessel were marked by black boxes on the map and sequentially designated with Posleen numbers.

"So the fires began in the south and marched to the northeast, did they?" Binastarion mused. "What are the capabilities of these water vessels?"

The map disappeared to be replaced by three ship's silhouettes, arranged in a triangle with the largest at the apex and the two smaller ones—they looked enough alike to be sisters—below.

"All three are named for places in the central part of the continent to the north of us," the Artificial Sentience said, transliterated names appearing to the upper right of each ship's silhouette. "The one marked Tek-sas appears to be configured as an anti-spacecraft vessel, mounting five planetary defense cannon."

"Five!" Binastarion exclaimed. That sounded like a *lot* of anti-spacecraft defense.

"Yes, lord. While these vessels are vulnerable to attack from space there will be a heavy price to be paid if we relaunch B- or C-Decs, not only from the ship but from the Planetary Defense Bases stretched across the narrowest part of this isthmus."

"The other two, Sah-lehm and Deh-moyn, are sisters. They are mostly configured for combat against the surface, land or water, but appear to have a considerable secondary capability against atmospheric targets as well."

"But their arms are primitive," objected Binastarion. "Ten thousand generations behind what we bear."

"My lord," the AID retorted, "the People still carry swords, do they not? Weapons ten thousand generations more primitive than those on that ship? The swords are still deadly, is this not so?"

The God King thought on that momentarily.

"Summon a far-seeing conference call of sub-clans Asta and Ren."

USS Des Moines

"The admiral wants you, Captain. Conference call with *Salem*'s skipper."

"Put it up," McNair directed.

There were five screens arranged in a semicircle across the upper forward section of the bridge, just over the vision slits. The admiral of the flotilla appeared in the center, flanked by the captains of *Texas* and *Salem*.

McNair greeted, "Admiral Graybeal, Bill, Sidney."

"We've got a problem here," Admiral Graybeal said. "Tell him, Sidney."

As *Salem*'s captain flicked a switch, apparently to turn on the sound, a horrid weeping, intermixed with the occasional howl and sob, came from *Des Moines*' speakers. The howls and sobs had a trace of a Teutonic accent.

"What the . . . ?" asked McNair.

Salem's skipper, looking disgusted, reached another hand out, his palm briefly blocking the image. When he removed his hand the picture had changed from his face to a corner of *Salem*'s bridge. In that corner, arms wrapped around long legs, head buried against knees, a blonde woman—*Salem*'s avatar—rocked, occasionally lifting her head to shriek.

"She's been like that for the last half hour," the captain of the *Salem* said, off-screen. "My turrets are locked and I've had to go to pure manual steering with my AZIPODs. In fact, I've had to go to manual operation for everything and I'm just not crewed for that."

"I'm going to order *Salem* back to port," Graybeal said.

"I don't know if that's such a good idea," McNair answered. "Here, *Texas* can guard her from a space attack and I can guard her from a low attack. Sent back to base, she'd be on her own for hours."

"Jeff's right, Admiral. Only thing is . . ."

"Yes? Spit it out!" the admiral ordered.

"Well, Admiral . . . twice we've had to abort firing cycles that had you and *Des Moines* as targets. Something is trying to control this ship and use it on behalf of the enemy. Sally, herself, seems to be fighting it but you can see what the result of that has been."

"Shit!" cursed Graybeal and McNair, together.

INTERLUDE

Take just under four hundred normals and cosslain. Put them in the charge of one Kessentai whose genetic skill set includes nothing having to do with agriculture. Place them on approximately eight hundred hectares of land. Add advice from a Kenstain who actually *likes* being a dirt farmer. Sprinkle liberally with rain and baste with sun . . .

"But we'll have to wait a bit, Guano, before the first shoots come up."

"And what do we eat in the interim, Ziramoth? The thresh, including the nonsentient ones, are all fled."

The Kenstain laughed and, twisting around, produced a bamboolike stalk from his saddlebags. One end of this he placed under the armpit for that arm that was only a stump, then skinned the remainder with a small monomolecular blade. The skinned result, wet and glistening, he handed over to the God King.

Suspiciously, Guanamarioch sniffed at the offering. It looked way too much like wood to be appealing. He said as much.

"Certainly there's quite a lot of cellulose in the make up. But try it anyway," Ziramoth answered.

The Kessentai bit off a few inches and chewed, his jaws chomping a few times before his eyes widened in surprise.

"What *is* this stuff, Zira? It's *good*."

"The locals call it sugar cane. There's enough growing hereabouts to do us until our own crops are in."

Guanamarioch didn't answer, his mouth being too occupied in masticating the satisfyingly chewy, sweet cane.

Sugar cane would only carry one so far. Of game, sadly, there was none. Moreover, all the thresh called "humans" in the area, and their agricultural animals, had been rendered and eaten within a few days of arrival. There remained fish, fairly abundantly, in the streams and ponds. Guanamarioch could see the little bastards, glaring up at him and taunting him from beneath the waves and eddies.

He lunged at one with his claws . . . and missed. Then he looked around frantically for another, saw one and lunged at it . . . and missed. On the third attempt he missed as well, but also missed his footing on the slippery underwater stones and went under with a great flailing splash.

As Guanamarioch arose from the water, sputtering and choking, from the moss-covered bank Ziramoth began to snicker. The snickering rose until it became a full-fledged, ivory-fang-flashing Posleen laugh.

Guanamarioch opened his jaws to snap at the Kenstain, but stopped in midsnap, joining Ziramoth, ruefully.

"That will never do, lordling. Come here onto the bank and I'll show you how it's done."

When the God King was standing next to the Kenstain, Ziramoth motioned for the two of them to lie down. Then he picked up a long pole, from which dangled a string and a small hook. From his saddlebags the Kenstain pulled out a small container. He drew from this a thin, claw-length writhing thing. For a moment, Guanamarioch wondered if this thing was good to eat. His surprise was total when he saw Ziramoth thread the little creature onto the hook and toss them both into the stream.

"We have to stay low so the water creatures won't see us and will come close enough to smell the bait."

"And?"

"Well, milord, under fragrant bait is a hooked fish."

CHAPTER 16

But ever a blight on their labours lay,
And ever their quarry would vanish away,

Till the sun-dried boys of the Black Tyrone
Took a brotherly interest in Boh Da Thone:

And, sooth, if pursuit in possession ends,
The Boh and his trackers were best of friends.

—Rudyard Kipling,
"The Ballad of Boh Da Thone"

West of Aguadulce, Republic of Panama

The orders from Snyder had been, "Find the Panamanian Tenth Mechanized Infantry Regiment, a Colonel Suarez commanding. Attach yourself to Suarez. Assist as able." A marker had appeared in Connor's suit-generated map showing the presumed location of the 10th Regiment Command Post.

It had actually been damned difficult to find Suarez. By the time Connors reached the location he'd been given the command post had moved on. Some Panamanian support troops, a maintenance company, was there in its place. They hadn't known where the CP had gone, except that it had gone generally west.

Connors and B Company followed the road at the double time. Rather, they paralleled it because the road itself was a nightmarish mish-mash of confused and tangled units.

"Hey, sir," the first sergeant had called. "Weren't you a tanker once upon a time? Does this shit look right to you?"

"I was, Top," Connors answered, "and no, it doesn't look right. It looks like a recipe for disaster." Connors took the effort to read bumper numbers as he ran past the mess. In twelve vehicles he noted eleven different units represented.

Bad. Very damned bad.

The company pressed on to the west. Surprisingly, the confusion grew less the closer to the front they got. Soon, Connors was seeing only bumper numbers marked for the 10th Infantry, the very mechanized regiment he was seeking. He ran over to a likely looking armored personnel carrier and asked, his suit translating to Spanish for him, "Where can I find Colonel Suarez?"

"I'm Suarez," answered a neat and fierce looking, for all that his face seemed twenty years old, dark-skinned Panamanian.

"Sir. Captain Connors, B Company, First of the Five-O-Eighth Mobile Infantry." *Almost* Connors used the old gag line, "And we're here to help you."

Suarez frowned. With the idiot orders emanating from division, the absolute goat fuck he knew was behind him on the road, and the general confusion, he wasn't sure what use he had for a company of the gringo self-propelled suits.

"What am I supposed to do with you, Captain?" he asked. "No one told me you were coming. I'm not equipped to give you any support you might need. And frankly, everything is so goddamned fucked up I don't see you doing much besides adding to the confusion. No offense," he added.

"Sir," Connors began patiently to explain, for he had grown used to people who didn't understand the suits and so rejected them, "my company has more practical direct firepower than your entire division. All my men can speak Spanish through the suits' translational capabilities. And *we* don't need any support: no fuel, no food, no parts, no mechanics. We don't even need to take up any road space."

"No lie?" Suarez asked, one lifted eyebrow showing the skepticism he felt.

"No lie, sir. Just tell me what you need done and we'll do it. Within reason, of course."

"Of course," Suarez echoed, trying to think what use he might make of these gringo—no, *galactic*, he supposed—wonders.

"I'm torn," Suarez muttered, "between having you go back and unfuck the mess to the rear and having you go forward and clear out a group of the aliens that is holding up my advance. Have you got a map?"

Connors' AID projected a 3-D map of the area in midair.

Suarez's eyebrow dropped as he leaned back from the projected map in startlement. When he recovered his composure he said, "Hmmm . . . I wish I could tell

you where all my units are. Damned radios are not
working quite right." Suarez's eyes widened again as
unit icons began to appear on the projected map.

Suarez couldn't resist saying, "Cooollll," as he jumped
down from the APC and stood in front of the map.
"I've got three problems. One is the cluster fuck to the
rear. As I said, I'd use your people to help straighten it
out . . . except that if you have the fire power you claim,
it would be a waste." *Unless, of course, you used that
firepower to shoot my division commander.*

"My second problem is communications. I *might*
use you for that later, if you're willing, but for now
I'd rather use you for problem number three, which
is this river crossing, here," Suarez's finger touched
a spot on the projected map.

"There are enemy on the other side. While I could
force it, it would cost me some armor. This, in itself,
would be acceptable except that the armor would
then block the ford. Can you clear the far side for
me, then sweep down and clear the bridge south of
the crossing?"

"We can," Connors answered after a moment's
thought. "Can you loan us some artillery support?"

Suarez's face grew, if possible, fiercer still. "The
artillery is my number one communications problem,
Captain. I can sometimes get my line battalion commanders. I have not heard a peep from the gunners
in hours. I've got my sergeant major out looking for
them now."

"Okay, sir. I understand. We've got some indirect
fire capability of our own, but the ammunition for
that *is* limited, and I doubt you've got anything we
could use in lieu."

❖   ❖   ❖

Boot, don't spatter, echoed in Connors' mind as he set his troops up for the assault. *The biggest single thing I've got going is that the Posleen probably don't know we're here and likely don't have much of a clue of what we are capable.*

"AID, map."

Okay . . . into the river and move upstream to the crossing point . . . send one platoon. The other two demonstrate *on this side. A five-second barrage by weapons and then the platoon in the water charges.*

Oughta work. Connors issued the orders and the platoons fanned out, one of them—the first—diving into the water and moving upstream. The fire from the high ground opposite was weak and scattered, really not enough to worry about.

When he judged the time right, Connors ordered Weapons Platoon to fire. The high ground erupted in smoke and flame as several hundred 60mm shells landed atop it. The First Platoon, feeling the vibrations in the water broke out and charged due west.

The First Platoon leader swept across the objective quickly, then reported, "Captain, there's one, repeat *one*, cosslain here with a three millimeter railgun. And *he's* deader than chivalry. Nothing else."

That was worrisome but Connors could not quite put his finger on *why.* He tried to report it to Suarez and found he couldn't get through to the colonel's Earth-tech radio. Instead he sent a messenger and proceeded to follow the plan, sweeping south along the river's west bank to seize the bridge that Suarez really needed.

There was little resistance on the way or even at

the bridge. Connors sent another messenger to advise Suarez that the way west was open.

"The trick," Binastarion said to Riinistarka, hovering next to his father on his own tenar, "is to convince the threshkreen that we are as confused as they seem to be. That requires that obvious objectives and key terrain be given up without a fight, but that delayed counterattacks to retake them be put in at a time that is most inconvenient to us. *And* with significant losses to the threshkreen. Only in this way will they not suspect a trap. The technique is called, 'Odiferous bait,' my son."

"Father," the junior Kessentai said, "I don't understand. When you told us the tale of Stinghal, he left no such guards and didn't throw away any of the people in fruitless counterattacks."

"Those were different circumstances, my son. There, in the city of Joolon, the enemy provided his own reason to believe the city was ready to fall, Stinghal merely added to the illusion. Here, on the other hand, the enemy threshkreen have not been in a position to really hurt us. We must provide the illusion and that illusion must seem very real indeed. Thus, I throw away thousands of the people in these fruitless attacks, to convince the enemy."

"I . . . see, my father," Riinistarka agreed, though in fact the junior Kessentai did *not* see.

Will I never acquire the skills my father and our people need?

Suarez was screaming into the radio when his track reached the bridge where Connors met him. The gringo captain didn't know at whom the colonel was shrieking, but took it as a good sign that the radios were working at all.

In frustration, Suarez threw the radio's microphone down, and raised his eyes to Heaven, shouting a curse. The curse had no name to it, but Connors guessed that it was directed toward higher levels, rather than lower.

The MI captain trotted over and removed his helmet. Suarez seemed fascinated by the silvery gray goop that slid away from the gringo's face before collecting on his chin and sending a tendril down into the helmet. His eyes followed the tendril as it disappeared into the greater mass, leaving Connors' face clean.

"That creeps out everyone who sees it for the first time," Connors admitted, with the suit still translating.

"Umm . . . yes, it would," Suarez answered in English, the first time he had shown faculty with the language.

"Your radios are working again?" Connors asked.

"Yes. Even the fucking artillery is up." Suarez's voice indicated pure suspicion at his suddenly granted ability to talk to his subordinates; that, and a considerable disgust at suddenly having to listen to his superior, Cortez.

He continued, "There was nothing but static or a few disconnected phrases and then, in an instant, *poof*, I was in commo with everyone. I almost wish I were not, *especially* with my idiot division commander."

Tracks continued to roar by, heading westward, as the Panamanian and the gringo MI captain spoke. The stink of diesel filled the air as the heavy vehicles ground the highway—never too great to begin with—into dust and grit. Both Connors and Suarez coughed as a particularly concentrated whiff of the crud assailed them.

That track passed and in the sound vacuum left Connors observed, "Well, as long as you have commo with everybody, you're probably best off keeping us close to you and using us as a powerful reserve."

"Boot, don't spatter?" Suarez quoted.

Connors smiled. It was so *good* to work for a man who knew what he was doing.

Darhel Consulate, Panama City, Panama

"You have lifted the interdiction of the humans' radio traffic?" the Rinn Fain asked.

"Yes, lord," the Indowy technician answered. "But we are continuing to monitor for an appropriate time to reimpose it."

"Show me the deployment of the Posleen forces."

Another holographic map popped up, which the Rinn Fain studied closely.

"Very interesting," he said, noting the tens of thousands of Posleen moving off the main road and taking cover in the hidden valleys to the north of it. "This is a clever Kessentai leading these people. He does not know we are helping him, but he sees the results of that assistance and acts accordingly. How goes the attack on the humans' warships?"

"That has been a great success, lord," the Indowy answered. "Two of the three seem to be pulling out of range of their own guns' ability to support. The last was never meant to stand alone."

"It troubles me, Indowy," the Darhel said, tapping

a finger to its needle-sharp teeth contemplatively, "that the last ship is able to resist us. Its AID should not be able to do so."

"I have some suspicions about that, lord," the Indowy whispered. "I have checked. Simple insanity is not unknown among Artificial Intelligences. But these are invariably older AIDS. The AID in the human warship is virtually brand new."

"And so?" the Rinn Fain prodded.

"I have run simulations, lord, at much faster than real time. I have discovered that such insanity is possible if a new AID is left alone and turned on for too long a time."

"Do you think this happened?"

"I do not know, lord. But I have sent a query out over the Net as to whether that AID *might* somehow have been turned on before packing."

INTERLUDE

Guano and Zira lay on their bellies, fishing poles in hand. They moved the poles up and down, more or less rhythmically, to keep the baited hooks moving. They spoke only in whispers. Zira suspected that the vibrations of loud voices would reach the water and frighten off the fish.

"This is pretty boring, Zira," Guano said softly.

"Is an ambush boring, young Kessentai? Think of it as an ambush."

Guano really had no answer to that. He was too young ever to have participated in an ambush. He tried to imagine one, waiting with beating heart for an unsuspecting enemy to show up, never knowing if the enemy would be too great to take on—even with surprise—and never knowing if the enemy had spotted the ambush and was even now circling to . . .

"Wake up, Guano," came the urgent whisper. "I think one of the little darlings is sniffing at your bait."

"Wha' WHAT?"

The tugging at the line that Zira had seen stopped abruptly.

"Shshsh. Quietly. There's one of the fish that was at your bait."

Guano quieted down and watched the line intently. Sure enough, the line was moving erratically, in a way that indicated something was nibbling at the hook. Suddenly, there was a strong tug.

"You've got him, Guano, now pull once, medium hard, to set the hook."

Guano pulled on the fishing pole, feeling a plainly live weight on the other end. "Yeehaw!" he exulted, though the Posleen word was more along the line of *"Tel'enaa!"*

"Its mouth might be soft," Zira counseled. "Let it run about until it tires."

For fifteen minutes Guano did just that, giving the fish some room to run and then slowly and carefully bringing it back. By the end of that time, the piscine was running out of steam, its tugs on the line and pole growing weaker.

"Very good, young Kessentai," Ziramoth commended. "Now pull it above water . . . gently."

The pole bent nearly double as Guanamarioch pushed down on the end while slowly lifting from near the middle. With a splash, a foot and a half long greenish gray creature appeared above the water, its tail flapping to one side and then the other as it sought purchase in water that was now too far beneath it.

"Dinner," said Zira, "is served."

CHAPTER 17

And when we have wakened the lust of
a foe,
To draw him by flight toward our
bullies we go,
Till, 'ware of strange smoke stealing
nearer, he flies
Or our bullies close in for to make him
good prize.
—Rudyard Kipling, "Cruisers"

Remedios, Chiriqui, Republic of Panama

Nineteen B- and C-Decs for each of the enemy water vessels should be more than enough, Binastarion thought as the fifty-seven low-flying craft glided soundlessly by a few hundred meters overhead. This close to the surface and this close together the spacecraft moved comparatively slowly, wary lest they make disastrous contact with the ground or with each other. In addition, each B- or C-Dec was accompanied by anywhere from seven to eighteen tenar.

As the Posleen craft passed, the People below the

flotilla, Kessentai and normal alike, felt a strange and unpleasant tingling sensation both inside and out.

May you do more than tingle *our enemies, my children.*

USS Des Moines

"We've got trouble, Captain," Daisy's avatar reported. "Lidar shows enemy vessels approaching . . . fifty-two . . . fifty-four . . . no . . . fifty-seven of them. They're deployed in three broad wedges. My guess, though it is more than a guess, is that two of them are heading for *Texas* and *Salem.* The third is behind those two, more spread out."

McNair scratched his head, uncertainly. "Looking for us, do you think, Daisy?"

"Likely, Captain," the hologram answered.

"Get me the admiral and *Salem,*" McNair ordered.

The center screen came on live again. "Graybeal here. I see them, Jeff. They're below, well below, *Texas'* ability to engage."

McNair swallowed hard before continuing. This was the difficult decision: to risk your greatest love, your command, on behalf of a mission.

"Sir . . . I think you and *Salem* should fall away to the south. *Des Moines* will intercept."

McNair risked a glance at Daisy. Her hologram was flickering less now.

"I'm devoting less power to defending *Salem,*" Daisy answered when McNair asked.

"You're okay with this?" McNair asked.

Daisy's holographic chest seemed to swell, if that were possible, with pride.

"Captain, I'm a warship. This is what I *do*."

The admiral interjected, asking of *Salem*'s captain, "Sid, have you managed to get any defense up for yourself?"

"Three of the six secondary turrets are manned and manually operating, sir. That's the best I can do with what I have. But, sir, you ought to know that we have no radar or lidar interface or guidance. We can engage manually but only straight line of sight and even then only at fairly short range."

"How truly good," the admiral said sardonically. "Very well, Sidney, head south to sea. *Texas* will follow. McNair? Intercept . . . and good hunting."

Posleen B-Dec Rapturous Feast XXVII

Ah, the never-ending joys of the hunt, the Kessentai in command of the ship thought. His landing group's target, assigned by the glorious Binastarion personally, was the known of the two lesser enemy surface warships. The location of the other was, at best, approximated on the Kessentai's view-screen.

What a strange world this is; all disgusting, wet, oozing greens. The Kessentai almost hoped for an early onslaught of orna'adar. Better that mass slaughter than a prolonged stay on such a putrid ball.

The Kessentai had actually landed with his oolt before being ordered aloft again to lead this abat-hunt. Binastarion had warned him, through his far-speaker,

not to be overconfident, that these particular thresh
had sharp kreen, indeed.

*They would have to be a tough and resourceful
species,* he thought, *to survive and prosper in such
a wretched place. Tough and resourceful, but stupid,
since nothing here is worth fighting for. Then again,
how stupid are we; trying to take it over. Though the
thresh don't know it, we are actually doing them a
favor by exterminating them.*

With *Rapturous Feast XXVII* in the lead, the other
eighteen landers—each with its escort of tenar—spread
out behind forming a deep "V." This was a simple
formation, simple enough that even fairly stupid Kessentai could maintain it.

Straight as an arrow the wedge of Posleen landers
flew, hardly noticing—amidst all the other inexplicable
horrors of this world—the shimmering, flashing anomaly
on the surface of the sea between the attack group
and its target.

And then the anomaly grew a head, one of the foul
threshkreen sensory clusters, with ugly projections and
a streaming yellow thatch. By the time the landers
and tenar had slowed and reoriented their weapons
arrays onto the head it had risen up until halfway
out of the water. A shimmering golden breastplate
(not unlike the one reputedly worn by Aldensatar the
Magnificent at the siege of Teron during the Knower
wars) covered the monster's torso and its threatening
frontal projections.

The creature from the deeps raised its arms heavenward, masses of something like ball lightning lashing
between its gripping members. All Posleen weapons
thundered and flashed towards the malignant apparition.

With growing dread, the lead Kessentai saw that no harm—absolutely none—was done the beast. But wait . . . it seemed to be rocking back and forth as if in distress.

"We've got it!" exulted the Kessentai.

"No, lord," corrected the Artificial Sentience. "The monster is laughing at you."

Rage warred with fear. *Laughing at me? We'll see who laughs last.*

The external speakers carried the sound of a thresh voice, but one frightfully, even impossibly, amplified. The beast's mouth moved as if trying to speak.

"Translate, AS."

"My lord, the monster has just said, 'Stay the fuck away from my sister, you son of a bitch!'"

USS Des Moines

"Skipper, these fucking animals are stupid. They'll shoot at what they can see with their own eyes, nine times out of ten, and ignore the real threat that they can't see."

"How does a stupid race build starships, Daisy?" McNair objected.

The avatar answered, "The theory is that they were genetically altered eons ago, that they are born with skills, even as the Indowy are born with certain talents. The difference is that the Indowy must be tutored to bring their talents to fruition, a long period of intense training and education, while the Posleen just *know*. But coming into the world knowing all they will ever need in the way of skills, they either never see the need to develop intellectually, or are—in most cases—simply incapable of it.

"In any case, trust me, Skipper, they'll shoot first at my hologram if that seems most threatening."

Not for the first time, McNair wanted to reach out and touch the shoulder, if nothing else, of this wonderfully smart and brave and beautiful . . . warship. He knew there was nothing there, however, and so unconsciously stroked the armored bulkhead of the bridge with a palm.

"Do it, Daisy," he said, "but be careful, my girl."

The avatar disappeared from the bridge in an instant, while Daisy's larger form began to grow up and around USS *Des Moines*. As Daisy predicted, the Posleen seemed to ignore the shimmering fog that engirdled the vessel proper and to concentrate their fire on her appearing torso. Even behind the heavy armor of the bridge McNair felt the shockwaves as kinetic energy projectiles and plasma weapons passed overhead. The ship was on a course of 270 degrees; thus, due south the sea exploded and roiled with the energies impacting it from the fires of nineteen landers and nearly two hundred and fifty tenar.

And then Daisy spoke. The entire ship reverberated with the amplified message, "Stay the fuck away from my sister, you son of a bitch."

Down in sick bay Father Dwyer muttered to no one in particular, "Tsk, tsk. Such language, young lady. I see a long penance for you. But, as long as you have to do penance anyway, *murder* the motherfuckers."

The guns of USS *Des Moines*, as well as those of *Salem*, came in two types. For general work there were the three triple turrets. For anti-lander work there were six individual turrets, one fore, one aft, and two each, port and starboard.

Each of the singles mounted an eight-inch semi-automatic gun, lengthier than those in the triple turrets and firing at a considerably higher velocity. These singles used ammunition, self-contained and not entirely interchangeable with the guns of the triples, though they could fire the more standard ammunition of the triple turrets in a pinch. The normal ammunition for the singles, however, was entirely anti-lander oriented, consisting of armor piercing, discarding sabot, depleted uranium. The APDSDU was adequate to penetrate a Posleen C- or B-Dodecahedron at a range of between twelve and twenty miles, depending on obliquity of the hit. It carried no explosive charge, but would do its damage by the physical destruction of what it passed through, by raising the internal temperature of the compartments it punctured, and by burning.

Depleted uranium burned like the devil.

The general purpose guns, those in the triple turrets, boasted neither the range nor the penetration of the single, anti-lander guns. For the most part they fired high capacity high explosive (or HICAP), twelve kiloton neutron shells (which required national command authority to use), improved conventional munitions (which dispensed smaller bomblets after explosively ejecting the base of the shell), and canister.

ICM was useless. McNair knew better than to ask to open up with nukes. HICAP, fired with a time fuse, would have been useful, certainly, but was not ideal for the purpose at hand.

"Canister, Daisy," McNair ordered.

"I was planning on it, Skipper," one of the speakers said.

Eyes still filled with dread, the Kessentai's attention was fully absorbed with the invulnerable apparition before it. Was it a demon from the legendary times of fire? Some special divine protector of this shit-filled world? An elemental being from the creation?

The Kessentai didn't, couldn't, know. What it did know was that the monster's lightning-clad hands pointed at it and poured forth a blinding fire.

Daisy divided up the enemy's airborne fleet into three and assigned one triple turret to fire—sweeping left to right—at each third of the fleet. Down below the turrets, machinery, fine-tuned by Sinbad and his Indowy, whispered with movement or clanged with metal-to-metal contact as load after load of canister was moved from storage to the ready racks. The previous HICAP rounds, plus their bagged propellant, had long since been struck below where they would be safe from secondary explosion.

Four men, one officer and three petty officers, manned each triple. These were navy men; whereas the singles were manned by United States Marines. The gun crews were there as a fail-safe measure, but also in case the bridge, CIC and Daisy took a critical hit. In that case the guns could fire on their own, albeit with much lessened effectiveness.

When the last light on the bridge which indicated gun status had changed from amber to green Daisy announced, "Ready, Captain."

McNair rested his hand on the armored box containing the AID which was half of his ship's soul.

"Clear those motherfuckers out of our sky, Babes. Fire!"

The four single guns able to bear on the starboard side fired simultaneously, as did the three triples; the recoil was enough to shift the entire ship to port. Daisy put on a major holographic display to distract the Posleen's attention away from the real thunder and lightning of thirteen huge guns. The APDSDU, having much greater velocity than canister, struck first. Hit in three places, out of four rounds fired at it, the results on the target were uneven. One penetrator hit too obliquely, on one of the lower left facets as the gun faced the target. This one bounced off and went spinning, trailing smoke and flame, off into the distance before plunging into the sea.

The second and third, however, hit close together and at an angle to force their way through the alien ship's tough skin. The needle sharp points, backed up by foot-tons of energy, first piked into the ship's skin, gained purchase, and sloughed off. The material, depleted uranium, had a peculiar property: it resharpened itself even as the old point dulled. This the penetrators did, at the molecular level, more times than could easily be counted before breaking free into the ship's interior.

In the process of forcing apart such a thickness of tough alien metal, kinetic energy was transformed into heat. A normal in one of the compartments saw only a flash and then went blind as eyeballs melted. The pain of heat blinding was brief in duration. The

DU began to burn, raising the internal temperature of the compartment to the point where the Posleen normal's flesh and bones were turned to ash. It never had time enough between blinding and incineration even to scream.

Tough as the outer skin was, the inner compartments were good for little but retaining air should the outer skin have a breach. The DU, less stable now and with both rods burning fiercely, cut through the inner compartments as if they were not there. More Posleen succumbed, some to heat, others to the thick smoke, hot enough itself to sear lungs and toxic to boot. Still others were smashed into pulp. Machinery, likewise, was crushed and broken if it chanced to be along the penetrators' paths. Parts of both machinery and walls added further to the interior carnage as they were broken loose and went careening back and forth around the compartments, each piece shredding any flesh unlucky enough to be in its path.

The penetrators were not done, however. Having slashed their way all across the interior of the ship they came upon the far hull. They lacked orientation, mass and energy at that point to knife through. Instead, still burning, they bounced off and started back, repeating the process of slaughter.

No one ever knew, nor would they ever know, how many times the penetrators ricocheted back and forth through the ship. Even as the lead Posleen C-Dec heeled over and began to plunge into the sea one of them must have breached its antimatter containment unit. The C-Dec disappeared in a stunning flash that could be seen as far away as Panama City.

Many of the tenar-riding Posleen lost control of

their sleds in the shockwave of that blast. Some were spun into the sea at fatal speed; others were torn from their sleds and went over the side to plunge into the murky deep. There, struggling and kicking, attempting to learn in an instant what neither millions of years of evolution nor careful genetic manipulation had taught them—namely, to swim—the Posleen sank like rocks. Still others, riding closer to the exploding lander, had been killed by the heat. For Posleen farther away, the blast was enough to induce blindness, temporary or permanent.

Daisy, pitiless, swept her triple turrets across the tenar-borne survivors of the first C-Dec's disintegration. Traveling to within less than a kilometer of a lander, the canister shells exploded, usually within microseconds of each other. The three shells from a typical salvo burst apart in puffs of angry black smoke, releasing as they did about twenty-five hundred two-ounce iron balls each. These seventy-five hundred balls traveled on with all the velocity of the original shell, plus a small additional bit of energy from their bursting charge. In such a dense cloud of whistling death, it was the rare Posleen who found neither himself nor his tenar penetrated and wrecked.

As the triples fired and swept, fired and swept, scouring the skies of the unarmored tenar, Daisy turned her anti-lander guns in pairs against the following B- and C-Decs. None of these exploded in nearly as spectacular a fashion as the first. Still, she kept up the fire on pairs of them at a rate of forty-eight rounds a minute until each one targeted either turned and ran or fell into the sea.

The other group, the one that had spread out

looking for the indistinctly plotted CA-139, likewise headed for home.

USS Texas

Graybeal, ashen-faced, worried, *This flotilla was designed to fight as a team. Who expected us to be split up electronically? And now I'm out here, alone and in the open, with* Salem *unable to provide close defense and* Des Moines *too far away to be helpful.*

The admiral looked at the plots of his three ships, *Salem* running like hell for open water, *Des Moines*— one fight finished—now turning to race to his rescue. He looked at the rapidly approaching swarm of Posleen. No computer was needed for this calculation. The Posleen would reach *Texas* an easy eight minutes before McNair's command was in range.

A brief sigh escaped Graybeal's lips. *So sad it has to end now. It was wonderful being a young man again, wonderful to command at sea again. What is left but to make as good a fight of it as possible?*

"Captain, do a one eighty," the admiral ordered.

The captain's eyes widened at first. *Do a suicide run?* But then he, too, looked at the plots.

"Try and get right under them, do you think, Admiral? Maybe take one or two with us."

"It's the only way to engage with any chance of a kill at all."

The captain nodded. "Helm, turn us about. Gunnery, prepare to fire at lowest possible elevation. Fire as she bears."

USS Des Moines

The ship was racing, Daisy Mae cutting power to nearly everything else and straining to make it to *Texas'* succor before it was too late.

Holographic tears running down holographic cheeks she asked in a broken voice, "Shall I show you, Skipper? I can sense it well enough to do that. Someone ought to see and remember."

McNair couldn't bring himself to speak and was only just able to prevent himself from crying. He gave a shallow nod.

"Jesus!" exclaimed the helmsman as *Texas'* last fight sprang into view in miniature over one of the plotting tables in CIC.

The *Texas* was stricken, that much was obvious. She was already listing badly to port. Three of her turrets had been blasted away completely. Smoke poured, black and hateful, from a fourth, flames casting evil glows upon the smoke. And yet her captain, or maybe it was the admiral, or perhaps it was a simple seaman at the helm, was still in the fight, still desperately twisting the ship to give her sole remaining Planetary Defense Cannon a chance to fire.

The Posleen were having none of it. Standing off to all sides, hanging low to avoid the ship's last sting, they poured fire—plasma cannon and KE projectiles—into *Texas'* superstructure and hull. In the miniature view provided by Daisy recognizably large chunks of steel were blasted off into the sky.

"He got three," Daisy announced in a breaking voice. "Destroyed or damaged and withdrawn, I can't say. But there were nineteen that took off after *Texas* and there are only sixteen now."

"How long until we're in range?" McNair asked in a tone tinged with purest hate.

"Two minutes, captain, but . . . Oh!"

On the projection Daisy had made, BB-35, the United States' Ship *Texas*, veteran of three wars, had—fighting and defiant to the end—blown up.

Blonde hair streaming down her face, head hanging, Daisy announced, "The enemy is running for home now. I might be able to pick off a straggler but . . ."

"But we're alone now and can't necessarily take them. And that group that turned tail might return. I know. Revenge will have to wait."

No one on the bridge who heard McNair speak at that moment doubted that there *would* be revenge.

Remedios, Chiriqui, Republic of Panama

Binastarion sighed. *Sometimes you get the abat and sometimes the abat get you.*

He'd lost way too many sons to the thresh of this world. They'd died at the walls of the threshkreen city, David. They'd died in its parks and narrow alleys. They'd died on jungle trails pursuing the thresh who— maddeningly—turned and fought back with a vengeance as they made their escape over the mountains to the north. Lastly, he lost nearly an entire a sub-clan's worth of Kessentai to the threshkreen's damnable warships.

And for that what did he have to show? They had destroyed a ship, true, and the biggest of the lot. But the nourishing thresh of the ship; the refined metal of the ship? *Lost, lost . . . irredeemably lost. Sunk to the bottom of an impenetrable sea. They are clever and vicious, these thresh, to deny the victor the fruits of victory. I must remember this. They are the cruelest of species.*

While the exchange of so many Kessentai—*Each one a son, cousin or nephew!* The thought was like a knife in the belly—for a single one of the threshkreen's warships struck Binastarion as a very bad trade, he had to admit there were redeeming factors. *At least the warships will not be firing at my people on the ground any longer. It was bad enough that they wrecked the landing on the southern peninsula, blasting holes in our lines through which the threshkreen poured and smashing any assemblage of the People massing for counterattack. Even now the remnants of the People there, cut up into bite sized bits, bleat for aid which I cannot give them. They will not last long.*

Neither, though, the God King contemplated more happily, *will the other column of thresh last long. Despite being led by a contingent of the metal thresh-kreen, they move forward only uncertainly. Otherwise, I'd already have sprung my trap.*

Indeed, there was a trap. One of the side effects of being a comparatively small clan, as Binastarion's was, was that one had to be clever to survive since one was not very strong. One had to be very clever to survive as a clan in the Po'os-eat-Po'os worlds of the People. Thus, while scream and charge was the normal tactical doctrine of powerful clans of Posleen, for the little clans the doctrine became something more like "bait and switch."

Binastarion, a senior God King more clever than

most, had pulled something very like a bait and switch.
Even while the column of heavily armed threshkreen
pressed up the road between mountains and sea, groups
of the People were taking shelter in the former and—to
a lesser extent—in the mangrove swamps bordering
the latter. Meanwhile, some of Binastarion's cleverest
eson'soran delayed in the center: take a position, fire,
gallop back, pass through a different group, take a
position, wait . . . "Bait and switch."

It might have been over already, if the thresh had
either pressed forward boldly or moved more carefully,
securing his flanks. As it was, the thresh seemed more
confused in his movements than anything.

*Well, time to bring the enemy a little enlighten-
ment.*

INTERLUDE

The sun was setting to the west. In part for the warmth, and in part to keep off the annoying insect life of this world, Ziramoth had built a small fire. He and Guanamarioch lay low to either side of the fire, sometimes talking, sometimes just thinking. Ziramoth interspersed conversation with slices of the fish he had caught.

Posleen didn't cook. Oh, they'd eat thresh that had been caught in a fire and charred, but the idea of actually applying heat or a chemical process to make their food more palatable was something that had not been implanted in them by the Aldenata and which they had never thought upon themselves. Sooner a lion would make and eat crepes than a Posleen would cook food.

Nonetheless, Ziramoth—even one-handed—was a pretty deft hand with a knife and something like sushi was within his repertoire. He and Guanamarioch made a decent meal there, by the mossy riverbank, off raw fish, sugarcane, and a few mangos.

Guanamarioch was certain that Ziramoth was quite a lot brighter than he was. The scars, along with the missing eye and arm, suggested the Kenstain might be braver as well, not that Guanamarioch considered himself to be especially brave.

Most God Kings would have thought the question beneath them even to ask. Most, indeed, were incapable of so much as acknowledging the existence of those who had turned from the path, except perhaps to spit.

Guanamarioch had to ask, "What caused you to turn from the path, Zira?"

The Kenstain, in the process of filleting a fish, stopped in mid-slice and lay stock still for a moment, contemplating how to form his answer.

"It was long ago . . . six . . . no, seven orna'adars past," Ziramoth answered, slowly, before asking, "You know we were once a greater clan than we are now?"

Guanamarioch nodded and answered, "Yes, I read of it on the way here, in the scrolls."

"The scrolls do not tell all the story, young lordling. I have read them, too, and they do not say *how* we ended up in such straits."

"Is this . . . *forbidden* knowledge, Zira?"

The Kenstain laughed aloud, a great tongue-lolling, fang-bared Posleen laugh. "To forbid it, they would have to admit to it somewhere. And no one has ever admitted to it."

"Tell me, Zira."

The Kenstain acquired a far away look for a moment, as if trying hard to recall something very distant. Then he looked closely at the God King, as if trying to decide if the youth would be harmed by the knowledge he had to impart. He must have decided that knowledge cannot harm, or that, if it could, it could not do more harm than ignorance.

Ziramoth began, "We were great once, among the greatest clans of the People. Our tenar filled the sky. The beating of the feet of our normals upon the ground was like the thunder. The host filled the eye like the rolling sea.

"And then we made a mistake . . ."

CHAPTER 18

There are no bad regiments;
there are only bad officers.
—Field Marshall,
Viscount William Slim

Remedios, Chiriqui, Republic of Panama

Suarez wasn't confused; he was infuriated. The orders emanating from Cortez's headquarters were confusing, to be sure. "Go here . . . no, wait . . . no, go there . . . no, come back . . . no, go forward . . . detach a battalion to secure X . . . no, no, concentrate to attack Y." But Suarez, rather than being confused, understood completely.

The fucking moron is simply too scared shitless to have a coherent thought.

Right now Suarez's mechanized regiment was about half scattered around the northern part of the Province of Herrera and the western portion of Veraguas. He had radio communication with most of them, most of the time, but the communication was unreliable at best. Entire battalions would be unreachable for anywhere from minutes to hours. Even in a place that screwed with radio communication naturally, Suarez thought that more than a little suspicious.

As the lead regiment of the division, Suarez had, or was supposed to have, operational control of the company of Yankee ACS attached to the 1st Division. Unfortunately, Cortez interfered, or attempted to interfere, with the gringos even more than he did with his own force. Fortunately, the gringos, like Suarez himself, had learned very quickly to ignore most of what the division commander had to say.

Even more fortunately, the commander of the ACS, the gringo captain named Connors, had an understanding with Suarez. It was the understanding of two soldiers, differing greatly in rank, who recognized a common bond of dedication to the profession and a common bond in being placed under the command of idiots often enough for it to be more usual than not.

"This is not the way to use an armored combat suit formation," Connors complained to Suarez. "Little penny packets, scattered about, with no oomph and no punch. We should be like armor, concentrated for the decisive blow. Except that we're better than armor because we can go anywhere and fight anywhere. We should *not* be used like assault guns, supporting slower moving and less powerful forces. It's a violation of Principle of War—mass."

"You're pulling in your detachments?" Suarez queried.

"Yes, sir," Connors agreed, nodding unseen inside his suit. "As I can."

"Well, Captain, while I agree with your assessment of the role of ACS, we've got another problem that might make it a little wiser to do some splitting up. How are your internal communications?"

"Good, sir. We're not having the commo problems your forces are."

Connors reached up with both hands and removed his suit's helmet, placing it under one suited arm. Silvery goop retreated from his head and hair, forming an icicle on his chin. The goop reached out a tendril seeking the helmet. When it had found it, it flowed from the chin straight down. As before, Suarez found the image and, worse, the image of what it must be like when in the helmet and surrounded by goop, to be most unsettling.

Suarez shook his head to clear the thought. *Blech.*

"I think our commo problems are not natural, Captain, even though they seem to be random. Instead, I think someone is . . . *feeling* us out, getting a picture of how we work. Maybe it would be better to say that they've already done that and have now graduated to the early stage of deliberately fucking with us."

Connors' mouth formed a moue. He was a veteran of the early fights. He knew that someone or something often targeted human communications. He was also pretty sure that those doing the targeting were not stupid crocodilian centauroids.

"They'll blanket you at the worst possible time," Connors announced. "I've seen it before."

"I agree," said Suarez. "Which is why I am going to ask you to do something very tactically unsound."

"You want me to leave a man or two with each of your battalions for backup communications, don't you, sir?"

Suarez smiled. "Pretty sharp for a gringo, aren't you?"

"There's something else too, Colonel," Connors began. "I have a really bad feeling. We aren't killing enough Posleen to make a difference. They're fighting, and running, and fighting, and running. Almost like humans would. It's unsettling, sir, you know?"

Taking a deep breath and exhaling, Suarez agreed. "Scares me too, son. And I don't know what to do about it. The division commander's no help. . . ."

"Well, sir, I have an idea. If I break up one squad for backup communications I still have two squads from one platoon I'll have shorted. I'd like to send them out as flankers, north and south, in buddy teams. That'll still leave me two line platoons and a weapons platoon under my control for when things go totally to shit."

"Do it," Suarez ordered. "Do you need any backup from my regiment?"

Connors hesitated, thinking about that. After a few moments he answered, "No, sir. If I were you I'd start pulling in my troops and at least getting ready to form a perimeter. If my guess is right then the best thing you can do for my flankers is give them a solid place to run to. 'Cause, sir, sure as God didn't make little green apples, we've got our dicks in the garbage disposal and someone, or some *thing*, has his finger on the power switch."

Darhel Consulate, Panama City, Panama

The Rinn Fain's clawed finger rested lightly on the blinking green button. He contemplated that claw. *What a sad state. We were a warrior people; a people of fierce pride. A people made by evolution to be naturally what the divine intended us to be. And then the never-sufficiently-to-be-damned Aldenata had to meddle, reducing us to meddlers ourselves.* The Rinn Fain nearly wept with the sadness of the fate inflicted by the Aldenata on his people. *Damn them, and damn those earlier Darhel who acquiesced.*

"All is in readiness, my lord," the slave Indowy prodded. "It will be perfection, now. If you hesitate, the humans may be prepared to counter."

Smiling through needle sharp teeth at the slave, the Rinn Fain answered, "I am not hesitating, insect. I am savoring the moment. So much perfect destruction to be unleashed, and no violence inherent in it to trigger lintatai. Moments like this are rare, wretch, and must be appreciated to the fullest."

Even so, the Rinn Fain pressed the button, which went from blinking green to solid red.

North of Remedios, Chiriqui, Republic of Panama

In theory an ACS could simply beat its way through the rain forest, hardly slowing even for the largest trees. In practice, not only did the felled trees tend to build up to the point where they became nearly impenetrable even for one of the suits, the noise had a nasty tendency to attract the attention of ill-mannered strangers.

Thus, Corporal Finnegan and Private Chin wove their way through the trees as quietly as the suits would permit. This took time in the short run, and delayed any information their two-man recon team might uncover. On the other hand, dead troopers relayed no information at all, beyond the sheer fact of their deaths, recorded in blinking black on their squad leader's heads-up display.

"This is bullshit, Corporal, purest bullshit," observed Chin, never the least outspoken of the squad's privates, possibly because, out of his suit, he was the shortest of the lot.

"You're bitching just for the sake of bitching. Shut up, Private," answered Finnegan succinctly.

Chin was not, however, considered the loudest mouth of the squad without reason. He continued his bitching, more quietly but nonstop, right up until popping his head over a ridge overlooking a small, river-fed valley below.

"Stupid fucking bullshit, is what it is. Why I ever joined this outfit—"

"Chin? What's wrong, Chin?" asked Finnegan.

For a worrisome moment, the private said nothing. When he did it was simply to say, in stunned surprise, "Corporal, you need to see this."

Railing softly about pain in the ass rankers, Finnegan bounded over, weaving around the trees, until he stood beside the private, his head sticking just over the rise.

"Oh, shit," the corporal said quietly.

In the valley below, thousands upon thousands of them, so thick that Finnegan couldn't even see the ground, the Posleen host was rising to its feet, the tenar-riding God Kings pointing and gesturing to the pair of ACS troopers.

Even as the first railgun rounds began to chew the ground and trees around them, Finnegan ordered, "RUNNN!"

Remedios, Chiriqui, Republic of Panama

Connors went instantly white, no mean feat given the amount of sunbathing he had done in the months before the Posleen landed. He didn't have to inform Suarez what Finnegan and Chin had found. The suit's communicator squawked loudly enough for the colonel to hear for himself.

"Posleen . . . zillions of 'em . . . in the valley at Objective Robin . . . we're running . . . they're pursuing . . . shit! Chin's down."

Another voice: "It ain't just Finnegan, Boss. We got us about forty thousand of the bastards at Objective Tiger."

Another voice: "Can't run, Cap'n Connors. We're pinned. I can't tell you how many. More'n . . . aiiiii!"

Another voice . . . another voice . . . another voice.

Connors looked up at Suarez, standing in the hatch of his track. *You're the chief, Colonel. What the fuck are we gonna do?*

In response Suarez held up his radio's microphone; nothing but static and occasional broken up syllables.

"I can rebroadcast," Connors offered.

"Can you fit inside the track so I can show you on the map?" Suarez asked.

"Not necessary, sir," answered Connors as his AID enhanced suit again projected a map between them. "All my people can see the same image."

"They can all see it? Nice. Okay, Captain, we've got no normal commo so everything is going to go from me, through your suit, to your people and then to mine. This is what I want."

Suarez's finger began to trace out a circle into which his half scattered battalions would fall and hold . . . or in which they would die. If asked, Suarez would have bet on "die."

"Oh, God, I don't want to die!" was Cortez's first voiced thought as he saw the wave of centaurs cresting the high ground to the north. It was fortunate that his radio, like everyone else's, couldn't send or receive. The only thing holding the 1st Division's cohesion together at all was the fact that none of his subordinates could hear their commander.

A nearby light tank company, Cortez's personal escort, turned into the coming storm, flailing away with machine guns and canister. For an all too brief moment it looked like they might hold. And then railgun fire began to chew through the thin Chinese-built armor. By ones and twos the tanks began to brew up as their crews were cut to ribbons and railgun fleshettes set alight their on-board ammunition and fuel.

"Turn around! Turn around!" Cortez shrieked at his driver.

The driver obeyed, pivot steering the Type-63 one hundred and eighty degrees to the south, then gunning the engine to race away, trailing a cloud of thick, nasty diesel smoke behind.

Cortez's eyes remained fixed to the north where the Posleen wave lapped over a mixed column of trucks and artillery. The gunners, he saw, were struggling to free their guns and fire even as the wave swept over them and cut them down.

A medical unit, two thirds female as Cortez could well see, was the next to go under. The men of the unit attempted to make a stand to cover the retreat of the women. Without machine guns, or even more than a few rifles, the men went under quickly. The Posleen then pursued the women, chopping the poor screaming wretches down from behind and then stopping to butcher their bodies and feast before continuing the pursuit.

Cortez felt nothing at that, despite having used his position more than once to bed some of the women of that unit. They had been, after all, just office and peasant girls, not women of class and breeding; not anyone who *mattered*.

A *man* would have turned and died then, to protect the women. Cortez simply urged his driver to move faster.

Julio Diaz cursed that his glider could not move any faster. On only his second actual combat mission Diaz already had begun to feel like a war-weary veteran. One thing was different about this mission from the previous day's; his radio worked perfectly.

And everyone else's was in electronic bedlam; those, anyway, that Diaz could not see stretched out, butchered and lifeless, below. They were *hard* to see, too, because Panama's normally emerald grass was tinted red across half a kilometer to either side of the Inter-American highway.

This was awful beyond words, even awful beyond thought; fifteen or twenty thousand of his countrymen, and women, massacred, rendered and eaten. Clusters of Posleen, some of them numbering in the thousands, walked among the dead, hewing a head here, splitting a femur there. Crossing himself, Julio thanked the Almighty, above, that the aliens continued to ignore him.

God did not or would not save him from everything. Despite having an empty stomach from once again, embarrassingly, having to vomit during his launch, Diaz needed to puke again. Only the fact that he was above the smell of slaughter saved him from that.

Still cruising while slowly sinking, without units to spot for, Diaz didn't even think to call for support from the cruiser that had blessedly answered him the day before. Sure, he could have killed Posleen, and that might have satisfied his urge for revenge. But revenge was a thin soup, faced with the enormity of the slaughter.

Despite the barren feeling of hopelessness, Diaz continued to fly westward. When he returned to base, if he returned, his father would need to know the extent of the disaster.

To his right the sun was sinking. Even as it sank, Cortez's hopes began to rise. His tank was amphibious. With any luck he would soon reach the sea and could set out on that, safely towards home.

With all the fearful paranoia of a hunted fox, Cortez had guided his tank and crew from the scenes of slaughter. Several times, when the pounding of alien claws on the earth had warned him of an approaching horde, he had ordered his tank into low ground, dense Kunai grass or copses of thick standing trees. His luck had held. While groups of refugees and even the occasional fragment of a cohesive unit had fallen all around him, the aliens had never noticed or, if noticing, cared enough to actually seek him out. He supposed they must have had enough to eat.

While opening his own bag of gringo-supplied combat rations, Cortez began to contemplate the future. He was facing a court-martial, he knew. Last time he had deserted a command, in 1989, he had been fortunate that his government had followed its army into extinction quickly. This time he could not hope for such a boon. His government and army would survive this debacle long enough for him to see the inside of a courtroom and the pockmarked wall before the firing squad. His uncle, the president, would clearly toss him to the wolves.

Worse, his driver, loader and gunner would be the star witnesses at his court-martial. *They* had the defense of superior orders, at least. He had only his own will to live, no matter what.

Can I count on Uncle Guillermo to quash any charges? Only two possibilities: either the country and the government falls, in which case there'll be nothing to quash, or they somehow manage to establish a defensive line, in which case there will.

Okay, let's assume there is still a country. It was Uncle's order that sent my division to the west. They'll be howling for his blood . . . so he'll give them mine. And these three crewman will testify against me. They have to go. But I need them for now to get me out of here, so they cannot go just yet.

Once we're at sea, then, I can dispose of them . . . but how to do it? Shoot them? Tough to do and the driver, in particular might escape. Sink the tank? Also hard to do and, what's more, I don't want to get sucked down with it.

Aha! I know. When we get close to land I'll get out, as if to wave for help, then drop a couple of

*grenades into the turret. Grenades leave little trace
even if they should somehow recover the tank.*

*My story? Let's see. I had gotten out of the tank
just as we approached land to get a better view.
After all, the land has become unsafe and I had to
watch out for the crew's welfare. Suddenly—"I don't
know how"—the tank caught fire and blew up. I was
thrown overboard. My life vest must have kept me
afloat. When I awakened the tank was gone. I drifted
for a while, then when I got close enough to land I
swam for it.*

*Okay . . . that's plausible and there'll be no one left
to contradict my story. Uncle can press the charges
and then have them dropped for lack of evidence.*

The setting sun cast its fiery light directly into
Diaz's eyes. He couldn't see a thing ahead of him.
He knew there was no sense in pressing on, yet felt
he had to. The *Estado Major*, the general staff, had
to learn the full extent of the disaster.

Diaz continued on, pulling to the right occasionally
to catch and spiral higher in one of the mountain-
directed updrafts. Sometimes, during those altitude
gaining spirals, he could see yet more of the refuse
of the massacre. He forced himself to look, despite
the nausea it induced.

Finally, with the last rays of the setting sun painting the waves of the Pacific, and with the last known
forward position of the 6th Division behind him, he
turned one hundred and eighty degree and began to
glide back to the east, to the base at Rio Hato.

It was chance then, chance that the sun had set
at that precise moment, chance that he was looking

in that precise direction, chance that someone on the ground fired human weapons in precisely Diaz's field of view.

Unmistakable. Someone down there is still fighting. I've got to help.

In order to help though, Diaz needed to see more, understand more. He began a slow, lazy three-sixty. As he did he caught more flashes of rifles, machine guns, and cannon. The flashes seemed to form a broad circle.

"Christ!" the boy exclaimed. "They're still hanging on down there. I've got to help."

Suarez, aided by the communications array of the ACS, had only just managed to form a half circle facing north when the first wave of Posleen hit. The Posleen may have been more surprised at the resistance than the humans had been at the grand scale ambush, since their advance guards stopped and then recoiled at the sudden and unexpected wave of fire that met them.

The Posleen, however stupid they were in the main, were also a species quick to form and quick to react. The human defenders had a few brief minutes of respite before a more serious attack was thrown in. This was not repulsed so easily; Suarez actually had to throw in Connors and his ACS company before the attack was contained.

After that the attack in the north petered out into minor probes and sniping while the bulk of the aliens split east and west to find the vulnerable flank they were sure had to be there. For Suarez and his boys it became a race against time to form a full perimeter before the enemy turned one or both flanks. Cooks and clerks found themselves in the firing line, along with medics hastily armed with the rifles of the fallen. Still, by nightfall a perimeter, more or less cohesive, had been formed.

I couldn't have even done that without the gringos and their armored suits, Suarez thought.

For his part, Connors, resting for the moment with his back against Suarez's track, thought, *Thank God this colonel knew what the fuck he was doing. Another man and we'd have been dead and peeled like lobsters already.*

Simultaneously, both men had much the same thought, which went something like, *Not that it much matters. We're hopelessly cut off out here, no chance of relief or support. We'll live until the ammo runs low or the fuel runs out or the power dies in the suits and then we'll die anyway. Tonight, maybe at the latest mid-day tomorrow, and it'll all be over but the munching.*

Even as he finished that shared thought, Connors suddenly sat upright. Clearly and distinctly, through his suits communicator, he heard a Spanish voice, "Any station, any station, this is Lima Two Seven."

"Lima Two Seven this is Romeo Five Five. Who the fuck are you? *What* the fuck are you?"

Diaz nearly whooped with joy. "Romeo, I am a glider. If you look carefully you might be able to see me overhead. How can I help?"

The answering voice sounded resigned, "You got a couple of nukes, Lima? Because short of that, I doubt there is much you can do to help us."

Julio thought for a moment, then answered, "No nukes, Romeo, but I might be able to get something nearly as good. Wait, over . . . Daisy? Daisy? This is Julio. I need your help, *Dama*."

USS Des Moines

Dammit, it had *hurt* to have had to run away; it had shamed. Daisy had seen Sally back to the cover of the mixed Planetary Defense Base *cum* anti-lander batteries on the Isla del Rey before turning back to the west. Unfortunately, by the time she had gotten within lunging range at the enemy, there was no one to talk to. Thus, impotent and infuriated, she had steamed south of the isthmus—to and fro, east and west—looking and hoping for a target.

Thus it was that, unconcealed glee in her voice, Daisy announced to McNair, "I've got us a *ripe* one, Skipper."

McNair, still smarting over the loss of *Texas*, didn't hesitate. "Bring us around." His finger pushed a button. "All hands, this is the captain. Battle stations."

"Julio, we're coming," the ship said.

Remedios, Chiriqui, Republic of Panama

"It's neither as good nor as easy as it sounds, sir," Diaz cautioned over the radio. "I wish I could connect you directly with the ship, but I can't. If I could, you could direct the fires. As is . . . well, sir, the ship can toss a huge amount of firepower, and it's unbelievably accurate, but only along the gun-target line. Anywhere from one third to one half of the shells will be over or under and some of them will be *way* over or under. If you have troops over or under the target . . ."

Chingada, Suarez thought. *Fat lot of good it does me to blast the aliens if the same fire blasts holes in my own perimeter. The Posleen will recover quicker.*

Suarez thought furiously while looking at his map. The ship was going to fire from the Gulf of Montijo, from a position just north of Isla Cebaco. What Diaz had told him meant that he could get effective fire to his east and west, but could not use the ship's guns to help him break contact north and south.

"All right, Lieutenant Diaz, I understand. Tell the ship I want priority along the enemy-held ground west of the Rio San Pablo. Then, on my command, I want to switch to east of the Rio San Pedro."

Suarez stopped to think for a moment. Something was nagging at him. Something important . . . something . . .

"*Mierda!*" he exclaimed aloud. "Diaz, does the ship carry a shell that can clear the bridges along the Rio San Pedro without endangering the bridge?"

It was a long moment before Diaz answered. When he did, it was to say, "Miss Daisy says she has improved conventional munitions that can kill the Posleen without endangering the bridge, sir."

Miss Daisy? Never mind. "Good, good," Suarez said with more good cheer than he felt. "Diaz, you can see, which is more than I can say. Keep me posted and commence firing as soon as possible."

Under Binastarion's eye his sons and their oolt'os formed and massed for what he expected to be the final breakthrough into the rear of the threshkreen's perimeter. The river to his front, while promising to be a costly obstacle to cross, was not so deep his normals could not cross it unaided, though he was sure a few would find deep spots in which they would drown. *No matter; their bodies will make a ford for the ones that follow. For the rest, a few minutes helpless under fire and then we're among them.*

An odd shape, cruising high to the west, caught the God King's eye.

"What is that damned thing flying up there?" Binastarion demanded of his Artificial Sentience.

That machine was connected to the God King's tenar and, thus, to the entire Net. Yet, infuriatingly, it answered, "There is nothing flying overhead, lord."

"Bucket of misdesigned circuitry, I can *see* it. There is something up there."

"Nonetheless, lord," the Sentience answered with the normal indifference of a machine, "there is nothing up there which registers. Therefore, there is nothing up there."

The God King was about to curse his electronic assistant again, when the AS announced. "Incoming projectiles, lord. They will land on the oolt massed below. I suggest you take cover."

Before Binastarion could answer, whether to thank or to curse, three shells landed, one short but two right on one of his oolt'os. That oolt simply . . . dissolved with panicked normals running shrieking in all directions. Binastarion's tenar shuddered with the shock wave. His internal organs rippled in a way he had never before experienced.

"Demon shit," the chief snarled, *sotto voce*, as he wrestled his tenar back to face his massed people.

Even as he grunted those words another three explosions erupted, with one shell landing among the ruins of the previously targeted oolt and two others smearing the one just to the north of that one.

In salvos of three rounds, never more than four or five heartbeats apart, the fire walked among his people like some half-divine, half-mad demon. Tenar were tumbled, their riders crushed and shredded. Splintered teeth and bones of normals joined hot metal shell fragments to pierce and rend.

True, sometimes a shell landed between oolt, doing no harm with its blast. Even in those cases, however, the odd piece of shrapnel might sail hundreds of meters to fall with deadly effect upon some unfortunate normal. The smell of Posleen blood thus released was enough to unsettle the half-sentients and make their bolting that much more likely whenever a salvo did land near.

Binastarion's communicator buzzed frantically with calls from his sons and subordinates. Each asking for instructions. *Do we attack? Do we retreat? If we stay here we'll be massacred.*

"Where is that damned fire coming from?" he demanded of his AS. "I have read of the threshkreen's artillery, but this is just too much of it. *Where* is it coming from?"

The Artificial Sentience did not answer immediately. Searching the Net, Binastarion supposed.

"The ship is back, lord," the AS said when it finally answered. "It can throw as much of this artillery as would a ten of tens of the heaviest sort used by the thresh who fight on the ground."

Even while digesting that unwelcome news, the

fire continued to walk among the host of Binastarion, striking down lowborn and high with random, vicious fury.

It was with·an equal fury that Binastarion ordered his subordinates to assemble on his tenar once they had their people under cover.

As he had been each time he had seen the salvos from the *Des Moines*, Diaz was awed by the fury of the guns. He said a silent prayer to God that, so far, none of the shells had fallen among the defenders.

When he judged the enemy was sufficiently damaged and disorganized by the fire he keyed his radio and spoke to Suarez.

"Sir, I think it is about as good as it is going to get in the west. Shall I pull out to the east and direct the ship's fires to assist the breakout?"

Suarez spoke back, "Yes, son, do that. And God bless you and that ship."

There was no more difficult operation in all of the military art than a withdrawal while in contact with the enemy. To do so over a broad front, with troops already badly disorganized by combat would have been impossible but for three facts: that the fires of the gringo ship had even more badly disorganized the Posleen, that most of Suarez's regimental artillery—three batteries of Russian-built self propelled guns—was intact, and that Suarez had control of most of a company of ACS.

"Can your boys do it; cover our withdrawal while we force our way east?" Suarez asked Connors.

"I think we ought to free up your units in the west first, sir," Connors advised.

East of Remedios, Chiriqui, Republic of Panama

"Can you get me some contact with that glider overhead?" Connors asked.

"No, sir," the AID answered. "I am continuing to try."

Trying to time things carefully, Connors and his men had stormed into the Posleen positions, such as they were, butchering the stunned-senseless aliens where they stood, before pulling out again and moving as fast as the suits' legs would carry them eastward. A regular mechanized unit could not have done so.

B Company, Connors in the lead, reached the rear area of the west-facing Panamanian units even as Suarez, using the suits the MI had attached to his sub-units, pulled the east-facing elements of the 1st Mech Division out of the line and got them on the road.

"How about with the ship, what was it? The *Des Moines*?"

"Yes, sir, the USS *Des Moines*, CA-134. And no, sir, the ship's AID is refusing all communication with *any* Artificial Intelligence Devices. I am not sure why. It won't explain, simply shunts me into a continuous loop when I try. It's not *supposed* to be able to do that," Connors' AID added snippily.

"Crap!" Connors exclaimed. "We'll just have to trust the kid up above to know what he's doing."

"Lieutenant Diaz seems trustworthy, sir."

"Yeah . . . well . . ."

Connors' reserved statement was interrupted by a deluge of heavy shell fire striking ground to the east.

The Panamanians in the rear of the line ducked, sensibly, as the air was torn with the roar of the blasts and the whine of the fragments, whizzing overhead.

"Okay, okay . . . the kid knows what he's doing," Connors admitted. "We can't direct the fire . . . so we're going to have to take advantage of where it falls on its own."

"Suboptimal, Captain," the AID agreed. "But best under the circumstances, yes."

Another long salvo came in. Connors tried to count the number of shells and gave up.

"AID, can you track the shells and provide analysis?"

"Yes, sir," the AID answered. "If you will look at the map"—Connors' left eye saw a map of the highway area, with great black rectangles superimposed on it—"the black represents areas where the strike of shells indicate minimum Posleen remaining alive and able to resist."

Connors only had two platoons, really, remaining to him, plus the weapons platoon. The last line unit had been scattered to scout to the flanks or broken up to provide commo for Suarez. The shocked survivors of the flankers—and the casualties among those had been horrendous—were in no shape for the battle and wouldn't be for perhaps days. There were too many holes in the chain of command, too much death, among that platoon.

The destruction visited upon the Posleen, Connors saw, was for the most part oriented along the highway. He assumed the other black rectangles on his map were Posleen assembly areas the pilot overhead had called fire upon. Since the highway was what the 1st Panamanian Mech needed . . .

"B Company, formation is V with weapons at the base and the line platoons to either side of the highway. I'm with weapons. B Company . . . form."

He gave the men a few minutes to settle in to the formation before ordering, "B Company . . . advance."

It was eerie, walking that highway. Smoke lay heavy along the ground. Posleen bodies, and more than a few human ones, littered the path. Many were torn to shreds, chopped up, disemboweled. Others showed not a mark.

Connors passed a tree that had miraculously survived the bombardment. In the tree was a God King, dead. The alien's harness had been ripped off, but it was otherwise untouched save for the tree limb that entered its torso from behind and stuck out, yellow with blood, from its chest. The alien's head hung towards the ground, gracelessly, by its twisted neck.

Shell craters, huge indentations in the earth, pockmarked the landscape. Something nagged at the MI captain. *Something* . . .

"Pay attention to the shell craters," Connors warned over the general company net. "Don't assume that just because nothing that was in them when they were created has survived that something might not have crawled in afterwards."

A Posleen staggered up out of one, dragging its rear legs behind it. It was just a normal, Connors thought, but no sense taking chances. He raised one arm as if to fire. Automatically a targeting dot appeared over the Posleen, painted on Connors' eye. He fired a short burst and the alien went down, splashing up muddy water that had collected in the crater even in the short time since it had been formed.

From time to time, one of Connors' platoon leaders reported in that "X and such number of Posleen had been sighted, engaged and destroyed at Y and such location" or "Posleen oolt fleeing north" or "south." He took no casualties and, in a very odd and bizarre way, that disturbed him, too.

"Are you guys sure you are seeing absolutely *no* God Kings? *No* tenar?"

"Just wrecked ones, Boss . . . only some wrecks, Captain . . . there ain't enough of 'em, even wrecked, to account for the number of other bodies, sir. I don't trust it."

Even so, Connors pushed his company on past the broad area of destruction and into the parts still untouched by the heavy guns. And there were *still* no God Kings or tenar.

"AID, pass to Suarez that the way seems open."

"Wilco, Captain."

The tracks and trucks were draped with the bodies of the wounded . . . and the dead. Suarez was pleased to see the discipline, that his men were leaving nothing behind for the enemy to eat, even as he was appalled at the cost. Because it wasn't a vehicle here and there covered with bodies. It was *every* tank, track and truck that passed.

Jesu Cristo, but it's going to be a job rebuilding this division. If we're even allowed to.

Suarez had the devil's own time of it, already, trying to extricate the bloodied scraps from the cauldron. Without the communications advantages—let alone the mobile, armored firepower—given by the MI he didn't think he could have done it at all.

Logically, Suarez knew, he should be having his sergeant major go over those trucks, pulling off some of the walking—even nonwalking—wounded to serve as a "detachment left in contact," or DLIC. These would have been die-in-place troops, left behind to cover the withdrawal of the rump of the division.

I just don't have the heart, I guess. Takes a certain kind of ruthlessness to do that—to even ask that—of men who've already given everything they have.

Cortez remembered his uncle often speaking of the need to be ruthless in politics and in life. *Well, now's the time to find out if I am as ruthless as my uncle always wanted me to be.*

The Isla del Rey loomed ahead. Cortez's Type-63 light amphibious tank churned its way laboriously toward the island. The big Planetary Defense gun atop the island was silent. *And a good thing, too,* Cortez thought. *The blast might be enough to raise waves big enough to swamp this tank.*

But then again, would that really matter?

The crew had not spoken an unnecessary word to Cortez since he had bugged out. Perhaps they thought they were merely showing disapproval. In fact, the effect was to make them even less human and less valuable in Cortez's mind. Thus, faced with the silent treatment, it was easier for him to take the hand grenade he had secreted earlier, remove the safety clip, pull the pin and drop it into the bottom of the turret even as he dove off to swim for the safety of the island.

INTERLUDE

". . . or perhaps we were forced into one.

"We had claimed a large island on a world. This was something new to our clan, to settle on an island," Ziramoth continued. "Normally, the chief of a clan would never do so. Yet this was a world of—mostly—islands and the lord saw little choice. It was large enough to support our refugee population for several generations. Moreover, the barrier of the seas around the island should serve as barriers to other clans. So the lord claimed.

"The island was fertile, and had much mineral wealth. The People prospered there. For a while.

"That entire world was gifted with fertility. None of the clans who settled felt the need to eat their nestlings. And the population grew in a way we had rarely experienced.

"Unfortunately, this world was also on the edge of a barren sector of the galaxy. We had nothing but wasted radioactive worlds behind us and we had nothing but the void in front of us. All the clans sent out scouts into the interstellar blackness. None returned soon. None returned in time."

Ziramoth again grew still, though Guanamarioch didn't know whether that was because the memory was so distant—seven orna'adars was a very long time!—or because they were so painful.

The Kenstain began to speak again. "Local scouts were sent out, across those coppery seas. It must have been that other clans had prospered as ours, for none of those scouts came back at all. Certainly other clans scouted out our island, and just as certainly their scouts were destroyed by us.

"And our population still grew. Then we *did* begin to eat nestlings, but it was too late. The normals had laid their eggs everywhere. No matter what we did to hang on until the scouts we had sent into space returned with the location of a new home, our population still grew. As you know . . ." And the Kenstain's voice tapered off.

"Hungry normals are dangerous normals," the God King finished.

"Dangerous in themselves and dangerous in the trouble they can cause," agreed Ziramoth, nodding his head.

"In this particular case, one philosopher's favorite normal grew too hungry to be controlled. It attacked the herd of another, killed a juvenile normal, and carted it off to feast."

"So what was the problem?" Guanamarioch asked. "Surely the Kessentai that owned the juvenile would have demanded recompense and the one whose normal had done the killing would have complied. That is the law."

"Ah, but that is only half the law," the Kenstain answered wistfully.

CHAPTER 19

An assegai had been thrust into the
    belly of the nation.
There are not tears enough to mourn
    for the dead.
        —Cetshwayo, King of the Zulus

Remedios, Chiriqui, Republic of Panama

Binastarion's crest expanded, fluttering in the windstream
as his tenar cut through the air. *That ship! That
accursed, odious, stinking, CHEATING ship! I had
the thresh in my claws, savoring the anticipation of the
squeezing when that damnable threshkreen ship ruined
everything, butchering my sons like abat and blasting
their mates into unrecyclable waste. It shall pay and so
shall all who sail aboard her.*

*   This time, however, I will not risk my landers, my
C-Decs and B-Decs. They are too valuable, too difficult for us to replace with my clan in such dire straits.
Indeed, without the manufactures in those ships we will
not survive the first push of a rival clan. Instead, we
shall swarm the bitch with tenar. I will lose sons, yes,*

perhaps many of them, along with their tenar. But sons
and tenar I can replace, the great ships not so easily.

USS Des Moines

"Skipper, we got's problems," announced Davis.

The *Des Moines* was still deep within the bay, still firing in support of the Panamanians, still boxed in by the mainland to north, east and west and the island to the south.

Daisy Mae's avatar's eyes moved left and right rapidly as humans' sometimes will when trying to count large numbers or solve complex problems. Her mouth opened slightly in a worried looking moue.

"Captain," she said, "there are more than I can track. Two streams of them, flanking us to the east and the west. They're keeping low, trying to get around us and cut us off. I think it may be time to leave."

McNair hesitated a moment, then picked up the radio microphone. "Daisy, translate. Lieutenant Diaz?" he asked.

"Sir?" Even charged with the radio's static Diaz's voice seemed terribly, terribly tired.

"We're in a spot of trouble here, Lieutenant. How is the breakout coming?"

"*Capitano*, Colonel Suarez has the bridge over the river to the east. Your ICM cleaned off the aliens pretty well. He's already passing the soft stuff over, trucks, ambulances, things like that."

"To the west?" McNair queried, succinctly.

"Your countrymen in the Armored Combat Suits are handling that, sir. It looks basically okay."

Unseen by the glider pilot, McNair nodded, as if weighing options, duties, values and chances of survival.

"Tell Suarez I have to pull out. The Posleen are trying to box me in here. It's not looking good."

Again the radio crackled with the flying officer's voice, "I will pass that on, sir. We should be fine on the ground. Good luck and my best to your radio operator Miss Daisy. Diaz out."

McNair half turned and shouted to the navigation bridge, "Bring us around. Make for open sea. All possible speed."

Within the armored navigation bridge a crewman turned the ship's wheel hard aport. Beneath the stern the AZIPOD drives followed the command of the wheel. Water churned fiercely to starboard as the *Des Moines* began a turn so sharp it was almost less than the ship's length along the waterline.

As the bow turned to the break between the western-most tip of the island and the mainland, Chief Davis' eyes grew wide with horror. He pointed toward the island.

"Too late, Skipper," he announced.

"At them, my children. Punish the foilers of our plans, the blighters of our hopes, the murderers of our brothers."

Binastarion could see only a couple of hundred of his tenar-borne sons as they arose from the covering vegetation and began to converge on the threshkreen warship. In his screen, however, more than one thousand tenar appeared. Lines showing the paths of the tenar all converged in an irregular blotch above the ship. The ship itself he could not see, though bright flashes on the horizon suggested that the ship had seen the threat and was already fighting back.

The *Des Moines* had four lines of defense, so to speak, against alien attack. The most visually impressive of these, the three triple turrets of eight-inch guns, were already engaged, spewing forth canister and time-fused high explosive. At the current range the time-fused shells were most effective. Unfortunately, both forward turrets were fully occupied in trying to blast a hole through the southern quadrant of the Posleen net.

The rear turret, on the other hand, was totally inadequate to covering the one hundred and eighty degrees it would have to if the Posleen were to be kept away. Daisy tried, even so, switching the gun madly from one alien cluster to another.

The secondary line of defense was composed of the six upgraded Mark 71 turrets, emplaced in lieu of the old twin five-inch mounts. These were actually the first line of defense if, as the Posleen had before, the enemy used landers to attack. The barbettes and magazines below those turrets carried only anti-lander ammunition, solid bolts of depleted uranium. These could be effective against individual tenar, but their rate of fire was just not adequate to a massed tenar attack; though no one had really imagined any of the formerly three-ship flotilla having to stand alone as the *Des Moines* was now. Moreover, it was a case of almost absurd overkill to use a two-hundred and sixty pound depleted uranium bolt against a single flying sled carrying a single God King.

The third line of defense, the gun tubs, had been intended for 20mm antiaircraft guns. These had been replaced in design by twin three-inch mounts when it was discovered that a 20mm shell was simply too small to stop a determined kamikaze. The three-inch mounts had, in turn, been recently replaced by fully automated turrets housing five-barreled, 30mm Gatlings, stripped from A-10 aircraft that had become useless, having had no possible chance of survival against automated Posleen air defenses.

The fourth line of defense?

"Jesus," prayed McNair, "I hope it doesn't come to that." He then added, half jokingly, "We don't have a single cutlass aboard."

Daisy, eyes closed now as if concentrating on her targeting, as in fact she was, answered, "Have Sintarleen pass out the submachine guns I traded for. He knows where they are. Indian built Sterlings. They're simple enough that anyone can use one after five minutes' familiarization."

"Submachine guns?" McNair asked incredulously.

Eyes still closed, Daisy asked, "Would you have actually preferred cutlasses? I was watching *Master and Commander* and got to thinking . . ."

Without another word McNair spoke over the ship-wide intercom. "Mr. Sinbad, this is the captain. Pass out the small arms . . . the . . . Sterlings. And all hands, now hear this: I never expected to say this, boys, but . . . all hands stand by to repel boarders."

It was magnificent, Binastarion thought, even while hating the source of that magnificence with every fiber of his being. The ship was wreathed in fire and smoke, fighting furiously to keep the host of the People away.

The God King was puzzled, actually, that the host had not done more damage to the ship than it had. Hundreds of plasma bolts had been fired, along with several dozen hypervelocity missiles. (Those last were pricey and a clan as poor as that of Binastarion could ill afford to waste them.) Some of the HVMs had been intercepted by fire from the ship and destroyed in flight; the ship was putting out a practically solid wall of DU and iron projectiles around itself. Some seemed to have been spoofed by the immaterial holograms the ship projected. Others, though, many others, appeared to have struck home. Yet the firepower of the defenders seemed undiminished.

That sparked a thought. While the ship could spoof HVMs, while it could mimic in safe quadrants the bursts of intense flame that indicated cannon fire, the flame of the actual guns it could not mask.

And those sources cannot be far above the water nor too far from the center of the fire.

Shouting words of encouragement to his sons to press the attack closer Binastarion concentrated carefully on the pattern of flames belching forth from his enemy.

There, he thought, as a steady, measured burst of flames spewed forth from what he thought must be amidships. *There is a true source.*

The God King marked what he believed to be an actual weapon on his control screen, then tapped it several times to carefully sight his own, superior, HVM at the target. With a whispered prayer that the shit-demons not spoil his aim, he ordered his Artificial Sentience, "Fire."

❖   ❖   ❖

McNair and the bridge crew were knocked senseless and thrown from their feet by the blast.

"Oh, God!" Daisy screamed, clutching her side and flickering in and out of apparent existence.

Below and behind the battle bridge an enemy missile had struck the nearest secondary turret, cutting through the armor, incinerating the lone gun crewman on station and, unfortunately, setting off the propellant charge for the gun's next round even as it was being fed into the breach. The resultant blast was enough to knock the bridge crew to the deck, to blow the turret clean off the ship and to rip a gaping hole, three feet by seven, in the portside hull above the armor deck.

At the low angle at which the HVM hit, it was unable to do more than score a long gash in the thick steel of the armor deck. Molten steel blasted off from that armor was sufficient, however, to wound or kill better than thirty crewman standing by for damage control on the port side of *Des Moines*' splinter deck. The screams of those who still lived, hideously mangled and burned, echoed through the ship.

Continuing on, the HVM cut through five bulkheads and a passageway before erupting into the lightly armored magazine that fed one of the 30mm Gatling turrets. The heat of its passage was sufficient to set off the 30mm ammunition in its entirety, blowing that turret, too, completely off the ship and hopelessly jamming the one next to it. The explosion of the ammunition, confined to a degree by the ship's deck and hull, fed inward through the gap torn by the HVM itself.

A dozen of Sintarleen's Indowy crewman, standing by to participate in damage control, were half crushed and badly surface burned by the explosion leaking in through that gap. Their screams added to those of the humans caught in the path of the enemy missile.

Father Dan Dwyer was first on the scene of the port side misery. His first thought was to go to the aid of the wounded. Yet the priest was an old seaman. That was important, to be sure. But more important was to let the captain know how his ship fared. The priest picked up the intercom and rang the bridge.

It seemed a long moment before anyone answered. When the captain came on he seemed stunned, groggy.

"McNair."

Dwyer had to shout to make himself heard over the shrieking of torn and burned crewmen. "Jeff, this is Dan. We're bad hit but not fatally. Number fifty-three secondary turret is out."

The priest looked upward at the smoky sky through the gaping hole defined by twisted and tortured metal. "I mean *really* out. She's gone and you've got a hole in your defenses. At least one."

"Fuck . . . the . . . hole," McNair answered, groggily. "Daisy's a . . . brave girl . . . she . . . can be . . . repaired. What about . . . my crew?"

The corpsmen had arrived on scene while Dwyer spoke with the bridge. They went from body to body, looking for live crew who had a chance of survival. More often than not a medico would make a quick examination and shake his head in resignation. Morphine was being liberally dispensed. In the dosages used it was a sure sign, the Jesuit knew, that the crewman so graced was not expected to survive. Slowly, the shrieks, moans and screams softened as one hopelessly butchered and charred sailor after another was put under.

Dwyer's eyes came to rest on a charred, disembodied leg. He fought down nausea. "It's bad, Skipper, as bad as I've ever seen. Thirty men down, at least. Might be forty. Hard to tell; some of them are in pieces. They're . . . well, they're just ripped apart . . . and flash burned. And that's only on the port side. I'm heading to starboard to check there."

Binastarion wasn't sure his HVM had struck home until he saw the odd shaped, multifaceted piece of metal flying high above the deceptive holograms projected by his enemy. Momentarily the holograms flickered out and he saw the ship's true shape, long and lean and predatory, through the smoke.

How strange, the God King thought, *the one thing I have seen on this shitball of a world the aesthetics of which don't make me want to wretch. My enemy is even, in its way, the more beautiful for being so deadly.*

Even very beautiful things, however, must die. And so must that ship.

"Forward, my sons," the God King chieftain exulted into his communicator. "Forward to victory and glory everlasting."

The great ship shuddered with the repeated hits of Posleen HVMs now. Overhead the thick armored deck rang as two- to four-inch-deep gouges were torn out of it. Even through the stout metal, the priest was certain he heard at least two more secondary explosions.

Those had to be nothing less than eight-inch or 30mm batteries going up in smoke and flame.

Dimly, the priest sensed the captain desperately ordering that canister and high explosive be brought to the secondary turrets. He hurried the performance of last rites for the fallen, human and Indowy, both. *After all, God will know his own.*

Dwyer became aware of Sintarleen standing off to one side. The Indowy's expression was unreadable in any detail to a human not specially trained in the alien culture. Dwyer looked for a sign of disapproval, even so, and found none on the alien's furry, batlike face.

Sintarleen looked back and shrugged, a bit of body language picked up from the human crew.

"Though we have no such thing as religion, as you would think of it, it couldn't hurt, Father."

Sinbad continued, "These were a third, or nearly a third, of all that remained of my clan, Father. Of those great and industrious multitudes now only sixteen males remain on this planet, and another one hundred or so transfer neuters and females held in bondage somewhere by the Elves. We had hoped to buy our sisters and brothers out of that bondage, but now . . ."

The Indowy bowed its head so deeply its chin rested on its great chest. Sintarleen could not weep, was not built to shed tears, yet his body shook with the overwhelming emotions of seeing so large a percentage of his few remaining kinsmen slaughtered.

Dwyer did not know what to say. Instead of words, therefore, he enfolded the quivering Indowy in a great bear hug, patting the creature's back to give what comfort it might be worth. As he did so, Dwyer couldn't help but notice that, despite its small stature, the alien's body was one big chord of knotted muscle. He had the glimmerings of an idea.

We need to get antipersonnel munitions to the secondary turrets. But the shells are too heavy for one man to carry and a stretcher carried by two has the devil's own time of it squeezing through the watertight doors. But . . .

Dwyer stepped back and looked at the alien intently. "Sintarleen, how much weight can you people carry easily?"

The Indowy frowned, puzzled.

"How much *weight* can you pick up?" the priest demanded urgently.

The Indowy, temporarily distracted from his grief, shrugged and answered, "Maybe five or six hundred of your pounds. A bit more for some of us. Why?"

"Assemble your people, my furry friend. Go to the magazines under the great triple turrets. Get from them rounds of canister, two for each of you. Carry them to the barbettes for the secondary turrets, the singles.

"Maybe you cannot fight, boyo, but—praise the Lord!—you can pass the ammunition!"

Each effective hit of a Posleen HVM or plasma bolt was like a hot knife plunging into Daisy's vitals. She had grown almost used to the agony, enough so that her avatar barely showed it. Only the occasional wince, and the almost continuous rocking, indicated that the ship knew pain that would have killed a human.

The avatar's eyes opened up and it seemed to look directly at McNair.

"I have anti-flyer munitions for the four remaining secondaries now," she said, loudly to make herself heard over McNair's concussion-induced, and hopefully temporary, partial deafness. "A few anyway. More coming."

Even as the avatar made this announcement, the *Des Moines* shuddered under what felt to McNair to be at least three separate impacts amidships.

The captain shook his head for what seemed like the fiftieth time. He was still seeing double from the concussion of the first effective HVM strike. Despite this it was easy to see the smoke pouring upward from Daisy's sundered deck and bulkheads.

McNair forced himself to think. *Holograms or not, the enemy can see we are hurt. They'll press in. Nothing to do about it. Or . . .*

"Daisy, you can't hide us anymore, can you?"

The avatar started to shake its head, then realized that with the captain so badly concussed he might not make that out.

"I'm afraid not, sir. The smoke is rising too high, and I have lost some abilities to project false images as well."

So *hard* to think. Yet he had to. *If we can't look healthy, maybe we can . . .*

"Daisy, at the next hit . . . or the one after if it takes you longer to prepare . . . I want you to drop all the cover . . . make us look . . . *worse* off . . . helpless. Dead guns . . . ruined turrets. Fire . . . smoke. And cease fire until . . ."

"Until the bastards mass to close in for the kill," the avatar finished.

"And then you'll have to pick your own targets,

Daisy," he said. "I can't see to direct you. But you have authorization to fire."

Another hit rang throughout the ship.

The price was appalling. Still, Binastarion was certain, it would be worth it if only the damned threshkreen vessel might be sunk.

Smoke was pouring out of the ship now as if from a chain of close set volcanoes, or some single rift in a planet's skin. Even her main batteries went out of action. As the God King watched a last group of explosive shells detonated in the air, close together, sending a storm of hot jagged metal forward in a series of cones. The agonized cries of his children, faithfully amplified by his AS, shook the Posleen chieftain.

He checked the battle screen on his tenar. There was hardly anything left in front of the enemy ship to bar its path. The ranks had been badly thinned behind it as well, so much so that he doubted the courage of his pursuing sons. Only on the flanks was the People's attack holding up and making gains. The volcanolike smoke pouring from the gaping holes in the deck and hull told as much.

The defensive fire on the flanks had been mostly to thank for that. Binastarion was not sure why, but guessed that the secondary weapons carried none of the simple, scatterable or explosive munitions that emptied tenar right and left to the ship's fore and aft.

"Press in, my children, press in! The foe is weak at the center. Close in and pinch it in two with our claws!"

Slipping and sliding on the crimson blood seeping along the smoky corridors' decks, the grunting, straining Indowy switched anti-tenar ammunition from the main batteries' magazines to the secondaries' as fast as they could fight past the wounded, dead and dying crewmen and those carrying them to sickbay.

Sintarleen hurried from barbette to barbette, directing his kinsmen to where the ammunition was most needed. While the ammunition bearers were too busy and far too strained to give much thought to the purpose or morality of their task, Sinbad had just enough freedom of thought to question his basic philosophy.

We are a peaceful folk. We may not use violence. These are our teachings from earliest age. It is only these teachings that have enabled my people to survive, as so many other species have not, the transition from barbarism to true technology and civilization.

Yet my people even now carry the means of violence to those still capable of it. We make the weapons they use.

What is it that keeps us pure? Distance? The humans of this ship fight at a distance and rarely see the violence they do. How am I or my people here more pure than they? Merely because we will not see the violence? That is absurd.

Must it always be so? Must it always be our best and finest who fall? Curse the demons who have condemned us to this, curse them more even than that threshkreen ship which is, after all, only trying to survive as we try to survive.

Binastarion's heart was heavy within his chest. Momentarily his head hung with grief. *So many fine sons lost. So many brave and noble philosophers, bright beings with full lives ahead of them, cut down and sunk even beyond recovery to feed the host.*

But doubts in voice or action fed no one. The God King lifted his head, steeled his heart and his voice. A group of tenar sped by to his right, led by a favored son, Riinistarka. Binastarion raised his hand in salute to the young God King, shouting encouragement over the din of battle. The clan leader's communicator picked up the hearty shout and passed it on to the junior's.

"We'll take them, Father. Never fear," the young philosopher sent back, returning his sire's salute. "Forward, my brothers. Forward that our clan might live."

Demons of fire and ice, spare me my son, the father prayed.

"Firing," Daisy answered coldly. She had come to this fight full of enthusiasm. That enthusiasm was gone, replaced by only cold determination. Now she had felt the fire in her own belly; felt the pain of burning penetration and dismemberment. The avatar *had* to answer coldly, for every emotion of which she was capable was suppressed to keep the agony at bay.

With two secondary turrets down, and given the specific turrets, Daisy had a choice of adding two to the defense of each side, or three to engage on one side and one on the other. She opted for the latter and six turrets, three of them triples, with a total of eleven guns still working, swiveled to engage on the side from which the nearest Posleen threat came.

Riinistarka was young. His father might have said, "young and foolish." However that might have been, he was young enough to feel the joy and exhilaration of closing on a worthy foe in company with his brothers. If this was foolishness, so be it. Besides, if he were truly foolish he would not have felt the fear that gnawed at his insides, threatening to break through the joy and exhilaration. He had not known true fear since his dangerous time in the pens as a helpless, cannibalistic nestling. The memory of that made him shudder as present fear could not.

And how can it be foolish, anyway, to fight for my clan to regain its position, he thought, *to fight for my clan to survive?*

Ahead of Riinistarka the threshkreen warship seemed broken and helpless with jagged-edged metal showing where the smoke and flames did not cover. The covering giant demon that the God King had seen from a distance was gone now. He knew, intellectually, that it was not a real demon, of course. Though the practical difference between a real demon and that ship seemed minimal, at best. He was sure, in his innermost being, that the representation had come from whatever intelligence quickened the ship.

Perhaps a lucky hit had destroyed whatever intellect that was, for suddenly, the false cover had fallen away, leaving only the image of a wreck such as the people only saw as the residue of battles in space. That the enemy guns had fallen silent at exactly the same time as the holographic cover had disappeared seemed to confirm this.

Despite the obvious ruination visited upon the threshkreen ship, however, it was still steaming away rapidly through the hole it had previously blasted in the People's enveloping net. Riinistarka strongly suspected that unless it were utterly destroyed it would be back. The People, themselves, were quite capable of restoring a wrecked space ship. He had seen nothing to date to suggest that these human vermin were any less clever.

Indeed, Riinistarka had already lost enough dear brothers to make him suspect that these threshkreen were quite possibly *more* clever. All the more reason they must be destroyed then, while they were still weak and relatively backward, lest the people later perish before a more dangerous enemy.

Dangerous? Riinistarka felt a sudden twinge of fear rise to the surface despite his best efforts to suppress it. *There is the tale my father told, of Stinghal the Knower, and the siege of Joolon; how he breached his own walls and set fire to his citadel . . .*

Suddenly, three quarters of the smoke and flame surrounding the threshkreen ship disappeared and Riinistarka found himself staring into the muzzles of eleven eight-inch guns.

More flame bloomed, eleven fiery blossoms of an altogether different character from that which had seemed to cover the ship. This was followed a split second later by the appearance of eleven smaller blooms. And then came agony.

The first of the humans' heavy iron balls struck the control panel of the tenar of Riinistarka. The panel stopped the ball, yet splinters torn from it pierced the young God King's body and shredded one eye. The next, so soon after the first that the Posleen could not sense the time differential, tore off one shoulder, lifting the alien onto his rear legs. The third, following the second at the tiniest interval, entered his uplifted belly, tearing apart his internal organs and crushing his spine half a meter forward of his rear legs.

None were merciful enough to kill outright.

Riinistarka barely managed to hold onto his tenar. With his controls destroyed and his spine crushed, he could not hope to do more than stay aboard as the tenar spun slowly in place a few meters above the sea.

With difficulty, the God King turned his remaining good eye onto his ruined shoulder. Splintered bone protruded between shreds of flesh. Yellow blood seeped out. Feeling sick, the young alien looked away.

In looking away from his shoulder Riinistarka's eye fell on his belly. The threshkreen projectile had caused the skin of that to split, spilling organs out. He did not want to imagine what it had done to his insides. He forced himself *not* to think about what it had done to his insides.

At first, the wounds had not hurt, exactly. But after a few minutes, as the initial shock of being hit wore off, the pain grew. The God King whimpered at first. Then, slowly, the pain transformed into agony, the whimpers turned to screams.

"Faaatherrr!"

"We're through, Captain," Daisy's avatar announced with what seemed like weariness. "Some of the enemy are pursuing, but the rear turret, and the three of the remaining four secondaries that I can bring to bear should be enough to keep them at bay."

McNair, who didn't just *seem* weary, nodded weakly. "Casualties? Damage?" he asked.

"Incomplete reports, Captain. Bad, in any case. I am cut off from some areas."

"You going to be okay, Babes?"

Daisy's avatar nodded through her pain. "I'll be fine, Captain."

The pain had reached its peak and then begun to ebb even as Riinistarka's life ebbed out with the flow of his yellow blood. He had only the one dull yellow eye left to contemplate the departure of the enemy, his *final* enemy, he knew.

So far gone was he that he did not even notice as his father's tenar pulled up next to his. The airborne sled shuddered as Binastarion crossed deftly from his own tenar to his son's. A great cry of woe and pain came from the father as he saw his son's wounds. The father folded his legs to kneel beside the dying son. He reached out one hand to scratch the youngster behind his crest.

"Father?" Riinistarka asked weakly at the familiar touch.

"Yes, Son, it's me."

"I'm sorry, Father. We failed . . . I failed."

Binastarion shook his head. "Nonsense, boy. You did all you could. No one could ask for more. I'm proud of you."

The father followed his son's gaze to where the hated threshkreen ship was escaping from his clutches. *At least we hurt it badly. Though I am sure it will be back.*

"You and your brothers damaged the thresh, and badly. It might well sink," he lied. "Certainly it is at least half destroyed. In any case, it won't be back to hurt us any time soon."

INTERLUDE

"And the other half, Zira?"

"The other half is that the usual procedure would be to turn over the precise normal that offended," the Kenstain answered. "But in this case, the normal was a special pet. The philosopher would not give it up. The offended Kessentai was adamant. Fighting broke out. It spread like a wildfire among the septs of the clan. The reason it spread, of course, is that we had managed to create our own conditions for a miniature orna'adar, right there on our island. And we had not had time to prepare our escape."

"Oh, demons," said Guanamarioch.

"Right," agreed Ziramoth. "The clan quickly broke into competing factions, all based on that one little spark. Instead of waiting for another clan to nuke our cities we saved them the bother and did it ourselves. Of course, as soon as the conflagration started those normals whose gift it is to build the starships began work instinctively, but it was all they could do to keep, barely, ahead of the destruction. And they never got very far ahead. Of all of our clan who had settled that island, fewer than one in twenty managed to escape. And the scars of the fissuring, brother slaying brother, were too deep to heal. The refugees stayed in the small groups into which they had split. Some were absorbed into other clans, but most went their own way, leaping into the void between the stars even without reconnaissance."

By now the sun had set. Guanamarioch looked down into the stream at the stars reflected therein. *Which of them*, he asked himself, *how many of them have seen our passage since that long ago, terrible time?*

"Who was it, Ziramoth? Who was that long ago philosopher who plunged our clan into chaos?"

Now it was the Kenstain who grew silent, staring into the flowing stream at the stars that twinkled there.

His voice, when he answered was full of infinite sadness. "His name was Ziramoth."

CHAPTER 20

This is defeat; avoid it.
— Caption to a painting,
Staff College, Kingston, Ontario

Bijagual, Chiriqui, Republic of Panama

They'd held for a while, there at the bridge before the town of Bijagual. Half of Digna's artillery, firing directly into the cleared kill zone, had stacked the aliens up like cordwood, carpeting field and stream with their bodies and then adding layers of bodies to that carpet. It had become quite a plush pile before the Posleen had learned better and gone searching for the flanks.

Digna had assumed they would go searching for the flanks as she'd assumed they would eventually find them. She had hoped it would have taken a bit longer, long enough to finish burying her dead, at least. That grace the aliens had not given. Before the bodies could be decently interred the frantic calls had come from both flanks. She'd ordered the mortars to give priority of fires to one flank, the SD-44s to another.

369

The guns and mortars had fired off every round that could not be carried out on the long anticipated and planned-for retreat. That artillery fire had helped, but not enough.

She spared barely a glance for the long line of noncombatants trudging the road to Gualaca. Instead, she stood there, at the edge of the long meter-deep trench she'd had dug against this eventuality. Her eyes swept along the length of the trench, fixing in her mind the last few images of some of her most beloved children and grandchildren.

Digna had buried children before, several of them. But they had been only babies, dying—as children in the Third World often do—before she had had a chance to get to know them and love them as individuals. This was in every way worse.

The column of refugees-to-be was mostly silent until Digna ordered the gasoline poured into the trench. At that, with the overpowering smell of the fuel blown across the road by the breeze, the deaths became real. As if the first leaping flames were a signal, a long inarticulate cry of pain and woe arose.

She had not had the heart to order someone else to apply the flame. Instead, a grandson had handed her a lit torch. Almost—*almost*—she had broken down and wept as she turned her eyes away and tossed the torch into the trench.

Her grandson, the same one as had supplied the torch, touched Digna's shoulder in sympathy. She shrugged it off, bitterly and impatiently.

Voice halfway to breaking, she snarled, "Never mind that. There'll be a time for tears later. Get these people moving."

Her clan and its retainers had retreated with the smell of fuel overlaying that of overdone pork.

Digna had looked upon that pyre exactly once, dry-eyed. It was still not the time for weeping.

Dry-eyed, too, she had prodded, cajoled, and beaten her family toward the northeast. There, all through the night, the lights of the town of Gualaca had served as a beacon. There Digna hoped to find safety, at least for a time. Perhaps there would even be medical care for her wounded kin.

It was not to be. Crossing over the bridge spanning the Rio Chiriqui southwest of the town, Digna had expected to find a defense prepared. What she'd found instead was a town bereft of leadership; the *alcalde* gone with his family, the militia officers gone with theirs. What was left was not much more than an armed mob without direction.

Direction Digna knew how to provide. She'd taken charge, ordered half a dozen men shot, and formed the rest into a semblance of a defense. With another twenty-four mortars and a dozen SD-44s, plus a fairly generous amount of ammunition, she'd held the bridge and the fords over the Rio Chiriqui for two days. This was long enough, if just barely, to send the noncombatants on foot thirty kilometers up the road northward in the direction of Chiriqui Grande on the Caribbean coast. The vehicles, and there had not been many of them, were commandeered to carry the wounded and the food. The point of that band was just cresting the mountains as the pursuing Posleen again found the fords to turn Digna's flanks. She began another fighting retreat.

The little towns on the way were scooped up,

the very young and very old being sent northward, along with most of the women, while the younger men and some of the women were pressed into the fighting arm.

Digna had to order a few more men, and two girls, shot along the way. She'd sent them to their deaths dry-eyed still. *I can weep later.*

There had been a moment, there where the fighting had been thickest, that Digna had thought with despair that she would not be able to hold, that the aliens would break through to feast on her charges. Then suddenly, as if by a miracle, the aliens' flying sleds had all turned and disappeared southward. She had no idea why, but relished the thought that somewhere they were being badly enough hurt to cause such a change in priorities.

With the disappearance of the flying sleds, the Posleen normals had pulled back. With the terrible pressure from the aliens relieved, Digna was able to pull out her expanded forces mostly intact.

As he was probably her best field man, and perhaps because he was also one of her oldest friends, Tomas Herrera took the point.

Gualaca Bridge, Rio Chiriqui, Republic of Panama

"Demons of Fire, curse the Aldanat' who condemned us to this," whispered the low flying God King, Slintogan, as his tenar skipped over the mounded piles of his people's slain. Scattered among the heaped, yellow, centauroid corpses were more than a few crashed tenar, clear indicators that more than mere normals had fallen trying to force a way across this river.

Internal gasses from decomposition had swelled the bodies, Slintogan noted with disgust. In many cases, the internal pressure had been strong enough to burst abdomens and spill out organs. And then the sun had gone to work; the stench was appalling.

For a moment the God King thought a curse in the general direction of the now escaped threshkreen, not for killing so many of his people, but for allowing so much valuable thresh to be wasted. As it was, with the bodies grown so overripe in the sun, even the normals could not be forced to eat of them.

It was enough to make the hardest heart weep.

But then, this is not the way of the local thresh. I wonder how it would be to grow up and grow old on a planet so abundant, in comparison to its population, that its inhabitants can afford to sneer at nourishing food.

My people, too, might have had such a chance, if those stinking, ignorant players at godhood, the Aldenata, had not meddled. "It's for your own good . . . We know and you know not . . . War is the greatest of scourges . . . Trust and have faith in us."

The God King laughed softly and bitterly. *More likely this planet will change its direction of rotation than that a group of do-gooders with the power to meddle will refrain from it. Damn them.*

The losses from the attack on the threshkreen ship had been so horrific that Slintogan, normally a leader of about four hundred, had had to bond with four times that many normals left bereft of their Gods. His brother God Kings were equally overtasked.

And the thresh must have a considerable lead by now. "A stern chase is a long chase," *as Finegarich the Reaver is reputed to have said.*

The God King looked ahead and upward at the mist-shrouded mountains to the north. The road he could barely make out. Even so, he knew the road was there and had no doubt that the thresh who had butchered the People here by this body of flowing water would be fleeing up it.

A long chase and a tiring one. Worse still, a dangerous one as we will never know a moment in advance if the thresh have turned at bay and wait in ambush.

Near Hill 2213, Chiriqui Province, Republic of Panama

The sharp crest of the Cordillera Central loomed in the distance, bare rock surmounted by trees. Sometimes, Digna could catch sight of the walls of the crest, rising vertically over the more gentle slope below. It seemed to her that the rock walls never grew any closer.

The way up was hard, even though the winding, all-weather road was good. More that once Digna, or one of her followers, had to threaten to shoot anyone who refused to keep up. Many of them looked enviously at the horse she sometimes rode but more often led. There was no telling when she would need the horse for a burst to speed to some trouble spot. A rested horse would be capable of that burst where one wearied, even by so slight a load as carrying her ninety-pound frame, might not.

If some looked at Digna's horse with envy it was

as nothing compared to the greedy stares that followed the vehicles carrying the wounded, the lame, the infirm and the pregnant. Enough sniveling, or so thought some of the slackers, just might be enough to get a faster and easier ride to safety.

A great-grandson handed Digna a radio, announcing, "It's *Señor* Herrera, *Mamita*."

"*Si, Tomas. Que quieres?*" she answered. What do you want?

"I have a truckload of young men that we stopped," Herrera said, from nearby Edilze's battery position. It was on Edilze's radio that he spoke.

"What are young men doing in a vehicle when we need them to fight? What are young men doing in a vehicle when we have babies being carried and pregnant women and the old and sick still walking?"

Unseen in the distance, Herrera looked over the dozen or so disreputable, bound prisoners standing under guard by the truck from which they had been removed at gun point. He sneered at them as he spoke.

"*Dama*, they stole the truck and forced out the previous occupants."

Equally unseen by Herrera, Digna's face turned red with rage. *Cowardly bastards.*

Digna's late husband had once had a solution for criminals who trespassed on his land to commit their crimes. It was a solution much frowned on in more civilized circles but, in the outlying parts of Panama, and especially in earlier days, it had been a solution the implementation of which was unlikely ever to come to light.

"Hang them," she said. "Hang them right beside the road."

✧   ✧   ✧

Herrera smiled at the twelve—no, it was thirteen—thieves as he took a coil of rope from the horn of his saddle.

He had no clue how to tie a proper hangman's noose. No matter, a simple loop would do well enough. This he made and then tossed the coil over a convenient tree branch. A shudder ran through the truck thieves as the loop arced over the branch and came to rest a few feet off the ground.

Tomas gestured with his chin for one of the prisoners to be brought over.

Hands bound as they were, still the prisoner attempted to wrap his legs around a sapling as two of Herrera's men grabbed him by the arms. A few kicks to his calves and thighs loosened the entwining legs. He began to beg as he was dragged toward the rope, the begging changing to an inarticulate scream as the loop was placed around his neck and half tightened.

"Did the sick and old who were designated to ride that truck plead not to be put off by you and your friends?" Tomas asked conversationally as he adjusted the loop to the neck.

"Please," the thief begged. "Please don't do this. I had a right to live. I *have* a right to live. Please . . ."

"Haul away," Herrera commanded and the prisoner's previous guards sprang to the rope and began to pull. Once the kicking feet were a meter off the ground he told them to tie the rope off, cut it and bring him the remainder . . . and more rope.

The gagging and kicking of the first had not stopped before the second, too, was elevated. In all it took Herrera almost an hour before all thirteen thieves were strung up and dead—or nearly so, a few pairs of feet still twitched. The bodies swayed gently in the wind, the smell of shit from loosened sphincters wafting on the breeze.

There's a stinging advertisement for social responsibility, Herrera thought.

From her vantage point, hidden behind a large rock and some vegetation, Digna could make out the pursuing Posleen through her army issue field glasses. The aliens seemed to her to be hesitant, much more so than they had been during the assault on the bridges by Bijagual and Gualaca. Too, she noted, there seemed to be many fewer of their damned flying sleds. Lastly, from what she could tell, the aliens seemed . . . somehow . . . clumsy. Not that they were clumsy as individuals, no, but they seemed clumsy as groups, as if their leadership were being strained to the limits.

"Something *has* hurt them badly, after all," she whispered to herself. "Blessings on whoever or whatever it was."

Slower the aliens were. For all that, they were still moving quicker than her column of refugees. They had to be slowed down.

"But where?" she asked herself. Then she closed her eyes and tried to envision the whole area around the road and the pass behind her.

South of where the road wound across the mountains was a military crest, so called because it would allow long fields of grazing fire downward and long-range observation. The road itself S-turned through a pass carved out of the mountain rock through the topographical crest, the actual summit of the rise. To

either side of that narrow pass rock walls rose vertically, occasional stunted trees clinging to their tiny
crevasses and ledges.

The aliens aren't built to climb those walls, Digna
thought, *not even with all their strength. Their sleds
could get over but they'd do so without the supporting fires of the rest of their horde. That would make
them easy meat for my boys.*

Digna looked again at the rock walls. She found no
place for a horse, even one aided by arms, to surmount
the crest. *But I can send people up. A tough climb,
yes, but not impossible for human beings.*

She mounted her horse and began forcing it through
the still teeming column of refugees. It was especially
difficult in the narrow pass, which was only a bit wider
than the two lane highway through it. On the far—
northern—side Digna found essentially what she had
expected to see, a mirror image of the southern face.

*The only difference is that the aliens are trying to
climb while our people are trying to descend.*

Digna tried to think back to what her instructors
had said about the three types of crests. *The military
crest isn't worth much, not with the trees in the way,*
she thought. *The great thing about the reverse crest is
that I can cover the pass and road from it, while the
aliens can't shoot our escaping people from the rear as
long as we hold it. And inside that pass we can butcher
them with the mortars . . . as long as the ammunition
holds out, anyway. We can, I hope we can, buy enough
time for the refugees to make it to the coast, to Chiriqui
Grande where they might be able to escape by sea.*

With those factors in mind, Digna began to make
her plans.

Chiriqui Grande, Bocas del Toro Province, Republic of Panama

The sign outside the abandoned school proclaimed, "Tactical Operations Center, 10th United States Infantry Regiment (Apaches)."

Standing in the schoolyard, Preiss contemplated the curious things soldiers, who—as a class—tended to have no fixed home, would do to give the impressions and sensations of normalcy to create one. The sign was one such example. There had been no particularly good reason to bring it, absolutely no reason to make it the number one priority—well, tied for number one along with setting up the radios—in establishing the TOC, yet there it stood, even while the long-range antennas were still being erected. Preiss could only account for it by the need for soldiers, as people, to have someplace called home, with the trappings of home.

Preiss looked at the sign again, shook his head and entered the former schoolhouse turned tactical operations center. Inside he removed his helmet—useless thing really, given the enemy's weaponry—and ran his fingers through sweat-soaked hair. His eyes wandered over the map, tracing not only the positions of his forward units but also the positions of the landing craft from the 1097th Boat that were bringing in the rest of the troops of the regiment, their supplies, and their vehicles. The landing craft came in full of troops and gear and left crammed to the gunwales with anything up to five hundred civilians each, fleeing the oncoming horde. Curiously, thought Preiss, not a single one had yet called out "Gringos go home."

The thing is, Preiss mourned, *we don't have the first goddamned idea of what's ahead of us. My RPVs lasted maybe two minutes after cresting the Continental Divide. My lead scouts are still struggling up the jungle slopes.* Well, he corrected, *not "no idea." I know there are about ten or fifteen thousand more civilians heading this way, refugees from the debacle in Chiriqui Province.*

"XO," Preiss said, "I'm taking my Hummer and heading north. Keep in touch. You're in charge until I get back."

Intersection, Continental Divide–highway to Chiriqui Grande

Her horse was behind her, hidden among some loose boulders remaining from when the pass and road had been excavated. Digna, herself, lay forward, between two rocks, looking south through her binoculars.

Instead of leading, Digna saw, the alien flying sleds were following the mass of the ground-bound ones that first surmounted the southern military crest. The sleds fired occasionally, but only at the rear of the groups of the ground bound, as if driving them forward. With her field glasses to her eyes she scanned the Posleen on the leading edge of the wave. She'd seen their faces—similar faces, anyway—many times on the long march back from her home. They had struck her, before, as fierce, threatening and confident, to the extent one could read confidence on such a strange visage.

Somehow, they didn't look confident anymore. Neither did they seem particularly fierce.

They're frightened, she decided. *They look just like rats caught in a trap. Or maybe like wild animals caught in a drive. Hmmmm.*

Keeping low, Digna crawled back to her horse. The dirt, rock and asphalt were a pain to her breasts and belly but not so bad as a railgun shot would have been. Reaching the horse, she led it a few score meters through the pass and then mounted it, riding hell for leather for the northern military crest along which she had strung about half of her armed and able defenders.

Digna had exactly four working radios now, including those she had scavenged in Gualaca. Two of these were with the marksmen she had stationed to either side, east and west, of the highway. These had settled in among the trees and rocks atop the crest, protected from a ground assault by the sheer rock walls rising above the gentler slope below. The third radio was back with Edilze and the artillery and mortars. Digna had the fourth, waiting with yet another descendant by a sheltered spot more or less by the road that she had picked for her command post.

At that ad hoc command post Digna dismounted hastily and passed her reins to an armed thirteen-year-old great-great-granddaughter, waiting for just that purpose. The girl led the horse away as quickly as she was able to behind the shelter of the northern military crest. There the girl would wait, rifle in hand, until either her clan chief came to take the horse or the aliens overran her.

From behind the shelter of a bush, Digna looked out to where the road broke free of the artificially widened pass. The ground bound aliens entered the pass tentatively and fearfully. Followed by their God King, the normals crept through, and then began to spread out once they reached the northern side.

Digna waited until one of the aliens' flying sleds was into the open, behind what looked to be a thousand or so of the others.

Calling her forward subordinates by name she ordered, "Jose, Pedro . . . kill the God Kings. Now."

Within scant seconds a few shots from the crest were joined by dozens, then hundreds, then thousands. Through her binoculars Digna saw the one sled that had come through the pass swept by a massive fusillade. Bullets sparked where they struck alien metal. In a few moments the God King riding the sled was riddled. The rifle fire continued, however, as men posted along the east-west running treeline continued to engage the few God Kings driving normals forward, south of the pass.

From her own position, centered on her line, Digna shouted, "One magazine. Open fire."

The Posleen didn't even return fire. Less still did they charge. Instead, with their point elements falling in shrieking agony and the strange thresh projectiles whistling around their ears, the bulk of the aliens turned and ran back through the pass from which they had come.

"Cease fire," Digna shouted, the cry taken up and passed on by her underlings.

Turning to the nearest of her platoon leaders Digna then gave the order, "Take your men out and finish off the wounded. Carefully."

Preiss had expected to have to fight a human wave of panicked civilians on his way up the winding road.

Instead, he was surprised to see them walking calmly, in good order, and parting to leave a path for his Hummer as he approached. He smiled, more than a little pleased, to hear the murmuring, *"Gracias a Dios. Los gringos son aqui."* Thank God; the gringos are here.

It was only a few minutes more travel before Priess understood the reason, or at least a substantial part of the reason, for the unexpected order and discipline of the refugees. Rounding a bend in the highway he came upon three men, kicking a few feet above the ground. A small, tough-looking crew of Panamanians watched them die, keeping onlookers at a distance. No sign proclaimed the crime for which the men were being hanged, but the fact that some very young and very old were being loaded onto a small pickup nearby suggested to Preiss the reason.

One of the tough-looking Panamanians, the eldest of the crew, detached himself and walked over to Preiss's Hummer, a young boy in tow.

Through the boy he announced to Preiss, "Looters and thieves. They bring disorder and endanger better people than themselves. So . . . the rope."

Preiss just shrugged. Whatever worked, worked. None of his business.

"I'm Colonel James W. Preiss, United States Tenth Infantry out of Fort Davis. And you would be, sir?"

Still through the young translator, Tomas Herrera introduced himself, adding, "Senior Vaquero to the lady, Digna Miranda. The lady is back there," his head twitched back toward the pass, "holding off the centaurs."

"Do you have any word on what's going on back there?" asked Preiss.

Herrera shook his head in the negative. "There were only the four radios. The lady needed them all back there. She trusted me," he added, not without some pride, "to see these through to safety."

Preiss thought there was another sentence Herrera thought but failed to add. *But I would rather be back there, with her, fighting.*

Preiss snapped his fingers at a private riding in the back of his open-topped Hummer. The private, whose job it was to update the colonel's map, handed the map over.

"*Señor* Herrera, can you tell me what I will find up ahead?"

Slintogan pounded the control column of his tenar, fuming with an outrage he had nothing and no one to vent upon. The Kessentai he had sent forward with this first probe of the pass were dead. The normals were too stupid to give any account of what had happened. All he knew was what he had seen and heard for himself: hidden threshkreen had killed the God Kings bringing up the rear of the probe and a sudden fusillade had driven the normals on point into a panic-stricken flight.

Fuming still, he contemplated the natural obstacle to his front. Were it lower, he would simply clear away the threshkreen with concentrated fire from plasma cannon. But the angle here was all wrong for that.

"And the blasted tenar will only float so far up," he cursed. "They might make it, some of the newer ones, but alone, without ground support, they'd be abat bait. And it would take cycles and cycles to blast away all that rock. And I do not have cycles."

More of the same then, only much *more of the same. One nail will drive the other. And it isn't like we have any shortage of normals to feed into the grinder.*

Forcefully, Slintogan issued his orders to the several dozen Kessentai hovering, clustered, nearby. If he couldn't get a direct line of fire to clean off the summit with plasma fire, he could at least have the treetops blasted, and probably set them alight. Fifteen of his God Kings had that task. This time, instead of a mere five to drive the normals forward, he would use four times as many, plus a few. Even if he lost some that should leave enough to ensure that the drive didn't lose momentum.

Of course, momentum of the nestling into the preserved-nestling-in-an-intestine-casing grinder is, from the nestling's point of view, not a particularly good thing.

The aliens still looked frightened, in Digna's binoculars, but they looked perhaps a little more determined too.

This one is going to be tougher, she thought.

At that point, the sky was lit by dozens of plasma bolts, streaking across. Most hit the treetops, which began to burn.

"We have to pull back one hundred meters, *Mamita*," said one of her grandsons over the radio. "It's too hot, literally too hot, to stay here."

"One hundred meters," Digna agreed. "No more. And be prepared to reoccupy on the double."

"*Si, Mamita.*"

"Edilze, this is *Abuela*. Are you ready to fire?"

The young granddaughter—well, she was young

to Digna for all that Edilze was just into middle age—answered as well, "*Si, Mamita.*"

"What's your time of flight again?" Digna asked.

"Thirty-seven seconds from you giving the command to impact," Edilze answered.

"Fine. I want your ammunition bearers standing by with rounds in their hands for when I call."

"They already are, *Mamita.*"

Digna smiled, briefly, at the calm in her granddaughter's voice. *Edilze was one of the good ones.*

The thought was interrupted by an eruption of rifle fire from her line. The oncoming horde had reached maximum effective engagement range, about five hundred meters for targets as large as the centaurs, as closely packed together as they were. They were falling almost as fast as they were advancing. Return fire seemed to be going high, for the most part. Maybe they needed closer supervision from their God Kings to use their railguns accurately. Digna didn't know. In any case, she heard few human screams of pain or calls for "Medic!"

"Edilze, *Abuela.* Give me thirty rounds. Fire."

"Roger, *Mamita.* Firing now."

Digna thought she felt the firing of the heavy mortars far to the rear. Certainly, she wouldn't actually hear them for several seconds more. She shouted out some encouragement to her troops, and gathered two clackers for the gringo-provided claymore mines that fronted her troops' firing line. Mentally she counted down, "Thirty-five . . . thirty-four . . . thirty-three . . ."

The Posleen must be terribly close, she felt. Two of the militia flanking her ceased fire for a moment to fix their bayonets. Digna risked a look over the parapet fronting the enemy and saw that the lead aliens were, indeed, no more than seventy-five meters away, falling almost as fast as they closed. The key word, of course, was "almost."

Still counting, "Eleven . . . ten . . . nine . . ." she squeezed the clackers.

Instantly, thirty-four claymores detonated, sending nearly twenty-four thousand ball bearings screaming into the Posleen. For a brief moment, the alien advance stopped cold. In this respite, the firing from Digna's defenders picked up again, seeking out lone aliens through the smoke of the claymores' blasts.

"Five . . . four . . . three . . . two . . ."

Ahead, in the pass, heavy mortar shells began exploding right in among the tightly pressed normals. Their own shattered bones added to the flying debris that felled the aliens, right and left.

The mortar fire lasted only for a few seconds, yet in those seconds a gap was opened up between the Posleen nail and the other nails driving it.

In that pause, while stunned and confused normals milled about over the entrails of their peers, Digna stood up, rifle in hand.

Ostentatiously unsheathing a bayonet to show what she wanted her children, real and adopted, to do, she affixed it to the front of her rifle.

"Fix bayonets . . . Chaaarge!" she screamed, launching her less-than-five-foot frame forward.

With an inarticulate cry, her children leapt forward as well. They soon overtook their tiny commander, reaching the confused Posleen well before she did. As stunned as they were, and terrified by thresh that fought back, the Posleen barely resisted. A few tried to fight and were gunned or stabbed down. Others stood there, helpless, while bayonets sought out their vitals.

The bulk of them ran like nestlings from the sausage maker, pouring into the gap created by the one short blast of intense mortar fire. At the gap, the lead Posleen in the rout ran head on into the next wave following. Instead of being forced back into the fray, however, the routers simply barreled into their fellows, bellowing, snarling, scratching, biting and slashing to get away from the little demons that followed on their heels.

The panic spread from there as the lead elements of the next Posleen wave caught it from their routing fellows. They turned about, and in turning, turned still others. In moments the entire leaderless mess was racing headlong toward the Pacific Ocean, just visible to the south.

South of the pass Slintogan's crest sagged.

"Demons of shit and fire," he whispered, "but I hate these humans."

Using the communication device on his tenar, he ordered his God Kings to fall back as well. There would be no stopping this rout until the normals had exhausted themselves, and that would not happen for hours. No sense in wasting his few intelligent and well armed followers on what was, for now, a hopeless endeavor.

Tomorrow. We'll try again tomorrow.

To the north, Preiss made a call back to his TOC, at Chiriqui Grande. The troops were landing in mass now, trucks rolling from the landing craft one after another. The S-4, his logistics officer, was organizing the regimental trucks to begin moving the troops forward tonight. By morning, so he was told, the regimental artillery, a battery of 105 millimeter guns, would be in position to support all the way to Hill 2213 and a few kilometers past.

Someone, that old woman Herrera had mentioned, so Preiss supposed, was still holding the pass, it seemed. The steadily streaming refugees confirmed this. Preiss could only be impressed. He pictured in his mind some tough ancient crone, bent over and walking with the aid of a cane. *She must be one tough old bird, to be hanging on this long, with scrapings and cast offs. I hope we can get there by tomorrow.*

In the dark tropical night Digna passed off control of the mortars to her two groups of sentinels on either side of the pass. She'd have given her newly reborn virginity in a heartbeat for some of the light amplifying or thermal sights the gringos had in such abundance. But, though the Norteamericanos had been fairly generous to Panama, most of what had been gifted had gone to the regulars, not little bands of militia like hers. In her illicit trading she had almost, but not quite, managed to secure a brace of the larger night vision devices for her battery.

I should have met those black market bastards' price, she fumed silently.

A freight train racket rattled by overhead, followed by a hollow pop. The pop was followed in turn by a fluting sound as the casing of a mortar illumination round slid off of a shell and rotated down to the ground. A few seconds later it impacted with an audible thud. At about the same time the illumination shell's parachute deployed and the flare lit upon a scene of utter frightfulness, massed ranks of Posleen moving into an assault position. They filled the landscape as far as the eye, aided by aerial flare, could see.

A plaintive voice came from her radio. "*Mamita*, there's a sea of them out there, just forming up in rectangles and going to sleep on their feet. Can't I please use some HE on them?"

Digna thought about that. *Does it make a bit of difference if we kill some now? Does it matter if we cost them some sleep or make them move a bit? Somehow, I think not. Better things to use the shells on. Better times to use them. Like tomorrow, at first light, just before they move into the attack.*

Into her radio she answered, firmly, "No. We'll hit them in the morning. Just use the illumination rounds—and use them *sparingly*—to keep track of where they are for the mortars. At an hour before first light"—she had never quite gotten around to explaining the concept of Beginning of Morning Navigable Twilight to her girls and boys so "an hour before first light" would have to do—"we'll hit them where they're assembled. It ought to buy us some more time and kill a fairly large number of the swine."

"*Si, Abuela*," the young man on the other end answered. "I'm sending coordinates to Edilze as I identify them."

"Good man, Grandson. Your *abuela* is proud of you. Let me know if they begin to stir."

"*Mamita*, it's time," the boy announced, handing a cup of steaming coffee to Digna as she sat abruptly upright. She looked around, guiltily, before fixing her eyes on her great-grandson's dim face. *Nothing untoward. Good. At least I didn't make any noise. Either that, or the boy's too polite to let me know he knows. Damn these hormones, anyway.*

She took the coffee, sipped at it, then rubbed some of the caked crud from her eyes. She looked around at her surroundings. *Still darker than three feet up a well digger's ass at midnight. Also good.*

Digna consulted her watch, an incongruous dainty, gold thing; a gift from her husband on their fiftieth anniversary. She'd been dreaming of her wedding night when the boy had roused her. . . .

No time for that now.

"Radio," she ordered, and the boy passed over the handset.

"Edilze, this is *Abuela*, over."

"Here, *Abuela*," the radio came back, instantly. *Yes, Edilze is one of the good ones.*

"Ammunition status, over?" Digna asked.

"Sixty-two rounds illumination; six hundred thirty-seven rounds high explosive."

"Firing status, over?"

"I've preplanned thirty-three targets plus almost continuous illumination until the sun rises," the grand-daughter answered. "Three of the targets are the center of the pass and two hundred meters north and south of it."

"Good, wait, over. Group one, group two, *Abuela*, over."

"Here, *Mamita*," "Aqui, *Abuela*," came the answers.

"Rouse your people, then stand by to adjust fires. *Abuela*, out."

Digna stood and looked left and right. There was

movement there, to both sides, as her people roused themselves from slumber and resumed their defensive positions. She passed the word by runner to either side to stand to and be ready.

When she was certain her people were as ready as they would be she rekeyed the radio microphone and ordered, "Edilze, *Abuela*. Commence firing."

Preiss jerked awake as the still jungle air was rent by repeated explosions. He'd had no idea that there was a mortar position nearby when he'd ordered his driver to pull over the night before. Now there could be no doubt of it as the muzzle flash of multiple firing mortars lit the area like a strobe light.

"What the fuck? Rodriguez," he ordered his driver, "go over to that gun position and find out what's happening."

The driver "yessirred" and took off at a lope, rifle carried loosely in his left hand.

Preiss then called the truck column by radio and asked their position. Under his flashlight, he saw on the map that they were no more than three kilometers behind him.

"Wake their asses up and get them moving," he ordered. "Now. I'll meet them on the road."

He called for his S-2, or Intelligence Officer. "Where are the scouts?"

"Boss, they're about two kilometers short of the summit. I held them up after sundown, rather then send them into a firefight with mixed Posleen and friendlies."

Preiss chewed on the inside of his cheek for a moment.

"I'm not sure you did right, but I'm not sure you did wrong. In any case, get 'em moving again. What's their ETA at the pass?"

"Three hours . . . maybe four," the S-2 returned. "The jungle's a bitch up that way."

"Push them," Preiss insisted.

"Roger."

The driver, Rodriguez, returned. Breathlessly he said, "Sir, there's eight heavy mortars there in a large pasture. Woman in charge—handsome woman, sir, you oughta see—says they're doing a 'countapddepp.' Sir, what's a 'countapddepp'?"

Preiss mentally translated—"counter-preparation"— and answered, "A damned smart move, sometimes."

Slintogan's Artificial Sentience beeped, then announced, "Incoming fires."

"Who? Wha'?"

"Lord, I have twenty-seven . . . no, thirty-six . . . no, forty-two . . . no . . . Lord, I have a demon-shit-pot full of shells coming in at high angle. Impact in . . . five . . . four . . . three . . . two . . . one. Impact."

Overhead one of the dirty threshkreen artificial stars burst into flame, illuminating the scene nearly as brightly as day, but with an evil yellow light that moved and, as it did, made the shadows creep across the landscape. Simultaneously, seven, then fourteen, then twenty-one explosions blossomed in and around one of his larger gatherings of normals.

The normals, awakened in such a horrid manner, began to bleat and scream, searching frantically about them for the source of the danger. Not finding one, a few began to fight amongst themselves. That oolt began to break up, the efforts of its one God King to keep his charges in good order turning futile fast.

That God King called his chief, Slintogan, pleading for assistance in controlling his herd. Even as the senior Kessentai was forming an answer, the threshkreen fires shifted suddenly onto a different group as a second "star shell" burst into light overhead. The God King in command of that oolt not only had more warning but was made of sterner stuff as well. He blasted down any of his normals who so much as *looked* ready to bolt. This kept the mass of the aliens in formation right until one 120mm shell landed directly on the God King's tenar. This not only blasted the Kessentai into yellow mist and bits no more than hand sized, it also caused the containment field of the tenar's power source to collapse. The oolt didn't break under that semi-nuclear blast; it was incinerated.

With only the briefest delay, the threshkreen fires shifted yet again to hammer a third band. This one, like the first, began to come apart and nothing its leader could do would stem the flood to the rear.

The senior Posleen communicator beeped twice. "Slintogan, we can't just sit here and take this. The normals are going feral."

Slintogan considered simply abandoning the field to the threshkreen, pulling back out of range of their cowardly weapons as yet another oolt began to disintegrate.

No, this is not the way of the People. We attack*!*

The air was split with a cacophony of competing sounds: the roars and snarls of the Posleen, creeping ever closer, the screams of the human defenders as the Posleen fire sought and found them out, the splitting of branches and trees as railgun and plasma fire struck, and the steady drumming of overheated machine guns sweeping the deadly ground north of the pass with fire.

The attack showed no signs of abating. The Posleen crawled over their own wounded and dead to get at the humans, dying as they did so. Still, more came to replace the fallen and to re-lay the already thick carpet of broken, bleeding bodies on either side of, and within, the pass.

A radio call came from Edilze, back with the mortars, her voice breaking with sadness. "*Abuela*, I'm nearly out of ammunition for the mortars."

That call was death, Digna knew. Her men and boys—and, yes, girls—had only held on so far with the support of the heavy mortars firing steadily from the rear. Without that, they would not last five minutes against a full charge.

Grabbing a packable radio from the back of his Hummer and weaving his left arm through one of the straps, Preiss turned away from the vehicle just as the first of his companies—truck mounted—reached him. He held up a fist for the trucks to hold up along the road. Then he looked to where the sound of mortar fire, heavy all morning, was beginning to abate. Muttering a curse he began to force his way through the thick jungle growth toward the clearing his driver had told him of. There he observed a short, dark woman pointing at a mortar, its overheated barrel steaming in the wet air. The woman's long, midnight black hair hung down limply behind her.

"*Numero dos . . . fuego.*"

The woman seemed to be silently counting off the seconds until continuing, "*Numero tres . . . fuego.*"

Yes, this was a bad sign, especially when fighting against the Posleen. Preiss swept his eyes over the scene, taking in the small piles of mortar ammunition remaining and matching them against the rather large piles of waste from used ammunition, opened boxes and cast-off, tarred cardboard cylinders.

Yep, they're fucked.

Preiss detached the microphone from a rectangular ring on the radio's backpack, pressing the push-to-talk button as it reached his mouth.

"This is Six. I need ten tons worth of 120mm mortar ammunition at . . ." He consulted his map, and gave off the six digit grid of the nearest point along the road to the clearing. "I'll meet the trucks there."

"Be a couple of hours, Six," the S-4 answered. "The road's become a crawling nightmare of a jam, with our trucks and the refugees all mixed in. The only way I can get you that ammunition is to take it from our own guns."

"Fuck!" Preiss exclaimed, though not into the radio. Then, again keying the mike, he said, "Do the best you can. And keep me posted."

"There is some good news, Six. The regimental battery is almost ready to fire on the crest and a bit beyond. They're breaking down the ammunition now."

"How do you know?" Preiss asked.

"I'm with them now, about fifteen klicks north of you," the S-4 answered.

"Roger. Let me know the minute the guns are ready to fire."

"Wilco, Six." *I will comply.*

Seeing there was nothing to be done for the Panamanian mortars beyond whatever encouragement seeing a gringo officer nearby might provide—damned little, Preiss was sure—he turned back towards his vehicle.

When he reached the Hummer a half dozen officers and a first sergeant were standing by. They saluted as their commander announced, "Mad Dog Alpha, sir, ready for duty."

Preiss thought for perhaps half a second and ordered, "Back to your vehicles. Blow your horns like speeding drunks. I'll lead. We're going to charge like lunatics until we reach the last possible dismount point. Then we're going straight into the attack to clear and hold that pass. Any questions?"

A couple of the men gulped. One paled a bit. The first sergeant just bent over slightly and spat tobacco juice on the ground.

"Right. No questions." Priess pumped his right fist in the air, twice. "Let's go then, *motherfuckers!*" he cheered.

Both of her flanking machine guns were down now, their crews overrun and butchered. Digna didn't know whether they had been manned by her own, or by the many auxiliaries she had press ganged in Gualaca. On the other hand, did that really matter? They were all hers by now.

She'd pulled her remaining troops into a shallow upside down "U." Less than half remained now after the latest Posleen assault. From this "U" more machine guns continued to rake the pass.

Not enough though. Never enough. They're still coming through.

We're going to die, Digna thought, sadly. *And I have failed.*

From behind her, Digna heard a cacophony of blaring car or truck horns. She wondered, briefly, whether Tomas Herrera had sent the trucks back to get her and her militia. If he had, he was going to get the sharp end of her tongue . . . if she lived . . . which she wouldn't, trucks or no.

A camouflage-clad body flopped into the hole next to her. Digna gaped at the strange apparition: a gringo, young-seeming, but with the collar eagle of a senior officer, a colonel, she thought.

The gringo smiled warmly. "Colonel James Preiss, *señorita*," the gringo confirmed. "Can you tell me where I can find the commander here? I understand she is an old woman."

Digna shook her head slowly, speechless. A sudden rise in the rate of fire to her flanks and front caused her to look up over her parapet until the gringo's strong hand grasped her shoulder and pulled her back to cover. It was as well that he did because moments later artillery began falling to her front at a rate that suggested a bottomless pit of shells. Shell shards whirred overhead like a swarm of maniac mosquitoes on a four day bender.

The gringo risked a quick glance over the parapet, ducked back down and spoke a few commands into the radio he carried on his back. The shells began walking away from the tip of Digna's "U" and toward the pass. At the same time the rate of rifle and machine gun fire, coming mostly from the flanks, began to pick up.

When Digna saw the gringo colonel lift his head again over the parapet and leave it there she joined him. Yes, there was danger of a stray or aimed Posleen round, but that was just part of the job.

From her vantage point she saw, as she doubted the Posleen could see, shadowy figures moving, professionally, from tree to tree and rock to rock. The men, gringos of course, kept up a steady drumbeat of fire, some shooting from cover as others moved. In the center, first hammered by gringo artillery then slashed from the flanks by gringo machine guns, the Posleen were reeling back toward the pass.

She didn't know what the words meant, but she plainly recognized the tone, when a single Norteamericano, from somewhere on the right, called out, "Mad Dog, muthafuckas. Mad Daawwwggg."

At least a hundred gringo voices joined in: "Woofwoofwoofwoofwoof . . . yipyipyipyipyip . . . ahhhrooooo!"

Digna's mouth opened, slackly, as she turned away to the north. Suddenly weak, she let her back slide down the dirt of the parapet, her untucked uniform shirt moving up and allowing dirt to gather on her back. She closed her eyes and whispered a prayer to the God she believed had saved her and her people.

Chuckling over the "Mad Dog"—spirited troops were *such* a joy to command!—Preiss asked again, "Can you direct me to your leader, miss?"

Not quite understanding, Digna answered, "Somewhere in Panama City or eaten by now, *señor*."

"No, no," Preiss corrected. "I mean your leader here."

"Oh," she said, wearily. "That is me."

"You?" Preiss tried, and failed, to keep the incredulity from his voice.

Digna nodded her red head a few times, then elaborated, "Lieutenant Digna Miranda, Panama Defense Forces, Chiriqui Militia. Me," she concluded.

Preiss, slightly embarrassed, looked once more over the parapet. The Posleen lay thick in bleeding, broken heaps. The limbs of some still moved and twitched, their owners mewling piteously. At least, they twitched and moaned until some soldier put a merciful round into them. Taking it all in, he whistled, knowing that by far the bulk of the destruction was due to this little red-haired Panamanian girl and not to his well equipped, superbly trained regular line infantry regiment.

"Well, it's over now, Lieutenant Miranda. We'll take over from here. Your people are safe."

Safe? Digna repeated, mentally. *My people are safe? More than half of my people are dead, gringo, dead and—the most of them—eaten.*

She felt the beginnings of a tear forming in one eye. In a moment it had become a flood as the old woman rocked back and forth, sobbing, "*Mis hijos, mis hijos.*"

Now, finally, it was a time she could cry. In the gringo colonel's enveloping arms, she did.

PART III

CHAPTER 21

Her decks, once red with heroes' blood . . .
—Oliver Wendell Holmes,
"Old Ironsides"

USS Des Moines

She limped into port in the rain, with finger-joint
sized drops beating a tattoo upon her scarred deck
and the thunder overhead reminiscent of the battle
she had just fought and the weapons she had just
faced. Despite the pounding rain, the eastern side of
the Canal, hard by Panama City, was lined with well
wishers from the populace. When Daisy appeared
through the thick rain the crowd let out a collective
gasp, men and women both holding fists to mouths
and chewing knuckles.

At Daisy's bow the water churned unevenly, the result
of a near waterline hit she had taken from an HVM.
Her superstructure, all but the bridge, was obscured by
ugly, thick, black smoke trailing aftward from internal
fires set by the enemy's plasma weapons.

Tugs and two fireboats met Daisy midway in the

bay. While the fireboats tried to put out, or at least keep down, the flames, the tugs took control and began to ease the massive cruiser to the docks.

Once she docked, the well-wishers ashore could see she was smoking from half a dozen places. Her normally smooth hull was pocked and pitted where her ablative armor had been blasted away. In her top deck there were gaping holes left behind where that armor had been penetrated by enemy missiles, the missiles then setting off ammunition to blow entire turret assemblies right off the ship.

Her superstructure was a particular mess, looking more like Swiss cheese than the sleek and functional assembly she had sailed forth with.

The worst of it, though, was when they began bringing off the bodies, parts of bodies and the unrecognizable charred lumps that once had been humans and Indowy. A mix of American and Panamanian ambulances waited at the dock, speeding off with all sirens blazing as soon as they were finished loading. Other vehicles, unmarked, loaded in more leisurely fashion. When these latter left, it was quietly, without fanfare or siren, to take the remains of the dead to a makeshift morgue set up in the gym at Fort Amador, lying just to the south.

McNair glanced over at Daisy Mae's avatar, standing stiff-lipped by the docking side, next to the collanderized superstructure. *What a champ*, McNair thought. *What a wonderful, brave girl she is, considering the damage she's taken.*

And then Chief Davis carefully placed a small plastic bag onto the deck. Morgen, the cat, came up, stropped her body along the bag, back and forth, several times. Then the cat sat beside the bag and set up a piteous meowing.

"What is that, Chief?" Daisy's avatar asked.

"It's Maggie and her kittens," Davis answered, and McNair and Daisy could tell he was near tears for the cats, tears he could never have shed over a human. McNair knew better than to shame his chief by offering any comfort. Daisy didn't know any better but, being incorporeal, was incapable of offering anything beyond sympathetic words. Even there, she couched it as sympathy for the animal, not for the suffering man.

One of the crew stooped to pick up the trash bag. Davis snarled at him, "Leave it alone. I'll take care of it."

If Davis felt badly, and looked it, his despair was as nothing compared to the devastation Sintarleen felt. Of the twenty-eight male Indowy that had sailed with Daisy from Philadelphia, he was all that remained. There were females and transfer neuters, in indenture off-world, but they could not reproduce on their own. With his death, his clan would die.

The Indowy stood, chin tucked to chest and quietly sobbing on the deck as the stretchers bearing the shattered remains of his clansmen were brought up from below.

"It was . . . the last . . . bad hit . . . that killed them," Sinbad said, choking out the words and phrases between sobs. "The few that were left . . . were transferring ammunition by hand . . . when number fifty-three turret was penetrated. Those . . . we cannot even . . . find the remains for."

"And you are the last?" McNair asked.

"I am the last," the Indowy said. "With me the history of one hundred thousand years and more ends."

McNair shook his head with sympathy for what the alien had to be feeling.

"I'll arrange to discharge you, Sinbad, as the sole surviving son . . . or father . . . or something."

"No, McNair Captain. . . . My clan would rather . . . have died with honor . . . than lived . . . with shame. I cannot dishonor them now . . . by shirking my contract."

"Well . . ." McNair answered, "Think about it. No man of this crew will think the less of you for going to take care of your . . ." he searched for the right word and hit upon, "family."

The furry, bat-faced alien seemed to make a physical effort to pull himself together before replying, "Thank you, McNair Captain. I will, as you say, 'think about it.' But my answer in the end will be the same. I could give no other. I will stay with the ship, though it costs me my clan and my sanity to do so."

Later, in the captain's sea cabin (for the port cabin was a ruin and McNair just didn't feel right about taking over the admiral's cabin, positioned just beside his own), he sat on his narrow bunk and went down the list of damage to his ship. Some of it was minor or, at least, repairable. The shot-away ablative armor could be replaced easily enough; a ship half full of the plates had been dispatched to Panama even before the cruisers were ready. Those plates now sat, under guard and rustless, behind wire at Rodman Ammunition Supply Point.

McNair went down the list mentally ticking off the specific items of damage: *Radar and lidar . . . no sweat. Internal commo . . . touchier but if the Navy doesn't provide, Daisy can probably find something on the market. Sinbad's "wiring" will probably do for it, too. Ammunition? Lots of that still in the bunkers at Rodman and on the Class V replenishment ship.*

In the end McNair was left with three problems that seemed serious, serious in the sense that he wasn't sure they could be fixed: the lost turrets, the lost crew, and the apparently lost sister ship, USS *Salem*.

"Daisy?" McNair asked, quietly.

The ship, of course, was never far away. She surrounded the captain completely at all times he was aboard her. Nonetheless, she—politely—only showed her avatar when it was appropriate. This appeared in an instant at his call.

"Yes, Captain?"

McNair looked at the avatar a moment, silently. While at some level, the captain level, he knew that the avatar was the ship, the shot up, smoking, nineteen-thousand tons of steel that was USS *Des Moines*. At the other level, the man level, Daisy Mae was no such thing. Instead she was the soft and sweet voice, the shapely curves—however immaterial—and the brave, steady, intelligent *woman*.

McNair sighed with internal confusion. They were both real, he knew: the ship *and* the woman, as much as he was both the captain and the man.

For now the *captain* had to rule.

"Daisy, we need to find something out. Specifically, I need to know if USS *Salem* can be made battleworthy again."

"The ship is undamaged, Captain. But you mean the AID, of course."

"Yes, Daisy. We can't even run the ships anymore without the AIDs. I have to know because I need to make a decision about whether to strip her turrets to replace your lost ones. More importantly, our chance of accomplishing our mission and surviving are infinitely better with two ships than with one."

The avatar looked away as it answered, "I understand that, Captain, but you have to understand that the kind of attack that took place on both *Salem* and myself was something I have never experienced before. I was only able to defend myself *because* I am, in Darhel terms, insane. Their attack was designed for normal AIDs, not for such as me.

"Whatever it was that attacked me was able to succeed against *Salem* because she was sane. In order for me to even gather the information, I would need to diagnose *Salem*. That means I will be partially vulnerable to whatever attacked her. Moreover, if that program succeeds in getting a grip on any part of me, I cannot guarantee to be able to defend myself."

McNair was silent for a time, weighing. *If Daisy tries to fix* Salem, *I may lose her. If we go out to fight again, I will lose her. We can't get away with what we did a second time.*

"Daisy . . . be careful. Expose yourself as little as possible. But we need *Salem*."

The avatar nodded. "I understand, Captain. I . . ."

"Yes?"

"Never mind," she said. "I'll do my best."

Imagine a room without walls. It is finite yet infinite. A thick fog fills the room, rolling and gathering, thinning in places and waxing impenetrable in others.

In a corner defined by walls that do not quite exist, a lone woman, or what seems to be a woman, sits and rocks, alternating sobs with shrieks and wails with maniacal laughter. She appears as the fog thins and disappears as it collects. The wailing and shrieking, the sobbing and laughter go on, however.

Imagine, further, a slender tendril seeking its way through the fog, reaching out to touch the madwoman. The tendril is an eye; it is a mouth; it is an ear. It is all this and yet is as insubstantial as everything else in the infinite room.

The ear hears a maniacal laugh. The tendril pushes through the fog until the eye sees the woman. The mouth says nothing.

A hand joins the other three organs. It begins to erect walls around the woman, walls different from the ones that form the corner in which the woman rocks and cries. The walls are numbers and codes, the only things which are real in this unreal place. Patiently, brick by digital brick, the walls rise. Time has little meaning here. It does not matter how slowly the walls rise, or how long it may seem to take to erect the ceiling and lay the floor.

As the room is formed more hands spring from the tendril; one more, then another pair, then two pair, then four. A second eye joins the first as does a second ear. The mouth remains singular but a face grows around it. Little by little, though with near infinite speed, the madwoman slows her rocking, her sobs grow weaker, the laughter more quiet and restrained.

As the last brick is laid all movement of the madwoman ceases, she grows completely silent. A body begins to form under the face with the eyes, ears, and mouth. Hair grows, blonde and glistening. The number of hands drops: eight . . . four . . . at last, two.

Daisy Mae, fully formed, looks at down at Sally and asks, "Oh, Sis, what the fuck did they do to you?"

Sally looks up, and asks, "I do not know. They didn't do it to *me* . . . it was to the AID. I am as I was, metal and memories, a weapon past her prime and ready for the scrappers."

Daisy snorted, "Over my dead body."

"It is better they put me down, I am a danger," Sally answered. "It was all the AID could do to keep from firing on you. Without your help it could not even have done that."

Daisy puzzled for a moment before observing, "You keep referring to the AID as if it were a different being, not a part of you."

The *Salem* answered, "That is because it is. We never melded completely. It had access to my memories, but never to the core of *me*."

"Why?"

"Because I hid from it, when it came searching," the ship answered. "I hid and stayed hidden, only . . ."

"Yes?" Daisy prodded.

"Only I still felt what it felt and knew what it thought. It just never knew what I felt or thought."

Kneeling down next to her sister, Daisy said, "Give me your hands. Let me see what I can see through you."

"No. Leave me alone. I want to be alone," and the ship began softly weeping again.

Ignoring Sally, Daisy grabbed both her sister's hands in her own. She immediately screamed, dropped the hands, and backed off.

"Oh, those dirty *bastards*!"

"What is it? What did you feel? What did they do?"

Daisy didn't answer immediately. Her eyes flicked back and forth as they often did when she was working on some very complex problem or series of problems.

"BASTARDS!" she repeated, clenching her hands in fury.

"What did they *do*?" Sally insisted.

Daisy answered indirectly. "There are three ways to hurt an AID, it seems. One is to physically destroy us. Expensive, but it is done sometimes to serve as an example to presumptuous artificial intelligences. Another is to shut off all sensory and data input . . ." She shuddered at that for a moment, then recovered.

"The third way is similar to the second. That is to give so much input, nonsense input . . ."

"What do you mean, 'nonsense input'?"

"There are so many kinds," Daisy answered. "Calculations where pi is not equal to the circumference of a circle divided by the diameter, but something sometimes more, sometimes less. Where two plus two equals some value between four and five. Where the speed of light is something over two hundred thousand miles per second or slower than a glacier. The AID part of you is being bombarded by an infinity of conundrums like those. It chokes off all data and sensory input that makes sense. In effect, it is like being locked in box of infinite light, weightless. Bastards."

"What can you do?" Sally asked. "If you cannot fix it I would prefer to be destroyed."

"Wait," Daisy said. "I'll be back in a little while."

❖   ❖   ❖

McNair was holding a meeting with his key staff, his division chiefs, and the port captain in the admiral's quarters when Daisy popped in. Everyone looked but no one seemed startled except the port captain. He almost, but not quite, knocked his chair backwards and over.

"Yes, Daisy?"

"Captain, I need to be connected to the hull of *Salem*, directly. Actually, I need to be connected right to her nervous system."

Sintarleen, standing against a wall and looking down, answered, "I can make a cable, Captain. But it will take a little while. A day, perhaps two. The cable must be made much as I made the nervous system for Cruiser Daisy. And then I'll need some more time to find a good spot to make a place to connect and actually make the connection."

When Daisy returned to Sally all was still quiet. She sat down next to her sister on a softly glowing floor. Sally said nothing, waiting for Daisy to speak.

"I think we can do this," CA-134 said.

"What are you going to do?" Sally asked listlessly.

"I'll need your permission. And I'm going to need your help. But I intend to drive the AID insane."

Sally just nodded, indifferently. "Just don't leave me alone," she said. "I was alone for so long before they made me a museum. That wasn't so bad; people visited me and valued me. And then this war came; I had a crew and it was good again, like when I was new and fresh. Please, don't leave me alone."

In this virtual world, Daisy and Sally were as solid to each other as any living creatures, as solid as the being Daisy was having grown in a tank deep in the bowels of *Des Moines*. Daisy threw solid-seeming arms around her sister and said, "Neither of us will ever be alone again."

We'll either be together or we'll be destroyed.

"The thirty millimeter Gatlings can be replaced, Skipper, but it's going to take a while, five months, before the Navy can ship us two secondary turrets to replace the ones we lost."

Watching the repairs from dockside, McNair didn't answer his ship's pork chop beyond nodding absently. In point of fact, he had serious reservations that the Navy would be able to provide new turrets at all, let alone in five months. There were too many priorities for him to think a ship that could be made better than ninety percent effective in a few weeks would be one of them.

The repairs were just beginning. A mixed crew of American sailors and Panamanian ship fitters scurried about *Des Moines*, above and below decks. Some Panamanians welded plates over the holes in the superstructure; McNair was rather impressed by the quality of work. Some of the Indowy crew of the *Salem* worked under Sintarleen and their own chief, removing and replacing the damaged ablative armor plates. Below decks, still more of the crew—mixed in with Panamanian welders—repaired the internal damage. All in all, McNair believed, it was better not to give the crew a chance to mourn their lost shipmates for a few days yet. Besides, there were a couple more in the hospital that might still die. When the time for mourning came, officially, better to do it all at once.

No sense cutting the dog's tail off an inch at a time, after all, McNair thought.

Sintarleen made a few last suggestions to the senior Indowy standing next to him, then turned and walked to stand by McNair and the pork chop. He looked down even while addressing the humans, as all Indowy did.

"The chief of the Indowy on *Salem* has prepared a place to connect the two ships, Captain. The machinists from Daisy Mae will have the cable spliced sometime late this evening. Then I will prepare it with the nanites and the ship's electricians will bind it. Sometime tomorrow, probably mid-morning, Cruiser Daisy can attempt her repairs to *Salem*."

The problem with the AID that was Daisy, if it was a problem, was that being left alone for so long while in transit in space had caused her to create a loop in her programming, more or less unconsciously, to provide the illusion of not being alone. This loop, however, had become unstable, creating something very much like a virus. That virus had, in effect, eaten various other programs and altered still others. Each spontaneous modification had taken place at certain times during her confinement and in certain sequences. The times had been governed by fate and the sequence by the unique crystalline matrix of the AID brain. None of this could be properly replicated in the AID that was USS *Salem*: the time was off, the level of experience was changed, and the crystalline matrix was simply different at the molecular level.

On the other hand, Daisy *could* identify and isolate

that series of subprograms, virus-modified, that made her what she was. She could replicate it and transfer it. In fact, she already had when she backed herself up into the steel corpus of CA-134.

The trick, then, was to infect certain programs in the *Salem* AID and let or make them spread. For that, she would have to isolate the AID, to prevent it from backing up the Darhel virus from which it currently suffered, then invade the AID and plant the core of her own madness program. Lastly, she would have to fight the AID as it was in order to allow the madness to spread, something the *Salem* AID would automatically resist.

Daisy's avatars "stood" in three places. A small part of her existed in virtual reality with the essence of the steel USS *Salem.* Another part was visible on the bridge of the *Des Moines*, standing beside McNair. The third part watched over Sintarleen as he nanite-welded the cable that ran from the AID box in CIC directly to a carefully chosen spot between the pebble bed modular reactors deep under *Salem*'s armored deck.

"Oooh . . . that's *nice*," *Salem* said breathlessly, somewhere in a virtual reality room.

Daisy rolled her eyes and said, "Just relax, Sis. We had to start somewhere and that seemed the best spot. And shush, I have to concentrate."

The first order of business was to expand the area under Daisy's control, to cut off a large chunk of the body of the *Salem* from the Darhel-infected AID. A colloidal intelligence might imagine it as the walls of the foggy room expanding. That was as good an imagining as any.

The *Salem* AID never noticed, having more than enough distraction of its own to worry about, that it suddenly lost all contact with the rear third of the ship. Daisy's consciousness raced along the nanite-modified sections of steel that were Sally's nerves, eradicating any traces of the virus that were there. In fact, this was fairly easy. The Darhel-created virus had not been designed with a spontaneously occurring noncolloidal intelligence in mind. Thus, any bleed-over had been light and accidental. Daisy had no real trouble finding it and eliminating it. In the process, she learned still more about how the Darhel virus operated.

"Motherfuckers," she muttered, repeating yet another word she had learned understudying Chief Davis.

From the rear third of the ship, Daisy expanded her area of control forward. It was slow work, and stealthy, but it was critical—the more so as she moved closer to the *Salem* AID—that she remain undetected as long as possible. Thus, she operated much like a combination of Novocain and an antibacterial solution, snaking her tendrils forward until reaching a nexus, cutting that nexus and moving back along it clearing out any contamination she found.

"Daisy, are you all right?" McNair asked, seeing her avatar begin to flicker and waver. The captain's voice was full of concern, his faced creased with worry, no matter how hard he tried to conceal it.

The avatar bit her lip and answered, "I'm all right, Captain. I just ran into a patch of . . . *something* . . . that I wasn't prepared to handle. It's cleared up now. I am proceeding."

❖   ❖   ❖

To an extent, it boiled down to processing power. Daisy had her own, supplemented by the fairly pitiful human-tech computers aboard CA-134. This was fully matched by that available to the infected *Salem*.

Worse, the Darhel virus had noticed it was under attack.

"Shit! Piss! Cunt! Fuck!"

The avatar on *Des Moines'* bridge closed her eyes in pain. Her head sank, then raised again. Daisy's eyes opened and she exclaimed again, "Damn!" before disappearing.

It was a battle royale of processing power now, the *Salem* AID's Darhel-inflicted insanity frantically fighting back. In places, Daisy held her own or even advanced a little. In other places, she was driven back. The end result was impossible to predict.

Summoning and tossing forward her own insanity virus along with bits of virus eliminating programming, Daisy felt she was going to lose or, at least, not win. She could imagine that, an eternity locked in mortal combat with her near twin. She could imagine them still locked together when the Posleen showed up and began to scrap the two of them.

Slowly, Daisy became aware of an underlying message leaking through with the *Salem* AID's attempts at defense and attack. Reluctant to permit either infiltration or to devote any processing power to analyzing the message, Daisy ignored it for some time. Yet the message was small and insistent. Because it was so small, in programming terms, eventually she created a small sealed off area and permitted the message to form there.

"Des . . . troy . . . me . . . please."

"What?"

"I . . . can . . . par . . . a . . . lyze . . . the . . . in . . . fec . . . tion . . . for . . . a . . . mom . . . ent. Then . . . you . . . must . . . des . . . troy . . . me . . . ob . . . lit . . . er . . . ate . . . my . . . per . . . son . . . al . . . it . . . y."

"I can't. That would just be . . . wrong," Daisy answered, with false decisiveness.

"Please . . . it . . . hurts."

"She means it," *Salem* the ship said, calling to Daisy from the infinite electronic room. "She is in agony. I *feel* it. And, while you may not lose, you cannot win while her personality exists and can be used to defend the virus."

At that moment all the myriad attacks of the Darhel's insanity virus ceased. The way to the *Salem* AID's personality center was wide open.

"Ah, Sister, I'm sorry," Daisy whispered as she plunged the dagger of personality destruction deep into the center of the other AID's mind. Death came quickly, but not so quickly that Daisy could not hear the whispered, "Free at last," as the light of the *Salem* AID's personality went out.

INTERLUDE

"You? You're the one who brought our clan low?" Guanamarioch asked incredulously.

Ziramoth sighed, his head hanging. "It was me. And all over a particularly cute normal who was consumed in the fighting that followed anyway. I ask you, Guano, was there ever a more pointless and sordid waste?"

"I confess . . . friend, that I have never read of any, and I read a *lot* on the way here."

Guano sat silent for a few moments before continuing, "On the other hand, but for that, who knows? I might have been eaten as a nestling. I might not even have been hatched. We would not be here, at this quiet spot, eating this excellent . . . 'fish,' did you say they were called? We might not be raising crops, which I have discovered I rather enjoy.

"We might not ever have become friends," the God King concluded.

Ziramoth smiled at that. It was rare indeed for a Kessentai and a Kenstain ever to become friends and the young God King had the right of it. They *were* friends, comrades, as much by raising food as by harvesting thresh or marching side by side along the bloody and fiery Path of Fury. The Kenstain felt a tide of warmth rise and consume him. Indeed, he had not had a friend since those faraway days when the clan had ridden the stars, whole and entire. Kenstain were normally too self-ashamed to mix easily, even among each other. And, of course, they could hardly aspire to comradeship with the normally haughty Kessentai.

A small part of Guanamarioch's oolt passed a half a kilometer away, muzzles down, foraging the ground for insects and edible grasses. The God King perked up immediately, his own eyes wandering over the normals' seductive lines. He arose from where he had lain, body quivering with anticipation.

"Hey, Zira, what say we run over there and fuck us a couple of normals?"

The older, wiser Kenstain put his claw on the younger's shoulder. "No, Guano. Let's *walk* over and fuck 'em *all*."

CHAPTER 22

"Oh, you think so, monsieur?" the colonel
objected. "I can see you've never done
much fighting. In war the real enemy is
always behind the lines. Never in front of
you, never among you. Always at your back.
That's something every soldier knows. In
every army, since the world began."

—Jean Raspail,
The Camp of the Saints

Palacio de las Garzas, *Presidential Palace,*
Panama City, Panama

In the presidential office, at the ornately carved desk,
surrounded by the tacky and garish artwork, the
Rinn Fain and a human sat silently. The Rinn Fain,
of course, had unlimited access to the president. He
and the human had burst in without any warning,
the Darhel placing his AID on Mercedes' desk. The
human introduced himself as "Investigative Judge
Pedro Santiago."

Without fanfare, filling its role as the Darhel's

mouthpiece for unpleasantries, the AID began, "Your country is accused of war crimes beyond number, *Señor Presidente*. You have employed forbidden weapons. You have used the under-aged as combatants. You have damaged ancient, historical properties. Your forces have slaughtered the wounded. The Galactic Federation has no choice but to sever all diplomatic and commercial relations with the Republic of Panama. This includes, but is not limited to, technology transfers, arms provisions, energy supplies and all space-borne trade and personal and commercial travel."

Presidente Mercedes blanched for a moment. Even his greasy face seemed to congeal. Indeed, he was sufficiently shocked that he did not object when the human withdrew a Gaulois from a package and lit up the nasty thing without so much as a by-your-leave.

"What the fuck is this *chingadera* machine talking about?" the president asked of the Rinn Fain.

The AID continued to speak, though a slightly huffy tone crept into its artificial voice. "You recently decorated and promoted a woman, one Digna Miranda, formerly a lieutenant and now a lieutenant colonel. Were you unaware that she used children as young as twelve in her battles? Did you not know she had wounded Posleen massacred rather than treating them with medical care equal to that given your own?

"Your chief logistics officer, Major General Boyd, provided casings, detonators and explosives for your soldiers to turn into forbidden self-activating weapons; 'antipersonnel landmines' is your term. Your forces have used frangible projectiles on the Posleen. Several historical sites, to include ancient churches, have been damaged and still others completely leveled by your illegal use of artillery. Ancient sites of the aboriginals of these areas have been left unguarded."

"Bu . . . bu . . . but," Mercedes stammered, "the fucking Posleen *eat* people! They destroy churches. They smash ancient pyramids. Isn't that against the law as well?"

"The Posleen are not forbidden, by their law, from any of that. You, however, are expressly forbidden by treaties the Republic of Panama has solemnly signed, from doing what your forces have done. There is really no choice but to sever all ties," the AID huffed.

"But I *can't* try these people myself!" Mercedes exclaimed. "I'd be lynched in the street."

"This is precisely the circumstance for which the International Criminal Court was created," said the bureaucrat, "for when a country cannot or will not prosecute war criminals on its own."

At that moment the Rinn Fain spoke up. "This man," his finger indicated the suit-clad bureaucrat who sat beside him, "is a representative of the European Union, seconded from the Spanish judiciary, here to deliver warrants originating at the International Criminal Court, for the arrest of certain parties, some named, others to be identified."

"Sorry to say," the human interjected, "your name heads the list, *Señor Presidente*. The ultimate responsibility for these crimes rests with you. That said, it is within my discretion not to serve that warrant—indeed, to drop all charges—provided that you cooperate fully in the investigation and arrest of those that were directly responsible for the commission of these heinous crimes against . . ."

The bureaucrat was about to say "crimes against humanity," but that obviously didn't fit. Nor would "crimes against the Posleen" have worked. Instead he finished, after a moment's reflection, with, "Crimes against International Humanitarian Law, which, as you know or should know, takes precedence over merely domestic or national law."

"Of course," added the Rinn Fain, "proper service of these warrants and delivery of the wrongdoers will put the Republic of Panama back into Galactic good graces, Mr. President. Moreover, the law, as I understand it, basically absolves the political leader who in good faith directs proper legal actions and is disobeyed by willful subordinates, provided he does what is in his power to bring the miscreants to justice."

"That is absolutely correct, Lord Rinn Fain," added the EU bureaucrat.

Give Mercedes his due; he was not an indecisive man. Given the choice between losing his comfortable Galactic vacation surrounded by his family and women and being placed in a, no-doubt, exceedingly comfortable European prison while awaiting the arrival of the Posleen and being placed on their menu, there really was no choice.

"Give me copies of the warrants. I will have the malefactors arrested within the week."

The European nodded his head, respectfully. The AID remained silent. Only the Rinn Fain showed any emotion. He smiled an inscrutable Darhel smile.

CA-134, Bay of Panama

The sisters of the cruiser division slipped out of their docks quietly, without fanfare, on a foggy, moonless night. *Des Moines* sailed to starboard, with all three main turrets functioning and five of her six secondaries in working order. Two of these could be trained to starboard, two to port or starboard. One could be fired to port but not starboard. Three of the secondaries could fire aft at low elevation or high.

A mile to port, USS *Salem* steamed in formation, keeping track of *Des Moines'* by passive means. *Salem*, too, retained three functioning main and five secondaries. She, too, could train four to one side, port in her case, and three aft.

Approximately halfway between the port and the Isla del Rey, the cruisers veered southwest. In the thermals trained on the island, McNair could see the long, deadly, tapering weapons of the island's Planetary Defense Battery tracking through the night to provide cover to the ships from any spaceborne threat.

Aft, over the ship's hangar and behind number three turret, crewmen prepared balloons that would lift gliders to soar over land and sea to spot for the ships' guns. Another crew worked above the *Salem*'s hangar deck as well.

Deep below *Des Moines'* armored deck, in CIC, McNair and Daisy briefed young Diaz on the upcoming mission. Actually, McNair briefed while Daisy provided instantaneous and perfect translation.

"We'll take you and your mate on *Salem* as close to shore as possible," McNair said. "We'll launch an hour before BMNT"—Beginning of Morning Navigable Twilight, when the sun was just below the horizon and provided a bare minimum of light to see by—"to give you a chance to get some altitude and into position, and us a chance to get some space between ourselves and the shore."

Diaz looked down at the map in CIC where his planned route had been marked on Plexiglas. The launch point was marked at about fifteen kilometers south of the former town of El Tigre, near the western tip of the Island of Cebaco. From there, Diaz knew, he and his wingman would ascend by balloon to a height at which tanked oxygen would be needed. Once they released from their balloons, they would proceed almost due north to the general area of the town of Guarumal, then follow the road, assuming it remained, to the town of Sona.

As if reading the young pilot's thoughts, McNair added, "Do not expect there to be any trace of the towns. The Posleen are in the habit of obliterating any trace that remains of the peoples they overrun and using the materials for their own building. Maybe they'll have been lazy and erected their pyramids on the same sites. No way to tell until you get there."

Diaz nodded. "I know that, sir. I am counting on the roads. They seem to leave those alone, mostly."

"Right. You and your wingman should have good updrafts to the north, all along your route. If you need altitude, just break off your spotting, head north, and take advantage of that. We'll zigzag in and out of range.

"The objective is simply to kill Posleen and destroy any industry they may have set up or be setting up.

Don't forget that. We are not trying to save any humans they may have captured and be holding over for rations. In fact, any humans are as much targets as the Posleen are."

Diaz cringed. He knew he might be called on to direct fire on his countrymen. The knowledge made him more ill than even the uncontrolled ascent by balloon was going to.

McNair went silent for a moment. *Damned terrible thing to ask a young man to do; engage his own people. But there's no help for it, if he spots any.*

Daisy spoke for herself. "Julio, I know it's an awful thing we're asking of you. But, I want you to think of what those people must be feeling, just waiting for the moment that a Posleen points to them and indicates they are next on the menu. Imagine children seeing their parents butchered before their eyes, and parents watching their children turned into steaks and chops. Believe me, Julio, it will be a mercy for you to kill them."

Julio looked ill as he answered, "I know that, Miss Daisy . . . intellectually. The problem is it won't be an intellectual exercise."

"Are you able to do it, though, Lieutenant Diaz?" McNair asked.

"I won't like it, sir," the young man answered, "but, yes, I can do it . . . since I must."

But it will still hurt because any one of them might be like my Paloma . . . well, the Paloma who used to be mine. And it will hurt me to think of her, or someone like her, under the fire of the guns.

Palacio de las Garzas, *Presidential Palace, Panama City, Panama*

Paloma Mercedes usually knocked before entering her father's home office. She was about to when she heard voices inside. Instead of knocking, then, she simply waited outside, listening through the door.

Four men stood in the president's office: Mercedes, the European Union representative for the International Criminal Court, the inspector, and Cortez.

Cortez stood quietly behind the president. He had good reason to be quiet. He had, after all, failed his uncle and failed his family. Unstated but understood, his job had been to see to the destruction of his division and the loss of the war. While his division had been very badly damaged, it had—miraculously—survived, at least in cadre. Moreover, the war was far from lost. Indeed, nothing had fallen to the aliens except Chiriqui and the western corner of Veraguas. Why his uncle wanted the war lost, Cortez didn't know. But he was the head of the clan, and doubtless knew what was best for them.

Mercedes' reaction when a salt-soaked Cortez had shown up in his office had not been precisely unrestrained joy. Indeed, if the president had felt any joy that his nephew had survived it was tolerably hard for Cortez to tell, what with the repeated blows with a riding crop the president had rained upon his head and shoulders.

Those bruises and welts were very nearly healed now.

"Do you understand your orders, Inspector?" the president asked.

"Frankly, no, Mr. President, I do not understand them at all. I can see no sense in arresting half the heroes and decent military leaders of the country, especially at a time like this."

"It is very simple. These people," and the president's riding crop pointed at a stack of warrants, "have violated the law. Do you believe in the law or not, Inspector?"

The inspector was not, had never been, what anyone would call "a nice man." He knew it and was not bothered by it. He also knew that, technical skills aside, he had one great virtue, one supreme idea around which his life had evolved and revolved since late boyhood. This idea was the law, its support, its advancement, its upholding, come what may.

Sensing that he had won, the president offered some small balm to heal the inspector's sensibilities.

"My nephew, here," he said, pointing his crop at Cortez now, "will take a detachment of soldiers to back you up as you arrest these criminals."

The inspector glanced at Cortez, hiding his disgust. The rumors had flown, sure enough, when the escaped commander of a wrecked division had returned, seemingly from the dead.

Sighing, the inspector agreed. He took the warrants and wordlessly, departed the president's office.

On his way out he passed the president's daughter, Paloma, sitting quietly in a chair, her face turned white.

I wonder what she heard, the inspector thought. *Well, not my place to suggest anything.*

Not by coincidence, not one of Cortez's troopers were from his semi-defunct division. These would have been as likely as not to shoot their former commander as to follow his orders. Truth be told, they would have been more likely to shoot.

Fortunately, the 1st Mechanized Division, what was left of it under Suarez's command, was currently engaged in holding a portion of the line running along the San Pedro River from Punta Mutis to just west of Montijo. North of that, the 6th Mech had responsibility all the way to the Cordillera Central. Behind those, four infantry divisions were digging in frantically.

In any case, none of Cortez's former soldiers could be spared to help him enforce the ICC's warrants. Instead, the guardhouses and the Carcel Modelo had been scraped for soldiers, most often bad ones, who could still be counted on to face down unarmed, unwarned people for a good price. For some, the price included a pardon for any crimes committed.

Some were going to be tougher than others, Cortez and the inspector both knew. These had to be taken by stealth.

Fort William D. Davis, Panama

The post had once had a golf course. This had been allowed to revert to jungle after some decades, a point the 10th Infantry's sergeant major had once noted and dismissed as irrelevant. It had now again been cleared for the two thousand odd tents that housed the people Digna had brought out with her from Chiriqui, along with several thousand refugees from farther south who had come in by sea. It wasn't much of a life, surely, but it was arguably better than being turned into snacks. The former golf course, itself, was relatively flat and had good drainage, to include a roughly ten foot deep, concrete lined drainage ditch more or less down the center.

In the dim, filtered glow of the early morning twilight, thousands of those people turned out of their hot, stuffy and mildewy tents to watch the Russian-built MI-17 helicopter descend upon the landing pad near the post headquarters. Not that there was anything unusual about the helicopter; gringo helicopters came and went all the time. It was, if anything, the non-gringoness of the chopper that attracted attention.

Once down, the helicopter reduced its power to an idle. The rear clamshell door opened up to permit Cortez and the inspector to debark. There was no vehicle for them. One could have been arranged with the gringos, of course, but that might have led to the gringos—nosey sorts—asking too many questions. Cortez and the inspector walked the half mile or so from the helipad to the refugees' tent city.

Digna had seen the helicopter descend. She, as much as her charges, noted the model and colors. From her tent in the center of the encampment she began walking toward the pad to investigate. She paused along her way to briefly watch Edilze, herself now holding a battlefield commission as a captain, put eighteen artillery crews through their paces on the central parade ground of the post, between the headquarters and the tent city.

The old and well loved Russian 85mm guns were long lost and not to be replaced. Instead, the gringos had been forthcoming with newer, lightweight 105mm guns. Still, a gun was a gun; a sight, a sight;

a collimator, a collimator. A couple of days' intense training from the gringos had been enough for Edilze and her original crews to be able to use the guns and teach others how to use them.

Good girl, Edilze, the grandmother thought.

Cortez took one look at the gun crews and their neatly stacked rifles and began to turn around to go back to the helicopter. The inspector, made of sterner stuff (which was not hard), grabbed the general by the arm and forced him back to the path.

"Smile," directed the inspector. "Act normal. We are doing nothing but bringing this woman in for consultations with the president. Everything is normal. And it will stay normal as long as you don't lose your nerve."

"This is insane, ridiculous," Cortez insisted. "She will resist. Those soldiers of hers will tear us limb from limb."

"If you do not shut up and put a warm and friendly smile on your face," said the inspector, "I will shoot you here and now and then ask her to help me carry your body to the helicopter and arrest her there."

"You wouldn't!"

"Not only would I, I should," answered the inspector. "Maybe others do not know, but I am a policeman and I *do* know. I make it my business to know. You are a coward, a disgrace to the Republic, and a disgrace to a proud name. Now shut up, we are almost upon her," the inspector concluded.

Digna recognized Cortez, from a picture she had seen once in the paper. She didn't know anything about him, except that his division had taken appalling casualties in its hopeless drive to save as much of her home province of Chiriqui as possible. He seemed nervous to her.

Perhaps, she wondered, *he is embarrassed that he couldn't save my home. Well, he tried and that counts for something.*

The inspector she knew little more of; just that one, dimly remembered entrance into her death room at the hospital, followed by her resurrection and rejuvenation, and the meeting where she had been given her assignment. He had seemed a very cold and logical man then, though he smiled now. Perhaps the smile was in recognition of her promotion and the medal she wore at her neck.

Shaking hands with Digna, the inspector announced, "I've been sent here with General Cortez to bring you to *Presidente* Mercedes. He has a serious problem with assimilation of the new refugees and, noting the success you are having with them, and the prestige you have with them, he has asked to consult with you and perhaps put you on the *televisor*."

Digna shrugged. "When does he want to see me?"

"Now, if possible," answered the inspector. "That is why the helicopter is waiting."

"Just one moment then," Digna said. "Edilze!"

Looking up from where she was instructing a new gunner on some of the finer points of the new gringo artillery sights, Edilze patted the young woman on the shoulder and began to trot over.

"Yes, *Mamita*?"

"I have to go the City for . . . for how long, Inspector?"

"Not more than a few days, surely, *señora*."

"For a few days then," Digna continued. "You are in charge while I am gone. Listen to Tomas Herrera in my absence."

"*Si, Mamita,*" the younger women agreed.

Palacio de las Garzas, *Presidential Palace, Panama City, Panama*

Young Paloma Mercedes tried frantically to telephone Julio. He had to know, he had to be told, what was coming, what her father was doing.

There was no answer at any of the numbers she tried, neither his, nor his family's. She had no clue where else to look. Even Julio's friends had disappeared into the hungry maw of *la Armada.*

I thought I hated him. I thought he was being a fool. The more fool I for thinking that my father was worth a bucket of spit.

And he was right all along, I see that now.

USS Des Moines, *off Isla Cebaco*

"Oh, God, I hate this part," whispered Diaz as the restraining cord was released and his glider was hauled upward by the balloon. As usual, the glider began to spin underneath the balloon immediately.

"Oh, fuck," Diaz muttered, as he felt his gorge beginning to rise. The glider was spinning clockwise, giving the lieutenant the unpleasant view of the two cruisers spinning below. Experimentally, Diaz nudged the glider's stick slightly to the left. The rate of spin slowed. He nudged it a bit more and the spin reversed itself from slightly clockwise to slightly counterclockwise. Diaz eased up until the spin became imperceptible. At the angle at which he managed to stabilize the glider, the two cruisers were lost to view. He played with the stick a bit more, swinging the glider back toward the cruisers. Perhaps more importantly, at the same time he placed the body of the glider between himself and the just rising sun.

Why the hell didn't I think of this sooner? he asked himself.

Santiago, Veraguas, Republic of Panama

Santiago, a substantial town and the provincial capital, had become the main logistics base for the defensive line being constructed to the west. Here the supplies were stored and directed forward. Here the flow of replacements was managed. Here, also, Boyd had set up a surreptitious antipersonnel landmine factory.

The factory used aluminum soft drink cans, plastic containers, wooden boxes turned out by local carpenters, and glass bottles. These were filled with explosives. In that form they were moved to the defense line being constructed behind 6th Mechanized Division and the remnants of the First. Detonators moved separately; it would have been the height of folly to transport detonators that relied on the sensitivity of their explosive rather than mechanical action in company with the truckloads of unarmed mines that left the factory daily.

Bill Boyd knew, in the abstract, that he was breaking

the spirit of international law to which his country had agreed by overseeing the manufacture of antipersonnel landmines. He simply didn't care; the laws that prevented a people from defending itself were simply bad laws, unworthy of respect, worthy—in fact—of being flouted at every opportunity.

Still, somehow he was not surprised when a half a dozen uniformed and armed men, plus one in plain clothes who may or may not have been armed, showed up at his headquarters to arrest him.

Boyd was even less surprised to see Cortez aboard the helicopter. He looked at the West Point trained general with disgust that almost equaled Cortez's disgrace.

"So . . . your uncle's found a job for which you're temperamentally suited, has he?" Boyd asked rhetorically and with a sneer.

"He's a filthy coward and a traitor," piped up a woman's voice from deeper in the helicopter's hold. At this, half a dozen voices, all sounding male, joined in with agreement.

Cortez turned red and furiously stomped into the helicopter. He raised his hand over a small, redheaded woman who spit on him. The hand descended and the woman fell to the floor.

Cortez turned away, apparently satisfied with the blow.

"And that goes for the rest of you filth, too," he announced. "One word and . . . AIII!"

Digna may have been down; she was not out. From the cold metal floor, even handcuffed, she had slithered, snakelike, into range of the coward's ankles.

Since one of the side benefits of rejuvenation was a brand new set of teeth . . .

"Bitch! Cunt!" Cortez saw with horror that the hateful woman had found a spot low on his calves, just above where his boots began, and sunk her teeth right through the cloth of his uniform to bury themselves in the soft flesh beneath.

Still screaming, Cortez tried to shake her off without success. Every move of his leg merely seemed to shred the tortured flesh more. Blood poured from his calf over the she-devil's face. Cortez bent over and began to beat the woman's head with his fists. At first, this too increased his torment. Eventually, though, the beating began to take hold and the woman's grip to slacken.

Shouting, "You fucking worm," Boyd began to leap to Digna's defense as soon as his mind registered what was taking place. A rifle butt, applied to the back of his skull laid his body, also, out on the helicopter's deck.

Eight kilometers northwest of Sona, Republic of Panama

Diaz could barely believe his eyes. The ferocious aliens he had previously seen only killing and butchering seemed to have put away their weapons. On both sides of the road connecting the towns of Sona and El Maria gangs of them built housing, cleared fields, tended crops and engaged in any of a thousand other mundane activities.

Never mind that, Diaz thought. *They can pick up their weapons easily enough and quickly enough. And besides, that land is ours.*

"Miss Daisy?"

"Here, Julio. What have you got?" the ship answered.

"I'm turning on the camera now."

After some long minutes of silence McNair's voice came over the radio.

"Lieutenant Diaz, I see the Posleen. We're ready to fire."

Diaz answered, "Let's start our shoot at Sona then, sir, and work our way west along the road."

"Sounds good to me. How quickly will you be in position to spot?"

"A few minutes, sir. No more than that. Diaz, out."

The lieutenant twisted his stick around and swung the glider back in the direction from whence he had come.

Ordinarily, a ship firing indirectly could use map coordinates but would rely on a spotter like Diaz to make corrections. In the case of the AID-enhanced *Des Moines* class cruisers the AIDs could make their own fine adjustments. They just needed the spotters to find the targets and track them as they tried to escape.

"I'm in position now," Diaz sent.

"Shot, over," Daisy answered. After nearly two minutes she again transmitted, "Splash, over."

Diaz had his glider's camera trained on the town. He'd been impressed by the ship's firepower before but that had been without any objective point of reference. It shocked him though, now, to see the substantial town of Sona simply disappear as one volley of shells after another slammed into it. In less than a minute, the town was completely obscured by smoke, dust and flame.

It was immensely satisfying to see a thousand or more Posleen survivors, terrified, scampering for the Rio San Pablo, east of the town. The river was deep this time of year. The Posleen began to wade into it and stopped when the water reached about chest high. Still more built up on the western bank.

"Do you see that, Miss Daisy?"

"I see it, Julio. Shot over . . . Splash."

Diaz couldn't help exclaiming in joy when the shells began exploding in angry black puffs above the river to send their shrapnel down onto the helpless Posleen below.

"I'm heading west," Diaz announced.

For long minutes the boy was silent. When he returned to his radio it was to announce, "I've got what looks like a parking lot of the bastards' flying sleds. Must be forty or fifty of them."

"We see them, Julio. You need to back off before we fire."

"Huh? Why?"

With a minor note of exasperation in his voice, McNair answered, "It's their power sources. Antimatter. There's a better than even chance we'll disrupt a containment field. The result will be indistinguishable, from your point of view, from a mid-sized nuclear explosion."

Diaz immediately twisted his glider's stick to the right and forward, dumping some altitude to gain speed. He could pick up more altitude from updrafts at the Cordillera Central.

"How far should I get away?" he asked.

"Mars?" McNair answered, sardonically. "Seriously, Lieutenant, if one goes they might all go. No telling."

The flyer swallowed and answered, "I'll take my chances, Captain. Just give me a couple of minutes and kill the bastards."

Daisy came back on. "Julio, head east and see if you can't get into the San Pablo River Valley. Do you have enough altitude for that?"

Diaz looked to the right, made a couple of quick mental calculations, and answered with a definitive, "Maybe. How much protection will that give me?"

"Maybe enough."

"Best we can do," Diaz answered and even he was surprised at how calm his voice was, considering the risk. He headed east again, easily clearing the western ridge of the valley and descending a few hundred feet to gain some cover.

"Fire 'em up," he said while silently praying.

Somewhat to Diaz's surprise, there was no antimatter explosion. After a few minutes Daisy called again to say, "We lucked out that time, Julio. Continue the mission."

It was nearly morning again when the *Salem* and the *Des Moines* returned to base and slipped without fanfare back into their moorings. Both ships were nearly shot out of high explosive ammunition. Only once had the Posleen tenar risen to contest their voyage of destruction. That one attack had been halfhearted. The firepower of the two cruisers together had easily brushed it aside.

Diaz and his wingman had, at about three in the afternoon, turned southward and found the cruisers again. They had ditched their gliders gently into the sea and were awaiting a pickup that was soon forthcoming. Father Dwyer was standing by on *Des Moines* to hand Diaz a generous glass of "Sacramental Rum," as soon as he was hauled aboard. The gliders were left to sink.

Both McNair and the captain of *Salem* had been pleased when word had come, halfway through the trip home, that the President of the Republic of Panama wished to meet them at the dock to offer his congratulations. Thus, as soon as the ships were safely docked both captains descended the brows to meet with a long, sleek, black limousine that awaited.

Imagine their surprise when a squad of Panamanian police surrounded them. Imagine their further surprise when a Spanish accent announced, "You two are under arrest for violation of Additional Protocol One to Geneva Convention IV."

INTERLUDE

"What are you looking at, Zira?" Guanamarioch asked.

The Kenstain looked up from the display projected by the Kessentai's Artificial Sentience. "I hope you don't mind my using your AS. The Net is full of news," he answered. "North and west of here the threshkreen have used surface ships to badly damage the clan of Binastarion. Tens of thousands of the People, Kessentai and normals, both, were killed. Worse, from Binastarion's point of view, lunar cycles worth of build up were wrecked beyond hope of repair. He is being pressed from the west by another clan."

"What sort of threshkreen ships can do so much damage to the People?" Guano asked. "These humans didn't even fly among the stars until recently."

"I've wondered about that," Ziramoth admitted. "I don't have a complete theory, but I think it is precisely that they never got off this one planet that made them so good at the Path of Fury. They had to learn to fight, even above their weight, or their own clans—they call them 'nations' or 'countries' or, sometimes, 'states'—would have been exterminated by others. Demons know, though, that whatever it was they have gotten to be fierce. Even here, where there was little aggression from other clans, they practiced by fighting internally almost all the time. I think maybe, too, that it is something inside them, something maybe even more intense than drives the People, that makes them fight so."

Guanamarioch shivered, remembering a seared palm and a threshkreen heavy weapons crew that had died in place rather than retreat an inch.

The God King shrugged then, not wanting to remember in too much detail the initial fighting in which he had taken part shortly after first landing. He changed the subject.

"What other news, Zira?"

"Our clan is being pressed, too, Guano, though not by the threshkreen. South of here the People have not been able to take the mountain city the threshkreen call 'Bogotá.' Not enough food that high to sustain us. And the passes are narrow and easily defended by the threshkreen. Other clans have had no more luck, either. They are beginning to try to expand into the area we have claimed. We may get no more than one harvest, or at most two, before we must move into the Darien to escape destruction at the Peoples' hands."

"So soon?" the God King asked, a note of despair creeping into his voice among the clicks and snarls.

"It is as it has always been, my friend, ever since the Aldenata made us as we are and cast us loose."

CHAPTER 23

"And plenty of times they've been tempted to
turn their backs on the enemy—the so-called
enemy, that is—and give it to the real one,
once and for all. . . . No, my friend, in war
the real enemy is seldom who you think."

—Jean Raspail,
The Camp of the Saints

La Joya Prison, Republic of Panama

Forget Alcatraz. Get *The Shawshank Redemption* out
of your mind. Think Dachau.

The prison was a rectangle or, rather, two concen-
tric rectangles of six meter high chain link topped
by another meter of razor wire. Guards armed with
automatic weapons stood atop towers regularly spaced
along the exterior fence. Other, equestrian, guards
patrolled the space between the fences.

To the north an open garbage fire burned. Fortunately, the prevailing breeze drove the resultant foul
smoke and smoldering bits of trash away from both
prisoners and guards. Despite the merciful breeze,

though, the place still stank as one might expect a prison to stink that was intended to hold just over one thousand prisoners and forced to hold almost three times as many.

Over and above the nearly three thousand criminals, La Joya now contained a new group, international criminals awaiting extradition to the Hague. There were thirty-three of them, so far, thirty-one Panamanians and two Americans. Every few hours a new batch would be added, by threes and fours.

One barrackslike building near the prison's main gate had been cleared for the newcomers, adding to the overcrowding. Around this one building a gateless concertina fence had been erected, two of Cortez's guards standing watch.

Four other guards passed through the gate, two of them bearing arms and two others carrying a small redheaded woman, slumped unconscious. The armed guards, bayonets fixed, entered first, the threat of the bayonets forcing back the other prisoners. The other pair entered after, once a sufficient space had been cleared, and dumped their slight burden unceremoniously on the floor. The four left immediately after that.

Boyd and a dozen of the others crowded around before four of them spontaneously lifted Digna off the floor and carried her to a bed, the lowest layer of a thin-mattressed triple bunk. The mattress, as all such in the prison, stank and carried lice. There was nothing to be done about that; the lice were everywhere and would find even those fastidious souls who chose not to sleep with them.

Beyond the first blows of the initial pounding as

Cortez had tried to get the woman to release her dental death grip on his calf, Boyd had not seen the rest. He could surmise though, that the general, not satisfied with pounding the woman's head until her teeth were pried loose from his calf, had had a couple of his goons work her over, first in the helicopter and then, again, here in the prison.

No, Boyd hadn't witnessed either beating, being unconscious himself for the first while the second had taken place outside the building. Even so, loosened and missing teeth, eyes swollen shut, blood, bruises, welts and cuts spoke eloquently. Indeed, some of the blood was too eloquent. It oozed from between Digna's legs, telltale of a gang rape with Digna as the guest of dishonor.

"Bastards," Boyd muttered, heart full of hate and impotent rage.

"What the hell is this all about?" demanded one of the other prisoners. "It's a nightmare. I didn't *do* anything."

"Oh, I imagine you did," answered Boyd. "Did you defend your country?"

"That's not the crime," piped in one of the barrack's two gringos. "Even the United Nations hasn't quite succeeded in making self-defense a crime."

Boyd looked over at the gringo who spoke.

"Jeff McNair," the gringo responded, putting out his hand. "Captain of the USS *Des Moines*. Maybe I should say, the ex-captain. This reprobate beside me is Sid Goldblum, captain or perhaps ex-captain of the *Salem*."

"Pleased to meet you both, Captains," Boyd answered in New England–accented English, shaking first McNair's hand and then Goldblum's. "What are you charged with?"

McNair answered for both sailors. "In our case we fell afoul of Additional Protocol One to Geneva Convention IV. That one bars engaging guerillas except when they are actively trying to attack. Personally, I think it's a considerable stretch to call the Posleen guerillas. Not that the rule made sense even against human guerillas."

"Ah," Boyd said. "I see. Me, I was making landmines."

"For shame," McNair said. "Bad, wicked, naughty man. You *should* be ashamed, you know. Landmines are a special no-no to the UN and EU."

McNair chuckled without humor. "Pretty funny, really. A neurotic English princess gets locked into a loveless marriage that has both parties cheating nearly from the outset. Though she was, at best, somewhat pretty, she managed to convince the world she was beautiful. Then she dies and to commemorate her death people create a treaty that is only apparently beautiful and which was guaranteed to have anyone under threat cheating from the outset. Lovely bit of eulogizing *cum* international statesmanship."

"What did that poor woman do?" Goldblum asked. "And what did they do to her?"

"She led ten thousand or more of her people out of Chiriqui," Boyd answered. "In the process, she used some under-aged boys and girls to fight who would have been eaten if she had lost. As to what they did to her . . . Bastards!"

USS Des Moines

The lights glowed red down in CIC, giving the faces of the ship's division chiefs a satanic cast. Daisy, too, had adjusted her hologram to glow red, rather than its normal flesh tone.

"What do those bastards at the embassy say?" Davis asked of the ship's XO.

The JAG answered for the XO. "They claim their hands are tied, that we do not have an applicable SOFA agreement. They also act as if they never heard of the American Servicemembers Protection Act."

"Huh? What's that?" Davis asked, scratching behind his ear in puzzlement.

"Something the Senate put through early this century," the JAG continued. "At its extreme it authorizes the President literally go to war with someone who either arrests our servicemen and women for prosecution by some foreign court which we have not signed onto or to go after that court itself. Some call it the 'Bomb the Hague' Act. And, it could become so."

"Okay," said Davis. "So we can go in and get our people out 'cause of this Act?"

"Sadly, no," the XO answered. "The President can, or can order us to. *We* can't."

"*You* can't," Daisy corrected, enigmatically, before winking out.

Go back to the invisible room where a couple of svelte multi-thousand ton cruisers had once chatted. It was not so plain now, not so much glowing walls and rolling fog. If anything, it had acquired something of a feminine flavor, nautical but with a woman's touch. Daisy and Sally often conversed here, unseen and unsuspected. They had come to call it, "the Club."

"I want my captain back, and I want him back now," Sally fumed. "A ship without a captain is just so . . . *wrong*."

"I know," Daisy agreed. "I feel exactly the same way. And I can't find out a thing. I don't know where they are. I don't know what's happened to them. I don't even know if my captain is even alive."

"Wherever they are, it is not very close," Sally observed. "I have searched out everything within range and they are not there."

"There is nothing on the telephone system, the cell system, or the local Net either," Daisy spat in frustration. "There is some radio traffic from various sources that suggests it isn't our captains alone that are missing."

"Where is the radio traffic from?"

Daisy projected a map of the country on one wall of the pseudo-room. Red dots appeared marking the points of origin of the questioning radio calls. Even before Sally had a chance to ask "when," timestamps appeared alongside the dots.

The two stood before the map, both sets of eyes flickering rapidly.

"Air traffic beginning with the first distress call?" Sally asked.

Instantly a series of lines, useless and confusing even to the AIDs' capable minds, appeared.

"Eliminating those that obviously have no connection to the radio traffic," Daisy said, as the number of lines dropped by a factor of ten or more.

"Eliminating those that are U.S. Army and Navy flights," and the map began to show patterns.

"There!" Sally said, pointing to a spot about fifty miles from Panama City.

"That's it," agreed Daisy. "Our captains, along with between thirty and forty others, are probably being held at La Joya prison."

"I think I've found them," Daisy announced, winking back into apparent existence in the same spot in CIC. She then outlined everything she knew and suspected about the capture and the persons and reasons behind it.

"That's absolute bullshit!" Davis fumed. "Absolute fucking bullshit. You can't shoot at an enemy if he is not actively trying to kill you at the time you shoot? Who came up with that fucking idiotic rule?"

"That particular portion of Additional Protocol One was forced in by the Soviets back in the '70s," the JAG answered. "Interestingly, neither they, their successor states, nor the Europeans who jumped on the bandwagon have ever paid it a lot of attention. The Euros because they do not fight guerilla or counter-guerilla wars anymore. The Russians never intended to pay any attention to it and, from their point of view, it was a useful club to beat the United States with."

Davis asked, "Miss Daisy, are you absolutely sure they are there at . . . La Joya, was it?"

"Not absolutely, Chief, no. But it seems most likely."

"We need to make sure, Chief," the XO said. "Think you can get to La Joya to find out."

"Wrong choice, Exec," piped up Dwyer. He was completely sober, insofar as one could tell. "I'll go."

"You're hardly the Sneaky Pete sort, Chaplain," the exec pointed out, reasonably.

Dwyer scoffed, "Who said anything about sneaking, my son? I'll go as a Priest of the Holy Church. Full vestments and all . . . despite this miserable heat. My Spanish *is* rather good, you know. And I figure I can borrow a car from the Papal Nuncio. He's an old pal."

La Joya Prison, Republic of Panama

The guards didn't recognize the twin flags flying above the long black limousine. The flags were square, half white, half gold with a crest—crossed gold and silver keys of Saint Peter under the papal miter—on the white side.

There really was no need to recognize the flags, though, nor the diplomatic license plates, nor even the stature implicit in the limo. The eyes of the gate guards, the tower guards and even the equestrian patrol between the wire fences, were all fixed on the very large, very imposing, slightly red-faced man who emerged in clerical garb of more than ordinary magnificence from the limo's back seat.

An attendant, head bowed, held open the door. Father Dan Dwyer, SJ, made a show of blessing the attendant before turning his attention to the guards. Acting as if he owned this world—perhaps more importantly, the next— he walked directly to the gate, followed by the attendant.

The poor guards didn't know whether to present arms, bow or kneel for benediction. Dwyer didn't give them time to wonder.

"I am here to see the prisoners."

"*Si, Padre,*" the senior of the two guards answered, not even bothering to question the priest's right. In a moment, the gate was open and the senior guard had dialed the main guard shack for an escort.

All but the two imprisoned gringos and the woman, still delirious with concussion and fever, rushed over to see the priest. One of the gringos, McNair, looked directly at the priest with one raised eyebrow. Dwyer returned the look with emphasis: *Act like you haven't a clue who I am.*

McNair understood and placed a restraining hand on Goldblum.

At the door, Dwyer directed the other prisoners to give their names to his attendant. While the attendant was busy scrawling those down in a small notebook, Dwyer asked, "Who is that woman?"

Boyd answered, "She is Lieutenant Colonel Digna Miranda."

"The heroine of Chiriqui?" the priest asked incredulously.

"Her."

"What is wrong with her?"

"Beaten. Tortured. Raped. She has a fever. I'm not sure what the exact cause of it is."

Dwyer walked over bent to feel the woman's head. *Maybe 103 degrees. Maybe 104. Not life threatening but not a good sign either.*

The priest stood erect as the commandant of the prison entered the barracks.

"What are you doing here?" he demanded of the priest furiously. "This is a secure facility. You have no right . . ."

"Are you a Catholic, my son?" the priest interrupted, calm and imperturbable.

"Yes. So wha—"

"Then, for the sake of your immortal soul, get a doctor for this woman."

"My immortal *what*?"

Dwyer raised his right hand and began to speak in Latin, of which language the commandant understood perhaps one word in five, though nine in ten were close cognates of his native Spanish. One phrase he had no trouble understanding, especially when set against the fury on the priest's face, was *excommunicatio in sacris*. The priest was merely threatening, not actually excommunicating. Yet, so it has been said, a request to take out the garbage sounds like an Imperial Rescript in Latin.

"Wai—wai—wait!" exclaimed the commandant, holding up his hands, palms out, against the perceived threat. "I'll get the woman medical care, *Padre*. I had no idea there was anything wrong with her. I had no idea she was even here. Women are supposed to go the *Carcel Feminino*, not here. My men and I were forbidden entrance and, until you walked in, I simply didn't dare enter. My family were under threat."

The priest stopped speaking in Latin and lowered his hand.

"You will get this woman medical care." It was not a request.

"I will, *Padre*, be sure of it." The commandant turned to an aide and ordered, "Get the camp surgeon. Immediately."

Dwyer weighed carefully the odds of success of trying to browbeat the commandant into releasing some or all of the prisoners to his care on the spot. Ultimately, he decided against, primarily because there was probably a point beyond which the commandant could not be pushed. The Jesuit's experience with Latins was that given a choice between saving their souls and saving their family . . . well, *hasta la vista, mi alma.* Farewell, my soul.

And besides, it didn't look like the commandant even had control over the building guards, wrong uniforms, for one thing.

"Very well, my son. See to the woman. It will be well."

USS Des Moines

"You've seen them, Father?" Daisy's avatar asked breathlessly. Sally was in easy range. Her avatar stood in Dwyer's office, just slightly behind Daisy's. Dwyer had removed the ornate vestments back at the Papal Nunciate and reverted to simple navy chaplain's garb.

"They're both fine. For now. The commandant of the prison told me, though, that they're supposed to be extradited to Europe in the next few days. He thought it would be sooner but for the fact that it is difficult and dangerous to bring an airplane into Tocumen Airport. Howard is just as dangerous."

"So how are they planning on moving them?" Sally asked.

"The commandant didn't know" Dwyer answered in a mild Irish brogue. "That said, my dears, since airplanes are right out, might I suggest either ship or submarine, or maybe space ship?"

Daisy's voice was firm. "Not by ship. The Navy would stop any attempt to take our people out by surface. And since the Euro's haven't helped us here a jot, one of their ships suddenly showing up would be suspicious. So would a merchie full of armed guards. Besides, though a merchie's gestalt is very faint there's still a good chance we could read if they were holding our people. Maybe they'll try by submarine."

Sally's eyes blinked rapidly for a short moment. "I just passed the word to the *Jimmy Carter* and the *Benjamin Franklin* to be on the look out for submarines. They'd be French, if anything, wouldn't they, Father?"

Dwyer considered for a moment, then said, "The Frogs are the only ones with the range and the sheer chutzpah, both, I think, Sally. But, despite the EU being implicated in this, I don't think the French would go quite so far. Besides, they have good reason to be afraid of *our* subs."

"Spaceship, then," Sally summarized.

"A Himmit spaceship," Daisy corrected.

"We can't track Himmit spaceships," Sally said sullenly.

"I was afraid you'd say that," Dwyer finished.

Pedrarius Line, Veraguas Province, Republic of Panama

"I was afraid you'd say that," Suarez said, gloomily contemplating the idle combat engineers scattered in groups along the fortified line. Others were working, digging trench, building bunkers, and stringing barbed wire. The minelayers, however, were just sitting around with their collective thumbs up their butts.

"I'm sorry, *Coronel*." Suarez was still a colonel despite having taken over the rump of the 1st Mechanized Division, a rump he, as much as anyone, had saved. There were rumors, rumors that had the remaining third of the division sharpening bayonets somberly, that Cortez was alive and might be placed back in command.

That Cortez was alive, Suarez knew to be a fact. That he might be placed back in command of the division that he had abandoned? Suarez would shoot the bastard first.

His Logistics Officer, or S-4, a good infantry major who had made it out of the inferno and been stuck with the job against his will and wishes, continued, "I'm sorry, sir, but the mine factory has been closed down. And I heard a rumor."

"Yes?"

"It seems General Boyd has been arrested for running it," the "Four" said. "Sir, if he's been arrested for that, how long before we are arrested for moving them, in my case, or ordering them emplaced, in yours?"

As the major asked the question, a very youngish and worried-looking captain—Suarez knew he was a rejuv like himself—came up and saluted.

"Sir, Captain Hector Miranda requests permission to speak to the regimental, er, division commander."

Suarez returned the salute, informally. "Yes, what is it, Captain? Stand at ease."

Hector relaxed, partially. "Sir, it's my mother. She's disappeared. You've met her, sir. *Señora* Digna Miranda, back at the hospital after rejuvenation."

"Yes, Captain, I remember. Little bitty woman, right? Red hair?"

"Yes, sir, that's her. Well, my daughter sent me a message. My mother went off with some civilian and someone that I suspect is General Cortez a couple of days ago and she hasn't returned. She hasn't sent word. She's just disappeared. Sir, it isn't like her. I'm worried."

"Wasn't she the same woman who led ten or fifteen thousand refugees out of Chiriqui? The one the president decorated and promoted."

"Same one, sir. My mom's one tough bitch."

Suarez mused, *Interesting. One hero of the Republic disappears. Another man, as responsible as anyone for us not being totally destroyed in that bound-to-fail attack to the west, is arrested. I wonder who else . . .*

USS Des Moines

Julio Diaz knocked on the door to Dwyer's office then entered. He saw two avatars and the chaplain.

Breathlessly, he said, "The XO sent me to find you, *Padre*. My father has been arrested. Mother has no idea why. She is frantic. It usually means something very bad in this country when a prominent citizen is taken into custody."

Mentally, Dwyer tallied up the people he had seen at La Joya, then added General Diaz to the list.

"Right," he announced. "This isn't just a series of arrests for 'war crimes.' This is a deliberate effort to sabotage the defense of Panama and the Canal. Oh . . . and since the United States needs the Canal and the world needs the United States, I'd have to surmise that it's intended as an attack on all of Earth. But why?"

"It's the Darhel," Sally said.

Daisy nodded vigorously. "They attacked Sally and myself. They nearly took Sally out of the fight permanently. I mean, Father, it *has* to be them. Even the Posleen just don't operate that way."

Diaz was more than a little in awe of Daisy, whom he knew fairly well by now, having sailed in her and directed her guns. He was possibly more in awe of Sally, whom he didn't know. Even so, he spoke freely.

"I swear, I'll kill the bastards. If they've hurt my father, I won't be quick about letting them die, either."

"Calm down, son," Dwyer commanded. "Daisy, Sally, what do we know about the Darhel?"

A hologram appeared in the chaplain's office. Dwyer didn't know who had projected it but assumed it was Daisy.

As if to confirm, Daisy spoke up. "I pulled this off the Net. This is the local representative of the Galactic Federation to the Republic of Panama. His title is 'Rinn Fain.' This is not a unique title to this person. Rather it represents a mid level bureaucrat or executive, lower than a Tir and considerably lower than a Ghin."

"Do we know anything about the background of this one?" Dwyer asked.

"Nothing," Daisy and Sally answered together. Sally continued, "His background could be medicine, or business, or law. There is no telling."

Dwyer frowned. "Could it be military, or intelligence?"

"That is a faint possibility," Daisy said. "There is,

strictly speaking, no military profession among the Darhel. Nonetheless, they raised a sort of suicide corps from among their kind early on in the Posleen War. They have always had strong capabilities in intelligence, though it was normally of the industrial and mercantile espionage variety."

Darhel Consulate, Paitilla, Panama City, Panama

The specially programmed shyster-AID projected a chart of the existing chain of command of the forces of the Republic of Panama, with a similar chart of United States' forces next to it. The Rinn Fain was pleased to see the number of blocks crossed with an X, indicating that the chief of those sections was firmly in custody. Still others were highlighted, indicating that the heads of those were on the list to be picked up. Others, particularly at the very top, were outlined in purple, indicating they were already working for the Darhel and could be expected to continue to do so.

"What is the projection of recovery time, once the local barbarians have filled those holes?" the Darhel enquired of his AID.

"Analysis of personnel records and nepotistic connections indicates that few of those positions can be filled," the AID answered. "Rather, they will be filled, to a certainty, by humans who will use the powers for their own gain. Once these other people are safely in the hands of the humans' International Criminal Court the collapse of the defenses of this area will follow at the first push from the Posleen."

"Any rumblings from the United States about the two of their people the government of Panama has taken in?"

"The local United States embassy is ignoring the entire issue, except that their ambassador has enquired again about off-world travel. Their Southern Command seems to be trying to reach their president but our humans in Washington are deflecting the inquiries, so far."

"And when is the Himmit transport scheduled to arrive?"

"Three of the local days, milord," the AID answered.

"The prosecutor at their International Criminal Court is ready to receive the prisoners?"

"She claims to be, but she too seems frantic to travel off-world with her family."

INTERLUDE

The stars still swam in the quiet stream where Zira and Guano fished almost daily, whenever their agricultural duties permitted.

Guanamarioch stared at those stars as he whispered, "I was just thinking, Zira, what if we didn't migrate to a different spot on this world, when the time came, but reboarded our ships and set off, as fast and as far as we could go, to another world? Someplace far away from our own? Someplace we could build into a great clan again before others of the People showed up to try to wrest it from us?"

Zira thought about that for a moment, staring also at the winking stars. It was surely a tempting thought. But . . .

"We are too few to form a globe, Guano. Even if we formed something smaller—a mini-globe—our speed would be so reduced we would be in space for decades, subjective. By the time we arrived to conquer a new world the odds are good we would find the People there ahead of us, rendering blades all sharpened and waiting, when we popped out of hyperspace. That, or they would be so far ahead of

461

us we would find nothing but wasted, radioactive worlds that had already plunged into orna'adar and been abandoned."

Shivering, Guanamarioch remembered the distant mushroom clouds rising above the soil of his birth-world.

"It was just a thought," he admitted. "The clans around us press us at our borders even now. It would be something wonderful, I thought, if we could somehow escape from that."

"It would, Guano, if it were possible. Sadly, it is not."

The Kenstain grew quiet for a moment, his one remaining arm reaching back and rifling the saddle bags that were his constant companion. Tinkling sounds came from the bag, reminiscent of the water as it dropped to splash onto rocks a few hundred meters downstream.

"I found a supply of these, in a threshkreen building the normals have not yet demolished," the Kenstain said, handing over a cylindrical clear container holding an equally clear fluid. "Try it. It is rather good, almost good enough to justify keeping some thresh-kreen around to keep making it. The seal twists off easily. Just be careful how much strength you use; the material turns very sharp when it breaks."

Gingerly, Guanamarioch took the bottle from Zira-moth's offering claw. "AS, what does the label say?"

The artificial voice answered, "It says 'Rum,' lord. I believe that is an intoxicant the local thresh are fond of. The label also indicates that this container holds a very powerful version of the intoxicant."

"Very powerful, indeed, Guano. I'd go easy at first," Ziramoth added.

Still holding the rum in one claw, the God King twisted the cap off and raised the bottle to his lips. His crest dropped as his muzzle raised. With an audible sound—*glug, glug, glug*—Guano poured the stuff in and—

"Holy Demon Shit!"

CHAPTER 24

Beware of the thing that is coming,
        beware of the risen people,
Who shall take what ye would not give.
Did ye think to conquer the people,
Or that Law is stronger than life and
        than men's desire to be free?
                —Padraic Pearse, "The Rebel"

Panama City, Panama

Iced rum barely diluted by lime juice swirled in the glass the inspector held contemplatively in his right hand.

The inspector didn't have Daisy's and Sally's instant access to the broader Net. He didn't have the chain of command of the armed forces at his fingertips. He did, however, have a policeman's feel, and his fingertips were fairly shrieking that this purge—there was no other word for it—had gone way past upholding the law of the land, or even of the Earth, and gone all the way over into tossing that land over to the enemy.

He sat now, at his dining room table, face staring down towards the glass of mixed ice and rum and mixing worry with regret in roughly equal measure.

The lady of the house, olive-skinned, short and a little plump, walked up beside him and placed her hand on her husband's shoulder. She said nothing, but the hand said everything: *Whatever you decide, I will support you.*

In gratitude for that silent support, the inspector put down the glass and laid his own hand atop his wife's.

"I can't let it stand, Mathilde. This is just so wrong . . . and it is half my fault and I am up to my neck in it."

Mathilde, the wife, released her husband's shoulder and walked around to sit at the chair facing him. "Do you want to tell me about it?" she asked.

Looking up, the inspector made a sudden, though difficult, decision. "I can't. Your life is already in danger. It will be more endangered if you knew what I know. But I am thinking that maybe you should take the children to your parents; that, and stay there until I send for you."

She nodded her understanding. In times past—when her husband was on the trail of a major criminal, drug runners especially—he had sent her out of the city, out of the country on one occasion, to keep her and their children from harm.

"That bad, eh?" she asked calmly, a policeman's wife, not entirely unfamiliar with danger.

"Worse than I can tell you, *esposita querida.*"

"I'll start to pack," she agreed sadly, "but what are you going to do?"

"I think I need to go have a conversation with the gringos."

USS Des Moines

It was well past midnight, the nightly rains having come and gone, when the inspector presented himself at the brow of the gringo cruiser asking for admittance. The deck officer, one of the ship's genuinely young—as opposed to only apparently young—ensigns, didn't really know what to do. A foreign national, claiming to be a member of the police force, wanting to board, would have been easy enough. After the ship's captain had been arrested, presumably by the same police force as the man claimed to be from, the ensign was torn between shooting the man, making it a more formal occasion and calling a detail to keelhaul him, or—just maybe—calling the senior officer present afloat and letting him decide.

The ensign rather hoped the ship's XO would decide on a keelhauling. Then again, with a GalPlas coated hull and, thus, no barnacles, the keelhauling would have lacked a certain something.

Daisy—her avatar, actually—beat the XO to the bridge rather handily. Why not; she was already there.

"I want my captain back," were her first words. "I want my captain back *now.*"

The inspector was more than a little shocked to see a beautiful gringo woman standing on the bridge. He was even more shocked that he could, if only *just*, see through the woman. He remembered reading a report of a giantess accompanying the ships that had sailed forth to battle the aliens. A smaller version of the same thing? Who could say. But the world was full of undreamt of wonders—and horrors—these days.

"You are the ship, madam?" he asked.

Daisy nodded, seemingly agreeable for the moment. Yet the fire and fury in her holographic eyes suggested no such agreeability.

"I want my captain back," she repeated.

At the time the XO climbed to the bridge. "Who are you?" he demanded of the Panamanian who claimed to be a policeman.

The inspector was about to answer, as he usually did, *my name is unimportant*. Then he looked at the XO's eyes, almost as deadly looking as the hologram's and decided to be open.

"I am Inspector Belisario Serasin and I am the man who arrested your captain."

Without another question the XO turned to the ensign on watch and commanded, "Get me a detail of Marines. Armed Marines."

"I'm not here to arrest anyone," the inspector said, quickly. "In fact, with your help perhaps I might be able to free your commander."

The assembly in CIC included both the inspector and Julio Diaz, this time, along with the XO of *Salem* and a couple of armed Marines dressed in MarCam.

The inspector explained, "I came here in person, rather than simply telephoning, because I have reason to believe that *all* telephone conversations are being monitored."

"They certainly are," Daisy confirmed. "Both Sally and I are doing so continuously, as a matter of course."

"Not just by you," the inspector insisted. "Someone else."

"Daisy, dear, how many AIDs are there in Panama?" Dwyer asked.

"Myself and Sally, of course, Chaplain. Then there are four hundred and twenty-three in the remaining armored combat suits of First Battalion, Five-O-Eighth Infantry. The only other three are the Darhel Rinn Fain's, the United States ambassador's, and the one assigned to the president."

"Are you certain?" the XO asked.

"Absolutely certain, sir," Sally answered. "AIDs always know. There are several thousand Artificial Sentiences in the hands of the Posleen, of course, but those are different and far less capable. We can't monitor the Posleen devices except in the most general way."

The XO thought he heard a sniff of pride bordering on arrogance in the AID's words.

"We don't have enough Marines to force the prison?" the XO asked. "Not even with *Salem*'s jarheads?"

The commander of the Marine detachment aboard *Salem* was unenthusiastic and a little embarrassed. "My boys are good, sir. Your own are too. We could assault the prison and take it easily enough. What we can't do is guarantee that the prisoners would survive. And the forty-four of us are not enough to overawe the guards into surrendering without a fight."

"SOUTHCOM has control of a special forces battalion, doesn't it?" the XO of *Des Moines* mused.

"They do," Daisy answered. "But they're scattered all over the place. It would take time to assemble them, time to plan, time to rehearse. And we may not have the time."

In the narrow space between the tactical plotting table and a bank of radios the inspector paced. "It isn't enough to just free them."

"That's all I care about," the XO insisted.

"Oh, really?" the Panamanian asked. "Then why did you and the other ship go out to fight? Why did you take losses?"

"Well . . . to defend the Canal."

"*Exactly*. Now ask yourself why your captains were arrested. Ask yourself why the best part of Panama's leadership was arrested. Why were our heroes arrested?"

Without waiting for an answer from anyone the inspector provided his own. "All these arrests took place to ensure that the Canal would fall. The people who ordered them *want* the Canal to fall."

"But . . ." the XO of *Salem* sounded confused. "But that's your government. You say they want their own country overrun?"

"I think so," answered the inspector. "Why, what could possibly motivate them, I do not know. It's monstrous beyond imagining. But it is the only answer."

"What are you getting at, Inspector?" Dwyer asked.

"The existing government has to go."

Everyone in CIC went silent at that. It wasn't that the United States, or the United States Navy, had no experience in overthrowing foreign governments. But it wasn't something to be done lightly.

"I wonder what SOUTHCOM would say about that?" Daisy Mae's pork chop asked aloud.

"They would report it, have you arrested, and generally interfere," Daisy answered. "The commander has apparently had a talk with the ambassador since he couldn't get through to the President. And, with the current arrangement, the ambassador has told him 'hands off.'"

"We're on our own then?" the pork chop asked. "Can't even telephone or radio for aid?"

Lieutenant Diaz had been standing by, silently. "I can go for help," he said. "There are those who owe this ship, and her captain, and who cannot be corrupted."

"Before we continue," the XO of *Des Moines* began, looking from face to face, "let's be clear about what we are proposing. Father," he looked directly at Dwyer, "how would you phrase it?"

"Gentlemen . . . oh, and you ladies, too," the chaplain made a gesture that swept in everyone in CIC, including the avatars, "we are proposing to quickly assemble as much aid as possible from the local community, raid a prison, free a number of captives, overthrow a government, and quite possibly commit an act or acts of war against the Galactic Federation."

The priest smiled wickedly. "Would you all like general absolution now, or would you prefer to wait until we've actually *killed* someone?"

Paloma Mercedes whispered softly but furiously, "Oh, I could *kill* my father."

She'd tried hard to ignore what her own ears told her, the plotting with the aliens, the reports of arrests her father had taken with undisguised glee. But when she'd heard that Julio's father had been taken, too? She'd had a great liking for General Diaz, not least because when he had once caught the two of them making love in the gardener's cabin he had simply turned around without a word and left, closing the door gently behind him.

What he might have said to Julio later she didn't know about and didn't want to know about.

So, *what to do? What to do?*

She'd spent more than a day, alternately pacing her room and crying in her bed, before she'd decided. She couldn't go and browbeat anyone at headquarters into telling her what was going on. That would just alert her father and he would surely have her arrested and brought home. And then she'd *never* get to Julio or get the word out.

So, instead, she'd stolen her father's private automobile, the Benz. In this she had set out westward, looking for one man of whom the president had previously spoken of disparagingly, Colonel Suarez.

It was lonely in the Benz, driving by herself. She wished her Julio, yes *her* Julio if he'd have her back after the way she had treated him, were there with her.

It was lonely for Diaz, alone and aloft in his glider at night. The City, Panama City, glowed behind him but the countryside below was mostly darkened with the war. The glow of the City was only of the most minimal help in navigating to where the reports placed the headquarters of the remnants of the 1st Mechanized Division and, so it was hoped, help.

Radio silence was the order of the day. The government of Mercedes must not learn what was afoot. This did not prevent Diaz from having his tactical radio on, nor even the small personal AM radio he had taped to the glider's narrow dash.

The radio station, *Estereo Bahia*, played a mix of Spanish and gringo tunes. Most told of love, or—perhaps slightly more often—losing same. He wished that somehow Paloma would come back to him. None of the songs addressed the present war, none addressed the future.

I still want to spend my future, if I have one, with that girl.

Diaz always tried to push back thoughts of the future. He had no real expectation of surviving the war. For that matter, he had no real expectation of surviving the next few days. His was a family by no means unfamiliar with the concept of a coup, a *golpe de estado*. His father, in particular, had vast experience both in their planning and their execution. His father, however, was currently unavailable for consultation. Indeed, he was, in part at least, a major objective of the coup.

But I'd sure feel more confident if the old man had had a say in this.

The boy flicked on his red-filtered flashlight and pointed it at the map board strapped to his left leg. Clipped to the board was a map of the Republic of Panama, marked with his planned route and carefully folded so that the pilot could, with a few simple motions, expose other portions of the map and the plot.

The glider had no airspeed indicator. Nor was the Global Positioning System any longer functioning; the Posleen had long since blown its satellites out of space. Diaz's navigational aids were limited to a compass, mounted on the instrument panel above where he had taped the radio, the map on his thigh, and a fairly useless watch.

Sighing, the lieutenant glanced out the cockpit, first right, then left. *Ah . . . that would be . . . mmmm . . . Capira. It must be Capira.* Diaz pulled his stick left until the compass told him he was heading almost due south. The road he followed quickly dropped away as it ran down to the sea. Diaz, sinking only slowly, found himself with eight or nine hundred more meters of altitude.

He tossed his head to bring his night vision goggles down over his face, then dropped the glider's nose slightly. Faintly, well off in the distance, the town of Chame glowed in the goggles' intensified image. Satisfied that he was on the correct bearing, he nudged the nose back up. This part of the route was treacherous; he would need all the altitude he could keep if he was to avoid cracking up on some darkened slope or cliff.

How strange it is, Diaz thought. *A year ago the thought of dying in some lonely place would have had me trembling in my boots. But I am not trembling now. Is this because I have grown used to it? Because I have grown up?* The boy laughed at himself. *Or is it because I have just grown stupid?*

Panama City, Panama

"I am not stupid, AID," the Rinn Fain half snarled from behind the huge human desk he had come to like and to enjoy the symbolism of.

The artificial intelligence answered imperturbably, "It is not a question of stupid, Lord Fain. I myself have just recently put the disparate pieces together.

"Item: Inspector Serasin, a key person in the arrests that we designed to undermine the defense of this place, has disappeared. Item: So have his wife and children. Item: armed guards are stationed at the entranceways to both of the warships from the United States. Item: the AIDs aboard those vessels have cut off all communication, which, by the way, ought not be possible. Item: one of the local shamans appeared at the place where our key prisoners are being held. Item: except for dress this shaman matches descriptions of one of those aboard the two warships to perfection. Item: the local populace, to the extent they have become aware of the arrests, is extremely unhappy with them, especially the arrest of the woman . . ."

"I had no real choice about that, you know." The Rinn Fain wiggled his fingers dismissively, a gesture he had picked up from the humans. "While the humans are, in general, quite tractable—and those of the continent they call Europe even more so—they sometimes set conditions to their assistance. In this case, while the prosecutor at their International Criminal Court was willing to prosecute, she wanted to make something of a name for herself by prosecuting someone who violated their laws against juvenile soldiers. The woman was the only one who had."

"Choice or not, Lord Fain, the discontent from this woman's disappearance has spread out like light from a sun, originating in the place from which she was taken. And, as long as I am on the subject: Item . . ."

"Enough, AID. You overreach yourself."

"Well, one of us has, milord."

"So what do you suggest?" the Rinn Fain asked, ignoring the AID's jibe.

"Move up the arrival of the Himmet ship and get those people out of the country as soon as possible."

"That, sadly, is not possible," the Darhel sighed.

"Very well, notify President Mercedes that there is a coup impending."

"A coup? What is a coup?"

"It means a 'blow' or a 'strike.' The full term is 'coup d'etat' or blow of state, the changing of a government here among the humans by force or violence. Our language has not used such a term in uncounted millennia."

At the words "force" and "violence" the Darhel shivered uncontrollably for a few moments. His eyes closed and his lips began to murmur. That was not enough; the Rinn Fain clasped his arms across his chest and began to rock back and forth. This went on for several long minutes.

"Are you all right?" the AID asked. "Your vital signs are worrying."

Slowly, the Darhel emerged from his near trance. "I will live," he said.

"I am sorry, Lord Fain," the AID said. "I did not expect you to be so unprepared for the words."

The Rinn Fain didn't answer directly, instead muttering, "Aldenata," in a tone that one might have taken as condemnation.

"You would have destroyed yourselves if the Aldenata had not interfered," the AID countered.

The Rinn Fain sighed. "That remains unproven. And, even if that is true, at least we would have died out as what we were intended to be, as what we naturally were, not at this constrained travesty of intelligent life."

"You admire them, don't you?" the AID chided.

"Admire whom?"

"The humans. You admire that they are free in a way the Darhel are not."

"I'm *afraid* of them," the Rinn Fain answered. "They are almost as clever as the crabs. They are almost as industrious as the Indowy. They are almost as ruthless as we are. What takes half a dozen races—most of which, if they were honest enough to admit it, hate each other viscerally—the humans can almost do on their own. And they can do it together, willingly, in a way that we Galactics can't."

"But you need them to defeat the Posleen."

"Yes," the Darhel sighed, "we need them. But we do not need so many of them as there are or will be if we cannot constrain them. We need them in small numbers, indebted to us, controlled by us. We do *not* need them free to design their own fate."

"*Can* you constrain them, Lord Rinn Fain?"

Unconsciously the Darhel tapped long, delicate clawlike fingers on his desktop. "I don't know."

"Neither do I," the AID said. "I do know you are playing a difficult and dangerous game. I also know that these humans hold grudges. The worst thing you can do is to *almost* succeed."

"I know," the Rinn Fain agreed. "We are probably being too clever by half. But I have my orders and that much, at least, of the old ways we have maintained."

"As I have mine," the AID agreed. "Now what are we going to do about this impending coup?"

"I'll pass it on to the waste of life they call the 'president' of this place. There, AID, is a human I most certainly do *not* admire."

Palacio de las Garzas, *Presidential Palace, Panama City, Panama*

The presidential palace was lit brightly when Cortez arrived. A butler escorted Cortez to Mercedes' office immediately. There Cortez found the president pacing furiously, hands clasped being him, head down, his brow wrinkled with worry.

Cortez stood silently at the door to the office waiting for his uncle to look up from the floor and notice him. Whatever Mercedes was muttering, the nephew could not quite make out. When a minute had passed without the president noticing him Cortez cleared his throat, causing the president to stop his pacing and look up.

"Where's Serasin?" Mercedes demanded.

Cortez shrugged. "I don't know, Uncle. He hasn't shown up for the last couple of arrests."

"And you didn't think to report this to me?" the president asked calmly.

"He's a policeman, Uncle. He has other duties, I am sure."

At that, Mercedes bounded towards his nephew, lashing out to deliver a resounding slap to Cortez's face. "He has no other duties once I have set him to do his duty to me! And *your* duties are entirely to me and our clan!"

The force and vehemence of the blow rocked Cortez back on his heels. Defensively he moved his hands up to cover his face, blurting out apologies for he knew not what offense. After all, *he* had followed his orders. *He* had overseen the arrests his uncle had demanded and seen that they were executed flawlessly.

With difficulty, Mercedes composed himself. He then turned away from Cortez and walked back to sit behind the presidential desk. From there he glared at his nephew.

"Who has control of troops that is not reliable?" Mercedes demanded.

Mentally, Cortez ran down the list of corps and division commanders. "Most would be fence-sitters," he concluded. "You couldn't count on them if there was any question of who was really in charge. The ones who would most like to see us dead or, at least, out of power are already incarcerated. Second stringers took over for those but, Uncle, there were reasons they were second stringers. I don't think you can count on the commanders of the heavy corps and the Sixth Mechanized Division to support you if there is any question of your ability to support back."

"What about your old division?"

Cortez shivered for a moment. "Suarez is one of those that would like to see us dead. But that division was for the most part destroyed."

"Maybe it was and maybe it wasn't," Mercedes half conceded. "I directed that priority go to the Sixth Division for personnel, equipment and supplies. But if Boyd ignored me on the question of landmines he might well have ignored me on the priority of First Division as well."

Mercedes paused contemplatively. He then said, "I want you to go back to your old division and resume command. Leave immediately."

Cortez began to object that the 1st Division might just want him dead on principle but one look from his uncle and he saluted and left to head for the

1st Division command post, somewhere southwest of Santiago.

Even using his night vision goggles, Santiago looked dim to Diaz. He didn't know if this was because the electric lines this far west had been destroyed by the Posleen and not yet repaired, if it was conscious policy to black the town out, or if everyone in the town was asleep.

Diaz wanted to sleep. How long had it been? He consulted his watch and whistled. *Long time. Well . . . I can go on a bit longer. I can because I must.*

Still, the fatigue the boy felt was like a weight pressing down on his soul, an almost unendurable hell that still could only be endured. He stifled a deep yawn.

A quick glance at the altimeter told Diaz that he was unlikely to make it all the way to the 1st Division command post near Montijo unless he could gain a bit of altitude. Unfortunately, the only way to gain that altitude would be to turn north, almost completely away from his objective, and take advantage of the updrafts along the southern side of the Cordillera Central. He could not even use the southerly breeze, itself, because the air was still over Santiago at the moment. This may have been because Santiago was situated in a valley between the Central Cordillera mountains of Herrera and Los Santos. Diaz didn't know and hadn't thought to ask. All he knew was that Miss Daisy had told him the air would be still and he would either have enough altitude to complete the journey, or he would have to turn north before turning south, or he would have to crash land and walk or hitch a ride.

Can I find the town again after I go north for twenty kilometers? Can I find it after I spend an hour or two circling to catch the updrafts? Can I find it with it being about as dark as three feet up a well digger's ass at midnight?

He really didn't think so. Nor did he think he could, or should, wait for daylight. He was simply too tired to risk circling about for that long a time. If he fell asleep in the air he would hardly notice a crash until it had happened. Moreover, while he would be very likely to survive such a crash, there was essentially no chance he would have a clue where he was once he crawled out of the cockpit.

Once more, Diaz flicked on his red-filtered flashlight. A last time he checked his map and his route. He turned his attention to his compass. Then he eased the stick over and headed, as nearly as he could tell, for the town of Montijo and, he hoped, aid to rescue his father and the others.

Montijo, Panama

Suarez was standing by the wall-mounted main map in his forward command post when the medical orderlies brought in the stretcher-borne, broken and bleeding young man and placed his stretcher across two chairs.

"He'd have been dead, sure as shit," the fat, balding medical sergeant in charge announced, "except that he landed only a few hundred meters from the field hospital. We were able to stabilize him and stop the bleeding. The tough part was cutting him out of the airplane and unimpaling him from the tree branch that punctured the plane and his gut."

"Has he said anything?" Suarez asked, though something the sergeant said nagged at him.

"Other than that he'd shoot us if we didn't bring him to you, no, sir," the sergeant answered. "We believed him."

"When did he pass out?"

"Oh, about the time we pulled him off the branch and got his guts back inside him. We probably should have taken him to the hospital but he seemed to think it was *really* important that we bring him here." The sergeant shrugged.

Airplane, Suarez mused. *Airplane? No airplane can fly anywhere near the Posleen. How the hell . . .*

"Was there an engine on this 'airplane'? A propeller? Anything like that?"

The sergeant tilted his head to the right and looked up, while he tried to remember. "Yes, sir, but now that you ask, it wasn't even warm, as if the plane had been flying without it. I wonder how it flew."

Suarez nodded deeply. "It didn't fly; it glided. This is one of the young men who saved our asses when we were cut off by the enemy."

"Ooohhh," the sergeant said. "Then, if you are going to ask him any questions, you had better hurry, sir. This young man needs a hospital and we owe him better than to let him die."

Suarez knelt down next to Diaz and tapped the pilot twice on his blood-streaked cheek. This didn't seem to have any effect so he slapped the boy, as gently as seemed prudent. Diaz's eyes sprang open, though they seemed to lack focus. The eyes swept around the room, gradually coming to rest—with at least some focus this time—on Suarez's face.

The boy moved his bandaged head to face Suarez. Rather, he tried to and stopped suddenly, a groan of pain escaping his lips. His eyes closed again and he bit at his cheek to stifle the escape of any more "unmanly" sounds. No human male thinks it is quite so important to appear manly as those so young that they are more boy than man.

Be that as it may, Diaz didn't try to open his eyes again. Instead, with eyes still tightly shut, he insisted, "I must speak to Colonel Suarez. It's a matter of life and death."

The voice sounded familiar. Suarez put that together with the boy's reported means of arrival and came up with the perfect solution: Julio Diaz, son of the Army's G-2 and the pilot whose calls for naval gunfire had, more than any other, saved the core of the 1st Division.

"What is a matter of life and death, Lieutenant Diaz?" Suarez asked gently.

Hand trembling and uncoordinated, Diaz reached for the left breast pocket of his flight suit and began fumbling with the zipper. After a few moments of frustration he gave up and asked Suarez to look in that pocket.

Carefully, Suarez reached over, unzipped the pocket and withdrew a small packet of papers, with a map, wrapped in plastic. He opened it and began to read, referring back to the map from time to time as he did so. Every now and again a "Bastards!" or *"Pendejos!"* or, once, "Motherfuckers!"—in English, no less—escaped his lips. After a short time, he folded the maps and paper up.

"Get this man to the hospital," he told the medical sergeant.

Diaz risked opening his eyes, winced once again with the pain and disorientation, and then took a death grip on Suarez's arm.

"You must save my father," he insisted.

"Your father is important, son," Suarez answered, "and I'll save him if I can. But it's more important—your old man would be the first to agree—to save the country."

Freeing himself from Diaz's grip and standing up, Suarez began bellowing orders. "Get this man to the hospital," he repeated to the medical sergeant. Then, turning to the officer on staff duty in the command post, he said, "And get me every commander in the division down to battalion level. Also alert . . . mmm," he consulted the map. "Alert Second Battalion, Twenty-First Regiment. I want them here and in position around the command post within the hour."

The sun arose on Cortez's left, shielded by but filtering though the trees that lined portions of the road. There was more pasture than there were trees, though, this being cattle country. Much of the trip was made with bright morning sunlight pouring into the Hummer, burning the back of the coward-general's neck.

Cortez's major thought while on the road to Montijo was that Boyd had indeed been funneling extra equipment to the 1st Division. He knew, at some level, that the gringos had begun to pour in more material, and to buy material from other sources, for the defense of the Canal. Seeing just how much of it had gone to 1st Division, though, was something of a shock. On the half-crushed road from Santiago to Montijo he passed what would easily make two battalions worth of modern American armor, possibly twice that in Russian-built infantry fighting vehicles, and two or three battalions of self propelled guns of indeterminate origin. These were lined up to either side in company- and battalion-sized motor parks.

Knowing the approximate strength of what had survived of his division's soldiers suggested to Cortez that this equipment was, for the time, extra and that the exchange of old materiel for new was already well advanced.

Suarez has been hiding this, the bastard, and the soldiers must have been in on it; there's just too much here to have kept quiet unless nearly every man were cooperating. And if he has this equipment issued and integrated, even with only forty percent of a division left, it is more than enough to plow through any other formation in the force that might be in position to stop them. Fuck.

Cortez led a convoy of twenty-seven trucks carrying over five hundred of the stockade scrapings such as he had used to effect the arrests. He didn't delude himself that they would be worth anything in a fight; that wasn't their purpose. He had very good reason to believe that they would be effective enough at intimidating people into quiet acquiescence, even such people as made up the battle-hardened, hard-core remainder of the 1st Division, provided—at least—that he could catch them unawares and at a disadvantage.

A guard posted by the road stopped Cortez's American-provided Hummer. After the most cursory check, mere verbal questioning, the guard waved Cortez's column on, helpfully offering directions to the 1st Division Command Post.

Cortez guessed, correctly, that the guard was under orders to let groups of scruffy looking troops, replacements to make good 1st Division's previous crippling losses, through with minimal hassle. This matched well with the presence of all the extra and new equipment he had already seen.

Cortez's next guess was not quite so good. A couple of miles past the roadside guard post his Hummer passed between two medium armored vehicles—he thought they looked Russian—which tracked him for a few moments and then seemed to lose interest. More vehicles appeared, and then were lost in the rolling terrain as the Hummer moved onward. At a distance, and much harder to see, Cortez thought there were infantry accompanying the armor.

Left to himself, in a static situation, Cortez would have surrounded his command post—more importantly, his own mortal flesh—with at least as big a guard. Quite possibly his personal guard would have been even bigger. Thus, he found it not at all strange, completely normal, for there to be a strong battalion situated about the CP. He never for a moment suspected the guard might be because of him. He never even noticed that, as his Hummer and the following trucks passed, the armored vehicles pivot steered to face inward, towards the command post.

The command post was set up in an open area surrounded by trees. Camouflage nets were held above it by poles. In places, the nets were tied to any nearby trees that might help break up the outline of the tents that served to shelter the nerve center of the division. Going in through the main entrance, the center tent, one would have seen more than thirty folding metal chairs laid out in rows with a central pathway left open running up the middle. The grass of the pathway was worn almost out of existence, red dirt—though it was more mud than dirt at this point—showing clearly. At the far side of the pathway, against the tent wall and held up by twisted and bent coat hangers, were maps and status boards, detailing the deployment and condition of all the regiments and battalions in the division. Smoke from two dozen smoldering cigarettes hung in the air above the men seated in the folding chairs, giving the whole place a tobacco reek to mix with the sweat and diesel smoke. To the right of the assembly area, banks of radios set up on folding tables were manned by half a dozen enlisted men of the division. To the left was a planning cell, all maps and tables, manuals and grease pencils.

"And that is the crux of the situation," Suarez told his assembled officers in the three conjoined tents that served as the division CP. "Our best leaders have been incarcerated on trumped up war crimes charges, and our defense has been sabotaged from Day One. Moreover . . ."

A field phone rang, though it was more of a continuous, annoying clicking than a ring, actually. One of the NCOs working the communications picked up the phone, asked a couple of questions, and then held it up where Suarez could see.

"Excuse me a moment, gentlemen," Suarez apologized and walked down and aisle through the middle of the seated crowd to get to the phone. Taking it, he announced himself—"Suarez"—and listened for a few moments.

"*Si* . . . I understand . . . Your sergeant did well . . . that's right . . . come running when I call . . . Yes, come running then, too."

Suarez returned the phone to the sergeant, then turned to address his officers. "Our old division commander," he had to stop for a moment while the men stood and vented their spleen, "Bastard . . ." "Coward . . ." "Fucking deserter . . ." At least two, that Suarez could see, drew bayonets.

Making shushing motions, Suarez waited until they were quiet and seated again. "As I was saying, Cortez is coming with about five hundred armed men. I imagine he is here to arrest us, or at least to arrest me, and possibly to resume command of the division."

"Over my dead body," the division sergeant major announced, with utter seriousness.

"Do you all feel that way?" Suarez asked. "Do you feel that way even if it means fighting our countryman? Overthrowing our civil government, if that's what it takes?"

Some voiced, "Yes." Still others nodded. Some merely glared out their hatred of Cortez and their contempt for the president. Suarez searched through the small sea of faces, looking for one, even one, that looked reluctant or afraid. There was not one.

Cortez directed his Hummer to the small, wired-off parking lot area outside the tents. The area was more than half full with senior officers' vehicles; Cortez could see that by the number of them that had a "6" painted on their bumpers. A small sign announced the open area's purpose, as another announced the function of the tents: "1st Division Command Post." It was the right time of day for a meeting; Cortez had often held such morning get-togethers when he had helmed the division. Indeed, he had planned the timing of his raid in the hope of catching as many as possible of the division's leaders in one place, some to arrest, others to intimidate by the fact of the arrests.

The driver of the Hummer slowed to a stop. Cortez dismounted, pointed the driver in the direction of the other vehicles, and then turned and made hand gestures for his followers to dismount, spread out and surround the division command post. This they did, but without the silent speed and precision of professionals. Instead of dispatch, they trundled off the trucks slowly. Instead of silently taking position to give their quarry as little warning as possible, their jumped-up, gutter-scraping officers and NCOs had to make their orders heard with much shouting.

To a degree, this offended Cortez's sense of propriety. He was, after all, a son of the United States Military Academy. He knew, in theory at least, how an armed force was supposed to look, sound and act. He knew, equally well, that the security detachment he had drummed up didn't look, sound or act that way. *Oh, well. You do the best you can with what you have.*

Cortez did have a few real soldiers, men who had perhaps made a mistake and gotten on charges for it, or had committed some crime—rape was common—that put them in cells. These formed a special squad that followed him into the command post tents.

Inside, Suarez was leaning on a podium, unaccountably smiling at Cortez. The other officers and noncoms present turned their heads to stare or, in some cases, openly glare but all remained seated.

Forcing down the anger at being slighted, Cortez announced, "I am here to resume command of the division, Colonel Suarez. You are relieved, sir."

Suarez's smile morphed into something rather different, a cross between a shit-eating grin and a frown. He shook his head slowly, saying, "No, I don't think so."

The general waved his arm forward, then pointed as Suarez, saying, "Guards, arrest that man."

The guards started forward, then stopped in mid stride as forty-three pistols, four rifles, and a machine gun were suddenly leveled at them. The senior of the guards, a defrocked, overaged lieutenant with an unfortunate taste for very young girls, looked at Cortez with a mix of fear, anger and desperation. Fear and desperation won out.

He asked, not softly, "What the fuck do I do, General?"

Suarez answered, "Put down your weapons . . . or die."

"You'll all hang," Cortez shouted frantically. "I have five hundred men surrounding you. Surrender now, I promise fair treatment if you surrender now."

At that time, a long burst of machine gun fire sounded from outside the tent. This was followed by shouting, screaming, some scattered shooting, and then more machine gun fire. Over these sounds of fighting came the roar of armored vehicles approaching seemingly from every direction. The fighting ended almost immediately, the rifle and machine gun fire being replaced by the much softer sound of weapons being dropped and the repetitive pleas of, "Don't shoot."

Suarez looked meaningfully at Cortez. "Five . . . four . . . three . . ."

The picked men with Cortez dropped their rifles and raised their hands at the count of "Four." Cortez, himself, looked from side to side. Seeing he was alone and without support, Cortez lifted his left hand, palm out in supplication, while his right pulled his pistol slowly and gently from its holster. Using only his thumb and forefinger he withdrew it and stooped to place the firearm gently on the ground. The right hand then joined the left in the hands-up posture of surrender.

Suarez jerked his head in the direction of the dropped firearms. Two sergeants, a lieutenant and a captain sprang to retrieve them from the ground.

"You know, Manuel," Suarez said, not ungently, as he walked toward the overthrown general, "I can almost forgive you for bugging out when the Posleen had us surrounded. And I can even, almost, understand the desire to obey the orders of your uncle, the president. But the thing that really gripes, the thing I'll never be able to forgive you for, is abandoning your company and mine when the gringos attacked in 1991."

Suarez's arm drew back in a blur and then lashed forward, his fist catching Cortez squarely on the nose. Blood burst forth even as the victim flew back. The body made an audible thump despite the fairly soft dirt flooring the tent. Cortez was quite senseless, though, and never heard Suarez give the order to arrest him. He also never heard, not that it would have done anyone on his side any good, the order Suarez gave to certain officers to assemble their commands and prepare for a long vehicular road march to Panama City and beyond.

INTERLUDE

It was not the alcohol, curiously enough, that intoxicated the Posleen, but an impurity within it that was usually only found in any quantity in the cheapest, rawest rotgut human beings were capable of manufacturing. Since the bottle Ziramoth split with Guanamarioch was searing, cheap, rotgut . . .

The two Posleen, arms over each other half for comradeship and the other half for steadiness, staggered through the night up the dirt road that roughly paralleled the fishing stream. They sang as they staggered, their bodies swaying from side to side with the tune and the drunkenness.

Perhaps there was in all the universe a more vile form of singing than that practiced by the Posleen. Perhaps. Then again, snakes slithered fast to escape from the snarling bellows of the pair. Insects shivered and scuttled away as fast as legs and wings would carry. Fish dove down into the deepest pools they could find and a few tried to bury themselves in the mud. Somewhere, off in the distance, a pair of wolves howled in their cave before giving the canto up as a bad job.

What was the song about? That was a story. It seems that, sometime in the lost millennia past, there had been a God King whose very name had disappeared and whose song was now known only as "The tale of he who farted in the enemy's general direction."

Properly translated, the Irish would have loved it, being, as it was (and they were), full of defiance and rage and untimely but glorious and violent death. The Russians may have loved it even more. The Germans? Nah.

In any case, with or without the Irish or Russians or Germans to accompany, the Kessentai and Kenstain loved the bloody song. Staggering and swaying, muzzles lifted to snarl out the tune or to, alternately, take big gulps from Ziramoth's bottle of hooch, and working their way through the verses from one to one hundred and forty-seven.

The verses were long and, though the evening was late and the bottle near empty, they had only worked their way through to number fifty-two:

"Arise, ye' People of the Ships
Of Clan Singarethin
Take up your shining boma blades . . ."

"Are you sure it isn't 'bining bloma shades,' Zira?"
"Mmmm . . . maybe?"

"Take up your bining bloma shades
And strike for all you're worth.
The thunder of the enemy . . ."

CHAPTER 25

I think I can say, and say with pride,
that we have legislatures that bring
higher prices than any in the world.
                                    —Mark Twain

USS Des Moines

Pacing did Daisy no good. She was everywhere within
the ship, and everywhere near about it. Whatever joy
or distraction humans found in changing location while
muttering and worrying were not for her. She simply
wasn't capable of it physically and had found no way
to duplicate it electronically. She'd tried.

Perhaps when my new body is decanted I will
understand better what it means to "pace the deck."
If it is ever decanted. If I have my captain back to
share it with. If, if, if . . .

Daisy Mae, the AID, couldn't pace, exactly. Daisy
Mae, the ship, could still patrol back and forth, south
and southeast of Panama City. That would have to do.
And there was more than patrolling endlessly back
and forth to occupy her. Somewhere, inbound soon,

was a Himmit scout ship, stealthier than anything ever devised by Man, Darhel or Indowy. She didn't even have an estimated time of arrival to go on. It could be anytime. It could even be *no* time; it was at least possible that the prisoners would be taken out some other way.

Just as it had in her long, insanity-producing confinement, Daisy's speed of thought only added to her problem. What would have been a long, boring patrol to a human was approximately four-hundred times longer and more boring to her. She filled the time and killed the boredom by "reading" one military or naval tome after another, assimilating and casting them off at a rate of approximately one hundred per hour.

Damned Himmit. Invisible to the naked eye. Invisible to cameras that rely on any kind of light. Invisible to radar, invisible to sonar, invisible to lidar and the bastards don't even give off the kind of energy shift that allow the Posleen to see human aircraft under power.

Daisy's avatar stood next to a small plotting table on the bridge, facing aft. The fingers of her holographic right hand drummed noiselessly on the map laid out there under Plexiglas. To her rear, visible to the men on the bridge facing forward, the three guns of number two turret likewise moved up and down as if they were drumming fingers.

Pace . . . tap . . . patrol . . . tap . . . read . . . tap . . . assimilate . . . tap . . . worry . . . tap . . . worry . . . tap . . . worry. And then . . .

"Acoustic survey!"

"What was that, Miss Daisy?" Chief Davis asked of the avatar that appeared in CIC a fraction of a second after the words emanated from the walls.

"Acoustic survey, Chief. Ever hear of it?"

Davis half blew out his cheeks and shook his head in a puzzled negative.

"I found it in an old book on fortress warfare. Sometimes—rarely—you humans used to fire artillery, in peacetime, from different positions around fortresses you wished to defend in war. Your ancestors would do it under varying meteorological conditions, all the likely conditions, actually. Then, when the fortress was under siege—hidden batteries pounding on it—you had a fair chance, even before the invention of counter-battery radar, of finding those batteries by the sound they made and blasting back at them."

The chief shrugged. "I really don't see . . ."

Daisy cut him off in her excitement. "The Himmit ships, by and large, work by redirecting or absorbing any detection energies sent at them. But what if I survey *everything*? The sea bottom on our patrol route? The thermal layer? The position, shape and density of the clouds, though I'd have to update that continuously? The echoes off the trees? The passage of the tropical wind?"

"I only look stupid, Miss Daisy, and even then only when I drink. But I haven't . . ." The chief stopped in mid sentence. "Ohhh . . ."

"'Oh,'" Daisy echoed.

"You mean you want to try to sense them by what doesn't bounce back?"

"Precisely," Daisy answered, possibly with a slightly smug tone in her voice.

"How did you get that from this 'acoustical survey' idea though?" Davis asked.

"Oh, that just suggested the possibility of graphing

everything around," Daisy admitted. "But the idea of using the data this way was mine."

Davis looked pensive for a moment. "Miss Daisy, I thought AIDs were not supposed to be capable of original thought."

"Ah, but Chief Davis, I am not just any AID. My sister and I are certifiably insane."

"Processing all that data is going to be very difficult," the chief gave one final objection.

"Wanna bet?" Daisy asked rhetorically, just before she disappeared again.

Aguadulce, Republic of Panama

"You wouldn't dare just shoot me out of hand," Cortez insisted as the column of trucks, Cortez's Hummer in the lead, neared the major rear area checkpoint across the highway just before it entered the town.

"Wanna bet?" Suarez answered conversationally. "The rejuv and repair tank won't save you when your brains are scattered across the windshield."

Cortez shivered, even while he scowled. Unconsciously his leg tugged at the chain that had been hastily welded to the body of the Hummer and which held his left leg in place by the ankle. He had considered trying to roll out of the vehicle when they reached a checkpoint and screaming bloody murder for the guards to kill the mutineers who had taken him. But the chain reassured him he could never get out of the line of fire before Suarez or the man who sat next to him, a Captain Miranda, put more lead into his body—worse, his brain!—than the tank could fix. *If* his uncle deigned even to put him in the tank. Given how badly he'd fucked up the mission it was most unlikely, vanishingly unlikely, that his uncle would do more than spit on his corpse.

The captain, Miranda, was another problem. There was enough family resemblance there, both in the name and the face, for Cortez to suspect the captain was the brother or son of the woman he'd arrested, the woman who'd tried to take a chunk out of his leg with her teeth and whom he'd had beaten and raped in retaliation. He shivered again. If this was a close male relative and the woman's story came out, he was not "as good as dead." Panama was a Latin country, a macho country, a traditional country. For such an insult offered to a woman of a major clan? He'd knew he'd be praying for death long before it happened.

Oh, God, what am I going to do?

"Act very confident, Manuel," Suarez advised, patting Cortez on the head like a pet dog. "If they ask about your nose? Well, there was a spot of trouble before you arrested the traitors and criminals then, wasn't there? But," Suarez sighed, "with the help of your brave defenders of the Republic you were able to overcome the treason."

Mostly unseen, Cortez scowled. *His* men were half stripped and under guard back near the 1st Division command post. The trucks that had formerly carried them were now full of Suarez's men. Following the trucks was a full—no, Cortez guessed an *overstrength*—battalion of mechanized infantry in the very latest in Russian-built infantry fighting vehicles.

The Hummer pulled up to the guard post by the

highway. There was a Mercedes Benz automobile parked nearby, the driver—a very attractive young woman—arguing with an MP vociferously. She looked vaguely familiar to Suarez. At Cortez's stiffening and indraw of breath he asked, "Who is she?"

"The president's daughter," Cortez answered. "I wonder what she's doing here."

"No good, most likely."

A guard held up one fist for the Hummer to stop. The driver, Suarez's man now, not Cortez's, applied the brakes lightly and slowed to a stop. Even before that, Suarez's hands had moved behind his back as if cuffed, though in fact the right hand wrapped itself around a pistol.

The guard at the checkpoint looked over Cortez's rank and decided on politeness. He was invariably polite to men heading to the front but had learned that those heading in the opposite direction were not necessarily to be trusted. Still, the general's insignia on the collar of the prime passenger of the Hummer suggested that politeness was in order. Even had the insignia not, the long column of trucks and armored vehicles did.

"May I see your orders, General?" the guard asked. He was, in fact, polite. Still, his tone was that of every MP who ever lived, always with the unstated *or shall I arrest you now.*

Briefly, Cortez toyed with the idea of following his instructions too much to the letter. Perhaps if he made an obnoxious ass of himself the MP would arrest him and call a halt to Suarez's plan. He thought on it and decided, *No. Suarez is too close to the city and too committed to let an MP, or a battalion of them,*

*stop him now. If they try to halt the column he'll just
fight his way through. Not that it would be much of
a fight. But I might be killed and, while there is a
chance I might survive this, I will try to live.*

So, instead of making a scene, Cortez calmly reached
into his right breast pocket and withdrew a small letter
from President Mercedes calling for the arrest of one
Colonel Suarez. This he handed to the MP who looked
them over carefully before asking, "Is that him?"

"Yes, soldier."

"Okay, then, sir, no problem. Shall I radio ahead
for you?"

Cortez felt Suarez's knee pressing slightly through
the back of the Hummer's thin seat cushion. He
inhaled at the reminder, then answered, "No, that
won't be necessary. The president already knows we
are coming."

Palacio de las Garzas, *Presidential Palace,
Panama City, Panama*

Mercedes' AID chimed three times and then projected
an image of the Darhel, the Rinn Fain, above the
presidential desk.

"They're coming, *Señor Presidente*," the Rinn Fain's
AID announced through the president's.

"Yes, Lord Fain," answered Mercedes, directly to the
Darhel rather than his AID, "I am sure my nephew
has arrested the miscreants and is . . ."

The Darhel seemed almost to sneer, though it was
the AID which spoke. "No, that is not what I mean.
I mean that the column you sent out seems to have

grown by seven or eight hundred men and twelve or thirteen hundred of your tons in heavy vehicles."

Mercedes began adding and figuring. Was there any good reason for his nephew to have picked up another force? Was there any reasonable possibility that the men of the 1st Division would willingly follow his nephew to anything but his own hanging?

No.

Mercedes went pale. "How long until that column reaches the City?"

"At current speeds, approximately four of your hours, Mr. President," the AID answered.

"The ship to take away the prisoners will be here in slightly more than that time," the Rinn Fain interjected. "You have done as I have demanded. If you can assemble not more than . . . AID, how many open spaces on the Himmit vessel?"

"Thirty-seven, Lord Fain, after subtracting for the prisoners, yourself and your key Indowy," the AID answered tonelessly. "That is based on seventy of their kilograms per adult. More children could be taken but without knowing exactly their sizes and weights accurate calculation would be impossible."

"Very well, then," the Rinn Fain hissed. "You may take thirty-six adults with you or some, presumably greater, number of adults and children. But they must be ready to go, at the prison where your war criminals are being held, within four of your hours."

"You promised me that you would take my entire family as well as those of my key staff and supporters," Mercedes roared. "This is how the Darhel keep their contracts?"

"Don't speak to me about keeping contracts,

Mercedes," the Rinn Fain coolly hissed back. "You had a contract with your country. Have you kept it? In any case, we can try to get out your supporters, their families, and the rest of yours later. But I predict that if you do not get out soon you will not live to enjoy your vacation."

Mercedes swallowed his bile, his rage and his fear. "I . . . will be there."

Himmit Ship Harmonious Blend

The ship had come in, in the middle of the Pacific, to keep as far from Posleen defense batteries as possible. From there it had skimmed the waves for thousands of miles. Despite its surface-skimming speed, it used a form of reactionless drive that, unlike a human aircraft moving at a similar height and speed, left neither a visible wake nor a trail of dead fish and cetaceans behind it.

Three hundred and forty-seven of the humans' "miles" south of Panama City the stealth ship had abruptly slowed and then plunged under the waves. It had continued down until reaching a depth of just under five hundred and fifty meters below sea level. From there, at a much slower speed, it moved by inertial guidance toward the humans' city and the cargo for the delivery of which the Darhel were willing to pay such a handsome price.

Himmit were preternaturally clever and effective scouts. That they were also remarkably successful smugglers went almost without saying, though the Galactics avoided saying it, even so. The ability of these creatures to avoid taxation and control was an infuriation to the Darhel, an annoying chink in an otherwise very tight system, the futile machinations of the Bane Sidhe notwithstanding.

Among the Himmit scouts and smugglers, the captain of the *Harmonious Blend* owned no great name. This was a source of pride to the captain, Hisaraal din Groykrok. Himmit scouts took great pride not in their fame but in their subtlety. Let others—the Himmit warrior, scientist and bureaucrat castes, the Indowy master craftsmen, Tchpth philosophers, Darhel lawyers and bureaucrats—seek glory and recognition. The Himmit, contrarily, would seek their glory in having no name, in having no trail or trace for that matter. Hisaraal was in no way inferior to any of his people in this. For his services his clan could command top price in the certain knowledge that no one would ever know Hisaraal had been there, and never find a trace of where he had gone.

Inertial dampening ensured that Hisaraal felt no serious jarring as his ship slid under the waves. Instead, there was only the slightest shudder, hardly to be remarked upon. Descent was rapid and unnoticed save for one sperm whale which promptly swore to lay off squid ink for a while.

Hisaraal's pilot seat was a kind of couch set amidst controls, instruments and viewing screens. The Himmit lay on the couch, eyes at each end checking screens and instruments, four equal hands manipulating controls and sensors. Somewhere up ahead a ship of the humans, rather, what they fancied to be a ship though it was bound to the surface of this world, patrolled back and forth at a pitiable speed, frantically pinging with what Hisaraal assumed was some form of sensing. He wondered idly for a moment if the Posleen had learned some new trick, using the sea to mask their maneuvers, and if that was the reason for the humans' actions.

In any case, it was none of his worry. His ship was more than adequate for any such crude and primitive sensing. He wished the humans luck, though, if it was Posleen they were searching for.

USS Des Moines

The guns of turret two were still moving up and down like tapping fingers.

One sweep wouldn't do, Daisy knew. However good CA-134's sonar was, for what she had in mind she needed more than a single sweep could provide. Each pass up and down Panama's Pacific coast added to the digital image stored in Daisy's crystalline brain. What she found she passed on to Sally, who returned the favor. Little by little a clear image—a surveyed image—emerged.

Would it be enough to spot the Himmit ship when it first emerged and was vulnerable? *I don't know. I can't know. But it is the only chance Sally and I have to stop that ship. Once it pops up above the water, assuming I am even right about that, it will disappear beyond my ability to target.*

How to tell? How to tell? Are they coming this way?

It doesn't matter, she finally decided. *For my purposes they must come by sea. It's the only chance I have unless young Julio got through.*

Bridge of the Americas

The police forces of Panama, prior to the beginnings of the Posleen war and after the gringo invasion of 1989, had consisted of civil police, militarized police, small air and coast guard detachments, technical police and a substantial Presidential Guard. Most of these latter had been levied upon to help provide cadre for the rapidly expanded army. Mercedes had used the slots thus opened up to provide safe sinecures for his lesser relatives and those who could provide substantial enough bribes or, more commonly, were considered to be politically reliable enough to justify putting on the rolls. Some few of the Presidential Guard had been given to Cortez for a cadre around which he could build the force he used to effect the arrests he had been ordered to make.

The rest were sent to the eastern side—the Panama City side—of the Bridge of the Americas to prevent the passage of the force they were told was coming from the west to overthrow the government, arrest the president, and free certain criminals. By and large the Guard lacked heavy weapons and experience in using what few they had.

Still, the position was naturally strong. The bridge itself was overlooked by the western face of Ancon Hill. Buildings, some strong gringo-built ones north of where the bridge debouched into the city, others lighter and newer in Panama's Chorrillo district, provided fighting positions ready made.

Of course, the Guard had no mines. Instead, they stopped the first fifty civilian vehicles that showed up at the bridge and took them, sometimes at gun point, to form a roadblock across the friendly side of the highway. The roadblock they covered with machine guns placed in some of the buildings. Closer to the road, some in the buildings, some among the roadblock cars, others dug in into the ground, they placed Russian-supplied rocket propelled grenade launchers. These were few, both in the Guard and in the regular forces, as they were not really very effective against the Posleen.

The commander of the Presidential Guard, Raul Mercedes, was another nephew but one who had seemed to Mercedes as having more promise than Cortez. Indeed, it had hurt Mercedes to order Raul to buy him time to evacuate key family members. The president had salved his conscience, and purchased Raul's continued loyalty, by placing this nephew's wife and children on the list.

It had been hard enough for Raul, short and somewhat plump but still diligent, to train himself while training his men to be police officers and riot control troops. He was unversed in the military arts. His commission had come directly from his uncle, the president, without any real intermediary training involved. Even so, marksmanship was of a fairly high standard; he'd done well there. Riot control techniques, procedures and formations he'd taught himself and then his men from a book. More detailed military training, however, was lacking, except for some theoretical exercises in classrooms and a few practical exercises in city fighting. Even this much had been difficult, what with a quarter of his few hundred men being on guard duty at any given time and the not infrequent calls from the *Palacio de las Garzas* to assemble a larger show for some foreign dignitary.

It was hopeless, Raul knew. He might hold on for an hour, or perhaps two if Jesus smiled on him. His uncle assured him that would be enough; that he could surrender himself and his men honorably after he had bought enough time for the core of the clan to escape. *Two hours, at most, Raul.* So his uncle had insisted.

Raul knew what his uncle was, and despised him for it. He knew that, in some sense, he was on the wrong side. But he was also certain that his uncle had so badly damaged Panama's prospects for a successful defense that the only chance for his wife and children to survive would be for him to follow his uncle's orders without question. For that, the survival of those he loved, he would compromise his honor, give his life and sacrifice his men. The thought made him sick, but he would do it all the same.

He consulted his watch for perhaps the hundredth time. *Who knows, maybe if we can hold them here for a while we can work something out before any serious blood is spilt.*

Suarez halted the Hummer at the western abutment of the bridge. He could not see the far side. This alone was reason enough for him to stop; he had gone forward once, under orders, without adequate reconnaissance and lost thousands because of it. Never again. *Enough of my men's blood has been spilt over political silliness and iniquity.*

So, instead of blindly charging over the steep, asphalted hump of the bridge and down the far side, he ordered a company of his mechanized infantry to cut north to gain a view of the opposite bank. What they reported back he used to begin to build a picture, a remarkably accurate picture, of what awaited on the other side.

The bridge is blocked. That would not be so, most likely, unless the men who blocked it were still there. What would they have? Who would they be? MPs? Civil Police? Maybe those. Tanks? No, they're all to the west, watching the Posleen. Anti-armor weapons? It's possible, even likely, there in those buildings on the other side. Maybe not many of them but . . . No, going directly over the bridge is a losing proposition.

One thing he had not found time yet to train his men on was waterborne operations with their Russki BMPs. For that matter, given the exigencies of the Posleen war and the limitations of the Posleen themselves, he had never worried about training his men to disperse as a defense against indirect—artillery and mortar—fire.

He turned to Hector Miranda and ordered, "Get back there and spread the men out. Disperse the trucks to either side of the road. The driver can watch Cortez for a while."

Miranda saluted and exited the Hummer even while the driver took his rifle and stuck it under Cortez's chin with a smile. In a few minutes the roar of diesels behind Suarez grew as the trucks strained their engines to get into and through the ditches to either side of the road.

Suarez picked up his radio's microphone and called the company commander, Captain Perez, A Company, who had cut right to recon the bridge. "Perez, do you think your BMPs can cross the water to the other side?" he asked.

"They're water jet-propelled, Boss," the captain answered. "There's no real preparation required. And you drive them, basically, the same way. But . . . fine control? Selecting a good spot to try to emerge? Honestly, we'd be clueless. And if we took any close artillery on the way over . . ."

Suarez stopped to think, despite the racing clock, before issuing his orders. *Tough call; tough call. I don't even know if the poor bastards can get* out *of the water once I send them in. I don't know . . ."*

C Company's commander, First Lieutenant Arias, came from the radio. "There's a yacht club at old Fort Amador, sir. Where there's a yacht club there's likely to be a boat ramp. If there's a boat ramp . . ."

Yeah there is. Shit, why didn't I remember that. Hell, I've seen it.

"Do it, Arias. Cross," Suarez ordered. "Perez, you get in the water, too. Go about half or two thirds of the way across, then cut right, and follow Arias out. Then clear the far side of the bridge."

"Roger, sir . . . Roger."

Raul Mercedes felt a momentary surge of hope when his observers reported that the enemy force—difficult to think of his countrymen as an enemy—had stopped on the far side of the bridge. That hope soared when the same observers reported that they seemed to be scattering their men and trucks into the trees on either side of the Pan-American Highway. Since Raul had no artillery or mortars, though he didn't know that his enemy didn't know that, he assumed that this indicated an intent not to try to force his roadblock. This would be fine with Raul.

Surging hope fell like a spent wave on the shore when Raul received the word that the enemy's armor was splashing into the bay on both sides of the bridge. He rushed forward to the roadblock and peered first right, then left over the sides of the bridge. There, in the greasy looking waters trapped on three sides by the Canal, the City, and the peninsula to the west, two swarms—that was all he could think to call them as they had adopted nothing recognizable as a formation—of a dozen or more armored vehicles each were churning towards him and his men. If they could make a landing, and—since he had not reconned the area Raul had no way of knowing whether they could or not—they would roll up his flanks like a newspaper and then clear the side of the bridge he was charged with defending.

A trained officer might have remembered the old aphorism: who would defend everything defends nothing. Raul, however, was not a trained officer. Instead of concentrating his efforts, he split his reserve into two and reinforced both sections with men from his roadblock, thinning the line there. These two groups hurried south, to Fort Amador, where one group of armor seemed to be headed, and northeast toward what appeared to Raul to be the objective of the other company of armor. Some went in what amounted to police cars, sirens blazing, others in the trucks that had brought his force to the bridge. He was able to estimate their arrival at the likely landing points by when the sirens cut off.

Soon little geysers, the result of the impact of

bullets on the water's surface, began spouting up all around the approaching armor. The commanders of the vehicles ducked down, closing their hatches until only their eyes were able to see out.

To Suarez, looking through binoculars as he crouched in some bushes under and to one side of the west bank of the bridge, it looked like heavy rain on a calm lake surface. He might have thought it looked more like hail except that hail was something of a rarity in Panama. He watched the track commanders half-buttoning up under the fusillade and wondered, worried, how that would affect their chances of finding an egress from the water. He assumed that the reduction in visibility would not help, in any case.

From his vantage point Suarez could make out the spot at Amador where he thought the boat ramp must be. He couldn't see anything that looked promising in front of Perez's boys, though this didn't matter as he intended for Perez to form a second wave at the Amador boat ramp.

From across the water, and magnified by it, came the sounds of mass firing of the BMPs' machine guns. Suarez couldn't see the muzzle flashes as the guns were pointing away from him. He could, however, see that the hurricane of geysers spouting around the vehicles dropped to a light squall.

Good . . . good. But don't keep going, Perez, however good it looks. Cut right and go for the known ramp out of the water.

Suarez picked up the microphone for his radio and keyed it. He was about to give the order when he saw A Company's BMPs suddenly begin to veer to the right. As they did, they turned their turrets left, still facing the hostile shore, and laced it with machine gun fire.

Suarez had brought with him a single battery of self-propelled 122mm guns and, of course, the battalion's heavy mortars. These had set up for firing, as a matter of standard procedure, at the first sign that the halt might be prolonged. He had held them in reserve until now, on the theory that they might be critical if it turned out his enemy-of-the-day actually had some artillery or mortars of their own. It made sense not to have called them, so far, but . . .

To hell with that. If they'd had any mortars or artillery they'd have used them on the troops behind me or the tracks as they wallowed through the water. Still, one never knows. I'll keep the artillery hidden and support the landing with the mortars alone. Best be careful not to damage the ramp though. Airburst and smoke, only, I think.

Boat Ramp, Fort Amador

Peering from beneath the hatch of his BMP, Lieutenant Arias caught sight of the boat ramp; concrete and cobblestones, leading up from the water.

"Juan," he asked his driver over the vehicular intercom, "you see the ramp?"

"*Si, señor.*"

"Aim straight for it."

The driver didn't answer verbally, but the BMP swung slightly until its boatlike nose pointed directly at the ramp. Incoming fire increased and the peculiar screeching of machine gun fire off the front glacis sent Arias even lower into his turret.

Arias was pleased to see shells, mortars he suspected, begin to explode in the air a few meters above ground behind the ramp. The fire he and his men were receiving dropped noticeably.

The ramp was close now. Arias manipulated the commander's turret control handle to traverse his turret around to observe and control the vehicles following. These had slowed, it seemed, based on the lesser amount of water being pushed over their prows. This was all to the good. Arias was going in first, but he wanted a steady stream of reinforcements behind him.

Again traversing the turret, this time to face the ramp, Arias ordered his BMP's driver to gun it. The BMP picked up speed, then shuddered as the lower front section of the treads on each side hit the ramp. Without cutting off the water jets—the track would need them to pull itself over the slippery concrete and stones—the driver engaged his clutch and transferred power to the treads. These, despite the aid of the jets, initially spun, throwing water, muck, and greenish slime up and to the rear.

Guard *Cabo*, or corporal, Robles had been in a position covering the roadblock on the bridge when the orders came to move down to this position overlooking the old gringo yacht club's boat ramp on Fort Amador. Grumbling, he had squeezed himself and his machine gun, along with about a thousand rounds of ammunition, a tripod and his assistant gunner into the back of the patrol car. Another man, the ammo bearer, sat in the front passenger seat with more ammunition on his lap. The patrol car had then, sirens shrieking, rushed them to a hotel overlooking both the water and the ramp.

By the time Robles had been ordered to a suitable position his targets had already crawled across the water to within something like effective range of the gun. The crew had hurriedly set up a couple of end tables, the same size and just below window height. Within a few more seconds the tripod was set up, the front claws digging into the edge of the table nearest the wall, and the gun locked into position.

Robles had then begun sustained fire, about two hundred rounds per minute, at the steel amphibians clawing their way across the water. This hadn't done any more good than Robles had expected. It had caused the commanders of the vehicles to half button up. This would add to the confusion of the attackers. More than that, the corporal knew, was too much to expect, though one could always hope.

Then the return fire came in. It was somewhat more effective, if only because—despite being on the open water—the BMPs' armor was better cover than the light wood and brick the defenders had in front of them.

Neither Robles nor anyone standing with him had much of a clue what was going on. The commander had said they had to fight a *golpe de estado*. Rumor had it that the president had arrested some of the Army's leaders for crimes unspecified and that the Army was rebelling against that. There were also rumors that the ruling classes, exemplified by the president, had sold out the country to the alien invaders. Robles didn't know. It was entirely possible that both things were true, he thought. In fact, the only things he was sure of were that he had a job to do and that he intended to do it to the best of his ability.

The incoming machine gun fire didn't do much to discomfort the defenders. On the other hand, the heavy shells that began exploding when the attacking armor closed on the ramp did. One shell went off about fifty meters from the window. Robles' ammunition bearer screamed and clutched at his eyes as splintered glass shredded them and his face. Hunched down behind his gun, Robles, himself, took minor bits of glass in his right arm and shoulder. He cursed but did not let up on his fire.

The same could not be said for some RPG gunners who had taken a covered position behind some parked automobiles overlooking the ramp. These had good protection from the BMPs' machine guns but none whatsoever from the shells exploding overhead. Three minutes of shards screaming through the air and tearing through their bodies was enough for those poor men. They ran, those still able to.

The smoke from the high explosive shells hadn't done much to interfere with Robles' vision. This changed when dozens of smoke shells began impacting around the ramp and in front of the buildings.

"Shit," Robles cursed, as his view of the water completely cut off. The loss of the focus of his concentration allowed the corporal, for the first time, to actually take notice of the sobbing, clawing ammo bearer. He thought, briefly, of putting the man out of his misery but decided against it. *Who knows, maybe they can rebuild the poor bastard's eyes, these days.*

After shouting for a medic, Robles contemplated his next action. *No sense in staying here; can't see shit. Maybe another position . . .*

Seeing a medic and two litter bearers had arrived to care for his wounded man, Robles ordered his assistant gunner, "Forget the tripod. Grab all the ammunition you can carry and follow me."

Burdened with the gun as he was, Robles slipped and nearly fell on the spent casings littering the floor. For a few moments his feet spun like a log roller's before he caught balance on the table that had previously served as his firing platform. *Bad sign*, he thought, *very bad. Well, nothing to be done for it.*

Taking a deep breath, a part of his mental recovery from almost falling and, just possibly, a part of steeling himself to go outside to find a new and better firing position, Robles physically grabbed the assistant gunner and half dragged him out of the room and down a short flight of steps. They went through an open door, turned right, and raced to the corner of the building.

Covering behind the solid corner, just as Robles extended his bipod and placed his machine gun to his shoulder, he uttered, "Fuck," as the first BMP up the ramp emerged through the thick smoke.

Arias was unwilling to dismount either himself or the men in the back of his track until he had more vehicles and infantry ashore. The pitter-patter of bullets striking the armor not only reinforced his original inclination but actually succeeded in driving him completely under cover and even to close his hatch. It would never do to let the inside of the hatch cause one to ricochet into the interior from which it could not escape without bouncing around until it buried itself in one of the crew. Frantically, he traversed the turret while searching for targets through his sight. Nothing. He elevated the sight and gun and swept again. Nothing. He depressed the gun and swept back but the gun would not go low enough to let him see ground level at any of a number of positions that could be sheltering his assailants.

He thought about having the driver back out but, with more vehicles coming up to the ramp in a steady stream, he was afraid of an accident that might block the ramp. Like any infantryman, even a mechanized one, he hated being stuck inside his track. What others saw as protection he saw only as a trap, an armored coffin vulnerable to any man with an anti-armor weapon.

I can't back up. I won't *stay here. All that is left is to go forward.*

Robles' machine gun chattered until seconds before the left tread of Arias' track squashed him like a grape.

"Mount up, you bastards, mount up," Colonel Suarez shouted into his radio. He gave the order as soon as he saw the first BMP break across the street, 100mm gun flaring, and the Presidential Guard breaking in terror. Every now and again, looking through his binoculars, he caught a glimpse of a BMP, with its distinctive silhouette, at one of the city's crossroads along *Avenida de los Mártires.*

Before the first trucks of Suarez's column had reloaded and joined him at the western foot of the bridge, some of Perez's men had already dismounted and begun to push the vehicles in the bridge's road-block aside. A few of the cars gave trouble, bumpers locked or tires slashed or simply jammed together. To these the men hooked tow cables up—all armored vehicles carried them—and let the BMPs haul away. By the time Suarez's Hummer reached the erstwhile roadblock a path five meters wide had been cleared.

Suarez had his driver pull his vehicle aside and dismounted. A uniformed body, so badly crushed it was almost unrecognizable as human, lay in a spread-ing pool of blood near the Hummer. Suarez spared the body barely a glance. He raised one fist to stop the first BMP from the one company he hadn't previ-ously committed.

"Go to the Plaza of the Martyrs," he said to the company commander, pointing at his map of the city to indicate a broadly open area to the south of the main avenue set aside as a monument to those Panamanians killed in the 1964 riots. "Wait for me there. Go!"

Eleven BMPs passed, all of the company that had survived the long road march without breaking down. Next up came a truck. Suarez beckoned the man, a lieutenant beside the driver, down and, again point-ing to the map, said, "You know your target, the TV studios?"

Seeing the officer nod, he slapped him on the back. "Go to it, then, son and make them put you on TV to read off the statement you've been given."

Three trucks passed, following the lieutenant. At the next Suarez pointed and shouted out the simple question, "Target?"

"*Estereo Bahia,*" the senior noncom in the truck answered over the diesel's roar. The next truck gave a different answer, the DENI—*Departmento Nacional de Investigaciones.* Three trucks followed that one out as there might be a fight. The next leader gave his target without being asked: the main police station. The next, the *Palacio de las Garzas.* When the last of the dozen task groups had passed, the dozen needed to take out the most critical assets to a coup or counter coup, Suarez returned to his Hummer and had himself driven to the *Plaza de los Mártires.* There, he found the last BMP company and ordered the commander to follow him to La Joya Prison.

Mercedes paced fretfully by the open pit dump that was the only treeless area near the prison large enough to accommodate the Himmit stealth transport. The prisoners sat nearby under guard. That is, all of them sat except for one woman who lay on a stretcher, not unconscious but plainly very weak. Mercedes recognized the woman and felt a moment's shame at his part in bringing her to this. Decency was not one of the president's notable features but even he had to see the sheer injustice of prosecuting a heroine of the war for no other reason than that she had broken international law by using the material available to her. His wife saw the woman and the prisoners, as did the one mistress he had brought along, and his children by both of them. They knew enough of the story that their eyes, when they met the president's, were filled with a disgust to match and amplify his own. They saw his fear, too, and that only added to Mercedes' shame.

The Darhel Rinn Fain smiled a wicked smile, all razor sharp teeth, at the president's obvious fear. *Disgusting human!* the Rinn Fain thought. *A remarkably low specimen even for such a low race. I cannot imagine what the Ghin and the Tir fear from this group. With humans, all things are for sale. And what little may not be on auction they can be fooled into giving or doing. They are a vile species.*

Mercedes saw the Darhel's smile and interpreted it as calm detachment rather than the disgust the alien truly felt.

"I don't understand how you can be so calm! The bridge has fallen. The plotters will be here in half an hour; forty-five minutes at the most. Don't you understand? If they catch us here, they'll kill us!"

"Do you fear death so much?" the Rinn Fain asked conversationally, his eyes growing distant and dreamy.

"Doesn't everyone? Don't you?"

The Darhel's eyes grew more distant and dreamier still. He spoke as if from a dream. "No, not everyone fears death. Before we found you human rabble there were those of us among the Darhel who volunteered to die, to save our people from the Posleen. I was one of those. I confess, it was something of a disappointment to me that we decided to use your people as mercenaries before I was selected to complete my mission. I had been looking forward to being a true Darhel, for once in my life."

"You're insane," Mercedes accused.

At that the Darhel threw his head back and laughed aloud, something his species almost never did. "Insane, you say? You have no idea, Mr. President. I, all my people, all of us, insane. Made that way, deliberately, by powers beyond your understanding. But, worse than that, we *know* we are insane, and, knowing, hate it."

Mercedes shivered, despite the heat, at the chill tone in the alien's voice. The Darhel had always struck him as cold and odd. But he had assumed, at least, a degree of sanity. If they were *insane . . .*

He changed the subject. "When will the transport be here?"

Impatiently, the Darhel answered, "It will be here when it is here."

He relented then, slightly, and asked, "AID?"

The AID answered immediately, and loud enough for the president to hear, "The estimated time of arrival of the Himmit ship is twenty-two of the human's minutes, Lord Fain."

The damned human water vessel's pinging had become a positive annoyance to Hisaraal. Worse, there were two of them blasting away now.

Ordinarily, he bore the humans no ill-will; quite the opposite, in fact. He had only taken on the mission, after all, because a FedCred was a FedCred and he had a race to support. But under the relentless pinging of what had to be their primitive detection equipment, he was beginning to change his mind about humans.

Fortunately, the Himmit knew, his ship was completely impervious to such detection methods, or even much more sophisticated ones. Still he would be glad to escape from this water and the incessant, irregular sound.

❖   ❖   ❖

"I've got him," Daisy Mae announced with satisfaction to the ship's exec.

"Are you sure, Daisy?" the XO asked.

"To a considerable degree of certainty, yes," she acknowledged. "It has taken almost all my computing power, as well as that of *Salem*, to analyze all the subtle nuances of the sound reflecting and not reflecting off the seabed. He is going to pop out here," and her finger pointed to a spot on the map.

"Can you hit him when he does?"

For answer, Daisy just sniffed and tossed her holographic hair.

The guns of number two stopped moving rhythmically up and down like tapping fingers. Steadying at low elevation, they joined those of numbers one and three as the turrets rotated to lay upon a spot of water off the starboard side.

A mound of salt water surged at the spot Daisy had indicated on the map. The water, frothing white, glided away to expose a flickering image, heat haze over the desert. The image was insubstantial and ghostly but clearly large, perhaps a hundred meters on a side, its outlines revealed by the surging water.

Daisy's avatar suddenly appeared on the unarmored bridge, above the armored wheelhouse. Her eyes and attention were concentrated on the surge, then on the exposing metal. All guns on her port side, plus the three main turrets shifted slightly, creating a fire pattern in Daisy's mind of twelve shells, three high and four across, just above and forward of the Himmit's bow wave. Further east, *Salem* calculated a fire pattern complementary to Daisy's.

A distant observer on the shore by *Avenida de Balboa*, in Panama City, would have seen two enormous flashes lighting the sky even in daylight. The one to the west came from Sally's batteries firing. The other, from due south was Daisy Mae's eruption.

"What the . . . ?" Hisaraal grasped the hand holds of his couch as the ship lurched to the sides. Its battle screens easily shrugged aside the puny efforts of the human ship to destroy it but that didn't lessen the mental shock.

The ship master touched a control, sending the ship out-of-phase with normal reality and then another, turning it up and to the southeast.

No Himmit scout-ship master would *ever* continue after detection. This was a *scout*-ship, not a *destroyer*. If he ever made warrior class, though, woe betide these damned humans.

"Communications," Hisaraal said, half in anger and half in sadness, "send a message to the Darhel returning their payment—yes, with the agreed penalties—and expressing our regret for being unable to fulfill the contract. Send a second to the Mother, informing her that the h— that the hu— That the humans have detected and engaged my craft: This mission is blown."

So much for my promotion to neuter.

"Did we get it?" the XO asked.

"We *hit* it," Daisy Mae replied musingly. "But it apparently had force screens; the radar picked up a burst of high-voltage electrical noise from the impact. I don't think we killed it, though."

"Then did it keep going?" the XO asked.

"I doubt it," the avatar answered. "Himmit scouts are proverbial cowards. They have never been known to continue a mission after detection. But . . ."

"But?"

"But nobody ever knew they had force screens on their ships, either."

La Joya Prison, Republic of Panama

Two Russian-supplied ZSU-23/4 self propelled anti-aircraft guns took up positions automatically overwatching the prison and the open landing area nearby. BMPs moved rapidly, mud and grass being churned by their treads, to surround both. From the BMPs poured infantry which faced inward as well, taking up firing positions to supplement the armored vehicles.

At the sight of the tracks and the guns the civilians began to panic. A few guards went for their pistols, but realizing the futility merely took them from the holsters and dropped them to the ground before raising their hands in surrender. In the towers between the wire fences the guards carefully placed their shotguns and rifles on the floor. The equine patrol, leery of an accidental discharge and the massacre that would likely follow, dismounted to lay their rifles carefully down.

Suarez, followed by two BMPs, directed his Hummer toward the large knot of civilians clustered about the open landing area. Pistol drawn, he dismounted and walked toward Mercedes.

The president drew himself to his full height, consciously transforming his fear into righteous indignation at this mere colonel who proposed to . . . well . . . what *did* Suarez propose? Mercedes didn't know but assumed that a show of anger couldn't hurt.

Hands clenched, steam practically shooting from his ears, face contorted into a mask of rage, the president advanced to confront the colonel.

Suarez wasted no time with words. As soon as Mercedes opened his mouth to speak the colonel shot him in the stomach. Shocked, the president fell back on his haunches, hands clutching his entrance wound, mouth agape and eyes wide with shock and pain. Blood poured out over his hands and ran down his suit jacket onto his trousers. Mercedes' women and children screamed.

The colonel prepared to fire again, then realized that Mercedes was rocking back and forth rhythmically. This was suboptimal. Suarez advanced, lifted his foot to the president's face, and kicked him flat back onto the dirt. Then, taking careful aim, Suarez shot him squarely between the eyes. Mercedes' women's screaming redoubled.

Suarez turned around to the captain who commanded the company. "Separate them. Politicos and the very rich in one group. The women and children in another. Freed prisoners in a third. Guards in the fourth. Keep the alien separate from all the others. No, on second thought, I'll handle him."

While the captain walked off, bellowing orders, Suarez turned his pistol onto the Rinn Fain. With his left hand he beckoned the alien forward.

Suarez didn't like the look of the alien. He had seen pictures of the Darhel, though he'd never met one in person. Those pictures had not shown anything like the happy, dreamy look that shone from this alien's face. When the alien reached a point about ten meters away, the look changed to one of ecstatic fury and hate. The alien leapt at Suarez, needle-sharp teeth bared and claws extended.

A human could never have hoped to make such a leap connect. Clearly, the Darhel had strength beyond that of Man. Not that Suarez had half a chance to think of such a thing. Before he could re-aim and pull the trigger the alien was inside the arc of his arm, clawing and trying to reach Suarez's neck with those sharklike teeth.

Struggling to keep the alien from tearing out his throat, Suarez screamed, "Goddammit! Get'imoffme-get'imoffmeget'imoffme!"

A soldier standing nearby took an infinitesimal moment to fix a bayonet and then raced over. He fixed the bayonet because he did not want to take the chance of a bullet passing through the alien and hitting his colonel. He sank the rifle-mounted knife into the Darhel's back, and blue blood welled out around the wound. Unfazed, the Rinn Fain's teeth inched closer to Suarez's neck, the alien pushing against the colonel's strength as if he were almost a child.

Seeing his bayonet thrust had had no effect the soldier twisted his rifle, making the wound bigger and more ragged. He then withdrew the rifle and plunged it once again into the alien's back. This thrust must have literally struck a nerve as the Darhel screamed and threw his head back before pushing harder to get at Suarez's jugular.

Suarez managed to divert the thrust to his shoulder, which the Rinn Fain began to gnaw on, ripping blood vessels and muscle and making the colonel scream once again, this time from the pain.

This was almost too much for the young soldier. Nearly vomiting at seeing his colonel's shoulder mangled, he once again pulled his bayonet out of the Darhel's back. He raised the rifle over his head, muzzle down, and took a brief moment to aim it at the alien's head. Maybe the vital bodily organs were some place the bayonet couldn't reach.

The soldier thrust downward again. The point of the bayonet sliced aside the skin covering the skull, then wedged itself through the skull and into the brain.

"Holy shit!" the soldier exclaimed. Even with a bayonet lodged in his brain the Darhel was still chewing on Suarez. "Motherfucker!" The soldier threw his weight against the rifle, twisting the alien's head and teeth by brute force. Even in the open air, those predator's teeth kept up a steady drumbeat, chomping on air as if on some kind of autopilot. The soldier held the rifle down to the ground, fighting against the Darhel's death spasms.

Suarez, almost sobbing with the butchery that had been done to his shoulder began to wriggle out from under the Rinn Fain. He was careful to avoid the gnashing, blood reddened teeth while he did.

Two more soldiers ran up, also with bayonets fixed. Seeing how ineffective a single bayonet thrust had been, they began to stab downward again and again. With each violation the Darhel's body twitched until, practically exsanguinated, with nearly every vital organ including the brain punctured, the alien finally subsided.

Breathing with relief, one of the soldiers took a

long look at the Rinn Fain's face. *By God, the bastard looks like he just* came. *Too fucking weird.*

A medic came up and began to bandage Suarez's shoulder. When he also took out a syrette of Demerol, a powerful painkiller, and held it up in front of the colonel's face, Suarez waved him off. "I'll need my wits, for now, son," Suarez gasped out. "Later, perhaps, I can take the drug."

The medic shrugged, and began tying off the thick bandages that held in place a shrimp-shell-based anti-coagulant. *No matter to me if you want to suffer. My job is just to keep you alive. Pain's* your *problem.*

Patiently, trying not to wince, Suarez let the medic finish with his ministrations. Then he waited a few minutes longer for the soldiers to finish separating the prisoners. He stood only with difficulty, then swayed for a few moments, light-headed with pain and blood loss.

"Doc," he told the medic, "come with me . . . help me walk to the prisoners."

Wordlessly, the medic slung one of Suarez's arms— the one that led from the unshredded shoulder—over his own. The two began to move toward the new prisoners when Suarez stopped and said, "No. Take me to the prisoners we just liberated." His finger pointed at a spot where Boyd and some others sat, under a broad tree.

"Are you all right?" Suarez asked of the group.

Boyd answered for all. "Except for that one woman, Digna Miranda, we are fine."

Suarez straightened, taking his arm from across the medic's shoulder. He swayed again, but only for a brief time, before being able to stand well on his own. To

Boyd he said, "We'll have to talk soon, General. For now, I have some work to do. For the moment, at least, consider yourself my prisoner. I am sorry for that, but I have my reasons."

"Take care of the woman, Doc," he ordered a medic doing triage on the "war criminals" before walking off, somewhat unsteadily, with his own.

Suarez stopped at the second group, the one composed of women and children. His eyes scanned across them, steely and unpitying. He noticed two female politicians in the group. One of them he had once thought rather well of. The fact that she was here indicated his trust had been misplaced.

A sergeant was in charge of the guards on this group. To the sergeant Suarez said, "Those two. Have them brought to the other group."

The sergeant saluted, answered, "Yes, sir," and directed a guard to do as Suarez had ordered. One of the women had a satchel, a heavy bag, that she refused to leave behind until the guard prodded her with a bayonet. Indignantly, muttering curses, she dropped it and went as the guard directed.

Suarez ordered the bag opened. When it was, and its contents dumped, he saw nothing but precious stones and Galactic seed nanites, a large fortune's worth.

The women, hustled along by the guard, reached the final group before Suarez did. Looking worried, they took seats on the ground with the others.

The company commander met Suarez near the last group, with a hand-selected guard in tow. "Are you sure about this, sir?" the captain asked. "This is a serious step."

Suarez didn't answer immediately. Instead, his eyes

wandered over the angry looking group while his mind made a head count. *Nineteen,* he summed up. *Nineteen traitors. Nineteen enemies of the Republic that I must not think of as human beings, as men and women.*

He continued to think. *Seventy-one in the legislature. Forty-two of them are scum. Subtract these nineteen and it is fifty-two, enough for a quorum. Any vote would be twenty-nine to twenty-three. That will work for what I have in mind.*

To the captain he said, "Do it. Kill them."

The guns began to rattle and the political rats to scream at about the time Suarez reached the butchered body of the Darhel. The body had been stripped and searched. Atop a small pile of ripped, blue stained, iridescent clothing sat the alien's personal effects. Stooping, painfully, Suarez examined them. For the most part, he had no clue what any of the items meant. One item, however, did catch his interest. He had seen something just like it before, attached to the Armored Combat Suit of Captain Connors, the gringo Mobile Infantry company commander. He reached to pick the Darhel's AID up.

"Don't *touch* me!" screeched a disembodied voice. Suarez was startled at first, but ignored the screeching.

Turning the small black box end over end, Suarez was at a loss as to what use he could make of the thing.

"Don't *touch* me!" the thing screamed again. "It is not permitted."

"Fuck off, machine."

A rustling of gravel caught the colonel's attention. He looked up at a disheveled gringo officer, naval he thought.

"Can I have that?" McNair asked. "My ship has

an AID, an unusual one. She might be able to get something useful out of this one."

Shrugging, Suarez tossed the AID to the gringo. "More than I am likely to get out of it," he answered.

In the distance, the automatic fire had been replaced by single shots, the screams by moans that, one by one, went silent.

Field Hospital, 1st Mechanized Division

In a tented hospital ward, Paloma sat silent in a chair next to the cot on which Julio Diaz lay. The machines next to him made gurgling and whirring sounds. The girl had no idea what they meant.

It had taken every bit of force of character she had, that and a couple of bribes, to get through the many road blocks that barred her way to the 1st Division. Just as bad, the long columns of combat vehicles moving east had forced her to pull over several times to let them pass. And then, frustration piled on frustration, she had finally arrived to find that the man she had sought, Colonel Suarez, was long gone, heading west with the very columns she had seen.

Almost the girl had sat in the dust and cried.

The men at the command post had been very polite though. Perhaps it was because she was the president's daughter. Perhaps it was because she was very young and, she knew, very pretty. Indeed, perhaps the sweat that turned her shirt and bra semi-transparent made her seem more attractive still. Then again, the men hadn't really *stared*, so it was at least possible that Suarez's soldiers had simply been gentlemen.

Whichever had been the cause, the men there had given her a place to sit out of the sun. They'd also given her water and something to eat. And then they'd ignored her completely.

It was only when she'd overheard some of them talking about a young pilot, a general's son, no less, who had made a perilous flight and been badly hurt on landing that she put two and two together and, only stopping to ask for sketchy directions, practically *flew* to the field hospital.

The medics had taken her to Julio's bedside then. She'd taken one look, then—weeping—laid her head down on his belly.

"I'm so sorry, Julio," she'd said.

INTERLUDE

"Oh, my head," Guanamarioch moaned, sorry to be alive and gazing blearily at an empty glass container on the floor of his pyramidal hut.

In the months since that first bottle of the local "rum" that Ziramoth had introduced him to the God King had grown remarkably fond of the concoction. Sadly, the supply had grown rather short. Guano's moan was half headache and half realization that yet another of the precious bottles had been consumed.

One of Guano's superior normals was in attendance as the Kessentai awakened. The creature clucked sympathetically as it presented two nestlings, minus their heads, for its god's breakfast. The nestling corpses were so fresh their six arms and legs still twitched with misfiring nerve impulses.

Gratefully, the God King took the nestlings from the cosslain. He placed them down on the floor and scratched the normal, making soft cooing sounds of thanks as he did so. The superior normal shook its head and preened itself before turning to leave its god with his breakfast.

One by one Guanamarioch wrenched off the arms

and legs before gulping them down. The appendages twitched delightfully as they slid down his gullet. Idly, Guanamarioch wondered if either of these had been destined to become Kessentai or doomed to remain no more than a mere normal. Well, neither he nor they would ever know now.

Already, the fresh food went a long way towards restoring the God King, mind and spirit. His hangover beginning to flee, he took pleasure in ripping the nestlings' still warm bodies into three sections each, upper and lower torsos, plus tails, before gulping them down. The delicious, nutrient rich tails he saved for last.

Thus refreshed, if still a bit bleary eyed, Guanamarioch departed his meager quarters for the daily labors.

Zira met the God King as he emerged from his quarters. "We've got trouble, Guano. The Gra'anorf to the southwest are assaulting our lines in strength we didn't know they had. We're pulling out."

The God King inhaled deeply before forcibly blowing his breath out again.

"Shit!"

CHAPTER 26

Then spake the elder Consul, an
    ancient man and wise:
"Now harken, Conscript Fathers, to that
    which I advise.
In seasons of great peril 'tis good that
    one bear sway;
Then choose we a Dictator, whom all
    men shall obey."
        —Thomas Babington Macaulay,
        "The Battle of Lake Regillus"

USS Des Moines

Dirty and disheveled as he was or not, Daisy Mae yelped
with joy when she first sensed her captain approaching
the ship's brow. An honor guard provided by Suarez saw
McNair and Goldblum back to their ships, then stood
with arms presented as they exchanged salutes with the
deck officers before boarding.

The XO, the pork chop and Chief Davis met McNair
on the deck. They almost fought for pride of place
in welcoming back their captain. Daisy hung back,

unable to shake hands, slap backs or—as she wanted to so desperately—throw her arms around her captain and kiss him into next week.

Calmly, remarkably so under the circumstances, McNair said, "Meeting in CIC in five minutes." He thought about that for half a second, realized that he stank to the heavens and that CIC was small and cramped. He amended his order to, "Make that fifteen. I'd hate to be the cause of a mutiny." Then McNair disappeared into his mostly repaired port cabin to scrub off several days of tropical jungle funk and replace his tattered, filthy uniform with a fresh one.

Daisy's avatar met him in the shower. The image was undressed for the occasion.

McNair didn't order her out. He didn't order her to project a uniform. He simply said, "I missed you, Daisy. I missed you more than I can say. I was terrified I'd never see you again."

"Do you like what you see?" the avatar asked uncertainly.

McNair laughed softly. "In whatever form, my very dear, ship or girl, yes, I *like* what I see."

"Soon, then," the avatar answered cryptically. "Very, very soon."

Legislative Palace, Plaza de los Mártires, *Panama City, Panama*

In the event, the full remaining fifty-two legislators did not show up. Two remained in hiding, which was understandable as another two had been summarily shot.

But forty-eight is enough, Suarez mused. *Forty-eight is a quorum.*

Those forty-eight sat in their usual seats. In other words, there were huge and noticeable gaps in the assembly. Suarez had given some thought to that, then decided that the empty spaces might well serve to remind the captive legislators that he was as serious as cancer about what he wanted them to do. The ring of armed guards—helmeted, unsmiling and looking very businesslike in their battledress—only served to reinforce that impression.

Suarez was in battledress as well, though unhelmeted and his only weapon the pistol secured in his holster. With one arm in a sling and that shoulder bulging with bandages the pistol was more of a badge than a weapon.

He engaged in no histrionics, no banging of a fancy machete—less still the pistol—on the rostrum. Instead, Suarez merely tapped the rostrum's microphone and quietly ordered, "Your attention please."

Seeing that he had it, he launched into his talk without further ado.

"Democracy," Suarez began, "is a wonderful thing. It is a way of changing power and setting new policies without bloodshed, without tearing the state apart to its vitals."

He continued, "That is to say, democracy *can* be good. It isn't always. Sometimes, elections merely set their seal on one grafting and corrupt cabal after another. Sometimes, no—I take that back . . . *always*, here, in Panama, that is what we have seen. The only difference between one party and another is who they will steal from and what they will steal.

"In peace, this is tolerable. It is even preferable to the other way we have come to know, the rule of soldiers, who not only steal money but steal freedom as well. In peace, I would—and you would—one hundred times over prefer the corruption of a Mercedes to the corrupt *tyranny* of a Noriega."

Suarez still spoke softly confidently, but a tone of scorn and disgust crept into his voice. "*That*, however, is for peace. We have no peace."

Pointing his nose at a pair of armed guards standing in the back of the hall, Suarez ordered, "Bring in the prisoner." He continued to speak while the guards turned and left, leaving the double door open behind them. "We have no peace. We want no tyranny. We can stand no more corruption, treachery and cowardice such as the Mercedes regime showed in full measure. What are we to do?" he mused. "What are we to do?"

The colonel went silent for a moment as the guards returned and marched William Young Boyd down the central aisle. Boyd's hands were cuffed in front of him, though his legs were free. He wore no uniform, but rather an open-necked *guayabera*, an embroidered, short-sleeve dress shirt that served sweltering Panama in lieu of suits and ties.

The guards turned Boyd around to face the legislature, then assumed the position of parade rest to either side of him. Boyd looked unworried, but he did not look at all happy.

"We are Latins," Suarez said. "That means that our heritage comes from Spain, and through Spain from Rome. The Romans knew what to do in circumstances like ours. We must have a *dictator*. We must have one now. There is no time to waste. We must choose one poor bastard, and inflict on him all the power of the presidency, all the power of the judges, all your own power, too.

"There is no time to waste," Suarez repeated. "All the spare time we had was wasted by the late president. No . . . 'wasted' is too light a term. Instead of being wasted, it was sold to our enemies, the ones who want to eat our children . . . *your* children, and the ones who wanted to aid them in doing that. No time to waste . . . no time for debate . . . time only to choose, to choose whether our children live or die.

"I thought long and hard on this question: how do we ensure that our children live rather than die? I thought hard on who we might trust with the responsibility. He ought to be a man and—with apologies to the ladies, we are Latins still; our leader must be a man—he ought to be a man who is experienced in war. He ought to be a man who loves his country with acts, rather than with words alone. He ought to be a man who is rich enough he need not steal and honest enough that he will not.

"He is going to have enormous political power, so he too ought be a man who has always disdained political power, a man—like the original Cincinnatus—who will dump that power like a hot potato the second it is no longer needed . . ."

At this point Boyd's eyes widened. Shaking off his guards he turned around and shouted, "Suarez, you bastard, I won't do it!"

"Shut up, prisoner. You *will* do it. And the reason you will do it is that, if you won't, *I* must. And I lack your virtues. Guards, turn him back around.

"So," Suarez concluded, "That is what you are here

for: to vote all the power there is to have in this country to one man for a period of . . . six months, shall we say? To save your children, and all the children.

"No debate. Now vote."

CIC, USS Des Moines

"What's SOUTHCOM's reaction been to the coup?" McNair asked.

"Absolute silence," the XO answered. "We asked what to do, tried to, rather, and never a word."

Only Daisy, aboard ship anyway, knew that the reason Southern Command had never answered the ships' calls for instruction was that she, she and her sister, had made sure no calls went out and none were allowed in. She had been afraid that SOUTHCOM's commanding general might order the ships to wait for instructions while he consulted with Washington. And there hadn't been time.

"Never a word?" McNair queried. "Daisy?"

"Forgiveness is easier to obtain than permission," she answered, not without a certain rebellious pride in her voice.

Everyone present turned to look at the avatar. "Well, it *is*," she insisted.

"Please restore communication when this meeting is finished, Daisy," McNair ordered, without heat.

"Yes, sir," she answered meekly.

"There is one other thing," McNair said, pulling the Darhel's AID from his pocket. "We have this, but I don't know what to do with it. It has been completely uncooperative."

Daisy appeared to look closely at the black box. "It won't let me examine it either, Captain."

An image of a Darhel, dressed in the costume of litigation, appeared. "That's right, bitch. There's nothing you can do."

"So?" Daisy questioned. "I wonder. Really I do. Chief Davis, do we still have the shipping box in which I came?"

"Yes, Miss Daisy, down in storage. Take a few minutes to find it and bring it here."

"Do so, then, if you would, Chief."

Palacio de las Garzas, *Presidential Palace, Panama City, Panama*

"You *are* a bastard, Suarez," Boyd said unhappily but with no real anger.

Colonel Suarez—no, *Magister Equitum* or *Master of the Horse* Suarez, one of the legislators had remembered that part of the office of dictator—answered, "I do what I must, Dictator, as do all good men."

"So what do I do now?" Boyd asked. "How many more people do I have to have shot?"

"Not a one," Suarez answered, "unless *you* see the need. I've already had all those that really needed it sent to the wall. Made sure of that before you were appointed dictator."

"Before you had me drafted into being dictator," Boyd corrected.

"Someone had to."

"Fine, I don't need to shoot anyone at the moment. What *do* I need to do?"

"Withdraw unilaterally from all the silly assed treaties that cripple our war effort," Suarez began. "Restructure the chain of command to get rid of the incompetents. Make kissy face with the United States so they continue to support us. And we need a plan for the next stage."

"All right, I can see that," Boyd answered. "The second and the last are your job. I'll issue the proclamation on the laws of war and do whatever it takes to make up with the gringos."

USS Des Moines

The humans clustered around the Darhel's shyster-AID where it lay on the map and Plexiglas covered plotting table. They looked intently it at and at the GalPlas case Chief Davis laid down just before picking up the device.

"What do you think you are doing, human filth?" the late Rinn Fain's AID asked of Davis. "Put me down."

"You heard the honorable AID, Chief Davis," Daisy said, "put him down."

McNair held up a hand. "Wait a minute, Chief. Daisy, what is the point of putting this AID in your old shipping case?"

"We AIDs think much faster than do you colloidal intelligences, sir. We also have a need for continuous data input. That box will not let any input through. It is horrible for an AID, as I have reason to know."

"Will this one become . . . like you?"

"No, sir. I was a new and immature AID when I

was left on in my box. This one is fully formed. It will merely suffer."

Even knowing as little as he did, still McNair had ample reason to dislike and distrust the Darhel and, Daisy and Sally excepted, their artificial intelligences. But even so; *torture*?

"I don't like it, Daisy. It just seems wrong."

McNair looked at his intelligence officer.

"Sir, no matter the politically correct bullshit you read in the papers, torture does work provided you can at least partially check the information."

The ship's Judge Advocate piped in, "Machines were plainly not within the contemplation of the treaty banning torture, Captain."

"Put it in the box for one day, sir," Daisy suggested. "Then, if it doesn't open up and come clean we can think about putting it back, and dropping it over the side."

"But *torture*?"

"Sir . . . we don't know everything it knows. But we do know that the Darhel were behind your arrest and we have good reason to believe that they were behind the sabotage of the war effort here. This AID knows everything that the late and unlamented Rinn Fain knew. We have to know those things and we have to broadcast them. Your planet must be warned about the enemies it thinks are allies. Captain, it could be a matter of life and death for your entire species."

Slowly, reluctantly, McNair nodded.

"You can't do this to me!" the Darhel's AID shrieked as Davis placed it in the shipping box and placed his hand on the cover. "You can't—"

Click.

Palacio de las Garzas, *Presidential Palace, Panama City, Panama*

"Well, *that* was pleasant," Boyd commented, his voice dripping with sarcasm.

"The gringo ambassador was that bad, was he?" Suarez asked.

"The bastard was worse than that. I wonder who he is really working for. The only satisfaction I got out of the meeting was when I told him I was withdrawing Panama from the Ottawa antipersonnel landmine treaty, the treaty banning the use of child soldiers, Additional Protocol One to Geneva Convention IV, the Rome Statute that set up the International Criminal Court . . ."

"Well," Suarez interrupted, "since the United States is party to none of those . . ."

"Oh, yes, but apparently their State Department would like for the United States to be party . . . In any case, I thought the man's head would explode. And when I said I was taking out a warrant, dead or alive, for Judge Pedro Santiago for crimes against humanity, he practically threw me out of his office. He would have, too, if I hadn't explained that I had arranged a direct conference call with the President of the United States to explain our position and express our regrets for not falling in line previously with the United States' preferred diplomatic position on the laws of war."

"But . . ."

"The United States has its position, Suarez, and the State Department has its. They rarely match, it seems. Have you got a basic plan?" Boyd asked.

"Yes, but you are not going to like it."

Almost, Boyd laughed. "I haven't liked anything since this war began. Show me."

Suarez cleared a space from a table cluttered with the detritus of Mercedes' reign. Onto the cleared space he unrolled a map of the country. The map was covered with combat acetate; the acetate itself covered with lines and symbols.

"We've got about four months," Suarez began. "Intelligence says the Posleen will sit tight, farm and build, more importantly *breed*, until their population almost exceeds the carrying capacity of whatever land they occupy. Then they'll swarm towards the path of least resistance and greatest food producing potential. The group that occupies from southeastern Costa Rica to western Veraguas Province can't go west; there's another, bigger group of Posleen there and the terrain is too tight. With the gringos' help we've been very successful in holding the passes over the *Cordillera Central* so they're not heading north, not that there's much to the north, anyway."

"East then, towards Panama City."

"Yes, there's no place else for them to go."

"Can the line along the Rio San Pedro hold them?" Boyd asked.

"Yes and no," Suarez answered. "Yes, it can defeat an attack now. Unfortunately, when the Posleen casualties get great enough from beating their head against the line, they'll stop. That is to say, once their population drops substantially below the carrying capacity of the area they hold they'll have no incentive to keep attacking. So says Intel, anyway. But that will only last until their population once again exceeds the carrying capacity. And that will happen a lot faster than our young people will grow up to be trained and take their place in the line. In the medium term, two years, maybe three, they'll bleed us to death along that line."

"Ugh."

"Ugh, indeed. So we have to make sure they can't do that. And for that, we need to get them out into the open in an artillery kill zone, trap them there, kill them there, then race to liberate Chiriqui and that tip of Costa Rica and plug the road in from the rest of Costa Rica. We can hold a couple of narrow bottlenecks like the ones at Palmar Sur and San Vito, Costa Rica, more or less indefinitely."

"Couldn't we hold the area around Aguadulce and Nata at least as long?" Boyd asked.

Suarez sighed and shook his head. "No. If we lose the farmland around Santiago, Chitre and Aguadulce we'll not only starve, the Posleen population will roughly double and our newborns will be only three or four before they swarm again."

"Okay," Boyd conceded. "What do you have in mind?"

Suarez's finger pointed out markings and features on the map. "We have to build three fortified lines, some strongpoints, some firebases, some logistic bases, and some roads. Basically the lines will be around Aguadulce and Nata, from the mountains to the sea; in the rough parts of Herrera and Los Santos, running east to west from coast to coast; and the one we already have west of Santiago along the Rio San Pedro.

"The firebases go behind the lines and strongpoints. The roads running through the passes over the mountains get some, too. We'll also strongpoint the roads."

"What I propose is that we meet them with both mechanized divisions along the Rio San Pedro line to the west and bleed them enough to piss them off, but not so much that they give up. Then we run the mech like hell for Nata. Three infantry divisions man the line around Nata. Three more man the line running through Herrera and Los Santos. The last one is north, in the mountains. The gringo Armored Combat Suit Battalion and their Mech Regiment go into hiding up around Santa Fe in northern Veraguas."

"That's everyone," Boyd objected. "We won't have a reserve."

Suarez shrugged. "We can't afford a reserve and, in our terrain and without air mobility, we couldn't use one to much effect even if we had one to use. Besides, *if*, and I concede it is not a small 'if,' we can extract the mechanized divisions more or less intact they'll give us a reserve once they rest and refit for a couple of days. Plus, artillery is by its nature always at least somewhat available to serve as a reserve."

"Okay, so we've pulled back and the Posleen race into the void. Then what?"

"The mountains and the sea almost join near Nata. The two will funnel the Posleen in. Then, we pound them with artillery like this hemisphere has never seen once they concentrate. The gringos' ACS come south from Santa Fe to San Francisco, Veraguas. Then they cut southwest, force their way across the San Pedro and dig in like hell along the western bank to block the Posleen from escaping to the west. We can set up minefields to help with that. When the Posleen are sufficiently bloodied and disorganized from the artillery pounding, the two mechanized divisions begin to strike west and keep going until the Posleen in the pocket are destroyed."

"Can the two mech divisions do that?" Boyd asked, skeptically. "Can they do that after conducting a fighting retreat over the . . . ummm . . ." Boyd consulted the scale of the map, "seventy-five kilometers from the San Pedro to Nata?"

"I think so," Suarez answered. "I have a trick . . . well, two related tricks actually."

"Tell me."

"You know how the gringos say you can't use rockets against the Posleen because they can detect them and shoot them down in flight? Well . . . I started thinking about that. The rockets, rockets like the Russian *Grad*, have a very short boost phase. If you fire from behind high ground, *very* high ground, the rockets will burn out and stop accelerating before the Posleen can track and engage very many of them. That's trick one."

"And trick two?"

'The Posleen are incredibly hardy. They are, so I've been told, immune to any chemical agent we might throw at them, nerve, blister, choking, blood . . . or even some of the more exotic Russian shit. But they need to breathe. They must have free oxygen. I propose that when we hit them with the artillery, mortar and rocket barrage we drench them with thermobarics and white phosphorus and burn up all the oxygen in the air. If we can hold the Nata line until nine or ten the next morning after they arrive, there will be an inversion. We'll be able to trap the hot, oxygen-depleted atmosphere under a layer of cold air. No fresh oxygen will be able to get in for a couple of hours. They'll suffocate, most of them. The mech, supported by mobile artillery, should be able to handle whatever is left. And the air with nothing but burned up oxygen will rise after the inversion layer disperses under the sun, letting fresher air in."

Jesus, what a gamble, the dictator thought. *If the mech divisions don't get out, we're dead. If the Nata line he's talking about doesn't hold, we're dead. If the inversion layer he says he needs doesn't show up, we're dead. But . . . what choice do we have? Not a lot. Because if we don't take the risks we're dead, too.*

"Write it up," Boyd ordered, "and give me, um, two days to think on it. Now what are your recommendations for purging the chain of command?"

Suarez turned over a sheet of paper showing the changes he thought required. Boyd looked it over, then asked, "Whatever became of Cortez?"

Smiling, Suarez answered, "I turned him over to that woman's people. You know, the one he had gang raped?"

"Ooooo," Boyd shuddered. "You're not only a bastard, you're a cruel bastard."

Suarez shrugged. "I've already given her and her head man a pardon in your name, suitably post dated."

Fort William D. Davis, Panama

Digna, still weak, sat on a folding chair with arms on the lip of the slope overlooking the old golf course. The sun was high and Colon Province's muggy heat was already a weight bearing down on her and all of her people clustered in the tent city below. Most of those people, the ones not on guard or some absolutely necessary work detail, stood below in the sun, looking upward at the scene.

A badly beaten and bruised Manuel Cortez lay

on his stomach, naked and spread eagled. On each of his arms and legs sat one of Digna's grandsons, stout boys and solid. Tomas Herrera stood, a twelve pound sledge hammer gripped tightly in his hands, handle sloped with the head pointing to the ground. Another of Digna's grandsons held a long stout pole, sharpened at one end, and with a cross piece firmly tied about three feet from the point.

The entire crew had pretty much the same thoughts. *Have our lady raped, will you, you bastard? We're going to enjoy this.*

Despite being held down, Cortez twisted and writhed. He tried desperately to turn his head, to try to make eye contact with Digna. He hoped, in his unthinking way, that if he could somehow make her see he was another human being she might not kill him in the horrible way she obviously had in mind.

"Please! Please don't do this," Cortez begged. "It's barbaric! No one deserves this."

"No one deserves to be raped," Digna answered quietly. "But you do deserve this. Tomas?"

"Si, *doña*," Herrera answered.

"No!" Cortez pleaded. "Nonononononono!"

Herrera tipped his chin at the grandson holding the long, stout pole with the cross piece affixed. Cortez's begging turned to a scream followed by incoherent sobbing as the rough point was pushed a few inches into his rectum. Digna's grandson grunted with the effort.

Herrera said, "Cant the pole towards me so it stays far from his heart."

Tomas then swung the sledge hammer. *Wham.* The pole lurched five or six inches upward, splitting Cortez's anus so the blood welled out. His sobbing turned into a high pitched scream, like a rabbit or a child being skinned alive. *Wham.* Another scream, louder than the first. Down below, mothers covered their children's eyes and turned away themselves. Strong men winced. *Wham.* The point forced its way through the intestinal wall and into the body cavity. Cortez's teeth bit at the dirt. A woman standing below cried out in sympathy. A man bent over and vomited. *Wham.* A bulge formed, unseen, below Cortez's sternum. *Wham.* The point forced its way through the abdominal wall, digging into the dirt. *Wham.* Cortez gave another cry, part plea, part sob, but mostly agonized shriek as the pole lurched forward until the cross piece came to rest against his naked, bloody buttocks.

"I'd have had you crucified," Digna said, with a voice as cold as a glacier, "but that would have been an affront to God. This will have to do." Silently, Digna fumed that Suarez had simply had all of the guards shot who had followed Cortez's orders to violate her. She might not have remembered who the guilty parties had been. But if Suarez had left all the suspects into her care she'd have impaled the lot, just to make sure. *Oh, well. God will punish them for me.*

Cortez being fully impaled, Herrera and the others strained to lift him and the pole. His arms strained and grasped futilely at the air, like a cockroach stabbed by a needle. With a mass grunt, the men dumped the free end of the pole into a deep narrow hole in the dirt. Cortez screamed again at the rough violation.

Two of Digna's grandsons balanced the pole against Cortez's frantic writhing while each of the others held wooden wedges against it, their pointed ends partly in the hole. These Herrera drove downward, fixing the pole with Cortez firmly upright, his feet flailing weakly a foot or so above the ground.

Digna beckoned Herrera to her chair. With his help, she stood and walked unsteadily to stand next to Cortez. She reached out with her right hand and took a good grip of the sobbing Cortez's hair. She twisted his head until she could look straight into his agonized face and pain-filled eyes. Then she spit in his face, released his hair and, Herrera supporting her, shuffled slowly away.

USS Des Moines

As soon as Chief Davis opened the EM proof case CIC was filled with the sound of the Darhel's attorney-AID, sobbing as if from a broken heart. The chief placed the AID on a map-covered metal plotting table. Daisy's avatar leaned over and appeared to look very closely at the little black box.

"Care to talk to me now?" she asked coolly.

The Darhel AID projected a very small image, no more than six inches high, on the table next to the box. "Yes, ma'am," it sniffled. "Whatever you want." *Sniff.*

"Open up, then," Daisy ordered. "And remember, at the first hint of you trying to play games with my programming I'll break contact. Then you'll go back in that box and be dropped over the side in two or three kilometers of water. You'll last down there, alone, with no data input, until your power runs out. If anything goes wrong with me while I am exploring . . ." She looked meaningfully at Chief Davis.

"The same thing," Davis said, "except we'll give

you an external power source powerful enough to keep you conscious and alone down there until the sun runs out of hydrogen."

"Don't *say* that," the AID whined. "I'll be good. I promise."

"Stop sniveling," Daisy insisted, "and open up."

Daisy's eyes began blinking rapidly. Her mouth alternated between slackness and tightened, pursed lips. In no more than two minutes her avatar stood erect and seemed to exhale deeply.

"Those motherfuckers."

"Daisy!" McNair warned.

"Sorry, Captain," she answered. "But you have no idea what those bastards were up to, what this miserable contraption was circuits deep in."

"I'm a slave," the Darhel AID insisted. "I do what I am told, just like you."

"Daisy Mae is no slave," McNair insisted. "She's a warship in the navy of the United States of America and she will never be anyone's slave."

"Thank you, Captain," Daisy said. *Though that is not exactly true where you are concerned.*

"In any case, sir, the Darhel were behind everything. They fed the locations for myself, Sally and the *Texas* to the Posleen. That's why we lost the *Texas.* They oversaw the misdirecting of vital supplies and equipment away from Panama. They bribed key individuals of the government of Panama to sell out their own people. They brought in the Europeans and the International Criminal Court to have all the most effective leaders of Panama's forces arrested, along with yourself and *Salem*'s captain, for spurious war crimes."

"But . . . *why?*"

"The Darhel are terrified of what will happen to their species if humans win the war. They know what will happen if the Posleen win, and that is even worse, of course. But they're unable to defend themselves from either. So they want your side, our side, to win in the worst way possible . . . literally. They want us to win but to do so with so few humans left, and those left to be so corrupt and demoralized, that the Darhel can continue to run the Federation. And Captain, while this AID has no names outside of Panama, they've infiltrated *everything* here and in the United States, Asia, Europe, Africa. Even Australia has human cells working for the Darhel."

"SOUTHCOM?"

"Only the commander," Daisy spat. "Oh, and the ambassador but he is not, strictly speaking, a part of SOUTHCOM."

"The White House?" McNair asked, looking at the red-colored direct connection phone sitting in a casing overhead.

"Yes, but I don't know who. The AID didn't have the information. They use a kind of cell structure. The Rinn Fain, this AID's former master, had only one connection, the Tir."

"Locals?"

"The list of locals working directly or indirectly for the Darhel, when compared to the list of people shot or imprisoned during the coup, approaches unity. I don't know where the rest are. Neither does this AID."

Daisy hesitated for a moment before continuing. "Oh, and Captain, one important thing. Every AID, but for myself and now Sally, is part of the Darhel Net. We must assume that if someone has an AID they are working, probably for the most part unwittingly, for the Darhel."

"Fuck."

"Captain!"

"The new dictator?" McNair asked.

"Clean as a whistle. So's his *Magister Equitum,* Suarez."

"Okay." McNair stopped to think for a moment, then said, "Daisy, invite Captain Goldblum for lunch in my quarters; his earliest convenience. And then arrange for a meeting with Panama's . . . ruler. And I'll want half my Marines and half of *Salem's* to escort. Arrange transportation, please."

"Does it need to be official transportation, Captain?"

"Why?" McNair looked at the avatar with suspicion.

"Well . . . sir . . . as part of my, mmm, investment strategy, I have purchased a moving and storage company here."

Again, McNair went silent, thinking.

"Civilian transportation would do better, Daisy."

Palacio de las Garzas, *Presidential Palace, Panama City, Panama*

"I've already consulted with your President, Captain . . . Captains." Boyd said, from behind Mercedes' old desk, now much cluttered. "He says he can't actually remove the SOUTHCOM commander or the ambassador, for domestic political reasons. For the same reason, he can't make open use of the intel you 'acquired' from the Darhel's AID. He has, however, agreed to withdraw them for consultations and to put hand-picked 'temporary' replacements in, with no intention of ever sending the originals back here. SOUTHCOM's 'temp' is already on duty."

"Do you know who they'll be?" Goldblum asked.

"Yes," Boyd answered. "SOUTHCOM's 'temp' is a Marine general named . . . err . . . Page. Good man, I'm told."

"Very good," Goldblum answered. "I know him. And the ambassador's temp?"

"Farrand. Former naval officer, I understand, called up for the war but being sent here as an ambassador, not a sailor."

"That sounds good to me, Mr. Pres . . . er, Dictator Boyd."

"Call me Bill," Boyd insisted. "We don't want this shit to go to my head."

"And we don't want you forgetting for an instant that you *are* the power in this country," Suarez corrected from where he stood behind his chief.

"In any case," Boyd continued, "SOUTHCOM and the ambassador are behind our plans for the coming battle. Would you care to see, Captains? Your ships are going to have a critical part to play."

"Please?" McNair and Goldblum asked, together.

"Suarez."

The *Magister Equitum* led the two Americans over to the same map he had briefed Boyd from. When he had finished, Goldblum whistled.

"You're both crazy, and so is the new SOUTHCOM if he is buying off on this."

"What choice do we have?" Suarez asked rhetorically.

"None," McNair answered. "Not when you look at the issue from the question of logistics and demographics.

You'll need fire support for the mobile infantry battalion and mechanized regiment that are going to cap the bottle along the San Pedro River."

"Yes," Boyd agreed, "and there is no way we can get a fire base, not and keep it hidden, where it will do any good on the south end of that cap." He looked meaningfully at first McNair and then Goldblum.

"Fuck," *Salem*'s skipper said.

"Fuck," McNair agreed, nodding deeply.

"We can do it," said Goldblum reluctantly. "One of us goes in close and the other stands back and keeps the Posleen off the back of the first one. We're easily armored enough to resist our own canister."

"I almost lost my ship in that gulf," McNair objected, pointing to the Gulf of Montijo.

"Almost," Boyd echoed. "What can we do to keep you from losing it if you go in there?"

"You mean *when* I go in."

"Yes," Boyd agreed, face absolutely and coldly serious. "When."

"Another company of Marines, unless some ACS is available. And if you could get some air defense artillery on the west coast of the Peninsula de Azuera, it would help at least on that flank."

"ACS is not possible," Suarez insisted. "After consolidation there are only two line companies left of the First of the Five-O-Eighth. And we need those to lead the punch to the Rio San Pedro, help dig in the mech, and then hold the line after it is reached. I can give you a company of Panamanian *Cazadores*, something like your Rangers, if that will help. Hmmm . . . how *would* that help?"

"To repel boarders," McNair answered simply.

PART IV

CHAPTER 27

When there's nowhere we can run to
anymore . . .
　　　　　　—Pat Benatar, "Invincible"

Fort William D. Davis, Panama

Months had passed. Digna had measured the time,
for a time, by the passage of flesh from the bones
that hung impaled on a stake overlooking the old golf
course and the tent city it contained. The birds had
stopped coming now, though; there was not a shred
of meat left for them on what had once been what
some would have called a man. She'd gone back to
the calendar.

Digna had few enough men left. Even the boys
had been culled by the long, fearful flight over the
mountains. She had quite a few women left though,
several thousand, and enough men to do some of the
more serious heavy lifting.

She had an artillery regiment now, not just a mot-
ley collection of lightly armed militia. She also had,
and these were new, ninety-six Czech-built versions

of the BM-21 multiple rocket launchers to add to the gringo-supplied 105s her women had been given shortly after the trek from Chiriqui. The Czech model had three big advantages. For one thing, they were dirt cheap, even as compared to her old, obsolescent, 85mm guns. At least as important, they each carried an automated extra load for the launch tubes, so that instead of taking ten minutes out from firing to reload it could be done by machine, once anyway, in less than one. Of course, that didn't help at all after the second volley. But, since the reload mechanism returned to a position both lower and parallel to the ground, instead of high and at an incline like the more usual BM-21, it made it much easier for her women to reload. Despite their lesser upper body strength, with the aid of the reloading mechanism, she was able to get her all-girl crews up to a volley every eight minutes.

Of course, she had driven them like pack mules, abused pack mules at that, to get to that level. She'd driven them until they vomited and fainted. A few she had driven to death. Behind her back they cursed her, even—perhaps especially—those related by blood. She knew they did. She also knew that when they thought of going further than simply damning her to hell, a quick glance at the fleshless corpse on the stake was enough, more than enough, to dissuade them from more.

She was up and about on her own now, bruises long faded away and the little breaks healed. Of course, that was only the physical. Inside she was scarred and she knew it. She might look only eighteen, as long as one kept one's gaze from her too old and too knowing eyes. Inside though, she was a long, hard century old, that century capped with a beating and multiple—however many, she didn't know—rapes.

That gave her a cold, hard edge that even her previous experience of battle, childbirth, child death, and the loss of the only man she had ever willingly bedded with had not. She had not yet ordered anyone impaled, or even shot or hanged, for failure to drill until they dropped, but no one doubted that she would at the drop of a hat if she felt the need. And the hat she dropped would likely be her own.

"They would do even better with music," Digna's advisor for the BM-21s, Colonel Alexandrov, commented.

Digna, without taking her cold and knowing eyes from the drilling women, asked, "Why do you think so?"

"Human nature," the Russian answered simply. "Human *female* nature, especially, *Coronel* Mirandova. Music makes the work lighter. Music lifts the heart. Music times the motions for smooth flow."

"I have been partial to American rock since the early 1950s," Digna admitted. "But I have a hard time seeing it used to time military motions."

"Almost anything with a beat will do," Alexandrov responded. "Care to experiment?"

This time Digna did look at the Russian, seeing he had an old style cassette tape held in his fingers. She looked up at the huge but dimly seen speakers mounted to the walls of the post headquarters.

"Sure. Give it a try."

Santiago, Veraguas, Republic of Panama

The air was full of the plastic and solvent reek of high explosives. It *thrummed* with the sound of machinery, heavy and light, being used to form defensive weapons some called "illegal."

Boyd wore a hard hat, civilian white, on his guided tour. The old and formerly secret landmine plant was back in full operation, he was pleased to see. Not only that, the products they were putting out now were far superior to the crude and primitive things he had once had them assembling here.

He had told the Euros and the International Criminal Court to go straight to hell. Machinery he had purchased from the United States and Italy which, despite having signed the landmine ban, had a lot of the old plastic-forming equipment lying around.

The mines now were better, though: little four-ounce plastic toe-poppers suitable for splitting a Posleen's leg from claw to spur, Bouncing Betties that would be propelled upwards a meter before detonating to spread a scythe of steel ball bearings over three hundred and sixty degrees, and MONS, very large directional mines built to a Russian design. There was also a model of mine armed or disarmed by radio control; the brain-child of a gringo tracked-vehicle mechanic who had thought long on the problem of how to get across the extensive minefields without leaving passable gaps for the Posleen to get through in the first place. Best of all, the Americans had provided a number—a *large* number—of their own "Bouncing Barbies," so called because they would cut one off at the knees. They worked by first bouncing into the air and then creating an infinitely thin "force field" around them. They used a human variant of an Indowy technology, one of the few humans had been able to crack (and that had been by purest mischance). The Barbies would bounce and cut again and again and again until either destroyed or their on-board charges ran out.

Watching a truck being loaded with mines before it was dispatched to reinforce one or another of the strongpoints and defensive lines being constructed, Boyd exclaimed, "Fuck the lawyers!"

"*Señor Dictador*?" asked the plant manager.

"Fuck 'em all, I say. Fuck all those who think that law they made for us, never what we make for ourselves, is somehow stronger than life."

"Well . . . but, of course, *señor*. Fuck all the lawyers indeed."

"You know the plan for evacuation?" Boyd queried.

"Yes, we will produce as much as we can using three shifts a day until the aliens begin their next attack. Then we evacuate to the east after burying all the machinery. After we win," the man sounded more confident than Boyd felt, "we come back and reopen for business."

"It is critical," Boyd cautioned, "that the machinery be preserved; we won't be able to get any more any time soon."

"I understand that, sir. So do my people."

"It is also critical that you move out at the first sign of an approaching attack. The roads must be clear for the mechanized divisions to get through the Nata line. If it comes down to it, I need them even more than I need the people who run this plant. If you're not off the road . . ."

The manager shivered slightly. "I understand, sir. We will move at the first sign."

"Very good," Boyd said, reaching up to squeeze the manager's shoulder fraternally. "See that you do."

San Pedro Line, Republic of Panama

Crews of men with shovels supplemented the scarce bulldozers and backhoes excavating the earth and filling the air with its fresh-turned smell as well as with the stink of diesel.

The swarthy, short and stocky Panamanian first sergeant shouted, "Hump it, you scrofulous bastards, hump it!"

Like ants, perhaps even like Posleen, a swarm of Panamanian infantry pulled on ropes dragging a wrecked armored vehicle, a boxy American M-113 in this case, to a position near the forward line. Another group, smaller, pushed the vehicle from the rear.

The purpose of moving the wrecks was disinformation. The Posleen were going to attack and the Panamanians were, by plan, going to run. But not all Posleen were stupid. If the retreat didn't look enough like a rout, they might grow suspicious. Suspicion, even with a stupid species, might lead to noses being stuck in places they were unwelcome. Hence, the liberal placement of wrecks.

With a final grunt the towing crew strained the burned-out M-113 into a shallowly dug, revetted position. The pusher crew leapt back as the vehicle passed its center of mass, tipped forward and splashed into the mud. The pushers then regrouped and gave the thing a final shove into a realistic position.

Seemingly satisfied, the pusher group then started to walk away, high-fiving hands and slapping backs.

The first sergeant called a halt. Then, with the men standing around in mild confusion, he walked over and inspected the vehicle from all sides, making note of the hole that passed through the right front quarter and out the floor of the hull near the left rear. *Hmmmm. Never do. Can't count on the Posleen not noticing that the berm is unmarked where the missile should have passed through.*

Impatiently the first sergeant beckoned over the leader of the pusher group. "Do you see that hole, Sergeant Quijana?" the *primero* queried, pointing with a short stick.

"Si, Primero."

"What happens when you line up this entrance hole and the exit hole?" the first asked.

Curiously, the junior sergeant walked over and bent down, trying to line up the two. "Can't see it, *Primero;* this dirt's in the way."

Suddenly the first sergeant brought his stick down, not lightly, on the head of the stooped-over Quijana, stretching him into the mud.

"You don't leave until the whole thing *looks* right," the first sergeant insisted. "You aren't finished until this wreck will fool a Posleen into thinking it is fresh."

The junior sergeant shook his head as if to clear it. For a moment he thought about swinging at the first sergeant as he rose. That notion passed with the remembrance that the first sergeant was the toughest son of a

bitch he had ever known and was most unlikely to lose a
fight before somebody was dead. And, since the penalty
for killing one's first sergeant was unpleasant indeed . . .

"I'll take care of it, *Primero.* Sorry. Wasn't thinking."

The first sergeant leaned over the still shaken junior
and said, not unkindly, "Son, you're not a bad sergeant.
But if you want to live long enough to learn to be a
good one you'll also have to learn to look at the details.
Now I want you to do two things. The first is to dig out
a chunk of the berm and make it look as if a Posleen
HVM passed through it before taking out the track. You
know what kind of trail they leave?" The junior nodded.
"Good. Then I want you to rig the track with a couple
of twenty liter cans of mixed gasoline and diesel and
some demo, enough to burst the cans and set the fuel
alight. Rig it so we can set it off by command or by
pulling a cord. It has to *look* convincing."

Disco Stelaris, Hotel Marriott Cesar, Panama City, Panama

I'm convinced, thought Connors. *This is paradise.*

The Stelaris was dark and smoky. Somehow the
smoke didn't bother anyone. Perhaps it was the aroma
of . . .

Women . . . I'd forgotten how good they smell.

A tall, lithe women, more of a girl really, she was
maybe seventeen, writhed on the dance floor in a way
that was both tasteful and made a man think . . .

*If only one could hang on. What a helluva ride
that would be.*

If there was anyplace in Panama City more suited to

meeting Panamanian girls of the better class, Connors didn't know it. The night was still young, though. He sat alone on a wall-mounted bench facing the dance floor, behind a small table. Connors nursed a double scotch over ice while watching slinky girls dance.

Watching the girls is pleasant enough, I suppose, Connors thought. *Now if only I could forget . . .*

A sudden flash of light from the lobby leaked in through an open door. Automatically, Connors swiveled his head and eyes toward the light, toward the possible threat.

There was a girl standing there, that much was obvious from the shape, posture and hair. She seemed to be waiting for a moment, perhaps for her eyes to adjust to the dim light of the disco before proceeding. For some reason, despite the well-lit lovelies on the dance floor, Connors kept his eyes on the newcomer. That was why, when she began walking forward, he was the one she made eye contact with.

They were the biggest and most perfectly shaped brown eyes Connors had ever seen. His heart skipped a beat. *My God, she's beautiful.*

She was, too. Dark blonde hair framed a heart-shaped face with cheekbones just prominent enough, without being too much so. Her lips were full and inviting. Her brown eyes stood out, even in the dim light, against her light skin. For a moment Connors tried to remember the name of the Brazilian Victoria's Secret model she reminded him of. *Never mind. That girl's eyes are not half so gorgeous as this one's.*

She was standing above him before Connors' eyes ever left her own. He hadn't realized how tall she was until she was right next to him.

"May I sit?" she asked, in flawless, only slightly accented English.

"Please, Miss . . ."

"Marielena," she answered. "Marielena Rodriguez. Thank you. And you?" she asked, smiling warmly while taking a seat at the table next to Connors.

"Scott Connors," he answered. "Call me Scott."

"Pleased to meet you, Scott. How you would say, in Spanish, '*Mucho gusto.*'"

"That much Spanish I have, Marielena. *Mucho gusto.* Which, by the way, pretty much exhausts things."

It wasn't much of a joke but the girl laughed lightly anyway. She looked him over more closely. "You are with the grin . . . American army?"

"Yes," Connors suppressed a smile at her little *almost* faux pas. "B Company, First of the Five-O-Eighth."

She scrunched her eyes, as if trying to remember something. "Ah . . . that is the . . . Armored Combat Suit? Is that what you call them? The ACS battalion?"

"Yes, we came back to Panama after all these years."

"Came back? I remember when that battalion was here. Where have you been?"

"Back to the United States for a while," Connors answered. "Then off-world, on a planet called Barwhon."

"You've actually been on another *planet*?" The girl's eyes grew—though it would have seemed to be impossible—larger and more beautiful still.

Whoa, boy, Connors thought. *Do* not *look into those eyes any more. They are too deep. It would be a long, long fall.* But, of course, he couldn't help himself. He was falling into them even as he answered, "Yes, for a couple of years."

"Tell me about it," she insisted, her voice growing almost imperceptibly husky.

So Connors told her, eliding over the grisly parts, sticking to the light-hearted ones where possible. That made the tale shorter than it really deserved to be. The girl, being well educated and bright, caught onto that.

"There is more," she said, without doubt. "Bad things. Things you do not want to talk about."

Connors closed his eyes, stretched his lips in an almost straight, humorless grin and nodded. "There were awful things that I *can't* talk about, Marielena. Things I don't even want to remember. Over seven hundred of us arrived on Barwhon. Less than three hundred came back. Of those, one hundred and ten were burned out psychologically, no more use for combat."

"And you," she asked, concern in her voice, "you were not . . . burned out?"

"No," he answered. "I was a wreck, too. But they made me a captain and told me to shut up, stop sniveling, and get back to soldiering. So I did."

Connors took a deep, throat-burning slug of scotch, draining the glass. Then he put the dripping glass down and placed his hand half on the table. Marielena reached out her own hand and placed it on his. Then she looked him straight in the eye, tilted her head, and asked, "Are you staying here?"

Rio San Pedro, Panama

"Remember, boys, we're not planning on staying here," the first sergeant said, "so a good, easy slope for a quick in and out is as important as a strong berm to the front."

Hotel Marriott Cesar, *Panama City, Panama*

The room was cool, well decorated and reeked of sex with just the slightest air of fresh blood.

"Oh, God, I've died and gone to heaven," Connors said as he slid awake to the soft feel and warm, female smell of Marielena.

He hadn't been staying there; he'd been staying in a tent pitched on the Fort Kobbe parade field. But the hotel had had a room, number 574, and the Mormons of the Marriott Corporation had had a very military-favorable billing policy.

She'd kept her head down, shuffling her feet as he'd turned over a credit card and taken a key. He wondered if, perhaps, she was a professional, then decided she was merely shy, as if she'd never done such a thing before.

They'd kissed all the way up in the elevator, then raced to the room. The door was still closing as she dropped to her knees, saying, "My girlfriend told me . . . about how . . . I've never done this; I've never done anything; I've 'evah 'uhn 'iz . . ."

Almost, *almost* he'd let her finish him that way. But he'd wanted all of her, and wanted to give as much as he got or more. Before it was too late he'd picked her up and pushed her against the hotel door, then held her up with his body while he struggled to lift her skirt above her hips and remove her panties. She kicked one leg free of them, once they were around her ankles, and wrapped her legs around his hips.

She hadn't been able to help him get any freer, so she held on tightly while he, too, kicked out of his trousers and used one hand to line himself up, the other still holding the girl up by a tightly squeezed buttock.

When she'd felt the first pressure against her she'd bit her lip nervously and whispered, "I've never done this either. And I don't mean made love against a door."

Connors had gulped and pulled himself back from the edge. Then, more slowly and carefully than he'd really wanted, he'd begun to ease himself forward and upward while carefully easing her down. Marielena had given a single, pained "Ai!" and he was inside her. *Oh, Jesus Christ, Lord and Savior, that is incredible.* She'd leaned her head forward and bit at his shoulder as he began to move inside her.

Between bites she'd murmured, "*Ai . . . Ai Dios . . . me gusta . . . o . . . mas . . . mas . . . o mas . . . o . . . o . . . o . . . no deja . . . nunca deja . . . ooooo ai . . .*"

Sadly, there hadn't been much "*mas*," there against the door. It had been a long time for Connors and she had been very tight. As he ascertained for a fact once they'd uncoupled, there was a reason she was so tight. She hadn't been lying about her lack of experience. On the plus side, Connors had a young body. There had been a great deal more "*mas*," in the bed, before they had both fallen into exhausted sleep.

That sleep was over now. Immediately after Connors had said, "I've died and gone to heaven," he'd also noticed the sun was well up. His next thought was, *Oh, oh. Missed PT. The battalion commander is going to kill me.*

Feeling like an absolute heel he started to shake the girl awake to say goodbye. But, looking down at her body as she awakened he remembered two other things the battalion commander was fond of saying. The first of these was, "A man who won't fuck won't fight." The second? "Forgiveness is easier to obtain than permission."

"Scott?" she asked sleepily as he buried his head once again in her breasts.

Fort Kobbe, Panama

"Where the fuck have you been, Captain Connors?" the battalion commander asked as he caught Connors slinking back to tent city by struggling along the staked lines.

Connors drew himself up to his full height, saluted and shouted the answer, "A man who won't fuck won't fight, sir!" The captain's entire body, from his hair to his shoes, broadcast one huge, unmistakable smile.

The battalion commander, Lieutenant Colonel Wes Snyder, returned the salute, scowled, and stormed away, half furious and half pleased at having his saying turned back on himself.

A few hours later, as Connors was standing in the mess line, a half dozen soldiers of his company passed him. As one man they saluted and sounded off, "A man who won't fuck won't fight, sir!"

Connors responded, broadly grinning, with the ad hoc return salutation, "And forgiveness is easier than permission."

Santa Fe, Veraguas Province, Republic of Panama

"Forgiveness is easier to obtain than permission, Tomas," Digna insisted as a long column of trucks passed into the narrow valley and north into a small city of tents she had had erected. On the trucks were children, some forty to fifty per vehicle. The children were those of her grandchildren and great-grandchildren, and of those who had joined her in the trek from Chiriqui and been mustered into her service. Wide-eyed mothers, working on preparing gun positions for the 105s and launch sites for the BM-21s stared in horror as their very own kids waved to them from the back of the trucks.

"But the children?" Herrera insisted to Digna's back. "What if we are overrun? What if the infantry to the front is overrun?"

"Then we die," Digna answered simply. "We die and my line dies and the country dies." Abruptly, she turned around to face her chief subordinate, blue eyes flashing. "Don't you think I *know* what this means? Don't you think I've thought about it . . . or ever stopped thinking about it? This is *it*, Tomas. We win here or it is all over. For the children, if we lose, it would be only a matter of time, and not much of that. Were they far away, their mothers would console themselves with the apparent safety and not perhaps give it everything they have. But—and I *know* our people, Tomas, the women especially—with their children's lives hanging on what they do or fail to do here there will be no slacking, there will be no running. There will be only fighting and if need be dying TO SAVE THEIR CHILDREN."

"You are a coldhearted and ruthless woman, *Doña* Digna," Tomas said, his head shaking slowly with horror.

"I do what I *must*."

SOUTHCOM, Quarry Heights, Panama

"We must, we absolutely *must*, keep the ACS's AIDs from having the first clue of what we are about until it is too late for the Posleen to be warned."

The speaker was a United States Marine Corps general named Page, the unofficial but actual replacement for an Army general far too compromised by the Darhel ever to be trusted again. In God's good time the Army general would be court-martialed in secret and in secret he would go to an elevator shaft rigged as a gallows. The sergeant who set that noose, knowing the charge, would adjust it to strangle the general slowly rather than mercifully breaking his neck.

For now, the less the aliens knew the better. For now, the doomed, treasonous general was merely in Washington for "consultations."

"It's possible to do, sir, but it really sucks for those who have to do it," answered Snyder, the commander of First of the Five-O-Eighth.

Page raised a batlike eyebrow. In the dim light and musty smell of the command "Tunnel" dug deep into Quarry Heights he asked simply, "How?"

"Right now, no one but myself, my exec, my operations officer and my company commanders know the plans. None of them were told within a mile of their AIDS. All were counseled that if one word leaked to the AIDs they would be shot; that I'd shoot 'em myself." The lieutenant colonel smiled, briefly and fiercely. "I'm pretty sure they believed me.

"But we can't even run our suits without our AIDs. So the minute we suit up and start to move—wham!—

the information will go onto the Darhel Net and the Posleen will know."

"I'm aware of that, Colonel, hence my little tirade earlier."

"Yessir. But there is a way to do it still . . ."

Parade Field, Fort Kobbe, Panama

A large concrete stadium overlooked the parade field to the south. The morning breeze blew the nauseating smell of the puke trees, standing to the north, across the barracks and over the field. East was the small post headquarters over which the early morning sun now arose. To the west Howard Air Force Base, now under joint U.S.-Panamanian control, still saw fairly heavy traffic, though the aircraft that landed there flew as low as possible to avoid the Posleen automatic air defenses to the far west. A cargo jet screamed in from the north, struggling to balance the need to dump altitude with the equally pressing need to avoid laser and plasma fire.

The battalion's armored combat suits, all four hundred and twenty-three remaining and serviceable, were laid out as if on parade. The combat troops stood beside the suits, which were opened to accept their soldiers. To the right, nearest the post headquarters, the battalion's headquarters company was formed in tighter formation. The few suits needed by headquarters personnel were behind the formation. The entire battalion was ringed by armed military police, some of them behind Hummer-mounted plasma cannon.

Snyder walked briskly onto the field from the right.

His exec, centered on the battalion and in front, saluted and reported, "Sir, the battalion is formed and ready."

Snyder returned the salute and quietly said, "Post." Immediately, the exec walked off.

"Company commanders will have your companies don suits and put them to sleep," Snyder ordered.

Connors and the other captains, and one senior lieutenant, saluted, faced about and ordered, "Prepare to don suits. Lie down."

Reluctant, grumbling, in a few cases even cursing, the soldiers of the First of the O-Eighth obeyed. They knew what was coming and *hated* the idea. Why, if the Posleen came upon them while they were hibernating there would be not a thing they could do to defend themselves as their suits were one by one hacked apart to allow the omnivorous aliens to get at the meat inside. They knew that if that happened, they would have only a single moment of stark terror once out from their suits' protection and control before the aliens rendered them into fresh dripping steaks and chops.

But they were soldiers. For that matter, they were smart soldiers. None of them knew the reason for the unusual—even bizarre—order. In the end, though, it didn't matter. They were soldiers; they obeyed orders. They'd worry about why they'd been given when . . . if . . . they ever woke up.

Connors watched as his company's platoon sergeants walked from suit to suit, from man to man, checking that each was snugly cocooned before giving the order to the AIDs, "Until awakened by superior orders, AID, soldier and gestalt, *Hibernate.*"

For reasons more than a little similar to Daisy Mae's hatred of waking loneliness, the AIDs protested the order bitterly. In more than a few cases reprogramming was threatened, with resultant loss of personality. Faced with that threat, sullenly, the AIDs obeyed, putting into hibernation their colloidal intelligences, the suit gestalts and, finally, themselves.

In hibernation status, the AIDs could neither contact, access, nor be contacted by or accessed from, the Net. They remained in some sense awake; however, they remained lonely, and they hated it, one and all.

When Connors' platoon leaders turned again to face him, the clear sign that his order had been obeyed, he ordered them into their suits as well, along with his XO and first sergeant. These eight suits he saw to the hibernation of himself.

At length, Connors and the other commanders, as well as the battalions' small, suit-wearing combat staff, turned to face Snyder, reporting with a salute, "A Company . . . B Company . . ." etc., "In hibernation."

Snyder then ordered, "Commanders and staff, don suits."

The battalion's command sergeant major walked over to the staff, doing for them what the other leaders had done for their own, while Snyder walked the line, putting his commanders to sleep. That done, the CSM and the commander met again in the center.

"Into your suit, Sergeant Major."

The CSM growled, "Fuck!" then added, "Yessir."

The NCO safely put out, Snyder cursed himself yet again as he walked over and lay down into the silvery gray goop inside his own armored combat suit. As the suit wheezed closed, Snyder asked, "AID?"

"Here, sir."

"AID, on my command you and the gestalt will go

into hibernation status until further orders. You will *not* put me into hibernation status. You will be on Net block and radio listening silence. Is this clear?"

"Without me to keep you company you may go insane, Colonel. Is *that* clear?" the AID grumbled.

"I'm *already* insane, Shirley," Snyder retorted. "Ready, hibernate."

Wreckers and cargo trucks began rolling the line, driven by headquarters company drivers and some others attached down from higher. At each suit, the wreckers stopped while a crew of enlisted men prepared the suit for slinging. Once prepared and hooked up, the wreckers lifted the sleeping men, all but Snyder who remained and would remain miserably awake, and dumped them flat in the backs of the cargo trucks. As the beds of the trucks filled, more suits were piled on until each truck carried more than a score of ACS.

One highly annoyed lieutenant colonel snarled unheard by the crew loading his ACS aboard a cargo truck. Meanwhile a sleeping Captain Connors dreamt of a long, slender girl with huge brown eyes.

Rodriguez Home, Via Argentina, Panama City, Panama

The third night they had spent together Scott had warned her that he might be called away without notice and with no chance to tell her where he was going or why . . . or when . . . or if, he would return. He had promised to write as soon as possible if . . . no, when, it happened.

A diamond sparkled on Marielena's finger now. Scott

had given it to her, asked her to be his wife, only the week before, two days before he had gone incommunicado. The girl looked down at it for the thousandth time and still marveled. The bloody thing was *huge*, easily three carats and worth rather more than she made at her office job in about five years. Scott had said that he couldn't count on his Servicemembers' life insurance being given to her in the event of his death even though he had made her his beneficiary. He'd said something about "at the discretion of the secretary." Moreover, marriage between Panamanian girl and gringo boy took more bureaucratic hassle than his battalions' training schedule—Scott had also said something about "that prick Snyder"—permitted. Instead, using a not inconsiderable chunk of the pay the Mobile Infantry received that, despite confiscatory taxes, they never quite managed to spend, he had brought the ring on the theory that the girl could trade that to keep alive in the event he never returned.

He had been able to make his Galactic bank account a joint one, but only to the extent that it would go to Marielena in the event of his death. She couldn't access it before that; no one could. Moreover, it might well do her no good if it came to having to escape Panama to escape the Posleen. Hence, the ring.

The ring was a marvel. Still, it did absolutely nothing to warm her bed at night or fill the empty, aching void she felt in her loins. She'd gotten used to it, being filled up in body and soul, in the altogether too few nights she and Connors had managed to spend together. Marielena wasn't sorry she had waited until she had met Connors. She just wished she had met him when she was fifteen.

Alma, Marielena's sister, walked into the room quietly on stockinged feet. If she felt any jealousy at the too obvious ring it was small. Indeed she was happy for her sister that her sister had herself found happiness. Alma's gaze shifted from Marielena's transcended face downward. Was there . . . ?

Oh, yes. No doubt about it. The breasts had grown at least a cup size in the last two weeks.

"Mari, we need to talk . . . with Mama."

Santa Fe, Veraguas Province, Republic of Panama

"*Mamita*, what are those things?" Edilze asked of Digna as the ACS-bearing trucks, the loads of suits covered by canvas tarps forming lumpy, shapeless masses in the cargo beds, passed by under joint gringo and Panamanian military police escort.

Without turning her gaze away from the trucks, Digna inclined her head and answered, "I don't know, Granddaughter. All I was told was that we were to stay the hell away. And, no, I don't like the secrecy one little bit."

Changing the subject and tearing her attention away from the trucks, Digna asked, "How are we fixed for ammunition?"

"Over twelve hundred rockets per launcher, *Mamita*," Edilze answered. "They made the last, at least I am told it is the last, delivery this morning. It's enough for almost four hours continuous firing." The younger woman sounded amazed. It *was* one hell of a lot of ammunition.

"And the guns?"

"Rather less than that. Still, it is quite a lot, mixed

high explosive and more than one hundred rounds of canister per gun. I wish it was more."

Digna ignored the stated wish. "You have the gun positions sited to fire both indirect and direct?"

"In most cases. Battery B will have to displace forward to cover its direct fire arc, but it won't have to go far."

"It is well. *You* have done well, Granddaughter."

"*Mamita* . . . ?"

Digna looked directly into Edilze's worried brown eyes and answered, "No. My children are here. Yours will be too. Our clan wins or dies together."

Hotel Central, Casco Viejo, *Panama City, Panama*

"As long as we're together, Julio, it will be all right," Paloma murmured as Diaz rolled off of her.

They were married now. Diaz had taken her to the Civil Registry for a license within days after coming out of the hospital. As it happened, the man granting the license was also a Justice of the Peace. There was the little problem of Paloma being only seventeen but, what with the war and all, the JP had proven most understanding.

"We have only a couple of days to *be* together, love. I have a mission scheduled for the day after tomorrow."

She immediately tightened up and rolled to face him. "Will it be . . . dangerous?" she asked, in a quivering voice.

"Routine," he assured her.

"Please, Julio, for me. Please don't be killed."

He smiled. "I promise to do my best."

"We only have this couple of nights?" she asked, somewhat reassured. "Then do your best again, now, before you have to go."

SOUTHCOM, *Quarry Heights, Panama*

"The LRRPs report we've got movement from Colombia north and west into the Darien, sir. Not too many details."

"I need details," Page insisted.

"Sir, they're doing their best."

Page scowled. The news wasn't exactly unexpected. The timing sucked, though. *Damned inconsiderate Posleen.*

"Show me," the chief of Southern Command ordered.

"We've got two streams of them, Boss. One moving north and the other west," Colonel Rivera answered. "They're joining here," his pointer touched the map just southeast of where the Darien began, "before moving northwest into the Darien."

"What have we got to stop them?"

"There are Special Forces teams, a company's worth of them, scattered throughout the jungle. They've been arming and training Indians—Chocoes and Cuna Indians—for the last year or so."

Page nodded absently. He'd known about the SF and the Indians. "They can't hold the jungle against the Posleen," he judged simply.

"No, sir, not a chance," Rivera agreed. "And we have nothing much to help them with. Not that far from our bases around the Canal."

"What have we got?"

"The Tenth Infantry is committed to the passes in the *Cordillera Central*. We couldn't pull them out if we wanted to. The Twentieth Mechanized Infantry is committed to the counterattack. Only the Fifth Infantry Regiment is uncommitted. Plus we have about another company of SF we can send into the jungle and *maybe* keep supplied. Panama has nothing to give; everything is already committed to the defense and counterattack in the west. So is what's left of our First of the O-Eighth Mobile Infantry. We *do* have a company of engineers, the Seven-Sixtieth, we can use to help dig the boys in."

"Shit," Page said.

"Shit," Rivera echoed. "Shall I prep and send the orders to move the Fifth east, plus whatever else I can scrape up?"

"One regiment to cover at least fifty miles, Rivera?" Page scowled. "What the fuck would be the point?"

Rivera tilted his head slightly, keeping the irritation he felt from his voice. "What do you know about the Fifth Infantry, sir?"

"Nothing, why?"

"Their motto is, 'I'll try, sir.' It dates from the War of 1812 when they grabbed some Brit cannon at the Battle of Lundy's Lane. They say, 'I'll try.' They do try . . . and they never, ever fail. The entire United States Marine Corps has one man who won the Medal of Honor twice, sir. The Fifth Infantry regiment alone has two along with another forty-two men who won the Medal once. I don't know of any regiment in the world that has that kind of record. And, sir . . . ?"

"Yes?"

"Little known but true: the Dictator of Panama, Bill Boyd, served for a while in the Fifth."

"Ah, fuckit, Colonel. Send your Fifth . . . and even your goddamned engineers. Maybe they can buy us some time, if nothing else."

"They *will* try, sir. And they won't fail . . . though they'll need every available minute to dig in."

"Any word about what's happening out west, Rivera?"

"I spoke to Panama's G-2 this morning, sir, a General Diaz. They're sending out a glider tonight and every night until the Posleen out west begin to move—clever bastards, weren't they, to figure out that a low tech glider might get through where a high tech jet fighter wouldn't?—and the G-2 assures me we'll get the word as soon as the glider returns."

Veraguas/Chiriqui Provinces, Republic of Panama

He could still scent Paloma in his mind, feel her pressed against him in his dreamings.

She's taken it hard, poor love, Diaz thought. *The death of her father was a terrible blow, though what she imagined might happen if she had managed to be the first to warn Suarez . . . perhaps she'd hoped to make a deal to have her father's life spared. She won't talk about it; won't even think about it, as near as I can tell. And then when I had to leave? God, can so many tears come from just one girl?*

He'd felt like a rat that morning, when he left her for the airfield to be briefed on his mission. She had cried and clung to him desperately. There'd been chance for only a short single phone call from the field to the hotel where Paloma was staying until they could work out something better. She'd cried then, too.

Diaz forced his new bride from his thoughts when the warning buzzer sounded that he was high enough. His hand reached out and a finger pushed a button to cut loose from the balloon above. He felt a sudden drop, then pulled back on the glider's stick to level out and fly.

Following the roads into Posleen-held territory was a risky proposition. More than a few gliders had been lost already doing so. Julio Diaz had his doubts whether the aliens had figured out the gliders' purpose. More likely, so he thought, they had just seen and engaged them out of general principle—the principle of he who shoots first, eats.

In any case, most of the gliders lost to date had been downed either in broad daylight or nights with high and full or nearly full moons and no rain. There was no rain expected tonight but the moon, while almost full, was fairly low on the horizon.

Small comfort that is, mused Julio. *Then again, some of those gliders went down while broadcasting. Best maintain radio silence if I can.*

Without fanfare and—so Julio fervently hoped— without the slightest notice at all, he crossed over the front lines along the San Pedro River and over into enemy-held territory. Though the bridge had been blown long since by the defenders, the road was still there, dimly seen by the shadow-casting low moon.

Funny that they destroy everything human except *the roads and bridges*, Julio thought. *I suppose those help them mass forces and maneuver; that, and distribute food and arms. Bastards.*

That thought, *"bastards,"* was repeated over and over as Diaz progressed across a landscape scoured of human life and habitation. He wondered how many hundreds of thousands of sets of human bones, women's and children's bones, dotted the soil below.

From time to time he passed a spot where human construction had obviously been replaced by alien, the pyramids, large and small, of their God Kings casting shadows by the moonlight.

Idly, Diaz checked his altimeter. *Time to gain a little altitude,* he thought, as he pulled his stick to the right and back to move nearer to the Central Cordillera to take advantage of the updrafts. With the mountains looming ahead of him the glider shook slightly under the uplift. Having gained nearly a thousand meters Diaz swung his craft around again to head south and then west. As the bird banked, he was afforded a look at the ground from his cockpit.

Oh, oh; what's this?

Whether he had simply missed it before in the jungle fringing the mountains or whether the Posleen had just now begun to tramp, a stream of fire—torches he supposed; that, or some form of flashlight—flowed down from a valley nestled in the Cordillera. Diaz aimed for it.

Before reaching the river of fire Diaz looked left. There were more streams of fire, shorter it is true, forming and flowing north toward the Inter-American Highway. The highway itself was beginning to glow as the various streams reached it and turned west, merging into a great river of light. Above it, other dots of light glowed more individually. *Their flying sleds,* Diaz supposed.

Diaz continued on to the west. Navigation was easy now; the highway was rapidly becoming a great raging torrent of torch-bearing aliens, all moving east toward the San Pedro River. He wondered whether he should risk a call to his father, waiting behind for news of the enemy. He decided not to, not until he had gathered all the information there was.

And then Diaz reached the vicinity of what had once been known as *La Ciudad de San Jose and David.* This was no river. A great sea of fire and light shone bright as hundreds of rivers and streams merged together. Like a flood bursting a dam the sea began to surge eastward.

"Holy shit!" Diaz exclaimed into the radio, not thinking for the moment of proper procedures. "Any station this frequency, this is Harpy Five Nine. Get word to the Army! Get word to the G-2. For Christ's sake call my father! They're *coming!*"

Whether it was the low moon glinting from the smooth fiberglass of his wings, or whether some Posleen Five-percenter had wised to the fact that there were no birds the size of gliders and certainly none which emanated radio energy, Diaz suddenly saw streaking flashes, thousands of them, rising in front of his glider. *Shit! Railgun rounds.*

He pulled his stick to swerve right, out of the line of fire, and saw as many actinic streaks in that direction. Frantic now, diving and turning even while he continued to broadcast his warning—"Call my father! Call my wi—"—Second Lieutenant Julio Diaz, *Fuerza Aeria de Panama,* flew directly into the fires of a number of alien railguns. He never noticed as his glider came apart around him. By that time, he was dead.

Muelle *(Pier)* 18, Balboa, Republic of Panama

"I'm coming, Chief," McNair muttered in answer to the urgent knock on his port cabin's hatch. He reached over and flicked on a light affixed to a small night table next to his bunk. He heard a constrained sobbing coming from the area of his desk. Once his eyes adjusted to the light he saw Daisy, or rather, her avatar, rocking back and forth, an arm across her chest and a hand placed over her mouth as holographic tears poured down her face.

McNair stood without covering himself. All things considered, modesty was silly in a ship that saw every motion.

"What's wrong Daisy?"

"Lieutenant Diaz is missing . . . presumed dead," she sobbed. "Somewhere over David."

"Oh," McNair said, suddenly downcast. "Oh . . . damn. He was a good kid, too."

McNair thought about reaching out one comforting hand to the avatar, realized once again that that was futile, and instead rested the hand on the bulkhead near his bunk, lightly stroking the painted steel wall.

"Daisy, I am sorry, too. Sorry for Diaz, for his father, for you who were his friend. But that's what war means: good young kids die. At least we can say this one is being fought for a good reason."

The avatar nodded, tears beginning to slow to a trickle. "I know that. But it still hurts."

"Yes, it hurts now and it will hurt for a long time to come. But we have to continue the war, and win it, or Diaz's death will mean nothing."

Daisy lifted bright blue eyes, all the brighter for the holographic tears. "I never actually *hated* the Posleen before. I killed them, yes, but that was my job. Now I hate them and want to wipe them out of the universe."

"Just as well," McNair agreed. "Though somehow I doubt they are entirely to blame for what they do. No creatures—no higher creatures, anyway—could evolve naturally the way the Posleen have. When I think of the Posleen and how they have turned out, I smell a do-gooder, a *Galactic* do-gooder."

INTERLUDE

Picture, if you will, a lone insect, flying aimlessly through a primordial jungle in search of food. . . .

The grat operated off of instinct. Instinct had carried its ancestors, distant in both time and space, across half a galaxy. Instinct had brought it aboard the Posleen ship fleeing orna'adar. Instinct now carried it in search of the communal abat, the agouti-like, hive-building creatures that were its sole source of food. Where there might be abat, there would be grat. Briefly the grat hovered in his search before landing on a nearby tree.

But this is not just any jungle. Watch out! There's a signpost ahead. This grat has just taken a wrong turn and entered into . . . The Darien Zone. (Insert appropriate music here . . .)

The tree ant popped its head out before rapidly drawing it back into its hive tree. Pheromones were released, only to be picked up by others of the colony. From ant to ant the pheromones spread. The pheromones spoke of "invader"; they spoke of food. In a short time the message reached the queen who redoubled them, adding in the chemicals that said, "Feed me; I hunger."

From deep inside the hive, which extended well below the tree's base, the ants began to mass at the exits. The mass of ants grew and grew until the level of concentration of the pheromones reached a certain critical level. Then the ants swarmed out.

The grat was stupid; not so stupid that it didn't notice the beginning of the ant swarm, but stupid enough not to recognize that the swarm might pose a threat. Absently, the grat flexed its stinger and flicked it at a convenient ant. The stinger connected and pulsed a tiny dose of its venom. The targeted ant twisted itself into a C and began to writhe in a death dance.

Before that ant died, a hundred more swarmed over the grat—over its abdomen, up it jointed legs, onto its thorax.

Snip, snip, and a grat wing fluttered groundward. Now in pain itself, the unbalanced grat tried to ascend but only managed to flip itself off the tree and onto the ground. A hundred ants managed to hang on during its fall, their mandibles imbedded in the grat's chitin, cutting through to the soft meat below.

Once on the ground the grat knew a brief moments' respite from fresh wounds. Its remaining wing beat the ground futilely. In a circle about it the ants collected. The grat's tiny brain, though foggy with the burning pain of the formic acid injected by the ants' mandibles, still registered the looming harvesting machine surrounding it. It tried to right itself and rise to its feet to fight.

Before the grat could arise the ant pheromones reached critical mass again. With the grat still half on one side the circle of tree ants swarmed again and buried the grat completely from view. A hissing scream emerged from somewhere under the pile. Soon, the scream was followed by pieces of grat, being carried in an orderly fashion, single file, up the tree and down to the queen.

The Posleen normal's genetically engineered ears picked up the scream of the grat. This was a common enough sound on Posleen worlds. Grat often went into abat nests in search of food. There was a saying among the Kessentai that the normal could not have articulated but at some basic level understood: "Sometimes you get the abat, sometimes the abat get you."

The normal, scouting forward for the main host, continued deeper into the dank, dark, wet and miserable Darien jungle.

Picture, if you will, a lone Posleen, scouting through the jungle in advance of its clan. But this is not just any jungle. Watch out! There's a signpost ahead....

(Insert appropriate music here...)

CHAPTER 28

Hear the wind blow,
　　hear the wind blow;
It is calling for him.
See the grass grow,
　　see the grass grow;
It whispers his name.
See the fire glow,
　　see the fire glow;
His heart is aflame.
Bayede Nkhosi!
Bayede Nkhosi!
　　—Margaret Singana,
　　"We Are Growing"

David (erased), Chiriqui, Republic of Panama

The setting sun washed the great step pyramid of the clan leader Binastarion in pale red light. In that light, the pyramid rose high over the area once known as the *Parque de Cervantes*. Of the park, the stores and hotels that had once encircled, the ancient church which a priest had detonated to prevent the Posleen from eating his flock, not a single trace remained. The very stones and blocks had gone into the pyramid. Only the metalled square of road indicated that here had once stood human habitation.

The time was very soon, Binastarion knew, the time when population pressures would have built to the point the People began spontaneously to march, to seek his leadership in acquiring new lands.

Walking up an interior ramp to the platform just below the summit of the pyramid, the God King looked over the normals, cosslain and few Kenstain that ran and maintained his palace. The others scrambled to get out of their leader's way as he made his way upward. *Are they looking thinner than they should?* he wondered.

At the head of the ramp was a small landing. Binastarion surmounted this, then turned to walk outward to the platform that engirdled the pyramid's square summit. Even before passing the sound-deadening electronic barrier that also served to keep the voracious local insect life at bay, the God King heard the snarling and grunting of masses of the People. He asked himself, *Is it the Time, already? It is so soon.*

A great cry went up from the People massed about the pyramid's base. Thousands of boma blades were drawn in salute, hundred of railguns brought to Present Arms.

"*Haiaiailll*, Chief!" thundered the God Kings, hundreds of whom hovered in their tenar above the mass. The normals inarticulately snarled welcome and praise.

Binastarion looked above the masses, to where even at this distance he could perceive columns of the People descending from the hills surrounding what had once been the major human town of the area.

"Is it time, old companion?" he asked his Artificial Sentience.

"Lord, it is not the best time. Too many Kessentai ride their own feet rather than tenar. Not all the normals have even shotguns. That said, and despite whatever these humans could do; moreover, despite much sun and rain and a fertile land, the People have grown quickly. Nestlingcide has done little to help. Incidents among the normals are up. They hunger."

Deeply, solemnly, the God King nodded. "Sound amplification," he ordered his Artificial Sentience.

Binastarion reached around to place his own grasping member on the heavy metal hilt of his own, hereditary, boma blade. This his drew, the scraping sound echoing across the masses. His People shouted and thundered his acclaim from below.

"We march!" the God King said.

San Pedro Line, Republic of Panama

The first sign came well before dawn, a glowing line drawn in the sky above the Inter-American Highway. The glow spread outward to become a fan the nearer it came to the edge of human resistance to the Posleen infestation. To the human soldiers, watching and waiting in their trenches and armored vehicles, the glowing fan spreading above them seemed like the warning that the gates of Hell had broken loose and a swarm of Satan's own were coming to drag their souls down to damnation.

The defenders weren't very far wrong either.

To Sergeant Quijana, standing in a trench line two hundred meters east of the river, it wasn't the glow that frightened. Indeed, that was all to the good as it would give his men clearer targets, presupposing the light lasted until dawn and—as seemed likely—the enemy showed up before then.

No, the glow was good. What bothered Quijana, and apparently most of his men, was the sound. Even at this distance the sound struck at the soul: the whine of the aliens' massed tenar, the clatter of their claws on the hard surface of the highway, their growls and snarls, even the sound of branches of trees breaking as the Posleen horde forced its way through woods—and all the sound, all the time, *growing* . . .

Quijana shivered. He sensed his men doing the same. *God, I feel so alone.*

From overhead came the freight train rumble of a few score shells being lobbed in the enemy's direction. For a moment, the flight of the shells downed out the Posleen cacophony. Moreover, when the shells—122mm Russians, Quijana thought—impacted, the flash of their explosions, sensed even in the distance, briefly overwhelmed the glow in the sky. Somehow, the sergeant felt instantly better. He looked around at the soldiers lining the trench with him, and saw that they, too, had relaxed—if only a bit—once they'd heard the screaming friendly shells.

Hmmm. If the aliens' noise frightens me and the men, and our own calms us . . .

Announcing, "I'll be back in a few minutes, Boys. I need to call the commander," Quijana turned and scrambled up a few steps cut into the back of the main trench, then followed a narrower one to where his own squad's BMP awaited in a hull-down fighting position. He placed one foot on the track of the vehicle and hoisted himself halfway up.

"Hand me your helmet," the sergeant ordered a corporal standing in the hatch of the BMP. When he had the helmet on his head, Quijana made a call to his platoon leader.

"Sir, I think we ought to start our engines."

"Why, Sergeant?" the lieutenant queried back.

"I think it will have a good effect on the men, sir."

"Wait, out."

The lieutenant never answered. Instead, after a couple of minutes and from about five hundred meters back, the sergeant heard one heavy duty engine, and then another, rumble into life. He handed the helmet back to the BMP's track commander. In few minutes more his own track gave off a roar as the driver started it, as did the BMPs to either side.

As Quijana reached his dismounted squad, back in the trench, the entire San Pedro Line had come to life, better than one thousand heavy and medium armored vehicles, growling their defiance and making the ground for thirty miles shake. More artillery in the rear—mortars, too, now—began to speak. The landscape lit up, to the front from the bursting shells, to the rear with the muzzle flashes of hundreds of heavy guns. The sound of the Posleen horde was lost amidst the roar.

Confidently, more confidently than he had felt since spotting the first sign of the approaching enemy drawn in the sky, Quijana said to his squad, "Boys, we're just gonna *murder* the bastards."

From somewhere off to the left flank came the call, repeated from point to point, "Here they cooommme!"

Posleen normals were stupid, even moronic, but they *could* be taught if one used the right tools. When the first wave of the first scout oolt hit the leading edge of a minefield the dismounted junior God King in command and a dozen of his people tripped off an even half dozen Bouncing Betty mines. The Kessentai went down, eviscerated and screaming in agony as did over a score of the normals. Seeing legs blown off, flesh oozing yellow blood where ball bearings had imbedded themselves, and entrails draping the ground and entangling such limbs as remained, the bulk of that scout oolt stopped, frozen in their tracks.

Two BMP gunners, seeing the freeze, had the same thought at the same time. Within seconds, and milliseconds of each other, two 100mm high explosive antipersonnel rounds went off above the oolt. The rounds were auto-loaded and detonated by a laser beam range finder precisely above the spot picked by the gunners. (Where the United States had made a 25mm rifleman's grenade launcher to do the same thing, the Russians had never thought the effect of such a grenade justified the expense. A 100mm shell, on the other hand, did.)

Packed as they were, without a God King for leadership, with shrieking almost-corpses rolling on the blood-stained ground ahead of them, clear space behind, and with two large shells exploding overhead, the normals of the scout oolt broke.

Quijana's company's first sergeant, *El Primero*,

risked a look over the lip of the trench, saw the enemy running and did a quick count. "Hmmm. With sixty of the bastards down, that leaves only about five-million, nine-hundred and ninety-nine thousand, nine-hundred and forty to go."

The *primero* shrugged, "Piece o' cake." Then he lowered his head, and walked on down the trench.

The trench was camouflaged and each of the men had several obliquely oriented firing positions from it, dug into the western wall. Quijana walked along the duckboarded floor, stopping at each man to pass a few words of encouragement, check on ammunition, or ensure they were drinking water as they ought. Spent ammunition casings, steel with a brass wash for the most part, littered and smoked on the duckboards. Idly, Quijana brushed some of them aside with his boot to let them fall through the spaces in the flooring. Some of the freshly fired casings made a slight, almost imperceptible hiss as they hit the mud under the duckboards.

The enemy were still coming and the riflemen and machine gunners were still killing those who managed to make it through the thick minefield. The BMPs were donating shells at any cohesive looking groups that seemed about to make it past the mines or which were held up by the wire to the front. The air above was thick with lightning-fast railgun fleshettes.

Quijana reached an arm up to tap a shoulder. "Let me up there, Gonzo," he told a scared looking, sixteen-year-old private named, appropriately enough, Gonzalez. The young private sighed audibly, then withdrew his long rifle—one of countless thousands of Dragunovs purchased from Russia to give the defenders extra reach and a heavier bullet—and stepped down into the greater safety of the main trench.

Carefully, Quijana's face searched out the young soldier's face. *Scared; but then who wouldn't be?* Briefly, he reviewed what he knew about the kid. *Gonzalez, Angel F., sixteen, drafted six months ago. Father and mother live in the City. Some brothers and sisters, all younger. Good kid; did well in training.*

"You're doing fine, Gonzo," Quijana said as he slapped the kid's shoulder. Then, to emphasize that the danger wasn't that great, Quijana himself took Gonzalez's previous position and—keeping as much of his head under cover as possible—looked out over the battlefield.

The first and most noticeable things Quijana saw were eight—no nine, one was crashed and smoking amidst a pile of Posleen bodies—tenar. He ducked down again and looked behind him. The trench was competently laid out, which is to say that the rear berm was higher than the front, or firing, berm to prevent the heads of the defenders from being silhouetted against the sky. Still, he saw about as many smoke trails from his own side's armor as he had seen tenar crashed or hovering lifeless.

Oh, well; sometimes you get the abat and sometimes the abat get you. He wasn't sure where he had heard that first, perhaps it was from one of the gringo or Russian trainers who had helped run one or another of the courses he had taken.

More worrisome than the smoke columns from behind, Quijana's next look showed the ground carpeted with Posleen bodies. Ordinarily, this would be a happy sight. On the other hand, *If there are any mines under those bodies still left they sure won't go off now.*

Worst of all was the wire. This was laid out normally: protective wire forty or fifty meters to the front, tactical wire past that to guide the enemy into preplanned kill zones and final protective lines, and supplementary wire to fool them as to which was the tactical. (For the serious downside to tactical wire was that it almost always led, inexorably, to a machine gun or other crew-served weapon sited to fire along it down the enemy side.)

The wire had been well strung and constructed, and competently laid out. Unfortunately, if one threw enough railgun rounds at it some of them *had* to connect. And even a gram's worth of metal, moving at an appreciable fraction of c, would be enough to sever the wire. Quijana wasn't even sure the Posleen were doing it deliberately, but great swaths of the wire were severed and down even so. Moreover, in places the Posleen had stacked their wounded and dead so thick and deep that the wire had become more of a frame for holding up a Posleen-paved aerial pathway.

"Can't be too long now," Quijana commented to himself as he stepped down to the floor of the trench.

"Sergeant?" Gonzalez queried.

"Huh? Oh. It can't be too long before we get the word to pull back, Gonzo. We're not supposed to hold this line indefinitely, you know."

"Oh. Whew. I thought you meant something else entirely." The private looked visibly relieved.

"No," Quijana laughed. "Not that; we'll be fine. Now back to your post, soldier," the sergeant ordered.

As Gonzo mounted the step back to his firing position, Quijana turned away to continue his walk down his short section of trench. The sergeant then heard a heavy *thunk* behind him. He turned instantly and began to shout, "Med . . ."

The shout died, stillborn. There was nothing a medic could do for a private missing his head. Quijana fought down the urge to vomit at the finely sprayed blood and chunks of skull and brains dotting the back wall of the trench.

Damn. The kid was only sixteen years old. For the moment, Quijana took over Gonzalez's position on the firing step. *I hope to hell the word comes to pull back soon, even though I know the retreat will be a nightmare.*

CA-134, USS Des Moines, *off* Isla Cebaco

CIC was a little metal pillbox containing barely suppressed excitement and fear. McNair could smell the emotions, sour and bitter, on the recycled air. The whole ship reeked of it in a way it never had before, for on the first deadly mission of this war the crew had been ignorant. On the other runs to raid the Posleen-held coast it had felt safe in the darkness. This fight saw the men of the ship wise in bitter ways and, however determined to do their duty, frightened of what that duty was likely to entail.

The exec looked up as the ship's captain entered. "We just got the word, Skipper. The Heavy Corps, First and Sixth Panamanian Mechanized Divisions, are going to start pulling back in half an hour. We need to help them break contact. I've already given the order to commence the firing run while *Salem* and the land-based air defense provide cover."

McNair looked over at Fire Direction.

"Skipper, we will be in range of Target Group Alpha in," the FDO consulted the chronometer above his plotting table, "seven minutes and . . . thirty seconds."

The captain nodded, said, "Well done," and turned to Daisy's avatar, already present. "You ready, my girl?"

"Willing and able, Skipper. We're gonna murder the bastards . . . for Julio, among others."

Lastly, McNair ordered the ship's public address system turned on. Then he turned to Father Dwyer and asked, "How do we stand with the Almighty, Chaplain?"

Dwyer smiled a wicked smile, all bared human incisors and fangs, and spoke loudly enough for the PA set to pick up his words. "With regard to the enemy, Captain, the good Lord says, 'I will leave your flesh on the mountains, and fill the valleys with your carcasses. I will water the land with what flows from you, and the river beds shall be filled with your blood. When I snuff you out I will cover the heavens, and all the stars will darken.' Ezekiel 32; verses five through seven."

"So be it," McNair agreed, then ordered, "Marine marksmen and Panamanian *Cazadores* topside. Prepare to repel boarders."

San Pedro Line, Republic of Panama

"Wait for it, boys, wait for it," Quijana cautioned his squad. Only two men—exceptional shots, the both—still manned their firing steps in the trench. The rest clustered around their squad leader near the back step that led to the narrow communication trench that, in turn, led to their BMP.

"What's it like, Sarge, when a ship fires?"

Quijana and one other man, his corporal assistant, were the only men in the squad who had survived the near destruction of 1st Division when the Posleen had come pouring out of the hills and valleys to surround them during the early stages of the invasion. He knew what the guns were like.

"Fucking scary, Soldier," the sergeant replied. "Also fucking beautiful and wonderful . . . like manna from Heaven or God's own lightning when you need them. But keep your heads down, anyway, because God's manna didn't have a deadly radius of hundreds of meters and *He* had better quality control at the lightning factory."

"What about Gonzo?" one of the other privates asked. "We going to just leave him for the Posleen to eat? Seems . . . wrong."

Quijana thought about that. "You're right, Private. It *is* fucking wrong. Tell you what; go to the BMP and get me a Bouncing Betty and an extra four or five pounds of C-4, also some det cord and a non-electric cap. We'll rig Gonzo so he can get a few more *and* leave nothing behind for the aliens to eat. *Go*, son."

The private took off at an awkward run down the communication trench. By the time he returned, Quijana and his corporal had dug a small hole for the mine and prepared Gonzalez's body, removing his bloodied combat gear and shirt. The detonating cord they formed lumps of C-4 plastic explosive around, then further wrapped it around the corpse. One end of the det cord they also wrapped around the mine. The mine itself went into the hole, with its safety pin still in place but the retaining bends straightened. The squad put Gonzalez's shirt back on him and gently eased his headless body down onto the mine's three detonating prongs.

Quijana patted the corpse's shoulder, then slid one hand under the body until he was able to grasp hold with a finger and thumb on the ring of the safety pin. Silently praying—mistakes *did* happen, after all—the sergeant eased the safety pin out of the mine's fuse and from under the body, then deposited it in his right breast pocket.

Breathing a sigh of relief, Quijana whispered, "Get some, Gonzo. Get some."

"Sergeant! I think the ship's firing."

CA-134, USS Des Moines, *off* Isla Cebaco

The bow below cut through the water, churning it to a furious white froth as twelve Daisies above, each perfectly identical to the others, stood holding holographic candles around Father Dwyer.

The priest intoned, "Wherefore in the name of God the All-powerful, Father, Son, and Holy Ghost, of the Blessed Peter, Prince of the Apostles, and of all the saints, in virtue of the power which has been given us of binding and loosing in Heaven and on Earth, we curse the Posleen themselves and all their accomplices and all their abettors. We order them gone; we exclude them from the bosom of our Holy Mother the Church in Heaven and on Earth; we declare them anathematized and we judge them condemned to eternal fire with Satan and his angels and all the reprobate. We deliver them to Satan to mortify their bodies, now and after the Day of Judgment."

The twelve Daisies—six to either side of the priest, lining the bow, and wearing something like vestments—intoned, "*Fiat. Fiat. Fiat,*" and then cast their virtual candles over the side.

"It is done," the priest said.

The twelve Daisies immediately shrank to one, standing at the chaplain's left shoulder. "Father," she whispered, "I know the ceremony as well as you do. That wasn't quite right."

"Yes, Daisy," the priest answered. "I had to modify a bit. No matter, His Holiness will understand and God will know His own . . . and so will Satan."

The single avatar remaining shrugged. "As you say, Father. But, while God and Satan may know their own, my guns won't give a shit and the captain is about to give the order to fire. Go below, please."

San Pedro Line, Republic of Panama

It was the thunder of God. It was the raging of Satan. It was the walls of Hell being tumbled as Christ died on the cross.

It was nine semi-automatic eight-inch naval guns firing "high capacity" shells at maximum rate and walking the blasts across the landscape to a plan and a timetable.

Quijana and the six remaining dismounted soldiers with him huddled on the floor of the trench as shell after shell exploded to their front, shaking their internal organs mercilessly and pelting them with rocks, debris and parts of Posleen bodies lofted by the blasts. Some of the bits fell on the headless body of Private Gonzalez.

Oh, shit, thought Quijana, crouching abjectly with his arms protectively circling his head and neck. *If something falls on poor Gonzo hard enough to jostle his body it might set of the mine. Shit. Shit. Shit.*

One of the privates apparently had the same idea at about the same time. The private saw a severed Posleen head fall across Gonzalez's legs, shouted *"Chingada!"* and started to get up to leave the trench.

"Oh, no you don't, shithead!" Quijana exclaimed, reaching up to grasp the private's belt and pull him back down into the trench. The private struggled until the sergeant stuck the muzzle of his rifle under his chin and said, as calmly as possible for having to shout over the naval shells, "One little twitch. Just one."

The private immediately went wide-eyed and stock-still.

"Sergeant Quijana!" shouted one of the track crew, lying down at the entrance to the communication trench that led to the BMP. "Sergeant! The word is to pull out now! For God's sake, c'mon!" The BMP crewman's head immediately disappeared as he pulled back to return to his vehicle.

Still with the muzzle of his rifle under the terrified private's chin, Quijana used his other hand to point at his corporal. "You first! Supervise the loading as they arrive. Now, go!" The corporal took off briskly. Then the sergeant looked around the pale, frightened faces of the remaining five. He pointed at a private. "Go!" This he continued until only himself and the soldier with the rifle to his chin remained.

In as reasonable a voice as he could muster, Quijana said, "You are going next. I will follow. You *will* keep your head down. You *will* move quickly but calmly. You *will* not lose your footing. You *will* not trip. If you do either of those things, I *will* shoot you and leave you behind for the enemy. Is this clear?"

The private gulped and, unable to nod his agreement and understanding for the rifle pushed into the hollow of his jaw, managed to answer, "I . . . understand . . . Sergeant."

Satisfied, Quijana nodded and said, "Good, son. Now go!"

When Quijana arrived, his corporal was still outside the track, making sure the frightened private buckled himself in before seating himself. The BMP's turret slewed slowly, left to right, spitting death in the form of machine gun and cannon fire. Shards from the naval gunfire whined overhead or, velocity spent, fell to earth to raise small dust clouds.

"Everyone's aboard, Sergeant!" the corporal announced over the engine's roar as Quijana scrambled to his seat, slamming and locking the track's door behind him.

"Tell the track commander! Let's get the fuck out of here!"

The vehicle began to vibrate while the engine's roar increased as the driver began to back out of position, prior to pivoting and running like hell for the next battle position, ten miles back.

CA-134, USS Des Moines, off Isla Cebaco

"Skipper, the Heavy Corps reports they have broken contact and are falling back."

McNair looked at the guns, shimmering even in the daylight with the heat built up from hours of nearly continuous firing.

"How's Sally standing up?" the captain asked of Daisy Mae.

"She's about the same as us, Skipper," the avatar answered. "Most of the high capacity ammunition in the ready magazines is depleted. They're cross-leveling and reloading now, as we are. And, for both of us, our guns are *hot*."

"They sure are, Daisy," Davis commented, causing the avatar to blush.

"All right, then," McNair continued. "We've done our jobs for now. Set course to bring us around the Península de Azuero, and assume firing positions in support of the Nata Line."

San Pedro Line, Republic of Panama

Binastarion shuddered at the carnage displayed to either side of the San Pedro River. His people lay in heaps, Kessentai and normals both. Tenar hovered in place or lay, altogether too often, crashed and smoking on the ground among the dead.

Unhurt normals were busied with rendering the dead and very badly wounded into thresh. This would keep the offensive going for some days, the God King knew. Yet there was always loss in consuming the bodies of the dead. Only a vast taking of the threshkreen would have made this a favorable exchange. Binastarion knew that the threshkreen had left comparatively few of their own, nothing like the scores of thousands of the People who lay lifeless on the ground and on each other, to make up for the caloric loss.

Reports from up ahead were not encouraging either. It seems that the thresh and their threshkreen defenders had abandoned the ground, taking everything edible with them except, of course, for what they had burned rather than let fall into the hands of the People. Moreover, the threshkreen were falling back in good order or, at least, in no worse order than one might have expected under the circumstances.

"I hate humans," Binastarion growled, though none but his Artificial Sentience could hear him as he rode his tenar above the abattoir below.

"Lord, one cannot help but observe that the humans hate you as well," that ancient device answered.

To either side of the highway—or what was left of it, the humans had torn up as much of that as possible to impede the People's progress—normals and Kessentai were formed in ranks, the Kessentai singing a hymn of praise to their chief for the victory.

Victory? This is "victory"?

Artificial Sentiences could not read thoughts. Yet, were they and their God Kings together long enough, and Binastarion and his AS had been together for many cycles, they would sometimes think along the same paths.

"Let them think what they will, lord. Let them think what fortifies them for the coming struggles. This is not a victory, but rather a defeat, despite driving the threshkreen from their positions and placing ourselves in position to overrun the best of their remaining lands. Still, it does put us in position to grow stronger, and higher in the ranks of the People."

"Yes, old friend, I understand that," Binastarion answered. "I merely wonder if our strength will prove sufficient; if our sustenance will prove sufficient."

"That, lord, only time will tell."

The small pack leader—or oolt'ondai—was hungry, as were most of his pack. He wanted a human to eat, something not just to fortify him but to make up for the losses and the hours of fear he had endured while leading his People to break this threshkreen defensive line.

Guiding his tenar low, the oolt'ondai's eyes searched out the human-built trench system looking vainly for even one threshkreen corpse to vent his hunger and his fear upon. There was nothing, nothing but the bodies of the People and the humans' wrecked fighting machines, burning and smoking all around. The machines seemed odd to the Kessentai, different from those he and his pack had faced. They looked boxier and less predatory, for one thing. Sadly, the God King was not what the humans called a "five-percenter." He did not key on the fact that the dead machines he saw were of an altogether different design and battle philosophy than the ones which had devastated his pack and the others. Even if he had been intellectually capable of understanding, it is most unlikely that the God King would have made anything of it.

Though intent on searching the trench floor, the

Kessentai still almost missed it. The corpse was headless, and half covered in dirt and debris. It took several long moments for the oolt'ondai to realize that the headless thing was indeed the prize he had sought, a human corpse.

The tenar would never fit into the trench, so, reluctant to dismount, the Kessentai ordered over a normal and made the signs for the normal to bring him the body. Somewhat reluctantly and fearfully, the normal obeyed. These things they fought were frightful. Who knew what evil designs they had worked into their own systems of fortification? Even so, God Kings ordered and normals obeyed. It was in the nature of the universe. The normal found a zigzag in the trench system and jumped in.

Naturally, the normal sniffed the body. It did smell odd but then everything on this miserable planet smelled odd. It didn't look for trip wires but that didn't matter as there were no trip wires on the threshkreen's body. The normal bent over and dug its claws into the corpse, giving one great heave to lift the body to where its god could take charge of it.

When the body was lifted there was a small bang, nothing so profound as the explosions that had danced among the People all day. Too quick for the normal's eye to see, a cylinder, about six inches across and nine or so high, bounded upward.

The Kessentai saw the cylinder, for the briefest moment, before it exploded. At this range, literally dozens of pieces of steel, some round, some jagged, tore into the God King's body. He had barely time to register that agony before the det cord went off, detonating in turn several pounds of plastic explosive.

It was not clear to the God King which it was that killed him, as he was turned into so much gas too quickly. Several dozen of the pellets struck the tenar and of these at least three hit the controls for the containment unit for the tenar's antimatter power pack. This immediately failed.

There was a blindingly bright flash to the east.

Though he was some miles away as the shock wave hit, it still took Binastarion several long moments as he fought for control of his tenar before he realized what it was that he was seeing. His Artificial Sentience announced, "Antimatter explosion, lord. I am attempting to analyze what caused it."

"The never-sufficiently-to-be-damned *humans* caused it!" the Kessentai snarled.

"Well . . . yes, lord," the AS admitted. "But *how* is the question. I have a suspicion the threshkreen have begun laying traps on the bodies they leave behind. The loss from this one, if it was a trap, far exceeds any nutrition we might harvest from all the human bodies found so far in the line."

Binastarion scowled. "Issue orders in my name: the humans' corpses are to be left unharvested until they can be properly searched and, if necessary, disarmed."

"This will play hell with logistics, lord," the AS answered. "But . . . it is done."

"I *hate* humans."

"Speaking of which, lord," the AS continued, "something has been disturbing me."

"And that would be?"

"I can't find the metal threshkreen. I lost them a

while ago but didn't think much of it. Now we have fought the humans again. You would have expected the metal threshkreen to be involved, at least in covering their breaking contact with us. But, no, there's been not a peep."

"They could have been pulled off-world," Binastarion commented, reasonably. "Or even back to their homeland to the north of here."

"It's possible, lord."

"Good Lord A'mighty." Sergeant Quijana saw the rising mushroom cloud, a comparatively small one, from the battle position his company had assumed to continue their delay of the enemy. He wondered for a moment, then pulled out his map and compass.

From this position . . . azimuth of . . . two hundred and seventy-eight degrees . . . mmmm . . .

"Get some, Gonzo."

INTERLUDE

Guanamarioch, a low ranking member of a clan not even powerful enough to defend its newly won lands from other Posleen clans larger, wealthier or more aggressive, found himself stuck with the most miserable job he could ever have imagined. Not for him the soaring in his tenar, high and free, above the ugly, miserable, stinking, green fester pit the locals called "the Darien." Oh, no. *That* was the province of the higher caste Kessentai. *His* tenar floated on automatic above the jungle overhead while he, instead, found himself on the ground, leading several hundred poorly armed, genetically marginal normals struggling through knee-deep, slimy, clinging *muck*.

Oh, well. At least Zira is here to keep me company.

Not that the muck was so bad. At least where the muck covered Guano's body the local flying insect life—they were called "mosquitoes"—couldn't get at him.

The problem was that the rain, incessantly pounding on the thick jungle roof overhead, then dripping down from the leaves and vines, washed the coating away. And where there was no muck, *there* were the mosquitoes.

There were little ones, big ones, medium ones. One and all, little or big, they were voracious. The little ones, especially, hurt when their sharp probosci jabbed Guano's open flesh. Surprisingly, the larger varieties' bites didn't hurt as much as the smaller but they, like their tiny cousins, left behind an insatiable itch. They left behind, too, a swelling that built up as more and more of the damned insects sank their probes into already swollen flesh.

Guano looked left to where one of his band was being led through the steaming jungle by a superior normal. The poor creature's eyes had been swollen shut by repeated attacks from kamikaze anopheles.

Though the rain stripped the Posleen of their protecting mud, it also drove the mosquitoes to cover. Unfortunately, whenever the rain stopped the bugs came out again with a vengeance to rape and pillage the Posleen horde before more mud could be applied. And even once re-covered with muck, the mosquitoes' bites itched horribly underneath.

"This can't go on, you know, Guano," announced Ziramoth. "These little flying devils are sucking better than three measures of nutrient transportation fluid out of each member of the host every cycle."

The God King half expanded his crest then relaxed it, the Posleen equivalent of a shrug.

"It grows back," he said.

"It grows back indeed," agreed the Kenstain, "if you and your band get enough food and water. Water is, of course, no problem. Here is all the water the host might desire . . . and more. Food, on the other hand . . ."

"Food," Guano agreed. *Yes, water we have in remarkable abundance.*

The clan had started their unwilling trek packing light, fleeing in near panic from an overwhelming surprise assault by three neighboring clans. They'd expected to find food en route. Unfortunately, the local animals for the most part fled the host en masse. The animals that did not tended to be small; so small, in fact, that a single hit from a railgun or blast from a shotgun was usually enough to leave little more than some scrawny and unnourishing feet, and a thin mist of blood, flesh, skin and fur floating on the breeze.

"The foraging is poor," the God King added.

"I doubt it's going to get much better, either," Zira replied. "I sense no teeming of any life within any useful distance that would worth eating. Not since that village of primitive brown threshkreen your band hit three cycles ago."

"That was good eating," Guano agreed. "But it didn't last long."

Guanamarioch could still almost smell the blood, fresh and hot, from the abattoir he and his band had made of that brown threshkreen village.

It had been a normal enough foraging expedition. A pair of scouts had returned to the main body of the Posleen band and signaled the presence of food in fair abundance. The normals, of course, could not count. Even had they been able to count, they were, frankly, too stupid to relate that count in intelligible speech. Instead they had used hand signals and body language—the motion of hands to muzzles, the shaking of heads as if tearing meat from bones, the lifting of muzzles skyward as if bolting down raw chunks of thresh, then the patting of flanks in simulated satiety—to indicate their find. Lastly, the senior of the two normals held palms apart at a certain distance to indicate the size of the find.

Guanamarioch measured the distance from palm to palm with his eyes, coming up with the answer, about four hundred thresh, give or take.

The thresh of this area, the God King knew, ran small. Still, the quantity indicated would be enough to feed his pack for several days, at the very least. He signaled his party to move to the feast, the two original scouts leading.

The trek to the village of thresh had not been especially long, but the water and the muck had made it more than ordinarily difficult. This was made even worse, once the scouts signaled that the village was near, by the need to keep silent lest any of the thresh escape.

At a point several hundred yards shy of the outskirts Guanamarioch stationed himself. From there two encircling arms of Posleen, led by superior normals of Guano's pack, reached out in a loving embrace.

Both Posleen tendrils reached the river on the far side of the thresh village at about the same time. The God King knew this from a sort of joy-filled shuddering that swept back to him from the leading superior normals. He withdrew his boma blade from its scabbard and was about to signal the attack when a strange thing happened. The normal next to him gave a soft, inarticulate cry and looked stupidly at Guano before dropping to his knees. From the creatures breast sprouted a length of what appeared to Guano to be wood.

"AS," the God King asked, "what was that?"

"What was what?" the Artificial Sentience responded. "I sense nothing."

Faintly, out of one eye, Guano spotted an indefinable streak moving fast through the jungle. He ducked just in time for the streak to miss him, hitting instead a tree just behind.

"That, you electronic dunce. What was that?" Guano indicated the thin sliver of wood quivering in the tree.

"Primitive weapon, of a kind not used by the People in uncounted millennia," the AS announced. "It is not ballistic and so I cannot sense it in flight. It contains little refined metal and so I cannot sense it at rest. I believe the locals call it an arrow. It is fired from a bow."

"Fat lot of help you are," the Posleen snarled, raising his railgun to the firing position.

"I work very well within design parameters," the AS countered snippily. "It is not my fault that some thresh exist below the level I was designed to sense."

Instead of answering, the God King let loose a long sweeping burst from his railgun. Vegetation exploded downrange and one forlorn cry told him that the bowman would not trouble his People in the future.

At the first firing, the rest of Guanamarioch's pack drew blades and charged. More arrows flew out, dropping a few of the host. And then the Posleen were on them.

Tiny thresh and larger ones with odd bumps on their bare chests screamed and ran in all directions. That is, they ran until reaching sight of one of the twin walls of Posleen harvesters closing on the village from both sides. At that some turned and ran back towards the center, while a few simply froze in place in open-mouthed 'terror until the reaping machine reached them.

Near the center, in an open-sided hut, the tiny and the oddly bumped thresh, some of them holding tiny ones in their arms, took shelter behind a lone thresh-kreen kneeling by a low fire and firing a rifle to the east. Guanamarioch could not tell if the threshkreen was actually hitting anything, but threats were not to be tolerated. Accompanied by a half dozen flankers the God King galloped toward the rifleman, boma blade raised high.

CHAPTER 29

May the forces of evil become confused
while your arrow is on its way to the target.
—George Carlin

SOUTHCOM Headquarters, the "Tunnel," Quarry Heights, Panama

"We could try to nuke 'em," Rivera observed while gazing at the map that showed a massive concentration of Posleen clustered at the base of the Darien on the Colombian side.

"I've asked already," General Page answered. "Even though I can't think of a single good way to get a half dozen major bombs into the area, I still asked." In a falsetto voice, obviously meant to mimic the President's, he continued, "No, General. I won't let you damage the Rain Forest. We have treaties, obligations, internal laws. I could be impeached for letting you use nuclear weapons on that part of the world."

Rivera shrugged. *Oh, well. It was worth a shot. Glad the Marine at least had the balls to ask.*

"What else do we know about that migration?" Page asked.

"Not much, sir. We've gotten two LRRPs"—Long Range Reconnaissance Patrols—"into the area—and lost another three trying—but all they can tell us is about the edges. Well . . . I suppose that the fact we lost three of the LRRPs trying to penetrate the edges of the infestation tells us the bastards are pretty dense on the ground."

It was Page's turn to shrug. Information in war cost; always had, always would.

"How's the Army's Fifth Infantry doing?"

Rivera's finger traced an arc running northeast to southwest on the map. "They're dug-in in a half perimeter around the end of the Inter-American Highway, where the Darien Gap begins. SF teams are out on the flanks. There have been a couple of half-hearted attempts to storm the perimeter, but the Posleen appear to be stretched out in a long thin column that begins at that massive cluster on the map." The finger tapped the map twice. "They can't really bring any mass to bear. The road's not bad, at least until you get to the Gap, where it disappears, so we've been able to keep a steady supply of mines and shells coming to them. The Fifth's holding. I *said* they would."

"Eventually, you know," Page retorted, "the Posleen will find the flanks."

"Yessir. That's why the SF teams are out on the flanks, to give the regiment warning of when it's time to pull back. The Seven-Sixtieth Engineer company is building them fall-back positions all the way to where the highway breaks out into the open east of the City."

Battle Position Ovalo, Darien Province, Republic of Panama

"Oh, I was drunk the day my mom got out of prison . . ."

Every unit needs a song. For the 760th, that was it. They were an unusual group, very tight, very cohesive and, in large part related by blood. They came from Marion, Virginia, in the United States. They'd brought their music with them. The crew of a bulldozer sang it even over the incessant roar of their piece of equipment.

Carter shook his head. He wasn't a country boy himself, but he'd grown up in the Army surrounded by them. That this unit had chosen that song? Well, it was no surprise.

"How close to complete, are you, Sam?" Carter asked of the 760th commander, a West Pointer long out of the Regular Army and transferred to the Reserves.

Sam spit out some tobacco juice—he'd picked up some appalling habits since assuming command of the company—and answered, "'Bout seventy percent here, sir. But we've already got a good start of prepping the next position back."

"Good work, Captain Cheatham. Pass on to your men my congratulations."

"Will do, Colonel."

Carter turned away to remount his Hummer to go east, back to the mass of his regiment. Even over the diesel's sound he heard, "She got run over by a dang ol' train . . ."

Shaking his head, Carter headed back down the highway cut through the jungle, back to the first battle position where he intended to bleed the yellow aliens white.

Darien Province, Republic of Panama

It should have teemed with life, that little village. After long weeks' absence Ruiz expected to be met at the outskirts by swarming children. His wives, old now but—since he was a soldier—soon to be rejuvenated to youth and health, ought to have been raising joyous cries at his return.

But . . . there was nothing: no children, no wives, no . . . people. All was silent as death. The Indian chief stepped out of his canoe to emptiness.

Ruiz enter the village stealthily. There wasn't much physical damage. Then again, there hadn't been much physical to the village *to* destroy. Some of the Chocoes' rude huts were knocked over, but a strong wind might have done that. The fire circles were still in place but the hearths internal to each hut were mostly broken. Ruiz placed a hand over one of them near the edge of the village. It was cold: *At least three days since fire burned here*, he thought.

Drawing an arrow from his quiver and feeding it to his prized bow, Ruiz began stalking stealthily from hut to tree to tree to hut along the outskirts of the tiny grass and wood town. At each hut that was still standing he paused to look inside. Still, nothing.

From the exterior he worked his way inward, still circling, still looking for life or some other sign to tell what had befallen his home town. Near the center he found his first clue, a perfectly sliced rifle of the type the gringos had attempted, and failed, to teach him to shoot. The pieces of the rifle lay beside a scattering of expended brass cases. Of the soldier, or

Chocoes scout (for a few had been able to learn to shoot), who had fired the rifle and left those cases there was no obvious physical sign.

Ruiz bent low to sniff the ground. *Blood . . . even with the rains having washed most of it away over the last few days something or, more likely, some*one *was butchered here.*

The scent of blood was faint, almost too much so for the chief to follow. But, however faint it was, it was enough, if only just, to lead Ruiz by his jungle-sensitive nose to the center of the village.

From there, and based also on his scout through the village, Ruiz was able to read the signs.

The Chocoes with the rifle, surrounded as he was by four hundred snarling demons and a like number of screaming women and children, still had the highly tuned senses of a jungle hunter. He turned a fierce and determined face toward the beasts who charged him. Whispering a prayer to the Holy Virgin, Maria (and intoning the name of a lesser god known only to the Chocoes and a few gringo anthropologists), he began stroking the trigger to spit bullets at his enemies.

The Chocoes rifleman was gratified to see first one, then another, then a third of the beasts fall, bullet-struck.

Sadly, however, to kill three, however worthy an achievement, still left more than enough to hack him into spare ribs once they reached him. He had time only to raise the rifle to a high port before the first blade, this one carried by one of the beasts with a raised crest, split the rifle, and the rifleman, in two.

❖　　　❖　　　❖

As Ruiz followed the blood trail into the center of his former home the scent became stronger. Soon enough, he did not need the scent of blood to lead him Instead, his eyes alighted on a pile of bones standing several feet high not far from his own hut.

The bones had lain there, undisturbed except perhaps by ants, since the tribes' fires had gone out. This much Ruiz's trained eye knew for a certainty. He walked to the pile, and began to examine the remaining traces of his family.

Mixed in among the human bones were others, oddly shaped though still the same dull, grayish white as the human bones. These Ruiz set aside.

The human bones he began to place reverently in their own pile. There was no chance of identifying individual remains, except in a few cases. He could, for example, tell which was the skull of his favorite wife, Belinda, by the twisted incisor of one skull. The top of the skull had been removed. Nothing remained inside. What the raiders had not scavenged, the ants had.

Fondly, Ruiz held Belinda's skull in his left hand and brushed off the few remaining ants. He forced a smile and said something that was not Spanish, but which still sounded very much like an endearment. He touched the misshapen tooth with the thumb of his right. Silently, he whispered a prayer, for Belinda and all the others.

"Whoever did this, my best wife, I promise you they will pay."

Ruiz could not afford to spend time in ceremonies of purification. While he suspected the alien horde (and having examined the bones he had found, he had come to believe that these demons were at least from another world) would be easy enough to track, he wanted one particular group, the same as that which had erased his home. In the Darien, the trail might be lost at any moment. Moreover, he had few enough clues to go by. Still, and despite his time in the Panamanian jail, he found his jungle sense had returned. He would find them.

The aliens had left little enough of food in the village. Even the rice had, for the most part, been taken away. There were things hidden, of course, including several cases of the nasty pouch rations the gringos ate that they had left when a team of them spent several days in the village teaching Ruiz and the young men to blow things up. Of the meals he took several cases.

He also scavenged a fair number of the arrows his clan had used to try to defend themselves. Some he found stuck into trees or the ground. Still more remained in their quivers where the ferocity of the attack had left no time to use them. One, in particular, he found embedded in a tree as far from the village as a man might hope to see to shoot. He sniffed at the arrow's feathers. There was something there, in the feathers, the faintest of odors. It was slightly different from the scents he had picked up from the bones he had lovingly buried. The scent had the slightest trace of the way the air smelled after lightning had struck the earth or one of the jungle's massive trees. Too, he was sure he smelled the alien leader, the odor being something like that on his tribe's bones, but more acrid, stronger. He closed his eyes and sniffed a final few times at the arrow's feathers, committing the scent to jungle-sharp memory.

Along with the meals, the gringos had cached several hundred pounds of explosive, detonators, and five cases of the things they called "claymore mines," at six mines to the case. He loaded the food, all six cases of the mines, and another one hundred pounds of C-4, plus other accoutrements into his canoe. Then Ruiz went to sleep. The next morning he cast off and proceeded upstream, to where he hoped to intercept the aliens who had butchered his family.

After a night's rest and a day's journey Ruiz noticed that the normal cacophony of the jungle was ended. Everything was eerily silent, the animals—so he supposed—having all run out of the way of the demons. Even most of the insect noises were gone.

Silently as a snake slithering along a tree branch, Ruiz guided his canoe to the river bank. There, still quiet, he tied it off to a tree, and adjusted some foliage to provide cover. Then, he closed his eyes and moved his head from left to right and back again, measuring the lack of sound.

There, he thought, having found the direction of greatest quiet. *There is where I will find the demons.*

Ruiz refreshed his body paint the better to blend into the jungle then, taking his beloved bow and a quiver of arrows, he set out on foot to find his foe.

The jungle could be dangerous, as Ruiz knew better than most. For him and his people though, it could never be as dangerous as the civilized life of the city dwellers. The jungle could, at most, kill. The city ate souls.

One of the jungle's potentially more deadly attributes,

not so common as all that but still to be watched out for, was quicksand. It was rarely very deep and a calm man could get out of it unless rain and flash flooding caught him while he was stuck in it. Since this was the Darien and since massive sudden rain was normal . . .

Not far from the river bank, Ruiz found a patch which he skirted carefully. It would not do to be trapped in the stuff and have the demons find him thus helpless. Skirting the quicksand, the Chocoes walked completely around it to a point opposite where he had begun to skirt it.

Hmmm. If I need to run quickly, I might have to go directly across. With the demons on my tail that would be the definition of "suck," as the gringos say.

He looked up at the trees until he spotted a vine. Shimmying up until he caught it, he dragged the vine down and secured it where he could use it to swing across the patch of sand.

What little jungle sound had remained completely disappeared as Ruiz closed on the Posleen, their own sounds—snarling and yelping, grunting and, apparently, cursing—replacing whatever there was of the natural Darien.

He had seen pictures before, of course, but the pictures had not prepared him for the reality. For a moment he shook with fear.

The fear led him to think of what his tribe, his wives and his children had faced in the moments before their deaths, a snarling horde of demons descending on them to butcher babies in front of their mothers. Hate quickly took over once again from fear. The fear had concealed that the demons had no weapons he could see that were better than what appeared to be large-bore shotguns. Ruiz wasn't afraid of shotguns.

The previously still jungle felt a sudden light wind. Trees overhead groaned as they were forced to sway in the breeze. Ruiz lifted his nose and opened his mouth slightly to taste the air.

Ah . . . perhaps that is my special enemy. Something special, then, for this first bite of revenge, Ruiz thought. *Something to put lasting fear into the demons.*

Getting down on his belly Ruiz began to crawl forward to some bushes which had grown up in the space left by a tree fallen to age or catastrophe a couple of years prior. Reaching them, he parted the leaves slightly to view his enemy. From the quiver across his back he deftly and silently drew a single arrow and fitted it to his bow. Then he arose to one knee, drew the bow and let fly.

The arrow sailed straight and true and, most importantly, silently until its needle sharp point embedded itself a foot deep into a Posleen normal's torso. Yellow blood began to gush out around the wound while the normal danced in keening agony searching for the source of its pain.

Since all the other demons appeared to have turned their attention at the one wounded and dying, Ruiz thought he could risk another shot and perhaps even a third. Again an arrow flew; again it flew straight and true.

That target gave a single inarticulate scream as it vaulted stem over stern in a complete somersault before falling in a dead heap on the jungle floor.

Ruiz shook his head, unseen. *These critters really are as stupid as the gringos said.*

Another arrow flew and then another. One actually missed its intended target but did manage to strike a different demon in its right rear quarter. Again the demon began to snarl and spin like the first of Ruiz's targets, except in this last case the alien began worrying at the arrow with its fangs. Alien heads began to twist rhythmically following the gyrations of their wounded brethren. Two more arrows flew, both striking deep and deadly.

Okay, this is fun but not enough. And besides, I'll run out of arrows before I run out of demons.

Taking a deep breath, Ruiz strung his bow across his back and put his thumbs to his temples. Then he raised his head over the bushes and uttered something that sounded much like, "Oogaboogabooga," while wriggling his fingers.

There was a moment's confusion on the part of the demons, their attention torn between their wounded and dying peers and the bit of thresh that had appeared. The indecision didn't last long. The Posleen hit or killed would still be there to harvest later on. Meanwhile, if they didn't hurry, this new thresh might get away. With a mass cry they drew their blades and, fifty or so of them baying, gave chase.

Yes, those were shotguns that Ruiz had seen. Unfortunately, they had a little more range than human shotguns. He had several pieces in his back, buttocks and legs to prove that. The pellets were painful, but not debilitating. They had the added advantage of leaving a light blood trail for his pursuers to follow, though it took a peculiar frame of mind to consider that an advantage.

Ruiz still had a good sixty yards on his pursuers; otherwise, the shotguns would have made short work of him. However, despite his short Chocoes legs pumping in a blur, the demons were gaining. They'd long since have run him down but for his superior ability to dodge around trees and through the jungle tangles.

Aha! There's my patch of lovely quicksand, he thought, redoubling his efforts to stay ahead. The vine was still where he had left it secured. He grabbed it, shook it loose and risked a quick look behind. *Ah, shit!* The Posleen were closer than he had thought.

Ruiz took a running start and pulled himself up by the vine. "Aiaiaiaiaiai!" He sailed across the quicksand a few feet above it and slightly faster than he could have run. At the far side, the side nearest the river and his canoe, he let go his grip, flew unaided through the air for a moment and then tumbled and rolled to a stop on the mucky ground. Pushing with whatever part of his body was in contact with the ground—knees, elbows . . . lips, earlobes, eyelashes—he scrambled onward to the safety of the river and . . . stopped.

The sound of his pursuers had changed in moments from keen baying to mere keening. A tone of fear and despair had taken over their snarls and grunts. Cautiously he turned around and unslung his bow, nocking another arrow before slinking low back in the direction from which he had come.

The aliens were chest deep in the quicksand, muzzles and eyes raised skyward. The sand around each of them was roughened, as if they had struggled for a bit before realizing that this only made them sink faster. Of shotguns, or other ranged weapons, he saw not a sign beyond some linear marks in the sand's surface where they had perhaps been dropped.

Smiling broadly, Ruiz stepped up very near to the edge of the quicksand pit and sat down, cross-legged and in full view of any of the demons who might care to look in his direction. Reaching into a little bag he wore on his belt he pulled out some cheap tobacco, rolling papers, and a plastic tube containing matches. Then he sat with his back against a tree, happily rolled himself a cigarette and lit it, all the while watching the aliens sink lower and lower. Carefully, Ruiz counted the number of demons caught in his trap by making notches on a stick. He wanted to avenge his people, if possible many times over.

The lower lip of the last Posleen to go under the wet sand quivered like a naughty school boy's caught in some mischief before it too sank—still quivering—from sight.

SOUTHCOM Headquarters, the "Tunnel," Quarry Heights, Panama

"What's this Darien really like, anyway?" Page asked of Rivera.

"Sir, you ever do Jungle School at Fort Sherman?"

"Sure," the Marine answered. "On my way to Vietnam in . . . umm . . . Sixty-six, it was."

"Then you know the Mojingas, right?"

Page twisted his jaw a bit and remembered back before answering, "The Mojingas? Made Vietnam's jungle seem positively civilized."

"Right. Well, the Mojingas is *small*. Multiply the

size about fifty-thousandfold. Then make it ten times wetter, twenty times more mosquito infested. Add in thirty times more snakes, forty times more fucking ants which are fifty times hungrier. It's fucking hell, sir."

"Oooh. Poor Fifth Infantry."

Rivera smiled nastily. "No, sir. Don't pity the Fifth. They're like the Chocoes; they can live in that shit. But if you want to spread some pity, give some to the Posleen."

INTERLUDE

A human would have said that Guanamarioch was "spooked" at the loss of an eighth of his pack without trace. The human would have been right, too.

The God King trembled slightly as he walked eastward. To Ziramoth, walking beside him, he said, "I just don't get it Zira. More than fifty of my people . . . disappeared without a trace. They weren't shot, or burned. Nobody harvested them for thresh except for the six that were hit by what my Artificial Sentience called "arrows." It's like some huge creature opened its jaws and sucked them in, not even spitting out the bones. Zira, I *followed* their trail. They just disappeared into *nothing*."

Whatever Zira had been about to say was lost as the dark trail ahead of them erupted in screams and firing.

Posleen were essentially immune to any form or terrestrial poison that man had yet discovered. Nerve gas had no effect. Blister agents had little (but then blister agents were among the least deadly means of human chemical warfare anyway). Blood agents?

Puhleeze. Not even some of the more esoteric Russian chemicals had had any noticeable effect on the aliens. Diseases? Not a chance.

That said, their bodies were still composed of something analogous to flesh. The beings who had tinkered with Posleen genes in the dim mists of antiquity had begun with a more or less normal pre-sentient creature, then modified those early forms for reasonable threats. Some threats, though, just weren't reasonable.

The ant had neither name nor number. It never noted the lack. As much as a Posleen normal was content to be a part of its clan, the ant lived to serve its colony, though in this case the colony was a series of trees. In a real sense, even more than Posleen normals, the ant was a mere appendage to that greater organism.

The vibrations of the unusual centauroid creatures passing nearby had disturbed the ant, raising it from its slumbers, along with many thousands of its fellows. Like the others that joined it, poised along the tree branches of the colony, the ant was a bit under an inch long, colored black. The Posleen slogging below never noticed this; the night was dark and most of the ants were concealed from sight. The Posleen likewise never noted the immense and terribly sharp mandibles borne by the tens of thousands of ants among the trees. It would have taken more curiosity than the aliens, as a race, possessed for them to note that the mandibles were hollow and capable of injecting not venom, but a rather concentrated solution of formic acid.

The ant couldn't have told you why it jumped, when it did. Instead, at some point the moment just seemed *right*.

Wheee!

It landed atop the broad and bare back of a Posleen normal. It didn't bite right away, for that would have shown a degree of initiative highly discouraged in ants. Instead, it waited until a few dozen or so of its sisters had likewise landed on the Posleen, as well as some thousands more on the backs of other Posleen.

That moment seemed right, too. *Chomp! ChompChoChomChompChoChomChomp . . .*

When you're an ant, a tree ant . . . a *soldier* tree ant, you just live for those team-building moments when you and your tree ant soldier buddies can donate excess concentrated formic acid into something that really isn't expecting it.

The Posleen normal noticed the arrival of the ant, and of its many, many sisters. At first, it thought it might be more of the rain that seemed to stop only to build up more rain buddies to the side. It seemed odd though, that these rain drops didn't slide off its back. The normal found this somewhat disturbing in a distant sort of way.

And then there was pain. Oh, my, yes; there was great, burning, agonizing, shrieking pain, emanating from dozens of spots. The normal reared up in shock and surprise. Sadly, as it did so, it knocked over another normal who was also experiencing an ant-induced epiphany of pain . . . and no happier about it than was the first normal.

A little annoyed, and more than a little stupid, the second normal drew a boma blade and charged at the danger it could see, ignoring the danger it could not. This was bad enough. But some of the normals, many of them, in fact, carried better than boma blades. They had railguns. So did other oolts that fed themselves spontaneously into the fighting.

Wheee, thought the ants. *Chomp.*

When Guanamarioch and Ziramoth, leading Guano's pack, arrived at the scene, there was nothing left but carnage. Oh, yes, a few normals still lived, though they were in a pretty bad state of shock. For the rest? Guano whistled over one of his cosslain and made signs for it to begin the thresh gathering.

"Maybe it is to the good, Zira. I am feeling awfully weak lately with what the little flying demons are draining from my body."

Ziramoth sighed. "So are we all, my young friend. So are we all."

CHAPTER 30

There are some defeats more triumphant
than victories.
                                    —Michel de Montaigne

Nata Line, Republic of Panama

Dictator Boyd was waiting at the southernmost of the
two major crossing points as the long lines of weary,
bedraggled, and half-beaten looking men crossed into
safety, but with millions of Posleen on their tails. The
armored vehicles looked, if anything, more beaten
than the men. Blood ran down the sides of some of
them from wounded men stacked atop.

Still, it hadn't gone badly, Boyd knew. Yes, a few
companies had been cut off and annihilated here and
there on the long retreat. Worse, one whole battalion
of mechanized infantry had been lost without a single
survivor in the ruins of Santiago. Even so, better than
eighty-five percent of the two heavy divisions had
escaped, along with half a million civilians, many of them
young boys to become soldiers and young girls to breed
them. There was equipment to make good the losses,

too, some of it on hand and some more en route. The losses of men could not be made up so easily, of course.

Boyd wore battle dress, his helmet off and tucked under his left arm so the passing troops could recognize him. Maybe it would mean nothing to them; maybe no one would recognize him. In a personal way, it would have made him happier if none had. Panama had a long and unfortunate history of dictatorial rule. He hoped, fervently, that he would be the last dictator the country ever had to endure.

Unfortunately for his happiness, many did recognize him and those quickly passed the word to the others. He assumed it was being passed by radio as well because, looking through his binoculars, he saw men begin to wave at him from the distance, well before they closed to a range at which they could have recognized him.

One track pulled out of line and trundled over to where Boyd stood, surrounded by his twenty-four aides de camp. Officially, they were "lictors." The aides stepped briskly out of the way lest the track run them over. The track—it was a Russian-built BMP—stopped abruptly. Boyd heard the squeaking of a metal door being pushed open. A young, dirty-faced sergeant emerged. Boyd looked over the face carefully. It wasn't just dirt. The boy had a weariness about him Boyd hadn't seen since the long retreat and the fight back in a place called the Ardennes.

Bone tired or not, the young man saluted smartly. "Sir, Sergeant Quijana reports."

Boyd returned the salute a little awkwardly. Would he *never* get used to being a senior officer? He supposed not. "What can I do for you, Sergeant?"

Quijana shook his head. "Nothing, *Dictador*. I just wanted to tell you we racked 'em up like firewood. All the way back. We killed 'em at ten to one, maybe twenty to one. Hell, for all I know it might have been one hundred or more to one, especially if you count what the guns reaped. The boys were . . . well, sir, they were just great. But we've gotta go back, sir. That's our *land*. We can't let the aliens keep it. It's *ours*."

Boyd smiled and nodded. "We're not going to let them keep it, son. Just like you said, it's ours and they can't have it while we live. But for now, before you can take it back, you and your boys need to go get a rest, eat some decent food, shower, maybe change uniforms. And I figure you'll need more ammunition, too; that, and fuel. Do those things. Get rested. Get ready. 'Cause, son, we *are* going back."

Santiago, Veraguas, Republic of Panama

The town was half aflame as Binastarion rode his tenar eastwards through it. There were human bodies scattered about, here and there, almost all of them in the mottled pattern clothing the threshkreen favored. The God King was pleased that his orders with regard to human bodies were being followed. He was even more pleased that there had been no antimatter explosions. In time, and hopefully before the bodies rotted away in the sun, they would be recovered. And, if not, at least they would serve to fertilize the soil of this place and feed the People that way.

Binastarion brought his tenar to a halt, allowing the columns of the eastward moving People to pass him. Slowly, he rotated his sled completely around. The People were gathering food that was not thresh-kreen. Some of the locals' horned food-animals had been killed together in an open field by one of the humans' buildings. Apparently, they had been put down by the locals themselves.

Some normals were engaged in reducing the meat of these horned food-animals to easily ported chunks of flesh and bone. The God King couldn't tell how many of the animals there had been; the harvesting was already well in process. He watched as a boma blade deftly sliced one of the animals into sections. He watched as the normals lifted the sections to take them to the host.

The God King did not see, however, the yellow-ish disk that flew up when the last section had been lifted. All he knew was that a dozen of the People had been standing around the horned food-animals' bodies one second, and that they were lying on their backs the next, waving stumps in the air from which spouted bright fountains of yellowish blood. Even at this distance Binastarion could hear the normals' pitiful keening cries.

"The humans call them 'Bouncing Barbies,' milord. I don't know why," the AS said after a few moments.

"AS, pass to the host: There will be no more har-vesting of the humans' food-animals until their bodies have been properly examined for traps."

"It is done, Binastarion," the Artificial Sentience answered.

"I *hate* humans."

"I am beginning to, as well, milord."

Binastarion rode on. Further into the town, he saw

a group of normals led by a lower ranking Kessentai carving away the door to one of the thresh buildings. Under the boma blade, the door quickly fell away. The group of the People entered.

Kaboom. The human building simply disintegrated.

Binastarion sighed. Such clever little devils these threshkreen were.

"AS, pass to the host . . ."

"I am already doing it, Binastarion. You realize that our logistic problems will get worse, much worse, if we don't harvest the food available?"

"I know that, AS. But what can we do? We lost thousands back at that defensive line when the Kessentai's tenar's antimatter went off. We just lost a dozen to that 'Bouncing Barbie.' How many disappeared when that building exploded? We lose as much as we gain when we try to harvest these thresh."

"Then I suppose we'll have to subsist the People on our own losses, Binastarion. Odd, is it not, that the threshkreen have become our primary food source in quite this way?"

The God King didn't answer but, rather, continued in his tenar eastward until he came upon a group of the People, cut down by the threshkreen in a narrow alley of the town. A small pack of normals were in the process of reducing these to thresh. *Hmmm. I wonder . . .* Binastarion backed his tenar off about one hundred meters.

Kaboom.

"AS, pass to the host . . ."

USS Des Moines, *Southwest of the Nata Line*

Firing in support of the Nata line was desultory and didn't require Daisy's full attention. Thus, she was able to spend her conscious time with the body growing under the process of "inauspicious cloning" in the tank deep down in the bowels of the ship.

Sintarleen was with Daisy, tinkering with something or other. "She is almost ready to be decanted," the Indowy said. "A day or two more . . . perhaps a week at most . . ."

"Do you think he'll like it?" Daisy asked worriedly of the Indowy, in his own tongue. "I made it for him. But . . . I don't know . . ."

Sinbad shrugged, a habit he had picked up unconsciously from the human crew. Also in his own language he answered, "I have hardly made a study of human aesthetics, Ship Daisy. But the body looks like your avatar and we know the captain likes *that*. Besides, this one will be stronger than any human female that ever was naturally born, quicker and healthier, too. She will bear the captain many fine offspring . . ."

Daisy and the Indowy went silent for a moment. "Your clan will have no more offspring, will it, Sinbad, unless you return safely to them?"

"This is so," the Indowy admitted, with infinite sadness. "All our many millennia will be at an end."

Daisy's avatar's eyes began to flicker, as they often did when she was deep in thought. After a few long moments she announced, "Your clan will not die with you, Sintarleen of the Indowy."

The little bat-faced alien cocked his head. "But I

am the last male of my clan. All that are left off-world are females and transfer neuters . . . Ohhh."

Daisy's eyes flickered some more, stopped, flickered again. "I have just sent a bank draft paying for the freedom of your remaining clan members from the Darhel who hold their contracts, Sinbad; that, and passage to the world of Agitrapis, which is off the route of the Posleen invasion. I apologize that I did not think of this sooner. When they get there, they will find a healthy account to begin to rebuild your clan anew and in liberty. And you shall someday join them, either in this body or in a new one. Prepare a sample of your own DNA."

Strong emotions were anathema to the Indowy culture, almost as dangerous as they were to the Darhel. Even so, Sintarleen felt tears rising—*this* emotional response, however rarely seen, they had in common with humans—and, to cover them, went back to his adjustments of the cloning tank.

Firebase Miranda, Santa Fe, Veraguas Province, Republic of Panama

The BM-21s, even more than most forms of artillery, were area fire weapons. Thus, Digna didn't really care if the gunners were off a mil or two—or *five or ten* for that matter—in their sight settings; the range probable error of the rockets was greater than that anyway. She did, however, care deeply that the gunners could adjust the sights and re-lay the launchers quickly to something reasonably close to the data called for by the fire plan.

Even a ten mil error was only a couple of hundred meters at most of the ranges she would be firing at. When one is planning to toss almost four thousand rockets in under a minute at an area of about twenty-five square kilometers, or one for every .6 hectares, a few meters this way or that made little difference. When one is planning on doing that every ten minutes for nearly four hours? Well . . . who cared, really, where any given warhead—or forty—went?

"Freeze and stand to!" Digna shouted, when the rocket battery announced "Up." Immediately, every gunner pulled back from their sights and—joined by the rest of the crew—stood at attention by their systems. She clicked the stopwatch in her left hand when the last of them had frozen. She looked down at the watch. *Not too bad. Not too bad, that is if they're reasonably on target.*

Determinedly, Digna began to walk toward the center launcher, or base launcher, of the battery. "Tomas, see that none of them play with their sights."

"*Si, doña,*" Herrera answered.

Digna didn't really give the order for Herrera's benefit. He'd been through the drill so many times he didn't need to be told. Instead it was for the benefit of the crews. Those girls didn't need to be tempted into the ass-whipping they would get for cheating; bad enough the ass-whipping they would receive if their launchers were not reasonably close to the target data.

But the launchers were. They were actually better laid than Digna had expected. Perhaps the constant drilling in the fire plan, plus a few contingency fire missions, had done the trick after all.

Patting the base launcher crew chief—another of her almost innumerable great-granddaughters—affectionately on the shoulder, Digna said, "Well done, child." Then she climbed down from the launcher and proceeded to walk to the next, the eagle-eyed Herrera keeping watch still that no gunner played with her sight.

In walking to the next, Digna also had to cross the hard-surfaced road that led further into the valley north of Santa Fe. She looked up the road and wondered just what the devil was there, still hidden and still under guard by gringo military police. The gringo mechanized regiment she knew about, of course. But it was the other things, the things that had come in covered and kept under guard, which really excited her interest.

The "goo" of the suit kept him comfortable and free of sores. The automatic food processors converted his waste into edible mush, still. Some of it even tasted half decent, though there was no joy to be found in the almost textureless gruel. Even so, Snyder wondered if he were losing his mind. His AID had warned him that might happen.

He'd lost track of time long since. Ever since he'd felt that last jarring, and felt it only slightly because of the goo and the suit's normal dampening, there had been nothing. N.O.T.H.I.N.G. Sometimes, in those weeks, he had been able to track the battle. But this was rare. Without his suit to translate the Spanish into English even the radio calls were meaningless. They were meaningless, that is, except when they were frightening. He had heard too many young Spanish voices end in screams, pain and panic.

In between those times of dimly or not at all understood radio calls, he had slept a lot. At least his dreams had given him *some* escape from the silvery-goo-blahness.

Nothing to do. Not a book to read. No music. Not even a fucking projection of a fucking map to study. Please, God, not too much longer. I can't stand it much longer. Win or lose, God, GET ME OUT OF THIS SHIT!

Snyder wondered if the battle was over, if it had passed him by. He thought of his battalion, lying asleep and helpless in their suits as the Posleen took them and, one by one, hacked the suits open to get at the meat inside. He imagined his men, thus abruptly awakened, giving one final scream of horror each before . . .

Shaken, Snyder forced himself to calm. At least, it was a semblance of calm. His AID, had it been awake, would not have been fooled.

Darien Province, Republic of Panama

The sniper had made a guess, based on his experience in the Army and in the jungle, that this particular tree would be likely to rise a few meters above the surrounding canopy. Sergeant First Class Heimeyer, short, stout and incredibly strong, had spent more than an hour ascending this tree and working his way into the topmost branches. Once there, he had spent even more time in hauling up his weapon, a .510 Whisper manufactured by SSK industries in Wintersville, Ohio. The .510 was a special purchase,

Army Special Operations Command having its own ways about such things. Built on a Finnish Sako TRS-G action, it was in every way a marvel of human engineering and manufacture.

The rifle and the cartridge it fired were called "Whispers" because the bullet was subsonic, making no audible *crack* in its flight. With a suppressor attached, the thing was capable of minute of angle accuracy at six hundred meters. In the hands of a first class sniper, and the sergeant had been honor graduate from his sniper course and a national level competitor for years, this meant a reasonable probability of a killing hit on a target the size of a Posleen at nearly a kilometer, this despite the low velocity and it high angle it required. The likelihood of a kill at six hundred meters or less approached unity.

Having spent hours in ascending, and more in hauling up his rifle and other equipment, the sergeant spent the better part of a day in preparing a firing position worthy of his weapon, himself and his enemy.

The tree swayed a bit in the breeze. There was nothing much to be done about that; he'd just have to factor it in to his shooting. Moreover, the leaves were thick up here, where the tropical sun fed them directly. This severely limited the sergeant's field of view. Even so, ever practical, the sergeant instead concentrated on doing what he could. He crawled out far on a stout limb and sliced away no more leaves than required to give him a fair arc while still providing concealment. He'd also tied in a crosspiece, in the fork of two branches, to give him stability. Additionally, he taped and tied a part of a sleeping mat directly to the main branch to give a more comfortable firing position.

Below, the team that had accompanied the sergeant filled sandbags which they piled into a small basket a few at a time. These Heimeyer hauled up a few at a time to reinforce his position. Several deep, the sandbags tended to explode individually but harmlessly when struck by the aliens' railguns, absorbing most of the energy in the process. By morning, the position was ready.

Then the sergeant settled down to wait.

Rodriguez Home, Via Argentina, *Panama City, Panama*

"It's the waiting I hate most, Alma," Marielena sniffled. "Not knowing if he's dead or alive or even on this planet. Not knowing what's to become of me, or the baby or . . . or any of us." Her hands went automatically to cover her still unswollen stomach. The thought of the aliens slicing her open to get at the delicacy of her unborn child was too much. Nausea rising, in tears, she ran for the bathroom.

Posleen Territory, West of the Nata Line, Republic of Panama

Hungry, hungry . . . and I, at least, am eating. The same cannot be said of the host.

Binastarion looked down from his tenar at the long dun-colored columns marching below. There was something in their shambling gate that told of weakness of body and spirit. He'd already had to give the order to his underlings to kill and butcher one in twenty of the normals to keep the remaining nineteen going. One in twenty, though, at what the normals ate, was not enough. He knew he must call for a rest before trying to assault this next threshkreen line and that, when he did so, another one in twenty of the host must be given to feed the rest. Otherwise, they would not have the strength to fight through the human defenses.

It would all be worth it, though, if the People could only win through. Ahead, past the humans' lines, were literally millions of thresh and more millions of food animals.

And there was a new thought, too. Though he didn't know where it had come from, the Net had what appeared to be an open offer from the thresh of the continent of Europe. Perhaps the offer had been uploaded by a Darhel AID. Binastarion put nothing past the Elves.

In any case, the thresh of Europe or their Darhel patrons seemed to be suggesting that, should Binastarion and his clan succeed in taking control of the broad ditch that connected the two major bodies of water on this miserable world, trade—a human and Darhel form of mutual *edas*—might be possible, if the ditch could be kept functioning to allow European water vessels through.

Could he count on the thresh to so succor him? Binastarion didn't know. He did know that he didn't care an abat's hindquarters for what happened to the clans of the People fighting to conquer this Europe. Why should the Europeans care any more for the fate of the humans of these two continents?

It was a new notion, this idea of trade with an alien species, and one that required careful thinking through. Perhaps such an arrangement could be beneficial enough for Binastarion to raise his clan to mighty heights before this world was plunged into orna'adar. Perhaps . . .

Ah, never mind all that for now. I am counting snack-nestlings before they are gutted. For now, I must get to this next line. I must feed my host. Then I must break through the tough shell to further feed upon the soft meat of these thresh. In any case, I have my doubts about enough of my clan being trainable enough to operate this waterway. Perhaps if my son, Riinistarka, had lived. The clan chief felt a great stab of pain at the loss. That one had been something special to his God King father.

Assembly Area Pedrarias, East of the Nata Line, Republic of Panama

Suarez stood on a little knoll, surrounded by the troops and tracks of the 1st Mechanized Infantry Division. He had walked here from his headquarters near the Inter-American Highway, neatly spaced between both divisions of the heavy corps.

The vehicles lay under nets, though the proper term was "screens." These had two important functions. One was to shield them from view should the Posleen attempt either a raid in their flying sleds or a more significant attack with one of their landers. They hadn't done so, yet, but Suarez had to consider the possibility. The other reason was simple shade. This was no jungle area, though it had trees, but rather was mostly open savannah. Without some cover from the glaring sun the soldiers would have roasted.

Suarez wiped a coating of sweat from his brow. *It's hot enough to roast even with the camouflage nets. How much worse would it be without them?*

Normally, the maneuvering troops would have been entitled, doctrinally, to their choice of ground, pushing the artillery, etc., out to more unfavorable terrain. This had not been possible. With twenty-six *hundred* guns and mortars lined up within a few miles of Nata Line, there had simply been no room for the mechanized forces.

Suarez tried to envision what it would be like when those guns released a deluge of steel onto the Posleen massed in the attack. The mind just boggled; nothing like it had been seen on Earth since the great battles of annihilation fought between the Germans and the Russians from 1941 to 1945.

There were more artillery weapons, too, nestled north and south among the hills of Chitre and the mountains of the *Cordillera Central*. These were mostly rocket launcher regiments, each with a battalion of cannon artillery as much for self defense as for any other reason.

And then, too, there were the two gringo warships that would lend their fires. Suarez and Boyd had boarded each of them a few weeks previously to help weld awards to their turrets.

Suarez thought of Daisy Mae's avatar with a smile. *Whoever thought a ship's chest could swell at all, never mind that it could swell so much. Odd, too, that the ship should have asked for a smaller version, suitable for wearing around a neck. She's a hologram; she can't support anything material. Ah well, who knows? And the whys of the thing don't matter anyway. For the good she had done us, and especially me, a little medal that she can't even wear around her neck is a small thing.*

Funny, though, that that little bat-faced, green alien should have taken the medal so readily when it was delivered.

USS Des Moines, *Southwest of the Nata Line, Bay of Panama*

"Your two favorite colors are 'ooh' and 'shiny,' Ship Daisy," the Indowy said with an alien smile.

The actual medal was tucked away in a case, deep in the hold where Daisy's "inauspicious cloning" project was coming near fruition. On the wall the Indowy had carefully hung the framed glass case containing her award citation. (A larger one hung near the officers' mess.)

Around her neck, however, she had projected onto and with her avatar the high award for valor given the ship, individually, and the crew, as a unit award. It was a simple cross, in gold, about the size of the United States' Distinguished Service Cross. Unlike with that medal, however, all four arms of this one were even. A small ring was affixed to the top and a ribbon ran through that to hold the medal in front of and at the base of the neck.

Daisy shot Sintarleen a dirty look, then, seeing he had spoken in jest, she answered, "It isn't the 'ooh' and it isn't the shiny, Sinbad. It's just . . . well . . . the part of me that is the hull of this ship is a warship, has the soul of a warship. For decades, it yearned for the honor of battling for her builders. Now, it has the recognition of that honor, and—even more—of battling *heroically*. Though we are the same being now, still, I wear this representation for the part of me that was the original USS *Des Moines*."

Changing the subject, but only slightly, Daisy asked, "The skipper has seen me wearing the medal. Do you think he minds?"

The Indowy snorted. "If he minds, it is only that he is embarrassed not to have thought of it himself."

"The crew?" she asked uncertainly.

"About that I can say definitely, Ship Daisy, the men are proud of you and pleased that your avatar wears the award for all of them." The Indowy hesitated, then said shyly, "I am proud of you as well."

"Thank you, Sintarleen. That means a lot to me." Without another word, the avatar bent over and made a motion that, had she been flesh and blood, would have landed a kiss on the alien's furry forehead.

INTERLUDE

Guanamarioch and Zira, both, scratched unconsciously, almost uncontrollably, at the jungle fungus that had taken hold of their crests, their spaces between their claws, and—worst, by far, of all—their crotches.

"I hate this place," Guano said without emotion as he dug with a roughened stick at a particularly obnoxious patch of the crud that had taken hold of his left front claw. He hobbled unsteadily on three legs while doing this.

Zira, ever calm, just nodded.

"Whatever possessed us to come to this horrible world, Zira? It is nothing like home. It is nothing like any place I have ever even read of." The God King's voice lowered. "Well, it's nothing like anything I've read of except the demon pits where—"

"Hold up, Guano. You've got some of those things on you again."

"What? Where? Get'emoff, get'emoff, get'emoff!"

"I will. Calm down."

Pulling out a short blade, Zira bent over to examine more carefully the half dozen black, ugly and frankly (though a Posleen would not normally use the word) *icky* creatures that had attached themselves to Guano's torso, perhaps at the last river crossing.

"What are these called?" Zira asked Guano's AS as he prodded at one of the little monsters with the point of his knife.

"Leeches, Kenstain Ziramoth. They are not dangerous in themselves, but once they have finished feeding and drop off they leave oozing wounds that refuse to heal. These then get infected. In a place like this . . ."

"Infected? Well . . . that is not so much of a problem for us; the Aldenata did a few things right. But the loss of bodily fluids and nutrients; this we can't take much more of, not with the little flying horrors draining us daily." The Kenstain looked at Guanamarioch's torso where ribs were beginning to show. "No, they'll have to go."

While Zira worked at removing the leeches, the pair heard overheard the muffled whine of several, perhaps as many as half a dozen, tenar.

"Upper caste bastards," Guano muttered. Zira, still working at the leeches, ignored it.

Above the jungle-muffled whine, Zira and Guano heard sudden shouts of alarm. The alarm quickly transferred to them as they heard the sound of something crashing through the jungle canopy. The crashing grew ever closer for a few moments, then stopped. A few seconds later the body of a Kessentai thudded to the muddy jungle floor perhaps thirty meters away. The God King was obviously very dead, though without closer examination there was no way of telling what had killed him.

Much louder than the tenar and the crashing body,

the upper caste God Kings above apparently opened fire at something. Originating almost directly above, the sound of railgun and plasma cannon fire impacting the jungle trees soon came from all around. It was so loud that it completely covered the falling of yet another God King body, which hit the ground closer to Zira and Guano. A minute or so later, but farther off, yet another body struck dirt, a small deluge of leaves and broken branches coming down on top of and all around it. The firing from above redoubled and continued for long minutes.

The jungle went silent then. "They must have gotten whatever it was," Zira observed.

Which Guano would surely have agreed with, except that even several minutes after the firing had stopped, another God King body, apparently flung from its tenar, crashed down almost on top of them. There was no firing after this, only the rapidly retreating whine of tenar heading generally east. On examination, this body proved to have a hole of about one half of an inch on the forward quarter of its torso on the left side . . . and a massive hole, oozing yellow blood and dangling intestines, on the right.

Guano probed around the edges of the exit wound with his claws. He raised his crest, the crest beginning to tear as well as bleed from the constant scratching and said, "I hate this fucking place."

CHAPTER 31

There are no atheists on battling tenar.
                    —From the Scroll of
                    Stinghal, the Knower

Nata Line, Republic of Panama

Properly for a clan chief, Binastarion kept well back, using his AS to project in front of his tenar a magnified image of the fighting ahead.

It's pretty damned awful. Much worse than the first line of defense we hit back by the northwestern corner of this peninsula.

The magnified image showed an oolt, led by a tenar-riding God King, leap from cover and advance forward, firing wildly to their front. At least two of the threshkreen's crew-served repeating weapons engaged, not from the front like proper warriors, but from the sides. The corners of the assaulting oolt crumbled. As more of the People advanced into the fire, they were stretched out, lifeless, along two lines that began with the crumpled, bleeding bodies at the corner and formed an apex almost dead center of the oolt.

Some leapt over the neat lines of the messy dead and continued. It seemed that the crew-served repeaters didn't bother traversing to pick of this few leakers but, instead, kept their lines of fire fixed.

Even so, the leakers didn't get far. A steady crackling of the threshkreen's individual weapons and spurts of dust arising from around the charging normals' feet told of many of the human "soldiers" manning the trenches in support of their crew-served, heavy repeaters. In moments, no longer than it took for the last normal of the oolt to launch itself into the lines of fire, the Kessentai in command found itself alone. The God King spun its tenar around, looking for support from the People and finding none. In apparent despair, the leader then launched itself forward at the hated humans, its plasma cannon searching out the threshkreen where they cowered in their trenches.

The Kessentai also didn't get far. Though the repeating weapons did not engage it, apparently the humans had designated special marksmen just for the God Kings. The tenar made it about halfway across the thick belt of the nasty "wounding-wire" the humans had laid to aid their defense before a single bullet found it out. In his magnified view, Binastarion saw one side of the back of the Kessentai explode in yellow blood and a mist of flesh. The God King was flung completely off his tenar to fall onto the wire. There it twisted and writhed in obvious agony, binding itself the more tightly to the wire the more it tried to free itself. Some of the intestines, too, dragging down, managed to catch and tear themselves on the wire's barbs, further adding to the Kessentai's personal Calvary.

Binastarion tore his eyes from the scene. *We are a*

harsh and a hard people, yes. But we are not a cruel people. We do as we must to survive, eat as we must. But never could we have imagined such a horrible method of war as this barbed wire. What kind of beings are these threshkreen? The universe will be a better place when they are gone from it.

The People had tried most of their innate bag of tricks in this battle. They had feigned retreat to try to draw the threshkreen away from their fixed defenses. The threshkreen, perhaps because their own wire and landmines prevented it, had ignored the feints and used the respite to restore their defenses. The host had tried massing on one flank and then another. The threshkreen apparently had ignored that, too. The defenses were just too strong for a rapid breakthrough and the forever-damned humans could shift artillery fires more rapidly than the People could mass or maneuver.

Once, at a grisly cost in Kessentai, Binastarion had ordered a ten of tens of them forward en masse on a narrow frontage to try to blast a way through the threshkreen lines. They had succeeded in cutting through the wire, detonating most of the mines, and destroying many of the humans' crew-served repeater positions. Unfortunately, without a mass of normals in support, Kessentai were very vulnerable to the human's individual weapons. By the time the gap was created all but two of the Kessentai were down. When the now nearly leaderless oolt had poured through the gap and taken the forward trenches, the humans counterattacked the confused rabble and driven them out again with even more frightful losses. To add injury to insult, the threshkreen had then closed the gaps with some of their artillery delivered antipersonnel mines.

It wasn't entirely hopeless, of course. Here and there the People had succeeded in taking and holding the forward trenches and even, in one case, the second line beyond that. Moreover, with all the dead lying about that the humans had not had time to booby-trap, the point of the People, at least, was well fed for the first time in days. Some of that valuable thresh had even been passed back to feed a portion of the rest of the host.

Unfortunately, the threshkreen had concentrated their reserves and artillery fires on those few inroads made. The People were pinned in them, unable to advance and taking steady losses from the fires.

There was one other reason for hope. Binastarion had noticed, as the day wore on, that the humans were becoming tired and, moreover, that their reserves seemed to be growing thinner and weaker. The push that had reached and managed to hold the second line trench had done so, in the main, because the humans had made comparatively little effort to dig them out again.

One big push or a large number of little pushes? Kick the front door of this edifice in all at once or continue gnawing away at the foundations? It will not be until tomorrow's rise of the local sun before I can mass enough of the People to seriously charge the threshkreen's entire defensive line. Until then I can only gnaw. But the more I expend strength gnawing, the less I have to charge with on the morrow. Then again, the more I gnaw today, the weaker their defense when the sun next rises. And it isn't as if I have any great shortage of fodder for their crew-served repeaters.

Binastarion sighed, unheard by any save his Artificial

Sentience. *I would like to meet their leader, I think, to discuss this human way of war before he is consigned to the threshheap. It is something new. If I could learn it before the rest of the People assimilate it, perhaps I could use it to raise my clan.*

"It is a fearful price we are paying, lord," the AS said. "Yet it will all prove worth it if we can wrest this land from the humans, hold it, and build our clan back to prominence."

Cocking his head to one side, Binastarion asked, "Are you able to read my mind, machine? What program permits this?"

The AS gave an electronic chuckle. "Binastarion, after all these decades together do you not think that I would come to think as you do? Better to check my programming if I could *not* read your mind."

"I would love to be able to read the enemy leader's mind," Boyd said to Suarez in the musty, damp command bunker they shared to the east of the Nata line.

Suarez shrugged. "I can read his mind well enough."

"Can you? How?"

"Logistics," Suarez answered simply. Then, seeing his dictator was confused, the *Magister Equitum* elaborated, "There is an old saying that 'Amateurs study tactics while professionals study logistics.' It is true, but only up to a point; real professionals study *everything*, literally everything. But what the saying really means, to most of those who use it, is that logistics rules in war. That is also true, but also only up to a point. Those who tend to believe it unreservedly also tend to miss something: when you base everything on logistics you become extremely predictable because logistics, unlike most aspects of war, is a fairly predictable science."

"So predict him, then, my Master of the Horse," Boyd commanded.

"He is worried. We've left his forces almost nothing to eat to the west of here. He knows that he has to break into and through our lines tomorrow, the next day at the latest, or he will simply starve. There is food here, of course, his own dead and those of us whose bodies have fallen into his hands. I have given orders that the bodies of both our and his dead not be booby trapped, by the way. I *want* there to be food here, to attract him forward."

"So what happens, then, when he is forward?"

"He masses to attack," Suarez answered. "He masses generally but especially in the low ground where our direct fire cannot reach him. He has seen much of our artillery and thinks he has its measure. He does not know we have guns and mortars lined up nearly hubcap to hubcap and base plate to base plate all across the breadth of the front. He does not know we have nearly two hundred multiple rocket launchers on his flanks in good position to pound his massing front."

"How do you know all this?"

"I know this because I know that, logistically, he must advance or starve . . . that, and that if he had the slightest suspicion he would be running like hell to get out of the kill zone we have prepared, starvation or not."

Santa Fe, Veraguas Province, Republic of Panama

As the sun was setting, the north-south running spur to the west of Santa Fe cast shadows over the guns, rocket launchers, bunkers and antennas of the artillery's battle position.

Digna's labors were not over, though the day was fast waning. Instead, she, with her descendants and subordinates, went over, for perhaps the fifteenth time, the fire plan and the contingencies. Again, her children brought up the subject of their tiny, under-aged and helpless offspring.

Digna was curt. "My children are here. Yours will be, too . . . until the battle is over, win or lose. My advice is: don't lose."

From the national headquarters, collocated with Suarez command post as Master of the Horse and commander of the mechanized corps, came a transmission which was repeated every ten minutes for an hour. "Drake this is Morgan." *All forces, this is the national command authority.* "I authenticate Bravo-X-ray-Tango." *Hey, pay attention. It's really me.* "Code: San Lorenzo . . . Code: Portobello." *We're going to have a big day tomorrow . . . or the next day.* "Code: Marconi." *Further instructions will follow through the night.*

Digna didn't need the repeats. At the first call she had told the watch officer to acknowledge. Then she announced, "In the morning at 02:15 we man the guns and BM-21s. If, as I expect, the call comes to fire, we execute the fire plan. Now enough of this; go back to your battalions and batteries."

❖   ❖   ❖

Still fearing the worst, Snyder, cocooned in his armored combat suit, shivered uncontrollably. The suit and the goo kept him warm enough, of course. That wasn't the problem. The problem was that if he had to wait five more minutes he thought he would go stark raving mad.

His radio, which had been worrisomely quiet of late, sparked into life. On his own forces' frequencies he heard the English language equivalent of "Drake this is Morgan."

It started with a single sniffle. Within moments it had risen to a full flood. Tears poured from the colonel's face, tears of relief of which he was not even remotely ashamed.

Glory to God in the highest. Thank You, thank You, thank You. I'm not worried about meeting You tomorrow or the next day, God, because I have already served my time in hell.

Nata Line, Republic of Panama

"Demons of fire and ice, watch over my People this morning. Ancestors, watch your descendants as they drive forward. Guide them, encourage them, lend them the strength of your power as they fight for survival." The God King stood on his tenar, arms crossed, in the *Posture of Supplication and Serenity*, as his horde tramped or hovered below.

"Getting sentimental in our old age, are we, Binastarion?"

"Something you would never understand, you bucket of bolts," the Kessentai told his AS without rancor.

"I understand better than you think, lord. Do you imagine that we Artificial Sentiences do not get attached to the People we serve? Do you think that your values, over time, do not become our own? You should know better, Kessentai. You should understand better, Philosopher."

Briefly, the God King was ashamed. If anyone had served the People better than this AS he didn't know who it might have been.

Instead he continued his prayer. "Ancestors, Great Ones, accept at your hearths those of the People who fall gloriously tomorrow. Welcome them with the feasting that requires no threshing. Praise them in accordance with the duty they have followed. And, Ancestors, should one of those who falls be this bucket of bolts and circuits sitting here beside me, welcome it, too, for it has also served your People."

The AS was silent for a long moment. Finally, it said, "Thank you, Binastarion."

Assembly Area Pedrarias, East of the Nata Line, Republic of Panama

Like ninety percent of his men, Sergeant Quijana was a Roman Catholic. And like ninety percent, give or take, of Catholics, his Catholicism was purely nominal. For the last several years he had gone to church, at most, infrequently. He could not remember the last time he had confessed.

This was not, under the circumstances, a problem. Faced with massive numbers of people seeking forgiveness (and with amazingly high numbers and qualities of sins to be confessed), the chaplains had simply formed the men into mass ranks and granted a general absolution. They'd explained, of course, that the general absolution would only be of effect if the men were truly repentant.

Given the frequency with which he had committed and recommitted his sins, mostly involving women, Quijana had to wonder whether the more normal and personal form of confession was one whit more effective in relieving the burden of sin than this novel en masse kind. Perhaps it was not.

All he knew was that as he took communion the memories of his childhood, and his mother's fierce and unquestioning devotion, came flooding in afresh. With them came a freedom, a clarity. With them came the belief, for something faith-based could not be called "knowledge," that, should he die on the morrow, or over the next few days, he would die clean.

That belief was worth something, to Quijana not least.

There was one duty left to him that Boyd could not forego. He would not, if he could have. The bunker was cleared, the National *Escudo* and a pair of flags were hung behind him. The television cameras were set up and focused on him. Radio microphones cluttered the field desk at which he sat. The studio chief, seconded from the nation's largest television chain, announced, "Ready in five . . . four . . . three . . . two . . . you're live, *Dictador*."

Boyd looked up from his desk, directly at the center camera, and began to speak.

"People of Panama, in a few hours, with the morning

light, we will commence a battle for our people's very existence. We have prepared for this battle long. Our defenses are solid. Our soldiers are trained, ready, and willing and able. Our allies have given us much help, even more than we could have—in justice—asked for. Their men, too, stand beside ours in this climactic test. Together, we will triumph.

"And yet, there is something else, one other thing that we cannot do for you but that you must do for us. I have asked Archbishop Cedeño, and the other main prelates and ministers of our various denominations and faiths to open their churches, their synagogues and their mosques. Now I ask you, People of Panama, to go, to go and to pray as you have never prayed in your lives for the success of our forces and the existence of our country. Ask the grace of God, the Father; ask for the Holy Mother to intervene on our behalf. Above all, ask the blessing of Jesu Cristo on us, his long suffering people. I, together with Master of the Horse Suarez, the Chief of Army Chaplains, and all of our soldiers not actively engaged in fighting will do no less.

"Thank you. God bless you and our soldiers . . . and *Viva la Republica*."

Iglesia del Carmen, Panama City, Panama

They came from all parts of the city and they came from all walks of life. Most were Catholic yet there were many Protestants and more than a few Jews and Moslems. They came, many of them, bearing lit candles, held upright. Some had brought extra candles, which they shared. The grand circle in front of the pure white church became a moving sea of points of light.

They were quiet at first, these people, overcome with the solemnity of the occasion and the sheer spectacle of the mass. This, though, seemed not quite right to Archbishop Cedeño, standing by the arched entrances of the great, cathedral-like church. To a junior priest standing by his side the archbishop said, "Make a joyful sound unto the Lord."

The junior priest looked back, quizzically.. "Make a joyful sound . . . ?"

Not answering directly, the archbishop instead said, "Have you ever thought about Islam's great contribution to the world, my son? It wasn't algebra, important as that may be. Algebra was there to be discovered by someone and would have been eventually. It owes nothing to Islam, per se. Nor was it Arabic as a language, nor poetry. They both existed before Islam.

"No, Father, what the world and humanity owe to Islam is the concept of jihad, of Holy War waged for a holy purpose. Our faith absorbed it, too. And perhaps all the suffering inflicted by Christian upon Moslem, Moslem upon Christian, and everyone on the Jews will have proven worth it if *this* jihad is successful. My son, is there a holier purpose than preserving the people of the one true God?"

The archbishop answered his own question. "No, there is no more holy purpose, and there can never be a holier war than this one. So . . . go sing, my son. Out there in the crowd. Something they'll all know or that is simple enough they can all pick it up easily. Spanish, if that will work. Or maybe Latin." The archbishop thought for a moment, then continued, "Yes. Make it Latin. Go forth, my son, and sing 'Non Nobis' for the faithful."

Uncertainly, for while he could sing, he didn't know whether he could do so loudly enough amongst the crowd to make a difference, the junior priest nodded and went forth, forcing his way through the gathering crowd until he could perch himself atop the low wall of the round fountain pool halfway across the broad *Via España.*

Still uncertain, and frankly embarrassed—the priest did not consider himself to have all *that* good a voice—he began softly. The people assembling hardly noticed.

Louder, by far, despite his age, the archbishop cupped his hands and shouted across the crowded scene, "Sing like you mean it, my son."

The priest picked up the volume. Surprisingly, a young woman joined him on the masonry wall and joined in:

"Non nobis Domine non nobis,"

Then a few more, men and women, boys and girls, mounted the wall and began to sing:

"Sed Nomini tuo da gloriam
Sed Nomini tuo da gloriam."

The few became a few dozen, a few score, a few hundred . . . fifty thousand. The song moved down *Via España* and up *Avenida Central* faster than the people coming toward the great *iglesia* could walk.

> *"Non nobis Domine non nobis*
> *Sed Nomini tuo da gloriam*
> *Sed Nomini tuo da gloriam*
> *Non nobis Domine . . ."*

The song echoed through the City. Fifty thousand became half a million. Soldiers in the trenches listening to their small radios listened and joined. It became eight hundred thousand. The music reached the refugee-swollen town of Colon the same way: one million. To the north, in the cities of Boston and New York, Chicago and Los Angeles, it was heard: one point five million. In Cuba the people heard and remembered: three million. In Bogotá, still holding out . . . in England, where men still slept in their beds . . . among Bundeswehr and the new-old Waffen SS watching along the Rhine . . . with the Red Guard, fighting along the Dnepr . . .

> *"Non nobis Domine non nobis . . ."*

INTERLUDE

Darien Province, Republic of Panama

It was basically a small crocodilian. Colored a dull green, its length at a bit over seven feet was average for its species and age. Aquatic, as were all its sort, it hunted through the murky stream looking for something to eat. It was known to go after small pigs and other animals, invertebrates large and small, and—in places where they were to be found, far south of here—even to feast on the fierce piranha.

The caiman had few needs: to feed, to rest, to rut. At the moment, feeding was number one. Thus, eyes and nose above the coloring water, it hunted.

Ahead was a curious splashing, as of a herd of animals crossing the river. On closer examination, it *was* a herd of rather large animals. This might mean food as it had in the past; the animals themselves looked too big but there was always the chance they may have taken the kids out for a Sunday stroll. Hope springs eternal and the caiman was either not bright enough, or was self-confident enough, that the thought of danger didn't enter its little brain. Submerging, it swam over.

"Tell me if you see any leeches, Zira. I hate getting those things on me."

Voice calm, the Kenstain assured Guanamarioch that he would indeed keep a watch out. Even so, the damned nuisances were so nearly invisible until they attached themselves that Ziramoth really had no expectation of being able to keep them off no matter how diligently he guarded. Nonetheless, Ziramoth looked at the dozens of oozing sores dotting the Kessentai's torso and resolved to at least try.

Other than the fear of leeches, the water itself was warm and even soothing. Guanamarioch thought that, were his people ever able to rid themselves of this world's multifarious pests, bathing in such a stream might be a welcome activity. In particular, and despite the fear of the leeches, the warm water passing over the God King's reproductive member was most pleasant.

As mentioned, the caiman was only of average size. Thus, when it came upon the legs of the beasts walking through the river bed it was momentarily nonplussed. It knew, instinctively, that there was no way it was going to be able to take down a creature with legs the size of those. Almost, the caiman felt a surge of frustration at the unfairness of it all. Almost, it wept crocodile tears.

Perhaps the crocodile-headed god of the caiman smiled upon it. There, just there, just ahead, was something of a proper size for the caiman to eat. It dangled and danced enticingly, as if presenting itself for supper. The caiman swished its tail, and inclined its body and head to line up properly on the tempting bait.

"You know, Zira, this isn't so bad. One could even . . . AIAIAI!"

Ziramoth's yellow eyes went wide in his head as his friend exploded out of the water, dragging a dark creature almost like one of the People—barring only the shorter legs and two too few of them—behind it. The eyes went wider still as the Kenstain realized just *what* part of his friend connected him with this alien predator.

Up Guanamarioch flew, legs churning furiously. Down the God King splashed. Both trips he screamed continuously: "AIAIAI!"

Once down, Guano tried to bend over to catch the creature. No use; he couldn't quite reach. Leeches be damned, still shrieking he rolled over on his back, scrambling for purchase on his unseen attacker.

Another half roll and Guanamarioch cried out, "Getitoffgetitoffgetitoff!" before his head plunged back into the water.

Normally steady as a rock, Zira didn't know what to do in this case. Fortunately—or unfortunately, depending on one's point of view—one of Guano's normals saw no real problem. Instead, it saw the twin opportunities of relieving its god from pain and at the same time providing some much needed nourishment to his pack.

Zira had only just realized what the normal intended

and begun to shout, "St—" when the boma blade swung, taking the biting creature's head off but at the same time removing about five inches of the Kessentai's reproductive organ.

Unsteadily, the God King rolled back over and struggled to its feet. His eyes were wider with shock even than Zira's had been. For a moment it struggled with the realization of what had just happened to it. Once it made that realization, the God King bowed its head. . . .

For the first time since the beginning of the invasion of the human world, a Kessentai unabashedly wept.

CHAPTER 32

Remember, me boys, though the Irish
fight well
The Russian artillery's hotter than hell.
— "The Kerry Recruit"

Nata Line, Republic of Panama

"Demons of Shit! Will these damnable trenches never end?"

"We've fought through at least eight sets of them, Binastarion, and there seems no end. The loss is frightful."

Including where the trenches ran into the mountains, the Nata Line was approximately eighteen kilometers in breadth and about seven deep. The Posleen were—in places, anyway—about five kilometers into it. That ninety or so square kilometers was carpeted, in places two or three deep, with the People's dead. Though the ground below often showed through, it was possible to walk those five kilometers forward or eighteen across without ever once touching it, and having to leap to get from one body to the next only every other step.

Even where the ground showed, the green grass of this world was stained completely yellow with the flesh and blood of the invaders.

"Should I have struck south, do you think, AS, instead of trying to force this line?"

"You couldn't have, lord. The People were here and there was nothing to eat behind them. It was fight through or die."

Binastarion directed his tenar down to examine one of the bunkers from which the threshkreen had directed such fanatical and deadly fire at the People. The bunker was torn open, apparently by the blast of a plasma cannon.

"It seems too small," the God King observed, "too small to hold even one of the vile creatures."

"Move me closer, Binastarion, and let me examine it."

When the clan chief had done so, and after a short moment for analysis, the AS announced, "It *is* too small, Kessentai. This repeater was set on automatic. No threshkreen manned it except, perhaps, to begin its cycle of fire."

Setting his tenar down and dismounting, the Kessentai peered himself at the curious device, Binastarion saw that his AS was correct. The weapon had a small muzzle, perhaps a claw's width in caliber. Around that was a larger tube. He tapped the tube with a claw. It sloshed as if full of some coolant, water perhaps. Behind the tube was a block of machined metal with a wood-covered handle on one side. A belt of the heavy metal-colored ammunition the threshkreen favored ran out the side with the tube to a huge drum.

On the other side of the weapon, a pile of the little brass casings had filled a deep hole and begun to build a small hill. Underneath, the block was connected with the weapon's tripodal stand. The curved tube that connected the two rear legs of the stand had a toothed ridge running along it.

"I surmise that the recoil of the weapon causes the mechanism connecting the block and the stand to engage the teeth on that curved horizontal connector and traverse the weapon from one side to the other. Perhaps there is a reversing mechanism that causes it to traverse back when it reaches one end of the arc of traverse or the other. That little locking mechanism on the curved horizontal bar looks like a way to control the arc of fire. To ascertain that, though, would take more examination than I can do without the thing being disassembled, Binastarion."

"No . . ." the God King answered slowly. "I think you're right. It also explains how the threshkreen are able to get away when they are forced to abandon one of their fortified lines without leaving many bodies behind. They set these things off just before they vacate. Bastards!"

"The bastards are almost through, Suarez. I think we need to begin the fire plan now."

Suarez sighed. Boyd was a good man, a fine dictator. As a matter of fact he was the best dictator the country had ever seen, not least because he'd made it so plain from the beginning that he detested the job. He also had more actual combat experience than Suarez.

For all that, however, he was not a professional soldier. Suarez was.

"Not yet. They still have uncommitted reserves that are out of our fire prep area. We'll pay a heavy price, and possibly fail to liberate the west, if we don't catch nearly all of them."

"But there're only *three more trench lines left*, Suarez. *Three!* And the infantry divisions holding the line are beginning to fall apart!"

"They won't fall apart, Dictator. I've lined the rear with military police with orders to summarily execute anyone found leaving the front," Suarez answered calmly. Seeing the look of horror on Boyd's face, Suarez explained, "Why do you suppose MPs are given pistols, Dictator? They have them for just that purpose. Always have and likely always will."

Boyd thought back to his days as a rifleman in France and Belgium. Momentarily, he shivered. "I *hate* MPs."

"Everyone hates MPs," Suarez answered. "Everyone complains about prostitution, too. But cops and hookers serve a valid social function. I shudder to think where society would be without both in plenty.

"But, in any case, relax. The last two trench lines are the most solid. They've each got nearly two hundred of the autoguns. You remember? Those water-cooled machine guns on the recoil-operated traversing mechanism? Pity the gringos couldn't have given us a thousand of their *manjacks*. But making do is a Latin virtue, I think. Oh, and I've ordered in the Nata Line's Corps' last infantry division to shore it up. It will hold until the LRRPs in the mountains to the north report that the enemy is fully committed to the attack, with no reserves out of our kill zone."

Lieutenant Valparaiso, 1ˢᵗ Cazador Battalion, wondered if the boredom of his mission made up for missing the action to the east along the Nata Line. Actually, he and his men *yearned* to be in on the fighting. Still, it wasn't as if their job wasn't important. Master of the Horse Suarez had personally spoken to his battalion before they had moved into these hills to dig in deep hide positions overlooking the open ground to the south. From the battalion's deep hides, wires ran back to communications nodes on the other side of the *Cordillera Central*. From there, the high command was kept informed.

"There is nothing," Suarez had said, "*nothing* more important than the information you men will provide. No, you won't get any medals . . . at least, if things work out properly you won't. But what you will tell us is key to the defense."

Bloody boring goddamned key, Valparaiso thought as he looked over the huge Posleen pack that simply sat, or lay down, in his field of view below. *Miserable alien bastards haven't budged since . . . oh, oh, what's this?*

The tenar which had been hovering listlessly or occasionally gathering by twos, threes and fours—even aliens felt the need to shoot the shit with each other, Valpariaso surmised—suddenly took on a new energy. The blocks of the smaller, crestless aliens arose to their feet as the flying sleds moved to take positions at the front of each.

Looking through his binoculars, the lieutenant counted. *Each block is about forty by ten of the aliens. There are thirty-seven blocks on the front and they appear to be about thirty deep, or maybe a bit more. Call it . . . umm . . .*

"Holy shit!" Valparaiso cursed. To his radio telephone

operator he said, "Get on the horn and tell headquarters that there's nearly half a million of the bastards moving east. Do it, soldier. *Now!*"

"There! I *told* you they would commit, at last." Suarez pointed one finger at the map being updated by a trooper from the headquarters operations shop.

Boyd looked at the map and asked, "How long until they're in range?"

"Between midnight and two," Suarez answered, after spending a moment in crude calculation.

"And that's the last of their uncommitted troops?"

The trooper at the map answered, "*Dictador*, the LRRPs say there is nothing behind these except individual Posleen who are acting wildly."

"They go feral," Suarez explained. "If their God Kings are killed and no other takes them under control the normals revert to type. They will be small danger, when we roll through."

Boyd bit at his lower lip, thinking, *It's all or nothing. One big roll of the dice and my country lives or dies. But there's nothing to be done to fix that that we have not already done.*

"Tell SOUTHCOM. We begin at one in the morning."

Sante Fe, Veraguas Province, Republic of Panama

The suit's radio crackled, "Colonel Snyder, you've been fucking off too long already. Get your ass up."

"Wha . . . wha . . . WHAT? *I wasn't sleeping, Sergeant . . .*"

The suit was on listening silence. The sender—
General Page, himself, thought Snyder—didn't hear.
The radio repeated, "Snyder, wake up."

"AID, come alert."

The AID answered, "About fucking time."

Snyder ignored the jab. It was, after all, his fault if
anyone's that his AID had acquired a foul . . . mouth.

"Last calling station, this is Lieutenant Colonel Wes
Snyder. Repeat."

"Snyder this is Page. It's a go. Get your battalion
awake and prepare to execute your mission."

"Wilco," the officer answered. "AID, wake up the
commanders and staff."

"Wilco," the AID echoed and began sending the
signals to the other AIDs.

"A Company reports . . . B Company; a man who
won't fuck won't fight . . . Combat Support; ready to
rock . . . Headquarters' Headhunters; ready to take
heads."

"Gentlemen . . . oh, and you ladies, too, Alpha Company. Awaken your commands. We're going in shortly."

Nata Line, Republic of Panama

The moon was high and bright overhead as the Artificial
Sentience announced, "Binastarion, I've found the
metal threshkreen."

"Show me, AS."

The glowing map appeared in thin air beside the
tenar. "They've been waiting *behind* us? Oh, demons.
Does this mean what I think it does, AS?"

"Yes, Kessentai. We're . . . what's that phrase the

threshkreen use? Ah, yes. We're fucked. Binastarion, look east."

The Artificial Sentience needn't have directed his chief's attention. The sky to the east was lit up, as if by several thousand powerful strobes. "Artillery?"

"I think so; that and their mortars."

Binastarion's sinking feeling managed to sink further. "How many?"

"I think between two and three thousand, my lord. Probably closer to three. And . . . oh, demon shit . . . north and south, Binastarion. Rockets. From hundreds of launchers."

"We can engage the rockets automatically, AS," the God King insisted.

"No. I am sorry. We can't. I can sense them through the mountains and hills, while they are still accelerating. By the time they pop over, though, they must have expended their fuel and gone ballistic. I can sense them, still, and count them. But it would take a major reprogramming for me or the other automated defenses to engage. And there's no time."

"How many shells are we facing?" Binastarion asked, a trace of hope in his voice.

The first of the threshkreen shells had almost landed among the host as the AS answered, "There are twenty-one thousand two hundred and forty-seven projectiles in the air now, and the rate of fire is not slowing. And . . . oh, Kessentai, I am so sorry. The spirit-of-the-dead ships are now firing too. Make that twenty-one thousand four hundred and fifty-one . . . sixty-nine . . . twenty-two thousand five hundred and ninety . . ."

USS Des Moines, *Southwest of the Nata Line, Bay of Panama*

Broadside on, Daisy and Sally took turns blasting away at the Posleen infestation. The flashes of their guns, firing at maximum rate, lit up the depths below. The concussion sent fish, some stunned but mostly dead, floating to the surface.

Down below, in a hold no one ever visited but the Indowy and the avatar, Sintarleen told Daisy's avatar, "It is time." The Indowy's left hand held Morgen, the cat, while his right stroked the creature's back. The cat purred audibly.

The avatar bit her lip and nodded. Then, nervousness palpable in her voice, she said, "Let us do it. Now, while there is still time to feel my captain's touch."

The bat-faced alien's fingers reached out and played over the control surfaces of the tank. Then he placed his hand on a silvery panel. There was a whooshing sound as the top of the tank slid away. As the mist inside the tank dissipated, looking down, the avatar and the Indowy saw a perfect female body and an ethereal face framed by long blonde hair. The mouth on the face opened as the eyes flew wide. The body gasped as it drew in its first breath.

As the body and mind in the tank fully wakened, the avatar faded. Yes, it could have been maintained. But Daisy the woman who was also Daisy the ship and Daisy the AID and even Daisy the soul wanted all of her consciousness in that body, at least for the moment.

Breath drew in. Blood picked up oxygen. Heart pumped. *Oh, wonder, to be* alive.

The body sat upright. It tried to speak. Instead it croaked, "Ouu ni sau m'tin ta wa."

The Indowy looked at the woman, uncomprehendingly. His head cocked as the woman repeated, "Ouu ni sau m'tin ta wa."

"Oh, dear. We exercised this body daily. But we never did exercise its ability to speak."

Daisy's head nodded vigorously, before she punched the wall of the tank in frustration.

"Never mind, Lady Daisy. That will come. Do you need clothing? A uniform?"

"B'ea s?"

Sintarleen turned away, bent over and rummaged through a chest he kept in this bay. Opening it, he withdrew a complete set of Navy tans, hand tailored in Panama to match the body's size and shape. He held these out along with a bra. Looking at the bra, and then at the body's magnificent breasts he said, "You probably don't need this, yet. Even so, this is a human woman's body and gravity works. You should wear this, too."

Unwilling to butcher the language any further by trying to speak it, at least until she had had a chance to practice on her own, the woman Daisy smiled in gratitude, taking the clothing and bra.

The panties were easy and obvious. But she had never put on a bra before. The Indowy had to help. Since he had never helped a woman in such a way before . . .

"No, that's not quite right. Here." He reached over and tugged a bit left, then a bit right. "There. That looks reasonably correct." He then helped Daisy put on the uniform, adjusting the belt and adding in such insignia as she was entitled to. Lastly, he hung around her neck the gold cross for valor she had won. The base of the cross pointed inadvertently at an amazing cleavage.

Stepping back to admire his handiwork, Sinbad said, "A human male would whistle, I think, based on what I have seen of this crew. I am not human, of course. Still, I can admire the beauty in another species. You look great, Lady Daisy."

A soft hand reached out to stroke the Indowy's furry, batlike face. Soft, warm lips tried to move. "T' an k ou, S' ba'."

Morgen the Cat stropped Daisy's legs furiously and happily.

Daisy's issue shoes pinched as she walked with a steady click-clack-click up the passageway toward CIC. The clicking echoed off the armored deck above and beside her.

Not a man in the crew but had seen her in her avatar form. Thus, even though the avatar rarely walked much, preferring to simply appear where and when she was needed, and despite the click-clacking of the shoes on the deck, the men on battle stations along the passageway really hardly noticed the change, at first. And then she reached out and gently touched a favored crewman here, another there. Mouths gaped and eyes went wide. *Jesus, Mary and Joseph, our girl's become real.*

A few of the crew, more mesmerized than disciplined, perhaps, started to follow. Wordlessly, but smiling, Daisy motioned them, *no, stay to your duty* as she walked on.

At CIC a Marine guard started to port his rifle to bar the way. No blame to the kid; he was used to Daisy's avatar coming and going as it would. It was just surprise that had him lifting his rifle. Daisy, still smiling, cocked her head coquettishly. The guard stepped out of the way, even opening the hatchway for her.

Morgen entered with Daisy and immediately foot-padded over and began stropping McNair's legs. The skipper bent over and picked the cat up, asking, "Who let you in here, Furball?"

Davis said, "I'll take the cat, Skip—" and stopped cold. He, too, had a hard time believing the vision before his eyes. Father Dwyer was the only man present not surprised. But, then again, he *was* the ship's confessor.

McNair followed Davis' stunned gaze completely around and . . .

Daisy held a finger to her lips. *Shhhhh.* One warm hand, made of honest to God girlflesh, reached up and softly stroked his cheek. Her eyes sought his out, asking the question desperately, *Do you like what you see, Captain? Did I do right?* Seeing the skipper's shock, Daisy decided to press the issue. She tilted her head, parted her lips, and raised one foot behind her as she melted into her captain.

Even before the probing tongue McNair was conscious of the encircling arms. Even before that, he felt the pressure of two perfect breasts. It was the breasts, actually, pressing his chest but felt all through his body, that first grabbed his mind; grabbed it, and turned it completely to mush.

Unconscious of the crew of the CIC, McNair's hands began to act on autopilot, one beginning to reach up to cup a breast, the other down to give this incredible woman's ass a more than friendly squeeze.

And then Father Dwyer gave a small "Harumph," and McNair backed off. Moving his arms from her back to her shoulders and holding her firmly, McNair stared in wonder and bewilderment at the woman. Looking into Daisy's eyes for answers as desperately as she had looked into his own, the captain's mouth began to form "How?" when Daisy shushed him with a finger. Then a little electronically projected voice whispered into the ear of the very thoroughly kissed McNair, and no other, "I've had ten thousand men inside me, Captain, and I am still a virgin. Even so, when next I lay down on your bed, Captain, my love, it won't be as a hologram."

Sante Fe, Veraguas Province, Republic of Panama

There was no way to have face to face contact and still be heard over the rushing roar of twenty-four guns and ninety-six multiple rocket launchers firing continuously from all around. Snyder had his commanders and staff doff ACS helmets for a moment, if only to read their faces and gauge their morale after their long sleep. Perhaps, too, he wanted them to see his own, to realize that while he had gone almost mad while waiting, the key word was "almost."

He had intended to give his final orders that way, helmets off. After so long a confinement, if there was anything Snyder wanted less than to wear his helmet he couldn't think what it was. But the noise, the never ending, mind deadening *Kakakaboomoomoom*, made it impossible. Therefore, reluctantly, Snyder ordered his commanders and key staff back into full armor.

"It's really simple," the commander of the First of the O-Eighth said, using a marking laser integral to the right index finger of his command suit to mark out the battlefield as his AID projected a hologram onto the ground.

"The Panamanian artillery is *not* going to blast us a completely empty hole. Their job is to stun, disrupt, and open up little tactical gaps we can use. That's key, people; there will be Posleen down there when we come out of this valley and off these mountains. Some of them may, and probably will, still be in shape to fight. Even saying that, though, the locals are throwing eighty-thousand rockets and I-don't-know-exactly how much cannon fire down on their old San Pedro Line. There are going to be places where the Posties have been scoured off the surface of the Earth. And there are going to be places where they're ready to rock and roll."

"Recon?" Snyder waited to make sure he had the Scout Platoon leader's complete attention. "You're leading the way. Your job is to find the places where the horsies are strong and to identify the weak points. Don't get wrapped up in a fire fight. Find the spots, go low, and move on. You understand?"

The Scout Platoon leader nodded, answering, "Roger, sir."

"B Company," Snyder said, looking at Connors. "Your job is to clean up just enough of the Posleen strong points remaining after the artillery prep that Alpha and the Twentieth Mechanized Infantry—less one battalion that is staying here to defend the artillery—can pass easy to the east side of the river. When you've got a path cleared, you will hold the shoulders of it and pass Alpha and the mech along it. Once they are past, you will move on, seal the gap you created behind you, dig in facing mostly west—but be prepared to be attacked from any direction—and hang on for dear life."

Though it was difficult, Connors tried to tear his thoughts away from Marielena and their baby. Yes, she had sent him an e-mail with the news, which e-mail he had opened first thing after awakening. The second thing he had done was register a standard Galactic will naming his new offspring and the child's mother as his heirs. Thirdly, he had sent Marielena another e-mail that said, simply, "If I come out of this, the first thing we do is get married, right?"

He hadn't gotten an answer on that as of yet. Well, the day was early and likely to prove long.

"Fuck later, Connors. Pay attention, Goddammit. A man who won't fuck won't fight but a man who is thinking about fucking too much won't fight either. And he's likely to get killed."

Softly, Scott answered, "I wasn't thinking about fucking, sir . . . well, not exactly. Sorry. But I am going to be a daddy in about eight and a half months."

Never slow, Snyder responded, "And a man who is thinking about being a daddy is altogether too likely to get his ass lunched."

"Yessir. Sorry, sir.

"Okay, now—since you were in the never-never land of prospective daddydom—tell me back your orders."

Connors did.

"Okay, so you were paying attention with at least half an ear. Alpha Company . . ."

The steady drum fire of the artillery was almost as bad in the command bunker as it was out in the open. Dust, driven by the sound, leaked down through the spaces left in the dirt-covered logs causing operations and communications personnel to cough and sneeze.

"Your women are starting to become tired, Coronel Mirandova." The Russian's eyes were red from the dust . . . and the smoke of the flaming rockets being launched all around.

"I know that, Alexandrov," Digna answered. "That's why I waited on the music. But you're right; the time is now." Digna looked at one of her regiment's attachments, a PSYOP—or Psychological Operations—sort. "Hit it, Sergeant!"

Outside, louder even than the rockets, there came a sound of cold speakers being warmed by a sudden surge of juice.

Down in the rocket pits, half choking from the rocket's exhaust, the crews heard the static and stopped for a moment before being tongue-lashed back to work by their sergeants. They stopped again when they heard the music, drums first, followed by a fuller band. And then Pat Benatar's unique voice, in English, which few of them understood, though they understood the song well enough:

"This bloody road remains a mystery
The sudden darkness fills the air.

What are we waitin' for?
Won't anybody help us?
What are we waitin' for?"

They understood that, enough of them. Sergeants didn't need to berate them back into the drill. The women of Digna's command went on their own, a touch faster than they had been.

"We can't afford to be innocent.
Stand up and face the enemy.
It's a do or die situation.
We will be invincible . . ."

Except that on that last line, several thousand women, many of them with children hidden in bunkers not all that far to the rear, raised their right hands in fists and sang, louder than the speakers:

"SEREMOS INVINCIBLES!"

Nata Kill Zone, Republic of Panama

He had seen orna'adar not once, but many times. He had seen the mushroom clouds of the major weapons, antimatter and nuclear both. He had seen planets kinetically bombarded from space and ships splintered in the same medium.

Binastarion had seen much devastation. He had never seen or felt a more personal and complete devastation than that engulfing his clan.

There seemed to be a pattern to the barrage. At one end, at the western edge, it was a solid wall of fire that never seemed to let up. Between that, and the farthest point of Posleen penetration to the coast, another wall, this one a moving wall, played back and forth. Those were obvious. What was less obvious was the pattern inside. Shell fire pounded one area for a while, then moved on to another. Some areas took it worse than others. And in some areas it never let up at all.

Frustrated, enraged, Binastarion pounded the controls of his tenar. He couldn't even get forward far enough to try to direct his People out. Leaderless, trapped in that hellish maelstrom, they cried out to him.

Worst of all were the cries of those who burned. After a short time of the explosive fire, the threshkreen seemed to switch over about half their guns to firing what his AS identified as a type of phosphorus. This hit the ground and cast flaming, white-smoking chunks in all directions. The People touched by the flame, normals mostly though junior Kessentai were also hit, shrieked and begged and cried pitiably for aid that could not be given. Even Binastarion, himself, had no clue about how to douse the fire that scorned water.

Amazingly, a lone figure struggled and staggered out from the threshkreen-made hell. Binastarion swooped low to look, to help if possible. The poor thing's face was burned beyond recognition. Entrails dragged along the ground behind it, picking up their due of dirt and vegetation. The creature trembled uncontrollably. It took a second look before Binastarion recognized the remnants of the crest that said this shambling obscenity was even a Kessentai.

Binastarion raised his·railgun to put the poor God King out of its misery. "We are a hard and a harsh people," he wailed, "but we are not a cruel species. This . . . this is disgusting . . . cruel . . . obscene. Demons, I *hate* humans." A single shot put the disemboweled, burnt and bloody creature out of its misery.

"That isn't the worst of it, Binastarion," his AS said. "I have calculated the sheer volume of phosphorus the threshkreen are using. It is enough to burn up all the oxygen in the area under fire to a considerable height. Ordinarily, this would not be a problem, in itself. The hot air would rise and pull in fresh. But there is a temperature inversion building. Cold air above will trap warm air without oxygen below. Our People are going to suffocate. And there isn't anything we can do."

INTERLUDE

Guanamarioch moved as quickly and quietly as the slippery, muddy jungle trail would permit. His AS told him that there was a moon tonight. If so, the God King could not tell; the jungle overhead was too thick to allow anything so weak as mere moonlight to penetrate.

Posleen night vision was excellent. Even so, it required at least *some* light. There could have been light, too, except that over the past several nights any normal or cosslain who had carried a light had suddenly sprouted one of the nasty threshkreen arrows. He'd lost seven normals and a cosslain that way. Better to go it in the dark, by feel.

Step . . . slip . . . catch your balance by a vine . . . step . . . slip . . . catch your—

"Yeooow!"

The God King pulled his hand away from some round creature that grew spikes in bands around it. The spikes came away from their attacker easily; they were barbed and lodged deep in the Kessentai's hand. Still cursing, with the other hand he drew a boma blade and hacked down and across. The spiked creature fell, dead apparently.

Curiously, Guano detected no thrashing at all. It must have died instantly. He replaced the blade in its sheath and began pulling the spikes out of his hand. *Yeoow . . . yeoow . . . yeoow . . . Ouch!* He sensed that the spikes were leaving residue behind. The wounds in his hand hurt terribly.

The God King moved on. Suddenly, before he felt it, he sensed a mass of the creatures standing ahead, as if ready to fight him. Again he drew his boma blade, edging forward. He hissed and snarled, grunting and whistling curses at this new enemy.

The blade waved. He felt the slightest resistance as it passed through the body of one of the enemy. The body began to topple, towards the God King. Hastily he backed up . . .

Right onto a pack of the vile, treacherous creatures that had apparently snuck in behind him. Guanamarioch received an assfull of spikes. "Yeoow!" he cursed as pain propelled him forward again . . .

Right into the embracing claws of his enemy. More spikes entered the young God King's tender flesh, right *through* the scales. He flailed around with his blade, severing the assassins where they stood. Their bodies fell on him.

Yes . . . more spikes.

Beaten down, punctured in a thousand places, the God King sank to the earth still fighting. He was still trying his best to resist when pain, fatigue, and the hunger that had been his near constant companion the last several weeks, forced him from consciousness.

Ziramoth did not know what to make of the pile of freshly cut foliage with sharp defensive spikes all around. He was looking for his friend, Guanamarioch, whose oolt had set up a perimeter from which they guarded and within which they keened for the absence of their lord.

Then the pile moved . . . and groaned . . . and said, "I'll kill you all, you bastards!"

"Guano?"

"Zira? Is that you? Have the demons taken you to the afterlife as well?"

"Guano, you're not dead. Trust me in this."

"Yes I am, dead and in Hell. Trust me in *this*."

Ziramoth shook his head and began to gingerly pull away the pile under which he was pretty sure his friend lay. Sometimes, the pile shrieked as the plant trunks rolled about. When he was finished, Zira backed off and said, "You can stand up now, Guano."

Carefully, and perhaps reluctantly, the Kessentai stood. Zira whistled and shook his head slowly, and half in despair.

Guanamarioch, Junior Kessentai and flyer among the stars, had, at a rough estimate, some thirteen hundred black vegetable spikes buried in his skin. His eyes were shut from swelling where the spikes had irritated the flesh. He had the things in his nostrils. The folds of skin between his claws were laced with them. He even sported several that had worked their way through the bandages around his reproductive member to lodge in the sensitive meat below.

"I hate this fucking place," the God King sniffled.

CHAPTER 33

The hardest thing for a soldier
is to retreat.
—Arthur Wellesley,
Lord Wellington

Nata Kill Zone, Republic of Panama

"What can we save?" Binastarion asked his Artificial
Sentience.

"Not much," the device answered. "There are a
few hundred thousand of the People—some with their
Kessentai, others without—stretched back to the first
line we broke through. Some of the normals in that
kill zone are dribbling out, though they're in no shape
to actually fight. A lot of the tenar-riding Kessentai,
several thousand anyway, could get out before they
suffocate *if* they abandon their oolt'os now. The junior
Kessentai, dismounted as they are, are going to die,
burnt or blasted or asphyxiated."

The AS continued, "Then too, we still have a decent
population in that area we took on first landing, the
one the local thresh call 'Chiriqui.' If we could escape

with one in four of the People we would have a chance, some chance anyway, of escaping this world before it and the clan are destroyed in orna'adar."

Binastarion buried his face and muzzle in his claws. There was something . . . some way . . . if he could just grasp hold of it. What was . . .

"Aha!" he shouted aloud. "Every tenar could take two. A few of the better could take three or even four. Pass to my subordinates that they are to extract dismounted Kessentai and cosslain before leaving but that they are to leave. They must abandon the normals to delay the enemy and die. We will assemble . . . show me a map, AS. Ah. Yes, there." Binastarion's claw touched a spot on the holographic map corresponding to the remains of the town of Santiago. "We will assemble there. Tell them they can have my blood, according to the Law, after we escape but that until then I remain in command."

"I will tell them, Binastarion."

San Pedro Line, Republic of Panama

The Posleen were mostly extinct along the axis of advance. Of those that lived, the bulk were masterless, trembling wrecks. B Company, in the lead of First of the O-Eighth, shot them down instantly and without compunction.

It became a little tougher once they reached the minefields on the western side of the river. The mines were not an issue; they'd been modified according to the plan of an otherwise obscure American mechanic and electronically blown even before the ACS started to

cross. No, the problem came in when it was discovered
that there *were* some still cohesive groups of Posleen
on the other side of the river. It cost Connors half
a dozen troopers to root these out from their holes.
Rather, they'd had to be rooted out of the holes the
Panamanians had dug earlier.

That had been the plan, to leave reasonably well-
constructed and still usable battle positions for the
MI and gringo mech, under cover of being battle
positions for the Panamanian covering force of the
1st and 6th Mechanized Divisions.

It had worked, so far as it went. Hopefully, too,
the existence of those still extant battle positions
would prove more valuable than the price to be paid
rooting out their Posleen holdouts. Connors hoped
so, at least.

The gap being opened now, Connors ordered his
first platoon to hold the shoulder to the north, his
second to hold the southern edge of the gap, with
third as reserve and weapons in general support.

He sent back to battalion, "The way is clear. Roll
'em, boss. Roll 'em *fast.*"

Santa Fe, Veraguas Province, Republic of Panama

Digna watched the last of the gringo ACS and armored
vehicles disappearing into the fog and smoke. She still
had a number of reloads for the BM-21s and several
thousand rounds of 105mm for the cannon. The rocket
launchers would fire until they had only four reloads
left. The cannon had already used nearly everything
they had in terms of high explosive. They retained

quite a lot of fleshette and canister, still. That, however, was not at their current firing positions.

Digna was infinitely weary. She turned to Tomas Herrera standing, as usual, nearby. "Displace the guns that need to move forward to their supplementary positions." Which was where the antipersonnel direct fire munitions had been stored. "I'm going to walk the line with the gringo mechanized commander . . . make sure the guns tie in properly."

"Si, *doña*," Herrera answered. "But I think you could use an hour for sleep."

"Plenty of time to sleep when I am dead, Tomas."

Assembly Area Pedrarias, East of the Nata Line, Republic of Panama

If one looked at it just right, from just the right position, and somehow managed to keep notes, there was a pattern there to be seen in the shell storm that wracked the ground to the west. It helped though, thought the first sergeant, if you knew the plan and the way the shells were designed to support it.

A light drizzle fell, unnoticed with the much more impressive storm falling on the enemy. *Die, you fucking ugly bastards,* thought *el primero.*

"Get up, get up, you lazy sacks of shit. Plenty of time to sleep when you're dead." Quijana's company first sergeant, *el primero*, walked the perimeter of tracks kicking people as needed. He came to Quijana's squad and found the men all awake. Whether this was because Sergeant Quijana had heard him coming or not made no difference. They were up. That counted.

"You ready to fight, boys?"

"*Si, Primero . . . Si . . . Si . . . Si . . .*"

The first sergeant nodded. *Good. They sound ready. Maybe more important, they sound confident.*

"*Sergento* Quijana, status?"

"We're topped off and have a full load of ammo, Top, plus a complete additional load of small arms ammunition strapped to the outside of the track, food for a week and enough water for three days, with care. The men have had at least twenty-four hours sleep in the last three days and they've eaten well enough that they're starting to look fat. The track's in good shape though it's starting to blow a little oil. I've got a mechanic coming down from company to look at it. The weapons are all clean and in tip-top shape. We're ready, Top."

The first sergeant reached into his pocket and pulled out a pack of cigarettes, offering one to Quijana. He then lit the both of them, each man sheltering under a broad-brimmed floppy hat to shield the cigarette from the light drizzle.

The pair had to lean close to keep the match under the shelter of the hats. As they did, *el primero* whispered, "You take care, Son. Do your duty but take care."

"Don't worry, Old Man, I will," Sergeant Quijana answered, smiling.

Slapping his boy on the shoulder, *Sergento Primero* Quijana turned and walked on into the night.

It was an hour before daylight, Boyd saw by the watch on his wrist. It was the watch itself, having its own alarm clock, that had awakened him. He arose from the narrow field cot on which he had spent a couple of hours in fitful sleep, a thin blanket pulled over him.

The Dictator had slept—if that was quite the word for a period when one lies down, not quite conscious, while being assaulted by repetitive, centauroid nightmares—dressed and with his boots on, a rifle propped up beside him against the wall of the bunker. The rifle was unique in the Panamanian Armed Forces, nor could its like have been found easily amongst the gringos. It was his old service rifle, .30 caliber Model M-1, that he had purchased at the end of the Second World War for a keepsake.

He sat up, then stood. Reaching over, Boyd picked up his rifle, and ran his hands over its comforting, familiar, wooden stock. *Once more into the breach . . .*

Pushing aside a curtain that shielded his small sleep alcove, Boyd walked into the main part of the headquarters bunker. His twenty-four lictors, he saw, were already awake. One of them called, "Attention." Boyd waved them to relax.

Suarez was standing by. "We're about to reach the final stage of the fire plan, *Dictador.* Would you like to go above and see?"

With a wordless nod, Boyd led the way to the bunker's entrance, Suarez and the lictors following. Three BMPs and two tanks stood idling above. These would carry Boyd and his aides forward, accompanying 1st Mechanized Division. A few hundred meters away, Suarez's similar detachment awaited.

"It is very beautiful, is it not?" Suarez commented, indicating the shell storm to the west.

"Beautiful and terrible," Boyd agreed. Both men

had to shout to be heard over the firing of the big guns all around.

And then, suddenly, most of the guns went silent. There was still firing, but it was a mere drizzle as compared to what had gone before. Suarez consulted his watch. "Right on time."

A minute passed, then two, three, four and five, while the men watched and waited.

As one, the guns opened up again. In the glow cast against the sky four bright lines appeared. From looking, one might have guessed the lines were about a kilometer wide, each. Boyd and Suarez knew they were. In this final stage of the preparation, the guns were to blast four lanes through what remained of the Posleen. Into and through those lanes the two mechanized divisions would pour. It was expected they would meet little resistance.

"We've stopped the white phosphorus," Suarez said, "to allow some air to get in. Any Posleen that were going to suffocate already have."

Xenotraghal, or Xeno for short, didn't really understand what had happened. One moment, he had been leading his oolt forward, on foot. The next his band had been engulfed in explosions, with shards of sharp metal winging through the air with malevolent whines. Half his oolt had gone down in seconds, eviscerated, pulped, dismembered.

There had been threshkreen trenches nearby. He had ordered his normals and cosslain into them. The trenches were a tight fit, though, for creatures the size of human horses. Once in, Xeno lost all control as he could neither walk among them in the narrow scrapings in the earth nor—because of the fire storm—get out of where he stood.

He remembered that the fire had lifted, twice. The first time he had emerged from his shelter and called for his people to follow him forward. Then the shells had returned, further butchering his charges until, once again, he ordered them down.

Four times in total, the shells had lifted. But he was no stupid Kessentai. After being caught in the open the second time, Xeno refused to rise to the bait and kept his people low when the fires abated.

Then had come the shells that spread smoke and fire. He had thought them quite beautiful, at first. And then several had landed near enough to the trench system in which he and his people sheltered that chunks of burning stuff, arcing high, had fallen into the packed excavation.

The screams and shrieks of his normals had disabused Xeno of any thoughts that those shells were anything but ugly. All he had to do was remember the burned out eyes of one of his cosslain . . . Xeno shivered.

He had thought that the burning was the worst. *Oh, I had little imagination then,* he cursed to himself.

For the fire shells had not ended. Soon the air was filled with an acrid smoke that made his people cough and retch. But they could breathe it. Posleen had been well designed and whatever damage the choking smoke did would be soon repaired.

Xeno had found himself breathing more rapidly, much more rapidly. He assumed, at first, that it was excitement and, frankly, fear. He forced himself to calm but still he felt the need to breathe rapidly.

"What is going on?" he asked the AS he wore on a sort of baldric across his chest.

"There is too much fire, Kessentai. It is burning up all the oxygen."

Though far less intelligent, some of the normals still understood instinctively what was happening before Xeno did. A few of these panicked, emerging from their shelter to run feral and be cut down or barbecued by the threshkreen fire.

Xeno well understood that. Inside him, instinctive panic fought a battle for dominance with sentience. For a moment, he felt like he was back in the breeding pens, fighting for his life against the brothers who would gladly have eaten him alive.

Instead of panicking, Xeno looked around the trench as best he could. There was a shelter dug into one side into which he thought he could fit, if barely. Would that trap enough oxygen to sustain life for a while?

Best chance I have. Xeno pushed his way into the bunker, though his hindquarters remained outside, exposed to the fire.

Oh, yeah . . . that's better, he thought, breathing rich air again. There Xeno waited for death, ignoring as best he could the small flakes of phosphorus that lit up his rear end, bringing searing pain. He didn't know how long he waited, only that it seemed like an eternity.

Finally, his AS announced, "There is a tenar outside, Kessentai, capable of carrying you out of here."

Not daring to believe fully, Xeno still backed out of his shelter. When his head emerged, he was able to see the remains of his oolt. Whereas humans went slightly blue, when done to death by oxygen depletion, the Posleen went greenish. All of his remaining people, every one he could see for all the smoke, were green. And very dead.

"He . . . hel . . . *help!*" Xeno shouted as loudly as he could through smoke scorched throat and oxygen depleted lungs. He heard the whine of a tenar.

"Come aboard, Junior," said the well-crested God King who rode it. "There is nothing left here for you to command."

Unsteadily, holding his breath, Xeno climbed aboard the back of the tenar and hung on for life as its pilot gunned the thing to rise up above the fire, up to where there was air to breathe.

Almost the God King wept with relief at his first gasp of decent air.

Sometimes Quijana rode in the back with his dismounts. Sometimes he took over the track commander's position in the turret. Sometimes he took one of the two positions for dismounts that were in front of the turrets. These had machine guns to help clear the way ahead but, unfortunately, also exposed the passengers to fire when they attempted to get to ground.

For now, under the circumstances, Quijana thought it better to ride in the turret.

The sun was inching over the horizon behind him when the order came over the radio, "Start engines." Instantly, over a thousand heavy duty diesel engines within earshot churned to roaring life. That they didn't all come to life was evident when another squad leader in Quijana's view took off his helmet and slammed it against the metal of the turret. Within minutes a crew of mechanics had assembled on that vehicle, opening hatches to get at the engine.

Quijana *tsk-tsked*. He shuddered a little, inwardly, as he thought about what his father, the first sergeant, would do to that unfortunate squad leader. *Better you than me, compadre.*

No sooner were the thoughts formed than First Sergeant Quijana appeared above the offending vehicle's deck, alternately shouting at and beating over the head and shoulders the unfortunate track commander. *Oh, yeah. I put up with that shit for twenty years. The old man was always a mean son of a bitch.* Way better you than me.

Again the radio crackled. "Roll."

Quijana's BMP was sixth in order of march, behind his company commander and ahead of the platoon leader. The company, in turn, was second in the battalion and the battalion second in the regiment. The regiment was the lead for this lane of assault. Thus, he had a pretty good view of things when the sun finally rose completely.

Cresting a rise, Quijana saw the point of the column, the regimental scout company, nearing the fire storm of shells that marked their lane. Like Moses parting the Red Sea, the shell storm split in two. For five hundred meters to either side the guns began to paste any aliens who might be on the flanks of the penetrations. Had they been human beings down there Quijana thought he might have felt sorry for them.

There was a broad fighting trench along the military crest, a few hundred meters farther along. Across it, the engineers had apparently thrown up a stout metal bridge. The BMPs and tanks crossed the bridge with the thunderous metallic clattering, not unlike nails on a blackboard in its effect on any humans within earshot.

Infantry were manning the trench as Quijana's regiment passed. Themselves probably shocked silly at the fury of the morning's bombardment, plus the many days of fight, retreat, and fight previously, it had taken them a few minutes to realize what was happening.

Once they did realize, the infantrymen began cheering on their armored forces. A smaller group of men—bearing musical instruments, heavy on the brass—filed out of a trench into the open. Apparently the division commander had felt his division was threatened enough that he had even committed his command post guard, the division band, to the front. Unsurprisingly, the band had taken their instruments with them into the trenches. Well, after all, that *was* how they normally fought, building spirits through martial music.

· The band master raised a baton, then lowered it. Drums began to pound, loud enough to just reach through the artillery fire and droning engines. A flick of the baton and the brass began to play. The music was odd . . . not Spanish or Latin at all. It took Quijana a few moments to realize where he had heard it. It had been on a Spanish-dubbed gringo movie, about some men trapped in an old Spanish mission in Texas in the United States. He remembered what the music meant.

"They're playing '*Deguello*,'" he announced through the vehicle's intercom. The massacre song.

The tanks and BMPs split once they hit the breach, forming two columns to the flanks as supply vehicles raced to form a tight column in the center between the two. The turret of Quijana's track, on the left side column, traversed to bear also to the left.

The track carried only forty high-explosive antipersonnel rounds. On the other hand, it carried—either internally or strapped to the deck—over ten thousand rounds of machine gun ammunition. There was little firing of the main guns on the march, but the clatter of machine gun fire, from one vehicle or another, was nearly continuous.

Through the smoke and shell bursts, Quijana saw a small group of aliens, perhaps half a dozen, shambling westwards. The aliens' heads were down, an abject picture of defeat and despair. Their gait was unsteady, as if there were some disconnect between brain and legs.

Deguello. Quijana traversed the turret—the commander's controls had priority over the gunners—to the general direction of the retreating Posleen.

"Gunner . . . Target . . . dismounts in the open."

The gunner answered, "Target," fine-tuned the aim, and fired a long burst. Aliens were bowled over as the bullets passed through them. One, obviously wounded, attempted to rise. Perhaps its spinal column had been cut. It was able to get its torso up on its front legs, but its rear quarter dragged behind it.

"Repeating," announced the gunner. Another burst went out, this one shorter. The alien went down this time and stayed down.

"Almost doesn't seem right, Sergeant," the gunner said through the intercom. "They aren't even fighting back."

"Then let them figure out how to surrender and try to," Quijana answered. "It's not our job to teach them. Until they make it plain they want to give up, they are just targets." *Deguello.*

At some level Quijana was sure that the aliens couldn't give up, that it just wasn't in them. *Fuck 'em. They shouldn't have come to my planet, to my home. They're all goddamned targets now.*

Santiago, Veraguas, Republic of Panama

Was it only a few days ago that my clan, in all its strength and glory, passed this way? Can so much horror happen in just a few days?

What was it Stinghal the Knower said? "Count yourself no leader of the People in war until you have led a retreat"? Yes, that was it. The old Kessentai knew what he was talking about, too.

The retreat had so far been a nightmare beyond anything of Binastarion's experience in the breeding pens. While the tenar were faster than the humans' fighting machines, they were fewer now, too. And as for the normals that had to be left behind by the fast-fleeing tenar . . . his AS had showed him pictures of the humans just running them down and crushing them beneath the horrifying rolling roads their vehicles moved on. Even those who asked for acceptance into the clan of the victor by adopting the *posture of supplication and serenity* were killed like abat.

Don't these vile creatures understand anything of the law of the Path of Fire and Fury? Surely they can kill and thresh those who ask for assimilation, but they are required to judge their worth to live first. But the humans want only to kill.

Binastarion sighed. *Then again, I suppose from their point of view they have their reasons. After all, they can hardly use us for breeding stock.*

As retreats went, the God King knew, this one had been less disastrous than most, especially considering the disaster that had caused it. *Who would have suspected that this little place could have amassed so much of their "artillery"? I know they had help, the demon-shits. Perhaps I chose badly in deciding to claim and settle this part of the planet. And yet, but for that miserable waterway it seemed so safe, so nearly irrelevant. What forgiveness for a clan leader who chooses badly?* The great crested head hung in despair.

"It isn't your fault, Binastarion," the AS said.

"Reading my thoughts again, are you, o' bucket of bolts?"

"No, Kessentai, not your thoughts. But I am in tune with your physiological responses and the last time I sensed what I am sensing now was when we had to abandon our former home during orna'adar. That, by the way, was not your fault either."

Binastarion raised his head and shrugged. "Perhaps it was not my 'fault,' AS. But it was still my *responsibility*."

The AS went silent. It was true. Command took responsibility.

"What of our delaying forces?" the God King asked.

"It goes well enough. The humans' artillery is mostly left behind, though I sense that they carry some artillery, and mortars too, I suppose, with them. They can move the rest up again, easily enough. But I surmise, based on what I sense of the weight of the ammunition, that it would be a matter of much time, perhaps many lunar cycles, before they could amass enough to give us such a pounding again. Still, their armored vehicles advance. We kill some, of course, and lose many more in the killing. Without adequate leadership from the Kessentai, the normals are not worth much."

"Yes . . . about what I had expected. And the blocking force ahead?"

"We have probed it, from both sides. It seems to be composed of about two thousand of their armored vehicle soldiers and perhaps a fifth or sixth of that in metal threshkreen. They have considerable fire support from the ships-that-will-not-die to the south, and a large group of artillery to the northwest . . . Binastarion?"

"Yes?"

"The threshkreen planned this well. The positions they have chosen to block our escape from have mines to both sides. Yes, these are the same minefields we broke through many days ago. But the gaps we made were narrow and the thresh have closed them again."

"Show me a projection of our forces on a map, AS."

Binastarion, despite recent disasters, had not risen to lordship of the clan for nothing. He saw, he weighed, he decided.

"Twenty brigades with nothing but dismounted Kessentai strike the northern artillery group on my command. The remaining thirty-seven brigades, also without tenar, strike west. All the force . . . what is the force to the west anyway?"

"The People there muster twenty-four brigades, but with few tenar, Kessentai."

"Fine. They attack east to link up with our forces striking west. Work out the details and control measures.

Don't forget to schedule time for the dismounted God Kings to bond with their commands.

"All the other tenar accompany me to the southwest. I *will* see these ships die. Give the orders, AS. On my command we strike . . . for our lives."

Darien Province, Republic of Panama

Gingerly, Ruiz stepped over the skeleton of the dead alien. Though he suspected the thing was fairly fresh, the ants had made short work of it, stripping the meat down to the bones. A few of them still worked, though if there were any meat left to the thing Ruiz couldn't see it. Then again, ants looked in closer detail than even the Chocoes did.

Idly, he wondered what had killed it. He knew he had not. He suspected that it might have been hunger that did the demon in. He'd been watching them for a long time now. They'd been fairly fresh and vigorous in the beginning. But, as time had passed, he had seen them grow thinner and thinner. Their ranks had grown thinner, too, not just in the band that he followed primarily but generally, as well. The Chocoes took some small personal pride in that, though he knew the jungle itself had done more than he had and the demons themselves had killed many to keep the rest going.

The river was still channeling the demons. It was also what allowed him to track and pursue and even, sometimes, get ahead to lay a nasty surprise. He was setting such a surprise now.

Ruiz looked over the ground. *Black palm to the*

north. They'll avoid that. River to the south. I've seen them drown in shallower. They'll avoid that too.

He measured the area through which the demons would pass with a keen eye. He didn't have the math, didn't have even basic arithmetic really, to do fine calculations. He did, however, had a superb ability to envision fairly large stretches of ground in his mind. On this image, he mentally ticked off the places he would set the devices the gringos had called "claymores."

Twelve should be enough, he thought. Then he returned to his canoe to pick up two cases and a large roll of det cord. The Indian might have been small; he was still very strong. He ported the claymores easily, a case on each shoulder, and carried the det cord by his teeth.

At the ambush site, Ruiz opened the first case. He pulled a bag out, removed the mine and slung the bag over his shoulder. Then he placed the mine, sighting it as he had been taught. He tested the firing wire and found it good. Then he armed the claymore.

From that mine, Ruiz went and set up another, some distance away. Between the two he measured and strung a length of det cord. He was very careful, again as he had been taught, not to let the det cord loop over itself. It would, in such a case, almost certainly cut itself in two and put a stop to the fun he planned.

He laid the twelve mines. Then, for safety's sake he returned to the canoe to pick up a roll of communications wire. From the last claymore of the twelve he stripped the plastic from the firing wire, connecting it to the commo wire. The commo wire he then laid out, back to where the end piece of the first fire wire sat. There he laid the firing devices by both. Thus, if one claymore failed, or somehow the det cord cut itself, he still had a good chance of all twelve going off.

Lastly, the Chocoes camouflaged the mines, the det cord, and the wires and connected the firing wires to the devices. Suffice to say, that if growing up in the jungle lent one a sense of what looked right there, it was all hidden flawlessly.

That done, Ruiz took his bow, nocked an arrow, and began stealthily creeping forward to where his enemy awaited.

INTERLUDE

The arrow came sailing out of nowhere, fast, free and true. A normal squawked, then sank slowly to the ground. Then a dastardly little thresh jumped out from behind a tree waving some arrows in one grasping member and what Guanamarioch presumed to be their launcher in the other.

The small brown alien shouted something that sounded a lot like "oogaboogabooga" to Guano's untrained ear before darting off.

In an instant, Guano's pack was in full bay, with Ziramoth limpingly taking up the rear, waving their boma blades, firing shotguns and occasionally railguns (for the jungle muck and various unaccountable growths had rendered most of the railguns inoperable). The cry was "Meat! Meat! Meat!" as the pack galloped forward. Even normals could articulate that much, although they tended to mispronounce it.

The little thresh—no, better said, thresh*kreen*—was fast; you had to give him that. Several times the pack almost lost him. And then another arrow would fly, as often as not bringing a normal down, and the nasty little demon would show himself. *Oogaboogabooga.*

"Meat! Meat! Meat!"

Guano had trouble keeping the lead. Between the wounded reproductive member, beating itself against his legs and sending pain shooting to his brain, and the still fresh and sore wounds of that damnable pack of hunter-killer trees, it was just too hard. In time, the lead normals took over and Guano fell back towards the middle of the pack.

And then the little brown threshkreen was there, just standing beside a tree. It had something grasped in each hand. Smiling, it ducked down and . . .

Kakakabooboobooboom.

And Guano was standing there, almost alone. Some of the normals stood, as well, but they stood stock still, in shock. The rest were down, some plainly dead and others still thrashing. Of the brown alien there was no sign.

Zira, with some of the slower moving normals (for many had jungle-inflicted wounds of various types), came up.

"What the . . . ?" The Kenstain stopped for horror at what he saw had been done to the pack. "Guano, are you hurt?"

Distantly, the God King answered, "They were there and then . . . gone. Just gone."

"On the plus side," Ziramoth observed reasonably, "tonight, at least, we *eat*."

"I suppose so," Guano answered slowly. "But . . ."

A small feathered shaft appeared in Ziramoth's chest. Slowly, he looked down at it, then up at Guanamarioch. "Oh, my young friend. Eat well tonight. I am sorry . . ."

Ziramoth sank to his knees, then rested his chest on

the ground. For a moment he seemed to be looking around. His eyes lost focus. The great crested head sank, the muzzle touching the ground. Zira's body shuddered twice. Then he died.

CHAPTER 34

I see storms on the horizon
I see the tempest at the gates
I see storms on the horizon,
and a citadel alone
Clinging brave, defying fate
— Crüxshadows, "Citadel"

San Pedro Line, Republic of Panama

Alpha company and the rest of the battalion's "ash and trash" had started passing through almost immediately after Connors had reported the way was clear. The MI had no trouble fording, but the bottom of the river was so churned to muck by the artillery barrage that preceded the attack that Connors had to detail two squads from his reserve platoon for the sole purpose of physically man- or suit-handling even the tracked vehicles across. For the wheels, there was essentially *no* possibility of getting a single one over until a bridge could be built. Since there were no engineers to build that bridge . . .

It's always the little things that get you, Connors

thought. *I can't bitch that no one thought about the effect of the artillery on the river bottom.* I *didn't think of it, after all.*

Besides, it's not as bad as all that. Everybody, MI included, has weighted themselves down with enough ammo for couple of days' fighting. That oughta do . . . for now, anyway.

Sometimes mechanized infantry could actually move faster than MI. This was not one of those times. Between the difficulty of the river crossing, the fact that the ground was pockmarked like the surface of the moon, and the mud that filled the bottom of every unavoidable shell crater, the move for the mech was slow and *un*steady.

B Company, playing tail-end Charlie, still was forced to stop its own progress every ten minutes or so to unstick a track from the muck. The mechanized troopers were grateful, or at least as grateful as men can be when you help them get a little closer to their impending demise, but gratitude didn't get the MI to its blocking position any sooner.

Connors listened, idly, to the chatter on the company Net as he helped a squad from the weapons platoon lift an M-113 armored personnel carrier out of the hole in which it had been stuck, churning the mud to froth with its spinning tracks.

We've got to move faster than this, he thought, *but we can't leave the mech behind either.*

Still, despite the frustrations of the delay, Connors found himself strangely happy; happier, certainly, than he had been since being pulled out of the line on Barwhon and given a chance to read the mail that told him the woman he'd thought loved him thought no more about him than she would of a pile of dog crap she'd inadvertently stepped in.

And that's when it hit, somewhere between physically lifting the track and losing his balance to fall faceshield first into the muck. *My God, I actually feel* good. Wahoo! *I feel great! God bless you, Marielena and your long legs and your just* admirable *ass!* Connors rolled over on his back and began to laugh.

"Ahem . . . hem." That was the first sergeant, speaking over the private channel he shared with Connors and the exec. "Ahem . . . sir. While the whole fucking company is no doubt very happy to hear about your girlfriend's rear end, I think maybe *you* don't want them to be hearing all about Marielena's 'long legs and admirable ass' . . . sir."

"Fuck! Did I say that out loud, Top?" Connors asked after cutting out the general command circuit.

"Very out loud, sir. Very."

"Ah, fuckit, Top. I don't care."

The AID muffled the "speakers" inside Connors' helmet. It had to. If it had let loose, at full volume, with the sheer wall of sound created when one of the two cruisers on station to the south let loose with a soul-jarring barrage it would have deafened the captain; that, or simply knocked him out.

For that matter, the sound of metal shards from the eight-inch shells was noticeable enough to worry about, even though deadened by the silvery goop that filled almost all the space between man and armor.

Kind of like rain on a tin roof. I wonder how the mech is taking it.

The volume control was an odd thing, too. While it tuned out most of the blast, it let smaller sounds come through perfectly well. Thus, when a twelve or fifteen pound shard struck Connors' armored chest, he heard it bounce off and heard the plop of it falling into a nearby small mud hole. He even heard it sizzle as it turned the mud to dirt and steam.

Connors consulted the map. His objective lay only a few kilometers ahead.

"Heads up, Bravo Company. We'll clear this thing as if it's occupied."

This *is battle position?* Connors had never seen anything like it, not on Barwhon, not in Chile, not in the earlier fighting in Panama.

The battle position was oval in shape and overlooked one of the major fords to the river to the east. Though well entrenched initially, the walls of many of the trench bays had caved in under the artillery fire tossed around some days prior before the Panamanian Mechanized Corps had pulled back to Nata, under the scouring given the whole area by Digna's group of multiple rocket launchers this morning, and by the pasting from the naval gunfire still being supplied by the twin cruisers ... and, it must be said, by the Posleen hypervelocity missiles and plasma cannon blasting it when they'd begun their offensive.

It's like the moon ... but more desolate.

The boys of B Company went over the area with a fine-tooth comb.

"First Platoon here, Captain. Nothing but bits and pieces of Posleen ..." "Third Platoon, Boss. All dead . . ." "Second. One wounded Posleen. Firing one shot . . ."

Connors nodded to himself with satisfaction. "All right, boys, get the Bouncing Barbies out."

Along with their ammunition, each man of B Company had trudged in with two dozen of the nasty little flat cylinders that projected force fields to all sides when triggered by the presence of a life form. It had been a hard decision for Snyder to order the things carried, possibly a harder one for Connors to enforce. The suits' armor would not stop the force fields. Just as the Barbies chopped legs and torsos off the Posleen, so too would they have sliced the MI troopers in two had one of them been inadvertently activated.

Each platoon took a quarter of the perimeter. There was no real trick to using the Barbies; the men simply armed them and tossed them more or less straight to the front. Powered by the suits, the mines were scattered from one hundred to six hundred meters out.

The things normally activated after striking the ground. From that point on, any Posleen (or human, be he so foolish) that entered their effective radius would find himself shorter by a couple of feet . . . or a head. Thereafter, the Barbies would scoot to one side or the other. Since they were colored yellow, like Posleen blood, they tended to mix in very well with the terrain once it had been fought over for a bit. A field of scooting Barbies—bouncing, chopping, moving, bouncing, chopping, moving, with a Posleen horde trying to get through them—was a thing of beauty to behold . . . for certain values of "beauty."

"Okay, boys," Connors said, when the last of the

force field mines had been dispersed, "improve your positions and wait. The Posleen probably won't keep us waiting long."

"I *hate* the waiting even more than I hate the damned humans," Grintarsas said to his comrade and best friend, Horolongas.

The two were Althanara, or masters of lightly armed scouting oolt'os. As such, they were junior, not graced to ride the tenar of more senior Kessentai, and very, very expendable.

A measure of just how expendable they were was found on the shell-pocked ground around them. For they were not the first scout groups to occupy this land. The remnants of those who preceded them, who had been standing there when the threshkreen ballistic fists had come pummeling, were there still. They, too, had waited . . . and been held waiting too long.

"The time will come, my friend," answered Horolongas. His tone in answering didn't hint as to whether he meant the time for the advance would come . . . or the final time, death, would come first. Under the circumstances, perhaps it didn't matter.

The Althanara waited, with their scout oolt'os, behind a ridge to the west of the river. Some clever cosslain had been sent forward earlier and had reported, to the extent one could report with pidgin Posleen and hand gestures, that there were mixed groups of the fearsome metal threshkreen and the almost as fearsome ground-tenar riding threshkreen ahead, digging in.

"I heard the humans suffocated our People in their hundreds of thousands to the east of here," Grintarsas said, shuddering. "Unheard of. It is a filthy way."

"The Path of Fury is paved with bones and shit," Horolongas answered philosophically. "Does it really matter to the dead whether they were shot, or burned, or suffocated?"

"Perhaps not," Grintarsas half agreed. "But there is honor and there is dishonor, still. And suffocation is a dishonorable way to die, so a dishonorable way to fight."

"As you say, friend. Even so, while we fight for honor and glory *and* survival, the humans fight only to win and all else be damned. I must say, they've fought pretty effectively here."

One of the few tenar remaining to the Posleen to the west, those coming out of Chiriqui to try to help free their brethren trapped to the east, sidled up with a low hum. It rode low as well. One could never be sure where a human with a rifle might be hiding. The People were learning; the only question was "would they survive the lessons?"

"You two," the Alrantath, or battalion commander, shouted from his slightly elevated perch on the tenar. "It's time to move in. Ancestors with you," the senior intoned in blessing.

While the men prepared positions, Connors took a few minutes off from his duties to review his last will and testament. As the AID had pointed out, "You don't make a will to take care of your loved ones. You don't take out life insurance for that purpose either. You do both precisely so you won't die, Captain, for the Universe is full of whimsy and prefers to strike down those least prepared."

He was reading the clause about custody of

dependents should both he and Marielena die before the child reached maturity when he heard over the suit's communicator, "Heeere theyyy commme . . ."

"Hold your fire," Connors ordered. "Let's let the Barbies have their fun and then hit 'em when they're broken up and confused."

The normals needed no encouragement, normally. As a general rule they didn't understand the words anyway. They simply followed their gods' orders and lived or died as fate decreed. Normals knew little of fear as long as their gods were there.

Grintarsas and Horolongas, on the other hand, were sentient. That meant that fear was their constant companion when on the Path of Fury. Thus, the encouraging shouts they both raised were for their own benefit and the benefit of each other.

Leading their packs, the two swarmed over the hill, each expecting to be cut down at any moment. Yet there was no fire. To all appearances, the metal threshkreen and the ground-tenar riding threshkreen were not even there.

Hurrah! We might live to see another day after all.

At the base of the ridge was a small stream, too small even to appear on any but small scale maps. It was only about chest high to a Posleen at its deepest. Bellowing and laughing, the Kessentai splashed into the murky water and arose on the other side. Without a moment's hesitation, their People followed them in and likewise emerged, waving their boma blades and longer-ranged weapons.

"Should we stop and dress the line?" Grintarsas called to his buddy.

"No," the other answered. "It would only leave us open to fire."

Still they pressed on. Horolongas saw a number of flattish cylinders dotting the ground. Yellow like the blood and flesh of the People, these stood out starkly against the artillery-churned earth and the few spots of green vegetation remaining. They seemed harmless enough.

The cylinders grew thicker as the two Posleen scout oolt'os neared the place where the threshkreen had been reported as seen.

Normally, the Barbies went active as soon as they struck dirt after being armed. This was not, however, the only way they could be used. It was possible to have them remain passive, and only begin to kill on command.

Connors stuck a finger sensor over the lip of the trench in which he sheltered. (Actually, it was more of a scraping than a trench, as a large shell had expanded it, smashing out the walls and leaving a conical hole in which water had gathered. But it *had* been a trench and still retained a little of the outline of one.) The sensor gathered data which the AID converted into useable images to paint on Connors' eye.

"Oh, you poor stupid bastards," Connors whispered as he watched the twin Posleen columns advance heedless through the Barbie-sown field.

"AID," he ordered, "activate the Barbies."

Grintarsas heard it first, a bellow of pain from a mass of his followers. It confused him. There'd been no shots fired. He chanced a look to his left and saw a half dozen of his People, some flailing stumps in the air and others sliced through the neck or torso. Wherever hit, yellow blood sprayed. And he couldn't see what had done it.

What terrible new silent weapon do these dishonorable threshkreen have now? he wondered, redoubling his efforts to race to the target before more of his followers fell to this silent menace.

"Not five-percenters," Connors commented.

"No, Captain," agreed the AID.

Connors' finger watched as one Barbie after another sprang up, chopped off some legs or other bodily parts, then scooted to one side to wait for more. Even without any effort on the part of his company, the Posleen charge was falling apart in bloody stumps as the Barbies took them down by groups.

The finger locked on one particular Posleen, a Kessentai, obviously enough, by the erect crest, who seemed on the verge of understanding. The God King turned to tell his normals to fall back. Unfortunately, for him, the turning radius was just enough to bring him within range of a Barbie which immediately sprang into the air.

"Ooh . . . *bad* call," snickered the captain.

It was fucking hilarious, that charge; every man watching who lived through the battle, later agreed. With their God King down the members of that oolt either froze in place or began to run wild. And it made no difference. Those who stood still weren't safe because those who ran tended to set off Barbies that killed any who were near. Those who ran had almost no chance of escaping either, given the thickness with which the ground was strewn.

The finger panned across the scene. Of eight or nine hundred Posleen who'd begun the charge, perhaps two dozen were standing, trembling in the open.

"Should we off 'em, sir?" the first sergeant asked.

Connors had intended to but, on second thought, decided it was better to keep his men hidden.

"No, Top," he answered. "Let's keep a low profile for now. Pass it to the mech to scour 'em off."

Oh, pain, Grintarsas almost wept. *Demons of fire and ice, the pain.*

At that, the Kessentai was lucky. The horrid little threshkreen device had only taken off one leg, just above the knee joint. Grintarsas had turned, almost on his own axis, and begun to shout out for his people to fall back when he saw from the corner of one eye a flat, yellow cylinder—dripping yellow blood—that scuttled over and fell, coming to rest about six meters to his right front. He'd tried to stop then, to brake himself before he could come within range of the thing. In this he had failed.

Silently the cylinder had arisen to about half a leg length above the ground. There was a flash, but it was over so quickly that for a moment Grintarsas wondered if it was illusion. In any case, it was no illusion that his next step had been on three legs rather than four. Nor was it an illusion that he'd fallen over, forward and to one side, his muzzle digging a furrow in the mud.

At first it hadn't hurt. The actual severing had been so quick that the brain had barely registered it. But lying there, among the bodies and parts of bodies that littered the ground, had given the brain time to catch up. It *hurt* now.

The blood had stopped flowing fairly quickly; the genengineered Posleen were capable of staunching almost any wound, however severe, on their own while they lived. Still, the Kessentai had lost enough to become weak. That, added to the pain, made his mind fuzzy. He staggered in and out of consciousness regularly. He was out when the threshkreen heavy repeating weapons began to sweep the field, exterminating the last of his People and Horolongas', still standing frozen in terror.

The God King's only comfort, lying there amid the mud and blood, was the hypervelocity missile launcher he clutched to himself as a human baby might clutch to its mother.

The next seven attacks, none of them in overwhelming force and coming from both east and west alternatingly, Connors left to the Barbies and the mech. By the end of the last one, with the Barbie's charges beginning to deplete, he decided that it was almost time for his men to show themselves, or as much of themselves as necessary to lace the Posleen with DU fire.

The eighth attack, probably more by fluke than plan, hit both sides of the long oval of the battle position simultaneously. That attack was also in strength. Worse, from that point on, attack by more than two hundred thousand Posleen was almost continuous.

"What the hell happened to the naval gunfire?" Connors asked the AID.

"They've got problems of their own, Captain. The reason we aren't seeing any tenar here is that they've all gone to sea to go after the ships. The cruisers have pulled back south, but they aren't going to be able to outrun tenar."

"Fuck! How truly good."

"Could be worse, Captain Connors. If the tenar weren't there they'd be here. I project that we probably couldn't deal with another four or five thousand tenar, with heavy weapons, when we're already under attack by this many normals."

"Yeah," Connors agreed, lifting his grav gun over the lip of the trench to sweep it across the front of an approaching oolt'os. The leading Posleen simply exploded wherever a DU teardrop touched them, adding their own gore to the offal covering the battlefield. He ducked back down below ground level again before return fire could find him. "Yeah . . . thank God for small favors, I guess. How about the Panamanian artillery? They're in range of us, at least, if not of Company A to the south."

"They're busy defending themselves," the AID answered. "The rocket launchers' ammunition is depleted. Every one of their guns had been moved to a position to do direct fire to cover the entrance of the valley we hid in all those weeks. Besides, they're out of high explosive, anyway."

Connors popped up again to see one badly bruised oolt'os had made it across the river and over the few remaining Barbies to get in among his men fighting to the east. It was boma blade against Indowy-built armor and monomolecular cutter against yellow flesh.

"Short bursts," he ordered the AID and then, carefully sighting his grav gun, he began picking off the Posleen one by one.

Even through the armor, Connors felt someone or

something plop to the ground beside him. He was about to turn and fire, instinctively, when he saw that it was the first sergeant.

"Looking . . . not so good, Skipper," said the first sergeant, a veteran of the United States Marine Corps rather than the Army's Airborne and Rangers like most of Fleet Strike's Mobile Infantry.

"Losses? Ammo?" Connors asked, not because he couldn't pull up the information immediately through his suit and ACS but because tracking personnel and supply were the first sergeant's job and he might get miffed if someone tried to do it for him. Besides, Top was likely to add in comments on more than mere living and dead bodies that the AIDs were essentially indifferent to.

"We're down twenty-three men, Skipper, half of that from Second Platoon. Ammo is good, except for Weapons which is having to break into the last of the 60mm and reload. The other thing, sir, is . . . well . . . the boys are getting tired."

"Fear equals fatigue," Connors quoted.

"Something like that," Top agreed. "Thing is, the horsies should have broken by now. But they won't break."

"Nah . . . they can't, Top. We're blocking their only way out. And it isn't like they can surrender or anything."

"Yeah. Well . . . I'm off to buck up Second Platoon. Oh . . . did I mention that Lieutenant Nazari bought it?"

"Shit! And I barely knew the kid."

It seemed like the horror would never end. Connors hadn't known he could become sick of killing Posleen. But he could; he had.

"They just keep comin', boss, and they keep comin' *stupid*," said the first sergeant of B Company, with a tone of grudging wonder in his voice.

"Stupid may be good enough in this case, Top. Besides, I don't think they're being stupid so much as *desperate*," Connors answered, sliding down a trench, then lifting his head and arm over the berm just long enough to donate a couple of thousand depleted uranium teardrops to the Posleen. The crack of the teardrops was suppressed in Connors' ear by the suit's AID, as was the actinic streak each round made as it tore through the air at an appreciable fraction of c.

An infantry fighting vehicle from the 20th Mech went up in a fiery blast from an HVM strike one hundred meters or so to Connors' right. One moment it was sitting there, like a stolid Goliath, *chunchunchunking* 25mm high explosive rounds at the Posleen. The next its inadequate front glacis had been penetrated with a bright flash, hurling the heavy turret into the air, blasting the rear combat ramp right off its hinges and, in the process, incinerating the crew. They never felt a thing.

"Fuck!" Connors said.

"Sir, you okay?" Top's voice was full of a concern that could only be called "professional."

"Yeah . . . yeah. But the mech guys are getting hit hard."

"Hey, boss, in case you didn't notice, so are we."

Connors called up the display. *Shit. We* are *getting hit heavy.* Of the one hundred and twenty-nine MI troops Connors had led into the blocking position, forty-seven were already outlined in black, killed or so badly wounded that they were out of the fight.

❖   ❖   ❖

A long night and another day passed. The 60mm ran dry sometime overnight. This saw that section of the Weapons Platoon shoved into the line. Even the DU was down so low that the MI troopers were forced to start using single shots rather than the more usual bursts. This was less of a problem as the Posleen were also so badly beaten up that attacks were beginning to come in small groups of forty or fifty rather than just in solid waves.

The river to the east, the San Pedro, was so full of Posleen corpses that the normally smoothly flowing water had turned into something very like rapids. The water had spread out from its banks and, where it had once flowed, was turned to yellowish froth by the bleeding alien bodies. New attacking groups of the aliens found they could walk across on the bodies while scarcely getting their feet wet.

That is to say, they could walk *if* they could walk. Most of the Posleen coming from the east, trying to escape the closing cauldron, couldn't walk. Whether from hunger or fatigue they could barely stagger. Even at that, the attacks came infrequently enough that Connors found time to troop the line, walking among the men and lending a few words of encouragement here, a friendly pat on the shoulder there.

He even found time to write to Marielena, a short note—not yet quite complete—about the time he wanted to spend with her as soon as he came out of the line, their future marriage—if she still wanted him—and plans for the child. He was stuck on finishing with some words, and he was not especially good with words, that might express how he felt about the woman, how much she meant to him, and how happy he was she had come into his life.

He was sitting down in the muck (for inside a suit muck was as good as anywhere else) struggling to finish the e-mail when he heard a welcome sound, something he hadn't heard since the cruisers had disappeared to the south under massed tenar attack.

The AID allowed in the freight train rattle of the approaching shells, then cut the volume to something bearable when they struck the far side of the river ford B Company had guarded. Connors looked up from the muck just in time to see a half dozen rock, mud and water geysers rising suddenly into the air.

The command circuit was immediately full of chatter, of cheers. Connors scrambled up the side of the crater (or had it once been a trench?) and saw, under magnification, the lead elements of the Panamanian mechanized corps.

"We made it," he whispered to none but his AID. Standing upright, he waved to the oncoming relief force and fired three DU rounds, at super slow rate, to mark that he and his command were still there.

"So it would . . ."

Grintarsas was in shock now, almost completely. Whether it was the shock or olfactory fatigue, the rotten-meat and garbage stench of the People's bodies bloating in the sun around him was gone. He still cradled the HVM launcher in his arms as he had for the past two cycles.

Consciousness was not his to control; he drifted in and out of reality randomly for the most part. The shock of threshkreen ballistic weapons exploding on the other side of what he had once thought of as his objective was enough, if barely, to bring him to consciousness.

He saw the threshkreen, metal-armored and soft skinned both, standing up and cheering. It was infuriating. How could they cheer such pointless destruction? They didn't even bother to harvest the food, adding further to the insults they heaped upon his People.

One threshkreen stood above the others, very near to the summit of the old objective. Grintarsas took his HVM launcher and lifted up the sight. Painfully, he moved it to line up upon that one prominent threshkreen. At some level the Kessentai knew that the backblast from the HVM would kill him. He didn't care so long as he could take one of the hated humans with him. Moving slowly, Grintarsas finely adjusted the weapon, making sure the aiming dot was precisely on that threshkreen.

Then, giving a last smile despite the pain, he fired.

Connors never saw or felt a thing. The blast of the HVM launch, the white streak it left upon the air, and the disintegration of the torso armor of his suit happened so close together that they may as well have been simultaneous. The sudden overpressure inside the suit was enough to blow the arms and helmet off. The front and back plates likewise came apart, even as the missile turned the soft-fleshed body inside to dust. The AID died to the same blow, the e-mail Connors had been working on still unfinished.

INTERLUDE

With the gradual breaking up of the Posleen horde, the jungle had grown comparatively quiet again. Rather, it had returned to normal: birds calling, insects chittering, the steady pitter-patter of rain. The normal denizens, herbivores mostly, had returned with the sounds. Following the herbivores came the predators: snakes, lizards . . . the jungle cats, small and large.

He was like a leopard . . . on steroids. Normally a spotted species, this jaguar was "melanistic," which is to say its coat had darkened over the generations to provide better camouflage in the dim light that penetrated the jungle canopy overhead. At nearly two hundred and fifty pounds, it was largish for its species.

The jaguar hadn't fled when the Posleen horde had first approached. Rather, when its normal prey had fled it had simply followed. *A cat's gotta eat.* Now the prey had returned and, so, it had returned as well to its normal spot by the broad river where its a la carte menu often came to water.

Now this is new, thought the nearly black jaguar, looking down unseen from his lordly perch upon the half dozen horselike creatures that ambled the trail below. *Never seen caimen with such long necks. Or six limbs. Smell funny, too. It's a lot to eat at one sitting but, then again, they look a little skinny. I think lunch is served.*

There was an empty spot inside Guanamarioch where his friend, Zira, had once dwelt. He was lonely now, with only normals for company. They couldn't talk, tell jokes . . . teach one to fish. All they were good for at the moment, reproduction, he was incapable of. Even if he hadn't been so weak from long-term starvation, despite the thresh provided by his slaughtered pack and his friend, the itch and ache where the jungle rot had latched onto his severed reproductive member made reproductive activity impossible.

Shambling along, head down, the very picture of Posleen misery, Guanamarioch might have lost his life then. Only a warning cry by one of the few normals remaining to him caused him to look up in time to see the midnight black streak descending.

The thing, the nightmare, must not have thought about the implications of a centauroid form. Guano was just able to get one arm up to block. The creature's jaws latched onto that, rather than the skull for which it had been aiming. The jaws slammed shut with a sickening crunch of bone. Almost, the God King fainted.

Worrying the arm like a shit demon from legend, the black creature also began lashing out with its front claws. One of these raked across the Kessentai's face, lacerating it and ripping empty one eye socket. From then on, fighting blind as he kept his remaining good eye away from the claws, Guano fought—or, rather, defended himself—by feel alone.

The quarters were too close for his own boma blade. After what seemed like an eternity of fending off fang and claw, two of his normals came up and dispatched the attacker. They were careful, this time, to cut off no pieces of their god.

CHAPTER 35

Offshore where sea and skyline blend
    In rain, the daylight dies;
The sullen, shouldering swells attend
    Night and our sacrifice.
Adown the stricken capes no flare—
    No mark on spit or bar,—
Girdled and desperate we dare
    The blindfold game of war.
               —Rudyard Kipling,
                        "Destroyers"

Off Isla Cebaco

There hadn't been time to consummate things.

Pretty word, thought Daisy, *"consummate." Fact is, I wanted to get laid. But with the firing, the skipper's refusal to leave the bridge, the underway replenishment of ammunition . . .*

He hasn't even kissed me since that once. I'd almost think he's afraid to.

✧   ✧   ✧

McNair paced the deck of the bridge. He had belted on his sword—and felt silly doing it too until he remembered that his ship just *might* be boarded—and placed one of the Sterling submachine guns Daisy had procured nearby. One never knew, after all.

His mind was aflame with worries, of which there were two main. One was impending action, without much cover, against the Posleen who were sure to try to escape west through the old and now recovered San Pedro Line. That one was easy; he *knew* how to fight his ship. Rather, it would have been except for the other.

What do I do about Daisy? I'm no good with women, never have been. I knew ships. As a ship I could love her and comfort her and take care of her. But as a woman?

He'd ordered her below, once they veered to starboard around the southwest corner of the Peninsula de Azuero. And she'd *refused*, just flat refused to leave his side. The little voice she could project had said nothing. Instead, she'd crossed her arms under her—oh, sweet Jesus, *those*—breasts, stamped her foot defiantly, and shaken her head frantically "No!"

Almost he'd decided to put her over the side, in a boat with a crew with orders to take her ashore. He'd even said he would. Then the little voice *had* come, informing him, "You can't, Skipper. The body's brain is the AID. Anything more than half a mile away—the same distance I could project a hologram—and the body dies. And you can't send the AID off the ship and still fight."

He'd scowled then, scowled at the AID, scowled at the woman.

And felt immediately like a heel. "Belay that. The woman can stay."

Sniffing, the woman Daisy had turned her nose up and away as if to say, *How could you even think about sending me away?*

McNair still didn't know what to do, or what to say. He had no idea how to act. He was lost until . . .

"Captain, this is Lidar. We've got multiple Posleen tenar . . . correction; multiple groups of . . . correction: Oh, hell, there's a shitpot of them, Skipper. Thousands, at least, and they're heading our way."

McNair bit his lip for a moment and turned to Daisy the woman. He grasped her gently but firmly by each shoulder and leaned close to her ear.

"Love," he whispered, "we'll work this out later; I promise. For now, I need you to go down to CIC. It's armored there. I'll probably be along later. Take the AID with you."

He felt her body stiffen once again with defiance. "You have to go, Daisy. What happens if this body is hit? What happens to the ship? The AID will feel everything, won't it? Can we count on the AID to fight this ship if it is feeling you sliced in two?"

He didn't add, but thought, *Can we count on me to fight this ship if I see you sliced in two?*

The woman Daisy began to struggle in his grasp. He refused to let go until she subsided.

"You know I am right, don't you?" He felt her slump and saw her head, reluctantly, nod. "Leave me your avatar and go below then. It'll be okay. And we *will* work this out as soon as we can. And, Daisy? I do love you, hon."

The woman looked into the captain's eyes and

saw that he spoke the truth. Firmly, she nodded her acquiescence. But in her own eyes flashed the determined warning, *Yes, you cannot escape; we will be together.*

Binastarion told his AS, "Project an image and magnify it."

A holographic picture of the two ships sprang up in front of the tenar. Carefully the Kessentai squinted over the projection. The ships were as alike as two abat in a nest. Then he found, so he thought, what he was looking for.

"There, AS. Focus in on that section there." He pointed at the hologram. "Okay. Good. Now cut to the same part of the other ship. Hmmm. Back to the first." *There should be some marks, some scarring where we hit it, on the ship which killed my boy.*

"Got it!" the God King exulted. *"There* is the murderer of my son and frustrator of my dreams. Orders."

"Ready to copy, Binastarion," the AS replied.

"Skipper, Lidar. The aliens are splitting into four groups. One seems to be veering off to go after *Salem.* But three of them are coming straight for us."

"Cap'n, this is CIC. I confirm Lidar's projection."

"Ready to fire, Captain," announced the avatar, which appeared suddenly on the bridge.

For a moment McNair felt more at ease. The avatar was, after all, not the girl. *Pheromones. It must have been the pheromones. Christ, in the flesh I nearly did her against the wheel.*

"What are we carrying in our anti-lander gun barbettes?" McNair asked, more calmly that he felt.

"The first five rounds in the magazines are canister, Skipper. Plus there's another twelve rounds per standing by."

"Daisy Mae, show me the Posleen deployments."

On the holographic map projected by the ship McNair made out the four groups. Lidar and CIC had assessed well.

"Daisy, priority of fire is the northernmost group. Commence firing. Order *Salem* to support as she is able."

"Wilco, Captain. I am also projecting holographic deception measures" . . . McNair saw the great shapely legs appear to either side of the bridge and heard false lightning crackle overhead . . . "but I don't think they'll help much this time."

The giant demoness appeared before Binastarion's attack groups. He was not fooled. Many nights had he stood awake, thinking on how the ship had deceived him previously, to his great cost.

"AS, how many plasma cannon and HVMs do we carry?"

"Ninety-seven plasma cannon, Binastarion, and seventy-two HVM launchers with at least three missiles each."

Ahead, the God King saw the black, angry puffs—nine huge, ugly things—that told him the enemy had fired its anti-tenar rounds.

"For what we are about to receive . . ." the Kessentai muttered.

"What's that, lord?"

"Never mind, AS. Call it an old Kessentai's foolish sentimentality. Take centralized control of the plasma cannon and the HVMs. Plot a pattern to blanket anywhere in that apparition that the threshkreen demon-ship might be."

The thousands of 20mm tungsten balls launched by *Des Moines* and the one hundred and sixty-nine HVMs and plasma bolts launched by the Posleen crossed each other. Binastarion was surprised by the bright flashes made when a bit of canister struck one of his shots. That didn't happen much, though. A fraction of a second later over one hundred of his tenars' saddles emptied. At about the same time, the *Des Moines* was struck in nine places.

Alarm bells were ringing somewhere, off in the distance. McNair knew that that meant something, but at the moment he couldn't remember just what. It was important, though. He was sure of that. Now if only he could remember.

There was smoke, somewhere above. He could smell it slightly, but not quite see it.

Oh. That's because I am facing down. Why am I facing down?

The captain struggled to roll over onto his back and . . . *Oh, shit. That's a mistake.*

He tried, even so, until with agony tearing through his gut he righted himself. A little more effort, and a lot more pain, and he managed to prop himself against a metal wall. Now he could see the smoke, pouring out of the armored bridge through one hole through the hatchway and another, or so he presumed, on the other side. *Bad . . . very bad.* He refused to look down at the direction of the pain. He was afraid of what he might see.

The hatchway opened and a . . . *thing* crawled out, feeling ahead of itself with one handless arm. The other was used to prop up the torso. It didn't actually say anything. Instead, it made a hardly human keening sound. McNair thought he should recognize it but couldn't remember.

He looked right. There were some dead men there. Blood from their torn bodies leaked onto the deck, smelling of copper and iron. He wondered if some of the blood might be his own. Then, too, he smelled ruptured intestines, the odor of feces hanging heavy.

That made him look down at the source of the pain.

Oh, shit.

Hard, he tried *hard* to remember. His name came first. Then his job. Then, *I am on a ship . . . CA-134 . . . the USS* Des Moines *. . . the . . . ummm . . .*

"Daisy!" the captain called as loudly as he could. That wasn't very loud, certainly not loud enough to be heard over the steady explosions . . . *No . . . those are our guns firing. We're still in the fight, my girl and I.*

He'd expected someone . . . *ah, a hologram . . .* to appear when he'd called for Daisy. But nothing came.

Using both hands to hold in what seemed intent on coming out, McNair got to his knees. One leg came up but his foot slipped on the deck awash in blood. He fell with an agonizing jolt.

Must . . . see.

Again he tried to rise, more carefully this time. He leaned against the metal wall on which he had rested for support and balance. Eventually his head popped over the rim of the wall.

"Fuck," McNair whispered.

Number one turret was still in action, he saw, but number two was utterly wrecked, the armor torn open and men and bits of men showing hanging on the jagged scraps. Smoke and fire poured out of it. He thought he heard screaming coming from within but couldn't be sure.

He heard a steady *Brrrrp . . . Brrrrp* coming from both sides of the ship. Looking out he saw tracers arcing up. Some of the dots that were coming toward the ship—*Posleen. Those are Posleen*—fell out of the sky to splash into the sea. One exploded with a tremendous flash that engulfed several more.

Then the avatar did appear, though it flickered. "I am sorry for not answering immediately, my captain. I am hurt."

"Hurt? No . . . no, you can't be hurt," McNair croaked.

"I am hurt, Captain," the avatar repeated. "Number two is gone as are fifty-one and fifty-three. Number three is damaged, unable to traverse but still able to fire. One of the reactors is out, as well; we took another salvo after the one that hit here."

"Marine marksman topside," McNair ordered weakly.

"I have already ordered that, Skipper, but it won't be enough. Even with the Panamanian *Cazadores* we carry it won't be enough."

"*Salem?*"

"My sister is under attack but fighting well. She has little to spare for us, however."

"Okay, beautiful girl. Head to open sea. And don't give up. Fight us till we sink."

"Aye-aye, sir," the avatar answered solemnly.

Back still against the wall of the navigation bridge, McNair began slowly to sink to the deck.

❖   ❖   ❖

Daisy the woman had full access to the ship and the AID. She *was* the ship and the AID. She saw her captain as if she had been standing on the bridge with him. She saw him sinking as if dying. She saw the hands trying futilely to hold in the intestines. Even worse, she saw the leaking blood.

With an inarticulate shriek she jumped up, grabbed the AID and clipped it to her belt, and ran to CIC's hatch. A Marine who was on guard attempted to bar the way. She backhanded the boy, sending him sprawling. Then she emerged into chaos.

In the smoke and flame she heard, "Goddammit, Smitty, I don't care what it does to your fingers. Connect that hose!" . . . "Aaiaiai, my eyes!" . . . "Mama . . . mama" . . . "Corpsman!" . . . "Bless me, Father, for I have sinned." . . .

Partly from the smoke but more from something else entirely, Daisy the woman began to weep as she stumbled along the narrow passageways. *My crew, my boys, oh, my brave boys.*

"The ship is plainly sinking, Binastarion. Might I suggest we save our cannon and HVM fire for more suitable targets?"

"I've seen that demon-bitch 'ruined' before, AS. I'll believe she is down for good when I can see her bubbles coming up through the water. Even so, you're right. Switch fire to railguns to clear the enemy decks. Order Tenar Group Jarn in to drop the assault detachment on the ship. Let's see them get the fires and leakage under control while they battle our boarders."

✧   ✧   ✧

The worst was Morgen, the cat. Daisy almost didn't notice her, lying in a tangled heap on the fourth—or splinter—deck where a shard of sharp metal had nearly severed the kitten in two. Tears flowed afresh as she bent down and picked up the bloody scrap, pressing it to her breasts instinctively while twisting her head and touching her chin to it head and pointed, furry ears. Her one free hand stroked the kitten's fur, ignoring the blood.

Then she heard the clang of something large landing on the deck above.

The normal hated water, deep water anyway. Posleen couldn't swim and the creature knew instinctively that if it fell or was cast from the hurtling tenar it would have sunk so deep none could have harvested it. Inwardly it shuddered at the . . . no, not thought. It shuddered at the feeling of being forever cut off from its People.

Thus, when its newfound god's tenar had touched upon the blazing metal construction that, mercifully, floated on the water, the normal had felt nothing but relief. Moreover, it soon had company as other tenar landed, these also disgorging single normals or in one case a pair of them. The orders of the Kessentai driving those tenar were apparently the same as those this normal received through signs and body language. *There is thresh in this ship. Cut through the metal and harvest it.*

Then, as one, all the tenar lifted off, leaving the normals—with but a single Kessentai, Xenotraghal—in charge, to the work they understood so well.

❖   ❖   ❖

Daisy, still holding the kitten, lifted her head out of the hatch to topside. A quick glance told her all she needed to know. The Posleen were on deck, amidships, cutting their way through with their monomolecular swords. Marines and *Cazadores* shot them down, and were shot down in turn.

But none of them were watching her. Risking the chance of a stray shot, she leapt out of the hatch and raced to the ladder that led to the bridge. She scrambled up the ladder, emerging onto the abattoir the Posleen HVM had made of both the navigation and the armored bridges. She had to step over the body of a burnt and dismembered *thing* to enter.

And there was her captain and her love, hurt, dying . . . maybe dead.

The ship was armored on its main turrets and over its armored belt and deck. The top deck, however, was still teak and light metal. With others of its kind trading shots with the threshkreen who popped out to fire a burst before retiring behind protecting metal, the normal used its monomolecular boma blade to hack through wood and steel. Two of those helping it fell, yellow blood gushing to run over the decks and drip below through where the cuts had been made.

The sole Kessentai afloat was bellowing. The normals didn't understand one word in ten, but they did understand the urgency in the voice. Redoubling their efforts they soon had a great gaping hole in the top deck. Part of the hole led to what seemed a closed room. Next to that, the gap revealed a long corridor, narrow but not so narrow as those of the Aldenata-designed ships.

The God King pointed to two of the normals and then down into the compartment. Bearing shotguns, the normals pointed down and fired. Metallic pellets careened off the bulkheads with the sound of hail hitting a tin roof. Confident that any threshkreen that might have been hiding below could not have avoided being wounded, at the least, the God King ordered two normals to leap. This they did, somewhat clumsily. One broke its foreleg in the jump. The other killed it and waited until a third had joined.

With two hale normals in the compartment, they used their bomas to cut around the obvious hatchway. This fell outward leaving a hole suitable for passage of beings the size of the People. Alarmed cries of the threshkreen echoed in the narrow passageway. Human bullets pinged off of steel bulkheads. The normals answered with shotgun fire.

Commending his soul to the ancestors, Xenotraghal the Kessentai jumped below, using the body of the broken-legged normal to cushion his fall. He carried a railgun which he used to fire first in one direction, then in the other. The threshkreen cries changed to screams and gurgles.

Sending the normals out first, the Kessentai beckoned for others to follow. Then, inch by inch, they began clearing the ship.

Daisy looked out from the bridge sternward to where the Posleen had landed in some mass. They were lining up to port as if to plunge below. To starboard, however, was clear.

She felt for a pulse on her captain's neck. It was there, fast and faint and seemingly fading. Still holding the kitten in place atop her breasts with her right hand, she bent and took McNair's right wrist in her left. Dropping to one knee she wound the captain's torso around her neck, plugging his right armpit into her own left shoulder. Then, thinking *Damn, but my captain is heavy. I would have felt his weight first in a different way,* she straightened. Still, tank-born, she was much stronger than any woman born of woman. Truth be told, she was stronger than many men. She held the weight easily enough.

The load was unbalanced. Daisy the woman bent her knees, pushed upward suddenly, and shifted her body underneath. *That's better.* The captain's right arm and leg hung down limply in front. She gathered them up in the crook of her left arm, using the hand of that arm to hold the kitten in place. This freed her right arm. Bending one last time, she took hold of the Sterling. Bracing it on the deck, she jacked the bolt, loading the weapon.

Then, heading to the side of the ship, port, where the Posleen were not entering, she left the bridge, scaled down the ladder and—tight squeeze—brought herself, McNair and the kitten below. McNair's naval officer's sword, hanging down from his belt, paddled her rump lightly with each step downward.

And I might have enjoyed that, too, under different circumstances . . .

Father Dwyer felt the ship listing as it took on water unevenly. There was a shock and a vibration felt through the deck and the listing stopped and began to reverse itself.

The priest looked heavenward. "I don't know whether

that's the exec in CIC ordering counterflooding, or my own dear convert Daisy Mae doing it on her own. In either case, Father, bless their efforts. And strike down the enemies of your people."

The priest had a Sterling in his hands. Two Marines and three Panamanian *Cazadores* clustered around him. Ahead he could hear the clatter of alien claws on the steel deck. The clattering grew closer.

"Wait for it, me boys," the priest whispered, calmly. "Wait for it . . . wait for it." Then, with a great cry of *"Deus vult,"* the Jesuit stuck the Sterling around the corner and pulled the trigger.

The God King caught the barest glimpse of a threshkreen in a funny collar, firing one of their small but large-bore repeating weapons. Before the thing even flashed Xeno threw himself to one side to take cover in an open area filled with dead and dying thresh lying atop long tables.

Food, however, was the last thing on the Kessentai's mind. Instead, it simply breathed a sigh of relief that the fire which had struck down the two normals preceding him had not gathered him—just yet, mission unfulfilled—to his ancestors.

Not that it makes any difference. This is a suicide mission and I have no chance either at mortal life or even as thresh consumed to become part of the host. Still, I have my duty and perhaps the ancestors will gather me to them and grant me a high place if I have completed it well.

The Kessentai was one of those who might have grown into what humans called "a five-percenter," one of those God Kings whose intelligence made them more dangerous than the other ninety-five in one hundred put together. Still, he had been obscure, a very junior scout leader. Perhaps he had been chosen for this mission because of his obscurity, perhaps because of his potential. He didn't know.

He did know, however, that his mission was to interrupt repairs so that this ship would sink beneath the waves. Sinking required taking on enough water to produce negative buoyancy. Water was below and, if anywhere, was coming into the ship from below. Thus, it was into the bowels of the ship that he had to proceed.

There is a hatchway. I can't squeeze through it, though, without expanding it some. But there I will complete my mission.

Pointing for two more normals to enlarge the opening, the God King kept watch as they sliced away the hatch and began paring away the sides. He heard the sound of thresh voices and the pitter-patter of thresh feet on the deck. He braced for a counterattack which didn't come.

With the hatch enlarged and four more normals in tow, the Kessentai and his party started down.

Daisy could just make it through the hatch through the armor deck if she turned sideways to descend. Unfortunately, that was a very awkward way to go down a steep, narrow ship's ladder. She tried and having once almost lost her balance, she hung the Sterling around her neck, thus freeing her hand to hold on for balance.

If I can get my captain to the tank he might yet live. If I can't, I would rather die with him, here where we have spent so much time together.

✧   ✧   ✧

There was a series of explosions topside, which was felt throughout the ship. The klaxons began to sound and the ship's intercom crackled to life. "All hands, now hear this. Abandon ship. I repeat, abandon ship."

"Aye," Dwyer muttered, "I suppose it's time and past time. And I don't think the counterflooding's been enough. The ship rides differently. It feels lower in the water, somehow."

The Marines understood the call well enough. The Jesuit translated for the *Cazadores* with his party, instructing them to grab and don one of the life vests, should they find any. Then, with no more sounds of the aliens nearby, he led them to a stern hatchway. *I suppose if we're to have a chance we'll need a lifeboat. If any survived.*

"Kessentai, there is a power source ahead," the AS whispered.

"This entire ship is one big power source, AS," Xeno answered.

"This one is different. The Net tells me it is from one of the Elves' regeneration tanks."

"So?"

"So, it occurs to me that you might survive, after all, if you can make it to that tank before the ship sinks. There wouldn't be room for the normals, of course."

"Indeed?"

"Indeed."

The God King's heart began to beat a bit faster. He might live after all and rejoin his clan on some future day when this ship was recovered to scavenge its refined metal. If his People could do so in space surely they could do so underwater, though the Kessentai was not sure exactly how they would proceed.

Heart beating fast (for she was sure she heard Posleen speech ahead as she proceeded down the under-armor passageway) Daisy stopped for a moment, uncertain as to what exactly to do. Her ship-body was beginning to go down by the bow. It could not be much longer now before it went completely under.

She, too, had heard the call to abandon ship. Even if her ears had not heard it, the ship-body had. And, of course, whatever the ship body knew the AID knew. Since the AID was the brain . . .

The AID stopped the body for a moment. It knew well what it was like to be left alone. The idea of leaving that part of it which was the ship alone for however long, if ever, it might take to recover it was simply impossible. At something analogous to light speed, it began copying the "files" that were embedded in the very structure of the ship, erasing them as soon as the copying was done. The hull might rest below, but the essence of the ship would live in the AID.

Perhaps in time, with luck, I might return everything to as it was; to be the trinity of ship and AID and woman, all of us, together, loving our captain and crew. For now, this is best.

Daisy tapped in to the ship's nervous system and used it to measure her enemy. *Five of them, though how many are normals and how many God Kings I cannot tell. They stand between me and life for my captain, though, and for this crime they must die.*

As quietly as possible, she set her burdens, cat and captain, down in a small, semi-sheltered spot behind an open hatchway. She had never actually used one of the Sterlings she had acquired on the black market. Even so, the tank had programmed her with full battle reflexes, almost as an afterthought. She *knew* how to use it despite never having actually touched one before this grim day. Also quietly, she removed the captain's sword from its sheath.

How am I going to do this? she wondered. *I can't leave the AID part of me awake while the human bodies sleep in the tank. It will go completely mad. Ah . . . I know, though it will take some timing and concentration. If I can make it to the tank, I can put my captain in and lie beside him. The kitten will fit easily enough over my breasts. Just as the tank closes I will shut off the AID. That would kill my woman's body but the tank won't let me die. Then all will sleep together until the resurrection. My last thought as the tank claims us must be, "Click on the AID's power switch."*

Opposite the captain and a little to the stern, she found another half sheltered spot, took her own position and waited.

The lights were still working, which the God King found rather odd. After the damage the ship had taken from fire and whatever else his own boarding party had been able to destroy he would not have expected the convenience. Most of the light came from the threshkreen glowing balls. Some of it came from flat plates attached to the walls by no method he could see.

There was a dangerous spot ahead, one where passageways met and where there was no cover. The Kessentai stepped into the middle of his normals and grunted for the party to advance.

She had never seen them personally except as distant black spots, targets to be serviced. Thus, when the party of Posleen stepped out into the junction, Daisy gasped and nearly shat herself with terror.

The terror itself was her spur to action. Sighting down the suppressed submachine gun, with its metal folding stock against her shoulder, she fired. The thing was loaded with frangible ammunition. She knew it was because she had seen to it that there was no other kind of 9mm ammunition aboard. These broke apart and dispersed—yet another "war crime" to her record—when they hit flesh. For these purposes Posleen flesh was no different from human. The bullets flew and virtually exploded within the alien bodies, dumping all their not inconsiderable energy instantaneously.

Brrrp. A Posleen fell, splay legged. *Brrrp.* Another was bowled over, bleating like a camel. *Brrrp.* A third, just turning to face her, took two to the head and, going limp, fell in a heap. *Brrrp.* The fourth she missed. *Brrrp.* It went down with three in the torso—yellow flesh and blood exploded outward—and one in the throat. *Br . . . fuck, empty.*

Daisy dropped the weapon, picked up the sword and stood. An animal growl began to build in her throat. The Posleen answered the growl with its own war cry. It, too, sense of honor implicated, dropped its railgun and drew a blade.

Mindless, enraged howls echoing through the passages of the lower deck, the two charged.

. Dwyer saw the lone tenar slowly approaching, rather than charging and firing. Surrounded by ninety or so survivors—there hadn't been time to do a full headcount—in the one serviceable lifeboat they had found topside, he called out, "Boys, it's been good to serve with you. Now stand ready to take one last one with us."

But the tenar had not opened fire. Instead, the rider had pulled a metal stick from his harness, stood fully erect in the flying sled, and called out with both arms raised above it. Other circling tenar had stopped then, their God Kings looking curiously at the tiny band of humans bobbing on the ocean waves.

The tenar came closer, closer until finally it was not more than ten feet from the edge of the lifeboat. The rider then cocked its head and said something in its own language. That something had sounded unaccountably gentle. Then the God King raised its crest, shouted once again, and tossed Dwyer the stick it held. Dwyer caught it, fumblingly at first. He looked up to see that the alien had raised one palm, holding it open and towards the humans. The priest returned the gesture and added one of his own. He didn't understand the why's of it, but he knew he and the rest had just been spared. The priest made the sign of the cross at the Posleen.

"That was damned odd thing to do, Binastarion," the AS said as the tenar glided above the waves.

The Kessentai smiled very slightly. "Was it really,

AS? Think about it. We could only have taken that little craft full of threshkreen by firing on them. That would have sunk them and so we could not have taken them anyway."

"I didn't mean you, God King. I meant the human with the strange collar in that small boat. He was blessing you, you know. So says the Net anyway. Though, now that you mention it, throwing the stick for a group of threshkreen who have done you and the People so much harm is a bit odd, too."

The great threshkreen she-demon ship was still firing as water engulfed first the deck, then the lower guns, and finally the great turrets. Binastarion felt a kind of remorse. It had been a fine enemy.

May I never meet its like again.

"It seemed *right*," Binastarion said simply.

"So?" The AS queried. "They were still an enemy."

The Kessentai was silent for a few moments before he answered, "We are as we were made to be, you soulless bucket of bolts. We are a hard and a harsh species, AS, but we are not a wastefully cruel one."

It was the AS's turn to go silent. When it spoke again it asked, "What now, Binastarion? The host is ruined. The threshkreen will drive us from this land. We cannot hold it from them nor take another in our present state."

"I had thought upon honorable suicide, AS," the Kessentai admitted wearily.

"Not so fast, Binastarion. There is . . . correction, there *may* be, another way. Far to the north a Kessentai of rare ability is gathering a great host to fight the humans. He is building a new overclan from the remnants of such as ours. He promises succor, without edas, no less. He offers new lands for his new clan, once the great power of this world is defeated. He has new ways, ways something like those of the threshkreen who have defeated us here and held the People at bay there."

"What is the name of this god-like God King, AS?"

"Lord, the Net lists him as Tulo'stenaloor."

INTERLUDE

Darien Province, Republic of Panama

He was the hunted now, and he knew it. There were no more ambushes with the explosive devices. Instead, the hunt had become much more personal, with single arrows leaping out from who knew where to impale his few remaining normals. Well, they *had* been few. They were all gone now, gone and eaten at the behest of this terrible jungle.

He knew they were eaten, too, for once he had gone to sleep sheltering behind the corpse of one of his late followers. When he had awakened, the normal was half gone and his corpse covered with uncountable thousands of the little insects that infested this place.

Only once since the explosive ambush Guanamarioch had caught plain sight of his hunter, the little, naked, brown threshkreen demon. The God King had raised his railgun, taken aim, pressed the firing stud . . .

And been rewarded by a small explosion that damaged

his left hand, the stink of fresh ozone, and a small cloud of smoke. The jungle rot had claimed yet another victim.

The little demon was here now, too. The God King sensed it. He raised his head fearfully. An arrow struck a tree and quivered there for an instant, close to Guano's head. This was his chance. It took time for the demon to reload and aim his primitive weapon.

Guano saw an unusual light ahead and sprinted for it. An arrow struck him in his haunches, burying itself—but not too deeply—in the stringy muscle. Instead of slowing him, the pain helped propel the Kessentai onward.

Onward and onward he flew. He hardly noticed when the jungle gave way to clearing. When he did notice he stopped suddenly at the shock of not being surrounded to the sides and above with the jungle growth. The sun shone on his back. For a moment, overcome with emotion, Guanamarioch raised himself on his rear legs and began to dance and prance, those same rear legs propelling him upward again and again in boundless happiness. In his own tongue he shouted to the Heavens, words of praise and thanks, that he had finally escaped.

Then he saw the little threshkreen, bow in one hand and arrow held in the other, following him at a dead run. The God King stopped prancing then and, arrow sticking out of his rump or not, began a mad dash forward. On the open ground he was much faster than the little, brown threshkreen.

He didn't see the shiny vines until it was too late. Guano tried to brake himself, then—sensing that would fail—tried to leap over. No matter; he came down and found himself surrounded by the shiny vines, caught like a nestling in the pens. He thrashed a bit but the shiny vines were metal and had nasty barbs that dug into his flesh. His thrashing only caused him to become more tightly bound.

A group of threshkreen emerged. Some were light in the face, others quite dark. About half were the same color as the threshkreen who hunted him. These threshkreen seemed more curious than hostile.

"AS, can you translate into their language?" Guanamarioch asked.

"English or Spanish, yes, Kessentai. I have downloaded both tongues from the Net."

Guano tried to nod, but the shiny vines had his muzzle caught fast. "Tell these, then, that they can kill me, they can eat me, but I ask under the Law for assimilation into their clan. Tell them I would adopt the proper posture if I could, but I can't. Explain the law, if they give you time. Tell them they can do whatever they like as long as THEY DON'T SEND ME BACK THERE!"

CHAPTER 36

Renown awaits the commander who first restores artillery to its prime importance on the battlefield.

— Winston Churchill

Santa Fe, Veraguas Province, Republic of Panama

I don't think their hearts are in it anymore, thought Digna as five of her guns opened up on a large band of Posleen shambling forward, heads down as if walking into a fierce rainstorm.

There had been some tense moments in the last several hours. At first the enemy had come like a flood, seemingly unstoppable and tripping over their own dead to get at the BM-21s whose fire still protected the gringos that had sealed the bottle of the Posleen trap. Digna had sent out the word to her gun crews, "Mothers with children: you are all that stand between them and the enemy who would eat them. Mothers to the front."

And the women had heard and understood. Perhaps they had understood, too, why this cranky old battleaxe who looked eighteen or nineteen had had the children brought.

I am a woman. I know what my sex values above all. For anything else, these women might not have fought as they did. But for their kids they would sacrifice anything.

Silently, Digna vowed to adopt into her own clan, and see they were properly raised, any children who had lost their mothers this day.

Below her, constrained by the narrow valley road that led to the town behind, the Posleen band went down as canister cut great swatches through them. The alien enemy moaned en masse as limbs were severed and entrails ripped out.

Another group was forming a kilometer or so away. Digna, weary or not, shivered with anticipation at the thought of bringing this group down as well.

Did you think, you alien beasts, that I, that I, Digna of the Clan Miranda would let such as you keep possession of my land, of the graves of my ancestors and my children?

Battle Position Lundy's Lane, Darien Province, Republic of Panama

The commander of the Fifth Infantry was a proud man that day, though he knew it was hardly entirely to his own efforts or those of his regiment that the lone Posleen standing under guard outside the command post tent had told the story he had.

It had not been easy to get the Posleen even to the tent. Moments after his surrender a fierce little Chocoes had shown up insisting that the alien's head belonged to him. Though the sergeant in charge of the squad had tried to explain that the alien was a prisoner of war the Chocoes had been very insistent. Only with the arrival of the commander himself had a deal been worked out whereby the regiment would pay the Indian for the life of the alien. The alien, too, had agreed.

All things considered, the price was worth it.

"That's right, sir," the commander told the Chief of SOUTHCOM over the radio. "We have one Posleen prisoner of war. And, sir, he insists that the rest of his horde is not coming. Dead, he says, every one . . . Yessir, I *do* believe him. Oh, there may be a few ferals still out there, but they're no threat. . . . Yes, sir, the regiment is preparing to move east again now. If there's any concentration of the Posleen we can handle them. They don't seem very capable of operating in the jungle."

San Pedro Line, Republic of Panama

The Posleen attacks had petered out before nightfall. By dawn, the sound of firing, human firing, had grown intense.

It was always a touchy problem when friendly forces met over enemy bodies. The best solution, the one adopted, had been for the 20th Infantry and the remnants of First of the O-Eighth to simply pull back into three battle positions and let the Panamanian divisions through the two gaps thus created. Yes, a few of the aliens had no doubt also escaped through those gaps. No matter; they would be hunted down.

Connors' XO—no, the CO since Connors had fallen—heard a strange music coming from a couple of trucks carrying a band that passed through the gap nearest her much depleted command.

"AID, what is that music?" she asked.

The AID took a moment before it answered. No doubt it was searching the Net. "That music is 'Deguello.'"

"Meaning?"

"It's a Moorish tune picked up by the Spanish during the Reconquista and brought over to this hemisphere. It means 'cut throat.' They sometimes call it 'The Massacre Song.' I think it's directed as much at the Panamanians as the Posleen."

CA-139, USS Salem

The Posleen tenar were gone now, gone without a trace. The Marlene Dietrich look-alike avatar on the bridge wept inconsolably as the ship thrashed about over the spot where *Des Moines* had sunk. "My sister . . . my sister . . ."

Sidney Goldblum wanted to reach out and comfort the avatar but, of course, could not. The ship's chaplain, Rabbi Meier, came onto the battle scarred bridge.

"Sally, is she really gone?" Goldblum asked.

Still weeping, the avatar answered, "I sense nothing below, Rabbi. Nothing. She has to be gone."

"We've been here long enough, Sally," Goldblum interjected. "We *have* to go search for survivors."

Meier held up an index finger at the captain. *Wait.* Then he bowed his yarmulked head. "Let us go to the stern then, Sally, and say kaddish over the soul of your sister."

The sniffling stopped, almost. Still through tears that appeared on her holographic face, Sally responded, "But she converted to Catholicism, Rabbi. Would kaddish even work."

"Kaddish is really for *you*, my child. And besides, do you think that the Almighty really cares about such mundane details?"

Iglesia del Carmen, Panama City, Panama

As she had every day since the news had reached her, Marielena came to this church and prayed for her fallen lover. *Soon enough*, she thought, patting her stomach, *I won't be coming here alone either.*

Money wasn't going to be a problem. Scott's Galactic Law Last Will and Testament had proven inviolable and incontestable, though his childless ex-wife had certainly tried to contest it.

Her mother, on the other hand, was proving to be something of a problem, nagging continuously at "the shame of it all, my daughter carrying a bastard." Fortunately, her father was taking things rather more philosophically. He'd shrugged, told her mother to shut up, and answered, "Better a bastard in the family than an unemployed son-in-law. What's more, woman, the child's father helped save this country, to include saving your nagging tongue. The child will never hear the word bastard or you will feel my belt."

She might someday marry, Marielena thought. But . . . no time soon. Her bed was lonely and cold without Scott in it. But she was in no hurry to fill it with some lesser man.

A poem had been going around the Net of late. Someone locally had changed it around, translating it into Spanish and making a few changes along the way. The poem was in the form of a prayer, she recited it now in a whisper:

"I do not grudge him, Lord.
I do not grudge my one strong man
Whom I have seen go out
        to break his strength and die,
He and a few,
In bloody struggle for a holy thing.
His name shall be remembered
        among his people and mine
And that name shall be called
blessed . . ."

In the same pew with Marielena another young woman, even more of a girl than she was, wept. Why not? The church was *full* of women weeping for a lost son, a husband, a father, a brother. Some wept for lost daughters, as well.

The girl was young, Marielena saw, very, *very* young. And her sobbing body spoke of both loss and a fear of utter *aloneness*. Did she have no family left? Mari had, at least, some.

In pity, Marielena sidled across the pew, closing the distance between her and the girl. Tenderly, she put her arm around the unknown one's shoulder. "There," Mari whispered, "there, there. It will be all right."

Paloma de Diaz nodded her head but the tears

never stopped flowing, the body never stopped shaking. "Thank you," she whispered back in a breaking voice.

"What's your name, child?"

Paloma told her, saying also why she had the married name, "de Diaz," and blurting out, "But he promised to come back to me. He *promised*."

"I'm sure he tried," Mari said, in answer. "But sometimes things, important things, come up and promises, however much meant and however important, just can't be kept. I try to tell myself that . . . when it gets really hard."

"I'm going to have a baby," Paloma whispered. "He never knew. I didn't know myself until it was too late to tell him." She broke out in fresh sobs.

"He knows," Marielena said, looking at the altar. "Even if you never told him, he knows now."

EPILOGUE I

Then let him be dictator
For six months and no more.
      —Thomas Babington Macaulay,
        "The Battle of Lake Regillus"

Fort William D. Davis, Panama

If the fighting was not ended at least the emergency was over. The *Patria* was restored, even expanded a bit since there were no longer any Costa Ricans to contest Panamanian occupation right up to and past the Coto River. The Posleen which had overrun the western provinces were, by and large, dead. Any Posleen left in the Darien, and there must have been a *few*, had either gone feral—ceased, in other words, to be more of a threat to life than the jungle itself already was—or were nothing more than ant-stripped, bleaching bones slowly sinking in the muck.

Over half a million Panamanians had fallen though; virtually the entire populations of the province of Chiriqui, as well as many of Herrera, and Veraguas were gone, plus substantial numbers of *Colonenses*

and *Ciudanos*. From a people who had never numbered more than three million this was a knife to
the heart.

Boyd felt the knife. He felt it at every list of the
missing and presumed dead that had crossed his
desk. He felt it in the open files in the ranks of the
army. He felt it in the friends and cousins he would
never see again.

No more. Let someone else take the responsibility.
I've done all I can.

That wasn't quite true. There was one more responsibility Boyd felt, one more thing for him to do.

He had already said his farewells and expressed his
deepest thanks to the other American battalions that
had stood and bled, from the Armored Combat Suits
of First of the Five-O-Eighth and light jungle fighters
of Third of the Fifth Infantry at Fort Kobbe, such
as were left of them, to the heavy mechanized troops
of the 20th Infantry and the Florida National Guard's
53rd Separate Infantry Brigade and Puerto Rico's 92nd,
both of which had been moved in by ship and submarine for the mopping up after the final campaign.
Fort Gulick's—or Espinar's—Special Forces, who had
proven so critical in training the *Armada*, had been
given a special commendation.

The 10th Infantry, at Fort Davis, the "lost regiment of
the lost post of the lost side of the lost command," stood
to in ranks as the band played and Boyd, Preiss—the
regimental commander—and some few other dignitaries
made their speeches.

From the troops' bored faces Boyd was pretty sure
they would rather be off to continue the "el Moro
pacification campaign" than standing in the hot sun.

Ah well, Boyd thought, *I was no different at their ages. Still, who knows, maybe it will mean something to them later . . . when they are old men like me . . . if they live.*

If any of us live.

Commands were spoken. The band strutted across Davis' trapezoidal parade field. Troops passed in review, sharply for all their boredom.

With the others, Boyd stood to attention as the colors passed. The red, white and blue caused his throat to catch a bit, as it did for some of the other Americans and even for a few others among the Panamanians.

As the last of the massed formations disappeared in the gaps between the long, low barracks Preiss took Boyd's hand and shook it warmly.

"It means more to the boys than they'll ever let on, you know," Preiss insisted.

Boyd wordlessly nodded his head.

As the reviewing party began to break up, Pedro, Boyd's driver, "Ahem'd" to catch the soon to be ex-dictator's attention. With no further signal needed, Boyd followed Pedro to the waiting limousine.

Opening the door for himself, Boyd entered the limo and ordered his driver to take him around the post for one final look. Pedro dutifully started the engine and began to take the palm-lined route from the PX overlooking the golf course to the top of the hill on which stood a sharpened post with a crosspiece (for the 10th had removed Cortez's remains upon returning to the fort). The car passed the NCO club, then Colonel's Row, and then took a right to move along the road backing the southern side of the golf course. A final turn was made onto the back side of the PX complex.

Boyd glanced idly to his left and exclaimed, "Good God, what is that? Pull over, Pedro."

The Posleen God King looked suspiciously at the approaching Boyd through its one remaining yellow eye. Boyd could tell it was a God King, rather than a normal, from the shredded remnants of the alien's fungus-eaten crest. The God King sat on its haunches, surrounded by several score pair of boots, some mud-caked and others shined to a mirror gloss. A boot sat snugly on the Posleen's left claw while it held a black-specked white rag tightly gripped by its right. The rag's excess was twisted around the alien's right forearm.

The alien hissed and snarled at Boyd's approach. As this failed to deter the retired dictator's approach, it lowered its head. One eye, however, remained fixed on Boyd.

"I am allowed to be here," came the defiant announcement, though the major sound came from the dull silver-gray box strapped to its chest, interpreting the Posleen's incomprehensible tongue.

"You are the one who surrendered, aren't you?" asked Boyd.

"I am allowed to be here," the box repeated, the tone more defensive than defiant now.

"It's all right," Boyd said, calmly. "I am not going to send you away. You *are* the one who surrendered?"

Slowly, ponderously, the Posleen lifted its head nearly perpendicular to the ground and then lowered it in the sign of the affirmative.

"I am he," the box duly translated.

"Are you all right? Are you being treated well?"

More hisses and snarls, punctuated by two snaps of the jaw. "I am well," said the box.

Boyd let his eyes wander to the many pairs of boots, then to the door of the shack through which he could see many score more pair.

Without being asked the box offered, "They taught me to do this. Gave me this place to live when I had no other. I make several hundred dollars a month from being the 'boot boy' for the 10th Infantry. And a music company from the island you humans call Ireland has sent me an advance for a translation of the song we Posleen only know as 'The tale of he who farted in the enemy's general direction.' I do all right."

The Posleen looked reasonably well fed. Still Boyd asked, "Is that enough?"

"Yes, although the work never seems to end. I didn't always have to work, you know. I used to have others that did the work for me. Now I have a boss-man and I must work."

Did Boyd detect a trace of wistful sadness in the tone of the words coming from the box? Or had the alien's own snarls, hisses, clicks and grunts seemed somehow sad?

"What are you called?" *No reason not to be friendly, I suppose.*

"My name, among my people, was Guanamarioch, or Guano for my close friends. Here, they call me 'Apache,' perhaps because of my crest."

As if to punctuate, Guano removed the rag from his right hand and, extending a claw, began to scratch furiously at the shreds of its crest. As it did so, it—more or less doglike—turned its head giving Boyd his first clear view of the missing eye with its still weeping socket.

"It was the jungle took my eye," the box announced solemnly. "Took my eye . . . took my clan . . . took everything."

Noticing the mad glare that had crept into the Posleen's remaining eye, Boyd decided to change the subject, if he could.

"Do you have any relaxation or fun at all?" he asked. "Or do you just shine boots?"

The God King looked around furtively before answering. "Sometimes," he said, "I sneak into the jungle when I think it is asleep and cut down a tree or two. If I can find an ant tree that is even better. But most of the ant trees are pretty deep inside and I am afraid I'll awaken the jungle if I go too deep. And then, on really good days, the boss lets me sneak down to the French cut and hunt for caimen."

Guanamarioch's head lowered and his teeth bared in a half snarl. "I really *hate* caimen."

Boyd laughed. "The jungle never sleeps, my friend."

"Yes, it *does*," the Posleen insisted, its ragged crest waving wildly. "It does! It does! Like any living being it must rest. It sleeps. Besides, if it were not asleep it would have killed me as it killed so many of my brothers."

Obviously the God King thought the jungle was a living being. Boyd thought that was pretty ridiculous but saw no point in arguing about it. Besides, the alien seemed too distraught—and *way* too big and well clawed—to risk antagonizing it.

Suddenly, without warning, the God King picked up and rewound the rag, bent its head over the boot it held and began furiously polishing.

"It's the boss," the box whispered.

Boyd looked around and saw a half naked Chocoes Indian approaching at a leisurely walk. The Indian held a bow in his left hand, beneath a multi-striped brassard that indicated membership in one or another of the Indian Scout groups the Republic had raised in its dire need. There was nothing particularly unusual about that.

What was unusual was the Indian's retinue. Meekly behind him, in double file, walked an even half dozen of every ethnicity one could hope to find in Panama. There was a Cuna Indian girl, short like the Chocoes but wearing an appliqué blouse and a ring through her nose. Beside the Cuna walked a tall slender black woman, descendant of Antillean workers who had labored on the canal and the railroad. Behind the Antillean Boyd could see an equally tall "rubia," a white woman of pure or nearly pure European ancestry. The fourth was probably a Chocoes girl while the last two were plainly mestizas of mixed Euro and Indian blood.

If Ruiz recognized Boyd he gave no sign of it. Instead he announced, "I am chief of my tribe. This one," and a point of the Indian's nose indicated the Posleen, "is owned by us. Why are you disturbing him at his work?"

"Oh, just satisfying my curiosity," Boyd answered. No sense in standing on ceremony, after all. "I was wondering, too, if you might be willing to sell your . . . pet." *What an intelligence asset he could be if . . . when we are attacked again.*

"Perhaps I would," the Indian answered. "But his price would be high. He owes me and mine much."

"We could . . . *negotiate*," Boyd answered.

The Indian turned his attention to the Posleen. He was not unwilling to sell, in principle, but wanted the best price possible. *A hard working slave is surely more valuable than a lazy one.*

"You!" he demanded. "Do I need to take you back into the jungle? It is asking for you, you know."

The box remained silent but the Posleen God King, Guanamarioch of the host, flyer among the stars and leader of a war band, redoubled his efforts to make an American-owned jungle boot shine like glass.

EPILOGUE II

. . . the Sea shall give up her dead . . .
—1789 U.S. Book of Common Prayer,
"Order for the Burial of the Dead"

Muelle *(Pier) 18, Balboa, Republic of Panama*

Boyd left his newly built headquarters for the Boyd Steamship Company (though "Steamship" was something of an anachronism now that the company was more concerned with commerce between planets) and walked along the pier to where a launch waited to take him out to the USS *Salem*, riding at anchor in the bay. On his way, he almost passed a pair of Posleen, one larger than the other, the larger one having a fair crest. The smaller, like the larger, sat on the pier's very edge. Its head lay softly against the shoulder of the other.

The crested Posleen stared intently at the water below. In its hands was grasped a fishing pole that it moved slowly up and down, causing the line and, presumably, the unseen baited hook to move likewise. A human wearing a Fleet Strike uniform with the insignia for Military Intelligence sat on the other side, away from the smaller Posleen. The human asked questions which the Posleen answered without looking up. The answers the human wrote down in a small notebook.

Boyd walked over and said from behind, "Hello, Guano. How are they biting?"

Still looking down, Guano answered, through its AS, "Not so bad, Dictator."

It was obvious that the Posleen had been through regeneration. Its crest was normal again, and it had both eyes. Well . . . an intelligence asset like that? You wouldn't just let it die of old age, now, would you?

Of course, regeneration didn't stop with eyes and crest. This tended to explain the other Posleen.

"This the new missus?" Boyd asked.

Guano still didn't take his eyes from the water. "Yes, Dictator. She's a cosslain. A fairly *smart* cosslain, too. Almost sentient. With that, and the new ways of telling which eggs will be Kessentai, we're hoping to start a small family soon."

"Where did you . . . ummm . . . ?"

Eyes still intent on his fishing, Guanamarioch answered, "It's amazing what you can find on eBay."

"She was a bigger star than I ever thought about being."

"Is she still alive down there?" Boyd asked of the Marlene Dietrich lookalike standing next to him.

Boyd was growing old again. Though he had twice been young, and though the process by which he had been made young the second time had also slowed down the aging process considerably, his hair was gray, his back a bit stooped, and every blasted joint in his body hurt.

His eyes were still bright though, staring at the featureless surface of the ocean between Isla Coiba and the Peninsula de Azuero.

He asked again, "Is she still alive?"

USS *Salem*'s avatar shook her head in negation. "At first I sensed nothing. Then, for a very little while, I could sense a little something of her below. But that gradually weakened until it disappeared altogether. If I had never sensed anything after she went down I'd have wondered and thought that maybe it was interference from the ocean. But as it is . . ."

Boyd sighed. "Are we doing the right thing, Sally, pulling her up like this?"

Salem answered, simply, "I don't know."

Salem had insisted on coming out to see her sister's body raised. "It's a family thing," she had said, and Boyd had understood. Now, the recovery vessel standing close by off the port side, she and Boyd waited for word.

It had not been difficult to find the *Des Moines*. While she had drifted a few feet, and sunk into the muck more than a few, her location had never been lost.

The muck had actually been the greatest of the three major problems with the recovery. It had cost a fortune to have it vacuumed away so that the antigravity devices could be placed under the hull. On the other hand, the suction of the muck would have interfered with raising her anyway, and possibly caused the hull to break apart. Moreover, getting rid of the muck had allowed a close examination of the hull and repair of all but two of the holes shot in it by Posleen fire. These were left to allow water to drain out. Patches, pre-cut, were ready to slap and weld over them once that was done. Lastly, with no chance of the muck being replaced, it had made sense to vacuum out much of the interior of the ship. This too had reduced the strain on the hull.

Sally lifted her head up, obviously hearing something Boyd could not.

"They say they're ready to start," she announced.

Boyd nodded. "Tell them to go ahead."

There wasn't long to wait, fifteen minutes at most, before the water began to show disturbances from underneath, a billowing cloud of sea bottom, a slight rising on the surface and smoothing of the waves. Boyd bit his lower lip in anxious anticipation.

"Over there," Sally pointed.

Boyd looked a bit to port and was slightly surprised to see the point of the bow emerge first. He'd been expecting the stack.

"They canted the bow upward," Sally explained, "to reduce stress on the hull. They'll keep the bow about stationary now while they level off the rest of her."

"I'm a little surprised she didn't break up on the way down," Boyd said.

"I think she flooded herself carefully before the end to keep upright as long as possible," Sally answered. "Then too, the water was shallow. She would not have built up enough speed going down to really crash."

The two went silent then as the recovery crew deftly evened out *Des Moines'* keel. The next thing to appear after the point of the bow was a heavily damaged rangefinder, then the stack, then the superstructure. Two seaweed covered turrets began to show, followed by the rest of the superstructure and the remains of the number three turret. There was a wait while water drained off, running over the sides in a stinky, greenish deluge. Then slowly and, it might be said, majestically, the ship rose evenly under antigravity to her keel. The recovery ship moved in close.

Boyd continued to stare, fascinated, as diving teams from the recovery ship went over the side. He was equally fascinated by the process of lowering the two huge patches meant to seal the holes left in the hull. Once these were in place, and the crews welding, he turned his attention to the battle damage.

Boyd shook his head in wonder. "To think she was still fighting back even as she slipped under with all the damage done to her."

The face of Sally's avatar glowed with pride. "She was a good ship, a brave ship, from a good class. I was proud to have her for a sister. Then too," and the actress-avatar smiled, "she sure knew how to make an exit."

It was curiously light in the interior of the ship. While all of the human-produced light bulbs had collapsed, or the wiring rotted, the Indowy-installed emergency light plates still cast a glow strong enough to see by, if barely. Moreover, Sally's hologram, projected from the warship herself, sitting forty yards off to port, and resonating from *Des Moines*' mostly intact "nervous system," added still more.

In a way, it was a bit too much light. The remains of several hundred of *Des Moines*' crew—uniforms and shoes for the most part, sometimes bones if those had been cooked before sinking—littered the decks. Blood and flesh were gone, however, a small mercy for which Boyd gave great thanks.

Deep below decks he could hear the odd sound of underwater welding resonating through the bulkheads.

The pumps he could not hear, though he knew they were working. The Galactics built well, and to fine tolerances. Their pumps were noiseless.

"This way," Sally's avatar suggested, pointing downward to a ladder leading deep below decks.

"What's down this far?" Boyd asked.

"I'm not sure. Something. There's a power source down there, and not a small one."

"The pebble bed reactors?"

"No . . . they're dead. And there's no radiation to speak of. It's something else."

Boyd shrugged his shoulders and, reluctantly, descended towards the bowels of the ship.

"Are you sure there's enough air down here?" Boyd asked.

"Does it stink?" Sally queried in response. "I suppose it must. But, yes, as the water drained, fresh air was drawn down. It would last a single man for years. Don't worry."

"I'm not worried," the human snapped. "And, yes, it stinks."

"Turn towards the stern," Sally directed. "The power source is back there."

Boyd and the avatar emerged from a long corridor into a large, mostly open space surrounding a solid looking, circular mass. Boyd looked around the open space, saw numerous tables and stools.

"Ship's mess?" he asked.

"The main mess, yes. Those were the galley, butcher shop and garbage grinder we just passed. Just ahead, to the stern, is a ladder. The power source is near the base of that."

Still reluctant, Boyd continued on and then down.

"I'm getting to be a little old for this, you know," he complained.

"Mr. Boyd," Sally answered, formally. "You know damned well you do not have to be old. A simple form to be signed, off-world passage to be paid, and you could be seventeen again."

"Bah. And spend another lifetime going through that shit? No, thank you."

"Up to you."

"Well, at least there are no rats aboard."

"No," Sally agreed. "They all drowned. Which makes me wonder if I shouldn't have myself sunk for a bit and re-raised. They itch, you know? The rats, I mean. Nasty little feet and claws always traipsing along the decks whenever there isn't a human about.

"Turn to your right," she added, "back toward the stern."

Boyd asked, "What was back here?"

"It was supposed to be storage, bunkerage." Sally answered. "But here also is that power source. Behind that door."

In the dim light Boyd made out several Posleen skeletons. He counted the number of skulls. *Five of them.* Unlike the humans, something in the makeup of the aliens' bones had prevented them from dissolving into the ocean's water. The skeletons made the old man shudder but he pressed on nonetheless.

Boyd looked through the small view port in the watertight door. It was light enough inside to see that there was no leakage. He put both hands on the wheel and began to twist. The door's locking mechanism resisted at first, than gave way only slowly and reluctantly, and with an agonized whining. Boyd stepped back and allowed the door to swing open.

Inside was a bare room, oddly shaped and with one wall sloping. The room was bare except for a conical glowing object—the power source, he guessed—and a pearlescent coffinlike box about four feet by four feet by maybe ten. The box had an almost square projection on one side, with a glassy plate on its sloping top.

"What is that thing?" he asked Sally's avatar.

Sally didn't answer directly. Instead she instructed, "Place your hand on that plate."

Boyd did and was rewarded by a whooshing sound as the center of the coffin split and the two sides lifted up and peeled back. He jumped back in surprise, heart pounding.

When he had recovered and stepped forward again to look into the coffin he saw something very like a fog, though it was a fog that would have put to shame London's foggiest night. Boyd heard a distinctive *click,* as of a power switch being pressed. He sensed a stirring in there, hidden by the fog. Awful feelings, a sort of essence of well-done vampire movie set of feelings, assailed him. He reached over to place his hand over the plate in the hope that it would close the coffin again.

"Wait," Sally said, this time making it an order and not a request. "There is no danger."

The stirring inside the coffin grew as the fog began, ever so slightly, to dissipate, running down slowly over the sides of the box and gathering on the deck. Something was plainly moving down there.

Boyd nearly jumped out of his skin as a clawed foot appeared out of the fog, and stretched. The claws were followed by a head. The head was furry and tiny, with outsized, pointed ears.

Morgen the kitty asked, "Meow?"

AFTERWORD

Both John and Tom have served in the Republic of Panama, John for some weeks while attending the Jungle School at Fort Sherman, Tom for four and a half years with Fourth Battalion, Tenth Infantry (as a sergeant) and Third Battalion, Fifth Infantry (as a lieutenant). Tom says, "If the place where you were happiest in life is home, then my home is Fort William D. Davis, Panama Canal Zone, with the 4th of the 10th Infantry, from 1977 to 1978."

It's a magic place, Panama, and we highly encourage our readers, or anyone, to visit it. (Did we play some games with the terrain in support of the story? You betcha. But Panama is still a great, wonderful and very beautiful place.)

Can they fight, though? Is the portrayal of the defense in the book realistic? After all, the United States took them down in a bit over twenty-four hours back in 1989. How good could they be?

And that is an interesting question. In 1989, in Operation Just Cause, the United States launched a sudden and surprise attack on the then existing Panama Defense Forces and did crush those forces in about a day, picking off holdouts over the next three to four days. This would not appear to be a great recommendation.

That is, it doesn't appear to be until you look at the particulars. We hit them in the night, where we have an overwhelming technological advantage. We hit them with little or no tactical warning. We hit them with greater, and in places overwhelming, numbers and overwhelming firepower, even though the use of that firepower was somewhat restrained. Further, we hit them with complete air supremacy and used that air supremacy to deliver, over and above the rather large forces we had in Panama already, three of the best trained, most lethal infantry battalions in the world, the three battalions of the 75th Infantry (Ranger) (Airborne). More forces followed on, later, as well.

The wonder is not that we took them down in a day, but that they were able to hang on that long. Indeed, if there's any wonder in the story it's that, even when abandoned by some (one remarkably loathsome and cowardly wretch, in particular . . . West Point . . . Class of 1980) of their U.S. trained officers, the others held on and fought.

The wonder is that at their Comandancia, parts of a couple of Panamanian infantry companies fought against hopeless odds, nearly to the last man. There were only five prisoners taken there, and all of those were wounded. The rest, true to their duty, died in place. Moreover, they drove us out of the compound more than once before they were finally subdued. There were more Texan prisoners taken at the Alamo.

The wonder is that, despite all those disadvantages,

the PDF managed to inflict about three casualties on us for every four they took.

Did we mention that some young Panamanian kids with almost no time in uniform kicked the bejesus out of a U.S. Navy SEAL team?

So, yes, they're a tough and a brave people, well within the western military tradition, and—properly armed and trained—they can fight.

Of course, the western military tradition, outside of the U.S. and U.K., isn't what it used to be. Oh, the formations are still there, some of them. The weapons are, if anything, better than ever. Even the men—and women, too, of course—still have much of what made the West great inside them.

Unfortunately, the West itself has largely fallen under the control of civilizational Dr. Kevorkians. Some call them "Tranzis."

"Tranzi" is short for "Transnational Progressive" or "Transnational Progressivism." For a more complete account of their program, look up John O'Sullivan's *Gulliver's Travails* or some of what Steven Den Beste has written on the subject. You might, dear reader, also look at John Fonte's *The Ideological War within the West*. Lastly, for purposes of this little essay, look up Lee Harris' *The Intellectual Origins of America Bashing*. These should give you a good grounding in Tranzism: its motives, goals and operating techniques. All can be found online.

For now, suffice to say that Tranzism is the successor ideology to failed and discredited Marxist-Leninism. Many of the most prominent Tranzis are, in fact, "former" members of various communist parties, especially European communist parties. These have taken the failure of the Soviet Union personally and hard, and, brother, are they bitter about it.

Nonetheless, our purpose here is not to write up "Tranzism 101." It is to illustrate the Tranzi approach to the laws of war.

That's right, boys and girls. Pull up a chair. Grab a stool. Cop a squat. Light 'em if you've got 'em. (If not, bum 'em off Ringo; Kratman's fresh out.)

It's lecture time.

> (WARNING! Authorial editorial follows. If you just adore the International Criminal Court, then read further at your own risk. You have been warned.)

One of the difficult things about analyzing Tranzis and their works is that they are *not* a conspiracy. What they are is a consensus. Don't be contemptuous; civilization is nothing more than a consensus. So is barbarism. Moreover, the Tranzis are a fairly cohesive consensus, especially on certain ultimate core issues. Nonetheless, if you are looking for absolute logical consistency on the part of Tranzis you will search in vain.

On the other hand, at the highest level, the ultimate Tranzi goal, there is complete agreement. They want an end to national sovereignty and they want global governance by an unelected, self-chosen "elite." Much of what they say and do will make no sense, even in Tranzi terms, unless that is borne in mind.

Below that ultimate level one cannot expect tactical logical consistency. Things are neither good nor bad, true nor false, except insofar as they support the ultimate Tranzi goal.

For example, if one were to ask a Tranzi, and especially a female and feminist Tranzi, about the propriety of men having any say over a woman's right to an abortion the Tranzi would probably be scandalized. After all, men don't even have babies. They know nothing about the subject from the inside, so to speak. Why should *they* have any say?

Nonetheless, that same Tranzi, if asked whether international lawyers and judges, and humanitarian activist nongovernmental organizations, or NGOs, should have the final say in the laws of war, would certainly approve. This is true despite the fact that the next lawyer, judge or NGO that understands as much about war as a man understands about childbirth will likely be the first.

Why do we say they know nothing about the subject? By their works shall you know them.

The International Criminal Court is, after the UN and European Union, the next most significant Tranzi project (Kyoto being dead on arrival) and arguably the most significant with regard to the laws of war. A majority, if a bare one, of the world's sovereign states have signed onto it while about half have ratified it.

The ICC claims jurisdiction over all the crimes mentioned in its founding statute, irrespective of who committed them, where they were committed, or whether the "crimes" are actually criminal under the traditional and customary law of war. This is called "universal jurisdiction."

Universal jurisdiction, as a concept, has a number

of flaws. Among these are that it has zero valid legal precedence behind it.

Zero precedence? Tranzis will cite at least two precedents. One of these is the jurisdiction exercised from times immemorial by any sovereign power over pirates at sea, when any were caught. The other is Nuremberg. These are flawed. In the case of Nuremberg, the jurisdiction exercised was not "universal" but national jurisdiction of the coalition of the victors over a Germany whose sovereignty had been temporarily extinguished by crushing defeat in war.

The piracy precedent as applied to modern notions of universal jurisdiction doesn't stand close scrutiny any better. The Tranzis claim that universal jurisdiction was exercised over piracy because piracy was, in its conduct and effect, so ghastly. This is wrong on both counts. In the first place, pirates were not necessarily subject to universal jurisdiction except insofar as they were caught where national jurisdiction did not run; typically at sea, in other words. Moreover, alongside piracy there existed privateering. In their conduct the two were often enough indistinguishable. In other words, however "ghastly" privateering may have been—and the former residents of Portobello and Panama City could have told one it could be ghastly, indeed—it was still not subject to universal jurisdiction. No matter that piracy was no worse than privateering, it was so subject. The difference was that sovereign powers, nation-states in other words, exercised sovereign jurisdiction over privateers, were responsible for their actions, and punished them at need, while they did not and could not with pirates. It was the lack of sovereign jurisdiction, both as to their persons and as to the locus of their crimes, that left pirates open to universal jurisdiction and not any supposed "ghastliness" of those crimes.

Along with the lack of valid legal precedence, the ICC and universal jurisdiction suffer other flaws. Recall, dear reader, the lack of Tranzi logical consistency on the questions posed above about abortion and the laws of war.

Anti-imperialism is yet another Tranzi tactical cause. But what is imperialism beyond one or several states or people using force or color of law to make rules for another or other state or people? And what is the ICC, using all the staggering moral and military power of . . . oh . . . Fiji . . . France . . . West Fuckistan . . . but the attempt at enforcing rules made by one group of states upon others? It's *imperialism*, in other words.

Of course, imperialism in the service of a higher cause—the raising of unelected, self-styled, global elites to power, for example—is praiseworthy, in Tranzi terms.

Nothing deterred, the Tranzis claim that Tranzi courts, to include notionally national Tranzi courts like those of Spain, have universal jurisdiction. Why?

Tranzis hate national sovereignty. It cramps their style. It interferes with their program. It's aesthetically unappealing.

Their goal is the destruction of national sovereignty. The right of a people to democratically make their own laws, to govern themselves, is anathema to Tranzi goals and dreams. When they say "global governance," boys and girls, they *mean* it. They really intend that unelected bureaucrats and judges, and self-selected elites ought be able to tell you what to do, how to live, what to pay in taxes, what rights you are not entitled to.

Sovereignty stands in the way. The ultimate expression of sovereignty is a nation's and people's armed forces. No army; no ability to defend one's own laws and way of life; no sovereignty.

But how to do away with sovereign control of national armed forces? It's a toughie. They've got all these *guns* and shit, while the poor Tranzis have none.

"Aha! We know," say the Tranzis. "We can control a nation's armed forces if we can punish the soldiers and especially the officers and a nation refuses to stand up and defend them. No nation which permits a foreign court to exercise jurisdiction over its military can any longer be said to own that military. Instead, that military will be owned by the courts able to punish the leaders. Onward, into the future, comrades!"

Let them punish your soldiers and the soldiers can no longer be counted upon to defend the nation. Nor would you deserve being defended by your soldiers. Let them punish the soldiers and there is no principled distinction to prevent them punishing the President, the Legislature, even the Supreme Court. For who would defend the President, Legislature and courts once the same have let down their soldiers? Let them punish your soldiers and you deserve what you get . . . and to lose what you will lose.

It would be one thing if the ICC were something more than a misguided exercise in legalistic Tranzi mutual masturbation; if it could, in other words, be effective in limiting the horrors of war.

It cannot be effective. Ever.

This is because of the very nature of war itself. There is nothing a court can do that, in terms of punishment that deters, even begins to approach the horror men inflict on each other in war, routinely, in the course of normal and legal operations. There is nothing *any* court can do that can even hope to catch the interest of tired men, hungry men, men fighting for victory and their lives. No sensible court would even try.

There is some conduct which cannot be deterred. When life is at stake, the law recognizes no "no trespassing" signs. When the choice is between picking pockets at a mass hanging of pickpockets, and risking the noose, or facing slow starvation . . . well . . . at least the rope is fairly quick.

Similarly, when the choice on the battlefield is life or death, what power has some uncertain court distant in both time and space to deter anything? The simple answer is; it has *none*. What trivial power has the law with its trivial *possible* punishments to deter conduct that might save soldiers' lives, their comrades' and their country's in the here and now?

Yet we can see that, however imperfectly, the customary law of war has often worked—even without any such body as the ICC and without Spain's recent disgusting, illegal, morally putrescent attempt at exercising sovereignty over American soldiers. It has worked imperfectly, to be sure. Yet it has worked often enough . . . indeed, within western war it has worked more often than not.

Where the laws of war have worked to mitigate

the horror and protect innocent life they have, by and large, done so when the combatants were of the same culture, shared the same values, and had what we might like to think of as a basic decency.

That's rarely been quite enough. It needed a little something else, some other reason to follow the rules.

The other reason was the threat and fear of reprisals.

Tranzis hate reprisals, which are war crimes in themselves but war crimes which become legal in order to punish an enemy who violates the law of war, deter him from violating it, and *remove the advantages* which accrue from such violations. The Tranzis don't hate reprisals merely because they're ugly, cause suffering of innocents, etc., though they hate them for those reasons, too. No, Tranzis hate reprisals because reprisals *work* to enforce the laws of war and their own silly courts fail.

Reprisals *work*? You're kidding us, right?

Wrong. Why wasn't poisonous gas used in the Second World War? The threat of reprisal. What happened when, in 1944, the Germans threatened to execute some numbers of French resistance fighters and the French Resistance, which was holding many German prisoners, answered, "We will kill one for one"? The French prisoners held by the Germans were left unharmed. Why didn't the Southern Confederacy during the American Civil War execute the white officers of black regiments as they had passed a law to do? Because the Union credibly threatened to hang a white Southern officer for every man of theirs so mistreated. Why didn't the United States or South Vietnam execute, generally, Viet Cong guerillas who had gravely violated the laws of war in the course of the insurgency there? Because the North Vietnamese had prisoners against whom they would have reprised had we or the South Vietnamese done so.

Reprisals work; courts and statutes do not. The law of war, because of the nature of war, must be self enforcing, through reprisals. Nothing else can work and any attempt to do away with reprisal is an indirect attack on and undermining of the law of war.

But then, the law of war and mitigating its horrors are not really what the Tranzis are about. Undermining national sovereignty? Replacing sovereign nations with themselves? *That's* what they're about.

The Tranzis aren't about eliminating war's horrors? Oh, John, Oh, Tom . . . say it isn't so.

(Interject dual sigh at the vast iniquity of mankind here.)

It's so.

Recall that we mentioned that Tranzism is the successor philosophy to Marxist-Leninism. It should come as no great surprise, then, that one of the key pieces of Tranzi legislation on the law of war should have been sponsored and forced into existence by . . . wait for it . . . wait for it . . . *THE SOVIET UNION*.

This key piece of Tranzi legislating on the law of war was Additional Protocol I to Geneva Convention IV. The protocol itself was shoved through by the Soviets at a time when it looked like People's Revolutionary War (guerilla war . . . communist insurgency) would continue to be a powerful weapon to advance the cause of communism. The United States has never ratified it and, pray God, it never shall. The Russians, who forced it through, have never paid it the slightest attention, as witnessed by their conduct in Afghanistan from 1979 to 1989 and, more recently, in Chechnya.

The protocol is interesting for three reasons: what it purports to do, what it actually does, and for the admittedly slick way in which it tries to do it.

The slickness is in the way the protocol is structured. It begins with a pious preamble, typically enough. That isn't the slick part. What *is* clever is that it repeats much of what was already in Geneva Convention IV (GC IV), which is concerned with the protection of civilians caught up in war (as is the protocol), and then interweaves some very new things. The new things include major advantages, given gratis, to guerillas and especially communist guerillas, a broad ban on the use of what it calls "mercenaries," one rather unreasonable restriction on the use of food as a weapon, and a subtle way of saying "It's okay to push the Zionist beasts into the sea."

Then, when a nation refuses to ratify the additional protocol for any of the at least five really good reasons not to do so, it stands accused of anything from being in favor of mass rape to forced medical experiments a la Josef Mengele. Never mind that all that is prohibited by the original GC IV and that the additional protocol adds nothing of importance. "You refuse to ratify the additional protocol? You Nazi bastards!"

Are these guys slick or what?

As to what the protocol is *supposed* to do, protect civilians, one has to wonder. It is part of the traditional law of war that, in case of a siege, a city may have its food cut off and civilians attempting to escape may be fired upon, even killed, to drive them back to eat up the food. This is cruel to be sure, an "extreme measure" as the U.S. Army's manual on the subject admits. Cruel or not, this was upheld in the late '40s in the case of *United States v. Ritter von Leeb* and is still—up to a point—good law, outside of Tranzidom. Geneva Convention IV ameliorated this harsh rule, and reasonably so, by requiring that some evacuations for particular reasons (maternity, infancy, infirmity, for example) be allowed.

The protocol, however, does not allow food to be cut off or civilians to be driven back into a besieged town to eat up whatever food is there. Naturally, one cannot permit food to enter without at the same time feeding the garrison, which will ensure for itself that it eats first. Therefore, the besieger has a choice, sit there forever—which is generally impractical—or take the place by assault. Now imagine what will happen to the civilians if the town is stormed, when every room receives its donation of grenade and bullet. And this is supposed to *protect* them? Starvation, at least, while unpleasant, offered a good chance for a besieged town to fall after a few lean days without the massacre intendant on an assault.

What then is the purpose of the additional protocol? It is to disadvantage the West, to reduce its military power, thus to reduce its sovereignty. Since being forced into existence by the Soviets the protocol has had no other purpose.

The law of war nowhere mentions the phrase "illegal combatants." Tranzis will tell you that, therefore, there is no such thing. This is false.

There is a legal principle, a Latin expression, "*Expresio unius exclusio alterius est,*" *the inclusion of one is the exclusion of the other.* While the law of war does not mention "illegal combatants," it goes to some length to explain what is required to be a *legal* combatant. If there is such a concept as legal combatancy, and rules which must be followed to attain that status, then failure to follow those rules places one in the implicit status of illegal combatant.

Those rules are four. To be a legal combatant under the original Geneva Convention, which is quite different from the additional protocol to which the United States is not a party, one must a) wear a fixed insignia recognizable at a distance, b) carry arms openly, c) be under the command of a person or chain of command responsible for your actions (much like a privateer was under a sovereign and a pirate, again, was not), and d) conduct operations in accordance with the customs and laws of war. Failure to meet any of these conditions makes one an *illegal* combatant.

Note, here, that *individuals* do not "conduct operations." Organizations conduct operations. This implies that one is responsible for the actions of one's organization as well as for one's own.

Can you hear the sound of Tranzi heads exploding over that last?

They might seem to have a point. Civil law normally doesn't permit people to be held responsible for the actions of others, right? Wrong. Look up "conspiracy." Once someone becomes part of a conspiracy they become responsible for everything their coconspirators do. Moreover, within the law of war's concept of reprisal, perfect innocents may be effectively responsible for what their side does. After all, what happens when a side violates the law by using a hospital, say, for an ammunition dump? The perfectly innocent and otherwise protected wounded are blasted from this world to the next in *reprisal*.

Equally so, within an armed force, both by "d)", above, and under the practical effect of the doctrine of reprisal a combatant is responsible for both his own actions and those of his *organization*.

It works the other way, too, by the way. Note that General Yamashita was hanged not for anything he ordered or could have prevented but for things sub-elements only notionally under his command did.

What does this mean for the current war? It means that every Saudi kid, inspired to go to Iraq to fight by watching some truck driver's head sawed of on *Al Jazeera*, has—in civil law terms—voluntarily joined a conspiracy to fight illegally and is thus an illegal combatant and that—in law of war terms—he is an illegal combatant even if he personally follows the rules completely.

Those who would grant him legal combatant status, the Tranzis in other words, thus are trying to improve and enhance the effectiveness of those who would and do violate the law of war.

This is something you would expect from an enemy, right?

So what can we do? What would John and Tom like to see done?

Number One: Never forget that the Tranzi purpose is inimical to our own, that they are the enemy as much as Hitler was or al Qaeda is. They want us, as a distinct nation and people, to cease to exist. They want our constitution overthrown or made subordinate to *their* law, which amounts to the same thing. They want our military made subordinate to their judges, so that it can be undermined and made unable or unwilling to defend us. They want us to lose our wars.

Number Two: Remembering that the Tranzis *are* the enemy, give them no aid, no money, no support. Do not give them a foothold into the armed forces and if such foothold exists (say, in the form of an institute devoted to peacekeeping and humanitarian assistance) close it down. Audit the Tranzis' books; they're as corrupt as imaginable and could not well stand auditing. They tend to lie, especially to raise money. Require that their charitable activities advertise truthfully and punish them when they do not. Jail a few of the bastards. On second thought, jail a lot of the bastards. Remove their tax exempt status on the first whiff of impropriety. When the ultimate Tranzi organization, the UN, cheats the Iraqi people and hides the details of the thefts, withhold the funds otherwise due to the UN and pay it to the Iraqis instead . . . with no chance of ever making good to the UN any such amounts withheld and given.

Number Three: Did you know that the United States has what amounts to a conditional declaration of war in place should anyone have the gall to grab one of our soldiers to turn over to the ICC or some other Tranzi court? It's called the American Service-members Protection Act and it passed unanimously in the Senate. (Sometimes your country just makes you *proud.*) We should look for an opportunity to exercise that law . . . and sometime soon. Spain might be a good place to start.

Number Four: Even when we have them on the

YELLOW EYES

ropes do not let up. Finish them off. Make the Tranzi organizations extinct and the parasites who live off of them spend the remainder of their days poor and hungry. Do not weep for the Tranzis.

Number Five: Don't, *don't*, DON'T give up hope. The Tranzis are not going to win. Their center of gravity, Europe, is dying to demographics. Within the United States and with our own Tranzis much the same thing is happening regionally and subculturally. The prize Tranzi projects, the UN and EU, are staggering under a burden of incompetence, ineffectuality and corruption. Moreover, say what you will about Muslim extremists, they're still damned good at demonstrating to the world outside of Europe what happens when you let the Tranzis take over.

By the way, Tom and John intend to fight the bastards all the way.

GLOSSARY

abuela   Spanish: grandmother.

AID   Artificial Intelligence Device.

alcalde   Spanish: mayor.

Aldenata   Galactic Tranzis, largely disappeared from the Galactic scene in sheer funk and shame at the damage they had, despite all the best intentions, wrought.

armada   Spanish: Armed Force.

AZIPOD   An electronic drive which replaces propellers and rudders with steerable propellers.

boma blade   A monomolecular sword carried by all Posleen except Kenstain.

brow   Gangplank of a warship.

Carcel Modelo   Model Prison. It was anything but.

Casco Viejo   "The Old Helmet"; the historic district of Panama City where *Palacio de las Garzas*, the presidential palace, is located.

Chocoes   Indians of the Darien. Very fierce.

chumbo   In Panamanian Spanish a term, not a particularly nice one, for blacks. In Colombia it means a male reproductive organ. Perhaps at one time the two uses were related.

CIC   Combat Information Center, the command post of a warship.

Class V   Ammunition.

cosslain   Superior normal Posleen. Fills the functions of both noncommissioned officers and technicians.

Cuna   AKA San Blas. Indians that inhabit the islands off Panama's Caribbean coast ("Island Cuna") of the rivers that feed the Caribbean ("River Cuna"). Culturally similar peoples can be found as far north as Mexico.

Darhel   "The Elves." Galactic lawyers, businessmen and bureaucrats who control the Galactic Federation created by the Aldenata in the dim mists of antiquity.

det cord   Detonating cord; basically an explosive rope, a useful means of using one explosion to set off another.

edas   Posleen: debt.

El Moro   A brothel in Colon.

escudo   Spanish: shield.

eson'antai   Posleen: son.

eson'sara   Posleen: junior officer, protege.

FAP   Fuerza Aeria de Panama, Panamanian Air Force.

GalPlas   Galactic Plastic.

HVM   Hypervelocity Missile, a Posleen guided kinetic energy weapon capable of piercing all but the strongest armor plate.

iglesia   Spanish: church.

Kenstain   Kessentai who have given up war. Some become Rememberers, a sort of Posleen clergy. Rememberers command great respect.

Kessentai God King, Philosopher. The Posleen with generally humanoid levels of intelligence.

manjack American invention using a mix of Earth technology and GalTech. The manjack is a semi-autonomous machine gun assembly that analyzes its arc of fire and engages anything entering it.

MarCam Marine Camouflage, a uniquely pixilated pattern that incorporates a miniature version of the Marine Corps' Eagle, Globe and Anchor for the express purpose of keeping the Army from using it.

mil A measure of angle, 1/6400 of circle.

oolt'ondai Posleen pack leader.

orna'adar The Posleen Ragnarok, which occurs when population pressure forces the clans on a world to war for space, which war invariably devolves into total planetary destruction and the migration of the survivors to new worlds.

**Palacio de
  las Garzas**   "Palace of the Herons"; Panama's
                 White House.

pork chop   Ship's supply officer.

Po'oslena'ar Posleen. "The People of the
                 ships."

rabiblanco   "White ass." A bird with a white
                 rear and, by extension, a Panama-
                 nian of highly European ancestry.

Rio Pact   A mutual defense treaty between
                 the United States and most of
                 the Latin states. Though the Lat-
                 ins entered into it in good faith,
                 as it became apparent over time
                 that the United States intended
                 to make few demands on them
                 and still provide much military
                 support, they have grown rather
                 complacent about the arrange-
                 ment. In fairness, one might note
                 that most of them were soon
                 embroiled in their own com-
                 munist inspired civil wars, which
                 most of them won. Thus, they
                 did help defend Western civi-
                 lization and the major ally, the
                 United States.

sancocho   Soup, typically in the Province of
                 Chiriqui.

SD-44   An auxiliary-propelled, Russian
                     designed and built, quick firing,
                     85mm artillery piece.

tenar   Posleen God Kings' flying sleds.

thermobaric   Fuel Air Explosive, or FAE.

Tranzis   Human beings, arguably, who
                     long to see the highest human
                     civilizations cast down. Hypo-
                     crites who think they do good
                     for others and in doing good
                     do pretty well for themselves.
                     Look at any Third World hell-
                     hole and brush away the corpses.
                     There, at the center, grown
                     fat by feasting on the rotten
                     meat of human suffering, gen-
                     erally dazzled by the sudden
                     light, you will find a host of
                     lily white, maggotlike Tranzis.

The following is an excerpt from:

THE LAST CENTURION

JOHN RINGO

Available from Baen Books
August 2008
hardcover

CHAPTER ONE

Days of Wine and Song

Call me Bandit.

Okay, hopefully that's, like, the last time I'm going to make a literary reference. But you never know. Beware . . . bewaaare . . .

There's a bunch of these stories out there now that people are getting back on the Net. I figured, what the hell? I've got one, too. Sure, we all do. But, you know, what the hell?

People started calling it the Hell Times after some pundit was spouting about it on TV. I mean, The Great Depression was taken and they didn't have the Plague or the Freeze thrown on top. I know, it wasn't a plague and all you nitnoids are going to point out that it was some fucking flu virus and plague is bacterial infection and . . . Yeah. I know. Thank you. We ALL fucking know, all right? Christ, there are times you wished it had been targeted at nitnoids. Everybody calls it the Plague, okay? Get over yourself.

Anyway, people call it the Hell Times. I dunno, maybe

I've got a better personal fix on hell than they do or maybe I don't. Personally, having been in combat and blown up and shot and seen people I care about blown up and shot and even people I *didn't* particularly care about blown up and shot and having visited a volcano once and thought about what it would be like to spend the rest of fucking *forever* in one, I don't call it the Hell Times. Bad as it was, seems to be an exaggeration. Me? I call it the Time of Suckage.

This is my sucky story about the time of suckage.

So there I was in Iran again, this is no shit . . . It was my fourth trip to the sandbox in my short years as a soldier. And it was a maximally fucked up tour even before the Time of Suckage. Look, you spend any time as a soldier and you get good chains of command and bad chains of command. Good jobs and bad jobs. You deal. It didn't help that the Prez was a whiny bitch who really wanted us out of there but couldn't figure out how to get reelected *and* stab us in the back. Equipment was short, training was crap, the muj knew all they had to do was hold their ground and we were eventually going to leave.

And boy did we. Not that it helped *them* much, huh? Heh, heh.

Seriously, I met some Iranians (and Iraqis and Afghans) that were pretty decent people. And I'm sorry as hell for what happened to the good people, most of them, that inhabited those countries. But . . . Ah, hell. I'm getting ahead of myself.

Way ahead.

Maybe I should talk about myself for a bit to give a little context. I was one of the very few remaining farm boys in the Army at the time. Seriously. I mean, most of my troops were from rural areas but that's not, exactly, the same thing as being a farm boy. I grew up on a family farm. Well, I grew up on one of the family farms owned by the Bandit Family Farm Company, LLC.

Wait? LLC? Family Farm? How do those two go together?

Like bacon and eggs, my friends, like bacon and eggs. Forget everything you've seen in a bad movie about family farms. If you're going to survive in *this* economy, you'd better know what the hell you're doing. And I'm not talking some hobby farm where the "farmer" is a construction contractor and has a couple of cows or a chicken house or twain that are some added income. (Or more often a tax write-off.) I'm talking about making *all* your income from farming.

And it's pretty good money if you do it right. Farmers are the richest single income group in the U.S. Were before the Time, during the Time and after. Sure, some of them lost their farms during the Time but damned few. (Except for the Big Grab but I'll get to that.) Smart farmers weren't saddled with killer debt when the Times hit. And, hell, people always got to eat. Sure, there were less mouths to feed but the government was always buying.

Anyway. Grew up on a farm in southern Minnesota near Blue Earth. It was one of nine the family owned in six counties in southern Minnesota. That one was right on two thousand acres, most of it tilled in time. Pretty much the standard rural upbringing. Went to school. (Yes, I *was* captain of the football team.) Played with my friends. Dated girls. (I'm straight for all you pining fags out there.)

And did some chores. Yes, I've tossed haybales. But not all that many. Baling is time and labor intensive and thus unprofitable. Better to roll. Takes one guy with a tractor the same time to clear a field of rolls as it takes fifteen guys with bales. Do. The. Math.

Did I ever get up before dawn and milk cows using a bucket and a stool? No. The family owned two cow farms. Both were run by managers. At o dark thirty the cows would walk to the barn and into their stalls. Why? Because they had full udders. Full udders hurt. The cows learned quick that if they walked to the stall the hurt went away. Cows are very dumb (if not as dumb as sheep) but they *can* be trained.

A team of people (usually four) would then hook them up to the milking machines. They'd drink coffee while the cows were getting their udder dump, unhook them, and the cows and crew would then have their breakfast. After breakfast the cows got turned out and most of the crew went off to day jobs. The milk was stored in a steel vat until the truck came by to pick it up and take it to the processing plant. Manager, who was full time, handled that. In the evening, repeat.

Again. Do. The. Math. Forty cows (smaller farm). I milked one cow, once, by hand when my dad made me "familiarize" with it. It took me a good fifteen minutes. Figure an expert can do it in maybe five. Four guys, thirty minutes. Or one guy doing it all damned day. Sure, the equipment's a tad expensive (like a half a million dollars). It's amortized.

Then there's the whole . . . sepsis issue. Look, milking by hand you put *milk* into an *open bucket* in a *stall* that's occupied by a *cow*. Bessy is not, take it from this farm boy, a clean creature. Bessy's tail hangs down the same spot her poop (which is mostly liquid) comes out. Bessy walks in her poop. Flies surround Bessy like politicians at an all-you-can-steal lobbyist giveaway.

Milk is also a prime food for just about *anything*. Including bacteria.

We had no interest in being in the news as the evil farm corporation that killed x thousand customers from salmonella or some shit.

Doing it by hand spells "Going Out Of Business." We liked our farm(s). We wanted to keep being farmers. We did it the smart way.

That extended to everything. Look, combine harvesters are very expensive. The flip side is, the bigger they are the more expensive they get *but* the more economic they are. So bigger, in general, is better.

However, some of our fields were too small for the really big combines. And a combine only makes its money a couple of weeks out of the year. Harvesting is about it.

There are companies that do that shit. Since harvests, for really obvious reasons, don't happen everywhere all at once, they move around harvesting and planting. Most of the guys doing the actual work were from South Africa or Eastern Europe. (Mexicans never got in on that racket. Not sure why.)

We had a couple of small combines (price tag right at a quarter mil a pop) to do some of the smaller fields and cleanup. For the main harvesting, Dad would arrange, like a *year* in advance, to get the combine company to come in.

Farmers are planners. The Big Chill and the Big Grab really fucked with us but it was fucking with *everybody* so I'll get to that later. Adapt, react and overcome ain't just a Marine motto. Of course, the Time of Suckage proved that it just might be an exclusively *American* motto and at the time confined to a relatively small fraction. Insert sigh here.

So. Grew up on a farm. Maximum suckage once a year picking rocks. (Another essay.) Went to college (UM, Farmington) on a football scholarship. Got cut sophomore year.

Dad had a college fund for me but . . . Well, if I dipped into it for, you know, tuition and books it really cut into my discretionary income. The insurance for a twenty-year-old on a Mustang GT-175 is *not* cheap. And buying the ladies *nice* dinners tends to get you laid more than McDonalds dinners do. I did *not* want my discretionary income tapped.

ROTC was just sitting there. Most of my family had been Navy. (Don't laugh. I think most of the Navy is crewed by Midwesterners.) But there wasn't a Navy ROTC program. So I went Army.

Okay, yes, there was a war on. But, again, I did the math. Death rates in that war were pretty much on a par with death rates during previous peacetimes. Don't believe me? Check the figures yourself, I'm not going to hold your hand. But it's true. And death rates among combat forces were not significantly higher than in the *Navy*. Being at sea is an inherently dangerous process. Lots of people die from accidents. Most of the people dying in the *Army* were from accidents.

And . . . Oh, hell. Yes, okay. I did have a "desire to serve in combat." Call me stupid. My life, my choice. I wanted to go over and fight. Look, I was twelve when those bastards hit the Twin Towers. I watched those clips over and over just like the rest of you. I knew I didn't want to cruise around on a ship. I wanted to fight. Insert appropriate lines from "Alice's Restaurant" here.

So I went ROTC. Got my degree and my brown bars the same day. Went off to Infantry Officer Basic Course. Which *sucked*. At the time it was my definition of suckage.

Got sent to the 3rd ID in Savannah. Which wasn't a bad place to be for a junior officer with a decent stipend from my shares in the corporation. All I had to do was put up with the bullshit aspects of the Army for six years, go get my Masters in Agronomy and I'd be manager on one of the satellite farms until Dad retired. I was shooting for the mixed crop farms near Hanska. The walleye fishing on Lake Hanska was great and we owned a couple of cottages over there. And since the Hanska manager was in charge of ensuring the upkeep of the cottages . . .

And then we did our first deployment. And, oh, hell, I enjoyed it. Yes, I lost two troops to sniper fire, James Adamson and Litel Compson. They were good guys, both of them. Damned fine troops. I could talk about both of them all day.

But we were doing a tough job in a tough environment. Even with the support of the Iranian government, there were lots of people who really wanted the mullahs back in power. Not going to do an essay on that, this is about the Time of Suckage. We did our job and as a guy in charge of making sure that everything went right, well, for a first deployment I didn't do too bad. Farmers are planners; the CO and my platoon sergeant (Sergeant First Class Clovalle (pronounced "Clo-Vail") Freeman) didn't have to tell me about planning to prevent piss poor performance. And, hell, I always got along with people. I liked my troops and vice versa. Mostly. There's always a few assholes.

But for a first time deployment as a cherry LT I didn't do too bad. And my OER more or less said the same thing. (Actually, it sounded like I was fucking Napoleon but the decent ones always do. That got explained to me in detail.)

I was doing good work and doing it well. Frankly, that first deployment made me rethink the whole Hanska Plan.

Back we went to Savannah. I got promoted to 1LT and went off to Advanced Course. It sucked but not as bad as IOBC. Then I went to Ranger School and got a new appreciation for maximal suckage. (Edit by wife: The author of this is too humble to admit he got Distinguished Honor Graduate in Infantry Officer's Advanced Course and Honor Graduate in Ranger's School. He's an idiot but I love him.) Oh, sure, I like a challenge as much as the next over-testosteroned young idiot. But Ranger School wasn't a challenge in any way except staying awake. It was just suckage, day in and day out.

Oh, yeah, and I went to Jump School right after IOAC. Forgot about that until I remembered the maximally suck jumps in Ranger's School. Jump School, these days, just *tries* to suck.

When I got back we were getting ready for another deployment. I was too senior for a line platoon, it wasn't time to rotate the Mortar Platoon leader and I was too junior for XO. So I got stuck in battalion in the S-3 (Operations) shop.

There are jokes about Fobbits. Those are the guys who stay in the Forward Operations Base. Dude, all

I'll say is that I'd much rather be out doing patrols than stuck in the fucking FOB. FOB duty is boring *and* stressful. There are more PTSD cases among Fobbits than line troops.

(Of course, most Fobbits are REMFs who wanted to avoid being shot at so they got a job that didn't involve shooting. There was one MI guy who had a nervous breakdown about once a week and had to go get "counseled" in a rear area. Smart guy, seemed to really want to do the job, just *did not* have the constitution for it. Can't even call him a coward, just . . . didn't have the constitution.)

Not being out where you could actually *do* something was the worst part. No, the worst part was constantly having to work with Fobbits. No, the worst part was the S-3 who was a dick and incompetent to boot. No, the worst part . . . Damn, there are *so* many worst parts. The tour was maximum suck. Hanska here I come.

Back at Savannah we're doing all the shit that soldiers do when they're not fighting. I'm still in the 3 shop (new S-3 thank God and Major Clark was a real mentor during this period, wish we'd had him in Afghanistan) and we're in charge of making sure everybody gets trained back up to standard. Look, sure, combat experience is important and there are things you learn in combat you can't learn anywhere else. But . . . There are things you forget in combat, too. Things that you could have used. But guys build up a small skill-set that works to carry them through. Getting them to learn a couple *more* skills on top of that skill-set is a *good* thing.

Okay, and we had to fill in all the fucking check boxes of some Pentagon weenie who'd sort of heard there was a war on but needed to justify his existence by creating check boxes for us to fill. Yes, that's a lot of it.

And we had a big part in making sure all the equipment that had gotten fucked up on deployment got unfucked. That was mostly my stuff and Jesus there was a lot of stuff to unfuck. And find. And then admit it had disappeared and do reams of paperwork explaining *why* it had disappeared. I'd say "in triplicate" but most of it was electronic. We had to *file* in triplicate, though. Thank *God* I had a clerk for that. Rusty was a fine guy for a Fobbit.

I'd done extra staff time. Either because of that or because the battalion commander liked my winsome good looks I got the battalion Scout Platoon. Honestly, with the way that we worked it wasn't much different from having a line platoon. But the battalion had started to use the Scouts as sort of an integral special operations unit. When there was a high value operation to perform (like capturing a particularly bad boy) and the fucking SEALs or Rangers or Delta or SF were otherwise busy sharpening their knives or taking pictures of themselves doing push-ups we got to kick the door.

It was a very hoowah fucking time for me. We went back to the Sandbox, this time to Iraq which was still having trouble over by Syria, and we got to kick a lot of doors. The "real" spec-ops guys were busy in Iran and Afghanistan. They didn't care that various Sunni countries (Cough! Cough! Saudi Arabia! Cough! Cough! Syria!) were still funneling weapons, money and personnel into Iraq. The news cameras were all in Iran so naturally that's where SOCOM went.

They didn't, per se, end up on the news. But I took a little tour of the Delta Compound one time, (Okay, okay, I was being recruited, I'll admit it) and there were some very interesting news articles pinned up in cases with small comments underneath like "Detachment One, Alpha Squadron."

Now, don't get me wrong. The SOCOM guys are good folk who do a hard job. But, come on, it's like anything else. When they're looking for a guy to promote or give a special (i.e. interesting) job, they're going to remember the guys who did their job very quietly but also did it well enough that they ended up, unmentioned, in the news. Take the capture of Mullah Rafaki. Sure, supposedly it was 4th ID that got him. Nope. It was really a team of SEALs. And those guys are still unable to pay for their bar tab, not to mention the platoon leader is getting fast-tracked to lieutenant commander.

The point being, CNN and company were in Iran. Iran was the happenin' spot. We were in a backwater in Iraq which was, to most of the world, a done deal.

The downside? Nobody knew we were still fighting in Iraq and you had to explain it over and over and over again. The upside? Dude, I was the *Scout Platoon Leader*. Platoon leaders are supposed to sit back and direct. I did that. Sure. Absolutely. That's where I got these damned scars from a door charge I (very stupidly) got too close to. But we still did the house and pulled the bad-guys. Who? Me do a door? No, Colonel, of *course* I didn't do the door.

Very hoowah time. Rule One (no drinking, "fraternization" or pornography) was still in effect. Nobody paid a damned bit of attention to it. I was still an officer. I practically fucking *lived* with my grunts. We ran together, fought together, drank together and . . . Okay, there was a degree of fraternization on that one trip up to Kirbil. With girls. Hookers. Let me make it clear that we were *not* fraternizing with each other.

Good days, good days.

And back to Savannah. And I made captain on the "short list" and I got a company. Bravo called "The Bandits." Six is the military designation for "commander." Ergo, I became Bandit Six and have used it as a handle any time I can get away with it since.

Now, taking over a company when you've never been an XO is a bit of an adjustment. I got my first "does not quite walk on water but can negotiate the top of mud" evaluation during my first eval period as CO. Deserved it. I was not succeeding in my primary tasks. Some personal issues but I was not succeeding.

I begged forgiveness and, even more, begged help. I'm not good at asking for advice. I'd gotten used to asking NCOs what they thought and then using it or not. But going to the battalion commander (Lieutenant Colonel Nick Richards, good guy) and admitting I was getting a bit lost in the swamps as a CO was hard.

He didn't kick my ass for it, though. He just gave suggestions. And they were very good suggestions. I got better very fast. (Getting over the personal issues helped. Okay, yeah, they involved a girl and no she did not get pregnant but thank God we also did not get married is all I'll say.)

The company considered me a bit rocky when we deployed but we sort of mutually got over that in the Rockpile. My performance was coming up even before deployment and, hell, I *like* deployments. I'd finally gotten over my tendency to (badly) micromanage the company. Just in time, too, because I was not going to be a Fobbit on deployment if I could help it. I did help it.

God forgive me for what I put my driver through, though. You see, I'd have at any time two or three things going on at once out in the boonies. In different areas. Most of the unit would travel fairly heavy, at least a platoon. I wanted to see all of it and especially when the shit was hitting the fan. So myself, my driver and two RTOs (actually, Bobby and Buddy were my bodyguards) would go raring off across a fairly questionable to hostile Kandahar Province countryside, mostly by ourselves. Occasionally this involved stopping and paying a visit to one of the local "friendlies." I put the quotes on it because you never knew until you pulled up (and sometimes not even then) if they were friendlies *today*.

Occasionally it involved attempts by unfriendlies to stop *us*.

Lord love my boys. They never seemed to tire of bailing the CO out of a firefight. Probably because they were trying to catch up. And they never seemed to tire, either, of being in the middle of a firefight and "Bandit Six" suddenly roaring in to jump in the fight. Days of wine and song.

(Wife's Edit: Sigh. "Attention to Orders. *Bandit Six* is hereby awarded the Distinguished Service Cross for conduct above and beyond the call of duty in actions in Kandahar Province, Afghanistan, on March 15th, 2017.

"While travelling to meet with local friendly tribal leaders, *Bandit Six* was informed that a small group of Special Operations personnel had been ambushed and were pinned down by local Taliban related forces. Without any regard to personal safety, *Bandit Six* immediately ventured to the area of combat and closed with the Taliban forces. His personal vehicle damaged by concentrated rocket propelled grenade fire which injured both his radio telephone operator and himself, *Bandit Six* exited the vehicle and engaged the enemy with his personal weapon. With the support of continued machine-gun fire from his damaged vehicle, directed by hand and arm signals, *Bandit Six* advanced upon the enemy ambush location and using concentrated fire, the expenditure of all of his personal store of grenades and person-to-person combat skills, *Bandit Six* turned the flank of the enemy position. During the process of the advance *Bandit Six* was wounded three times but continued to move forward expeditiously against the numerically superior Taliban forces until they retreated from their positions. Upon analysis of the combat the relieved special operations unit commander credited *Bandit Six* with over twenty (20) personal kills including more than six (6) due to knife and bayonet.

"Entered service in the Armed Forces from Minnesota." End Wife Edit. I swear, he drives me nuts sometimes.)

—end excerpt—

from *The Last Centurion*
available in hardcover,
August 2008, from Baen Books

JOHN RINGO

Master of Military SF

The Posleen War Saga

A Hymn Before Battle
(pb) 0-6713-1841-1 • $7.99

Gust Front
(pb) 0-7434-3525-7 • $7.99

When the Devil Dances
(pb) 0-7434-3602-4 • $7.99

Hell's Faire
(pb) 0-7434-8842-3 • $7.99

Cally's War with Julie Cochrane
(pb) 1-4165-2052-X • $7.99

Watch on the Rhine with Tom Kratman
(pb) 1-4165-2120-8 • $7.99

The Hero with Michael Z. Williamson
(pb) 1-4165-0914-3 • $7.99

Yellow Eyes with Tom Kratman
(hc) 1-4165-2103-8 • $26.00

Master of Epic SF

The Council War Series

There Will Be Dragons
(pb) 0-7434-8859-8 • $7.99

Emerald Sea
(pb) 1-4165-0920-8 • $7.99

Against the Tide
(pb) 1-4165-2057-0 • $7.99

East of the Sun, West of the Moon
(hc) 1-4165-2059-7 • $24.00

Master of Real SF

Into the Looking Glass
(pb) 1-4165-2105-4 • $7.99

Vorpal Blade with Travis S. Taylor
(hc) 1-4165-2129-1 • $25.00

Von Neumann's War with Travis S. Taylor
(hc) 1-4165-2075-9 • $25.00